13
SHORT
HORROR
NOVELS

ABOUT THE EDITORS

MARTIN H. GREENBERG, who has been called "the king of the anthologists," now has some 150 to his credit. Greenberg is professor of regional analysis and political science at the University of Wisconsin–Green Bay, where he teaches a course in American foreign and defense policy. He is also co-editor, with Charles G. Waugh and others, of *Baker's Dozen: 13 Short Fantasy Novels* and *Baker's Dozen: 13 Short Science Fiction Novels*; and, with Bill Pronzini and others, of *Baker's Dozen: 13 Short Mystery Novels* and *101 Mystery Stories*.

CHARLES G. WAUGH is a leading authority on science fiction and fantasy who has published more than 115 anthologies and single-author collections. He lives with his family in Winthrop, Maine.

BAKER'S DOZEN

13 SHORT HORROR NOVELS

Edited by
Charles G. Waugh
and
Martin H. Greenberg

BONANZA BOOKS
New York

Grateful acknowledgment for permission to reprint material is hereby given to the following:
Jerusalem's Lot—From *Nightshift* by Stephen King. Copyright © 1978 by Stephen King. Reprinted by permission of Doubleday & Company, Inc.
Fearful Rock—Copyright 1939 by Manly Wade Wellman; renewed © 1967 by Manly Wade Wellman. Reprinted by permission of Frances Wellman.
Sardonicus—Copyright © 1960 by Ray Russell. First published in *Playboy*. Reprinted by permission of the author.
Nightflyers—by George R. R. Martin. Copyright © 1980 by the Condé Nast Publications, Inc. Reprinted by permission of the author.
Horrible Imaginings—Copyright © 1982 by Fritz Leiber. Reprinted by permission of Richard Curtis Associates, Inc.
Jane Brown's Body—Copyright 1938, 1951 by Cornell Woolrich. Reprinted by permission of the agents for the author's Estate, the Scott Meredith Literary Agency, Inc., 845 Third Avenue, New York, NY 10022.
Killdozer—by Theodore Sturgeon. Copyright 1944 by Street & Smith Publications, Inc.; renewed © 1972 by Theodore Sturgeon. Reprinted by permission of Kirby McCauley, Ltd.
The Shadow Out of Time—by H. P. Lovecraft. Copyright 1936 by Street & Smith Publications, Inc. Reprinted by permission of the agents for the author's Estate, the Scott Meredith Literary Agency, Inc., 845 Third Avenue, New York, NY 10022.
The Stains—Copyright © 1980 by Robert Aickman. Reprinted by permission of Kirby McCauley, Ltd.
The Horror from the Hills—Copyright 1931 by Frank Belknap Long; renewed © 1959 by Frank Belknap Long. Reprinted by permission of Richard Curtis Associates, Inc.
The Children of the Kingdom—Copyright © 1980 by Ted Klein. Reprinted by permission of Kirby McCauley, Ltd.
Frost and Fire—Copyright 1946 by Ray Bradbury; renewed © 1973 by Ray Bradbury. Reprinted by permission of Don Congdon Associates, Inc.

First published in 1987 by Bonanza Books, distributed by
Crown Publishers, Inc., 225 Park Avenue South,
New York, New York 10003

Baker's Dozen is a trademark of OBC, Inc.

Printed and Bound in the United States of America

Library of Congress Cataloging-in-Publication Data
Baker's dozen.

1. Horror tales, American. 2. Horror tales, English.
I. Waugh, Charles. II. Greenberg, Martin Harry.
PS648.H6B34 1987 823'.0872'08 86-26418
ISBN 0-517-63171-7

h g f e d c b a

CONTENTS

INTRODUCTION

The storm howls outside, the house groans inside. You are alone, the lights are low, and midnight nears. Somewhat apprehensive, you open this book for distraction. What a mistake! Now each tick of the grandfather clock vibrates gong-like. The windows rattle and the doors creak as if someone seeks entry. Or could he be inside already, stealthily creeping, creeping toward your chair, bloody knife in upraised hand, poised to rush if noticed?

Get control of yourself, you say. This surely is a fantasy: your overactive imagination spurred on by circumstances. How you'll laugh about it later! And yet . . . what if you're right?

Pretend to read. Looking up could bring instantaneous death. But not looking up brings death too—agonizingly slow and terrifying—as you feel him drawing nearer, ever nearer.

As a shadow strikes the page, your eyes roll up to its source and a memory flashes through your mind. It is a story told one night on a camping trip as you huddled near the fire. It is about two teenagers. They are parked on a lonely, wooded road, celebrating the wonders of their love, when they hear an announcement on the radio: A homicidal maniac has escaped from the state asylum nearby after severely slashing two attendants with his horrible weapon, a large hook worn in place of a hand. For the girl, joy is dead. She detects menace in every sound. The boy says, "Come on, sweetheart, don't freeze like that, he's not around here." "No, stop," she says, "I'm frightened. Take me home right now." She will not budge. So, in fury, he starts the engine, throws the car in gear, and burns tread to her house. He stops, throws open his door, and stalks around the car. His hand reaches for her door,

vii

but trembles to a halt. In the gleaming moonlight he can see the handle, and swinging gently on it a large, bloody hook.

* * *

Not surprisingly, this is the type of introduction likely to be found in most horror anthologies. For the primary purpose of a horror story is, quite simply, to deliver a good emotional punch and nothing else. As such, it discards long-term goals for the immediacy of entertainment. So it's obvious anthologists should highlight those situations most likely to enhance the reader's immediate enjoyment, right?

Well . . . not always. For horror stories can be surprisingly utilitarian. It's a phenomenon of which I first became aware as a sophomore in college. A young woman I was taking on a first date said she'd like to see *The Haunting of Hill House.* During scary scenes, she jumped into my lap, and by show's end was lingering there. Several years later, I discovered why. It's called the Ovid-Horowitz Hypothesis, named for the noted Roman poet and an obscure nineteenth-century social scientist. According to the Hypothesis, joy, anger, fear, love, and other states of emotional arousal are physiologically not all that different. Often the emotions felt depend upon the labels used to describe the stimulus. If I think I am aroused by the horror, I decide I'm frightened, and scream. But if I think I am aroused by a woman, I decide I'm in love, and smooch. (Ah, where was *The Texas Chainsaw Massacre* when I really needed it?)

Hey, I know it sounds loony. But it's supported by research. For example, in one experiment, a beautiful woman initiated interviews with college men on two campus bridges. A low, sturdy bridge provided little external arousal. A high, swaying suspension bridge provided much more. In the latter condition, subjects reported feeling a greater attraction to the woman.

That's why Ovid counseled keeping fast chariots outside the Coliseum. Watch the gladiators pound each other, then whisk your date home before she (or he) cools off. That's the logic behind chaotic fraternity parties. Drink, dance, be overwhelmed by noise, and maybe you'll decide it's Henry (or Harriet) who's exciting you.

So, in summary, don't hibernate inside, reading this book to yourself. Make a date, preferably on a suspension bridge, where you can while away the time (Oh, that wile!) reading the stories out loud (minus the introduction, of course), before moving on to better things. (Hopefully.) For you urbanites without access to suspension bridges, civil libertarians have, thoughtfully, transformed parks and subways into more-than-adequate substitutes.

But please forgive me. I must stop. My lovely wife has passed by, and there are some galleys here I'm going to read to her. I'm sure you understand.

Winthrop, Maine   CHARLES G. WAUGH
1987

STEPHEN KING
Jerusalem's Lot

DEAR BONES,

How good it was to step into the cold, draughty hall here at Chapelwaite, every bone in an ache from that abominable coach, in need of instant relief from my distended bladder—and to see a letter addressed in your own inimitable scrawl propped on the obscene little cherry-wood table beside the door! Be assured that I set to deciphering it as soon as the needs of the body were attended to (in a coldly ornate downstairs bathroom where I could see my breath rising before my eyes).

I'm glad to hear that you are recovered from the *miasma* that has so long set in your lungs, although I assure you that I do sympathize with the moral dilemma the cure has affected you with. An ailing abolitionist healed by the sunny climes of slave-struck Florida! Still and all, Bones, I ask you as a friend who has also walked in the valley of the shadow, *to take care of yourself* and venture not back to Massachusetts until your body gives you leave. Your fine mind and incisive pen cannot serve us if you are clay, and if the Southern zone is a healing one, is there not poetic justice in that?

Yes, the house is quite as fine as I had been led to believe by my cousin's executors, but rather more sinister. It sits atop a huge and jutting point of land perhaps three miles north of Falmouth and nine miles north of Portland. Behind it are some four acres of grounds, gone back to the wild in the most formidable manner imaginable—junipers, scrub vines, brushes, and various forms of creeper climb wildly over the picturesque stone walls that separate

3

the estate from the town domain. Awful imitations of Greek statuary peer blindly through the wrack from atop various hillocks—they seem, in most cases, about to lunge at the passer-by. My cousin Stephen's tastes seem to have run the gamut from the unacceptable to the downright horrific. There is an odd little summer house which has been nearly buried in scarlet sumac and a grotesque sundial in the midst of what must once have been a garden. It adds the final lunatic touch.

But the view from the parlour more than excuses this; I command a dizzying view of the rocks at the foot of Chapelwaite Head and the Atlantic itself. A huge, bellied bay window looks out on this, and a huge, toadlike secretary stands beside it. It will do nicely for the start of that novel which I have talked of so long [and no doubt tiresomely].

To-day has been gray with occasional splatters of rain. As I look out all seems to be a study in slate—the rocks, old and worn as Time itself, the sky, and of course the sea, which crashes against the granite fangs below with a sound which is not precisely sound but vibration—I can feel the waves with my feet even as I write. The sensation is not a wholly unpleasant one.

I know you disapprove my solitary habits, dear Bones, but I assure you that I am fine and happy. Calvin is with me, as practical, silent, and as dependable as ever, and by midweek I am sure that between the two of us we shall have straightened our affairs and made arrangement for necessary deliveries from town—and a company of cleaning women to begin blowing the dust from this place!

I will close—there are so many things as yet to be seen, rooms to explore, and doubtless a thousand pieces of execrable furniture to be viewed by these tender eyes. Once again, my thanks for the touch of familiar brought by your letter, and for your continuing regard.

Give my love to your wife, as you both have mine.

CHARLES.

Oct. 6, 1850

DEAR BONES,

Such a place this is!

It continues to amaze me—as do the reactions of the townfolk in the closest village to my occupancy. That is a queer little place

with the picturesque name of Preacher's Corners. It was there that
Calvin contracted for the weekly provisions. The other errand,
that of securing a sufficient supply of cordwood for the winter,
was likewise taken care of. But Cal returned with gloomy countenance, and when I asked him what the trouble was, he replied
grimly enough:

"They think you mad, Mr. Boone!"

I laughed and said that perhaps they had heard of the brain
fever I suffered after my Sarah died—certainly I spoke madly
enough at that time, as you could attest.

But Cal protested that no one knew anything of me except
through my cousin Stephen, who contracted for the same services
as I have now made provision for. "What was said, sir, was that
anyone who would live in Chapelwaite must be either a lunatic
or run the risk of becoming one."

This left me utterly perplexed, as you may imagine, and I asked
who had given him this amazing communication. He told me
that he had been referred to a sullen and rather besotted pulp-
logger named Thompson, who owns four hundred acres of pine,
birch, and spruce, and who logs it with the help of his five sons,
for sale to the mills in Portland and to householders in the
immediate area.

When Cal, all unknowing of his queer prejudice, gave him the
location to which the wood was to be brought, this Thompson
stared at him with his mouth ajaw and said that he would send
his sons with the wood, in the good light of the day, and by the
sea road.

Calvin, apparently misreading my bemusement for distress hastened to say that the man reeked of cheap whiskey and that he
had then lapsed into some kind of nonsense about a deserted
village and cousin Stephen's relations—and worms! Calvin finished
his business with one of Thompson's boys, who, I take it, was
rather surly and none too sober or freshly scented himself. I take
it there has been some of this reaction in Preacher's Corners itself,
at the general store where Cal spoke with the shop-keeper, although
this was more of the gossipy, behind-the-hand type.

None of this has bothered me much; we know how rustics
dearly love to enrich their lives with the smell of scandal and
myth, and I suppose poor Stephen and his side of the family are
fair game. As I told Cal, a man who has fallen to his death almost

from his own front porch is more likely to stir talk.

The house itself is a constant amazement. Twenty-three rooms, Bones! The wainscotting which panels the upper floors and the portrait gallery is mildewed but still stout. While I stood in my late cousin's upstairs bedroom I could hear the rats scuttering behind it, and big ones they must be, from the sound they make— almost like people walking there. I should hate to encounter one in the dark; or even in the light, for that matter. Still, I have noted neither holes nor droppings. Odd.

The upper gallery is lined with bad portraits in frames which must be worth a fortune. Some bear a resemblance to Stephen as I remember him. I believe I have correctly identified my Uncle Henry Boone and his wife Judith; the others are unfamiliar. I suppose one of them may be my own notorious grandfather, Robert. But Stephen's side of the family is all but unknown to me, for which I am heartily sorry. The same good humour that shone in Stephen's letters to Sarah and me, the same light of high intellect, shines in these portraits, bad as they are. For what foolish reasons families fall out! A rifled *escritoire,* hard words between brothers now dead three generations, and blameless descendants are needlessly estranged. I cannot help reflecting upon how fortunate it was that you and John Petty succeeded in contacting Stephen when it seemed I might follow my Sarah through the Gates—and upon how unfortunate it was that chance should have robbed us of a face-to-face meeting. How I would have loved to hear him defend the ancestral statuary and furnishings!

But do not let me denigrate the place to an extreme. Stephen's taste was not my own, true, but beneath the veneer of his additions there are pieces [a number of them shrouded by dust-covers in the upper chambers] which are true masterworks. There are beds, tables, and heavy, dark scrollings done in teak and mahogany, and many of the bedrooms and receiving chambers, the upper study and small parlour, hold a somber charm. The floors are rich pine that glow with an inner and secret light. There is dignity here; dignity and the weight of years. I cannot yet say I like it, but I do respect it. I am eager to watch it change as we revolve through the changes of this northern clime.

Lord, I run on! Write soon, Bones. Tell me what progress you make, and what news you hear from Petty and the rest. And please do not make the mistake of trying to persuade any new

Southern acquaintances as to your views *too forcibly*—I understand that not all are content to answer merely with their mouths, as is our long-winded *friend,* Mr. Calhoun.

Yr. affectionate friend,
CHARLES.

Oct. 16, 1850.

DEAR RICHARD,

Hello, and how are you? I have thought about you often since I have taken up residence here at Chapelwaite, and had half-expected to hear from you—and now I receive a letter from Bones telling me that I'd forgotten to leave my address at the club! Rest assured that I would have written eventually anyway, as it sometimes seems that my true and loyal friends are all I have left in the world that is sure and completely normal. And, Lord, how spread we've become! You in Boston, writing faithfully for *The Liberator* [to which I have also sent my address, incidentally], Hanson in England on another of his confounded *jaunts,* and poor old Bones in the very *lions' lair,* recovering his lungs.

It goes as well as can be expected here, Dick, and be assured I will render you a full account when I am not quite as pressed by certain events which are extant here—I think your legal mind may be quite intrigued by certain happenings at Chapelwaite and in the area about it.

But in the meantime I have a favour to ask, if you will entertain it. Do you remember the historian you introduced me to at Mr. Clary's fund-raising dinner for the cause? I believe his name was Bigelow. At any rate, he mentioned that he made a hobby of collecting odd bits of historical lore which pertained to the very area in which I am now living. My favour, then, is this: Would you contact him and ask him what facts, bits of folklore, or *general rumour*—if any—he may be conversant with about a small, deserted village called JERUSALEM'S LOT, near a township called Preacher's Corners, on the Royal River? The stream itself is a tributary of the Androscoggin, and flows into that river approximately eleven miles above that river's emptying place near Chapelwaite. It would gratify me intensely, and, more important, may be a matter of some moment.

In looking over this letter I feel I have been a bit short with you, Dick, for which I am heartily sorry. But be assured I will explain myself shortly, and until that time I send my warmest regards to your wife, two fine sons, and, of course, to yourself.

Yr. affectionate friend,
CHARLES.

Oct. 16, 1850.

DEAR BONES,

I have a tale to tell you which seems a little strange [and even disquieting] to both Cal and me—see what you think. If nothing else, it may serve to amuse you while you battle the mosquitoes!

Two days after I mailed my last to you, a group of four young ladies arrived from the Corners under the supervision of an elderly lady of intimidatingly competent visage named Mrs. Cloris, to set the place in order and to remove some of the dust that had been causing me to sneeze seemingly at every other step. They all seemed a little nervous as they went about their chores; indeed, one flighty miss uttered a small screech when I entered the upstairs parlour as she dusted.

I asked Mrs. Cloris about this [she was dusting the downstairs hall with grim determination that would have quite amazed you, her hair done up in an old faded bandanna], and she turned to me and said with an air of determination: "They don't like the house, and I don't like the house, sir, because it has always been a *bad* house."

My jaw dropped at this unexpected bit, and she went on in a kindlier tone: "I do not mean to say that Stephen Boone was not a fine man, for he was; I cleaned for him every second Thursday all the time he was here, as I cleaned for his father, Mr. Randolph Boone, until he and his wife disappeared in eighteen and sixteen. Mr. Stephen was a good and kindly man, and so you seem, sir (if you will pardon my bluntness; I know no other way to speak), but the house is *bad* and it always *has been,* and no Boone has ever been happy here since your grandfather Robert and his brother Philip fell out over stolen [and here she paused, almost guiltily] items in seventeen and eighty-nine."

Such memories these folks have, Bones!

Mrs. Cloris continued: "The house was built in unhappiness, has been lived in with unhappiness, there has been blood spilt on its floors [as you may or may not know, Bones, my Uncle Randolph was involved in an accident on the cellar stairs which took the life of his daughter Marcella; he then took his own life in a fit of remorse. The incident is related in one of Stephen's letters to me, on the sad occasion of his dead sister's birthday], there has been disappearance and accident.

"I have worked here, Mr. Boone, and I am neither blind nor deaf. I've heard awful sounds in the walls, sir, awful sounds— thumpings and crashings and once a strange wailing that was half-laughter. It fair made my blood curdle. It's a dark place, sir." And there she halted, perhaps afraid she had spoken too much.

As for myself, I hardly knew whether to be offended or amused, curious or merely matter-of-fact. I'm afraid that amusement won the day. "And what do you suspect, Mrs. Cloris? Ghosts rattling chains?"

But she only looked at me oddly. "Ghosts there may be. But it's not ghosts in the walls. It's not ghosts that wail and blubber like the damned and crash and blunder away in the darkness. It's—"

"Come, Mrs. Cloris," I prompted her. "You've come this far. Now can you finish what you've begun?"

The strangest expression of terror, pique, and—I would swear to it—religious awe passed over her face. "Some die not," she whispered. "Some live in the twilight shadows Between to serve— Him!"

And that was the end. For some minutes I continued to tax her, but she grew only more obstinate and would say no more. At last I desisted, fearing she might gather herself up and quit the premises.

This is the end of one episode, but a second occurred the following evening. Calvin had laid a fire downstairs and I was sitting in the living-room, drowsing over a copy of *The Intelligencer* and listening to the sound of wind-driven rain on the large bay window. I felt comfortable as only one can on such a night, when all is miserable outside and all is warmth and comfort inside; but a moment later Cal appeared at the door, looking excited and a bit nervous.

"Are you awake, sir?" he asked.

"Barely," I said. "What is it?"

"I've found something upstairs I think you should see," he responded, with the same air of suppressed excitement.

I got up and followed him. As we climbed the wide stairs,

Calvin said: "I was reading a book in the upstairs study—a rather strange one—when I heard a noise in the wall."

"Rats," I said. "Is that all?"

He paused on the landing, looking at me solemnly. The lamp he held cast weird, lurking shadows on the dark draperies and on the half-seen portraits that seemed now to leer rather than smile. Outside the wind rose to a brief scream and then subsided grudgingly.

"Not rats," Cal said. "There was a kind of blundering, thudding sound from behind the book-cases, and then a horrible gurgling—horrible, sir. And scratching, as if something were struggling to get out . . . to get at me!"

You can imagine my amazement, Bones. Calvin is not the type to give way to hysterical flights of imagination. It began to seem that there was a mystery here after all—and perhaps an ugly one indeed.

"What then?" I asked him. We had resumed down the hall, and I could see the light from the study spilling forth onto the floor of the gallery. I viewed it with some trepidation; the night seemed no longer comfortable.

"The scratching noise stopped. After a moment the thudding, shuffling sounds began again, this time moving away from me. It paused once, and I swear I heard a strange, almost inaudible laugh! I went to the book-case and began to push and pull, thinking there might be a partition, or a secret door."

"You found one?"

Cal paused at the door to the study. "No—but I found this!"

We stepped in and I saw a square black hole in the left case. The books at that point were nothing but dummies, and what Cal had found was a small hiding place. I flashed my lamp within it and saw nothing but a thick fall of dust, dust which must have been decades old.

"There was only this," Cal said quietly, and handed me a yellowed foolscap. The thing was a map, drawn in spider-thin strokes of black ink—the map of a town or village. There were perhaps seven buildings, and one, clearly marked with a steeple, bore this legend beneath it: *The Worm That Doth Corrupt.*

In the upper left corner, to what would have been the northwest of this little village, an arrow pointed. Inscribed beneath it: *Chapelwaite.*

Calvin said: "In town, sir, someone rather superstitiously mentioned a deserted village called Jerusalem's Lot. It's a place they steer clear of."

"But this?" I asked, fingering the odd legend below the steeple. "I don't know."

A memory of Mrs. Cloris, adamant yet fearful, passed through my mind. "The Worm . . ." I muttered.

"Do you know something, Mr. Boone?"

"Perhaps . . . it might be amusing to have a look for this town tomorrow, do you think, Cal?"

He nodded, eyes lighting. We spent almost an hour after this looking for some breach in the wall behind the cubbyhole Cal had found, but with no success. Nor was there a recurrence of the noises Cal had described.

We retired with no further adventure that night.

On the following morning Calvin and I set out on our ramble through the woods. The rain of the night before had ceased, but the sky was somber and lowering. I could see Cal looking at me with some doubtfulness and I hastened to reassure him that should I tire, or the journey prove too far, I would not hesitate to call a halt to the affair. We had equipped ourselves with a picnic lunch, a fine Buckwhite compass, and, of course, the odd and ancient map of Jerusalem's Lot.

It was a strange and brooding day; not a bird seemed to sing nor an animal to move as we made our way through the great and gloomy stands of pine to the south and east. The only sounds were those of our own feet and the steady pound of the Atlantic against the headlands. The smell of the sea, almost preternaturally heavy, was our constant companion.

We had gone no more than two miles when we struck an overgrown road of what I believe were once called the "corduroy" variety; this tended in our general direction and we struck off along it, making brisk time. We spoke little. The day, with its still and ominous quality, weighed heavily on our spirits.

At about eleven o'clock we heard the sound of rushing water. The remnant of road took a hard turn to the left, and on the other side of a boiling, slaty little stream, like an apparition, was Jerusalem's Lot!

The stream was perhaps eight feet across, spanned by a moss-grown footbridge. On the far side, Bones, stood the most perfect little village you might imagine, understandably weathered, but amazingly preserved. Several houses, done in that austere yet commanding form for which the Puritans were justly famous, stood clustered near the steeply sheared bank. Further beyond, along a weed-grown thoroughfare, stood three or four of what might have been primitive business establishments, and beyond that, the spire of the church marked on the map, rising up to the gray sky and looking grim beyond description with its peeled paint and tarnished, leaning cross.

"The town is well named," Cal said softly beside me.

We crossed to the town and began to poke through it—and this is where my story grows slightly amazing, Bones, so prepare yourself!

The air seemed leaden as we walked among the buildings; weighted, if you will. The edifices were in a state of decay— shutters torn off, roofs crumbled under the weight of heavy snows gone by, windows dusty and leering. Shadows from odd corners and warped angles seemed to sit in sinister pools.

We entered an old and rotting tavern first—somehow it did not seem right that we should invade any of those houses to which people had retired when they wished privacy. An old and weather-scrubbed sign above the splintered door announced that this had been the BOAR'S HEAD INN AND TAVERN. The door creaked hellishly on its one remaining hinge, and we stepped into the shadowed interior. The smell of rot and mould was vaporous and nearly overpowering. And beneath it seemed to lie an even deeper smell, a slimy and pestiferous smell, a smell of ages and the decay of ages. Such a stench as might issue from corrupt coffins or violated tombs. I held my handkerchief to my nose and Cal did likewise. We surveyed the place.

"My God, sir—" Cal said faintly.

"It's never been touched," I finished for him.

As indeed it had not. Tables and chairs stood about like ghostly guardians of the watch, dusty, warped by the extreme changes in temperature which the New England climate is known for, but otherwise perfect—as if they had waited through the silent, echoing decades for those long gone to enter once more, to call for a pint or a dram, to deal cards and light clay pipes. A small square mirror hung beside the rules of the tavern, *unbroken*. Do you see the significance, Bones? Small boys are noted for exploration and vandalism; there is not a "haunted" house which stands with windows intact, no matter how fearsome the eldritch inhabitants are rumoured to be; not a shadowy graveyard without at least one tombstone upended by young pranksters. Certainly there must be a score of young pranksters in Preacher's Corners, not two miles from Jerusalem's Lot. Yet the inn-keeper's glass [which must have cost him a nice sum] was intact—as were the other fragile items we found in our pokings. The only damage in Jerusalem's Lot has been done by impersonal Nature. The implication is obvious: Jerusalem's Lot is a shunned town. But why? I have a notion, but before I even dare hint at it, I must proceed to the unsettling conclusion of our visit.

We went up to the sleeping quarters and found beds made up, pewter water-pitchers neatly placed beside them. The kitchen was likewise untouched by anything save the dust of the years and that horrible, sunken stench of decay. The tavern alone would be an antiquarian's paradise; the wondrously queer kitchen stove alone would fetch a pretty price at Boston auction.

"What do you think, Cal?" I asked when we had emerged again into the uncertain daylight.

"I think it's bad business, Mr. Boone," he replied in his doteful way, "and that we must see more to know more."

We gave the other shops scant notice—there was a hostelry with mouldering leather goods still hung on rusted flatnails, a chandler's, a warehouse with oak and pine still stacked within, a smithy.

We entered two houses as we made our way toward the church at the center of the village. Both were perfectly in the Puritan mode, full of items a collector would give his arm for, both deserted and full of the same rotten scent.

Nothing seemed to live or move in all of this but ourselves. We saw no insects, no birds, not even a cobweb fashioned in a window corner. Only dust.

At last we reached the church. It reared above us, grim, un-inviting, cold. Its windows were black with the shadows inside, and any Godliness or sanctity had departed from it long ago. Of that I am certain. We mounted the steps, and I placed my hand on the large iron door-pull. A set, dark look passed from myself to Calvin and back again. I opened the portal. How long since that door had been touched? I would say with confidence that mine was the first in fifty years; perhaps longer. Rust-clogged hinges screamed as I opened it. The smell of rot and decay which smote us was nearly palpable. Cal made a gagging sound in his throat and twisted his head involuntarily for clearer air.

"Sir," he asked, "are you sure that you are—?"

"I'm fine," I said calmly. But I did not feel calm, Bones, no more than I do now. I believe, with Moses, with Jereboam, with Increase Mather, and with our own Hanson [when he is in a philosophical *temperament*], that there are spiritually noxious places, buildings where the milk of the cosmos has become sour and rancid. This church is such a place; I would swear to it.

We stepped into a long vestibule equipped with a dusty coat rack and shelved hymnals. It was windowless. Oil-lamps stood in niches here and there. An unremarkable room, I thought, until I heard Calvin's sharp gasp and saw what he had already noticed.

It was an obscenity.

I daren't describe that elaborately framed picture further than this: that it was done after the fleshy style of Rubens; that it contained a grotesque travesty of a madonna and child; that strange, half-shadowed creatures sported and crawled in the background.

"Lord," I whispered.

"There's no Lord here," Calvin said, and his words seemed to hang in the air. I opened the door leading into the church itself, and the odor became a miasma, nearly overpowering.

In the glimmering half-light of afternoon the pews stretched ghostlike to the altar. Above them was a high, oaken pulpit and a shadow-struck narthex from which gold glimmered.

With a half-sob Calvin, that devout Protestant, made the Holy Sign, and I followed suit. For the gold was a large, beautifully wrought cross—but it was hung upside-down, symbol of Satan's Mass.

"We must be calm," I heard myself saying. "We must be calm, Calvin. We must be calm."

But a shadow had touched my heart, and I was afraid as I had never been. I have walked beneath death's umbrella and thought there was none darker. But there is. There is.

We walked down the aisle, our footfalls echoing above and around us. We left tracks in the dust. And at the altar there were other tenebrous *objets d'art*. I will not, cannot, let my mind dwell upon them.

I began to mount to the pulpit itself.

"Don't, Mr. Boone!" Cal cried suddenly. "I'm afraid—"

But I had gained it. A huge book lay open upon the stand, writ both in Latin and crabbed runes which looked, to my unpractised eye, either Druidic or pre-Celtic. I enclose a card with several of the symbols, redrawn from memory.

I closed the book and looked at the words stamped into the leather: *De Vermis Mysteriis*. My Latin is rusty, but serviceable enough to translate: *The Mysteries of the Worm*.

As I touched it, that accursed church and Calvin's white, upturned face seemed to swim before me. It seemed that I heard low, chanting voices, full of hideous yet eager fear—and below that sound, another, filling the bowels of the earth. An hallucination, I doubt it not—but at the same moment, the church was filled with a very real sound, which I can only describe as a huge and macabre *turning* beneath my feet. The pulpit trembled beneath my fingers; the desecrated cross trembled on the wall.

We exited together, Cal and I, leaving the place to its own darkness, and neither of us dared look back until we had crossed the rude planks spanning the stream. I will not say we defiled the nineteen hundred years man has spent climbing upward from a hunkering and superstitious savage by actually running; but I would be a liar to say that we strolled.

That is my tale. You mustn't shadow your recovery by fearing that the fever has touched me again; Cal can attest to all in these pages, up to and including the hideous *noise*.

So I close, saying only that I wish I might see you [knowing that much of my bewilderment would drop away immediately], and that I remain your friend and admirer,

CHARLES.

Oct. 17, 1850.

DEAR GENTLEMEN:

In the most recent edition of your catalogue of household items (i.e., Summer, 1850), I noticed a preparation which is titled Rat's Bane. I should like to purchase one (1) 5-pound tin of this preparation at your stated price of thirty cents ($.30). I enclose

return postage. Please mail to: Calvin McCann, Chapelwaite, Preacher's Corners, Cumberland County, Maine.
Thank you for your attention in this matter.

> I remain, dear Gentlemen,
> CALVIN MCCANN.

Oct. 19, 1850.

DEAR BONES,

Developments of a disquieting nature.

The noises in the house have intensified, and I am growing more to the conclusion that rats are not all that move within our walls. Calvin and I went on another fruitless search for hidden crannies or passages, but found nothing. How poorly we would fit into one of Mrs. Radcliffe's romances! Cal claims, however, that much of the sound emanates from the cellar, and it is there we intend to explore tomorrow. It makes me no easier to know that Cousin Stephen's sister met her unfortunate end there.

Her portrait, by the by, hangs in the upstairs gallery. Marcella Boone was a sadly pretty thing, if the artist got her right, and I do know she never married. At times I think that Mrs. Cloris was right, that it *is* a bad house. It has certainly held nothing but gloom for its past inhabitants.

But I have more to say of the redoubtable Mrs. Cloris, for I have had this day a second interview with her. As the most levelheaded person from the Corners that I have met thus far, I sought her out this afternoon, after an unpleasant interview which I will relate.

The wood was to have been delivered this morning, and when noon came and passed and no wood with it, I decided to take my daily walk into the town itself. My object was to visit Thompson, the man with whom Cal did business.

It has been a lovely day, full of the crisp snap of bright autumn, and by the time I reached the Thompsons' homestead [Cal, who remained home to poke further through Uncle Stephen's library, gave me adequate directions] I felt in the best mood that these last few days have seen, and quite prepared to forgive Thompson's tardiness with the wood.

The place was a massive tangle of weeds and fallen-down buildings in need of paint; to the left of the barn a huge sow, ready for November butchering, grunted and wallowed in a muddy sty, and in the littered yard between house and out-buildings a woman in a tattered gingham dress was feeding chickens from her apron. When I hailed her, she turned a pale and vapid face toward me.

The sudden change in expression from utter, doltish emptiness to one of frenzied terror was quite wonderful to behold. I can only think she took me for Stephen himself, for she raised her hand in the prong-fingered sign of the evil eye and screamed. The chicken-feed scattered on the ground and the fowls fluttered away, squawking.

Before I could utter a sound, a huge, hulking figure of a man clad only in long-handled underwear lumbered out of the house with a squirrel-rifle in one hand and a jug in the other. From the red light in his eye and unsteady manner of walking, I judged that this was Thompson the Woodcutter himself.

"A Boone!" he roared. "G— d—n your eyes!" He dropped the jug a-rolling and also made the Sign.

"I've come," I said with as much equanimity as I could muster under the circumstances, "because the wood has not. According to the agreement you struck with my man—"

"G— d—n your man too, say I!" And for the first time I noticed that beneath his bluff and bluster he was deadly afraid. I began seriously to wonder if he mightn't actually use his rifle against me in his excitement.

I began carefully: "As a gesture of courtesy, you might—"

"G— d—n your courtesy!"

"Very well, then," I said with as much dignity as I could muster. "I bid you good day until you are more in control of yourself." And with this I turned away and began down the road to the village.

"Don'tchee come back!" he screamed after me. "Stick wi' your evil up there! Cursed! Cursed! Cursed!" He pelted a stone at me, which struck my shoulder. I would not give him the satisfaction of dodging.

So I sought out Mrs. Cloris, determined to solve the mystery of Thompson's enmity, at least. She is a widow [and none of your confounded *matchmaking,* Bones; she is easily fifteen years my senior, and I'll not see forty again] and lives by herself in a charming little cottage at the ocean's very doorstep. I found the lady hanging out her wash, and she seemed genuinely pleased to see me. I found this a great relief; it is vexing almost beyond words to be branded pariah for no understandable reason.

"Mr. Boone," said she, offering a half-curtsey. "If you've come about washing, I take none in past September. My rheumatiz pains me so that it's trouble enough to do my own."

"I wish laundry *was* the subject of my visit. I've come for help, Mrs. Cloris. I must know all you can tell me about Chapelwaite and Jerusalem's Lot and why the townfolk regard me with such fear and suspicion!"

"Jerusalem's Lot! You know about *that,* then."

"Yes," I replied, "and visited it with my companion a week ago."

"God!" She went pale as milk, and tottered. I put out a hand to steady her. Her eyes rolled horribly, and for a moment I was sure she would swoon.

"Mrs. Cloris, I am sorry if I have said anything to—"

"Come inside," she said. "You must know. Sweet Jesu, the evil days have come again!"

She would not speak more until she had brewed strong tea in her sunshiny kitchen. When it was before us, she looked pensively out at the ocean for a time. Inevitably, her eyes and mine were drawn to the jutting brow of Chapelwaite Head, where the house looked out over the water. The large bay window glittered in the rays of the westering sun like a diamond. The view was beautiful but strangely disturbing. She suddenly turned to me and declared vehemently:

"Mr. Boone, you must leave Chapelwaite immediately!"

I was flabbergasted.

"There has been an evil breath in the air since you took up residence. In the last week—since you set foot in the accursed place—there have been omens and portents. A caul over the face of the moon; flocks of whippoorwills which roost in the cemeteries; an unnatural birth. You *must* leave!"

When I found my tongue, I spoke as gently as I could. "Mrs. Cloris, these things are dreams. You must know that."

"Is it a dream that Barbara Brown gave birth to a child with no eyes? Or that Clifton Brockett found a flat, pressed trail five feet wide in the woods beyond Chapelwaite *where all had withered and gone white?* And can you, who have visited Jerusalem's Lot, say with truth that nothing still lives there?"

I could not answer; the scene in that hideous church sprang before my eyes.

She clamped her gnarled hands together in an effort to calm herself. "I know of these things only from my mother and her mother before her. Do you know the history of your family as it applies to Chapelwaite?"

"Vaguely," I said. "The house has been the home of Philip Boone's line since the 1780s; his brother Robert, my grandfather, located in Massachusetts after an argument over stolen papers. Of Philip's side I know little, except that an unhappy shadow fell over it, extending from father to son to grandchildren—Marcella died in a tragic accident and Stephen fell to his death. It was his wish that Chapelwaite become the home of me and mine, and that the family rift thus be mended."

"Never to be mended," she whispered. "You know nothing of the original quarrel?"

"Robert Boone was discovered rifling his brother's desk."

"Philip Boone was mad," she said. "A man who trafficked with the unholy. The thing which Robert Boone *attempted* to remove was a profane Bible writ in the old tongues—Latin, Druidic, others. A hell-book."

"De Vermis Mysteriis."

She recoiled as if struck. "You know of it?"

"I have seen it . . . touched it." It seemed again she might swoon. A hand went to her mouth as if to stifle an outcry. "Yes; in Jerusalem's Lot. On the pulpit of a corrupt and desecrated church."

"Still there; still there, then." She rocked in her chair. "I had hoped God in His wisdom had cast it into the pit of hell."

"What relation had Philip Boone to Jerusalem's Lot?"

"Blood relation," she said darkly. "The Mark of the Beast was on him, although he walked in the clothes of the Lamb. And on the night of October 31, 1789, Philip Boone disappeared . . . and the entire populace of that damned village with him."

She would say little more; in fact, seemed to know little more. She would only reiterate her pleas that I leave, giving as reason something about "blood calling to blood" and muttering about "those who *watch* and those who *guard.*" As twilight drew on she seemed to grow more agitated rather than less, and to placate her

I promised that her wishes would be taken under strong consideration.

I walked home through lengthening, gloomy shadows, my good mood quite dissipated and my head spinning with questions which still plague me. Cal greeted me with the news that our noises in the walls have grown worse still—as I can attest at this moment. I try to tell myself that I hear only rats, but then I see the terrified, earnest face of Mrs. Cloris.

The moon has risen over the sea, bloated, full, the colour of blood, staining the ocean with a noxious shade. My mind turns to that church again and

(here a line is struck out)

But you shall not see that, Bones. It is too mad. It is time I slept, I think. My thoughts go out to you.

Regards,
CHARLES.

(The following is from the pocket journal of Calvin McCann.)

Oct. 20, '50

Took the liberty this morning of forcing the lock which binds the book closed; did it before Mr. Boone arose. No help; it is all in cypher. A simple one, I believe. Perhaps I may break it as easily as the lock. A diary, I am certain, the hand oddly like Mr. Boone's own. Whose book, shelved in the most obscure corner of this library and locked across the pages? It seems old, but how to tell? The corrupting air has largely been kept from its pages. More later, if time; Mr. Boone set upon looking about the cellar. Am afraid these dreadful goings-on will be too much for his chancy health yet. I must try to persuade him—

But he comes.

Oct. 20, 1850.

BONES,

I can't write   I can't [*sic*] write of this yet   I   I   I

(From the pocket journal of Calvin McCann)

Oct. 20, '50

As I had feared, his health has broken—
Dear God, our Father Who art in Heaven!

Cannot bear to think of it; yet it is planted, burned on my brain like a tin-type; that horror in the cellar—!

Alone now; half-past eight o'clock; house silent but—

Found him swooned over his writing table; he still sleeps; yet for those few moments how nobly he acquitted himself while I stood paralyzed and shattered!

His skin is waxy, cool. Not the fever again, God be thanked. I daren't move him or leave him to go to the village. And if I did go, who would return with me to aid him? Who would come to this cursed house?

O, the cellar! The things in the cellar that have haunted our walls!

Oct. 22, 1850.

DEAR BONES.

I am myself again, although weak, after thirty-six hours of unconsciousness. Myself again . . . what a grim and bitter joke! I shall never be myself again, never. I have come face to face with an insanity and a horror beyond the limits of human expression. And the end is not yet.

If it were not for Cal, I believe I should end my life this minute. He is one island of sanity in all this madness.

You shall know it all.

We had equipped ourselves with candles for our cellar exploration, and they threw a strong glow that was quite adequate—hellishly adequate! Calvin tried to dissuade me, citing my recent illness, saying that the most we should probably find would be some healthy rats to mark for poisoning.

I remained determined, however; Calvin fetched a sigh and answered: "Have it as you must, then, Mr. Boone."

The entrance to the cellar is by means of a trap in the kitchen floor [which Cal assures me he has since stoutly boarded over], and we raised it only with a great deal of straining and lifting.

A foetid, overpowering smell came up out of the darkness, not unlike that which pervaded the deserted town across the Royal River. The candle I held shed its glow on a steeply slanting flight of stairs leading down into darkness. They were in a terrible state of repair—in one place an entire riser missing, leaving only a black hole—and it was easy enough to see how the unfortunate Marcella might have come to her end there.

"Be careful, Mr. Boone!" Cal said; I told him I had no intention of being anything but, and we made the descent.

The floor was earthen, the walls of stout granite, and hardly wet. The place did not look like a rat haven at all, for there were none of the things rats like to make their nests in, such as old boxes, discarded furniture, piles of paper, and the like. We lifted our candles, gaining a small circle of light, but still able to see little. The floor had a gradual slope which seemed to run beneath the main living-room and the dining-room—i.e., to the west. It was in this direction we walked. All was in utter silence. The stench in the air grew steadily stronger, and the dark about us seemed to press like wool, as if jealous of the light which had temporarily deposed it after so many years of undisputed dominion.

At the far end, the granite walls gave way to a polished wood which seemed totally black and without reflective properties. Here the cellar ended, leaving what seemed to be an alcove off the main chamber. It was positioned at an angle which made inspection impossible without stepping around the corner.

Calvin and I did so.

It was as if a rotten spectre of this dwelling's sinister past had risen before us. A single chair stood in this alcove, and above it, fastened from a hook in one of the stout overhead beams, was a decayed noose of hemp.

"Then it was here that he hung himself," Cal muttered. "God!"

"Yes . . . with the corpse of his daughter lying at the foot of the stairs behind him."

Cal began to speak; then I saw his eyes jerked to a spot behind me; then his words became a scream.

How, Bones, can I describe the sight which fell upon our eyes? How can I tell you of the hideous tenants within our walls?

The far wall swung back, and from that darkness a face leered— a face with eyes as ebon as the Styx itself. Its mouth yawned in a toothless, agonized grin; one yellow, rotted hand stretched itself out to us. It made a hideous, mewling sound and took a shambling step forward. The light from my candle fell upon it—

And I saw the livid rope-burn about its neck!

From beyond it something else moved, something I shall dream of until the day when all dreams cease: a girl with a pallid, mouldering face and a corpse-grin; a girl whose head lolled at a lunatic angle.

They wanted us; I know it. And I know they would have drawn

us into that darkness and made us their own, had I not thrown my candle directly at the thing in the partition, and followed it with the chair beneath that noose.

After that, all is confused darkness. My mind has drawn the curtain. I awoke, as I have said, in my room with Cal at my side.

If I could leave, I should fly from this house of horror with my nightdress flapping at my heels. But I cannot. I have become a pawn in a deeper, darker drama. Do not ask how I know; I only do. Mrs. Cloris was right when she spoke of blood calling to blood; and how horribly right when she spoke of those who *watch* and those who *guard*. I fear that I have wakened a Force which has slept in the tenebrous village of 'Salem's Lot for half a century, a Force which has slain my ancestors and taken them in unholy bondage as *nosferatu*—the Undead. And I have greater fears than these, Bones, but I still see only in part. If I knew . . . if I only knew all!

CHARLES.

Postscriptum—And of course I write this only for myself; we are isolated from Preacher's Corners. I daren't cary my taint there to post this, and Calvin will not leave me. Perhaps, if God is good, this will reach you in some manner.

C.

(From the pocket journal of Calvin McCann)

Oct. 23, '50

He is stronger to-day; we talked briefly of the *apparitions* in the cellar; agreed they were neither hallucinations or of an *ectoplasmic* origin, but *real*. Does Mr. Boone suspect, as I do, that they have gone? Perhaps; the noises are still; yet all is ominous yet, o'ercast with a dark pall. It seems we wait in the deceptive Eye of the Storm . . .

Have found a packet of papers in an upstairs bedroom, lying in the bottom drawer of an old roll-top desk. Some correspondence & receipted bills lead me to believe the room was Robert Boone's. Yet the most interesting document is a few jottings on the back of an advertisement for gentlemen's beaver hats. At the top is writ:

Blessed are the meek.

Below, the following apparent nonsense is writ:

bkedshdermtheseak
elmsoerareshamded

I believe 'tis the key of the locked and coded book in the library. The cypher above is certainly a rustic one used in the War for Independence known as the *Fence-Rail*. When one removes the "nulls" from the second bit of scribble, the following is obtained:

besdrteek
lseaehme

Read up and down rather than across, the result is the original quotation from the Beatitudes.

Before I dare show this to Mr. Boone, I must be sure of the book's contents . . .

Oct. 24, 1850.

DEAR BONES,

An amazing occurrence—Cal, always close-mouthed until absolutely sure of himself [a rare and admirable human trait!], has found the diary of my grandfather Robert. The document was in a code which Cal himself has broken. He modestly declares that the discovery was an accident, but I suspect that perseverance and hard work had rather more to do with it.

At any rate, what a somber light it sheds on our mysteries here! The first entry is dated June 1, 1789, the last October 27, 1789— four days before the cataclysmic disappearance of which Mrs. Cloris spoke. It tells a tale of deepening obsession—nay, of madness—and makes hideously clear the relationship between Great-uncle Philip, the town of Jerusalem's Lot, and the book which rests in that desecrated church.

The town itself, according to Robert Boone, pre-dates Chapelwaite (built in 1782) and Preacher's Corners (known in those days as Preacher's Rest and founded in 1741); it was founded by a splinter group of the Puritan faith in 1710, a sect headed by a dour religious fanatic named James Boon. What a start that name gave me! That this Boon bore relation to my family can hardly be doubted, I believe. Mrs. Cloris could not have been more right in her superstitious belief that familial blood-line is of crucial importance in this matter; and I recall with terror her answer to my question about Philip and *his* relationship to 'Salem's Lot. "Blood relation," said she, and I fear that it is so.

The town became a settled community built around the church where Boon preached—or held court. My grandfather intimates that he also held commerce with any number of ladies from the town, assuring them that this was God's way and will. As a result, the town became an anomaly which could only have existed in those isolated and queer days when belief in witches and the Virgin Birth existed hand in hand: an interbred, rather degenerate religious village controlled by a half-mad preacher whose twin gospels were the Bible and de Goudge's sinister *Demon Dwellings;* a community in which rites of exorcism were held regularly; a community of incest and the insanity and physical defects which so often accompany that sin. I suspect [and believe Robert Boone must have also] that one of Boon's bastard offspring must have left [or have been spirited away from] Jerusalem's Lot to seek his fortune to the south—and thus founded our present lineage. I do know, by my own family reckoning, that our clan supposedly originated in that part of Massachusetts which has so lately become this Sovereign State of Maine. My great-grandfather, Kenneth Boone, became a rich man as a result of the then-flourishing fur trade. It was his money, increased by time and wise investment, which built this ancestral home long after his death in 1763. His sons, Philip and Robert, built Chapelwaite. *Blood calls to blood,* Mrs. Cloris said. Could it be that Kenneth was born of James Boon, fled the madness of his father and his father's town, only to have his sons, all-unknowing, build the Boone home *not two miles from the Boon beginnings?* If 'tis true, does it not seem that some huge and invisible Hand has guided us?

According to Robert's diary, James Boon was ancient in 1789— and he must have been. Granting him an age of twenty-five in the year of the town's founding, he would have been one hundred and four, a prodigious age. The following is quoted direct from Robert Boone's diary:

August 4, 1789.
To-day for the first time I met this Man with whom my Brother has been so unhealthily taken; I must admit this Boon controls a strange Magnetism which upset me Greatly.

He is a veritable Ancient, white-bearded, and dresses in a black Cassock which struck me as somehow obscene. More disturbing yet was the Fact that he was surrounded by Women, as a Sultan would be surrounded by his Harem; and P. assures me he is active yet, although at least an Octogenarian . . .
The Village itself I had visited only once before, and will not visit again; its Streets are silent and filled with the Fear the old Man inspires from his Pulpit: I fear also that Like has mated with Like, as so many of the Faces are similar. It seemed that each way I turned I beheld the old Man's Visage . . . all are so wan; they seem Lack-Luster, as if sucked dry of all Vitality, I beheld Eyeless and Noseless Children, Women who wept and gibbered and pointed at the Sky for no Reason, and garbled talk from the Scriptures with talk of Demons; . . . P. wished me to stay for Services, but the thought of that sinister Ancient in the Pulpit before an Audience of this Town's interbred Populace repulsed me and I made an Excuse . . .

The entries preceding and following this tell of Philip's growing fascination with James Boon. On September 1, 1789, Philip was baptized into Boon's church. His brother says: "I am aghast with Amaze and Horror—my Brother has changed before my very Eyes—he even seems to grow to resemble the wretched Man."

First mention of the book occurs on July 23. Robert's diary records it only briefly: "P. returned from the smaller Village tonight with, I thought, a rather wild Visage. Would not speak until Bedtime, when he said that Boon had enquired after a Book titled *Mysteries of the Worm.* To please P. I promised to write Johns & Goodfellow a letter of enquiry; P. almost fawningly Grateful."

On August 12, this notation: "Rec'd two Letters in the Post today . . . one from Johns & Goodfellow in Boston. They have Note of the Tome in which P. has expressed an Interest. Only five Copies extant in this Country. The Letter is rather cool; odd indeed. Have known Henry Goodfellow for Years."

August 13:

P. insanely excited by Goodfellow's letter; refuses to say why. He would only say that Boon is exceedingly anxious *to obtain a Copy. Cannot think why, since by the Title it seems only a harmless gardening Treatise . . .*

Am worried for Philip; he grows stranger to me Daily. I wish now we had not returned to Chapelwaite. The Summer is hot, oppressive, and filled with Omens . . .

There are only two further mentions of the infamous book in Robert's diary [he seems not to have realized the true importance of it, even at the end]. From the entry of September 4:

I have petitioned Goodfellow to act as P.'s Agent in the matter of the Purchase, although my better Judgement cries against it. What use to demur? Has he not his own Money, should I refuse? And in return I have extracted a Promise from Philip to recant this noisome Baptism . . . yet he is so Hectic; nearly Feverish; I do not trust him. I am hopelessly at Sea in this Matter . . .

Finally, September 16:

The Book arrived to-day, with a note from Goodfellow saying he wishes no more of my Trade . . . P. was excited to an unnatural Degree; all but snatched the Book from my Hands. It is writ in bastard Latin and a Runic Script of which I can read Nothing. The Thing seemed almost warm to the Touch, and to vibrate in my Hands, as if it contained a huge Power . . . I reminded P. of his Promise to Recant and he only laughed in an ugly, crazed Fashion and waved that Book in my Face, crying over and over again: "We have it! We have it! The Worm! The Secret of the Worm!"
He is now fled, I suppose to his mad Benefactor, and I have not seen him more this Day . . .

Of the book there is no more, but I have made certain deductions which seem at least probable. First, that this book was, as Mrs. Cloris has said, the subject of the falling-out between Robert and Philip; second, that it is a repository of unholy incantation, possibly of Druidic origin [many of the Druidic blood-rituals were preserved in print by the Roman conquerors of Britain in the name of scholarship, and many of these infernal cook-books are among the world's forbidden literature]; third, that Boon and Philip intended to use the book for their own ends. Perhaps, in some twisted way, they intended good, but I do not believe it. I believe they had long before bound themselves over to whatever faceless powers exist beyond the rim of the Universe; powers which may exist beyond the very fabric of Time. The last entries of Robert Boone's diary lend a dim glow of approbation to these speculations, and I allow them to speak for themselves:

October 26, 1789

A terrific Babble in Preacher's Corners to-day; Frawley, the Blacksmith, seized my Arm and demanded to know "What your Brother and that mad Antichrist are into up there." Goody Randall claims there have been Signs in the Sky of great impending Disaster. A Cow has been born with two Heads.

As for Myself, I know not what impends; perhaps 'tis my Brother's Insanity. His Hair has gone Gray almost Overnight, his Eyes are great bloodshot Circles from which the pleasing light of Sanity seems to have departed. He grins and whispers, and, for some Reason of his Own, has begun to haunt our Cellar when not in Jerusalem's Lot.

The Whippoorwills congregate about the House and upon the Grass; their combined Calling from the Mist blends with the Sea into an unearthly Shriek that precludes all thought of Sleep.

October 27, 1789

Followed P. this Evening when he departed for Jerusalem's Lot, keeping a safe Distance to avoid Discovery. The cursed Whippoorwills flock through the Woods, filling all with a deathly, psycho-pompotic Chant. I dared not cross the Bridge; the Town all dark except for the Church, which was litten with a ghastly red Glare that seemed to transform the high, peak'd Windows into the Eyes of the Inferno. Voices rose and fell in a Devil's Litany, sometimes laughing, sometimes sobbing. The very Ground seem'd to swell and groan beneath me, as if it bore an awful Weight, and I fled, amaz'd and full of Terror, the hellish, screaming Cries of the Whippoorwills

*dinning in my ears as I ran through those shadow-riven
Woods.*

*All tends to the Climax, yet unforeseen. I dare not sleep for
the Dreams that come, yet not remain awake for what lunatic
Terrors may come. The night is full of awful Sounds and I
fear—*

*And yet I feel the urge to go again, to watch, to see. It seems
that Philip himself calls me, and the old Man.
The Birds
cursed cursed cursed*

Here the diary of Robert Boone ends.

Yet you must notice, Bones, near the conclusion, that he claims
Philip himself seemed to call him. My final conclusion is formed
by these lines, by the talk of Mrs. Cloris and the others, but most
of all by those terrifying figures in the cellar, dead yet alive. Our
line is yet an unfortunate one, Bones. There is a curse over us
which refuses to be buried; it lives a hideous shadow-life in this
house and that town. And the culmination of the cycle is drawing
close again. I am the last of the Boone blood. I fear that something
knows this, and that I am at the nexus of an evil endeavor beyond
all sane understanding. The anniversary is All Saints' Eve, one
week from to-day.

How shall I proceed? If only you were here to counsel me, to
help me! If only you were here!

I must know all; I must return to the shunned town. May God
support me!

CHARLES.

(From the pocket journal of Calvin McCann)

Oct. 25, '50

Mr. Boone has slept nearly all this day. His face is pallid
and much thinner. I fear recurrence of his fever is inevitable.

While refreshing his water carafe I caught sight of two
unmailed letters to Mr. Granson in Florida. He plans to
return to Jerusalem's Lot; 'twill be the killing of him if I
allow it. Dare I steal away to Preacher's Corners and hire a

buggy? I must, and yet what if he wakes? If I should return and find him gone?

The noises have begun in our walls again. Thank God he still sleeps! My mind shudders from the import of this.

Later

I brought him his dinner on a tray. He plans on rising later, and despite his evasions, I know what he plans; yet I go to Preacher's Corners. Several of the sleeping-powders prescribed to him during his late illness remained with my things; he drank one with his tea, all-unknowing. He sleeps again.

To leave him with the Things that shamble behind our walls terrifies me; to let him continue even one more day within these walls terrifies me even more greatly. I have locked him in.

God grant he should still be there, safe and sleeping, when I return with the buggy!

Still later

Stoned me! Stoned me like a wild and rabid dog! Monsters and fiends! These, that call themselves *men!* We are prisoners here—

The birds, the whippoorwills, have begun to gather.

October 26, 1850.

DEAR BONES,

It is nearly dusk, and I have just wakened, having slept nearly the last twenty-four hours away. Although Cal has said nothing, I suspect he put a sleeping-powder in my tea, having gleaned my intentions. He is a good and faithful friend, intending only the best, and I shall say nothing.

Yet my mind is set. Tomorrow is the day. I am calm, resolved, but also seem to feel the subtle onset of the fever again. If it is so, it *must* be tomorrow. Perhaps tonight would be better still; yet not even the fires of Hell itself could induce me to set foot in that village by shadowlight.

Should I write no more, may God bless and keep you, Bones.

CHARLES.

Postscriptum—The birds have set up their cry, and the horrible shuffling sounds have begun again. Cal does not think I hear, but I do.

C.

(From the pocket journal of Calvin McCann)

Oct. 27, '50
5 A.M.

He is impersuadable. Very well. I go with him.

November 4, 1850.

DEAR BONES,

Weak, yet lucid. I am not sure of the date, yet my almanac assures me by tide and sunset that it must be correct. I sit at my desk, where I sat when I first wrote you from Chapelwaite, and look out over the dark sea from which the last of the light is rapidly fading. I shall never see more. This night is my night; I leave it for whatever shadows be.

How it heaves itself at the rocks, this sea! It throws clouds of sea-foam at the darkling sky in banners, making the floor beneath me tremble. In the window-glass I see my reflection, pallid as any vampire's. I have been without nourishment since the twenty-seventh of October, and should have been without water, had not Calvin left the carafe beside my bed on that day.

O, Cal! He is no more, Bones. He is gone in my place, in the place of this wretch with his pipestem arms and skull face who I see reflected back in the darkened glass. And yet he may be the more fortunate; for no dreams haunt him as they have haunted me these last days—twisted shapes that lurk in the nightmare corridors of delirium. Even now my hands tremble; I have splotched the page with ink.

Calvin confronted me on that morning just as I was about to slip away—and I thinking I had been so crafty. I had told him that I had decided we must leave, and asked him if he would go to Tandrell, some ten miles distant, and hire a trap where we were less notorious. He agreed to make the hike and I watched him leave by the sea-road. When he was out of sight I quickly made myself ready, donning both coat and muffler [for the weather had turned frosty; the first touch of coming winter was on that morning's cutting breeze]. I wished briefly for a gun, then laughed at myself for the wish. What avail guns in such a matter?

I let myself out by the pantry-way, pausing for a last look at sea and sky; for the smell of the fresh air against the putrescence I knew I should smell soon enough; for the sight of a foraging gull wheeling below the clouds.

I turned—and there stood Calvin McCann.

"You shall not go alone," said he; and his face was as grim as ever I have seen it.

"But Calvin—" I began.

"No, Not a word! We go together and do what we must, or I return you bodily to the house. You are not well. You shall not go alone."

It is impossible to describe the conflicting emotions that swept over me: confusion, pique, gratefulness—yet the greatest of them was love.

We made our way silently past the summer house and the sundial, down the weed-covered verge and into the woods. All was dead still—not a bird sang nor a wood-cricket chirruped. The world seemed cupped in a silent pall. There was only the ever-present smell of salt, and from far away, the faint tang of wood-smoke. The woods were a blazoned riot of colour, but, to my eye, scarlet seemed to predominate all.

Soon the scent of salt passed, and another, more sinister odour took its place; that rottenness which I have mentioned. When we came to the leaning bridge which spanned the Royal, I expected Cal to ask me again to defer, but he did not. He paused, looked at that grim spire which seemed to mock the blue sky above it, and then looked at me. We went on.

We proceeded with quick yet dread footsteps to James Boon's church. The door still hung ajar from our latter exit, and the darkness within seemed to leer at us. As we mounted the steps, brass seemed to fill my heart; my hand trembled as it touched the doorhandle and pulled it. The smell within was greater, more noxious than ever.

We stepped into the shadowy anteroom and, with no pause, into the main chamber.

It was a shambles.

Something vast had been at work in there, and a mighty destruction had taken place. Pews were overturned and heaped like jackstraws. The wicked cross lay against the east wall, and a jagged hole in the plaster above it testified to the force with which it had been hurled. The oil-lamps had been ripped from their high fixtures, and the reek of whale-oil mingled with the terrible stink which pervaded the town. And down the center aisle, like a ghastly bridal path, was a trail of black ichor, mingled with sinister tendrils of blood. Our eyes followed it to the pulpit—the only untouched thing in view. Atop it, staring at us from across that blasphemous Book with glazed eyes, was the butchered body of a lamb.

"God," Calvin whispered.

We approached, keeping clear of the slime on the floor. The room echoed back our footsteps and seemed to transmute them into the sound of gigantic laughter.

We mounted the narthex together. The lamb had not been torn or eaten; it appeared, rather, to have been *squeezed* until its blood-vessels had forcibly ruptured. Blood lay in thick and noisome puddles on the lectern itself, and about the base of it . . . *yet on the book it was transparent, and the crabbed runes could be read through it, as through coloured glass!*

"Must we touch it?" Cal asked, unfaltering.

"Yes. I must have it."

"What will you do?"

"What should have been done sixty years ago. I am going to destroy it."

We rolled the lamb's corpse away from the book; it struck the floor with a hideous, lolling thud. The blood-stained pages now seemed alive with a scarlet glow of their own.

My ears began to ring and hum; a low chant seemed to emanate from the walls themselves. From the twisted look on Cal's face I knew he heard the same. The floor beneath us trembled, as if the familiar which haunted this church came now unto us, to protect its own. The fabric of sane space and time seemed to twist and crack; the church seemed filled with spectres and litten with the hell-glow of eternal cold fire. It seemed that I saw James Boon, hideous and misshapen, cavorting around the supine body of a woman, and my Grand-uncle Philip behind him, an acolyte in a black, hooded cassock, who held a knife and a bowl.

"Deum vobiscum magna vermis—"

The words shuddered and writhed on the page before me, soaked in the blood of sacrifice, prize of a creature that shambles beyond the stars—

A blind, interbred congregation swaying in mindless, daemoniac praise; deformed faces filled with hungering, nameless anticipation—

And the Latin was replaced by an older tongue, ancient when Egypt was young and the Pyramids unbuilt, ancient when this Earth still hung in an unformed, boiling firmament of empty gas:

"Gyyagin vardar Yogsoggoth! Verminis! Gyyagin! Gyyagin! Gyyagin!"

The pulpit began to rend and split, pushing upward—

Calvin screamed and lifted an arm to shield his face. The narthex trembled with a huge, tenebrous motion like a ship wracked in a gale. I snatched up the book and held it away from me; it seemed filied with the heat of the sun and I felt that I should be cindered, blinded.

"Run!" Calvin screamed. "Run!"

But I stood frozen and the alien presence filled me like an ancient vessel that had waited for years—for generations!

"Gyyagin vardar!" I screamed. "Servant of Yogsoggoth, the Nameless One! The Worm from beyond Space! Star-Eater! Blinder of Time! Verminis! Now comes the Hour of Filling, the Time of Rending! Verminis! Alyah! Alyah! Gyyagin!"

Calvin pushed me and I tottered, the church whirling before me, and fell to the floor. My head crashed against the edge of an upturned pew, and red fire filled my head—yet seemed to clear it.

I groped for the sulphur matches I had brought.

Subterranean thunder filled the place. Plaster fell. The rusted bell in the steeple pealed a choked devil's carillon in sympathetic vibration.

My match flared. I touched it to the book just as the pulpit exploded upward in a rending explosion of wood. A huge black maw was discovered beneath; Cal tottered on the edge, his hands held out, his face distended in a wordless scream that I shall hear forever.

And then there was a huge surge of gray, vibrating flesh. The smell became a nightmare tide. It was a huge outpouring of a viscid, pustulant jelly, a huge and awful form that seemed to skyrocket from the very bowels of the ground. And yet, with a sudden horrible comprehension which no man can have known, I perceived *that it was but one ring, one segment, of a monster worm that had existed eyeless for years in the chambered darkness beneath that abominated church!*

The book flared alight in my hands, and the Thing seemed to scream soundlessly above me. Calvin was struck glancingly and flung the length of the church like a doll with a broken neck.

It subsided—the thing subsided, leaving only a huge and shattered hole surrounded with black slime, and a great screaming, mewling sound that seemed to fade through colossal distances and was gone.

I looked down. The book was ashes.

I began to laugh, then to howl like a struck beast.

All sanity left me, and I sat on the floor with blood streaming from my temple, screaming and gibbering into those unhallowed shadows while Calvin sprawled in the far corner, staring at me with glazing, horror-struck eyes.

I have no idea how long I existed in that state. It is beyond all telling. But when I came again to my faculties, shadows had drawn long paths around me and I sat in twilight. Movement had caught my eye, movement from the shattered hole in the narthex floor.

A hand groped its way over the riven floorboards.

My mad laughter choked in my throat. All hysteria melted into numb bloodlessness.

With terrible, vengeful slowness, a wracked figure pulled itself up from darkness, and a half-skull peered at me. Beetles crawled over the fleshless forehead. A rotted cassock clung to the askew hollows of mouldered collarbones. Only the eyes lived—red, insane pits that glared at me with more than lunacy; they glared with the empty life of the pathless wastes beyond the edges of the Universe.

It came to take me down to darkness.

That was when I fled, screeching, leaving the body of my lifelong friend unheeded in that place of dread. I ran until the air seemed to burst like magma in my lungs and brain. I ran until I had gained this possessed and tainted house again, and my room, where I collapsed and have lain like a dead man until to-day. I ran because even in my crazed state, and even in the shattered ruin of that dead-yet-animated shape, *I had seen the family resemblance.* Yet not of Philip or of Robert, whose likenesses hang in the upstairs gallery. *That rotted visage belonged to James Boon, Keeper of the Worm!*

He still lives somewhere in the twisted, lightless wanderings beneath Jerusalem's Lot and Chapelwaite—and *It* still lives. The burning of the book thwarted *It,* but there are other copies.

Yet I am the gateway, and I am the last of the Boone blood. For the good of all humanity I must die . . . and break the chain forever.

I go to the sea now, Bones. My journey, like my story, is at an end. May God rest you and grant you all peace.

CHARLES.

The odd series of papers above was eventually received by Mr. Everett Granson, to whom they had been addressed. It is assumed that a recurrence of the unfortunate brain fever which struck him originally following the death of his wife in 1848 caused Charles Boone to lose his sanity and murder his companion and longtime friend, Mr. Calvin McCann.

The entries in Mr. McCann's pocket journal are a fascinating exercise in forgery, undoubtedly perpetrated by Charles Boone in an effort to reinforce his own paranoid delusions.

In at least two particulars, however, Charles Boone is proved wrong. First, when the town of Jerusalem's Lot was "rediscovered" (I use the term historically, of course), the floor of the narthex, although rotted, showed no sign of explosion or huge damage. Although the ancient pews *were* overturned and several windows shattered, this can be assumed to be the work of vandals from neighboring towns over the years. Among the older residents of Preacher's Corners and Tandrell there is still some idle rumor about Jerusalem's Lot (perhaps, in his day, it was this kind of harmless folk legend which started Charles Boone's mind on its fatal course), but this seems hardly relevant.

Second, Charles Boone was not the last of his line. His grandfather, Robert Boone, sired at least two bastards. One died in infancy. The second took the Boone name and located in the town of Central Falls, Rhode Island. I am the final descendant of this offshoot of the Boone line; Charles Boone's second cousin, removed by three generations. These papers have been in my committal for ten years. I offer them for publication on the occasion of my residence in the Boone ancestral home, Chapelwaite, in the hope that the reader will find sympathy in his heart for Charles Boone's poor, misguided soul. So far as I can tell, he was correct about only one thing: this place badly needs the services of an exterminator.

There are some huge rats in the walls, by the sound.

Signed,
JAMES ROBERT BOONE
October 2, 1971.

ARTHUR CONAN DOYLE
The Parasite

1

MARCH 24. The spring is fairly with us now. Outside my laboratory window the great chestnut tree is all covered with the big, glutinous, gummy buds, some of which have already begun to break into little green shuttlecocks. As you walk down the lanes you are conscious of the rich, silent forces of nature working all around you. The wet earth smells fruitful and luscious. Green shoots are peeping out everywhere. The twigs are stiff with their sap; and the moist, heavy English air is laden with a faintly resinous perfume. Buds in the hedges, lambs beneath them—everywhere the work of reproduction going forward!

I can see it without, and I can feel it within. We also have our spring when the little arterioles dilate, the lymph flows in a brisker stream, the glands work harder, winnowing and straining. Every year nature readjusts the whole machine. I can feel the ferment in my blood at this very moment, and as the cool sunshine pours through my window I could dance about in it like a gnat. So I should, only that Charles Sadler would rush upstairs to know what was the matter. Besides, I must remember that I am Professor Gilroy. An old professor may afford to be natural, but when fortune has given one of the first chairs in the university to a man of four-and-thirty he must try and act the part consistently.

What a fellow Wilson is! If I could only throw the same enthusiasm into physiology that he does into psychology, I should become a Claude Bernard at the least. His whole life and soul and energy work to one end. He drops to sleep collating his results of the past day, and he wakes to plan his researches for the coming one. And yet, outside the narrow circle who follow his proceedings, he gets so little credit for it. Physiology is a recognized science. If I add even a brick to the edifice, everyone sees and applauds it. But Wilson is trying to dig the foundations for a science of the future. His work is underground and does not show. Yet he goes on uncomplainingly, corresponding with a hundred semi-maniacs in the hope of finding one reliable witness, sifting a hundred lies on the chance of gaining one little speck of truth, collating old books, devouring new ones, experimenting, lecturing, trying to light up in others the fiery interest which is consuming him. I am filled with wonder and admiration when I think of him, and yet, when he asks me to associate myself with his researches, I am compelled to tell him that, in their present state, they offer little attraction to a man who is devoted to exact science. If he could show me something positive and objective, I might then be tempted to approach the question from its physiological side. So long as half his subjects are tainted with *charlatanerie* and the other half with hysteria we physiologists must content ourselves with the body and leave the mind to our descendants.

No doubt I am a materialist. Agatha says that I am a rank one. I tell her that is an excellent reason for shortening our engagement, since I am in such urgent need of her spirituality. And yet I may claim to be a curious example of the effect of education upon temperament, for by nature I am, unless I deceive myself, a highly psychic man. I was a nervous, sensitive boy, a dreamer, a somnambulist, full of impressions and intuitions. My black hair, my dark eyes, my thin, olive face, my tapering fingers, are all characteristic of my real temperament, and cause experts like Wilson to claim me as their own. But my brain is soaked with exact knowledge. I have trained myself to deal only with fact and with proof. Surmise and fancy have no place in my scheme of thought. Show me what I can see with my microscope, cut with my scalpel, weigh in my balance, and I will devote a lifetime to its investigation. But when you ask me to study feelings, impressions, suggestions, you ask me to do what is distasteful and even demoralizing. A departure from pure reason affects me like an evil smell or a musical discord.

Which is a very sufficient reason why I am a little loath to go to Professor Wilson's tonight. Still I feel that I could hardly get out of the invitation without positive rudeness, and, now that Mrs. Marden and Agatha are going, of course I would not if I could. But I had rather meet them anywhere else. I know that Wilson would draw me into this nebulous semi-science of his if he could. In his enthusiasm he is perfectly impervious to hints or remonstrances. Nothing short of a positive quarrel will make him realize my aversion to the whole business. I have no doubt that he has some new mesmerist or clairvoyant or medium or trickster of some sort whom he is going to exhibit to us, for even his entertainments bear upon his hobby. Well, it will be a treat for Agatha, at any rate. She is interested in it, as woman usually is in whatever is vague and mystical and indefinite.

10:50 P.M. This diary-keeping of mine is, I fancy, the outcome of that scientific habit of mind about which I wrote this morning. I like to register impressions while they are fresh. Once a day at least I endeavor to define my own mental position. It is a useful piece of self-analysis, and has, I fancy, a steadying effect upon the character. Frankly, I must confess that my own needs what stiffening I can give it. I fear that, after all, much of my neurotic temperament survives, and that I am far from that cool, calm precision which characterizes Murdoch or Pratt-Haldane. Otherwise, why should the tomfoolery which I have witnessed this evening have set my nerves thrilling so that even now I am all unstrung? My only comfort is that neither Wilson nor Miss Penclosa nor even Agatha could have possibly known my weakness.

And what in the world was there to excite me? Nothing, or so little that it will seem ludicrous when I set it down.

The Mardens got to Wilson's before me. In fact, I was one of the last to arrive and found the room crowded. I had hardly time to say a word to Mrs. Marden and to Agatha, who was looking charming in white and pink, with glittering wheat-ears in her hair, when Wilson came twitching at my sleeve.

"You want something positive, Gilroy," said he, drawing me apart into a corner. "My dear fellow, I have a phenomenon—a phenomenon!"

I should have been more impressed had I not heard the same before. His sanguine spirit turns every firefly into a star.

"No possible question about the *bona fides* this time," said he, in answer, perhaps, to some little gleam of amusement in my eyes. "My wife has known her for many years. They both come from Trinidad, you know. Miss Penclosa has only been in England a month or two, and knows no one outside the university circle, but I assure you that the things she has told us suffice in themselves to establish clairvoyance upon an absolutely scientific basis. There is nothing like her, amateur or professional. Come and be introduced!"

I like none of these mystery-mongers, but the amateur least of all. With the paid performer you may pounce upon him and expose him the instant that you have seen through his trick. He is there to deceive you, and you are there to find him out. But what are you to do with the friend of your host's wife? Are you to turn on a light suddenly and expose her slapping a surreptitious banjo? Or are you to hurl cochineal over her evening frock when she steals round with her phosphorus bottle and her supernatural platitude? There would be a scene, and you would be looked upon as a brute. So you have your choice of being that or a dupe. I was in no very good humor as I followed Wilson to the lady.

Anyone less like my idea of a West Indian could not be imagined. She was a small, frail creature, well over forty, I should say, with a pale, peaky face, and hair of a very light shade of chestnut. Her presence was insignificant and her manner retiring. In any group of ten women she would have been the last whom one would have picked out. Her eyes were perhaps her most remarkable, and also, I am compelled to say, her least pleasant, feature. They were gray in color—gray with a shade of green— and their expression struck me as being decidedly furtive. I wonder if furtive is the word, or should I have said fierce? On second thoughts, feline would have expressed it better. A crutch leaning against the wall told me what was painfully evident when she rose: that one of her legs was crippled.

So I was introduced to Miss Penclosa, and it did not escape me that as my name was mentioned she glanced across at Agatha. Wilson had evidently been talking. And presently, no doubt, thought I, she will inform me by occult means that I am engaged to a young lady with wheat-ears in her hair. I wondered how much more Wilson had been telling her about me.

"Professor Gilroy is a terrible skeptic," said he; "I hope, Miss Penclosa, that you will be able to convert him."

She looked keenly up at me.

"Professor Gilroy is quite right to be skeptical if he has not seen anything convincing," said she. "I should have thought," she added, "that you would yourself have been an excellent subject."

"For what, may I ask?" said I.

"Well, for mesmerism, for example."

"My experience has been that mesmerists go for their subjects to those who are mentally unsound. All their results are vitiated, as it seems to me, by the fact that they are dealing with abnormal organisms."

"Which of these ladies would you say possessed a normal organism?" she asked. "I should like you to select the one who seems to you to have the best balanced mind. Should we say the girl in pink and white?—Miss Agatha Marden, I think the name is."

"Yes, I should attach weight to any results from her."

"I have never tried how far she is impressionable. Of course some people respond much more rapidly than others. May I ask how far your skepticism extends? I suppose that you admit the mesmeric sleep and the power of suggestion."

"I admit nothing, Miss Penclosa."

"Dear me, I thought science had got further than that. Of course I know nothing about the scientific side of it. I only know what I can do. You see the girl in red, for example, over near the Japanese jar. I shall will that she come across to us."

She bent forward as she spoke and dropped her fan upon the floor. The girl whisked round and came straight toward us, with an enquiring look upon her face, as if someone had called her.

"What do you think of that, Gilroy?" cried Wilson, in a kind of ecstasy.

I did not dare to tell him what I thought of it. To me it was the most barefaced, shameless piece of imposture that I had ever witnessed. The collusion and the signal had really been too obvious.

"Professor Gilroy is not satisfied," said she, glancing up at me with her strange little eyes. "My poor fan is to get the credit of that experiment. Well, we must try something else. Miss Marden, would you have any objection to my putting you off?"

"Oh, I should love it!" cried Agatha.

By this time all the company had gathered round us in a circle, the shirt-fronted men, and the white-throated women, some awed, some critical, as though it were something between a religious ceremony and a conjurer's entertainment. A red velvet armchair had been pushed into the center, and Agatha lay back in it, a little flushed and trembling slightly from excitement. I could see it from the vibration of the wheat-ears. Miss Penclosa rose from her seat and stood over her, leaning upon her crutch.

And there was a change in the woman. She no longer seemed

small or insignificant. Twenty years were gone from her age. Her eyes were shining, a tinge of color had come into her sallow cheeks, her whole figure had expanded. So I have seen a dull-eyed, listless lad change in an instant into briskness and life when given a task of which he felt himself master. She looked down at Agatha with an expression which I resented from the bottom of my soul—the expression with which a Roman empress might have looked at her kneeling slave. Then with a quick, commanding gesture she tossed up her arms and swept them slowly down in front of her.

I was watching Agatha narrowly. During three passes she seemed to be simply amused. At the fourth I observed a slight glazing of her eyes, accompanied by some dilation of her pupils. At the sixth there was a momentary rigor. At the seventh her lids began to droop. At the tenth her eyes were closed, and her breathing was slower and fuller than usual. I tried as I watched to preserve my scientific calm, but a foolish, causeless agitation convulsed me. I trust that I hid it, but I felt as a child feels in the dark. I could not have believed that I was still open to such weakness.

"She is in the trance," said Miss Penclosa.

"She is sleeping!" I cried.

"Wake her, then!"

I pulled her by the arm and shouted in her ear. She might have been dead for all the impression that I could make. Her body was there on the velvet chair. Her organs were acting—her heart, her lungs. But her soul! It had slipped from beyond our ken. Whither had it gone? What power had dispossessed it? I was puzzled and disconcerted.

"So much for the mesmeric sleep," said Miss Penclosa. "As regards suggestion, whatever I may suggest Miss Marden will infallibly do, whether it be now or after she has awakened from her trance. Do you demand proof of it?"

"Certainly," said I.

"You shall have it." I saw a smile pass over her face, as though an amusing thought had struck her. She stooped and whispered earnestly into her subject's ear. Agatha, who had been so deaf to me, nodded her head as she listened.

"Awake!" cried Miss Penclosa, with a sharp tap of her crutch upon the floor. The eyes opened, the glazing cleared slowly away, and the soul looked out once more after its strange eclipse.

We went away early. Agatha was none the worse for her strange excursion, but I was nervous and unstrung, unable to listen to or answer the stream of comments which Wilson was pouring out for my benefit. As I bade her good night Miss Penclosa slipped a piece of paper into my hand.

"Pray forgive me," said she, "if I take means to overcome your skepticism. Open this note at ten o'clock tomorrow morning. It is a little private test."

I can't imagine what she means, but there is the note, and it shall be opened as she directs. My head is aching, and I have written enough for tonight. Tomorrow I dare say that what seems so inexplicable will take quite another complexion. I shall not surrender my convictions without a struggle.

MARCH 25. I am amazed, confounded. It is clear that I must reconsider my opinion upon this matter. But first let me place on record what has occurred.

I had finished breakfast, and was looking over some diagrams with which my lecture is to be illustrated, when my housekeeper entered to tell me that Agatha was in my study and wished to see me immediately. I glanced at the clock and saw with surprise that it was only half past nine.

When I entered the room, she was standing on the hearth rug facing me. Something in her pose chilled me and checked the words which were rising to my lips. Her veil was half down, but I could see that she was pale and that her expression was constrained.

"Austin," she said, "I have come to tell you that our engagement is at an end."

I staggered. I believe that I literally did stagger. I know that I found myself leaning against the bookcase for support.

"But—but—" I stammered. "This is very sudden, Agatha."

"Yes, Austin, I have come here to tell you that our engagement is at an end."

"But surely," I cried, "you will give me some reason! This is unlike you, Agatha. Tell me how I have been unfortunate enough to offend you."

"It is all over, Austin."

"But why? You must be under some delusion, Agatha. Perhaps you have been told some falsehood about me. Or you may have misunderstood something that I have said to you. Only let me know what it is, and a word may set it all right."

"We must consider it all at an end."

"But you left me last night without a hint at any disagreement. What could have occurred in the interval to change you so? It must have been something that happened last night. You have been thinking it over and you have disapproved of my conduct. Was it the mesmerism? Did you blame me for letting that woman exercise her power over you? You know that at the least sign I should have interfered."

"It is useless, Austin. All is over."

Her voice was cold and measured; her manner strangely formal and hard. It seemed to me that she was absolutely resolved not to be drawn into any argument or explanation. As for me, I was shaking with agitation, and I turned my face aside, so ashamed was I that she should see my want of control.

"You must know what this means to me!" I cried. "It is the blasting of all my hopes and the ruin of my life! You surely will not inflict such a punishment upon me unheard. You will let me know what is the matter. Consider how impossible it would be for me, under any circumstances, to treat you so. For God's sake, Agatha, let me know what I have done!"

She walked past me without a word and opened the door.

"It is quite useless, Austin," said she. "You must consider our engagement at an end." An instant later she was gone, and, before I could recover myself sufficiently to follow her, I heard the hall door close behind her.

I rushed into my room to change my coat, with the idea of hurrying round to Mrs. Marden's to learn from her what the cause of my misfortune might be. So shaken was I that I could hardly lace my boots. Never shall I forget those horrible ten minutes. I had just pulled on my overcoat when the clock upon the mantelpiece struck ten.

Ten! I associated the idea with Miss Penclosa's note. It was lying before me on the table, and I tore it open. It was scribbled in pencil in a peculiarly angular handwriting.

"MY DEAR PROFESSOR GILROY [it said]: Pray excuse the personal nature of the test which I am giving you. Professor Wilson happened to mention the relations between you and my subject of this evening, and it struck me that nothing could be more convincing to you than if I were to suggest to Miss Marden that she should call upon you at half past nine tomorrow morning and suspend your engagement for half an hour or so. Science is so exacting that it is difficult to give a satisfying test, but I am convinced that this at least will be an action which she would be most unlikely to do of her own free will. Forget anything that she may have said, as she has really nothing whatever to do with it, and will certainly not recollect anything about it. I write this note to shorten your anxiety, and to beg you to forgive me for the momentary unhappiness which my suggestion must have caused you.

> "Yours faithfully,
> "HELEN PENCLOSA"

Really, when I had read the note, I was too relieved to be angry. It was a liberty. Certainly it was a very great liberty indeed on the part of a lady whom I had only met once. But after all, I had challenged her by my skepticism. It may have been, as she said, a little difficult to devise a test which would satisfy me.

And she had done that. There could be no question at all upon the point. For me hypnotic suggestion was finally established. It took its place from now onward as one of the facts of life. That Agatha, who of all women of my acquaintance has the best balanced mind, had been reduced to a condition of automatism appeared to be certain. A person at a distance had worked her as an engineer on the shore might guide a Brennan torpedo. A second soul had stepped in, as it were, had pushed her own aside, and had seized her nervous mechanism, saying: "I will work this for half an hour." And Agatha must have been unconscious as she came and as she returned. Could she make her way in safety through the streets in such a state? I put on my hat and hurried round to see if all was well with her.

Yes. She was at home. I was shown into the drawing room and found her sitting with a book upon her lap.

"You are an early visitor, Austin," said she, smiling.

"And you have been an even earlier one," I answered.

She looked puzzled. "What do you mean?" she asked.

"You have not been out today?"

"No, certainly not."

"Agatha," said I seriously, "would you mind telling me exactly what you have done this morning?"

She laughed at my earnestness.

"You've got on your professional look, Austin. See what comes of being engaged to a man of science. However, I will tell you, though I can't image what you want to know for. I got up at eight. I breakfasted at half past. I came into this room at ten minutes past nine and began to read the 'Memoirs of Mme. de Remusat.' In a few minutes I did the French lady the bad compliment of dropping to sleep over her pages, and I did you, sir, the very flattering one of dreaming about you. It is only a few minutes since I woke up."

"And found yourself where you had been before?"

"Why, where else should I find myself?"

"Would you mind telling me, Agatha, what it was that you dreamed about me? It really is not mere curiosity on my part."

"I merely had a vague impression that you came into it. I cannot recall anything definite."

"If you have not been out today, Agatha, how is it that your shoes are dusty?"

A pained look came over her face.

"Really, Austin, I do not know what is the matter with you this morning. One would almost think that you doubted my word. If my boots are dusty, it must be, of course, that I have put on a pair which the maid had not cleaned."

It was perfectly evident that she knew nothing whatever about the matter, and I reflected that, after all, perhaps it was better that I should not enlighten her. It might frighten her, and could serve no good purpose that I could see. I said no more about it, therefore, and left shortly afterward to give my lecture.

But I am immensely impressed. My horizon of scientific possibilities has suddenly been enormously extended. I no longer wonder at Wilson's demonic energy and enthusiasm. Who would not work hard who had a vast virgin field ready to his hand? Why, I have known the novel shape of a nucleolus, or a trifling peculiarity of striped muscular fiber seen under a 300-diameter lens, fill me with exultation. How petty do such researches seem when compared with this one which strikes at the very roots of life and the nature of the soul! I had always looked upon spirit as a product of matter. The brain, I thought, secreted the mind, as the liver does the bile. But how can this be when I see mind working from a distance and playing upon matter as a musician might upon a violin? The body does not give rise to the soul, then, but is rather the rough instrument by which the spirit manifests itself. The windmill does not give rise to the wind, but only indicates it. It was opposed to my whole habit of thought, and yet it was undeniably possible and worthy of investigation.

And why should I not investigate it? I see that under yesterday's date I said: "If I could see something positive and objective, I might be tempted to approach it from the physiological aspect." Well, I have got my test. I shall be as good as my word. The investigation would, I am sure, be of immense interest. Some of my colleagues might look askance at it, for science is full of unreasoning prejudices, but if Wilson has the courage of his convictions, I can afford to have it also. I shall go to him tomorrow morning—to him and to Miss Penclosa. If she can show us so much, it is probable that she can show us more.

2

MARCH 26. Wilson was, as I had anticipated, very exultant over my conversion, and Miss Penclosa was also demurely pleased at the result of her experiment. Strange what a silent, colorless creature she is save only when she exercises her power! Even talking about it gives her color and life. She seems to take a singular interest in me. I cannot help observing how her eyes follow me about the room.

We had the most interesting conversation about her own powers. It is just as well to put her views on record, though they cannot, of course, claim any scientific weight.

"You are on the very fringe of the subject," said she, when I had expressed wonder at the remarkable instance of suggestion which she had shown me. "I had no direct influence upon Miss Marden when she came round to you. I was not even thinking of her that morning. What I did was to set her mind as I might set the alarm of a clock so that at the hour named it would go off of its own accord. If six months instead of twelve hours had been suggested, it would have been the same."

"And if the suggestion had been to assassinate me?"

"She would most inevitably have done so."

"But this is a terrible power!" I cried.

"It is, as you say, a terrible power," she answered gravely, "and the more you know of it the more terrible will it seem to you."

"May I ask," said I, "what you meant when you said that this matter of suggestion is only at the fringe of it? What do you consider the essential?"

"I had rather not tell you."

I was surprised at the decision of her answer.

"You understand," said I, "that it is not out of curiosity I ask, but in the hope that I may find some scientific explanation for the facts with which you furnish me."

"Frankly, Professor Gilroy," said she, "I am not at all interested in science, nor do I care whether it can or cannot classify these powers."

"But I was hoping—"

"Ah, that is quite another thing. If you make it a personal matter," said she, with the pleasantest of smiles, "I shall be only too happy to tell you anything you wish to know. Let me see; what was it you asked me? Oh, about the further powers. Professor Wilson won't believe in them, but they are quite true all the same. For example, it is possible for an operator to gain complete command over his subject—presuming that the latter is a good one. Without any previous suggestion he may make him do whatever he likes."

"Without the subject's knowledge?"

"That depends. If the force were strongly exerted, he would know no more about it than Miss Marden did when she came round and frightened you so. Or, if the influence was less powerful, he might be conscious of what he was doing, but be quite unable to prevent himself from doing it."

"Would he have lost his own will power, then?"

"It would be overridden by another stronger one."

"Have you ever exercised this power yourself?"

"Several times."

"Is your own will so strong, then?"

"Well, it does not entirely depend upon that. Many have strong wills which are not detachable from themselves. The thing is to have the gift of projecting it into another person and superseding his own. I find that the power varies with my own strength and health."

"Practically, you send your soul into another person's body."

"Well, you might put it that way."

"And what does your own body do?"

"It merely feels lethargic."

"Well, but is there no danger to your own health?" I asked.

"There might be a little. You have to be careful never to let your own consciousness absolutely go; otherwise, you might experience some difficulty in finding your way back again. You must always preserve the connection, as it were. I am afraid I express myself very badly, Professor Gilroy, but of course I don't know how to put these things in a scientific way. I am just giving you my own experiences and my own explanations."

Well, I read this over now at my leisure, and I marvel at myself! Is this Austin Gilroy, the man who has won his way to the front by his hard reasoning power and by his devotion to fact? Here I am gravely retailing the gossip of a woman who tells me how her soul may be projected from her body, and how, while she lies in a lethargy, she can control the actions of people at a distance. Do I accept it? Certainly not. She must prove and re-prove before I yield a point. But if I am still a skeptic, I have at least ceased to be a scoffer. We are to have a sitting this evening, and she is to try if she can produce any mesmeric effect upon me. If she can, it will make an excellent starting point for our investigation. No one can accuse *me,* at any rate, of complicity. If she cannot, we must try and find some subject who will be like Caesar's wife. Wilson is perfectly impervious.

10 P.M. I believe that I am on the threshold of an epoch-making investigation. To have the power of examining these phenomena from inside—to have an organism which will respond, and at the same time a brain which will appreciate and criticize—that is surely a unique advantage. I am quite sure that Wilson would give five years of his life to be as susceptible as I have proved myself to be.

There was no one present except Wilson and his wife. I was seated with my head leaning back, and Miss Penclosa, standing in front and a little to the left, used the same long, sweeping strokes as with Agatha. At each of them a warm current of air seemed to strike me, and to suffuse a thrill and glow all through me from head to foot. My eyes were fixed upon Miss Penclosa's face, but as I gazed the features seemed to blur and to fade away. I was conscious only of her own eyes looking down at me, gray, deep, inscrutable. Larger they grew and larger, until they changed suddenly into two mountain lakes toward which I seemed to be falling with horrible rapidity. I shuddered, and as I did so some deeper stratum of thought told me that the shudder represented the rigor which I had observed in Agatha. An instant later I struck the surface of the lakes, now joined into one and down I went beneath the water with a fullness in my head and a buzzing in my ears. Down I went, down, down, and then with a swoop up again until I could see the light streaming brightly through the green water. I was almost at the surface when the word "Awake!" rang through my head, and, with a start, I found myself back in the armchair, with Miss Penclosa leaning on her crutch, and Wilson, his notebook in his hand, peeping over her shoulder. No heaviness or weariness was left behind. On the contrary, though it is only an hour or so since the experiment, I feel so wakeful that I am more inclined for my study than my bedroom. I see quite a vista of interesting experiments extending before us, and am all impatience to begin upon them.

MARCH 27. A blank day, as Miss Penclosa goes with Wilson and his wife to the Suttons'. Have begun Binet and Ferre's "Animal Magnetism." What strange, deep waters these are! Results, results, results—and the cause an absolute mystery. It is stimulating to the imagination, but I must be on my guard against that. Let us have no inferences nor deductions, and nothing but solid facts. I *know* that the mesmeric trance is true; I *know* that mesmeric suggestion is true; I *know* that I am myself sensitive to this force. That is my present position. I have a large new notebook which shall be devoted entirely to scientific detail.

Long talk with Agatha and Mrs. Marden in the evening about our marriage. We think that the summer vac. (the beginning of it) would be the best time for the wedding. Why should we delay? I grudge even those few months. Still, as Mrs. Marden says, there are a good many things to be arranged.

MARCH 28. Mesmerized again by Miss Penclosa. Experience much the same as before, save that insensibility came on more quickly. See Notebook A for temperature of room, barometric pressure, pulse, and respiration as taken by Professor Wilson.

MARCH 29. Mesmerized again. Details in Notebook A.

MARCH 30. Sunday, and a blank day. I grudge any interruption of our experiments. At present they merely embrace the physical signs which go with slight, with complete, and with extreme insensibility. Afterward we hope to pass on to the phenomena of suggestion and of lucidity. Professors have demonstrated these things upon women at Nancy and at the Salpetriere. It will be more convincing when a woman demonstrates it upon a professor, with a second professor as a witness. And that I should be the subject—I, the skeptic, the materialist! At least, I have shown that my devotion to science is greater than to my own personal consistency. The eating of our own words is the greatest sacrifice which truth ever requires of us.

My neighbor, Charles Sadler, the handsome young demonstrator of anatomy, came in this evening to return a volume of Virchow's "Archives" which I had lent him. I call him young, but, as a matter of fact, he is a year older than I am.

"I understand, Gilroy," said he, "that you are being experimented upon by Miss Penclosa.

"Well," he went on, when I had acknowledged it, "if I were you, I should not let it go any further. You will think me very impertinent, no doubt, but, none the less, I feel it to be my duty to advise you to have no more to do with her."

Of course I asked him why.

"I am so placed that I cannot enter into particulars as freely as I could wish," said he. "Miss Penclosa is the friend of my friend, and my position is a delicate one. I can only say this; that I have myself been the subject of some of the woman's experiments, and that they have left a most unpleasant impression upon my mind."

He could hardly expect me to be satisfied with that, and I tried hard to get something more definite out of him, but without success. Is it conceivable that he could be jealous at my having superseded him? Or is he one of those men of science who feel personally injured when facts run counter to their preconceived opinions? He cannot seriously suppose that because he has some vague grievance I am, therefore, to abandon a series of experiments which promise to be so fruitful of results. He appeared to be annoyed at the light way in which I treated his shadowy warnings, and we parted with some little coldness on both sides.

MARCH 31. Mesmerized by Miss P.

APRIL 1.   Mesmerized by Miss P. (Notebook A.)

APRIL 2.   Mesmerized by Miss P. (Sphygmographic chart taken by Professor Wilson.)

APRIL 3.   It is possible that this course of mesmerism may be a little trying to the general constitution. Agatha says that I am thinner and darker under the eyes. I am conscious of a nervous irritability which I had not observed in myself before. The least noise, for example, makes me start, and the stupidity of a student causes me exasperation instead of amusement. Agatha wishes me to stop, but I tell her that every course of study is trying, and that one can never attain a result without paying some price for it. When she sees the sensation which my forthcoming paper on "The Relation between Mind and Matter" may make, she will understand that it is worth a little nervous wear and tear. I should not be surprised if I got my F.R.S. over it.

Mesmerized again in the evening. The effect is produced more rapidly now, and the subjective visions are less marked. I keep full notes of each sitting. Wilson is leaving for town for a week or ten days, but we shall not interrupt the experiments, which depend for their value as much upon my sensations as on his observations.

APRIL 4.   I must be carefully on my guard. A complication has crept into our experiments which I had not reckoned upon. In my eagerness for scientific facts I have been foolishly blind to the human relations between Miss Penclosa and myself. I can write here what I would not breathe to a living soul. The unhappy woman appears to have formed an attachment for me.

I should not say such a thing, even in the privacy of my own intimate journal, if it had not come to such a pass that it is impossible to ignore it. For some time—that is, for the last week—there have been signs which I have brushed aside and refused to think of. Her brightness when I come, her dejection when I go, her eagerness that I should come often, the expression of her eyes, the tone of her voice—I tried to think that they meant nothing, and were, perhaps, only her ardent West Indian manner. But last night, as I awoke from the mesmeric sleep, I put out my hand, unconsciously, involuntarily, and clasped hers. When I came fully to myself, we were sitting with them locked, she looking up at me with an expectant smile. And the horrible thing was that I felt impelled to say what she expected me to say. What a false wretch I should have been! How I should have loathed myself today had I yielded to the temptation of that moment! But, thank God, I was strong enough to spring up and hurry from the room. I was rude, I fear, but I could not, no, I *could* not, trust myself another moment. I, a gentleman, a man of honor, engaged to one of the sweetest girls in England—and yet in a moment of reasonless passion I nearly professed love for this woman whom I hardly know. She is far older than myself and a cripple. It is monstrous, odious; and yet the impulse was so strong that, had I stayed another minute in her presence, I should have committed myself. What was it? I have to teach others the workings of our organism, and what do I know of it myself? Was it the sudden upcropping of some lower stratum in my nature—a brutal primitive instinct suddenly asserting itself? I could almost believe the tales of obsession by evil spirits, so overmastering was the feeling.

Well, the incident places me in a most unfortunate position. On the one hand, I am very loath to abandon a series of experiments which have already gone so far, and which promise such brilliant results. On the other, if this unhappy woman has conceived a passion for me—But surely even now I must have made some hideous mistake. She, with her age and her deformity! It is impossible. And then she knew about Agatha. She understood how I was placed. She only smiled out of amusement, perhaps, when in my dazed state I seized her hand. It was my half-mesmerized brain which gave it a meaning, and sprang with such bestial swiftness to meet it. I wish I could persuade myself that it was indeed so. On the whole, perhaps, my wisest plan would be to postpone our other experiments until Wilson's return. I have written a note to Miss Penclosa, therefore, making no allusion to last night, but saying that a press of work would cause me to interrupt our sittings for a few days. She has answered, formally enough, to say that if I should change my mind I should find her at home at the usual hour.

10 P.M. Well, well, what a thing of straw I am! I am coming to know myself better of late, and the more I know the lower I fall in my own estimation. Surely I was not always so weak as this. At four o'clock I should have smiled had anyone told me that I should go to Miss Penclosa's tonight, and yet, at eight, I was at Wilson's door as usual. I don't know how it occurred. The influence of habit, I suppose. Perhaps there is a mesmeric craze as there is an opium craze, and I am a victim to it. I only know that as I worked in my study I became more and more uneasy. I fidgeted. I worried. I could not concentrate my mind upon the papers in front of me. And then, at last, almost before I knew what I was doing, I seized my hat and hurried round to keep my usual appointment.

We had an interesting evening. Mrs. Wilson was present during most of the time, which prevented the embarrassment which one at least of us must have felt. Miss Penclosa's manner was quite the same as usual, and she expressed no surprise at my having come in spite of my note. There was nothing in her bearing to show that yesterday's incident had made any impression upon her, and so I am inclined to hope that I overrated it.

APRIL 5 (EVENING). No, no, no, I did not overrate it. I can no longer attempt to conceal from myself that this woman has conceived a passion for me. It is monstrous, but it is true. Again, tonight, I awoke from the mesmeric trance to find my hand in hers, and to suffer that odious feeling which urges me to throw away my honor, my career, everything, for the sake of this creature who, as I can plainly see when I am away from her influence, possesses no single charm upon earth. But when I am near her, I do not feel this. She rouses something in me, something evil, something I had rather not think of. She paralyzes my better nature, too, at the moment when she stimulates my worse. Decidedly it is not good for me to be near her.

Last night was worse than before. Instead of flying I actually sat for some time with my hand in hers talking over the most intimate subjects with her. We spoke of Agatha, among other things. What could I have been dreaming of? Miss Penclosa said that she was conventional, and I agreed with her. She spoke once or twice in a disparaging way of her, and I did not protest. What a creature I have been!

Weak as I have proved myself to be, I am still strong enough to bring this sort of thing to an end. It shall not happen again. I have sense enough to fly when I cannot fight. From this Sunday night onward I shall never sit with Miss Penclosa again. Never! Let the experiments go, let the research come to an end; anything is better than facing this monstrous temptation which drags me so low. I have said nothing to Miss Penclosa, but I shall simply stay away. She can tell the reason without any words of mine.

APRIL 6. Have stayed away as I said. It is a pity to ruin such an interesting investigation, but it would be a greater pity still to ruin my life, and I *know* that I can not trust myself with that woman.

11 P.M. God help me! What is the matter with me? Am I going mad? Let me try and be calm and reason with myself. First of all I shall set down exactly what occurred.

It was nearly eight when I wrote the lines with which this day begins. Feeling strangely restless and uneasy, I left my rooms and walked round to spend the evening with Agatha and her mother. They both remarked that I was pale and haggard. About nine Professor Pratt-Haldane came in, and we played a game of whist. I tried hard to concentrate my attention upon the cards, but the feeling of restlessness grew and grew until I found it impossible to struggle against it. I simply *could* not sit still at the table. At last, in the very middle of a hand, I threw my cards down and, with some sort of an incoherent apology about having an appointment, I rushed from the room. As if in a dream I have a vague recollection of tearing through the hall, snatching my hat from the stand, and slamming the door behind me. As in a dream, too, I have the impression of the double line of gas lamps, and my bespattered boots tell me that I must have run down the middle of the road. It was all misty and strange and unnatural. I came to Wilson's house; I saw Mrs. Wilson and I saw Miss Penclosa. I hardly recall what we talked about, but I do remember that Miss P. shook the head of her crutch at me in a playful way, and accused me of being late and of losing interest in our experiments. There was no mesmerism, but I stayed some time and have only just returned.

My brain is quite clear again now, and I can think over what has occurred. It is absurd to suppose that it is merely weakness and force of habit. I tried to explain it in that way the other night, but it will no longer suffice. It is something much deeper and more terrible than that. Why, when I was at the Mardens' whist table, I was dragged away as if the noose of a rope had been cast round me. I can no longer disguise it from myself. The woman has her grip upon me. I am in her clutch. But I must keep my head and reason it out and see what is best to be done.

But what a blind fool I have been! In my enthusiasm over my research I have walked straight into the pit, although it lay gaping before me. Did she not herself warn me? Did she not tell me, as I can read in my own journal, that when she has acquired power over a subject she can make him do her will? And she has acquired that power over me. I am for the moment at the beck and call of this creature with the crutch. I must come when she wills it. I must do as she wills. Worst of all, I must feel as she wills. I loathe her and fear her, yet, while I am under the spell, she can doubtless make me love her.

There is some consolation in the thought, then, that those odious impulses for which I have blamed myself do not really come from me at all. They are all transferred from her, little as I could have guessed it at the time. I feel cleaner and lighter for the thought.

APRIL 7. Yes, now, in broad daylight, writing coolly and with time for reflection, I am compelled to confirm everything which I wrote in my journal last night. I am in a horrible position, but, above all, I must not lose my head. I must pit my intellect against her powers. After all, I am no silly puppet, to dance at the end of a string. I have energy, brains, courage. For all her devil's tricks I may beat her yet. May! I *must,* or what is to become of me?

Let me try to reason it out! This woman, by her own explanation, can dominate my nervous organism. She can project herself into my body and take command of it. She has a parasite soul; yes, she is a parasite, a monstrous parasite. She creeps into my frame as the hermit crab does into the whelk's shell. I am powerless. What can I do? I am dealing with forces of which I know nothing. And I can tell no one of my trouble. They would set me down as a madman. Certainly, if it got noised abroad, the university would say that they had no need of a devil-ridden professor. And Agatha! No, no, I must face it alone.

3

I READ over my notes of what the woman said when she spoke about her powers. There is one point which fills me with dismay. She implies that when the influence is slight the subject knows what he is doing, but cannot control himself, whereas when it is strongly exerted, he is absolutely unconscious. Now, I have always known what I did, though less so last night than on the previous occasions. That seems to mean that she has never yet exerted her full powers upon me. Was ever a man so placed before?

Yes, perhaps there was, and very near me, too. Charles Sadler must know something of this! His vague words of warning take a meaning now. Oh, if I had only listened to him then, before I helped by these repeated sittings to forge the links of the chain which binds me! But I will see him today. I will apologize to him for having treated his warning so lightly. I will see if he can advise me.

4 P.M. No, he cannot. I have talked with him, and he showed such surprise at the first words in which I tried to express my unspeakable secret that I went no further. As far as I can gather (by hints and inferences rather than by any statement), his own experience was limited to some words or looks such as I have myself endured. His abandonment of Miss Penclosa is in itself a sign that he was never really in her toils. Oh, if he only knew his escape! He has to thank his phlegmatic Saxon temperament for it. I am black and Celtic, and this hag's clutch is deep in my nerves. Shall I ever get it out? Shall I ever be the same man that I was just one short fortnight ago?

Let me consider what I had better do. I cannot leave the university in the middle of the term. If I were free, my course would be obvious. I should start at once and travel in Persia. But would she allow me to start? And could her influence not reach me in Persia, and bring me back to within touch of her crutch? I can only find out the limits of this hellish power by my own bitter experience. I will fight and fight and fight—and what can I do more?

I know very well that about eight o'clock tonight that craving for her society, that irresistible restlessness, will come upon me. How shall I overcome it? What shall I do? I must make it impossible for me to leave the room. I shall lock the door and throw the key out of the window. But, then, what am I do do in the morning? Never mind about the morning. I must at all costs break this chain which holds me.

APRIL 8. Victory! I have done splendidly! At seven o'clock last night I took a hasty dinner, and then locked myself up in my bedroom and dropped the key into the garden. I chose a cheery novel, and lay in bed for three hours trying to read it, but really in a horrible state of trepidation, expecting every instant that I should become conscious of the impulse. Nothing of the sort occurred, however, and I awoke this morning with the feeling that a black nightmare had been lifted off me. Perhaps the creature realized what I had done, and understood that it was useless to try to influence me. At any rate, I have beaten her once, and if I can do it once, I can do it again.

It was most awkward about the key in the morning. Luckily, there was an under-gardener below, and I asked him to throw it up. No doubt he thought I had just dropped it. I will have doors and windows screwed up and six stout men to hold me down in my bed before I surrender myself to be hag-ridden in this way.

I had a note from Mrs. Marden this afternoon asking me to go round and see her. I intended to do so in any case, but had not expected to find bad news waiting for me. It seems that the Armstrongs, from whom Agatha has expectations, are due home from Adelaide in the *Aurora,* and that they have written to Mrs. Marden and her to meet them in town. They will probably be away for a month or six weeks, and, as the *Aurora* is due on Wednesday, they must go at once—tomorrow, if they are ready in time. My consolation is that when we meet again there will be no more parting between Agatha and me.

"I want you to do one thing, Agatha," said I, when we were alone together. "If you should happen to meet Miss Penclosa, either in town or here, you must promise me never again to allow her to mesmerize you."

Agatha opened her eyes.

"Why, it was only the other day that you were saying how interesting it all was, and how determined you were to finish your experiments."

"I know, but I have changed my mind since then."

"And you won't have it any more?"

"No."

"I am so glad, Austin. You can't think how pale and worn you have been lately. It was really our principal objection to going to London now that we did not wish to leave you when you were so pulled down. And your manner has been so strange occasionally—especially that night when you left poor Professor Pratt-Haldane to play dummy. I am convinced that these experiments are very bad for your nerves."

"I think so, too, dear."

"And for Miss Penclosa's nerves as well. You have heard that she is ill?"

"No."

"Mrs. Wilson told us so last night. She described it as a nervous fever. Professor Wilson is coming back this week, and of course Mrs. Wilson is very anxious that Miss Penclosa should be well again then, for he has quite a program of experiments which he is anxious to carry out."

I was glad to have Agatha's promise, for it was enough that this woman should have one of us in her clutch. On the other hand, I was disturbed to hear about Miss Penclosa's illness. It rather discounts the victory which I appeared to win last night. I remember that she said that loss of health interfered with her power. That may be why I was able to hold my own so easily. Well, well, I must take the same precautions tonight and see what comes of it. I am childishly frightened when I think of her.

APRIL 9. All went very well last night. I was amused at the gardener's face when I had again to hail him this morning and to ask him to throw up my key. I shall get a name among the servants if this sort of thing goes on. But the great point is that I stayed in my room without the slightest inclination to leave it. I do believe that I am shaking myself clear of this incredible bond—or is it only that the woman's power is in abeyance until she recovers her strength? I can but pray for the best.

The Mardens left this morning, and the brightness seems to have gone out of the spring sunshine. And yet it is very beautiful also as it gleams on the green chestnuts opposite my windows, and gives a touch of gaiety to the heavy, lichen-mottled walls of the old colleges. How sweet and gentle and soothing is Nature! Who would think that there lurked in her also such vile forces, such odious possibilities! For of course I understand that this dreadful thing which has sprung out at me is neither supernatural nor even preternatural. No, it is a natural force which this woman can use and society is ignorant of. The mere fact that it ebbs with her strength shows how entirely it is subject to physical laws. If I had time, I might probe it to the bottom and lay my hands upon its antidote. But you cannot tame the tiger when you are beneath his claws. You can but try to writhe away from him. Ah, when I look in the glass and see my own dark eyes and clear-cut Spanish face, I long for a vitriol splash or a bout of the smallpox. One or the other might have saved me from this calamity.

I am inclined to think that I may have trouble tonight. There are two things which make me fear so. One is that I met Mrs. Wilson in the street, and that she tells me that Miss Penclosa is better, though still weak. I find myself wishing in my heart that the illness had been her last. The other is that Professor Wilson comes back in a day or two, and his presence would act as a constraint upon her. I should not fear our interviews if a third person were present. For both these reasons I have a presentiment of trouble tonight, and I shall take the same precautions as before.

APRIL 10. No, thank God, all went well last night. I really could not face the gardener again. I locked my door and thrust the key underneath it, so that I had to ask the maid to let me out in the morning. But the precaution was really not needed, for I never had any inclination to go out at all. Three evenings in succession at home! I am surely near the end of my troubles, for Wilson will be home again either today or tomorrow. Shall I tell him of what I have gone through or not? I am convinced that I should not have the slightest sympathy from him. He would look upon me as an interesting case, and read a paper about me at the next meeting of the Psychical Society, in which he would gravely discuss the possibility of my being a deliberate liar, and weigh it against the chances of my being in an early stage of lunacy. No, I shall get no comfort out of Wilson.

I am feeling wonderfully fit and well. I don't think I ever lectured with greater spirit. Oh, if I could only get this shadow off my life, how happy I should be! Young, fairly wealthy, in the front rank of my profession, engaged to a beautiful and charming girl—have I not everything which a man could ask for? Only one thing to trouble me, but what a thing it is!

MIDNIGHT. I shall go mad. Yes, that will be the end of it. I shall go mad. I am not far from it now. My head throbs as I rest it on my hot hand. I am quivering all over like a scared horse. Oh, what a night I have had! And yet I have some cause to be satisfied also.

At the risk of becoming the laughing-stock of my own servant, I again slipped my key under the door, imprisoning myself for the night. Then, finding it too early to go to bed, I lay down with my clothes on and began to read one of Dumas's novels. Suddenly I was gripped—gripped and dragged from the couch. It is only thus that I can describe the overpowering nature of the force which pounced upon me. I clawed at the coverlet. I clung to the woodwork. I believe that I screamed out in my frenzy. It was all useless, hopeless. I *must* go. There was no way out of it. It was only at the outset that I resisted. The force soon became too overmastering for that. I thank goodness that there were no watchers there to interfere with me. I could not have answered for myself if there had been. And, besides the determination to get out, there came to me, also, the keenest and coolest judgment in choosing my means. I lit a candle and endeavored, kneeling in front of the door, to pull the key through with the feather-end of a quill pen. It was just too short and pushed it further away. Then with quiet persistence I got a paper-knife out of one of the drawers, and with that I managed to draw the key back. I opened the door, stepped into my study, took a photograph of myself from the bureau, wrote something across it, placed it in the inside pocket of my coat, and then started off for Wilson's.

It was all wonderfully clear, and yet disassociated from the rest of my life, as the incidents of even the most vivid dream might be. A peculiar double consciousness possessed me. There was the predominant alien will, which was bent upon drawing me to the side of its owner, and there was the feebler protesting personality, which I recognized as being myself, tugging feebly at the overmastering impulse as a led terrier might at its chain. I can remember recognizing these two conflicting forces, but I recall nothing of my walk, nor of how I was admitted to the house.

Very vivid, however, is my recollection of how I met Miss Penclosa. She was reclining on the sofa in the little boudoir in which our experiments had usually been carried out. Her head was rested on her hand, and a tiger-skin rug had been partly drawn over her. She looked up expectantly as I entered, and, as the lamplight fell upon her face, I could see that she was very pale and thin, with dark hollows under her eyes. She smiled at me, and pointed to a stool beside her. It was with her left hand that she pointed, and I, running eagerly forward, seized it—I loathe myself as I think of it—and pressed it passionately to my lips. Then, seating myself upon the stool, and still retaining her hand, I gave her the photograph which I had brought with me, and talked and talked and talked—of my love for her, of my grief over her illness, of my joy at her recovery, of the misery it was to me to be absent a single evening from her side. She lay quietly looking down at me with imperious eyes and her provocative smile. Once I remember that she passed her hand over my hair as one caresses a dog; and it gave me pleasure—the caress. I thrilled under it. I was her slave, body and soul, and for the moment I rejoiced in my slavery.

And then came the blessed change. Never tell me that there is not a Providence! I was on the brink of perdition. My feet were on the edge. Was it a coincidence that at that very instant help should come? No, no, no; there is a Providence, and its hand has drawn me back. There is something in the universe stronger than this devil woman with her tricks. Ah, what a balm to my heart it is to think so!

As I looked up at her I was conscious of a change in her. Her face, which had been pale before, was now ghastly. Her eyes were dull, and the lids dropped heavily over them. Above all, the look of a serene confidence had gone from her features. Her mouth had weakened. Her forehead had puckered. She was frightened and undecided. And as I watched the change my own spirit fluttered and struggled, trying hard to tear itself from the grip which held it—a grip which, from moment to moment, grew less secure.

"Austin," she whispered, "I have tried to do too much. I was not strong enough. I have not recovered yet from my illness. But I could not live longer without seeing you. You won't leave me, Austin? This is only a passing weakness. If you will only give me five minutes, I shall be myself again. Give me the small decanter from the table in the window."

But I had regained my soul. With her waning strength the influence had cleared away from me and left me free. And I was aggressive—bitterly, fiercely aggressive. For once at least I could make this woman understand what my real feelings toward her were. My soul was filled with a hatred as bestial as the love against which it was a reaction. It was the savage, murderous passion of the revolted serf. I could have taken the crutch from her side and beaten her face in with it. She threw her hands up, as if to avoid a blow, and cowered away from me into the corner of the settee.

"The brandy!" she gasped. "The brandy!"

I took the decanter and poured it over the roots of a palm in the window. Then I snatched the photograph from her hand and tore it into a hundred pieces.

"You vile woman," I said, "if I did my duty to society, you would never leave this room alive!"

"I love you, Austin; I love you!" she wailed.

"Yes," I cried, "and Charles Sadler before. And how many others before that?"

"Charles Sadler!" she gasped. "He has spoken to you? So, Charles Sadler, Charles Sadler!" Her voice came through her white lips like a snake's hiss.

"Yes, I know you, and others shall know you, too. You shameless creature! You knew how I stood. And yet you used your vile power to bring me to your side. You may, perhaps, do so again, but at least you will remember that you have heard me say that I love Miss Marden from the bottom of my soul, and that I loathe you, abhor you! The very sight of you and the sound of your voice fill me with horror and disgust. The thought of you is repulsive. That is how I feel toward you, and if it pleases you by your tricks to draw me again to your side as you have done tonight, you will at least, I should think, have little satisfaction in trying to make a lover out of a man who has told you his real opinion of you. You may put what words you will into my mouth, but you cannot help remembering—"

I stopped, for the woman's head had fallen back, and she had fainted. She could not bear to hear what I had to say to her! What a glow of satisfaction it gives me to think that, come what may, in the future she can never misunderstand my true feelings toward her. But what will occur in the future? What will she do next? I dare not think of it. Oh, if only I could hope that she will leave me alone! But when I think of what I said to her— Never mind; I have been stronger than she for once.

APRIL 11. I hardly slept last night, and found myself in the morning so unstrung and feverish that I was compelled to ask Pratt-Haldane to do my lecture for me. It is the first that I have ever missed. I rose at midday, but my head is aching, my hands quivering, and my nerves in a pitiable state.

Who should come round this evening but Wilson. He has just come back from London, where he has lectured, read papers, convened meetings, exposed a medium, conducted a series of experiments on thought transference, entertained Professor Richet of Paris, spent hours gazing into a crystal, and obtained some evidence as to the passage of matter through matter. All this he poured into my ears in a single gust.

"But you!" he cried at last. "You are not looking well. And Miss Penclosa is quite prostrated today. How about the experiments?"

"I have abandoned them."

"Tut, tut! Why?"

"The subject seems to me to be a dangerous one."

Out came his big brown notebook.

"That is of great interest," said he. "What are your grounds for saying that it is a dangerous one? Please give your facts in chronological order, with approximate dates and names of reliable witnesses with their permanent addresses."

"First of all," I asked, "would you tell me whether you have collected any cases where the mesmerist has gained a command over the subject and has used it for evil purposes?"

"Dozens!" he cried exultantly. "Crime by suggestion—"

"I don't mean suggestion. I mean where a sudden impulse comes from a person at a distance—an uncontrollable impulse."

"Obsession!" he shrieked, in an ecstasy of delight. "It is the rarest condition. We have eight cases, five well attested. You don't mean to say—" His exultation made him hardly articulate.

"No, I don't," said I. "Good evening! You will excuse me, but I am not very well tonight." And so at last I got rid of him, still brandishing his pencil and his notebook. My troubles may be bad to bear, but at least it is better to hug them to myself than to have myself exhibited by Wilson, like a freak at a fair. He has lost sight of human beings. Everything to him is a case and a phenomenon. I will die before I speak to him again upon the matter.

APRIL 12.   Yesterday was a blessed day of quiet, and I enjoyed an uneventful night. Wilson's presence is a great consolation. What can the woman do now? Surely, when she has heard me say what

I have said, she will conceive the same disgust for me which I have for her. She could not, no, she *could* not, desire to have a lover who had insulted her so. No, I believe I am free from her love—but how about her hate? Might she not use these powers of hers for revenge? Tut! why should I frighten myself over shadows? She will forget about me, and I shall forget about her, and all will be well.

APRIL 13.   My nerves have quite recovered their tone. I really believe that I have conquered the creature. But I must confess to living in some suspense. She is well again, for I hear that she was driving with Mrs. Wilson in the High Street in the afternoon.

APRIL 14.   I do wish I could get away from the place altogether. I shall fly to Agatha's side the very day that the term closes. I suppose it is pitiably weak of me, but this woman gets upon my nerves most terribly. I have seen her again, and I have spoken with her.

It was just after lunch, and I was smoking a cigarette in my study, when I heard the step of my servant Murray in the passage. I was languidly conscious that a second step was audible behind, and had hardly troubled myself to speculate who it might be, when suddenly a slight noise brought me out of my chair with my skin creeping with apprehension. I had never particularly observed before what sort of sound the tapping of a crutch was, but my quivering nerves told me that I heard it now in the sharp wooden clack which alternated with the muffled thud of the footfall. Another instant and my servant had shown her in.

I did not attempt the usual conventions of society, nor did she. I simply stood with the smouldering cigarette in my hand, and gazed at her. She in her turn looked silently at me, and at her look I remembered how in these very pages I had tried to define the expression of her eyes, whether they were furtive or fierce. Today they were fierce—coldly and inexorably so.

"Well," said she at last, "are you still of the same mind as when I saw you last?"

"I have always been of the same mind."

"Let us understand each other, Professor Gilroy," said she slowly. "I am not a very safe person to trifle with, as you should realize by now. It was you who asked me to enter into a series of experiments with you, it was you who won my affections, it was you who professed your love for me, it was you who brought me your own photograph with words of affection upon it, and, finally, it was you who on the very same evening thought fit to insult me most outrageously, addressing me as no man has ever dared to speak to me yet. Tell me that those words came from you in a moment of passion and I am prepared to forget and to forgive them. You did not mean what you said, Austin? You do not really hate me?"

I might have pitied this deformed woman—such a longing for love broke suddenly through the menace of her eyes. But then I thought of what I had gone through, and my heart set like flint.

"If ever you heard me speak of love," said I, "you know very well that it was your voice which spoke, and not mine. The only words of truth which I have ever been able to say to you are those which you heard when last we met."

"I know. Someone has set you against me. It was he!" She tapped with her crutch upon the floor. "Well, you know very well that I could bring you this instant crouching like a spaniel to my feet. You will not find me again in my hour of weakness, when you can insult me with impunity. Have a care what you are doing, Professor Gilroy. You stand in a terrible position. You have not yet realized the hold which I have upon you."

I shrugged my shoulders and turned away.

"Well," said she, after a pause, "if you despise my love, I must see what can be done with fear. You smile, but the day will come when you will come screaming to me for pardon. Yes, you will grovel on the ground before me, proud as you are, and you will curse the day that ever you turned me from your best friend into your most bitter enemy. Have a care, Professor Gilroy!" I saw a white hand shaking in the air, and a face which was scarcely human, so convulsed was it with passion. An instant later she was gone, and I heard the quick hobble and tap receding down the passage.

But she has left a weight upon my heart. Vague presentiments of coming misfortune lie heavy upon me. I try in vain to persuade myself that these are only words of empty anger. I can remember those relentless eyes too clearly to think so. What shall I do—ah, what shall I do? I am no longer master of my own soul. At any moment this loathsome parasite may creep into me, and then— I must tell someone my hideous secret—I must tell it or go mad. If I had someone to sympathize and advise! Wilson is out of the question. Charles Sadler would understand me only so far as his own experience carries him. Pratt-Haldane! He is a well-balanced man, a man of great common sense and resource. I will go to him. I will tell him everything. God grant that he may be able to advise me!

4

6:45 P.M. No, it is useless. There is no human help for me; I must fight this out single-handed. Two courses lie before me. I might become this woman's lover. Or I must endure such persecutions as she can inflict upon me. Even if none come, I shall live in a well of apprehension. But she may torture me, she may drive me mad, she may kill me: I will never, never, never give in. What can she inflict which would be worse than the loss of Agatha, and the knowledge that I am a perjured liar, and have forfeited the name of gentleman?

Pratt-Haldane was most amiable, and listened with all politeness to my story. But when I looked at his heavy set features, his slow eyes, and the ponderous study furniture which surrounded him, I could hardly tell him what I had come to say. It was all so substantial, so material. And, besides, what would I myself have said a short month ago if one of my colleagues had come to me with a story of demonic possession? Perhaps I should have been less patient than he was. As it was, he took notes of my statement, asked me how much tea I drank, how many hours I slept, whether I had been overworking much, had I had sudden pains in the head, evil dreams, singing in the ears, flashes before the eyes—all questions which pointed to his belief that brain congestion was at the bottom of my trouble. Finally he dismissed me with a great many platitudes about open-air exercise, and avoidance of nervous excitement. His prescription, which was for chloral and bromide, I rolled up and threw into the gutter.

No, I can look for no help from any human being. If I consult anymore, they may put their heads together and I may find myself in an asylum. I can but grip my courage with both hands, and pray that an honest man may not be abandoned.

APRIL 15. It is the sweetest spring within the memory of man. So green, so mild, so beautiful! Ah, what a contrast between nature without and my own soul so torn with doubt and terror! It has been an uneventful day, but I know that I am on the edge of an abyss. I know it, and yet I go on with the routine of my life. The one bright spot is that Agatha is happy and well and out of all danger. If this creature had a hand on each of us, what might she not do?

APRIL 16. The woman is ingenious in her torments. She knows how fond I am of my work, and how highly my lectures are thought of. So it is from that point that she now attacks me. It will end, I can see, in my losing my professorship, but I will fight to the finish. She shall not drive me out of it without a struggle.

I was not conscious of any change during my lecture this morning save that for a minute or two I had a dizziness and swimminess which rapidly passed away. On the contrary, I congratulated myself upon having made my subject (the functions of the red corpuscles) both interesting and clear. I was surprised, therefore, when a student came into my laboratory immediately after the lecture, and complained of being puzzled by the discrepancy between my statements and those in the textbooks. He showed me his notebook, in which I was reported as having in one portion of the lecture championed the most outrageous and unscientific heresies. Of course I denied it, and declared that he had misunderstood me, but on comparing his notes with those of his companions, it became clear that he was right, and that I really had made some most preposterous statements. Of course I shall explain it away as being the result of a moment of aberration, but I feel only too sure that it will be the first of a series. It is but a month now to the end of the session, and I pray that I may be able to hold out until then.

APRIL 26. Ten days have elapsed since I have had the heart to make any entry in my journal. Why should I record my own humiliation and degradation? I had vowed never to open it again. And yet the force of habit is strong, and here I find myself taking up once more the record of my own dreadful experiences—in much the same spirit in which a suicide has been known to take notes of the effects of the poison which killed him.

Well, the crash which I had foreseen has come—and that no further back than yesterday. The university authorities have taken my lectureship from me. It has been done in the most delicate way, purporting to be a temporary measure to relieve me from the effects of overwork, and to give me the opportunity of recovering my health. None the less, it has been done, and I am no longer Professor Gilroy. The laboratory is still in my charge, but I have little doubt that that also will soon go.

The fact is that my lectures had become the laughing-stock of the university. My class was crowded with students who came to see and hear what the eccentric professor would do or say next. I cannot go into the detail of my humiliation. Oh, that devilish woman! There is no depth of buffoonery and imbecility to which she has not forced me. I would begin my lecture clearly and well, but always with the sense of a coming eclipse. Then as I felt the influence I would struggle against it, striving with clenched hands and beads of sweat upon my brow to get the better of it, while the students, hearing my incoherent words and watching my contortions, would roar with laughter at the antics of their professor. And then, when she had once fairly mastered me, out would come the most outrageous things—silly jokes, sentiments as though I were proposing a toast, snatches of ballads, personal abuse even against some member of my class. And then in a moment my brain would clear again, and my lecture would proceed decorously to the end. No wonder that my conduct has been the talk of the colleges. No wonder that the University Senate has been compelled to take official notice of such a scandal. Oh, that devilish woman!

And the most dreadful part of it all is my own loneliness. Here I sit in a commonplace English bow-window, looking out upon a commonplace English street with its garish buses and its lounging policeman, and behind me there hangs a shadow which is out of all keeping with the age and place. In the home of knowledge I am weighed down and tortured by a power of which science knows nothing. No magistrate would listen to me. No paper would discuss my case. No doctor would believe my symptoms. My own most intimate friends would only look upon it as a sign of brain derangement. I am out of all touch with my kind. Oh, that devilish woman! Let her have a care! She may push me too far. When the law cannot help a man, he may make a law for himself.

She met me in the High Street yesterday evening and spoke to me. It was as well for her, perhaps, that it was not between the hedges of a lonely country road. She asked me with her cold smile whether I had been chastened yet. I did not deign to answer her. "We must try another turn of the screw," said she. Have a care, my lady, have a care! I had her at my mercy once. Perhaps another chance may come.

APRIL 28.   The suspension of my lectureship has had the effect also of taking away her means of annoying me, and so I have enjoyed two blessed days of peace. After all, there is no reason to despair. Sympathy pours in to me from all sides, and everyone agrees that it is my devotion to science and the arduous nature of my researches which have shaken my nervous system. I have had the kindest message from the council advising me to travel abroad, and expressing the confident hope that I may be able to resume all my duties by the beginning of the summer term. Nothing could be more flattering than their allusions to my career and to my services to the university. It is only in misfortune that one can test one's own popularity. This creature may weary of tormenting me, and then all may yet be well. May God grant it!

APRIL 29.   Our sleepy little town has had a small sensation. The only knowledge of crime which we ever have is when a rowdy undergraduate breaks a few lamps or comes to blows with a policeman. Last night, however, there was an attempt made to break into the branch of the Bank of England, and we are all in a flutter in consequence.

Parkenson, the manager, is an intimate friend of mine, and I found him very much excited when I walked round there after breakfast. Had the thieves broken into the counting house, they would still have had the safes to reckon with, so that the defense was considerably stronger than the attack. Indeed, the latter does not appear to have ever been very formidable. Two of the lower windows have marks as if a chisel or some such instrument had been pushed under them to force them open. The police should have a good clue, for the woodwork had been done with green paint only the day before, and from the smears it is evident that some of it has found its way on to the criminal's hands or clothes.

4:30 P.M.   Ah, that accursed woman! That thrice accursed woman! Never mind! She shall not beat me! No, she shall not! But, oh, the she-devil! She has taken my professorship. Now she would take my honor. Is there nothing I can do against her, nothing save—Ah, but, hard pushed as I am, I cannot bring myself to think of that!

It was about an hour ago that I went into my bedroom, and was brushing my hair before the glass, when suddenly my eyes lit upon something which left me so sick and cold that I sat down upon the edge of the bed and began to cry. It is many a long year since I shed tears, but all my nerve was gone, and I could but sob and sob in impotent grief and anger. There was my house jacket, the coat I usually wear after dinner, hanging on its peg by the wardrobe, with the right sleeve thickly crusted from wrist to elbow with daubs of green paint.

So this was what she meant by another turn of the screw! She had made a public imbecile of me. Now she would brand me as a criminal. This time she has failed. But how about the next? I dare not think of it—and of Agatha and my poor old mother! I wish that I were dead!

Yes, this is the other turn of the screw. And this is also what she meant, no doubt, when she said that I had not realized yet the power she has over me. I look back at my account of my conversation with her, and I see how she declared that with a slight exertion of her will her subject would be conscious, and with a stronger one unconscious. Last night I was unconscious. I could have sworn that I slept soundly in my bed without so much as a dream. And yet those stains tell me that I dressed, made my way out, attempted to open the bank windows, and returned. Was I observed? Is it possible that someone saw me do it and followed me home? Ah, what a hell my life has become! I have no peace, no rest. But my patience is nearing its end.

10 P.M. I have cleaned my coat with turpentine. I do not think that anyone could have seen me. It was with my screwdriver that I made the marks. I found it all crusted with paint, and I have cleaned it. My head aches as if it would burst, and I have taken five grains of antipyrine. If it were not for Agatha, I should have taken fifty and had an end of it.

MAY 3. Three quiet days. This hell fiend is like a cat with a mouse. She lets me loose only to pounce upon me again. I am never so frightened as when everything is still. My physical state is deplorable—perpetual hiccough and ptosis of the left eyelid.

I have heard from the Mardens that they will be back the day after tomorrow. I do not know whether I am glad or sorry. They were safe in London. Once here they may be drawn into the miserable network in which I am myself struggling. And I must tell them of it. I cannot marry Agatha so long as I know that I am not responsible for my own actions. Yes, I must tell them, even if it brings everything to an end between us.

Tonight is the university ball, and I must go. God knows I never felt less in the humor for festivity, but I must not have it said that I am unfit to appear in public. If I am seen there, and have speech with some of the elders of the university it will go a long way toward showing them that it would be unjust to take my chair away from me.

11:30 P.M. I have been to the ball. Charles Sadler and I went together, but I have come away before him. I shall wait up for him, however, for, indeed, I fear to go to sleep these nights. He is a cheery, practical fellow, and a chat with him will steady my nerves. On the whole, the evening was a great success. I talked to everyone who has influence, and I think that I made them realize that my chair is not vacant quite yet. The creature was at the ball—unable to dance, of course, but sitting with Mrs. Wilson. Again and again her eyes rested upon me. They were almost the last things I saw before I left the room. Once, as I sat sideways to her, I watched her, and saw that her gaze was following someone else. It was Sadler, who was dancing at the time with the second Miss Thurston. To judge by her expression, it is well for him that he is not in her grip as I am. He does not know the escape he has had. I think I hear his step in the street now, and I will go down and let him in. If he will—

MAY 4. Why did I break off in this way last night? I never went downstairs, after all—at least, I have no recollection of doing so. But, on the other hand, I cannot remember going to bed. One of my hands is greatly swollen this morning, and yet I have no remembrance of injuring it yesterday. Otherwise, I am feeling all the better for last night's festivity. But I cannot understand how it is that I did not meet Charles Sadler when I so fully intended to do so. Is it possible—My God, it is only too probable! Has she been leading me some devil's dance again? I will go down to Sadler and ask him.

MIDDAY. The thing has come to a crisis. My life is not worth living. But, if I am to die, then she shall come also. I will not leave her behind, to drive some other man mad as she has me. No, I have come to the limit of my endurance. She has made me as desperate and dangerous a man as walks the earth. God knows I have never had the heart to hurt a fly, and yet, if I had my hands now upon that woman, she should never leave this room alive. I shall see her this very day, and she shall learn what she has to expect from me.

I went to Sadler and found him, to my surprise, in bed. As I entered he sat up and turned a face toward me which sickened me as I looked at it.

"Why, Sadler, what has happened?" I cried, but my heart turned cold as I said it.

"Gilroy," he answered, mumbling with his swollen lips, "I have for some weeks been under the impression that you are a madman. Now I know it, and that you are a dangerous one as well. If it were not that I am unwilling to make a scandal in the college, you would now be in the hands of the police."

"Do you mean—" I cried.

"I mean that as I opened the door last night you rushed out upon me, struck me with both your fists in the face, knocked me down, kicked me furiously in the side, and left me lying almost unconscious in the street. Look at your own hand bearing witness against you."

Yes, there it was, puffed up, with sponge-like knuckles, as after some terrific blow. What could I do? Though he put me down as a madman, I must tell him all. I sat by his bed and went over all my troubles from the beginning. I poured them out with quivering hands and burning words which might have carried conviction to the most skeptical. "She hates you and she hates me!" I cried. "She revenged herself last night on both of us at once. She saw me leave the ball, and she must have seen you also. She knew how long it would take you to reach home. Then she had but to use her wicked will. Ah, your bruised face is a small thing beside my bruised soul!"

He was struck by my story. That was evident. "Yes, yes, she watched me out of the room," he muttered. "She is capable of it. But is it possible that she has really reduced you to this? What do you intend to do?"

"To stop it!" I cried. "I am perfectly desperate; I shall give her fair warning today, and the next time will be the last."

"Do nothing rash," said he.

"Rash!" I cried. "The only rash thing is that I should postpone it another hour." With that I rushed to my room, and here I am on the eve of what may be the great crisis of my life. I shall start at once. I have gained one thing today, for I have made one man, at least, realize the truth of this monstrous experience of mine. And, if the worst should happen, this diary remains as a proof of the goad that has driven me.

EVENING. When I came to Wilson's, I was shown up, and found that he was sitting with Miss Penclosa. For half an hour I had to endure his fussy talk about his recent research into the exact nature of the spiritualistic rap, while the creature and I sat in silence looking across the room at each other. I read a sinister amusement in her eyes, and she must have seen hatred and menace in mine. I had almost despaired of having speech with her when he was called from the room, and we were left for a few moments together.

"Well, Professor Gilroy—or is it Mr. Gilroy?" said she, with that bitter smile of hers. "How is your friend Mr. Charles Sadler after the ball?"

"You fiend!" I cried. "You have come to the end of your tricks now. I will have no more of them. Listen to what I say." I strode across and shook her roughly by the shoulder. "As sure as there is a God in heaven, I swear that if you try another of your deviltries upon me, I will have your life for it. Come what may, I will have your life. I have come to the end of what a man can endure."

"Accounts are not quite settled between us," said she, with a passion that equaled my own. "I can love, and I can hate. You had your choice. You chose to spurn the first; now you must test the other. It will take a little more to break your spirit, I see, but broken it shall be. Miss Marden comes back tomorrow, as I understand."

"What has that to do with you?" I cried. "It is a pollution that you should dare even to think of her. If I thought that you would harm her—"

She was frightened, I could see, though she tried to brazen it out. She read the black thought in my mind, and cowered away from me.

"She is fortunate in having such a champion," said she. "He actually dares to threaten a lonely woman. I must really congratulate Miss Marden upon her protector."

The words were bitter, but the voice and manner were more acid still.

"There is no use talking," said I. "I only came here to tell you—and to tell you most solemnly—that your next outrage upon me will be your last." With that, as I heard Wilson's step upon the stair, I walked from the room. Ay, she may look venomous and deadly, but, for all that, she is beginning to see now that she has as much to fear from me as I can have from her. Murder! It has an ugly sound. But you don't talk of murdering a snake or of murdering a tiger. Let her have a care now.

MAY 5. I met Agatha and her mother at the station at eleven o'clock. She is looking so bright, so happy, so beautiful. And she was so overjoyed to see me. What have I done to deserve such love? I went back home with them, and we lunched together. All the troubles seem in a moment to have been shredded back from my life. She tells me that I am looking pale and worried and ill. The dear child puts it down to my loneliness and the perfunctory attentions of a housekeeper. I pray that she may never know the truth! May the shadow, if shadow there must be, lie ever black across my life and leave hers in the sunshine. I have just come back from them, feeling a new man. With her by my side I think that I could show a bold face to anything which life might send.

5 P.M. Now, let me try to be accurate. Let me try to say exactly how it occurred. It is fresh in my mind, and I can set it down correctly, though it is not likely that the time will ever come when I shall forget the doings of today.

I had returned from the Mardens' after lunch, and was cutting some microscopic sections in my freezing microtome, when in an instant I lost consciousness in the sudden hateful fashion which has become only too familiar to me of late.

When my senses came back to me I was sitting in a small chamber, very different from the one in which I had been working. It was cozy and bright, with chintz-covered settees, colored hangings, and a thousand pretty little trifles upon the wall. A small ornamental clock ticked in front of me, and the hands pointed to half past three. It was all quite familiar to me, and yet I stared about for a moment in a half-dazed way until my eyes fell upon a cabinet photograph of myself upon the top of the piano. On the other side stood one of Mrs. Marden. Then, of course, I remembered where I was. It was Agatha's boudoir.

But how came I there, and what did I want? A horrible sinking came to my heart. Had I been sent here on some devilish errand? Had that errand already been done? Surely it must; otherwise, why should I be allowed to come back to consciousness? Oh, the agony of that moment! What had I done? I sprang to my feet in my despair, and as I did so a small glass bottle fell from my knees onto the carpet.

It was unbroken, and I picked it up. Outside was written "Sulphuric Acid. Fort." When I drew the round glass stopper, a thick fume rose slowly up, and a pungent, choking smell pervaded the room. I recognized it as one which I kept for chemical testing in my chambers. But why had I brought a bottle of vitriol into Agatha's chamber? Was it not this thick, reeking liquid with which jealous women had been known to mar the beauty of their rivals? My heart stood still as I held the bottle to the light. Thank God, it was full! No mischief had been done as yet. But had Agatha come in a minute sooner, was it not certain that the hellish parasite within me would have dashed the stuff into her—Ah, it will not bear to be thought of! But it must have been for that. Why else should I have brought it? At the thought of what I might have done my worn nerves broke down, and I sat shivering and twitching, the pitiable wreck of a man.

It was the sound of Agatha's voice and the rustle of her dress which restored me. I looked up, and saw her blue eyes, so full of tenderness and pity, gazing down at me.

"We must take you away to the country, Austin," she said. "You want rest and quiet. You look wretchedly ill."

"Oh, it is nothing!" said I, trying to smile. "It was only a momentary weakness. I am all right again now."

"I am so sorry to keep you waiting. Poor boy, you must have been here quite half an hour! The vicar was in the drawing room, and, as I knew that you did not care for him, I thought it better that Jane should show you up here. I thought the man would never go!"

"Thank God he stayed! Thank God he stayed!" I cried hysterically.

"Why, what is the matter with you, Austin?" she asked, holding my arm as I staggered up from the chair. "Why are you glad that the vicar stayed? And what is this little bottle in your hand?"

"Nothing," I cried, thrusting it into my pocket. "But I must go. I have something important to do."

"How stern you look, Austin! I have never seen your face like that. You are angry?"

"Yes, I am angry."

"But not with me?"

"No, no my darling! You would not understand."

"But you have not told me why you came."

"I came to ask you whether you would always love me—no matter what I did, or what shadow might fall on my name. Would you believe in me and trust me however black appearances might be against me?"

"You know that I would, Austin."

"Yes, I know that you would. What I do I shall do for you. I am driven to it. There is no other way out, my darling!" I kissed her and rushed from the room.

The time for indecision was at an end. As long as the creature threatened my own prospects and my honor there might be a question as to what I should do. But now, when Agatha—my innocent Agatha—was endangered, my duty lay before me like a turnpike road. I had no weapon, but I never paused for that. What weapon should I need, when I felt every muscle quivering with the strength of a frenzied man? I ran through the streets, so set upon what I had to do that I was only dimly conscious of the faces of friends whom I met—dimly conscious also that Professor Wilson met me, running with equal precipitance in the opposite direction. Breathless but resolute I reached the house and rang the bell. A white-cheeked maid opened the door, and turned whiter yet when she saw the face that looked in at her.

"Show me up at once to Miss Penclosa," I demanded.

"Sir," she gasped, "Miss Penclosa died this afternoon at half past three!"

MANLY WADE WELLMAN
Fearful Rock

1

THE SACRIFICE

ENID MANDIFER tried to stand up under what she had just heard. She managed it, but her ears rang, her eyes misted. She felt as if she were drowning.

The voice of Persil Mandifer came through the fog, level and slow, with the hint of that foreign accent which nobody could identify:

"Now that you know that you are not really my daughter, perhaps you are curious as to why I adopted you."

Curious . . . was that the word to use? But this man who was not her father after all, he delighted in understatements. Enid's eyes had grown clearer now. She was able to move, to obey Persil Mandifer's invitation to seat herself. She saw him, half sprawling in his rocking chair against the plastered wall of the parlor, under the painting of his ancient friend Aaron Burr. Was the rumor true, she mused, that Burr had not really died, that he still lived and planned ambitiously to make himself a throne in America? But Aaron Burr would have to be an old, old man—a hundred years old, or more than a hundred.

Persil Mandifer's own age might have been anything, but probably he was nearer seventy than fifty. Physically he was the narrowest of men, in shoulders, hips, temples and legs alike, so that he appeared distorted and compressed. White hair, like combed thistledown, fitted itself in ordered streaks to his high skull. His eyes, dull and dark as musket balls, peered expressionlessly above the nose like a stiletto, the chin like the pointed toe of a fancy boot. The fleshlessness of his legs was accentuated by tight trousers, strapped under the insteps. At his throat sprouted a frill of lace, after a fashion twenty-five years old.

At his left, on a stool, crouched his enormous son Larue. Larue's body was a collection of soft-looking globes and bladders—a tremendous belly, round-kneed short legs, puffy hands, a gross bald head between fat shoulders. His white linen suit was only a shade paler than his skin, and his loose, faded-pink lips moved incessantly. Once Enid had heard him talking to himself, had been close enough to distinguish the words. Over and over he had said: "I'll kill you. I'll kill you. I'll kill you."

These two men had reared her from babyhood, here in this low, spacious manor of brick and timber in the Ozark country. Sixteen or eighteen years ago there had been Indians hereabouts, but they were gone, and the few settlers were on remote farms. The Mandifers dwelt alone with their slaves, who were unusually solemn and taciturn for Negroes.

Persil Mandifer was continuing: "I have brought you up as a gentleman would bring up his real daughter—for the sole and simple end of making her a good wife. That explains, my dear, the governess, the finishing-school at St. Louis, the books, the journeys we have undertaken to New Orleans and elsewhere. I regret that this distressing war between the states," and he paused to draw from his pocket his enameled snuff-box, "should have made recent junkets impracticable. However, the time has come, and you are not to be despised. Your marriage is now to befall you."

"Marriage," mumbled Larue, in a voice that Enid was barely able to hear. His fingers interlaced, like fat white worms in a jumble. His eyes were for Enid, his ears for his father.

Enid saw that she must respond. She did so: "You have— chosen a husband for me?"

Persil Mandifer's lips crawled into a smile, very wide on his narrow blade of a face, and he took a pinch of snuff. "Your husband, my dear, was chosen before ever you came into this world," he replied. The smile grew broader, but Enid did not think it cheerful. "Does your mirror do you justice?" he teased her. "Enid, my foster-daughter, does it tell you truly that you are a beauty, with a face all lustrous and oval, eyes full of tender fire, a cascade of golden-brown curls to frame the whole?" His gaze wandered upon her body, and his eyelids drooped. "Does it convince you, Enid, that your figure combines rarely those traits of fragility and rondure that are never so desirable as when they occur together? Ah, Enid, had I myself met you, or one like you, thirty years ago—"

"Father!" growled Larue, as though at sacrilege. Persil Mandifer chuckled. His left hand, white and slender with a dark cameo upon the forefinger, extended and patted Larue's repellent bald pate, in superior affection.

"Never fear, son," crooned Persil Mandifer. "Enid shall go a pure bride to him who waits her." His other hand crept into the breast of his coat and drew forth something on a chain. It looked like a crucifix.

"Tell me," pleaded the girl, "tell me, fa—" She broke off, for she could not call him father. "What is the name of the one I am to marry?"

"His name?" said Larue, as though aghast at her ignorance.

"His name?" repeated the lean man in the rocking chair. The crucifix-like object in his hands began to swing idly and rhythmically, while he paid out chain to make its pendulum motion wider and slower. "He has no name."

Enid felt her lips grow cold and dry. "He has no—"

"He is the Nameless One," said Persil Mandifer, and she could discern the capital letters in the last two words he spoke.

"Look," said Larue, out of the corner of his weak mouth that was nearest his father. "She thinks that she is getting ready to run."

"She will not run," assured Persil Mandifer. "She will sit and listen, and watch what I have here in my hand." The object of the chain seemed to be growing in size and clarity of outline. Enid felt that it might not be a crucifix, after all.

"The Nameless One is also ageless," continued Persil Mandifer. "My dear, I dislike telling you all about him, and it is not really necessary. All you need know is that we—my fathers and I—have served him here, and in Europe, since the days when France was Gaul. Yes, and before that."

The swinging object really was increasing in her sight. And the basic cross was no cross, but a three-armed thing like a capital T. Nor was the body-like figure spiked to it; it seemed to twine and clamber upon that T-shape, like a monkey on a bracket. Like a monkey, it was grotesque, disproportionate, a mockery. That climbing creature was made of gold, or of something gilded over. The T-shaped support was as black and bright as jet.

Enid thought that the golden creature was dull, as if tarnished, and that it appeared to move; an effect created, perhaps, by the rhythmic swinging on the chain.

"Our profits from the association have been great," Persil Mandifer droned. "Yet we have given greatly. Four times in each hundred years must a bride be offered."

Mist was gathering once more, in Enid's eyes and brain, a thicker mist than the one that had come from the shock of hearing that she was an adopted orphan. Yet through it all she saw the swinging device, the monkey-like climber upon the T. And through it all she heard Mandifer's voice:

"When my real daughter, the last female of my race, went to the Nameless One, I wondered where our next bride would come from. And so, twenty years ago, I took you from a foundling asylum at Nashville."

It was becoming plausible to her now. There was a power to be worshipped, to be feared, to be fed with young women. She must go—no, this sort of belief was wrong. It had no element of decency in it, it was only beaten into her by the spell of the pendulum-swinging charm. Yet she had heard certain directions, orders as to what to do.

"You will act in the manner I have described, and say the things I have repeated, tonight at sundown," Mandifer informed her, as though from a great distance. "You will surrender yourself to the Nameless One, as it was ordained when first you came into my possession."

"No," she tried to say, but her lips would not even stir. Something had crept into her, a will not her own, which was forcing her to accept defeat. She knew she must go—where?

"To Fearful Rock," said the voice of Mandifer, as though he had heard and answered the question she had not spoken. "Go there, to that house where once my father lived and worshipped, that house which, upon the occasion of his rather mysterious death, I left. It is now our place of devotion and sacrifice. Go there, Enid, tonight at sundown, in the manner I have prescribed. . . ."

2

LIEUTENANT KANE LANARK was one of those strange and vicious heritage-anomalies of one of the most paradoxical of wars—a war where a great Virginian was high in Northern command, and a great Pennsylvanian stubbornly defended one of the South's principal strongholds; where the two presidents were both born in Kentucky, indeed within scant miles of each other; where father strove against son, and brother against brother, even more frequently and tragically than in all the jangly verses and fustian dramas of the day.

Lanark's birthplace was a Maryland farm, moderately prosperous. His education had been completed at the Virginia Military Institute, where he was one of a very few who were inspired by a quiet, bearded professor of mathematics who later became the Stonewall of the Confederacy, perhaps the continent's greatest tactician. The older Lanark was strongly for state's rights and mildly for slavery, though he possessed no Negro chattels. Kane, the younger of two sons, had carried those same attitudes with him as much as seven miles past the Kansas border, whither he had gone in 1861 to look for employment and adventure.

At that lonely point he met with Southern guerrillas, certain loose-shirted, weapon-laden gentry whose leader, a gaunt man with large, worried eyes, bore the craggy name of Quantrill and was to be called by a later historian the bloodiest man in American history. Young Kane Lanark, surrounded by sudden leveled guns, protested his sympathy with the South by birth, education and personal preference. Quantrill replied, rather sententiously, that while this might be true, Lanark's horse and money-belt had a Yankee look to them, and would be taken as prisoners of war.

After the guerrillas had galloped away, with a derisive laugh hanging in the air behind them, Lanark trudged back to the border and a little settlement, where he begged a ride by freight wagon to St. Joseph, Missouri. There he enlisted with a Union cavalry regiment just then in the forming, and his starkness of manner, with evidences about him of military education and good sense, caused his fellow recruits to elect him a sergeant.

Late that year, Lanark rode with a patrol through southern Missouri, where fortune brought him and his comrades face to face with Quantrill's guerrillas, the same that had plundered Lanark. The lieutenant in charge of the Federal cavalry set a most hysterical example for flight, and died of six Southern bullets placed accurately between his shoulder blades; but Lanark, as ranking non-commissioned officer, rallied the others, succeeded in withdrawing them in order before the superior force. As he rode last of the retreat, he had the fierce pleasure of engaging and sabering an overzealous guerrilla, who had caught up with him. The patrol rejoined its regiment with only two lost, the colonel was pleased to voice congratulations and Sergeant Lanark became Lieutenant Lanark, vice the slain officer.

In April of 1862, General Curtis, recently the victor in the desperately fought battle of Pea Ridge, showed trust and understanding when he gave Lieutenant Lanark a scouting party of twenty picked riders, with orders to seek yet another encounter with the marauding Quantrill. Few Union officers wanted anything to do with Quantrill, but Lanark, remembering his harsh treatment at those avaricious hands, yearned to kill the guerrilla chieftain with his own proper sword. On the afternoon of April fifth, beneath a sun bright but none too warm, the scouting patrol rode down a trail at the bottom of a great, trough-like valley just south of the Missouri-Arkansas border. Two pairs of men, those with the surest-footed mounts, acted as flanking parties high on the opposite slopes, and a watchful corporal by the name of Googan walked his horse well in advance of the main body. The others rode two and two, with Lanark at the head and Sergeant Jaeger, heavy-set and morosely keen of eye, at the rear.

A photograph survives of Lieutenant Kane Lanark as he appeared that very spring—his breadth of shoulder and slimness of waist accentuated by the snug blue cavalry jacket that terminated at his sword-belt, his ruddy, beak-nosed face shaded by a wide black hat with a gold cord. He wore a mustache, trim but not gay, and his long chin alone of all his command went smooth-shaven. To these details be it added that he rode his bay gelding easily, with a light, sure hand on the reins, and that he had the air of one who knew his present business.

The valley opened at length upon a wide level platter of land among high, pine-tufted hills. The flat expanse was no more than half timbered, though clever enemies might advance unseen across it if they exercised caution and foresight enough to slip from one belt or clump of trees to the next. Almost at the center of the level, a good five miles from where Lanark now halted his command, stood a single great chimney or finger of rock, its lean tip more than twice the height of the tallest tree within view.

To this geologic curiosity the eyes of Lieutenant Lanark snapped at once.

"Sergeant!" he called, and Jaeger sidled his horse close.

"We'll head for that rock, and stop there," Lanark announced. "It's a natural watch-tower, and from the top of it we can see everything, even better than we could if we rode clear across flat ground to those hills. And if Quantrill is west of us, which I'm sure he is, I'd like to see him coming a long way off, so as to know whether to fight or run."

"I agree with you, sir," said Jaeger. He peered through narrow, puffy lids at the pinnacle, and gnawed his shaggy lower lip. "I shall lift up mine eyes unto the rocks, from whence cometh my help," he misquoted reverently. The sergeant was full of garbled Scripture, and the men called him "Bible" Jaeger behind that wide back of his. This did not mean that he was soft, dreamy or easily fooled; Curtis had chosen him as sagely as he had chosen Lanark.

Staying in the open as much as possible, the party advanced upon the rock. They found it standing above a soft, grassy hollow, which in turn ran eastward from the base of the rock to a considerable ravine, dark and full of timber. As they spread out to the approach, they found something else; a house stood in the hollow, shadowed by the great pinnacle.

"It looks deserted, sir," volunteered Jaeger, at Lanark's bridle-elbow. "No sign of life."

"Perhaps," said Lanark. "Deploy the men, and we'll close in from all sides. Then you, with one man, enter the back door. I'll take another and enter the front."

"Good, sir." The sergeant kneed his horse into a faster walk, passing from one to another of the three corporals with muttered orders. Within sixty seconds the patrol closed upon the house like a twenty-fingered hand. Lanark saw that the building had once been pretentious—two stories, stoutly made of good lumber that must have been carted from a distance, with shuttered windows and a high peaked roof. Now it was a paint-starved gray, with deep veins and traceries of dirty black upon its clapboards. He dismounted before the piazza with its four pillar-like posts, and threw his reins to a trooper.

"Suggs!" he called, and obediently his own personal orderly, a plump blond youth, dropped out of the saddle. Together they walked up on the resounding planks of the piazza. Lanark, his ungloved right hand swinging free beside his holster, knocked at the heavy front door with his left fist. There was no answer. He tried the knob, and after a moment of shoving, the hinges creaked and the door went open.

They walked into a dark front hall, then into a parlor with dust upon the rug and the fine furniture, and rectangles of pallor upon the walls where pictures had once hung for years. They could hear echoes of their every movement, as anyone will hear in a house to which he is not accustomed. Beyond the parlor, they came to an ornate chandelier with crystal pendants, and at the rear stood a sideboard of dark, hard wood. Its drawers all hung half open, as if the silver and linen had been hastily removed. Above it hung plate-racks, also empty.

Feet sounded in a room to the rear, and then Jaeger's voice, asking if his lieutenant were inside. Lanark met him in the kitchen, conferred; then together they mounted the stairs in the front hall.

Several musty bedrooms, darkened by closed shutters, occupied the second floor. The beds had dirty mattresses, but no sheets or blankets.

"All clear in the house," pronounced Lanark. "Jaeger, go and detail a squad to reconnoiter in that little ravine east of here—we want no rebel sharpshooters sneaking up on us from that point. Then leave a picket there, put a man on top of the rock, and guards at the front and rear of this house. And have some of the others police up the house itself. We may stay here for two days, even longer."

The sergeant saluted, then went to bellow his orders, and troopers dashed hither and thither to obey. In a moment the sound of sweeping arose from the parlor. Lanark, to whom it suggested spring cleaning, sneezed at thought of the dust, then gave Suggs directions about the care of his bay. Unbuckling his saber, he hung it upon the saddle, but his revolver he retained. "You're in charge, Jaeger," he called, and sauntered away toward the wooded cleft.

His legs needed the exercise; he could feel them straightening by degrees after their long clamping to his saddle-flaps. He was uncomfortably dusty, too, and there must be water at the bottom of the ravine. Walking into the shade of the trees, he heard, or fancied he heard, a trickling sound. The slope was steep here, and he walked fast to maintain an easy balance upon it, for a minute and then two. There was water ahead, all right, for it gleamed through the leafage. And something else gleamed, something pink.

That pinkness was certainly flesh. His right hand dropped quickly to his revolver-butt, and he moved forward carefully. Stooping, he took advantage of the bushy cover, at the same time avoiding a touch that might snap or rustle the foliage. He could hear a voice now, soft and rhythmic. Lanark frowned. A woman's voice? His right hand still at his weapon, his left caught and carefully drew down a spray of willow. He gazed into an open space beyond.

It was a woman, all right, within twenty yards of him. She stood ankle-deep in a swift, narrow rush of brook-water, and her fine body was nude, every graceful curve of it, with a cascade of golden-brown hair falling and floating about her shoulders. She seemed to be praying, but her eyes were not lifted. They stared at a hand-mirror, that she held up to catch the last flash of the setting sun.

3

THE IMAGE IN THE CELLAR

LANARK, A young, serious-minded bachelor in an era when women swaddled themselves inches deep in fabric, had never seen such a sight before; and to his credit be it said that his first and strongest emotion was proper embarrassment for the girl in the stream. He had a momentary impulse to slip back and away. Then he remembered that he had ordered a patrol to explore this place; it would be here within moments.

Therefore he stepped into the open, wondering at the time, as well as later, if he did well.

"Miss," he said gently. "Miss, you'd better put on your things. My men—"

She stared, squeaked in fear, dropped the mirror and stood motionless. Then she seemed to gather herself for flight. Lanark realized that the trees beyond her were thick and might hide enemies, that she was probably a resident of this rebel-inclined region and might be a decoy for such as himself. He whipped out his revolver, holding it at the ready but not pointing it.

"Don't run," he warned her sharply. "Are those your clothes beside you? Put them on at once."

She caught up a dress of flowered calico and fairly flung it on over her head. His embarrassment subsided a little, and he came another pace or two into the open. She was pushing her feet—very small feet they were—into heelless shoes. Her hands quickly gathered up some underthings and wadded them into a bundle. She gazed at him apprehensively, questioningly. Her hastily donned dress remained unfastened at the throat, and he could see the panicky stir of her heart in her half-bared bosom.

"I'm sorry," he went on, "but I think you'd better come up to the house with me."

"House?" she repeated fearfully, and her dark, wide eyes turned to look beyond him. Plainly she knew which house he meant. "You—live there?"

"I'm staying there at this time."

"You—came for me?" Apparently she had expected someone to come.

But instead of answering, he put a question of his own. "To whom were you talking just now? I could hear you."

"I—I said the words. The words my fath—" She broke off, wretchedly, and Lanark was forced to think how pretty she was in her confusion. "The words that Persil Mandifer told me to say." Her eyes on his, she continued softly: "I came to meet the Nameless One. Are you the—Nameless One?"

"I am certainly not nameless," he replied. "I am Lieutenant Lanark, of the Federal Army of the Frontier, at your service." He bowed slightly, which made it more formal. "Now, come along with me."

He took her by the wrist, which shook in his big left hand. Together they went back eastward through the ravine, in the direction of the house.

Before they reached it, she told him her name, and that the big natural pillar was called Fearful Rock. She also assured him that she knew nothing of Quantrill and his guerrillas; and a fourth item of news shook Lanark to his spurred heels, the first non-military matter that had impressed him in more than a year.

An hour later, Lanark and Jaeger finished an interview with her in the parlor. They called Suggs, who conducted the young woman up to one of the bedrooms. Then lieutenant and sergeant faced each other. The light was dim, but each saw bafflement and uneasiness in the face of the other.

"Well?" challenged Lanark.

Jaeger produced a clasp-knife, opened it, and pared thoughtfully at a thumbnail. "I'll take my oath," he ventured, "that this Miss Enid Mandifer is telling the gospel truth.

"Truth!" exploded Lanark scornfully. "Mountain-folk ignorance, I call it. Nobody believes in those devil-things these days."

"Oh, yes, somebody does," said Jaeger, mildly but definitely. "I do." He put away his knife and fumbled within his blue army shirt. "Look here, Lieutenant."

It was a small book he held out, little more than a pamphlet in size and thickness. On its cover of gray paper appeared the smudged woodcut of an owl against a full moon, and the title:

John George Hohman's
POW-WOWS
or
LONG LOST FRIEND

"I got it when I was a young lad in Pennsylvania," explained Jaeger, almost reverently. "Lots of Pennsylvania people carry this book, as I do." He opened the little volume, and read from the back of the title page:

" 'Whosoever carries this book with him is safe from all his enemies, visible or invisible; and whoever has this book with him cannot die without the holy corpse of Jesus Christ, nor drown in any water nor burn up in any fire, nor can any unjust sentence be passed upon him.' "

Lanark put out his hand for the book, and Jaeger surrendered it, somewhat hesitantly. "I've heard of supposed witches in Pennsylvania," said the officer. "Hexes, I believe they're called. Is this a witch book?"

"No, sir. Nothing about black magic. See the cross on that page? It's a protection against witches."

"I thought that only Catholics used the cross," said Lanark.

"No. Not only Catholics."

"Hmm." Lanark passed the thing back. "Superstition, I call it. Nevertheless, you speak this much truth: that girl is in earnest, she believes what she told us. Her father, or stepfather, or whoever he is, sent her up here on some ridiculous errand—perhaps a dangerous one." He paused. "Or I may be misjudging her. It may be a clever scheme, Jaeger—a scheme to get a spy in among us."

The sergeant's big bearded head wagged negation. "No, sir. If

she was telling a lie, it'd be a more believable one, wouldn't it?"
He opened his talisman book again. "If the lieutenant please,
there's a charm in here, against being shot or stabbed. It might
be a good thing, seeing there's a war going on—perhaps the
lieutenant would like me to copy it out?"

"No, thanks." Lanark drew forth his own charm against evil
and nervousness, a leather case that contained cheroots. Jaeger,
who had convictions against the use of tobacco, turned away
disapprovingly as his superior bit off the end of a fragrant brown
cylinder and kindled a match.

"Let me look at that what-do-you-call-it book again," he requested, and for a second time Jaeger passed the little volume
over, then saluted and retired.

Darkness was gathering early, what with the position of the
house in the grassy hollow, and the pinnacle of Fearful Rock
standing between it and the sinking sun to westward. Lanark called
for Suggs to bring a candle, and, when the orderly obeyed, directed
him to take some kind of supper upstairs to Enid Mandifer. Left
alone, the young officer seated himself in a newly dusted armchair
of massive dark wood, emitted a cloud of blue tobacco smoke,
and opened the *Long Lost Friend.*

It had no publication date, but John George Hohman, the
author, dated his preface from Berks County, Pennsylvania, on
July 31, 1819. In the secondary preface filled with testimonials as
to the success of Hohman's miraculous cures, was included the
pious ejaculation: "The Lord bless the beginning and the end of
this little work, and be with us, that we may not misuse it, and
thus commit a heavy sin!"

"Amen to that!" said Lanark to himself, quite soberly. Despite
his assured remarks to Jaeger, he was somewhat repelled and
nervous because of the things Enid Mandifer had told him.

Was there, then, potentiality for such supernatural evil in this
enlightened Nineteenth Century, even in the pages of the book
he held? He read further, and came upon a charm to be recited
against violence and danger, perhaps the very one Jaeger had
offered to copy for him. It began rather sonorously: "The peace
of our Lord Jesus Christ be with me. Oh shot, stand still! In the
name of the mighty prophets Agtion and Elias, and do not kill
me. . . ."

Lanark remembered the name of Elias from his boyhood Sunday
schooling, but Agtion's identity, as a prophet or otherwise, escaped

him. He resolved to ask Jaeger; and, as though the thought had acted as a summons, Jaeger came almost running into the room.

"Lieutenant, sir! Lieutenant!" he said hoarsely.

"Yes, Sergeant Jaeger?" Lanark rose, stared questioningly, and held out the book. Jaeger took it automatically, and as automatically stowed it inside his shirt.

"I can prove, sir, that there's a real devil here," he mouthed unsteadily.

"What?" demanded Lanark. "Do you realize what you're saying, man? Explain yourself."

"Come, sir," Jaeger almost pleaded, and led the way into the kitchen. "It's down in the cellar."

From a little heap on a table he picked up a candle, and then opened a door full of darkness.

The stairs to the cellar were shaky to Lanark's feet, and beneath him was solid black shadow, smelling strongly of damp earth. Jaeger, stamping heavily ahead, looked back and upward. That broad, bearded face, that had not lost its full-blooded flush in the hottest fighting at Pea Ridge, had grown so pallid as almost to give off sickly light. Lanark began to wonder if all this theatrical approach would not make the promised devil seem ridiculous, anticlimactic—the flutter of an owl, the scamper of a rat, or something of that sort.

"You have the candle, sergeant," he reminded, and the echo of his voice momentarily startled him. "Strike a match, will you?"

"Yes, sir." Jaeger had raised a knee to tighten his stripe-sided trousers. A snapping scrape, a burst of flame, and the candle glow illuminated them both. It revealed, too, the cellar, walled with stones but floored with clay. As they finished the descent, Lanark could feel the soft grittiness of that clay under his bootsoles. All around them lay rubbish—boxes, casks, stacks of broken pots and dishes, bundles of kindling.

"Here," Jaeger was saying, "here is what I found."

He walked around the foot of the stairs. Beneath the slope of the flight lay a long, narrow case, made of plain, heavy boards. It was unpainted and appeared ancient. As Jaeger lowered the light in his hand, Lanark saw that the joinings were secured with huge nails, apparently forged by hand. Such nails had been used in building the older sheds on his father's Maryland estate. Now there was a creak of wooden protest as Jaeger pried up the loosened lid of the coffin-like box.

Inside lay something long and ruddy. Lanark saw a head and shoulders, and started violently. Jaeger spoke again:

"An image, sir. A heathen image." The light made grotesque the sergeant's face, one heavy half fully illumined, the other secret and lost in the black shadow. "Look at it."

Lanark, too, stooped for a closer examination. The form was of human length, or rather more; but it was not finished, was neither divided into legs below nor extended into arms at the roughly shaped shoulders. The head, too, had been molded without features, though from either side, where the ears should have been it sprouted up-curved horns like a bison's. Lanark felt a chill creep upon him, whence he knew not.

"It's Satan's own image," Jaeger was mouthing deeply. " 'Thou shalt not make unto thee any graven image—' "

With one foot he turned the coffin-box upon its side. Lanark took a quick stride backward, just in time to prevent the ruddy form from dropping out upon his toes. A moment later, Jaeger had spurned the thing. It broke, with a crashing sound like crockery, and two more trampling kicks of the sergeant's heavy boots smashed it to bits.

"Stop!" cried Lanark, too late. "Why did you break it? I wanted to have a good look at the thing."

"But it is not good for men to look upon the devil's works," responded Jaeger, almost pontifically.

"Don't advise me, sergeant," said Lanark bleakly. "Remember that I am your officer, and that I don't need instruction as to what I may look at." He looked down at the fragments. "Hmm, the thing was hollow, and quite brittle. It seems to have been stuffed with straw—no, excelsior. Wood shavings, anyway." He investigated the fluffy inner mass with a toe. "Hullo, there's something inside of the stuff."

"I wouldn't touch it, sir," warned Jaeger, but this time it was he who spoke too late. Lanark's boot-toe had nudged the object into plain sight, and Lanark had put down his gauntleted left hand and picked it up.

"What is this?" he asked himself aloud. "Looks like some sort of strongbox—foreign, I'd say, and quite old. Jaeger, we'll go upstairs."

In the kitchen, with a strong light from several candles, they examined the find quite closely. It was a dark oblong, like a small dispatch-case or, as Lanark had commented, a strongbox. Though as hard as iron, it was not iron, nor any metal either of them had ever known.

"How does it open?" was Lanark's next question, turning the case over in his hands. "It doesn't seem to have hinges on it. Is this the lid—or this?"

"I couldn't say." Jaeger peered, his eyes growing narrow with perplexity. "No hinges, as the lieutenant just said."

"None visible, nor yet a lock." Lanark thumped the box experimentally, and proved it hollow. Then he lifted it close to his ear and shook it. There was a faint rustle, as of papers loosely rolled or folded. "Perhaps," the officer went on, "this separate slice isn't a lid at all. There may be a spring to press, or something that slides back and lets another plate come loose."

But Suggs was entering from the front of the house. "Lieutenant, sir! Something's happened to Newton—he was watching on the rock. Will the lieutenant come? And Sergeant Jaeger, too."

The suggestion of duty brought back the color and self-control that Jaeger had lost. "What's happened to Newton?" he demanded at once, and hurried away with Suggs.

Lanark waited in the kitchen for only a moment. He wanted to leave the box, but did not want his troopers meddling with it. He spied, beside the heavy iron stove, a fireplace, and in its side the metal door to an old brick oven. He pulled that door open, thrust the box in, closed the door again, and followed Suggs and Jaeger.

They had gone out upon the front porch. There, with Corporal Gray and a blank-faced trooper on guard, lay the silent form of Newton, its face covered with a newspaper.

Almost every man of the gathered patrol knew a corpse when he saw one, and it took no second glance to know that Newton was quite dead.

4

THE MANDIFERS

JAEGER, BENDING, lifted the newspaper and then dropped it back. He said something that, for all his religiosity, might have been an oath.

"What's the matter, sergeant?" demanded Lanark.

Jaeger's brows were clamped in a tense frown, and his beard was actually trembling. "His face, sir. It's terrible.

"A wound?" asked Lanark, and lifted the paper in turn. He, too, let it fall back, and his exclamation of horror and amazement was unquestionably profane.

"There ain't no wound on him, Lieutenant Lanark," offered Suggs, pushing his wan, plump face to the forefront of the troopers. "We heard Newton yell—heard him from the top of the rock yonder."

All eyes turned gingerly toward the promontory.

"That's right, sir," added Corporal Gray. "I'd just sent Newton up, to relieve Josserand."

"You heard him yell," prompted Lanark. "Go on, what happened?"

"I hailed him back," said the corporal, "but he said nothing. So I climbed up—that north side's the easiest to climb. Newton was standing at the top, standing straight up with his carbine at the ready. He must have been dead right then."

"You mean, he was struck somehow as you watched?"

Gray shook his head. "No, sir. I think he was dead as he stood up. He didn't move or speak, and when I touched him he sort of coiled down—like an empty coat falling off a clothesline." Gray's hand made a downward-floating gesture in illustration. "When I turned him over I saw his face, all twisted and scared-looking, like—like what the lieutenant has seen. And I sung out for Suggs and McSween to come up and help me bring him down."

Lanark gazed at Newton's body. "He was looking which way?"

"Over yonder, eastward." Gray pointed unsteadily. "Like it might have been beyond the draw and them trees in it."

Lanark and Jaeger peered into the waning light, that was now dusk. Jaeger mumbled what Lanark had already been thinking—that Newton had died without wounds, at or near the moment when the horned image had been shattered upon the cellar floor.

Lanark nodded, and dismissed several vague but disturbing inspirations. "You say he died standing up, Gray. Was he leaning on his gun?"

"No, sir. He stood on his two feet, and held his carbine at the ready. Sounds impossible, a dead man standing up like that, but that's how it was."

"Bring his blanket and cover him up," said Lanark. "Put a

guard over him, and we'll bury him tomorrow. Don't let any of the men look at his face. We've got to give him some kind of funeral." He turned to Jaeger. "Have you a prayer book, sergeant?"

Jaeger had fished out the *Long Lost Friend* volume. He was reading something aloud, as though it were a prayer: ". . . and be and remain with us on the water and upon the land," he pattered out. "May the Eternal Godhead also—"

"Stop that heathen nonsense," Lanark almost roared. "You're supposed to be an example to the men, sergeant. Put that book away."

Jaeger obeyed, his big face reproachful. "It was a spell against evil spirits," he explained, and for a moment Lanark wished that he had waited for the end. He shrugged and issued further orders.

"I want all the lamps lighted in the house, and perhaps a fire out here in the yard," he told the men. "We'll keep guard both here and in that gulley to the east. If there is a mystery, we'll solve it."

"Pardon me, sir," volunteered a well-bred voice, in which one felt rather than heard the tiny touch of foreign accent. "I can solve the mystery for you, though you may not thank me."

Two men had come into view, were drawing up beside the little knot of troopers. How had they approached? Through the patroled brush of the ravine? Around the corner of the house? Nobody had seen them coming, and Lanark, at least, started violently. He glowered at this new enigma.

The man who had spoken paused at the foot of the porch steps, so that lamplight shone upon him through the open front door. He was skeleton-gaunt, in face and body, and even his bones were small. His eyes burned forth from deep pits in his narrow, high skull, and his clothing was that of a dandy of the forties. In his twig-like fingers he clasped bunches of herbs.

His companion stood to one side in the shadow, and could be seen only as a huge coarse lump of a man.

"I am Persil Mandifer," the thin creature introduced himself. "I came here to gather from the gardens," and he held out his handfuls of leaves and stalks. "You, sir, you are in command of these soldiers, are you not? Then know that you are trespassing."

"The expediencies of war," replied Lanark easily, for he had seen Suggs and Corporal Gray bring their carbines forward in their hands. "You'll have to forgive our intrusion."

A scornful mouth opened in the emaciated face, and a soft,

superior chuckle made itself heard. "Oh, but this is not my estate. I am allowed here, yes—but it is not mine. The real Master—" The gaunt figure shrugged, and the voice paused for a moment. The bright eyes sought Newton's body. "From what I see and what I heard as I came up to you, there has been trouble. You have transgressed somehow, and have begun to suffer."

"To you Southerners, all Union soldiers are trespassers and transgressors," suggested Lanark, but the other laughed and shook his fleshless white head.

"You misunderstand, I fear. I care nothing about this war, except that I am amused to see so many people killed. I bear no part in it. Of course, when I came to pluck herbs, and saw your sentry at the top of Fearful Rock—" Persil Mandifer eyed again the corpse of Newton. "There he lies, eh? It was my privilege and power to project a vision up to him in his loneliness that, I think, put an end to his part of this puerile strife."

Lanark's own face grew hard. "Mr. Mandifer," he said bleakly, "you seem to be enjoying a quiet laugh at our expense. But I should point out that we greatly outnumber you, and are armed. I'm greatly tempted to place you under arrest."

"Then resist temptation," advised Mandifer urbanely. "It might be disastrous to you if we became enemies."

"Then be kind enough to explain what you're talking about," commanded Lanark. Something swam into the forefront of his consciousness. "You say that your name is Mandifer. We found a girl named Enid Mandifer in the gulley yonder. She told us a very strange story. Are you her stepfather? The one who mesmerized her and—"

"She talked to you?" Mandifer's soft voice suddenly shifted to a windy roar that broke Lanark's questioning abruptly in two. "She came, and did not make the sacrifice of herself? She shall expiate, sir, and you with her!"

Lanark had had enough of this high-handed civilian's airs. He made a motion with his left hand to Corporal Gray, whose carbine-barrel glinted in the light from the house as it leveled itself at Mandifer's skull-head.

"You're under arrest," Lanark informed the two men.

The bigger one growled, the first sound he had made. He threw his enormous body forward in a sudden leaping stride, his gross hands extended as though to clutch Lanark. Jaeger, at the lieutenant's side, quickly drew his revolver and fired from the hip.

The enormous body fell, rolled over and subsided.

"You have killed my son!" shrieked Mandifer.

"Take hold of him, you two," ordered Lanark, and Suggs and Josserand obeyed.

The gaunt form of Mandifer achieved one explosive struggle, then fell tautly motionless with the big hands of the troopers upon his elbows.

"Thanks, Jaeger," continued Lanark. "That was done quickly and well. Some of you drag this body up on the porch and cover it. Gray, tumble upstairs and bring down that girl we found."

While waiting for the corporal to return, Lanark ordered further that a bonfire be built to banish a patch of the deepening darkness. It was beginning to shoot up its bright tongues as the corporal ushered Enid Mandifer out upon the porch.

She had arranged her disordered clothing, and even contrived to put up her hair somehow, loosely but attractively. The firelight brought out a certain strength of line and angle in her face, and made her eyes shine darkly. She was manifestly frightened at the sight of her stepfather and the blanket-covered corpses to one side; but she faced determinedly a flood of half-understandable invectives from the emaciated man. She answered him, too; Lanark did not know what she meant by most of the things she said, but gathered correctly that she was refusing, finally and completely, to do something.

"Then I shall say no more," gritted out the spidery Mandifer, and his bared teeth were of the flat, chalky white of long-dead bone. "I place this matter in the hands of the Nameless One. He will not forgive, will not forget."

Enid moved a step toward Lanark, who put out a hand and touched her arm reassuringly. The mounting flame of the bonfire lighted up all who watched and listened—the withered, glaring mummy that was Persil Mandifer, the frightened but defiant shapeliness of Enid in her flower-patterned gown, Lanark in his sudden attitude of protection, the ring of troopers in their dusty blue blouses. With the half-lighted front of the weathered old house like a stage set behind them, and alternate red lights and sooty shadows playing over all, they might have been a tableau in some highly melodramatic opera.

"Silence," Lanark was grating. "For the last time, Mr. Mandifer, let me remind you that I have placed you under arrest. If you don't calm down immediately and speak only when you're spoken to, I'll have my men tie you flat to four stakes and put a gag in your mouth."

Mandifer subsided at once, just as he was on the point of hurling another harsh threat at Enid.

"That's much better," said Lanark. "Sergeant Jaeger, it strikes me that we'd better get our pickets out to guard this position."

Mandifer cleared his throat with actual diffidence. "Lieutenant Lanark—that is your name, I gather," he said in the soft voice which he had employed when he had first appeared. "Permit me, sir, to say but two words." He peered as though to be sure of consent. "I have it in my mind that it is too late, useless, to place any kind of guard against surprise."

"What do you mean?" asked Lanark.

"It is all of a piece with your offending of him who owns this house and the land which encompasses it," continued Mandifer. "I believe that a body of your enemies, mounted men of the Southern forces, are upon you. That man who died upon the brow of Fearful Rock might have seen them coming, but he was brought down sightless and voiceless, and nobody was assigned in his place."

He spoke truth. Gray, in his agitation, had not posted a fresh sentry. Lanark drew his lips tight beneath his mustache.

"Once more you feel that it is a time to joke with us, Mr. Mandifer," he growled. "I have already suggested gagging you and staking you out."

"But listen," Mandifer urged him.

Suddenly hoofs thundered, men yelled a double-noted defiance, high and savage—*"Yee-hee!"*

It was the rebel yell.

Quantrill's guerrillas rode out of the dark and upon them.

5

BLOOD IN THE NIGHT

NEITHER LANARK nor the others remembered that they began to fight for their lives; they only knew all at once that they were doing it. There was a prolonged harsh rattle of gunshots like a blast of hail upon hard wood; Lanark, by chance or unconscious choice, snatched at and drew his sword instead of his revolver.

A horse's flying shoulder struck him, throwing him backward but not down. As he reeled to save his footing, he saved also his own life; for the rider, a form all cascading black beard and slouch hat, thrust a pistol almost into the lieutenant's face and fired. The flash was blinding, the ball ripped Lanark's cheek like a whiplash, and then the saber in his hand swung, like a scythe reaping wheat. By luck rather than design, the edge bit the guerrilla's gun-wrist. Lanark saw the hand fly away as though on wings, its fingers still clutching the pistol, all agleam in the firelight. Blood gushed from the stump of the rider's right arm, like water from a fountain, and Lanark felt upon himself a spatter as of hot rain. He threw himself in, clutched the man's legs with his free arm and, as the body sagged heavily from above upon his head and shoulder, he heaved it clear out of the saddle.

The horse was plunging and whinnying, but Lanark clutched its reins and got his foot into the stirrup. The bonfire seemed to be growing strangely brighter, and the mounted guerrillas were plainly discernible, raging and trampling among his disorganized men. Corporal Gray went down, dying almost under Lanark's feet. Amid the deafening drum roll of shots, Sergeant Jaeger's bull-like voice could be heard: "Stop, thieves and horsemen, in the name of God!" It sounded like an exorcism, as though the Confederate raiders were devils.

Lanark had managed to climb into the saddle of his captured mount. He dropped the bridle upon his pommel, reached across his belly with his left hand, and dragged free his revolver. At a little distance, beyond the tossing heads of several horses, he thought he saw the visage of Quantrill, clean-shaven and fierce. He fired at it, but he had no faith in his own left-handed snap-shooting. He felt the horse frantic and unguided, shoving and striving against another horse. Quarters were too close for a saber-stroke, and he fired again with his revolver. The guerrilla spun out of the saddle. Lanark had a glimpse he would never forget, of great bulging eyes and a sharp-pointed mustache.

Again the rebel yell, flying from mouth to bearded mouth, and then an answering shout, deeper and more sustained; some troopers had run out of the house and, standing on the porch, were firing with their carbines. It was growing lighter, with a blue light. Lanark did not understand that.

Quantrill did not understand it, either. He and Lanark had come almost within striking distance of each other, but the guerrilla chief was gazing past his enemy, in the direction of the house. His mouth was open, with strain-lines around it. His eyes glowed. He feared what he saw.

"Remember me, you thieving swine!" yelled Lanark, and tried to thrust with his saber. But Quantrill had reined back and away, not from the sword but from the light that was growing stronger and bluer. He thundered an order, something that Lanark could not catch but which the guerrillas understood and obeyed. Then Quantrill was fleeing. Some guerrillas dashed between him and Lanark. They, too, were in flight. All the guerrillas were in flight. Somebody roared in triumph and fired with a carbine—it sounded like Sergeant Jaeger. The battle was over, within moments of its beginning.

Lanark managed to catch his reins, in the tips of the fingers that held his revolver, and brought the horse to a standstill before it followed Quantrill's men into the dark. One of his own party caught and held the bits, and Lanark dismounted. At last he had time to look at the house.

It was afire, every wall and sill and timber of it, burning all at once, and completely. And it burnt deep blue, as though seen through the glass of an old-fashioned bitters bottle. It was falling to pieces with the consuming heat, and they had to draw back from it. Lanark stared around to reckon his losses.

Nearest the piazza lay three bodies, trampled and broken-looking. Some men ran in and dragged them out of danger; they were Persil Mandifer, badly battered by horses' feet, and the two who had held him, Josserand and Lanark's orderly, Suggs. Both the troopers had been shot through the head, probably at the first volley from the guerrillas.

Corporal Gray was stone-dead, with five or six bullets in him, and three more troopers had been killed, while four were wounded, but not critically. Jaeger, examining them, pronounced that they could all ride if the lieutenant wished it.

"I wish it, all right," said Lanark ruefully. "We leave first thing in the morning. Hmm, six dead and four hurt, not counting poor Newton, who's there in the fire. Half my command—and, the way I forgot the first principles of military vigilance, I don't deserve as much luck as that. I think the burning house is what frightened the guerrillas. What began it?"

Nobody knew. They had all been fighting too desperately to have any idea. The three men who had been picketing the gulley, and who had dashed back to assault the guerrillas on the flank, had seen the blue flames burst out, as it were from a hundred places; that was the best view anybody had.

"All the killing wasn't done by Quantrill," Jaeger comforted his lieutenant. "Five dead guerrillas, sir—no, six. One was picked up a little way off, where he'd been dragged by his foot in the stirrup. Others got wounded, I'll be bound. Pretty even thing, all in all."

"And we still have one prisoner," supplemented Corporal Googan.

He jerked his head toward Enid Mandifer, who stood unhurt, unruffled almost, gazing raptly at the great geyser of blue flame that had been the house and temple of her stepfather's nameless deity.

It was a gray morning, and from the first streaks of it Sergeant Jaeger had kept the unwounded troopers busy, making a trench-like grave halfway between the spot where the house had stood and the gulley to the east. When the bodies were counted again, there were only twelve; Persil Mandifer's was missing, and the only explanation was that it had been caught somehow in the flames. The ruins of the house, that still smoked with a choking vapor as of sulfur gas, gave up a few crisped bones that apparently had been Newton, the sentry who had died from unknown causes; but no giant skeleton was found to remind one of the passing of Persil Mandifer's son.

"No matter," said Lanark to Jaeger. "We know that they were both dead, and past our worrying about. Put the other bodies in—our men at this end, the guerrillas at the other."

The order was carried out. Once again Lanark asked about a prayer book. A lad by the name of Duckin said that he had owned one, but that it had been burned with the rest of his kit in the blue flame that destroyed the house.

"Then I'll have to do it from memory," decided Lanark.

He drew up the surviving ten men at the side of the trench. Jaeger took a position beside him, and, just behind the sergeant, Enid Mandifer stood.

Lanark self-consciously turned over his clutter of thoughts, searching for odds and ends of his youthful religious teachings. " 'Man that is born of woman hath but short time to live, and is full of misery,' " he managed to repeat. " 'He cometh up, and is cut down, like a flower.' " As he said the words "cut down," he remembered his saber-stroke of the night before, and how he had shorn away a man's hand. That man, with his heavy black beard, lay in this trench before them, with the severed hand under him. Lanark was barely able to beat down a shudder. " 'In the midst of life,' " he went on, " 'we are in death.' "

There he was obliged to pause. Sergeant Jaeger, on inspiration, took one pace forward and threw into the trench a handful of gritty earth.

" 'Ashes to ashes, dust to dust,' " remembered Lanark. " 'Unto Almighty God we commit these bodies' "—he was sure that that was a misquotation worthy of Jaeger himself, and made shift to finish with one more tag from his memory: " '. . . in sure and certain hope of the Resurrection unto eternal life.' "

He faced toward the file of men. Four of them had been told to fall in under arms, and at his order they raised their carbines and fired a volley into the air. After that, the trench was filled in.

Jaeger then cleared his throat and began to give orders concerning horses, saddles and what possessions had been spared by the fire. Lanark walked aside, and found Enid Mandifer keeping pace with him.

"You are going back to your army?" she asked.

"Yes, at once. I was sent here to see if I could find and damage Quantrill's band. I found him, and gave at least as good as I got."

"Thank you," she said, "for everything you've done for me."

He smiled deprecatingly, and it hurt his bullet-burnt cheek.

"I did nothing," he protested, and both of them realized that it was the truth. "All that has happened—it just happened."

He drew his eyes into narrow gashes, as if brooding over the past twelve hours.

"I'm halfway inclined to believe what your stepfather said about a supernatural influence here. But what about you, Miss Mandifer?"

She tried to smile in turn, not very successfully.

"I can go back to my home. I'll be alone there."

"Alone?"

"I have a few servants."

"You'll be safe?"

"As safe as anywhere."

He clasped his hands behind him. "I don't know how to say

it, but I have begun to feel responsible for you. I want to know that all will be well."

"Thank you," she said a second time. "You owe me nothing."

"Perhaps not. We do not know each other. We have spoken together only three or four times. Yet you will be in my mind. I want to make a promise."

"Yes?"

They had paused in their little stroll, almost beside the newly filled grave trench. Lanark was frowning, Enid Mandifer nervous and expectant.

"This war," he said weightily, "is going to last much longer than people thought at first. We—the Union—have done pretty well in the West here, but Lee is making fools of our generals back East. We may have to fight for years, and even then we may not win."

"I hope, Mr.—I mean, Lieutenant Lanark," stammered the girl, "I hope that you will live safely through it."

"I hope so, too. And if I am spared, if I am alive and well when peace comes, I swear that I shall return to this place. I shall make sure that you, too, are alive and well."

He finished, very certain that he could not have used stiffer, more stupid words; but Enid Mandifer smiled now, radiantly and gratefully.

"I shall pray for you, Lieutenant Lanark. Now, your men are ready to leave. Go, and I shall watch."

"No," he demurred. "Go yourself, get away from this dreadful place."

She bowed her head in assent, and walked quickly away. At some distance she paused, turned, and waved her hand above her head.

Lanark took off his broad, black hat and waved in answer. Then he faced about, strode smartly back into the yard beside the charred ruins. Mounting his bay gelding, he gave the order to depart.

6

IT WAS spring again, the warm, bright spring of the year 1866, when Kane Lanark rode again into the Fearful Rock country.

His horse was a roan gray this time; the bay gelding had been shot under him, along with two other horses, during the hard-fought three days at Westport, the "Gettysburg of the West," when a few regulars and the Kansas militia turned back General Sterling Price's raid through Missouri. Lanark had been a captain then, and a major thereafter, leading a cavalry expedition into Kentucky. He narrowly missed being in at the finish of Quantrill, whose death by the hand of another he bitterly resented. Early in 1865 he was badly wounded in a skirmish with Confederate horsemen under General Basil Duke. Thereafter he could ride as well as ever, but when he walked he limped.

Lanark's uniform had been replaced by a soft hat and black frock coat, his face was browner and his mustache thicker, and his cheek bore the jaggedly healed scar of the guerrilla pistol-bullet. He was richer, too; the death of his older brother, Captain Douglas Lanark of the Confederate artillery, at Chancellorsville, had left him his father's only heir. Yet he was recognizable as the young lieutenant who had ridden into this district four years gone.

Approaching from the east instead of the north, he came upon the plain with its grass levels, its clumps of bushes and trees, from another and lower point. Far away on the northward horizon rose a sharp little finger; that would be Fearful Rock, on top of which Trooper Newton had once died, horrified and unwounded. Now, then, which way would lie the house he sought for? He idled his roan along the trail, and encountered at last an aged, ragged Negro on a mule.

"Hello, uncle," Lanark greeted him, and they both reined up. "Which way is the Mandifer place?"

"Mandifuh?" repeated the slow, high voice of the old man. "Mandifuh, suh, cap'n? Ah doan know no Mandifuh."

"Nonsense, uncle," said Lanark, but without sharpness, for he liked Negroes. "The Mandifer family has lived around here for years. Didn't you ever know Mr. Persil Mandifer and his step-daughter, Miss Enid?"

"Puhsil Mandifuh?" It was plain that the old fellow had heard and spoken the name before, else he would have stumbled over its unfamiliarities. "No, suh, cap'n. Ah doan nevah heah tella such gemman."

Lanark gazed past the mule and its tattered rider. "Isn't that a little house among those willows?"

The kinky head turned and peered. "Yes, suh, cap'n. Dat place b'long to Pahson Jaguh."

"Who?" demanded Lanark, almost standing up in his stirrups in his sudden interest. "Did you say Jaeger? What kind of man is he?"

"He jes a pahson—Yankee pahson," replied the Negro, a trifle nervous at this display of excitement. "Big man, suh, got red face. He Yankee. You ain' no Yankee, cap'n, suh. Whaffo you want Pahson Jaguh?"

"Never mind," said Lanark, and thrust a silver quarter into the withered brown palm. He also handed over one of his long, fragrant cheroots. "Thanks, uncle," he added briskly, then spurred his horse and rode on past.

Reaching the patch of willows, he found that the trees formed an open curve that faced the road, and that within this curve stood a rough but snug-looking cabin, built of sawn, unpainted planks and home-split shingles. Among the brush to the rear stood a smaller shed, apparently a stable, and a pen for chickens or a pig. Lanark reined up in front, swung out of his saddle, and tethered his horse to a thorny shrub at the trailside. As he drew tight the knot of the halter-rope, the door of heavy boards opened with a creak. His old sergeant stepped into view.

Jaeger was a few pounds heavier, if anything, than when Lanark had last seen him. His hair was longer, and his beard had grown to the center of his broad chest. He wore blue jeans tucked into worn old cavalry boots, a collarless checked shirt fastened with big brass studs, and leather suspenders. He stared somewhat blankly as Lanark called him by name and walked up to the doorstep, favoring his injured leg.

"It's Captain Lanark, isn't it?" Jaeger hazarded. "My eyes—" He paused, fished in a hip pocket and produced steel-rimmed spectacles. When he donned them, they appeared to aid his vision. "Indeed it is Captain Lanark! Or Major Lanark—yes, you were promoted—"

"I'm Mr. Lanark now," smiled back the visitor. "The war's over, Jaeger. Only this minute did I hear of you in the country. How does it happen that you settled in this place?"

"Come in, sir." Jaeger pushed the door wide open, and ushered Lanark into an unfinished front room, well lighted by windows on three sides. "It's not a strange story," he went on as he brought forward a well-mended wooden chair for the guest, and himself sat on a small keg. "You will remember, sir, that the land hereabouts is under a most unhallowed influence. When the war came to an end, I felt strong upon me the call to another conflict—a crusade against evil." He turned up his eyes, as though to subpoena the powers of heaven as witnesses to his devotion. "I preach here, the gospels and the true godly life."

"What is your denomination?" asked Lanark.

Jaeger coughed, as though abashed. "To my sorrow, I am ordained of no church; yet might this not be part of heaven's plan? I may be here to lead a strong new movement against hell's legions."

Lanark nodded as though to agree with this surmise, and studied Jaeger anew. There was nothing left in manner or speech to suggest that here had been a fierce fighter and model soldier, but the old rude power was not gone. Lanark then asked about the community, and learned that there were but seven white families within a twenty-mile radius. To these Jaeger habitually preached of a Sunday morning, at one farm home or another, and in the afternoon he was wont to exhort the more numerous Negroes.

Lanark had by now the opening for his important question. "What about the Mandifer place? Remember the girl we met, and her stepfather?"

"Enid Mandifer!" breathed Jaeger huskily, and his right hand fluttered up. Lanark remembered that Jaeger had once assured him that not only Catholics warded off evil with the sign of the cross.

"Yes, Enid Mandifer." Lanark leaned forward. "Long ago, Jaeger, I made a promise that I would come and make sure that she prospered. Just now I met an old Negro who swore that he had never heard the name."

Jaeger began to talk, steadily but with a sort of breathless awe, about what went on in the Fearful Rock country. It was not merely that men died—the death of men was not sufficient to horrify folk around whom a war had raged. But corpses, when found, held grimaces that nobody cared to look upon, and no blood remained in their bodies. Cattle, too, had been slain, mangled dreadfully—perhaps by the strange, unidentifiable creatures that prowled by moonlight and chattered in voices that sounded human. One farmer of the vicinity, who had ridden with Quantrill, had twice met strollers after dusk, and had recognized them for comrades whom he knew to be dead.

"And the center of this devil's business," concluded Jaeger, "is the farm that belonged to Persil Mandifer." He drew a deep, tired-sounding breath. "As the desert and the habitation of dragons, so is it with that farm. No trees live, and no grass. From a distance, one can see a woman. It is Enid Mandifer."

"Where is the place?" asked Lanark directly.

Jaeger looked at him for long moments without answering. When he did speak, it was an effort to change the subject. "You will eat here with me at noon," he said. "I have a Negro servant, and he is a good cook."

"I ate a very late breakfast at a farmhouse east of here," Lanark put him off. Then he repeated, "Where is the Mandifer place?"

"Let me speak this once," Jaeger temporized. "As you have said, we are no longer at war—no longer officer and man. We are equals, and I am able to refuse to guide you."

Lanark got up from his chair. "That is true, but you will not be acting the part of a friend."

"I will tell you the way, on one condition." Jaeger's eyes and voice pleaded. "Say that you will return to this house for supper and a bed, and that you will be within my door by sundown."

"All right," said Lanark. "I agree. Now, which way does that farm lie?"

Jaeger led him to the door. He pointed. "This trail joins a road beyond, an old road that is seldom used. Turn north upon it, and you will come to a part which is grown up in weeds. Nobody passes that way. Follow on until you find an old house, built low, with the earth dry and bare around it. That is the dwelling-place of Enid Mandifer."

Lanark found himself biting his lip. He started to step across the threshold, but Jaeger put a detaining hand on his arm. "Carry this as you go."

He was holding out a little book with a gray paper cover. It has seen usage and trouble since last Lanark had noticed it in Jaeger's hands; its back was mended with a pasted strip of dark cloth, and its edges were frayed and gnawed-looking, as though rats had been at it. But the front cover still said plainly:

John George Hohman's
POW-WOWS
or
LONG LOST FRIEND

"Carry this," said Jaeger again, and then quoted glibly: " 'Whoever carries this book with him is safe from all his enemies, visible or invisible; and whoever has this book with him cannot die without the holy corpse of Jesus Christ, nor drown in any water, nor burn up in any fire, nor can any unjust sentence be passed upon him.' "

Lanark grinned in spite of himself and his new concern. "Is this the kind of protection that a minister of God should offer me?" he inquired, half jokingly.

"I have told you long ago that the *Long Lost Friend* is a good book, and a blessed one." Jaeger thrust it into Lanark's right-hand coat pocket. His guest let it remain, and held out his own hand in friendly termination of the visit.

"Good-bye," said Lanark. "I'll come back before sundown, if that will please you."

He limped out to his horse, untied it and mounted. Then, following Jaeger's instructions, he rode forward until he reached the old road, turned north and proceeded past the point where weeds had covered the unused surface. Before the sun had fallen far in the sky, he was come to his destination.

It was a squat, specious house, the bricks of its trimming weathered and the dark brown paint of its timbers beginning to crack. Behind it stood unrepaired stables, seemingly empty. In the yard stood what had been wide-branched trees, now leafless and lean as skeleton paws held up to a relentless heaven. And there was no grass. The earth was utterly sterile and hard, as though rain had not fallen since the beginning of time.

Enid Mandifer had been watching him from the open door. When she saw that his eyes had found her, she called him by name.

7

THEN THERE was silence. Lanark sat his tired roan and gazed at Enid, rather hungrily, but only a segment of his attention was for her. The silence crowded in upon him. His unconscious awareness grew conscious—conscious of that blunt, pure absence of sound. There was no twitter of birds, no hum of insects. Not a breath of wind stirred in the leafless branches of the trees. Not even echoes came from afar. The air was dead, as water is dead in a still, stale pond.

He dismounted then, and the creak of his saddle and the scrape of his bootsole upon the bald earth came sharp and shocking to his quiet-filled ears. A hitching-rail stood there, old-seeming to be in so new a country as this. Lanark tethered his horse, pausing to touch its nose reassuringly—it, too, felt uneasy in the thick silence. Then he limped up a gravel-faced path and stepped upon a porch that rang to his feet like a great drum.

Enid Mandifer came through the door and closed it behind her. Plainly she did not want him to come inside. She was dressed in brown alpaca, high-necked, long-sleeved, tight above the waist and voluminous below. Otherwise she looked exactly as she had looked when she bade him good-bye beside the ravine, even to the strained, sleepless look that made sorrowful her fine oval face.

"Here I am," said Lanark. "I promised that I'd come, you remember."

She was gazing into his eyes, as though she hoped to discover something there. "You came," she replied, "because you could not rest in another part of the country."

"That's right," he nodded, and smiled, but she did not smile back.

"We are doomed, all of us," she went on, in a low voice. "Mr. Jaeger—the big man who was one of your soldiers—"

"I know. He lives not far from here."

"Yes. He, too, had to return. And I live—here." She lifted her hands a trifle, in hopeless inclusion of the dreary scene. "I wonder why I do not run away, or why, remaining, I do not go mad. But I do neither."

"Tell me," he urged, and touched her elbow. She let him take her arm and lead her from the porch into the yard that was like a surface of tile. The spring sun comforted them, and he knew

that it had been cold, so near to the closed front door of Persil
Mandifer's old house.

She moved with him to a little rustic bench under one of the
dead trees. Still holding her by the arm, he could feel at the tips
of his fingers the shock of her footfalls, as though she trod stiffly.
She, in turn, quite evidently was aware of his limp, and felt
distress; but, tactfully, she did not inquire about it. When they
sat down together, she spoke.

"When I came home that day," she began, "I made a hunt
through all of my stepfather's desks and cupboards. I found many
papers, but nothing that told me of the things that so shocked us
both. I did find money, a small chest filled with French and
American gold coins. In the evening I called the slaves together
and told them that their master and his son were dead.

"Next morning, when I wakened, I found that every slave had
run off, except one old woman. She, nearly a hundred years old
and very feeble, told me that fear had come to them in the night,
and that they had run like rabbits. With them had gone the horses,
and all but one cow."

"They deserted you!" cried Lanark hotly.

"If they truly felt the fear that came here to make its dwelling-
place!" Enid Mandifer smiled sadly, as if in forgiveness of the
fugitives. "But to resume; the old aunty and I made out here
somehow. The war went on, but it seemed far away. We watched
the grass die before June, the leaves fall, the beauty of this place
vanish."

"I am wondering about that death of grass and leaves," put in
Lanark. "You connect it, somehow, with the unholiness at Fearful
Rock; yet things grow there."

"Nobody is being punished there," she reminded succinctly.
"Well, we had the chickens and the cow, but no crops would
grow. If they had, we needed hands to farm them. Last winter
aunty died, too. I buried her myself, in the back yard."

"With nobody to help you?"

"I found out that nobody cared or dared to help." Enid said
that very slowly, and did not elaborate upon it. "One Negro, who
lives down the road a mile, has had some mercy. When I need
anything, I carry one of my gold pieces to him. He buys for me,
and in a day or so I seek him out and get whatever it is. He
keeps the change for his trouble."

Lanark, who had thought it cold upon the porch of the house, now mopped his brow as though it were a day in August. "You must leave here," he said.

"I have no place to go," she replied, "and if I had I would not dare."

"You would not dare?" he echoed uncomprehendingly.

"I must tell you something else. It is that my stepfather and Larue—his son—are still here."

"What do you mean? They were killed," Lanark protested. "I saw them fall. I myself examined their bodies."

"They were killed, yes. But they are here, perhaps within ear-shot."

It was his turn to gaze searchingly into her eyes. He looked for madness, but he found none. She was apparently sane and truthful.

"I do not see them," she was saying, "or, at most, I see only their sliding shadows in the evening. But I know of them, just around a corner or behind a chair. Have you never known and recognized someone just behind you, before you looked? Some-times they sneer or smile. Have you," she asked, "ever felt someone smiling at you, even though you could not see him?"

Lanark knew what she meant. "But stop and think," he urged, trying to hearten her, "that nothing has happened to you—nothing too dreadful—although so much was promised when you failed to go through with that ceremony."

She smiled, very thinly. "You think that nothing has happened to me? You do not know the curse of living here, alone and haunted. You do not understand the sense I have of something tightening and thickening about me; tightening and thickening inside of me, too." Her hand touched her breast, and trembled. "I have said that I have not gone mad. That does not mean that I shall never go mad."

"Do not be resigned to any such idea," said Lanark, almost roughly, so earnest was he in trying to win her from the thought.

"Madness may come—in the good time of those who may wish it. My mind will die. And things will feed upon it, as buzzards would feed upon my dead body."

Her thin smile faded away. Lanark felt his throat growing as dry as lime, and cleared it noisily. Silence was still dense around them. He asked her, quite formally, what she found to do.

"My stepfather had many books, most of them old," was her answer. "At night I light one lamp—I must husband my oil— and sit well within its circle of light. Nothing ever comes into

that circle. And I read books. Every night I read also a chapter
from a Bible that belonged to my old aunty. When I sleep, I hold
that Bible against my heart."

He rose nervously, and she rose with him. "Must you go so
soon?" she asked, like a courteous hostess.

Lanark bit his mustache. "Enid Mandifer, come out of here
with me."

"I can't."

"You can. You shall. My horse will carry both of us."

She shook her head, and the smile was back, sad and tender
this time. "Perhaps you cannot understand, and I know that I
cannot tell you. But if I stay here, the evil stays here with me.
If I go, it will follow and infect the world. Go away alone."

She meant it, and he did not know what to say or do.

"I shall go," he agreed finally, with an air of bafflement, "but
I shall be back."

Suddenly he kissed her. Then he turned and limped rapidly
away, raging at the feeling of defeat that had him by the back of
the neck. Then, as he reached his horse he found himself glad to
be leaving the spot, even though Enid Mandifer remained behind,
alone. He cursed with a vehemence that made the roan flinch,
untied the halter and mounted. Away he rode, to the magnified
clatter of hoofs. He looked back, not once but several times. Each
time he saw Enid Mandifer, smaller and smaller, standing beside
the bench under the naked tree. She was gazing, not along the
road after him, but at the spot where he had mounted his horse.
It was as though he had vanished from her sight at that point.

Lanark damned himself as one who retreated before an enemy,
but he felt that it was not as simple as that. Helplessness, not
fear, had routed him. He was leaving Enid Mandifer, but again
he promised in his heart to return.

Somewhere along the weed-teemed road, the silence fell from
him like a heavy garment slipping away, and the world hummed
and sighed again.

After some time he drew rein and fumbled in his saddlebag.
He had lied to Jaeger about his late breakfast, and now he was
grown hungry. His fingers touched and drew out two hardtacks—
they were plentiful and cheap, so recently was the war finished
and the army demobilized—and a bit of raw bacon. He sandwiched
the streaky smoked flesh between the big square crackers and ate
without dismounting. Often, he considered, he had been content

with worse fare. Then his thoughts went to the place he had quitted, the girl he had left there. Finally he skimmed the horizon with his eye.

To north and east he saw the spire of Fearful Rock, like a dark threatening finger lifted against him. The challenge of it was too much to ignore.

He turned his horse off the road and headed in that direction. It was a longer journey than he had thought, perhaps because he had to ride slowly through some dark swampground with a smell of rotten grass about it. When he came near enough, he slanted his course to the east, and so came to the point from which he first approached the rock and the house that had then stood in its shadow.

A crow flapped overhead, cawing lonesomely. Lanark's horse seemed to falter in its stride, as though it had seen a snake on the path, and he had to spur it along toward its destination. He could make out the inequalities of the rock, as clearly as though they had been sketched in with a pen, and the new spring greenery of the brush and trees in the gulley beyond to the westward; but the tumbledown ruins of the house were somehow blurred, as though a gray mist or cloud hung there.

Lanark wished that his old command rode with him, at least that he had coaxed Jaeger along; but he was close to the spot now, and would go in, however uneasily, for a closer look.

The roan stopped suddenly, and Lanark's spur made it sidle without advancing. He scolded it in an undertone, slid out of the saddle and threaded his left arm through the reins. Pulling the beast along, he limped toward the spot where the house had once stood.

The sun seemed to be going down.

8

THE GRAPPLE BY THE GRAVE

LANARK STUMPED for a furlong or more, to the yard of the old house, and the horse followed unwillingly—so unwillingly that had there been a tree or a stump at hand, Lanark would have tethered and left it. When he paused at last, under the lee of the great natural obelisk that was Fearful Rock, the twilight was upon him. Yet he could see pretty plainly the collapsed, blackened ruins of the dwelling that four years gone had burned before his eyes in devil-blue flame.

He came close to the brink of the foundation-hollow, and gazed narrowly into it. Part of the chimney still stood, broken off at about a level with the surface of the ground, the rubbish that had been its upper part lying in jagged heaps about its base. Chill seemed to rise from that littered depression, something like the chill he had guessed at rather than felt when he had faced Enid Mandifer upon her porch. The chill came slowly, almost stealthily, about his legs and thighs, creeping snake-like under his clothing to tingle the skin upon his belly. He shuddered despite himself, and the roan nuzzled his shoulder in sympathy. Lanark lifted a hand and stroked the beast's cheek, then moved back from where the house had stood.

He gazed westward, in the direction of the gulley. There, midway between the foundation-hollow and the natural one, was a much smaller opening in the earth, a pit filled with shadow. He remembered ordering a grave dug there, a grave for twelve men. Well, it seemed to be open now, or partially open.

He plodded toward it, reached it and gazed down in the fading light. He judged that the dead of his own command still lay where their comrades had put them, in a close row of six toward the east. It was the westward end of the trench that had been dug up, the place where the guerrillas had been laid. Perhaps the burial had been spied upon, and the Southerners had returned to recover their fallen friends.

Yet there was something below there, something pallid and flabby-looking. Lanark had come to make sure of things, and he stooped, then climbed down, favoring his old wound. It was darker in the ditch than above; yet he judged by the looseness of earth under his feet that in one spot, at least, there had been fresh digging—or, perhaps, some other person walking and examining. And the pallid patch was in reality two pallid patches, like discarded cloaks or jackets. Still holding the end of his horse's bridle, he put down his free hand to investigate.

Human hair tickled his fingers, and he snatched them back with an exclamation. Then he dug in his pocket, brought out a match, and snapped it aglow on the edge of his thumbnail.

He gazed downward for a full second before he dropped the

light. It went out before it touched the bottom of the hole. But Lanark had seen enough.

Two human skins lay there—white, empty human skins. The legs of them sprawled like discarded court stockings, the hands of them like forgotten gauntlets. And tousled hair covered the collapsed heads of them. . . .

He felt light-headed and sick. Frantically he struggled up out of that grave, and barely had he come to his knees on the ground above, when his horse snorted and jerked its bridle free from his grasp. Lanark sprang up, tingling all over. Across the trench, black and broad, stood a human—or semi-human—figure.

Lanark felt a certain draining cold at cheek and brow. Yet his voice was steady as he spoke, challengingly:

"What do you want?"

The creature opposite stooped, then bent its thick legs. It was going to jump across the ditch. Lanark took a quick backward step toward his horse—an old Colt's revolver was tucked into his right saddlebag.

But the sudden move on his part was too much for the jangled nerves of the beast. It whickered, squealed, and jerked around. A moment later it bolted away toward the east.

At the same time, the form on the other side of the open grave lunged forward, cleared the space, and came at Lanark.

But it was attacking one who had been in close fights before, and emerged the victor. Lanark, though partially a cripple, had lost nothing of a cavalryman's toughness and resolution. He sprang backward, let his assailant's charge slow before it reached him, then lashed out with his left fist. His gloved knuckles touched soft flesh at what seemed to be the side of the face, flesh that gave under them. Lanark brought over his right, missed with it, and fell violently against the body of the other. For a moment he smelled corruption, and then found his feet and retreated again.

The black shape drew itself stoopingly down, as though to muster and concentrate its volume of vigor. It launched itself at Lanark's legs, with two arms extended. The veteran tried to dodge again, this time sidewise, but his lameness made him slow. Hands reached and fastened upon him, one clutching his thigh, the other clawing at the left-hand pocket of his coat.

But in the moment of capture, the foul-smelling thing seemed to shudder and snatch itself away, as though the touch of Lanark had burned it. A moan came from somewhere in its direction.

The crouched body straightened, the arms lifted in cringing protection of the face. Lanark, mystified but desperately glad, himself advanced to the attack. As he came close he threw his weight. It bowled the other backward and over, and he fell hard upon it. His own hands, sinewy and sure, groped quickly upon dank, sticky-seeming garments, found a rumpled collar and then a throat.

That throat appeared to be muddy, or at any rate slippery and foul. With an effort Lanark sank his fingertips into it, throttling grimly and with honest intention to kill. There was no resistance, only a quivering of the body under his knee. The arms that screened the face fell quivering away to either side. At that moment a bright moon shimmered from behind a passing veil of cloud. Lanark gazed down into the face of his enemy.

A puffy, livid, filth-clotted face—but he knew it. Those spiked mustaches, those bulging eyes, the shape, contour and complexion. . . .

"You're one of Quantrill's—" accused Lanark between clenched teeth. Then his voice blocked itself, and his hands jerked away from their stranglehold. His mouth gaped open.

"I killed you once!" he cried.

Between him and the body he had pinned down there drifted a wild whirl of vision. He saw again the fight in the blue fireglow, the assailant who spurred against him, the flash of his own revolver, the limp collapse of the other. He saw, too, the burial next morning—blue-coated troopers shoveling loam down upon a silent row of figures; and, ere clods hid it, a face peeping through a disarranged blanket, a face with staring eyes and mustaches like twin knife-points.

Then his eyes were clear again, and he was on his feet and running. His stiff leg gave him pain, but he slackened speed no whit. Once he looked back. A strange blueness, like a dim reflection of the fire long ago, hung around the base of Fearful Rock. In the midst of it, he saw not one but several figures. They were not moving—not walking, anyway—but he could swear that they gazed after him.

Something tripped him, a root or a fallen branch. He rose, neither quickly nor confidently, aching in all his limbs. The moon had come up, he took time to realize. Then he suddenly turned dizzy and faint all over, as never in any battle he had seen, not even Pea Ridge and Westport; for something bulky and dark was moving toward and against him.

Then it whinnied softly, and his heart stole down from his throat—it was his runaway horse.

Lanark was fain to stand for long seconds, with his arm across the saddle, before he mounted. Then he turned the animal's head southward and shook the bridle to make it walk. At last he was able to examine himself for injuries.

Though winded, he was not bruised or hurt, but he was covered with earth and mold, and his side pocket had been almost ripped from his coat. That had happened when the—the creature yonder had tried to grapple him. He wondered how it had been forced to retreat so suddenly. He put his hand in the pocket.

He touched a little book there, and drew it forth.

It was Jaeger's *Long Lost Friend.*

A good hour later, Lanark rode into the yard of his ex-sergeant. The moon was high, and Jaeger was sitting upon the front stoop.

Silently the owner of the little house rose, took Lanark's bridle rein and held the horse while Lanark dismounted. Then he led the beast around to the rear yard, where the little shed stood. In front of this he helped Lanark unbridle and unsaddle the roan.

A Negro boy appeared, diffident in his mute offer of help, and Jaeger directed him to rub the beast down with a wisp of hay before giving it water or grain. Then he led Lanark to the front of the house.

Jaeger spoke at the threshold: "I thank God you are come back safely."

9

DEBATE AND DECISION

JAEGER'S NEGRO servant was quite as good a cook as promised. Lanark, eating chicken stew and biscuits, reflected that only twice before had he been so ravenous—upon receiving the news of Lee's surrender at Appomattox, and after the funeral of his mother. When he had finished, he drew forth a cheroot. His hand shook as he lighted it. Jaeger gave him one of the old looks of respectful disapproval, but did not comment. Instead he led Lanark to the most comfortable chair in the parlor and seated himself upon the keg. Then he said: "Tell me."

Lanark told him, rather less coherently than here set down, the

adventures of the evening. Again and again he groped in his mind
for explanations, but not once found any to offer.

"It is fit for the devil," pronounced Jaeger when his old com-
mander had finished. "Did I not say that you should have stayed
away from that woman? You're well out of the business."

"I'm well into it you mean," Lanark fairly snapped back. "What
can you think of me, Jaeger, when you suggest that I might let
things stand as they are?"

The frontier preacher massaged his shaggy jowl with thoughtful
knuckles. "You have been a man of war and an officer of death,"
he said heavily. "God taught your hands to fight. Yet your enemies
are not those who perish by the sword." He held out his hand.
"You say you still have the book I lent you?"

From his torn pocket Lanark drew Hohman's *Long Lost Friend*.
Jaeger took it and stared at the cover. "The marks of fingers,"
he muttered, in something like awe. He examined the smudges
closely, putting on his spectacles to do so, then lifted the book
to his nose. His nostrils wrinkled, as if in distaste, and he passed
the thing back. "Smell it," he directed.

Lanark did so. About the slimy-looking prints on the cover
hung a sickening odor of decayed flesh.

"The demon that attacked you, that touched this book, died
long ago," went on Jaeger. "You know as much—you killed him
with your own hand. Yet he fights you this very night."

"Maybe you have a suggestion," Lanark flung out, impatient
at the assured and almost snobbish air of mystery that colored
the manner of his old comrade in arms. "If this is a piece of hell
broke loose, perhaps you did the breaking. Remember that image—
that idol-thing with horns—that you smashed in the cellar? You
probably freed all the evil upon the world when you did that."

Jaeger frowned, but pursued his lecture. "This very book, this
Long Lost Friend, saved you from the demon's clutch," he said.
"It is a notable talisman and shield. But with the shield one must
have a sword, with which to attack in turn."

"All right," challenged Lanark. "Where is your sword?"

"It is a product of a mighty pen," Jaeger informed him sententiously. He turned in his seat and drew from a box against the
wall a book. Like the *Long Lost Friend*, it was bound in paper,
but of a cream color. Its title stood forth in bold black letters:

THE SECRETS
OF
ALBERTUS MAGNUS

"A translation from the German and the Latin," explained Jaeger. "Printed, I think, in New York. This book is full of wisdom, although I wonder if it is evil, unlawful wisdom."

"I don't care if it is." Lanark almost snatched the book. "Any weapon must be used. And I doubt if Albertus Magnus was evil. Wasn't he a churchman, and didn't he teach Saint Thomas Aquinas?" He leafed through the beginning of the book. "Here's a charm, Jaeger, to be spoken in the name of God. That doesn't sound unholy."

"Satan can recite scripture to his own ends," misquoted Jaeger. "I don't remember who said that, but—"

"Shakespeare said it, or something very like it," Lanark informed him. "Look here, Jaeger, farther on. Here's a spell against witchcraft and evil spirits."

"I have counted at least thirty such in that book," responded the other. "Are you coming to believe in them, sir?"

Lanark looked up from the page. His face was earnest and, in a way, humble.

"I'm constrained to believe in many unbelievable things. If my experience tonight truly befell me, then I must believe in charms of safety. Supernatural evil like that must have its contrary supernatural good."

Jaeger pushed his spectacles up on his forehead and smiled in his beard. "I have heard it told," he said, "that charms and spells work only when one believes in them."

"You sound confident of that, at least," Lanark smiled back. "Maybe you will help me, after all."

"Maybe I will."

The two gazed into each other's eyes, and then their hands came out, at the same moment. Lanark's lean fingers crushed Jaeger's coarser ones.

"Let's be gone," urged Lanark at once, but the preacher shook his head emphatically.

"Slowly, slowly," he temporized. "Cool your spirit, and take council. He that ruleth his temper is greater than he that taketh a city." Once more he put out his hand for the cream-colored volume of Albertus Magnus, and began to search through it.

"Do you think to comfort me from that book?" asked Lanark.

"It has more than comfort," Jaeger assured him. "It has guidance." He found what he was looking for, pulled down his spectacles again, and read aloud:

" 'Two wicked eyes have overshadowed me, but three other eyes are overshadowing me—the one of God the Father, the second of God the Son, the third of God the Holy Spirit; they watch my body and soul, my blood and bone; I shall be protected in the name of God.' "

His voice was that of a prayerful man reading Scripture, and Lanark felt moved despite himself. Jaeger closed the book gently and kept it in his hand.

"Albertus Magnus has many such charms and assurances," he volunteered. "In this small book, less than two hundred pages, I find a score and more of ways for punishing and thwarting evil spirits, or those who summon evil spirits." He shook his head, as if in sudden wrath, and turned up his spectacled eyes. "O Lord!" he muttered. "How long must devils plague us for our sins?"

Growing calmer once more, he read again from the book of Albertus Magnus. There was a recipe for invisibility, which involved the making of a thumb-stall from the ear of a black cat boiled in the milk of a black cow; an invocation to "Bedgoblin and all ye evil spirits"; several strange rituals, similar to those Lanark remembered from the *Long Lost Friend,* to render one immune to wounds received in battle; and a rime to speak while cutting and preparing a forked stick of hazel to use in hunting for water or treasure. As a boy, Lanark had once seen water "witched," and now he wondered if the rod-bearer had gained his knowledge from Albertus Magnus.

" 'Take an earthen pot, not glazed,' " Jaeger was reading on, " 'and yarn spun by a girl not seven years old'—"

He broke off abruptly, with a little inarticulate gasp. The book slammed shut between his hands. His eyes were bright and hot, and his face pale to the roots of his beard. When he spoke, it was in a hoarse whisper:

"That was a spell to control witches, in the name of Lucifer, king of hell. Didn't I say that this book was evil?"

"You must forget that," Lanark counseled him soberly. "I will admit that the book might cause sorrow and wickedness, if it were in wicked hands; but I do not think that you are anything but a good man."

"Thank you," said Jaeger simply. He rose and went to his table, then returned with an iron inkpot and a stump of a pen. "Let me have your right hand."

Lanark held out his palm, as though to a fortune-teller. Upon the skin Jaeger traced slowly, in heavy capital letters, a square of five words:

$$\begin{array}{ccccc} S & A & T & O & R \\ A & R & E & P & O \\ T & E & N & E & T \\ O & P & E & R & A \\ R & O & T & A & S \end{array}$$

Under this, very boldly, three crosses:

$$X \quad X \quad X$$

"A charm," the preacher told Lanark as he labored with the pen. "These mystic words and the crosses will defend you in your slumber, from all wicked spirits. So says Albertus Magnus, and Hohman as well."

"What do they mean?"

"I do not know that." Jaeger blew hotly upon Lanark's palm to dry the ink. "Will you now write the same thing for me, in my right hand?"

"If you wish." Lanark, in turn, dipped in the inkpot and began to copy the diagram. "*Opera* is a word I know," he observed, "and *tenet* is another. *Sator* may be some form of the old pagan word, *satyr*—a kind of horned human monster—"

He finished the work in silence. Then he lighted another cigar. His hand was as steady as a gun-rest this time, and the match did not even flicker in his fingertips. He felt somehow stronger, better, more confident.

"You'll give me a place to sleep for the night?" he suggested.

"Yes. I have only pallets, but you and I have slept on harder couches before this."

Within half an hour both men were sound asleep.

10

THE SILENCE was not so deadly the following noon as Lanark and Jaeger dismounted at the hitching-rack in front of Enid Mandifer's; perhaps this was because there were two horses to stamp and snort, two bridles to jingle, two saddles to creak, two pairs of boots to spurn the pathway toward the door.

Enid Mandifer, with a home-sewn sunbonnet of calico upon her head, came around the side of the house just as the two men were about to step upon the porch. She called out to them, anxiously polite, and stood with one hand clutched upon her wide skirt of brown alpaca.

"Mr. Lanark," she ventured, "I hoped that you would come again. I have something to show you."

It was Jaeger who spoke in reply: "Miss Mandifer, perhaps you may remember me. I'm Parson Jaeger, I live south of here. Look." He held out something—the *Long Lost Friend* book. "Did you ever see anything of this sort?"

She took it without hesitation, gazing interestedly at the cover. Lanark saw her soft pink lips move, silently framing the odd words of the title. Then she opened it and studied the first page. After a moment she turned several leaves, and a little frown of perplexity touched her bonnet-shaded brow. "These are receipts—recipes—of some kind," she said slowly. "Why do you show them to me, Mr. Jaeger?"

The ex-sergeant had been watching her closely, his hands upon his heavy hips, his beard thrust forward and his head tilted back. He put forth his hand and received back the *Long Lost Friend*.

"Excuse me, Miss Mandifer, if I have suspected you unjustly," he said handsomely if cryptically. Then he glanced sidewise at Lanark, as though to refresh a memory that needed no refreshing— a memory of a living-dead horror that had recoiled at very touch of the little volume.

Enid Mandifer was speaking once more: "Mr. Lanark, I had a dreadful night after you left. Dreams . . . or maybe not dreams. I felt things come and stand by my bed. This morning, on a bit of paper that lay on the floor—"

From a pocket in the folds of her skirt, she produced a white scrap. Lanark accepted it from her. Jaeger came close to look.

"Writing," growled Jaeger. "In what language is that?"

"It's English," pronounced Lanark, "but set down backward—from right to left, as Leonardo da Vinci wrote."

The young woman nodded eagerly at this, as though to say that she had already seen as much.

"Have you a mirror?" Jaeger asked her, then came to a simpler solution. He took the paper and held it up to the light, written side away from him. "Now it shows through," he announced. "Will one of you try to read? I haven't my glasses with me."

Lanark squinted and made shift to read:

" 'Any man may look lightly into heaven, to the highest star; but who dares require of the bowels of Earth their abysmal secrets?' "

"That is my stepfather's handwriting," whispered Enid, her head close to Lanark's shoulder.

He read on: " 'The rewards of Good are unproven; but the revenges of Evil are great, and manifest on all sides. Fear will always vanquish love.' "

He grinned slightly, harshly. Jaeger remembered having seen that grin in the old army days, before a battle.

"I think we're being warned," Lanark said to his old sergeant. "It's a challenge, meant to frighten us. But challenges have always drawn me."

"I can't believe," said Enid, "that fear will vanquish love." She blushed suddenly and rosily, as if embarrassed by her own words. "That is probably beside the point," she resumed. "What I began to say was that the sight of my stepfather's writing—why is it reversed like that?—the sight, anyway, has brought things back into my mind."

"What things?" Jaeger demanded eagerly. "Come into the house, Miss Mandifer, and tell us."

"Oh, not into the house," she demurred at once. "It's dark in there—damp and cold. Let's go out here, to the seat under the tree."

She conducted them to the bench whither Lanark had accompanied her the day before.

"Now," Jaeger prompted her, and she began:

"I remember of hearing him, when I was a child, as he talked to his son Larue and they thought I did not listen or did not comprehend. He told of these very things, these views he has written. He said, as if teaching Larue, 'Fear is stronger than love; where love can but plead, fear can command.' "

"A devil's doctrine!" grunted Jaeger, and Lanark nodded agreement.

"He said more," went on Enid. "He spoke of 'Those Below,' and of how they 'rule by fear, and therefore are stronger than Those on High, who rule by weak love.' "

"Blasphemy," commented Jaeger, in his beard.

"Those statements fit what I remember of his talk," Lanark put in. "He spoke, just before we fought the guerrillas, of some great evil to come from flouting Those Below."

"I remember," nodded Jaeger. "Go on, young woman."

"Then there was the box."

"The box?" repeated both men quickly.

"Yes. It was a small case, of dark grey metal, or stone—or something. This, too, was when I was little. He offered it to Larue, and laughed when Larue could not open it."

Jaeger and Lanark darted looks at each other. They were remembering such a box.

"My stepfather then took it back," Enid related, "and said that it held his fate and fortune; that he would live and prosper until the secret writing within it should be taken forth and destroyed."

"I remember where that box is," Lanark said breathlessly to Jaeger. "In the old oven, at—"

"We could not open it, either," interrupted the preacher.

"He spoke of that, too," Enid told them. "It would never open, he told Larue, save in the 'place of the Nameless One'—that must be where the house burned—and at midnight under a full moon."

"A full moon!" exclaimed Lanark.

"There is a full moon tonight," said Jaeger.

11

RETURN OF THE SACRIFICE

THROUGH THE cross-hatching of new-leafed branches the full moon shone down from its zenith. Lanark and Enid Mandifer walked gingerly through the night-filled timber in the gulley beyond which, they knew, lay the ruins of the house where so much repellent mystery had been born.

"It's just eleven o'clock," whispered Lanark, looking at his big silver watch. He was dressed in white shirt and dark trousers, without coat, hat or gloves. His revolver rode in the front of his waistband, and as he limped along, the sheath of Jaeger's old cavalry saber thumped and rasped his left boot-top. "We must be almost there."

"We are there," replied Enid. "Here's the clearing, and the little brook of water."

She was right. They had come to the open space where first they had met. The moonlight made the ground and its new grass pallid, and struck frosty-gold lights from the runlet in the very center of the clearing. Beyond, to the west, lay menacing shadows.

Enid stooped and laid upon the ground the hand-mirror she carried. "Stand to one side," she said, "and please don't look."

Lanark obeyed, and the girl began to undress.

The young man felt dew at his mustache, and a chill in his heart that was not from dew. He stared into the trees beyond the clearing, trying to have faith in Jaeger's plan. "We must make the devils come forth and face us," the sergeant-preacher had argued. "Miss Mandifer shall be our decoy, to draw them out where we can get at them. All is very strange, but this much we know—the unholy worship did go on; Miss Mandifer was to be sacrificed as part of it; and, when the sacrifice was not completed, all these evil things happened. We have the hauntings, the blue fire of the house, the creature that attacked Mr. Lanark, and a host of other mysteries to credit to these causes. Let us profit by what little we have found out, and put an end to the Devil's rule in this country."

It had all sounded logical, but Lanark, listening, had been hesitant until Enid herself agreed. Then it was that Jaeger, strengthening his self-assumed position of leadership, had made the assignments. Enid would make the journey, as before, from her house to the gulley, there strip and say the words with which her stepfather had charged her four springs ago. Lanark, armed, would accompany her as guard. Jaeger himself would circle far to the east and approach the ruins from the opposite direction, observing, and, if need be, attacking.

These preparations Lanark reviewed mentally, while he heard Enid's bare feet splashing timidly in the water. It came to him, a bit too late, that the arms he bore might not avail against supernatural enemies. Yet Jaeger had seemed confident. . . . Enid was speaking, apparently repeating the ritual that was supposed to summon the unnamed god-demon of Persil Mandifer:

"A maid, alone and pure, I stand, not upon water nor on land; I hold a mirror in my hand, in which to see what Fate may send. . . ." She broke off and screamed.

Lanark whipped around. The girl stood, misty-pale in the wash of moonlight, all crouched and curved together like a bow.

"It was coming!" she quavered. "I saw it in the mirror—over yonder, among those trees—"

Lanark glared across the little strip of water and the moonlit grass beyond. Ten paces away, between two trunks, something shone in the shadows—shone darkly, like tar; though the filtered moon-rays did not touch it. He saw nothing of the shape, save that it moved and lived—and watched.

He drew his revolver and fired, twice. There was a crash of twigs, as though something had flinched backward at the reports.

Lanark splashed through the water and, despite his limp, charged at the place where the presence lurked.

12

JAEGER

IT HAD been some minutes before eleven o'clock when Jaeger reined in his old black horse at a distance of two miles from Fearful Rock.

Most of those now alive who knew Jaeger personally are apt to describe him as he was when they were young and he was old—a burly graybeard, a notable preacher and exhorter, particularly at funerals. He preferred the New Testament to the Old, though he was apt to misquote his texts from either; and he loved children, and once preached a telling sermon against the proposition of infant damnation. His tombstone, at Fort Smith, Arkansas, bears as epitaph a verse from the third chapter of the first book of Samuel: *Here am I, for thou didst call me.*

Jaeger when young is harder to study and to visualize. However, the diary of a long-dead farmer's wife of Pennsylvania records that the "Jaeger boy" was dull but serious at school, and that his appetite for mince pie amounted to a passion. In Topeka, Kansas, lives a retired railroad conductor whose father, on the pre-Rebellion frontier, once heard Jaeger defy Southern hoodlums to shoot him for voting Free-state in a territorial election. Ex-Major Kane Lanark mentioned Jaeger frequently and with admiration in the remarkable pen-and-ink memoir on which the present narrative is based.

How he approached Fearful Rock, and what he encountered there, he himself often described verbally to such of his friends as pretended that they believed him.

The moonlight showed him a stunted tree, with one gnarled root looping up out of the earth, and to that root he tethered his animal. Then, like Lanark, he threw off his coat, strapping it to the cantle of his saddle, and unfastened his "hickory" blue shirt at the throat. From a saddlebag he drew a trusty-looking revolver, its barrel sawed off. Turning its butt toward the moon, he spun the cylinder to make sure that it was loaded. Then he thrust it into his belt without benefit of holster, and started on foot toward the rock and its remains of a house.

Approaching, he sought by instinct the cover of trees and bush clumps, moving smoothly and noiselessly; Jaeger had been noted during his service in the Army of the Frontier for his ability to scout at night, an ability which he credited to the fact that he had been born in the darkest hours. He made almost as good progress as though he had been moving in broad daylight. At eleven o'clock sharp, as he guessed—like many men who never carry watches, he had become good at judging the time—he was within two hundred yards of the rock itself, and cover had run out. There he paused, chin-deep in a clump of early weeds.

Lanark and the girl as he surmised, must be well into the gulley by this time. He, Jaeger, smiled as he remembered with what alacrity Lanark had accepted the assignment of bodyguard to Enid Mandifer. Those two young people acted as if they were on the brink of falling in love, and no mistake. . . .

His eyes were making out details of the scene ahead. Was even the full moon so bright as all this? He could not see very clearly the ruined foundations, for they sat in a depression of the earth. Yet there seemed to be a clinging blue light at about that point, a feeble but undeniable blue. Mentally he compared it to deep, still water, then to the poorest of skimmed milk. Jaeger remembered the flames that once had burned there, blue as amethyst.

But the blue light was not solid, and it had no heat. Within it, dimmed as though by mist, stood and moved—figures. They were human, at least they were upright; and they stood in a row, like soldiers, all but two. That pair was dark-seeming, and one was grossly thick, the other thin as an exclamation point. The line moved, bent, formed a weaving circle which spread as its units opened their order. Jaeger had never seen such a maneuver in four years of army service.

Now the circle was moving, rolling around; the figures were tramping counterclockwise—"withershins" was the old-fashioned word for that kind of motion, as Jaeger remembered from his boyhood in Pennsylvania. The two darker figures, the ones that had stood separate, were nowhere to be seen; perhaps they were inclosed in the center of the turning circle, the moving shapes of which numbered six. There had been six of Quantrill's guerrillas that died in almost that spot.

The ground was bare except for spring grass, but Jaeger made shift to crawl forward on hands and knees, his eyes fixed on the group ahead, his beard bristling nervously upon his set chin. He crept ten yards, twenty yards, forty. Some high stalks of grass, killed but not leveled by winter, afforded him a bit of cover, and he paused again, taking care not to rustle the dry stems. He could see the maneuvering creatures more plainly.

They were men, all right, standing each upon two legs, waving each two arms. No, one of them had only an arm and a stump. Had not one of Quantrill's men—yes! It came to the back of Jaeger's mind that Lanark himself had cut away an enemy's pistol hand with a stroke of his saber. Again he reflected that there had been six dead guerrillas, and that six were the forms treading so strange a measure yonder. He began to crawl forward again. Sweat made a slow, cold trickle along his spine.

But the two that had stood separate from the six were not to be seen anywhere, inside the circle or out. And Jaeger began to fancy that his first far glimpse had shown him something strange about that pair of dark forms, something inhuman or sub-human.

Then a shot rang out, clear and sharp. It came from beyond the circle of creatures and the blue-misted ruins. A second shot followed it.

Jaeger almost rose into plain view in the moonlight, but fell flat a moment later. Indeed, he might well have been seen by those he spied upon, had they not all turned in the direction whence the shots had sounded. Jaeger heard voices, a murmur of them with nothing that sounded like articulate words. He made bold to rise on his hands for a closer look. The six figures were moving eastward, as though to investigate.

Jaeger lifted himself to hands and knees, then rose to a crouch.

He ran forward, drawing his gun as he did so. The great uneven shaft that was Fearful Rock gave him a bar of shadow into which he plunged gratefully, and a moment later he was at the edge of the ruin-filled foundation hole, perhaps at the same point where Lanark had stood the night before.

From that pit rose the diluted blue radiance that seemed to involve this quarter. Staring thus closely, Jaeger found the light similar to that given off by rotten wood, or fungi, or certain brands of lucifer matches. It was like an echo of light, he pondered rather absently, and almost grinned at his own malapropism. But he was not here to make jokes with himself.

He listened, peered about, then began moving cautiously along the lip of the foundation hole. Another shot he heard, and a loud, defiant yell that sounded like Lanark; then an answering burst of laughter, throaty and muffled, that seemed to come from several mouths at once. Jaeger felt a new and fiercer chill. He, an earnest Protestant from birth, signed himself with the cross—signed himself with the right hand that clutched his revolver.

Yet there was no doubt as to which way lay his duty. He skirted the open foundation of the ruined house, moved eastward over the trampled earth where the six things had formed their open-order circle. Like Lanark, he saw the opened grave-trench. He paused and gazed down.

Two sack-like blotches of pallor lay there—Lanark had described them correctly: they were empty human skins. Jaeger paused. There was no sound from ahead; he peered and saw the ravine to eastward, filled with trees and gloom. He hesitated at plunging in, the place was so ideal an ambush. Even as he paused, his toes at the brink of the opened grave, he heard a smashing, rustling noise. Bodies were returning through the twigs and leafage of the ravine, returning swiftly.

Had they met Lanark and vanquished him? Had they spied or sensed Jaeger in their rear?

He was beside the grave, and since the first year of the war he had known what to do, with enemy approaching and a deep hole at hand. He dived in, head first like a chipmunk into its burrow, and landed on the bottom on all fours.

His first act was to shake his revolver, lest sand had stopped the muzzle.

A charm from the *Long Lost Friend* book whispered itself through his brain, a marksman's charm to bring accuracy with the gun. He repeated it, half audibly, without knowing what the words might mean:

"Ut nemo in sense tentant, descendre nemo; at precendenti spectatur mantica tergo."

At that instant his eyes fell upon the nearest of the two pallid, empty skins, which lay full in the moonlight. He forgot everything else. For he knew that collapsed face, even without the sharp stiletto-like bone of the nose to jut forth in its center. He knew that narrowness through the jowls and temples, that height of brow, that hair white as thistledown.

Persil Mandifer's skull had been inside. It must have been there, and living, recently. Jaeger's left hand crept out, and drew quickly back as though it had touched a snake. The texture of the skin was soft, clammy, moist . . . *fresh!*

And the other pallidity like a great empty bladder—that could have fitted no other body than the gross one of Larue Mandifer.

Thus, Jaeger realized, had Lanark entered the grave on the night before, and found these same two skins. Looking up, Lanark had found a horrid enemy waiting to grapple him.

Jaeger, too, looked up.

A towering silhouette shut out half the starry sky overhead.

13

LANARK

THE COMBINATION of pluck and common sense is something of a rarity, and men who possess that combination are apt to go far. Kane Lanark was such a man, and though he charged unhesitatingly across the little strip of water and at the unknown thing in the trees, he was not outrunning his discretion.

He had seen men die in his time, many of them in abject flight, with bullets overtaking them in the spine or the back of the head. It was nothing pleasant to watch, but it crystallized within his mind the realization that dread of death is no armor against danger, and that an enemy attacked is far less formidable than an enemy attacking. That brace of maxims comforted him and bore him up in more tight places than one.

And General Blunt of the Army of the Frontier, an officer who was all that his name implies and who was never given to overstatement, once so unbent as to say in official writing that Captain Kane Lanark was an ornament to any combat force.

And so his rush was nothing frantic. All that faltered was his lame leg. He meant to destroy the thing that had showed itself, but fully as definitely he meant not to be destroyed by it. As he ran, he flung his revolver across to his left hand and dragged free the saber that danced at his side.

But the creature he wanted to meet did not bide his coming. He heard another crash and rattle—it had backed into some shrubs or bushes farther in among the trees. He paused under the branches of the first belt of timber, well aware that he was probably a fair mark for a bullet. Yet he did not expect a gun in the hands of whatever lurked ahead; he was not sure at all that it even had hands.

Of a sudden he felt, rather than saw, motion upon his left flank. He pivoted upon the heel of his sound right foot and, lifting the saber, spat professionally between hilt and palm. He meant killing, did Lanark, but nothing presented itself. A chuckle drifted to him, a contemptuous burble of sound; he thought of what Enid had said about divining her stepfather's mockery. Again the cackle, dying away toward the left.

But up ahead came more noise of motion, and this was identifiable as feet—heavy, measured tramping of feet. New and stupid recruits walked like that, in their first drills. So did tired soldiers on the march. And the feet were coming his way.

Lanark's first reaction to this realization was of relief. Marching men, even enemies, would be welcome because he knew how to deal with them. Then he thought of Enid behind him, probably in retreat out of the gulley. He must give her time to get away. He moved westward, toward the approaching party, but with caution and silence.

The moonlight came patchily down through the lattice-like mass of branches and twigs, and again Lanark saw motion. This time it was directly ahead. He counted five, then six figures, quite human. The moonlight, when they moved in it, gave him glimpses of butternut shirts, white faces. One had a great waterfall of beard.

Lanark drew a deep breath. "Stand!" he shouted, and with his left hand leveled his pistol.

They stood, but only for a moment. Each figure's attitude shifted ever so slightly as Lanark moved a pace forward. The trees were sparse around him, and the moon shone stronger through their branches. He recognized the man with the great beard—he did not need to see that one arm was hewed away halfway between wrist and elbow. Another face was equally familiar, with its sharp mustaches and wide eyes; he had stared into it no longer ago than last night.

The six guerrillas stirred into motion again, approaching and closing in. Lanark had them before him in a semi-circle.

"Stand!" he said again, and when they did not he fired, full for the center of that black beard in the forefront. The body of the guerrilla started and staggered—no more. It had been hit, but it was not going to fall. Lanark knew a sudden damp closeness about him, as though he stood in a small room full of sweaty garments. The six figures were converging, like beasts seeking a common trough or manger.

He did not shoot again. The man he had shot was not bleeding. Six pairs of eyes fixed themselves upon him, with a steadiness that was more than unwinking. He wondered, inconsequentially, if those eyes had lids. . . . Now they were within reach.

He fell quickly on guard with his saber, whirling it to left and then to right, the old moulinets he had learned in the fencing-room at the Virginia Military Institute. Again the half-dozen approachers came to an abrupt stop, one or two flinching back from the twinkling tongue of steel. Lanark extended his arm, made a wider horizontal sweep with his point, and the space before him widened. The two forms at the horns of the semi-circle began to slip forward and outward, as though to pass him and take him in the rear.

"That won't do," Lanark said aloud, and hopped quickly forward, then lunged at the blackbeard. His point met flesh, or at least a soft substance. No bones impeded it. A moment later his basket-hilt thudded against the butternut shirt front, the figure reeled backward from the force of the blow. With a practiced wrench, Lanark cleared his weapon, cutting fiercely at another who was moving upon him with an unnerving lightness. His edge came home, and he drew it vigorously toward himself—a bread-slicing maneuver that would surely lay flesh open to the bone, disable one assailant. But the creature only tottered and came in again, and Lanark saw that the face he had hacked almost in two was the one with bulge eyes and spike mustaches.

All he could do was side-step and then retreat—retreat eastward in the direction of Fearful Rock. The black-bearded thing was down, stumbled or swooning, and he sprang across it. As he did so the body writhed just beneath him, clutching with one hand upward. Hooked by an ankle, Lanark fell sprawling at full length, losing his revolver but not his sword. He twisted over at his left side, hacking murderously in the direction of his feet. As once before, he cut away a hand and wrist and was free. He surged to his feet, and found the blackbeard also up, thrusting its hairy, fishy-white face at him. With dark rage swelling his every muscle, Lanark carried his right arm back across his chest, his right hand with the hilt going over his left shoulder. Then he struck at the hairy head with all the power of arm and shoulder and, turning his body, thrust in its weight behind the blow. The head flew from the shoulders, as though it had been stuck there ever so lightly.

Then the others were pushing around and upon him. Lanark smelled blood, rot, dampness, filth. He heard, for the first time, soft snickering voices, that spoke no words but seemed to be sneering at him for the entertainment of one another. The work was too close to thrust; he hacked and hewed, and struck with the curved guard as with brass knuckles. And they fell back from him, all but one form that could not see.

It tottered heavily and gropingly toward him, hunching its headless shoulders and holding out its handless arms, as though it played with him a game of blind-man's buff. And from that horrid truncated enemy Lanark fled, fled like a deer for all his lameness.

They followed, but they made slow, stupid work of it. Lanark's sword, which could not kill, had wounded them all. He was well ahead, coming to rising ground, toiling upward out of the gulley, into the open country shadowed by Fearful Rock.

He paused there, clear of the trees, wiped his clammy brow with the sleeve of his left arm. The moon was so bright overhead that it almost blinded him. He became aware of a kneading, clasping sensation at his right ankle, and looked down to see what caused it.

A hand clung there, a hand without arm or body. It was a pale hand that moved and crawled, as if trying to mount his boot-leg and get at his belly—his heart—his throat. The bright moon showed him the strained tendons of it, and the scant coarse hair upon its wide back.

Lanark opened his lips to scream like any woman, but no sound came. With his other foot he scraped the thing loose and away.

Its fingers quitted their hold grudgingly, and under the sole of his boot they curled and writhed upward, like the legs of an overturned crab. They fastened upon his instep.

When, with the point of his saber, he forced the thing free again, still he saw that it lived and groped for a hold upon him. With his lip clenched bloodily between his teeth, he chopped and minced at the horrid little thing, and even then its severed fingers humped and inched upon the ground, like worms.

"It won't die," Lanark murmured hoarsely, aloud; often in the past he had thought that speaking thus, when one was alone, presaged insanity. "It won't die—not though I chop it into atoms until the evil is driven away."

Then he wondered, for the first time since he had left Enid, where Jaeger was. He turned in the direction of the rock and the ruined house, and walked wearily for perhaps twenty paces. He was swimming in sweat, and blood throbbed in his ears.

Then he found himself looking into the open grave where the guerrillas had lain, whence they had issued to fight once more. At the bottom he saw the two palenesses that were empty skins.

He saw something else—a dark form that was trying to scramble out. Once again he tightened his grip upon the hilt of his saber.

At the same instant he knew that still another creature was hurrying out of the gulley and at him from behind.

14

ENID

LANARK'S GUESS was wrong; Enid Mandifer had not retreated westward up the gulley.

She had stared, all in a heart-stopping chill, as Lanark made for the thing that terrified her. As though of themselves, her hands reached down to the earth, found her dress, and pulled it over her head. She thrust her feet into her shoes. Then she moved, at only a fast walk, after Lanark.

There was really nothing else she could have done, and Lanark might have known that, had he been able to take thought in the moments that followed. Had she fled, she would have had no place to go save to the house where once her stepfather had lived; and it would be no refuge, but a place of whispering horror. Too, she would be alone, dreadfully alone. It took no meditation on her part to settle the fact that Lanark was her one hope of protection. As a matter of simple fact, he would have done well to remain with her, on the defensive; but then, he could not have foreseen what was waiting in the shadowed woods beyond.

She did carry something that might serve as a weapon—the hand-mirror. And in a pocket of her dress lay the Bible, of which she had once told Lanark. She had read much in it, driven by terror, and I daresay it was as much a talisman to her as was the *Long Lost Friend* to Jaeger. Her lips pattered a verse from it: "Deliver me from mine enemies, O my God . . . for lo, they lie in wait for my soul."

It was hard for her to decide what she had expected to find within the rim of trees beyond the clearing. Lanark was not in sight, but a commotion had risen some little distance ahead. Enid moved onward, because she must.

She heard Lanark's pistol shot, and then what sounded like several men struggling. She tried to peer and see, but there was only a swirl of violent motion, and through it the flash of steel— that would be Lanark's saber. She crouched behind a wide trunk.

"That is useless," said an accented voice she knew, close at her elbow.

She spun around, stared and sprang away. It was not her stepfather that stood there. The form was human to some degree— it had arms and legs, and a featureless head; but its nakedness was slimy wet and dark, and about it clung a smell of blood.

"That is useless," muttered once more the voice of Persil Mandifer. "You do not hide from the power that rules this place."

Behind the first dark slimness came a second shape, a gross immensity, equally black and foul and shiny. Larue?

"You have offered yourself," said Persil Mandifer, though Enid could see no lips move in the filthy-seeming shadow that should have been a face. "I think you will be accepted this time. Of course, it cannot profit me—what I am now, I shall be always. Perhaps you, too—"

Larue's voice chuckled, and Enid ran, toward where Lanark had been fighting. That would be more endurable than this mad dream forced upon her. Anything would be more endurable. Twigs and thorns plucked at her skirt like spiteful fingers, but she ripped away from them and ran. She came into another clearing, a small one. The moon, striking between the boughs, made here a pool of light and touched up something of metal.

It was Lanark's revolver. Enid bent and seized it. A few feet away rested something else, something rather like a strangely shaggy cabbage. As Enid touched the gun, she saw what that fringed rondure was. A head, but living, as though its owner had been buried to his bearded chin.

"What—" she began to ask aloud. It was surely living, its eyebrows arched and scowled and its gleaming eyes moved. Its tongue crawled out and licked grinning, hairy lips. She saw its smile, hard and brief as a knife flashed for a moment from its scabbard.

Enid Mandifer almost dropped the revolver. She had become sickeningly aware that the head possessed no body.

"There is the rest of him," spoke Persil Mandifer, again behind her shoulder. And she saw a heart-shaking terror, staggering and groping between the trees, a body without a head or hands.

She ran again, but slowly and painfully, as though this were in truth a nightmare. The headless hulk seemed to divine her effort at retreat, for it dragged itself clumsily across, as though to cut her off. It held out its handless stumps of arms.

"No use to shoot," came Persil Mandifer's mocking comment— he was following swiftly. "That poor creature cannot be killed again."

Other shapes were approaching from all sides, shapes dressed in filthy, ragged clothes. The face of one was divided by a dark cleft, as though Lanark's saber had split it, but no blood showed. Another seemed to have no lower jaw; the remaining top of his face jutted forward, like the short visage of a snake lifted to strike. These things had eyes, turned unblinkingly upon her; they could see and approach.

The headless torso blundered at her again, went past by inches. It recovered itself and turned. It knew, somehow, that she was there; it was trying to capture her. She shrank away, staring around for an avenue of escape.

"Be thankful," droned Persil Mandifer from somewhere. "These are no more than dead men, whipped into a mockery of life. They will prepare you a little for the wonders to come."

But Enid had commanded her shuddering muscles. She ran. One of the things caught her sleeve, but the cloth tore and she won free. She heard sounds that could hardly be called voices, from the mouths of such as had mouths. And Persil Mandifer laughed quietly, and said something in a language Enid had never heard before. The thick voice of his son Larue answered him in the same tongue, then called out in English:

"Enid, you only run in the direction we want you to run!"

It was true, and there was nothing that she could do about it. The entities behind her were following, not very fast, like herdsmen leisurely driving a sheep in the way it should go. And she knew that the sides of the gulley, to north and south, could never be climbed. There was only the slope ahead to the eastward, up which Lanark must have gone. The thought of him strengthened her. If the two of them found the king-horror, the Nameless One, at the base of Fearful Rock, they could face it together.

She was aware that she had come out of the timber of the ravine.

All was moonlight here, painted by the soft pallor in grays and silvers and shadow-blacks. There was the rock lifted among the stars, there the stretch of clump-dotted plain—and here, almost before her, Lanark.

He stood poised above a hole in the ground, his saber lifted above his head as though to begin a downward sweep. Something burly was climbing up out of that hole. But, even as he tightened his sinews to strike, Lanark whirled around, and his eyes glared murderously at Enid.

15

EVIL'S END

"DON'T!" ENID screamed. "Don't, it's only I—"

Lanark growled, and spun back to face what was now hoisting itself above ground level.

"And be careful of me, too," said the object. "It's Jaeger, Mr. Lanark."

The point of the saber lowered. The three of them were standing close together on the edge of the opened grave. Lanark looked down. He saw at the bottom the two areas of loose white.

"Are those the—"

"Yes," Jaeger replied without waiting for him to finish. "Two human skins. They are fresh; soft and damp." Enid was listening, but she was past shuddering. "One of them," continued Jaeger, "was taken from Persil Mandifer. I know his face."

He made a scuffing kick-motion with one boot. Clods flew into the grave, falling with a dull plop, as upon wet blankets. He kicked more earth down, swiftly and savagely.

"Help me," he said to the others. "Salt should be thrown on those skins—that's what the old legends say—but we have no salt. Dirt will have to do. Don't you see?" he almost shrieked. "Somewhere near here, two bodies are hiding, or moving about, without these skins to cover them."

Both Lanark and Enid knew they had seen those bodies. In a moment three pairs of feet were thrusting earth down into the grave.

"Don't!" It was a wail from the trees in the ravine, a wail in the voice of Persil Mandifer. "We must return to those skins before dawn!"

Two black silhouettes, wetly shiny in the moonlight, had come into the open. Behind them straggled six more, the guerrillas.

"Don't!" came the cry again, this time a command. "You cannot destroy us now. It is midnight, the hour of the Nameless One."

At the word "midnight" an idea fairly exploded itself in Lanark's brain. He thrust his sword into the hands of his old sergeant.

"Guard against them," he said in the old tone of command. "That book of yours may serve as shield, and Enid's Bible. I have something else to do."

He turned and ran around the edge of the grave, then toward the hole that was filled with the ruins of the old house; the hole that emitted a glow of weak blue light.

Into it he flung himself, wondering if this diluted gleam of the old unearthly blaze would burn him. It did not; his booted legs felt warmth like that of a hot stove, no more. From above he heard the voice of Jaeger, shouting, tensely and masterfully, a formula from the *Long Lost Friend:*

"Ye evil things, stand and look upon me for a moment, while I charm three drops of blood from you, which you have forfeited. The first from your teeth, the second from your lungs, the third from your heart's own main." Louder went his voice, and higher, as though he had to fight to keep down his hysteria: "God bid me vanquish you all!"

Lanark had reached the upward column of the broken chimney. All about his feet lay fragments, glowing blue. He shoved at them with his toe. There was an oblong of metal. He touched it—yes, that had been a door to an old brick oven. He lifted it. Underneath lay what he had hidden four years ago—a case of unknown construction.

But as he picked it up, he saw that it had a lid. What had Enid overheard from her stepfather, so long ago? ". . . that he would live and prosper until the secret writing should be taken forth and destroyed . . . it would never open, save at the place of the Nameless One, at midnight under a full moon."

With his thumbnail he pried at the lid, and it came open easily. The box seemed full of darkness, and when he thrust in his hands he felt something crumble, like paper burned to ashes. That was what it was—ashes. He turned the case over, and let the flakes fall out, like strange black snow.

From somewhere resounded a shriek, or chorus of shrieks. Then a woman weeping—that would be Enid—and a cry of "God be thanked!" unmistakably from Jaeger. The blue light died away all around Lanark, and his legs were cool. The old basement had fallen strangely dark. Then he was aware of great fatigue, the trembling of his hands, the ropy weakness of his lamed leg. And he could not climb out again, until Jaeger came and put down a hand.

At rosy dawn the three sat on the front stoop of Jaeger's cabin. Enid was pouring coffee from a serviceable old black pot.

"We shall never know all that happened and portended," said Jaeger, taking a mouthful of home-made bread, "but what we have seen will tell us all that we should know."

"This much is plain," added Lanark. "Persil Mandifer worshipped an evil spirit, and that evil spirit had life and power."

"Perhaps we would know everything, if the paper in the box had not burned in the fire," went on Jaeger. "That is probably as well—that it burned, I mean. Some secrets are just as well never told." He fell thoughtful, pulled his beard, and went on. "Even burned, the power of that document worked; but when the ashes fell from their case, all was over. The bodies of the guerrillas were dry bones on the instant, and as for the skinless things that moved and spoke as Mandifer and his son—"

He broke off, for Enid had turned deathly pale at memory of that part of the business.

"We shall go back when the sun is well up," said Lanark, "and put those things back to rest in their grave."

He sat for a moment, coffee-cup in hand, and gazed into the brightening sky.

To the two items he had spoken of as plainly indicated, he mentally added a third; the worship carried on by Persil Mandifer—was that name French, perhaps Main-de-Fer?—was tremendously old. He, Persil, must have received teachings in it from a former votary, his father perhaps, and most have conducted a complex and secret ritual for decades.

The attempted sacrifice rite for which Enid had been destined was something the world would never know, not as regards the climax. For a little band of Yankee horsemen, with himself at their head, had blundered into the situation, throwing it completely out of order and spelling for it the beginning of the end.

The end had come. Lanark was sure of that. How much of the power and motivity of the worship had been exerted by the Nameless One that now must continue nameless, how much of it was Persil Mandifer's doing, how much was accident of nature and horror-hallucination of witnesses, nobody could now decide. As Jaeger had suggested, it was probably as well that part of the mystery would remain. Things being as they were, one might pick up the threads of his normal human existence, and be happy and fearless.

But he could not forget what he had seen. The two Mandifers, able to live or to counterfeit life by creeping from their skins at night, had perished as inexplicably as they had been resurrected. The guerrillas, too, whose corpses had challenged him, must be finding a grateful rest now that the awful semblance of life had quitted their slack, butchered limbs. And the blue fire that had burst forth in the midst of the old battle, to linger ghostwise for years; the horned image that Jaeger had broken; the seeming powers of the *Long Lost Friend,* as an amulet and a storehouse of charms—these were items in the strange fabric. He would remember them forever, without rationalizing them.

He drank coffee, into which someone, probably Enid, had dropped sugar while he mused. Rationalization, he decided, was not enough, had never been enough. To judge a large and dark mystery by what vestigal portions touched one, was to err like the blind men in the old doggerel who, groping at an elephant here and there, called it in turn a snake, a spear, a tree, a fan, a wall. Better not to brood or ponder upon what had happened. Try to be thankful, and forget.

"I shall build my church under Fearful Rock," Jaeger was saying, "and it shall be called Fearful Rock no more, but Welcome Rock."

Lanark looked up. Enid had come and seated herself beside him. He studied her profile. Suddenly he could read her thoughts, as plainly as though they were written upon her cheek.

She was thinking that grass would grown anew in her front yard, and that she would marry Kane Lanark as soon as he asked her.

RAY RUSSELL
Sardonicus

1

AN "S" OF VULGAR PRETENTION

IN THE late summer of the year 18—, a gratifying series of professional successes had brought me to a state of such fatigue that I had begun seriously to contemplate a long rest on the Continent. I had not enjoyed a proper holiday in nearly three years, for, in addition to my regular practice, I had been deeply involved in a program of research, and so rewarding had been my progress in this special work (it concerned the ligaments and muscles, and could, it was my hope, be beneficially applied to certain varieties of paralysis) that I was loath to leave the city for more than a week at a time. Being unmarried, I lacked a solicitous wife who might have expressed concern over my health; thus it was that I had over-worked myself to a point that a holiday had become absolutely essential to my well-being; hence, the letter which was put in my hand one morning near the end of that summer was not welcome.

When it was first presented to me by my valet, at breakfast, I turned it over and over, feeling the weight of its fine paper which was almost of the heaviness and stiffness of parchment; pondering the large seal of scarlet wax upon which was imprinted a device of such complexity that it was difficult to decipher; examining finally the hand in which the address had been written: *Sir Robert Cargrave, Harley Street, London.* It was a feminine hand, that much was certain, and there was a curious touch of familiarity to its delicacy as well as to its clearness (this last an admirable quality far too uncommon in the handwriting of ladies). The fresh clarity of that hand—and where had I seen it before?—bespoke

151

a directness that seemed contrary to the well-nigh unfathomable ornamentation of the seal, which, upon closer and more concentrated perusal, I at length concluded to be no more than a single "S," but an "S" whose writhing curls seemed almost to grin presumptuously at one, an "S" which seemed to be constructed of little else than these grins, an "S" of such vulgar pretension that I admit to having felt vexed for an instant, and then, in the next instant, foolish at my own vexation—for surely, I admonished myself, there are things a deal more vexing than a seal which you have encountered without distemper?

Smiling at my foible, I continued to weigh the letter in my hand, searching my mind for a friend or acquaintance whose name began with "S." There was old Shipley of the College of Surgeons; there was Lord Henry Stanton, my waggish and witty friend; and that was the extent of it. Was it Harry? He was seldom in one place for very long and was a faithful and gifted letter writer. Yet Harry's bold hand was far from effeminate, and, moreover, he would not use such a seal—unless it were as a lark, as an antic jest between friends. My valet had told me, when he put the letter in my hand, that it had come not by the post but by special messenger, and although this intelligence had not struck me as remarkable at the time, it now fed my curiosity and I broke that vexing seal and unfolded the stiff, crackling paper.

The message within was written in the same clear, faintly familiar hand. My eye first travelled to the end to find the signature, but that signature—*Madam S.*—told me nothing, for I knew of no Madam S. among my circle.

I read the letter. It is before me now as I set down this account, and I shall copy it out verbatim:

"MY DEAR SIR ROBERT,

"It has been close to seven years since we last met—indeed, at that time you were not yet Sir Robert at all, but plain Robert Cargrave (although some talk of imminent knighthood was in the air), and so I wonder if you will remember Maude Randall?"

Remember Maude Randall! Dear Maude of the bell-like voice, of the chestnut hair and large brown eyes, of a temperament of such sweetness and vivacity that the young men of London had eyes for no one else. She was of good family, but during a stay in Paris there had been something about injudicious speculation by her father that had diminished the family fortunes to such an extent that the wretched man had taken his own life and the Randalls had vanished from London society, altogether. Maude, or so I had heard, had married a foreign gentleman and had remained in Europe. It had been sad news, for no young man of London had ever had more doting eyes for Maude than had I, and it had pleased my fancy to think that my feelings were, at least in part, reciprocated. Remember Maude Randall? Yes, yes, I almost said aloud. And now, seven years later, she was "Madam S.," writing in the same hand I had seen countless times on invitations. I continued to read:

"I often think of you, for—although it may not be seemly to say it—the company of few gentlemen used to please me so much as yours, and the London soirées given by my dear mother, at which you were present, are among my most cherished recollections now. But there! Frankness was always my failing, as Mother used to remind me. She, dear kind lady, survived less than a year after my poor father died, but I suppose you know this.

"I am quite well, and we live in great comfort here, although we receive but rarely and are content with our own company most of the time. Mr. S. is a gracious gentleman, but of quiet and retiring disposition, and throngs of people, parties, balls, &c., are retrograde to his temperament; thus it is a special joy to me that he has expressly asked me to invite you here to the castle for a fortnight—or, if I may give you his exact words: 'For a fortnight at least, but howsoever long as it please Sir Robert to stay among such drab folk as he will think us.' (You see, I told you he was gracious!)"

I must have frowned while reading, for the words of Mr. S. were not so much gracious, I thought, as egregious, and as vulgar as his absurd seal. Still, I held these feelings in check, for I knew that my emotions towards this man were not a little colored by jealousy. He, after all, had wooed and won Maude Randall, a young lady of discernment and fine sensibilities: could she have been capable of wedding an obsequious boor? I thought it not likely. And a castle! Such romantic grandeur! ". . . Invite you here to the castle . . ." she had written, but where was "here"? The letter's cover, since it had not come by the post, offered no clue; therefore I read on:

"It was, indeed, only yesterday, in the course of conversation, that I was recalling my old life in London, and mentioned your name. Mr. S., I thought, was, of a sudden, interested. 'Robert Cargrave?' he said. 'There is a well-known physician of that name, but I do not imagine it is the same gentleman.' I laughed and told him it *was* the same gentleman, and that I had known you before you had become so illustrious. 'Did you know him well?' Mr. S. then asked me, and you will think me silly, but I must tell you that for a moment I assumed him to be jealous! Such was not the case, however, as further conversation proved. I told him you had been a friend of my family's and a frequent guest at our house. 'This is a most happy coincidence,' he said. 'I have long desired to meet Sir Robert Cargrave, and your past friendship with him furnishes you with an excellent opportunity to invite him here for a holiday.'

"And so, Sir Robert, I am complying with his request—and at the same time obeying the dictates of my own inclination—by most cordially inviting you to visit us for as long as you choose. I entreat you to come, for we see so few people here and it would be a great pleasure to talk with someone from the old days and to hear the latest London gossip. Suffer me, then, to receive a letter from you at once. Mr. S. does not trust the post, hence I have sent this by a servant of ours who was to be in London on special business; please relay your answer by way of him—"

I rang for my man. "Is the messenger who delivered this letter waiting for a reply?" I asked.

"He is sitting in the vestibule, Sir Robert," he said.

"You should have told me."

"Yes, sir."

"At any rate, send him in now. I wish to see him."

My man left, and it took me but a minute to dash off a quick note of acceptance. It was ready for the messenger when he was

ushered into the room. I addressed him: "You are in the employ
of Madam——" I realized for the first time that I did not know
her husband's name.

The servant—a taciturn fellow with Slavic features—spoke in a
thick accent: "I am in the employ of Mr. Sardonicus, sir."

Sardonicus! A name as flamboyant as the seal, I thought to
myself. "Then deliver this note, if you please, to Madam Sardonicus, immediately you return."

He bowed slightly and took the note from my hand. "I shall
deliver it to my master straightaway, sir," he said.

His manner nettled me. I corrected him. "To your mistress,"
I said coldly.

"Madam Sardonicus will receive your message, sir," he said.

I dismissed him, and only then did it strike me that I had not
the faintest idea where the castle of Mr. Sardonicus was located.
I referred once again to Maude's letter:

> ". . . Please relay your answer by way of him and pray
> make it affirmative, for I do hope to make your stay in—
> ——a pleasant one."

I consulted an atlas. The locality she mentioned, I discovered,
was a district in a remote and mountainous region of Bohemia.

Filled with anticipation, I finished my breakfast with renewed
appetite, and that very afternoon began to make arrangements for
my journey.

2

THE SIGHT OF A GIANT SKULL

I AM NOT—as my friend Harry Stanton is—fond of travel for its
own sake. Harry has often chided me on this account, calling me
a dry-as-dust academician and "an incorrigible Londoner"—which
I suppose I am. For, in point of fact, few things are more tiresome
to me than ships and trains and carriages; and although I have
found deep enjoyment and spiritual profit in foreign cites, having
arrived, the tedium of travel itself has often made me think twice
before starting out on a long voyage.

Still, in less than a month after I had answered Maude's invitation, I found myself in her adopted homeland. Sojourning from London to Paris, thence to Berlin, finally to Bohemia, I was met at———by a coachman who spoke imperfect English but who managed, in his solemn fashion, to make known to me that he was a member of the staff at Castle Sardonicus. He placed at my disposal a coach drawn by two horses, and, after taking my bags, proceeded to drive me on the last leg of my journey.

Alone in the coach, I shivered, for the air was brisk and I was very tired. The road was full of ruts and stones, and the trip was far from smooth. Neither did I derive much pleasure by bending my glance to the view afforded by the windows, for the night was dark, and the country was, at any rate, wild and raw, not made for serene contemplation. The only sounds were the clatter of hooves and wheels, the creak of the coach, and the harsh, unmusical cries of unseen birds.

"We receive but rarely," Maude had written, and now I told myself—little wonder! in this ragged and, one might say, uninhabitable place, far from the graces of civilized society, who indeed is there to *be* received, or, for the matter of that, to receive one? I sighed, for the desolate landscape and the thought of what might prove a holiday devoid of refreshing incident, had combined to cloak my already wearied spirit in a melancholic humor.

It was when I was in this condition that Castle Sardonicus met my eye—a dense, hunched outline at first, then, with an instantaneous flicker of moonlight, a great gaping death's head, the sight of which made me inhale sharply. With the exhalation, I chuckled at myself. "Come, come, Sir Robert," I inwardly chided, "it is, after all, but a castle, and you are not a green girl who starts at shadows and quails at midnight stories!"

The castle is situated at the terminus of a long and upward-winding mountain road. It presents a somewhat forbidding aspect to the world, for there is little about it to suggest gaiety or warmth or any of those qualities that might assure the wayfarer of welcome. Rather, this vast edifice of stone exudes an austerity, cold and repellent, a hint of ancient mysteries long buried, an effluvium of medieval dankness and decay. At night, and most particularly on nights when the moon is slim or cloud-enshrouded, it is a heavy blot upon the horizon, a shadow only, without feature save for its many-turreted outline; and should the moon be temporarily released from her cloudy confinement, her fugitive rays lend scant comfort, for they but serve to throw the castle into sudden, startling chiaroscuro, its windows fleetingly assuming the appearance of sightless though all-seeing orbs, its portcullis becoming for an instant a gaping mouth, its entire form striking the physical and the mental eye as would the sight of a giant skull.

But, though the castle had revealed itself to my sight, it was a full quarter of an hour before the coach had creaked its way up the steep and tortuous road to the great gate that barred the castle grounds from intruders. Of iron the gate was wrought—black it seemed in the scant illumination—and composed of intricate twists that led, every one of them, to a central, huge device, of many curves, which in the infrequent glints of moonglow appeared to smile metallically down, but which, upon gathering my reason about me, I made out to be no more than an enlarged edition of that presumptuous seal: a massive single "S." Behind it, at the end of the rutted road, stood the castle itself—dark, save for lights in two of its many windows.

Some words in a foreign tongue passed between my coachman and a person behind the gate. The gate was unlocked from within and swung open slowly, with a long rising shriek of rusted hinges; and the coach passed through.

As we drew near, the door of the castle was flung open and cheery light spilled out upon the road. The portcullis, which I had previously marked, was evidently a remnant from older days and now inactive. The coach drew to a halt, and I was greeted with great gravity by a butler whom I saw to be he who carried Maude's invitation to London. I proffered him a nod of recognition. He acknowledged this and said, "Sir Robert, Madam Sardonicus awaits you, and if you will be good enough to follow me, I will take you to her presence." The coachman took charge of my bags, and I followed the butler into the castle.

It dated, I thought, to the twelfth or thirteenth century. Suits of armor—priceless relics, I ascertained them to be—stood about the vast halls; tapestries were in evidence throughout; strong, heavy, richly carved furniture was everywhere. The walls were of time-defying stone, great grey blocks of it. I was led into a kind of salon, with comfortable chairs, a tea table, and a spinet. Maude rose to greet me.

"Sir Robert," she said softly, without smiling. "How good to see you at last."

I took her hand. "Dear lady," said I, "we meet again."

"You are looking well and prosperous," she said.

"I am in good health, but just now rather tired from the journey."

She gave me leave to sit, and did so herself, venturing the opinion that a meal and some wine would soon restore me. "Mr. Sardonicus will join us soon," she added.

I spoke of her appearance, saying that she looked not a day older than when I last saw her in London. This was true, in regard to her physical self, for her face bore not a line, her skin was of the same freshness, and her glorious chestnut hair was still rich in color and gleaming with health. But what I did not speak of was the change in her spirit. She who had been so gay and vivacious, the delight of soirées, was now distant and aloof, of serious mien, unsmiling. I was sorry to see this, but attributed it to the seven years that had passed since her carefree girlhood, to the loss of her loved parents, and even to the secluded life she now spent in this place.

"I am eager to meet your husband," I said.

"And he, Sir Robert, is quite eager to meet you," Maude assured me. "He will be down presently. Meanwhile, do tell me how you have fared in the world."

I spoke, with some modesty, I hope, of my successes in my chosen field, of the knighthood I had received from the Crown; I described my London apartment, laboratory and office; I made mention of certain mutual friends, and generally gave her news of London life, speaking particularly of the theatre (for I knew Maude had loved it) and describing Mr. Macready's farewell appearance as Macbeth at The Haymarket. When Maude had last been in London, there had been rumors of making an opera house out of Covent Garden theatre, and I told her that those plans had been carried through. I spoke of the London premiere of Mr. Verdi's latest *oeuvre* at Her Majesty's. At my mention of these theatres and performances, her eyes lit up, but she was not moved to comment until I spoke of the opera.

"The opera!" she sighed. "Oh, Sir Robert, if you could but know how I miss it. The excitement of a premiere, the ladies and gentlemen in their finery, the thrilling sounds of the overture, and then the curtain rising—" She broke off, as if ashamed of her momentary transport. "But I receive all the latest scores, and derive great satisfaction from playing and singing them to myself. I must order the new Verdi from Rome. It is called *Ernani,* you say?"

I nodded, adding, "With your permission, I will attempt to play some of the more distinctive airs."

"Oh, pray do, Sir Robert!" she said.

"You will find them, perhaps, excessively modern and disonant." I sat down at the spinet and played—just passably, I fear, and with some improvisation when I could not remember the exact notes—a potpourri of melodies from the opera.

She applauded my playing. I urged her to play also, for she was an accomplished keyboard artist and possessed an agreeable voice, as well. She complied by playing the minuet from *Don Giovanni* and then singing the *Voi che sapete* from *Le Nozze di Figaro.* As I stood over her, watching her delicate hands move over the keys, hearing the pure, clear tones of her voice, all my old feelings washed over me in a rush, and my eyes smarted at the unalloyed sweetness and goodness of this lady. When she asked me to join her in the duet, *Là ci darem la mano,* I agreed to do it, although my voice is less than ordinary. On the second singing of the word *"mano"*—"hand"—I was seized by a vagrant impulse and took her left hand in my own. Her playing was hampered, of course, and the music limped for a few measures; and then, my face burning, I released her hand and we finished out the duet. Wisely, she neither rebuked me for my action nor gave me encouragement; rather, she acted as if the rash gesture had never been committed.

To mask my embarrassment, I now embarked upon some light chatter, designed to ease whatever tension existed between us; I spoke of many things, foolish things, for the most part, and even asked if Mr. Sardonicus had later demonstrated any of the jealousy she had said, in her letter, that she had erroneously thought him to have exhibited. She laughed at this—and it brightened the room, for it was the first time her face had abandoned its grave expression; indeed, I was taken by the thought that this was the first display of human merriment I had marked since stepping into the coach— and she said, "Oh, no! To the contary, Mr. Sardonicus said that the closer we had been in the old days, the more he would be pleased."

This seemed an odd and even coarse thing for a man to say to his wife, and I jovially replied: "I hope Mr. Sardonicus was smiling when he said that."

At once, Maude's own smile vanished from her face. She looked away from me and began to talk of other things. I was dumbfounded. Had my innocent remark given offense? It seemed not possible. A moment later, however, I knew the reason for her strange action, for a tall gentleman entered the room with a gliding step, and one look at him explained many things.

3

HE WHO MUST SMILE FOREVER

"SIR ROBERT CARGRAVE?" he asked, but he spoke with difficulty certain sounds—such as the *b* in Robert and the *v* in Cargrave—being almost impossible for him to utter. To shape these sounds, the lips must be used, and the gentleman before me was the victim of some terrible affliction that had caused his lips to be pulled perpetually apart from each other, baring his teeth in a continuous ghastly smile. It was the same humorless grin I had seen once before: on the face of a person in the last throes of lockjaw. We physicians have a name for that chilling grimace, a Latin name, and as it entered my mind, it seemed to dispel yet another mystery, for the term we use to describe the lockjaw smile is: *Risus sardonicus*. A pallor approaching phosphorescence completed his astonishing appearance.

"Yes," I replied, covering my shock at the sight of his face. "Do I have the pleasure of addressing Mr. Sardonicus?"

We shook hands. After an exchange of courtesies, he said, "I have ordered dinner to be served in the large dining hall one hour hence. In the meantime, my valet will show you to your rooms, for I am sure you will wish to refresh yourself after your journey."

"You are most kind." The valet appeared—a man of grave countenance, like the butler and the coachman—and I followed him up a long flight of stone stairs. As I walked behind him, I reflected on the unsmiling faces in this castle, and no longer were they things of wonder. For who would be disposed to smile under the same roof with him who must smile forever? The most spontaneous of smiles would seem a mockery in the presence of that afflicted face. I was filled with pity for Maude's husband: of all God's creatures, man alone is blessed with the ability to smile; but for the master of Castle Sardonicus, God's great blessing had become a terrible curse. As a physician, my pity was tempered with professional curiosity. His smile resembled the *risus* of lockjaw, but lockjaw is a mortal disease, and Mr. Sardonicus, his skullish grin notwithstanding, was very much alive. I felt shame for some of my earlier uncharitable thoughts towards this gentleman, for surely such an unfortunate could be forgiven much. What bitterness must fester in his breast; what sharp despair gnaw at his innards!

My rooms were spacious and certainly as comfortable as this dank stone housing could afford. A hot tub was prepared, for which my tired and dusty frame was most grateful. As I lay in it, I began to experience the pleasant pangs of appetite. I looked forward to dinner. After my bath, I put on fresh linen and a suit of evening clothes. Then, taking from my bag two small gifts for my host and hostess—a bottle of scent for Maude, a box of cigars for her husband—I left my rooms.

I was not so foolish as to expect to find my way, unaided, to the main dining hall; but since I was early, I intended to wander a bit and let the ancient magnificence of the castle impress itself upon me.

Tapestries bearing my host's "S" were frequently displayed. They were remarkably new, their colors fresh, unlike the faded grandeur of their fellow tapestries. From this—and from Mr. Sardonicus' lack of title—I deduced that the castle had not been inherited through a family line, but merely purchased by him, probably from an impoverished nobleman. Though not titled, Mr. Sardonicus evidently possessed enormous wealth. I pondered its source. My ponderings were interrupted by the sound of Maude's voice.

I looked up. The acoustical effects in old castles are often strange—I had marked them in our own English castles—and though I stood near neither room nor door of any kind, I could hear Maude speaking in a distressed tone. I was standing at an open window which overlooked a kind of courtyard. Across this court, a window was likewise open. I took this to be the window of Maude's room; her voice was in some way being amplified and transported by the circumstantial shape of the courtyard and the positions of the two windows. By listening very attentively, I could make out most of her words.

She was saying, "I shan't. You must not ask me. It is unseemly." And then the voice of her husband replied: "You shall and will, madam. In my castle, it is I who decide what is seemly or unseemly. Not you." I was embarrassed at overhearing this private discussion on what was obviously a painful subject, so I made to draw away from the window that I might hear no more, but was restrained by the sound of my own name on Maude's lips. "I have treated Sir Robert with courtesy," she said. "You must treat him with more than courtesy," Mr. Sardonicus responded. "You must treat him with warmth. You must rekindle in his breast those affections he felt for you in other days . . ."

I could listen no longer. The exchange was vile. I drew away from the window. What manner of creature was this Sardonicus who threw his wife into the arms of other men? As a practitioner of medicine, a man dedicated to healing the ills of humankind, I had brought myself to learn many things about the minds of men, as well as about their bodies. I fully believed that, in some future time, physicians would heal the body by way of the mind, for it is in that *terra incognita* that all secrets lie hidden. I knew that love has many masks; masks of submission and of oppression; and even more terrible masks that make Nature a stranger to herself and "turn the truth of God into a lie," as St. Paul wrote. There is even a kind of love, if it can be elevated by that name, that derives its keenest pleasure from the sight of the beloved in the arms of another. These are unpleasant observations, which may one day be codified and studied by healers, but which, until then, may not be thought on for too long, lest the mind grow morbid and stagger under its load of repugnance.

With a heavy heart, I sought out a servant and asked to be taken to the dining hall. It was some distance away, and by the time I arrived there, Sardonicus and his lady were already at table, awaiting me. He arose, and with that revolting smile, indicated a chair; she also arose, and took my arm, addressing me as "Dear Sir Robert" and leading me to my place. Her touch, which at any previous time would have gladdened me, I now found distinctly not to my liking.

A hollow joviality hung over the dinner table throughout the meal. Maude's laughter struck me as giddy and false; Sardonicus drank too much wine and his speech became even more indistinct. I contrived to talk on trivial subjects, repeating some anecdotes about the London theatre which I had hitherto related to Maude, and describing Mr. Macready's interpretation of Macbeth.

"Some actors," said Sardonicus, "interpret the Scottish chieftain as a creature compounded of pure evil, unmingled with good qualities of any kind. Such interpretations are often criticized by those who feel no human being can be so unremittingly evil. Do you agree, Sir Robert?"

"No," I said, evenly; then, looking Sardonicus full in the face, I added, "I believe it is entirely possible for a man to possess not a single one of the virtues, to be a demon in human flesh." Quickly, I embarked upon a discussion of the character of Iago, who took ghoulish delight in tormenting his fellow man.

The dinner was, I suppose, first rate, and the wine an honorable vintage, but I confess to tasting little of what was placed before me. At the end of the meal, Maude left us for a time and Sardonicus escorted me into the library, whither he ordered brandy to be brought. He opened the box of cigars, expressed his admiration of them and gratitude for them, and offered them to me. I took one and we both smoked. The smoking of the cigar made Sardonicus look even more grotesque: being unable to hold it in his lips, he clenched it in his constantly visible teeth, creating an unique spectacle. Brandy was served; I partook of it freely, though I am not customarily given to heavy drinking, for I now deemed it to be beneficial to my dampened spirits.

"You used the word 'ghoulish' a few moments ago, Sir Robert," said Sardonicus. "It is one of those words one uses so easily in conversation—one utters it without stopping to think of its meaning. But, in my opinion, it is not a word to be used lightly. When one uses it, one should have in one's mind a firm, unwavering picture of a ghoul."

"Perhaps I did," I said.

"Perhaps," he admitted. "And perhaps not. Let us obtain a precise definition of the word." He arose and walked to one of the bookcases that lined the room's walls. He reached for a large two-volume dictionary. "Let me see," he murmured. "We desire Volume One, from A to M, do we not? Now then: 'ghee' . . . 'gherkin' . . . 'ghetto' . . . 'ghoom' (an odd word, eh, Sir Robert? 'To search for game in the dark') . . . 'ghost' . . . ah, 'ghoul!'

'Among Eastern nations, an imaginary evil being who robs graves and feeds upon corpses.' One might say, then, that he ghooms?" Sardonicus chuckled. He returned to his chair and helped himself to more brandy. "When you described Iago's actions as 'ghoulish,' " he continued, "did you think of him as the inhabitant of an Eastern nation? Or an imaginary being as against the reality of Othello and Desdemona? And did you mean seriously to suggest that it was his custom to rob graves and then to feed upon the disgusting nourishment he found therein?"

"I used the word in a figurative sense," I replied.

"Ah," said Sardonicus. "That is because you are English and do not believe in ghouls. Were you a Middle-European, as am I, you would believe in their existence, and would not be tempted to use the word other than literally. In my country—I was born in Poland—we understood such things. I, in point of fact, have known a ghoul." He paused for a moment and looked at me, then said, "You English are so blasé. Nothing shocks you. I sit here and tell you a thing of dreadful import and you do not even blink your eyes. Can it be because you do not believe me?"

"It would be churlish to doubt the word of my host," I replied.

"And an Englishman may be many things, but never a churl, eh, Sir Robert? Let me refill your glass, my friend, and then let me tell you about ghouls—which, by the way, are by no means imaginary, as that stupid lexicon would have us think, and which are not restricted to Eastern nations. Neither do they—necessarily—feed upon carrion flesh, although they are interested, *most* interested, in the repellent contents of graves. Let me tell you a story from my own country, Sir Robert, a story that—if I have any gift at all as a spinner of tales—will create in you a profound belief in ghouls. You will be entertained, I hope, but I also hope you will add to your learning. You will learn, for example, how low a human being can sink, how truly *monstrous* a man can become."

4

"YOU MUST transport your mind," said Sardonicus, "back a few years and to a rural region of my homeland. You must become acquainted with a family of country folk—hard-working, law-abiding, God-fearing, of moderate means—the head of which was a simple, good man named Tadeusz Boleslawski. He was an even-tempered personage, kindly disposed to all men, the loving husband of a devoted wife and father of five strong boys. He was also a firm churchman, seldom even taking the Lord's name in vain. The painted women who plied their trade in certain elaborate houses of the nearest large city, Warsaw, held no attraction for him, though several of his masculine neighbors, on their visits to the metropolis, succumbed to such blandishments with tidal regularity. Neither did he drink in excess: a glass of beer with his evening meal, a toast or two in wine on special occasions. No: hard liquor, strong language, fast women—these were not the weaknesses of Tadeusz Boleslawski. His weakness was gambling.

"Every month he would make the trip to Warsaw, to sell his produce at the markets and to buy certain necessaries for his home. While his comrades visited the drinking and wenching houses, Tadeusz would attend strictly to business affairs—except for one minor deviation. He would purchase a lottery ticket, place it securely in a small, tight pocket of his best waistcoat—which he wore only on Sundays and on his trips to the city—then put it completely out of his mind until the following month, when, on reaching the city, he would remove it from his pocket and closely scan the posted list of winners. Then, after methodically tearing the ticket to shreds (for Tadeusz never lived to win a lottery), he would purchase another. This was a ritual with him; he performed it every month for twenty-three years, and the fact that he never won did not discourage him. His wife knew of this habit, but since it was the good man's only flaw, she never remarked upon it."

Outside, I could hear the wind howling dismally. I took more brandy as Sardonicus continued:

"Years passed; three of the five sons married; two (Henryk and Marek, the youngest) were still living with their parents, when Tadeusz—who had been of sturdy health—collapsed one day in the fields and died. I will spare you an account of the family's grief; how the married sons returned with their wives to attend the obsequies; of the burial in the small graveyard of that community. The good man had left few possessions, but these few were divided, according to his written wish, among his survivors, with the largest share going, of course, to the eldest son. Though this was custom, the other sons could not help feeling a trifle disgruntled, but they held their peace for the most part—especially the youngest, Marek, who was perhaps the most amiable of them and a lad who was by nature quiet and interested in improving his lot through the learning he found in books.

"Imagine, sir, the amazement of the widow when, a full three weeks after the interment of her husband, she received word by men returning from Warsaw that the lottery ticket Tadeusz had purchased had now been selected as the winner. It was a remarkable irony, of course, but conditions had grown hard for the poor woman, and would grow harder with her husband dead, so she had no time to reflect upon that irony. She set about looking through her husband's possessions for the lottery ticket. Drawers were emptied upon the floor; boxes and cupboards were ransacked; the family Bible was shaken out; years before, Tadeusz had been in the habit of temporarily hiding money under a loose floorboard in the bedroom—this cavity was thoroughly but vainly plumbed. The sons were sent for: among the few personal effects they had been bequeathed, did the ticket languish there? In the snuff box? In any article of clothing?

"And at that, Sir Robert, the eldest son leapt up. 'An article of clothing!' he cried. 'Father always wore his Sunday waistcoat to the city when he purchased the lottery tickets—the very waistcoat in which he was buried!'

" 'Yes, yes!' the other sons chorused, saving Marek, and plans began to be laid for the exhuming of the dead man. But the widow spoke firmly: 'Your father rests peacefully,' she said. 'He must not be disturbed. No amount of gold would soothe our hearts if we disturbed him.' The sons protested with vehemence, but the widow stood her ground. 'No son of mine will profane his father's grave—unless he first kills his mother!' Grumbling, the sons withdrew their plans. But that night, Marek awoke to find his mother gone from the house. He was frightened, for this was not like her. Intuition sent him to the graveyard, where he found her, keeping a lonely vigil over the grave of her husband, protecting him from the greed of grave robbers. Marek implored her to come out of the cold, to return home; she at first refused; only when Marek offered to keep vigil all night himself did she relent and return home, leaving her youngest son to guard the grave from profanation.

"Marek waited a full hour. Then he produced from under his shirt a small shovel. He was a strong boy, and the greed of a youngest son who has been deprived of inheritance lent added strength to his arms. He dug relentlessly, stopping seldom for rest, until finally the coffin was uncovered. He raised the creaking lid. An overpowering fetor filled his nostrils and nearly made him faint. Gathering courage, he searched the pockets of the mouldering waistcoat.

"The moon proved to be his undoing, Sir Robert. For suddenly its rays, hitherto hidden, struck the face of his father, and at the sight of that face, the boy recoiled and went reeling against the wall of the grave, the breath forced from his body. Now, you must know that the mere sight of his father—even in an advanced state of decomposition—he had steeled himself to withstand; but what he had *not* foreseen—"

Here, Sardonicus leaned close to me and his pallid, grinning head filled my vision. "What he had not foreseen, my dear sir, was that the face of his father, in the rigor of death, would look directly and hideously upon him." Sardonicus' voice became an ophidian hiss. "And, Sir Robert," he added, "most terrible and most unforeseen of all, the dead lips were drawn back from the teeth *in a constant and soul-shattering smile!*"

5

THE REMEMBRANCE OF THAT NIGHT

I KNOW not whether it was the ghastliness of his story, or the sight of his hideous face so close to mine, or the cheerless keening of the wind outside, or the brandy I had consumed, or all of these in combination; but when Sardonicus uttered those last words, my heart was clutched by a cold hand, and for a moment— a long moment ripped from the texture of time—I was convinced beyond doubt and beyond logic that the face I looked into was the face of that cadaver, reanimated by obscure arts, to walk among the living, dead though not dead.

The moment of horror passed, at length, and reason triumphed. Sardonicus, considerably affected by his own tale, sat back in his chair, trembling. Before too long, he spoke again:

"The remembrance of that night, Sir Robert, though it is now many years past, fills me still with dread. You will appreciate this when I tell you what you have perhaps already guessed—that *I* am that ghoulish son, Marek."

I had not guessed it; but since I had no wish to tell him I had for an instant thought he was the dead father, I said nothing.

"When my senses returned," said Sardonicus, "I scrambled out of the grave and ran as swiftly as my limbs would carry me. I had reached the gate of the graveyard when I was smitten by the fact I had not accomplished the purpose of my mission—the lottery ticket remained in my father's pocket!"

"But surely—" I started to say.

"Surely I ignored the fact and continued to run? No, Sir Robert. My terror notwithstanding, I halted, and forced myself to retrace those hasty steps. My fear notwithstanding, I descended once more into that noisome grave. My disgust notwithstanding, I reached into the pocket of my decaying father's waistcoat and extracted the ticket! I need hardly add that, this time, I averted my eyes from his face.

"But the horror was not behind me. Indeed, it had only begun. I reached my home at a late hour, and my family was asleep. For this I was grateful, since my clothes were covered with soil and I still trembled from my fearful experience. I quietly poured water into a basin and prepared to wash some of the graveyard dirt from my face and hands. In performing my ablutions, I looked up into a mirror—*and screamed so loudly as to wake the entire house!*

"My face was as you see it now, a replica of my dead father's: the lips drawn back in a perpetual, mocking grin. I tried to close my mouth. I could not. The muscles were immovable, as if held in the gelid rigor of death. I could hear my family stirring at my scream, and since I did not wish them to look upon me, I ran from the house—never, Sir Robert, to return.

"As I wandered the rural roads, my mind sought the cause of

the affliction that had been visited upon me. Though but a country lad, I had read much and I had a blunt, rational mind that was not susceptible to the easy explanations of the supernatural. I would not believe that God had placed a malediction upon me to punish me for my act. I would not believe that some black force from beyond the grave had reached out to stamp my face. At length, I began to believe it was the massive shock that had forced my face to its present state, and that my great guilt had helped to shape it even as my father's dead face was shaped. Shock and guilt: strong powers not from God above or the Fiend below, but from within my own breast, my own brain, my own soul.

"Let me bring this history to a hasty close, Sir Robert. You need only know that, despite my blighted face, I redeemed the lottery ticket and thus gained an amount of money that will not seem large to you, but which was more than I had ever seen before that time. It was the fulcrum from which I plied the lever that was to make me, by dint of shrewd speculation, one of the richest men in Central Europe. Naturally, I sought out physicians and begged them to restore my face to its previous state. None succeeded, though I offered them vast sums. My face remained fixed in this damnable unceasing smile, and my heart knew the most profound despair imaginable. I could not even pronounce my own name! By a dreadful irony, the initial letters of my first and last names were impossible for my frozen lips to form. This seemed the final indignity. I will admit to you that, at this period, I was perilously near the brink of self-destruction. But the spirit of preservation prevailed, and I was saved from that course. I changed my name. I had read of the *Risus sardonicus,* and its horrible aptness appealed to my bitter mind, so I became Sardonicus—a name I can pronounce with no difficulty."

Sardonicus paused and sipped his brandy. "You are wondering," he then said, "in what way my story concerns you."

I could guess, but I said: "I am."

"Sir Robert," he said, "you are known throughout the medical world. Most laymen, perhaps, have not heard of you; but a layman such as I, a layman who avidly follows the medical journals for tidings of any recent discoveries in the curing for paralyzed muscles, has heard of you again and again. Your researches into these problems have earned you high professional regard; indeed, they have earned you a knighthood. For some time, it has been in my mind to visit London and seek you out. I have consulted many physicians, renowned men—Keller in Berlin, Morignac in Paris, Buonagente in Milan—and none have been able to help me. My despair has been utter. It prevented me from making the long journey to England. But when I heard—sublime coincidence!—that my own wife had been acquainted with you, I took heart. Sir Robert, I entreat you to heal me, to lift from me this curse, to make me look once more like a man, that I may walk in the sun again, among my fellow human beings, as one of them, rather than as a fearsome gargoyle to be shunned and feared and ridiculed. Surely you cannot, *will* not deny me?"

My feelings for Sardonicus, pendulumlike, again swung towards his favor. His story, his plight, had rent my heart, and I reverted to my earlier opinion that such a man should be forgiven much. The strange overheard conversation between Maude and him was momentarily forgotten. I said, "I will examine you, Mr. Sardonicus. You were right to ask me. We must never abandon hope."

He clasped his hands together. "Ah, sir! May you be blessed forever!"

I performed the examination then and there. Although I did not tell him this, never had I encountered muscles as rigid as those of his face. They could only be compared to stone, so inflexible were they. Still, I said, "Tomorrow we will begin treatment. Heat and massage."

"These have been tried," he said, hopelessly.

"Massage differs from one pair of hands to another," I replied. "I have had success with my own techniques, and therefore place faith in them. Be comforted then, sir, and share my faith."

He seized my hand in his. "I do," he said. "I must. For if you—if even *you,* Sir Robert Cargrave, fail me . . ." He did not complete the sentence, but his eyes assumed an aspect so bitter, so full of hate, so strangely cold yet flaming, that they floated in my dreams that night.

6

I SLEPT not well, awakening many times in a fever compounded of drink and turbulent emotions. When the first rays of morning crept on to my pillow, I arose, little refreshed. After a cold tub and a light breakfast in my room, I went below to the salon whence music issued. Maude was already there, playing a pretty little piece upon the spinet. She looked up and greeted me. "Good morning, Sir Robert. Do you know the music of Mr. Gottschalk? He is an American pianist: this is his *Maiden's Blush*. Amiable, is it not?"

"Most amiable," I replied, dutifully although I was in no mood for the embroideries of *politesse*.

Maude soon finished the piece and closed the album. She turned to me and said, in a serious tone, "I have been told what you are going to do for my poor husband, Sir Robert, I can scarce express my gratitude."

"There is no need to express it," I assured her. "As a physician— as well as your old friend—I could not do less. I hope you understand, however, that a cure is not a certainty. I will try, and I will try to the limit of my powers, but beyond that I can promise nothing."

Her eyes shone with supplication: "Oh, cure him, Sir Robert! That I beg of you!"

"I understand your feelings, madam," I said. "It is fitting that you should hope so fervently for his recovery; a devoted wife could feel no other way."

"Oh, sir," she said, and into her voice crept now a harshness, "you misunderstand. My fervent hope springs from unalloyed selfishness."

"How may that be?" I asked.

"If you do not succeed in curing him," she told me, "I will suffer."

"I understand that, but—"

"No, you do not understand," she said. "But I can tell you little more without offending. Some things are better left unspoken. Suffice it to be said that, in order to urge you towards an ultimate effort, to the 'limit of your powers' as you have just said, my husband intends to hold over your head the threat of my punishment."

"This is monstrous!" I cried. "It cannot be tolerated. But in what manner, pray, would he dare punish you? Surely he would not beat you?"

"I wish he would be content with a mere beating," she groaned, "but his cleverness knows a keener torture. No, he holds over me—and over you, through me—a punishment far greater; a punishment (believe me!) so loathsome to the sensibilities, so unequivocally vile and degraded, that my mind shrinks from contemplating it. Spare me your further questions, sir, I enjoin you; for to describe it would plunge me into an abyss of humiliation and shame!"

She broke into sobbing, and tears coursed down her cheeks. No longer able to restrain my tender feelings for her, I flew to her side and took her hands in mine. "Maude," I said, "may I call you that? In the past I addressed you only as Miss Randall; at present I may only call you Madam Sardonicus; but in my heart—then as now—you are, you always have been, you always will be, simply Maude, my own dear Maude!"

"Robert," she sighed; "dearest Robert. I have yearned to hear my Christian name from your lips all these long years."

"The warmth we feel," I said, "may never, with honor, reach fulfillment. But—trust me, dearest Maude!—I will in some wise deliver you from the tyranny of that creature: this I vow!"

"I have no hope," she said, "save in you. Whether I go on as I am, or am subjected to an unspeakable horror, rests with you. My fate is in your hands—these strong, healing hands, Robert." Her voice dropped to a whisper: "Fail me not! oh fail me not!"

"Govern your fears," I said. "Return to your music. Be of good spirits; or, if you cannot, make a show of it. I go now to treat your husband, and also to confront him with what you have told me."

"Do not!" she cried. "Do not, I beseech you, Robert; lest, in the event of your failure, he devise foul embellishments upon the agonies into which he will cast me!"

"Very well," I said, "I will not speak of this to him. But my heart aches to learn the nature of the torments you fear."

"Ask no more, Robert," she said, turning away. "Go to my husband. Cure him. Then I will no longer fear those torments."

I pressed her dear hand and left the salon.

Sardonicus awaited me in his chambers. Thither, quantities of hot water and stacks of towels had been brought by the servants, upon my orders. Sardonicus was stripped to the waist, displaying a trunk strong and of good musculature, but with the same near-phosphorescent pallor of his face. It was, I now understood, the pallor of one who has avoided daylight for years. "As you see, sir," he greeted me, "I am ready for your ministrations."

I bade him recline upon his couch, and began the treatment. Never have I worked so long with so little reward. After alternating applications of heat and of massage, over a period of three and a quarter hours, I had made no progress. The muscles of his face were still as stiff as marble; they had not relaxed for an instant. I was mortally tired. He ordered our luncheon brought to us in his chambers, and after a short respite, I began again. The clock tolled six when I at last sank into a chair, shaking with exhaustion and strain. His face was exactly as before.

"What remains to be done, sir?" he asked me.

"I will not deceive you," I said. "It is beyond my skill to alleviate your condition. I can do no more."

He rose swiftly from the couch. "You *must* do more!" he shrieked. "You are my last hope!"

"Sir," I said, "new medical discoveries are ever being made. Place your trust in Him who created you—"

"Cease that detestable gibberish at once!" he snapped. "Your puling sentiments sicken me! Resume the treatment."

I refused. "I have applied all my knowledge, all my art, to your affliction," I assured him. "To resume the treatment would be idle and foolish, for—as you have divined—the condition is a product of your own mind."

"At dinner last night," countered Sardonicus, "we spoke of the character of Macbeth. Do you not remember the words he addressed to *his* doctor?—

" 'Canst thou not minister to a mind diseas'd;
Pluck from the memory a rooted sorrow;
Raze out the written troubles of the brain;
And with some sweet oblivious antidote
Cleanse the stuff'd bosom of that perilous stuff
Which weighs upon the heart?' "

"I remember them," I said; "and I remember, as well, the doctors reply: *'Therein the patient must minister to himself.'*" I arose and started for the door.

"One moment, Sir Robert," he said. I turned. "Forgive my precipitate outburst a moment ago. However, the mental nature of my affliction notwithstanding, and even though this mode of treatment has failed, surely there are other treatments?"

"None," I said, "that have been sufficiently tested. None I would venture to use upon a human body."

"Ah!" he cried. "Then other treatments *do* exist!"

I shrugged. "Think not of them, sir. They are at present unavailable to you." I pitied him, and added: "I am sorry."

"Doctor!" he said; "I implore you to use whatever treatments exist, be they ever so untried!"

"They are fraught with danger," I said.

"Danger?" He laughed. "Danger of what? Of disfigurement? Surely no man has ever been more disfigured than I! Of death? I am willing to gamble my life!"

"*I* am not willing to gamble your life," I said. "All lives are precious. Even yours."

"Sir Robert, I will pay you a thousand pounds."

"This is not a question of money."

"Five thousand pounds, Sir Robert, *ten* thousand!"

"No."

He sank on to the couch. "Very well," he said. "Then I will offer you the ultimate inducement."

"Were it a million pounds," I said, "you could not sway me."

"The inducement I speak of," he said, "is not money. Will you hear?"

I sat down. "Speak, sir," I said, "since that is your wish. But nothing will persuade me to use a treatment that might cost you your life."

"Sir Robert," he said, after a pause, "yestereve, when I came down to meet you for the first time, I heard happy sounds in the salon. You were singing a charming melody with my wife. Later, I could not help but notice the character of your glances towards her . . ."

"They were not reciprocated, sir," I told him, "and herewith I offer you a most abject apology for my unbecoming conduct."

"You obscure my point," he said. "You are a friend of hers,

from the old days in London; at that period, you felt an ardent affection for her, I would guess. This is not surprising: for she is a lady whose face and form promise voluptuous delights and yet a lady whose manner is most decorous and correct. I would guess further: that your ardor has not diminished over the years; that, at the sight of her, the embers have burst into a flame. No, sir, hear me out. What would you say, Sir Robert, were I to tell you— that you may quench that flame?"

I frowned. "Your meaning, sir—?"

"Must I speak even more plainly? I am offering you a golden opportunity to requite the love that burns in your heart."

"Scoundrel!" I roared, leaping up.

He heeded me not, but went on speaking: ". . . As my guest, Sir Robert! I offer you a veritable Oriental paradise of unlimited raptures!"

"Enough!" I cried. "I will hear no more of your foulness." I strode to the door.

"Yes, you will, Sir Robert," he said immediately. "You will hear a good deal more of my foulness. You will hear what I plan to do to your beloved Maude, should you fail to relieve me of this deformity."

Again, I stopped and turned. I said nothing, but waited for him to speak further.

"I perceive that I have caught your interest," he said. "Hear me: for if you think I spoke foully before, you will soon be forced to agree that my earlier words were, by comparison, as blameless as The Book of Common Prayer. If rewards do not tempt you, then threats may coerce you. In fine, Maude will be punished if you fail, Sir Robert."

"She is an innocent."

"Just so. Hence, the more exquisite and insupportable to you should be the thought of her punishment."

My mind reeled. I could not believe such words were being uttered.

"Deep in the bowels of this old castle," said Sardonicus, "are dungeons. Suppose I were to tell you that my intention is to drag my wife thither and stretch her smooth body to unendurable length upon the rack—"

"You would not dare!" I cried.

"My daring or lack of it is not the issue here. I speak of the rack only that I may go on to assure you that Maude would *infinitely prefer* that dreadful machine to the punishment I have in truth designed for her. I will describe it to you. You will wish to be seated, I think."

7

ENTERTAINMENT FOR A MONSTER

"I WILL stand," I said.

"As you please," Sardonicus himself sat down. "Perhaps you have marveled at the very fact of Maude's marriage to me. When the world was so full of personable men—men like yourself, who adored her—why did she choose to wed a monster, a creature abhorrent to the eyes and who did not, moreover, have any redeeming grace of spiritual beauty, or kindness, or charm?

"I first met Maude Randall in Paris. I say 'met,' but it would be truer to simply say I saw her—from my hotel window, in fact. Even in Paris society, which abounds in ladies of remarkable pulchritude, she was to be remarked upon. You perhaps would say I fell in love with her, but I dislike that word 'love,' and will merely say that the sight of her smote my senses with most agreeable emphasis. I decided to make her mine. But how? By presenting my irresistibly handsome face to her view? Hardly. I began methodically: I hired secret operatives to find out everything about her and about her mother and father—both of whom were then alive. I discovered that her father was in the habit of speculating, so I saw to it that he received some supposedly trustworthy but very bad advice. He speculated heavily and was instantly ruined. I must admit I had not planned his consequent suicide, but when that melancholy event occurred, I rejoiced, for it worked to my advantage. I presented myself to the bereaved widow and daughter, telling them the excellent qualities of Mr. Randall were widely known in the world of affairs and that I considered myself almost a close friend. I offered to help them in any possible way. By dint of excessive humility and persuasiveness, I won their trust and succeeded in diminishing their aversion to my face. This, you must understand, from first to last, occupied a period of many months. I spoke nothing of marriage, made no sign of affection towards the daughter for at least six of these months; when I did—again, with great respect and restraint—she gently refused me. I retreated gracefully, saying only that I hoped I might remain her and her mother's friend. She replied that she sincerely shared that hope, for, although she could never look upon me as an object of love, she indeed considered me a true friend. The mother, who pined excessively after the death of the father, soon expired: another incident unplanned but welcomed by me. Now the lovely child was alone in the world in a foreign city, with no money, no one to guide her, no one to fall back upon—save kindly Mr. Sardonicus. I waited many weeks, then I proposed marriage again. For several days, she continued to decline the offer, but her declinations grew weaker and weaker until, at length, on one day, she said this to me:

" 'Sir, I esteem you highly as a friend and benefactor, but my other feelings toward you have not changed. If you could be satisfied with such a singular condition; if you could agree to enter into marriage with a lady and yet look upon her as no more than a companion of kindred spirit; if the prospect of a dispassionate and childless marriage does not repulse you—as well it might— then, sir, my unhappy circumstances would compel me to accept your kind offer.'

"Instantly, I told her my regard for her was of the purest and most elevated variety; that the urgings of the flesh were unknown to me; that I lived on a spiritual plane and desired only her sweet and stimulating companionship through the years. All this, of course, was a lie. The diametric opposite was true. But I hoped, by this falsehood, to lure her into marriage; after which, by slow and strategic process, I could bring about her submission and my rapture. She still was hesitant; for, as she frankly told me, she believed that love was a noble and integral part of marriage; and that marriage without it could be only a hollow thing; and that though I knew not the urgings of the flesh, she could not with honesty say the same of herself. Yet she reiterated that, so far as my own person was concerned, a platonic relationship was all that could ever exist between us. I calmed her misgivings. We were married not long after.

"And now, Sir Robert, I will tell you a surprising thing. Not once in the years of our marriage—not once, I say—have I been able to persuade or cajole my wife into relenting and breaking the stringent terms of our marriage agreement. Each time I have attempted, she has recoiled from me with horror and disgust. This is not because of an abhorrence of all fleshly things—by her own admission—but because of my monstrous face.

"Perhaps now you will better understand the vital necessity for this cure. And perhaps also you will understand the full extent of Maude's suffering should you fail to effect that cure. For, mark me well: if you fail, my wife will be made to become a true wife to me—by main force."

I had been shocked into silence. I could only look upon him with disbelief. He spoke again:

"If you deem it a light punishment, Sir Robert, then you do not know the depth of her loathing for my person, you do not know the revulsion that wells up inside her when I but place my fingers upon her arm, you do not know what mastery of her very gorge is required of her when I kiss her hand. Think, then; think of the abomination she would feel were my attentions to grow more ardent, more demanding! It would unseat her mind, sir; of that I am sure, for she would as soon embrace a reptile."

Sardonicus arose and put on his shirt. "I suggest we both begin dressing for dinner," he said. "Whilst you are dressing, reflect. Ask yourself, Sir Robert: could you ever again look upon yourself with other than shame and loathing if you were to sacrifice the beautiful and blameless Maude Randall on an altar of the grossest depravity? Consider how ill you would sleep in your London bed, night after night, knowing what she was suffering at that very moment; suffering because *you* abandoned her, because *you* allowed her to become an entertainment for a monster."

8

A TOKEN OF DETESTATION

THE DAYS that passed after that time were, in the main, tedious yet filled with anxiety. During them, certain supplies were being brought from London and other places; Sardonicus spared no expense in procuring for me everything I said was necessary to the treatment. I avoided his society as much as I could, shunning even his table, and instructing the servants to bring my meals to my rooms. On the other hand, I sought out the company of Maude, endeavoring to comfort her and allay her fears. In those hours when her husband was occupied with business affairs, we talked together in the salon, and played music. Thus, they were days spotted with small pleasures that seemed the greater for having been snatched in the shadow of wretchedness.

I grew to know Maude, in that time, better than I had ever known her in London. Adversity stripped the layers of ceremony from our congress, and we spoke directly. I came to know her warmth, but I came to know her strength, too. I spoke outright of my love, though in the next breath I assured her I was aware of the hopelessness of that love. I did not tell her of the "reward" her husband had offered me—and which I had refused—and I was gladdened to learn (as I did by indirection) that Sardonicus, though he had abjured her to be excessively cordial to me, had not revealed the ultimate and ignoble purpose of that cordiality.

"Robert," she said once, "is it likely that he will be cured?"

I did not tell her how unlikely it was. "For your sake, Maude," I said, "I will persevere more than I have ever done in my life."

At length, a day arrived when all the necessaries had been gathered: some plants from the New World, certain equipment from London, and a vital instrument from Scotland. I worked long and late, in complete solitude, distilling a needed liquor from the plants. The next day, dogs were brought to me alive, and carried out dead. Three days after that, a dog left my laboratory alive and my distilling labors came to an end.

I informed Sardonicus that I was ready to administer the treatment. He came to my laboratory, and I imagined there was almost a gloating triumph in his immobile smile. "Such are the fruits of concentrated effort," he said. "Man is an indolent creature, but light the fire of fear under him, and of what miracles is he not capable!"

"Speak not of miracles," I said, "though prayers would do you no harm now, for you will soon be in peril of your life." I motioned him towards a table and bade him lie upon it. He did so, and I commenced explaining the treatment to him. "The explorer Magellan," I said, "wrote of a substance used on darts by the savage inhabitants of the South American continent. It killed instantly, dropping large animals in their tracks. The substance was derived from certain plants, and is, in essence, the same substance I have been occupied in extracting these past days."

"A poison, Sir Robert?" he asked, wryly.

"When used full strength," I said, "it kills by bringing about a *total* relaxation of the muscles—particularly the muscles of the lungs and heart. I have long thought that a dilution of that poison might beneficially slacken the rigidly tensed muscles of paralyzed patients."

"Most ingenious, sir," he said.

"I must warn you," I went on, "that this distillment has never been used on a human subject. It may kill you. I must, perforce, urge you again not to insist upon its use; to accept your lot; and to remove the threat of punishment you now hold over your wife's head."

"You seek to frighten me, Doctor," chuckled Sardonicus; "to plant distrust in my bosom. But I fear you not—an English knight and a respected physician would never do a deed so dishonorable as to wittingly kill a patient under his care. You would be hamstrung by your gentleman's code as well as by your professional oath. Your virtues are, in short, my vices' best ally."

I bristled. "I am no murderer such as you," I said. "If you force me to use this treatment, I will do everything in my power to insure its success. But I cannot conceal from you the possibility of your death."

"See to it that I live," he said flatly, "for if I die, my men will kill both you and my wife. They will not kill you quickly. See to it, also, that I am cured—lest Maude be subjected to a fate she fears more than the slowest of tortures." I said nothing. "Then bring me this elixir straightway," he said, "and let me drink it off and make an end of this!"

"It is not to be drunk," I told him.

He laughed. "Is it your plan to smear it on darts, like the savages?"

"Your jest is most apposite," I said. "I indeed plan to introduce it into your body by means of a sharp instrument—a new instrument not yet widely known, that was sent me from Scotland. The original suggestion was put forth in the University of Oxford some two hundred years ago by Dr. Christopher Wren, but only recently, through development by my friend, Dr. Wood of Edinburgh, has it seemed practical. It is no more than a syringe"—I showed him the instrument—"attached to a needle; but the needle is hollow, so that, when it punctures the skin, it may carry healing drugs directly into the bloodstream."

"The medical arts will never cease earning my admiration," said Sardonicus.

I filled the syringe. My patient said, "Wait."

"Are you afraid?" I asked.

"Since that memorable night in my father's grave," he replied, "I have not known fear. I had a surfeit of it then; it will last out my lifetime. No: I simply wish to give instructions to one of my men." He arose from the table, and, going to the door, told one of his helots to bring Madam Sardonicus to the laboratory.

"Why must she be here?" I asked.

"The sight of her," he said, "may serve you as a remembrancer of what awaits her in the event of my death, or of that other punishment she may expect should your treatment prove ineffectual."

Maude was brought into our presence. She looked upon my equipment—the bubbling retorts and tubes, the pointed syringe—with amazement and fright. I began to explain the principle of the treatment to her, but Sardonicus interrupted: "Madam is not one of your students, Sir Robert; it is not necessary she know these details. Delay no longer; begin at once!"

He stretched out upon the table again, fixing his eyes upon me. I proffered Maude a comforting look, and walked over to my patient. He did not wince as I drove the needle of the syringe into the left, and then the right, side of his face. "Now, sir," I said—and the tremor in my voice surprised me—"we must wait a period of ten minutes." I joined Maude, and talked to her in low tones, keeping my eyes always upon my patient. He stared at the ceiling; his face remained solidified in that unholy grin. Precisely ten minutes later, a short gasp escaped him; I rushed to his side, and Maude followed close behind me.

We watched with consuming fascination as that clenched face slowly softened, relaxed, changed; the lips drawing closer and closer to each other, gradually covering those naked teeth and gums, the graven creases unfolding and becoming smooth. Before a minute had passed, we were looking down upon the face of a serenely handsome man. His eyes flashed with pleasure, and he made as if to speak.

"No," I said, "do not attempt speech yet. The muscles of your face are so slackened that it is beyond your power, at present, to move your lips. This condition will pass." My voice rang with exultation, and for the moment our enmity was forgotten. He nodded, then leapt from the table and dashed to a mirror which hung on a wall nearby. Though his face could not yet express his joy, his whole body seemed to unfurl in a great gesture of triumph and a muffled cry of happiness burst in his throat.

He turned and seized my hand; then he looked full into Maude's face. After a moment, she said, "I am happy for you, sir," and looked away. A rasping laugh sounded in his throat, and he walked to my work bench, tore a leaf from one of my notebooks, and scribbled upon it. This he handed to Maude, who read it and passed it over to me. The writing said: *Fear not, lady. You will not be obliged to endure my embraces. I know full well that the restored beauty of my face will weigh not a jot in the balance of your attraction and repugnance. By this document, I dissolve our pristine marriage. You who have been a wife only in name are no longer even that. I give you your freedom.*

I looked up from my reading. Sardonicus had been writing again. He ripped another leaf from the notebook and handed it directly to me. It read: *This paper is your safe conduct out of the castle and into the village. Gold is yours for the asking, but I doubt if your English scruples will countenance the accepting of my money. I will expect you to have quit these premises before morning, taking her with you.*

"We will be gone within the hour," I told him, and guided Maude towards the door. Before we left the room, I turned for the last time to Sardonicus.

"For your unclean threats," I said; "for the indirect but no less vicious murder of this lady's parents; for the defiling of your own father's grave; for the greed and inhumanity that moved you even before your blighted face provided you with an excuse for your conduct; for these and for what crimes unknown to me blacken your ledger—accept this token of my censure and detestation." I struck him forcibly on the face. He did not respond. He was standing there in the laboratory when I left the room with Maude.

9

THIS STRANGE account should probably end here. No more can be said of its central character, for neither Maude nor I saw him or heard of him after that night. And of us two, nothing need be imparted other than the happy knowledge that we have been most contentedly married for the past twelve years and are the parents of a sturdy boy and two girls who are the lovely images of their mother.

However, I have mentioned my friend Lord Henry Stanton, the inveterate traveler and faithful letter writer, and I must copy out now a portion of a missive I received from him only a week since, and which, in point of fact, has been the agent that has prompted me to unfold this whole history of Mr. Sardonicus:

". . . But, my dear Bobbie," wrote Stanton, "in truth there is small pleasure to be found in this part of the world, and I shall be glad to see London again. The excitements and the drama have all departed (if, indeed, they ever existed) and one must content one's self with the stories told at the hearthstones of inns, with the flames crackling and the mulled wine agreeably stinging one's throat. The natives here are most fond of harrowing stories, tales of gore and grue, of ghosts and ghouls and ghastly events, and I must confess a partiality to such entertainments myself. They will show you a stain on a wall and tell you it is the blood of a murdered innocent who met her death there fifty years before: no amount of washing will ever remove that stain, they tell you in sepulchral tones, and indeed it deepens and darkens on a certain day of the year, the anniversary of her violent passing. One is expected to nod gravely, of course, and one does, if one wishes to encourage the telling of more stories. Back in the eleventh century, you will be apprised, a battalion of foreign invaders were vanquished by the skeletons of long-dead patriots who arose from their tombs to defend their homeland and then returned to the earth when the enemy had been driven from their borders. (And since they are able to show you the very graves of these lively bones, how can one disbelieve them, Bobbie?) Or they will point to a desolate skull of a castle (the country here abounds in such depressing piles) and tell you of the spectral tyrant who, a scant dozen years before, despaired and died alone there. Deserted by the minions who had always hated him, the frightening creature roamed the village, livid and emaciated, his mind shattered, mutely imploring the succour of even the lowliest beggars, I say *mutely,* and that is the best part of this tall tale: for, as they tell it around the fire, these inventive folk, this poor unfortunate could not speak, could not eat, and could not drink. You ask why? For the simple reason that, though he clawed most horribly at his own face, and though he enlisted the aid of strong men—he was absolutely unable to open his mouth. Cursed by Lucifer, they say, he thirsted and starved in the midst of plenty, surrounded by kegs of drink and tables full of the choicest viands, suffering the tortures of Tantalus, until he finally died. Ah, Bobbie! the efforts of our novelists are pale stuff compared to this! English litterateurs have not the shameless wild imaginations of these people! I will never again read Mrs. Radcliffe with pleasure, I assure you, and the ghost of King Hamlet will, from this day hence, strike no terror to my soul, and will fill my heart with but paltry pity. Still, I have journeyed in foreign climes quite enough for one trip, and I long for England and that good English dullness which is relieved only by you and your dear lady (to whom you must commend me most warmly). Until next month, I remain,

> "Your wayward friend,
> "HARRY STANTON
> "(Bohemia, March, 18—)"

Now, it would not be a difficult feat for the mind to instantly assume that the unfortunate man in that last tale was Sardonicus—indeed, it is for that reason that I have not yet shown Stanton's letter to Maude: for she, albeit she deeply loathed Sardonicus, is of such a compassionate and susceptible nature that she would grieve to hear of him suffering a death so horrible. But I am a man of science, and I do not form conclusions on such gossamer evidence. Harry did not mention the province of Bohemia that is supposed to have been the stage of that terrible drama; and his letter, though written in Bohemia, was not mailed by Harry until he reached Berlin, so the postmark tells me nothing. Castles like that of Sardonicus are not singular in Bohemia—Harry himself says the country "abounds in such depressing piles"—so I plan to suspend conclusive thoughts on the matter until I welcome Harry home and can elicit from him details of the precise locality.

For if that "desolate skull of a castle" *is* Castle Sardonicus, and if the story of the starving man is to be believed, then I will be struck by an awesome and curious thing:

Five days I occupied myself in extracting a liquor from the South American plants. During those days, dogs were carried dead from my laboratory. I had deliberately killed the poor creatures with the undiluted poison, in order to impress Sardonicus with its deadliness. I never intended to—and, in fact, never did—prepare a safe dilution of that lethal drug, for its properties were too unknown, its potentiality too dangerous. The liquid I injected into Sardonicus was pure, distilled water—nothing more. This had always been my plan. The ordering of *materia medica* from far-flung lands was but an elaborate facade designed to work not upon the physical part of Sardonicus, but upon his mind; for after Keller, Morignac, Buonagente, and my own massaging techniques had failed, I was convinced that it was only through his mind that his body could be cured. It was necessary to persuade him, however, that he was receiving a powerful medicament. His mind, I had hoped, would provide the rest—as, in truth, it did.

If the tale of the "spectral tyrant" proved true, then we must look upon the human mind with wonderment and terror. For, in that case, there was nothing—nothing corporeal—to prevent the wretched creature from opening his mouth and eating his fill. Alone in that castle, food aplenty at his fingertips, he had suffered a dire punishment which came upon him—to paraphrase Sardonicus' very words—*not from God above or the Fiend below, but from within his own breast, his own brain, his own soul.*

GEORGE R. R. MARTIN
Nightflyers

WHEN JESUS OF NAZARETH hung dying on his cross, the *volcryn* passed within a light-year of his agony, headed outward. When the Fire Wars raged on Earth, the *volcryn* sailed near Old Poseidon, where the seas were still unnamed and unfished. By the time the stardrive had transformed the Federated Nations of Earth into the Federal Empire, the *volcryn* had moved into the fringes of Hrangan space. The Hrangans never knew it. Like us they were children of the small bright worlds that circled their scattered suns, with little interest and less knowledge of the things that moved in the gulfs between.

War flamed for a thousand years and the *volcryn* passed through it, unknowing and untouched, safe in a place where no fires could ever burn. Afterwards the Federal Empire was shattered and gone, and the Hrangans vanished in the dark of the Collapse, but it was no darker for the *volcryn*.

When Kleronomas took his survey ship out from Avalon, the *volcryn* came within ten light-years of him. Kleronomas found many things, but he did not find the *volcryn*. Not then did he and not on his return to Avalon a lifetime later.

When I was a child of three, Kleronomas was dust, as distant and dead as Jesus of Nazareth, and the *volcryn* passed close to Daronne. That season all the Crey sensitives grew strange and sat staring at the stars with luminous, flickering eyes.

When I was grown, the *volcryn* had sailed beyond Tara, past the range of even the Crey, still heading outward.

And now I am old and the *volcryn* will soon pierce the Tempter's

189

Veil where it hangs like a black mist between the stars. And we
follow, we follow. Through the dark gulfs where no one goes,
through the emptiness, through the silence that goes on and on,
my *Nightflyer* and I give chase.

From the hour the *Nightflyer* slipped into stardrive, Royd Eris
watched his passengers.

Nine riders had boarded at the orbital docks above Avalon; five
women and four men, each an Academy scholar, their backgrounds
as diverse as their fields of study. Yet, to Royd, they dressed alike,
looked alike, even sounded alike. On Avalon, most cosmopolitan
of worlds, they had become as one in their quest for knowledge.

The *Nightflyer* was a trader, not a passenger vessel. It offered
one double cabin, one closet-sized single. The other academicians
rigged sleepwebs in the four great cargo holds, some in close
confinement with the instruments and computer systems they had
packed on board. When restive, they could wander two short
corridors, one leading from the driveroom and the main airlock
up past the cabins to a well-appointed lounge-library-kitchen, the
other looping down to the cargo holds. Ultimately it did not matter
where they wandered. Even in the sanitary stations, Royd had
eyes and ears.

And always and everywhere, Royd watched.

Concepts like a right of privacy did not concern him, but he
knew they might concern his passengers, if they knew of his
activities. He made certain that they did not.

Royd's own quarters, three spacious chambers forward of the
passenger lounge, were sealed and inviolate; he never left them.
To his riders, he was a disembodied voice over the communicators
that sometimes called them for long conversations, and a holographic specter that joined them for meals in the lounge. His ghost
was a lithe, pale-eyed young man with white hair who dressed in
filmy pastel clothing twenty years out of date, and it had the
disconcerting habit of looking past the person Royd was addressing,
or in the wrong direction altogether, but after a few days the
academicians grew accustomed to it. The holograph walked only
in the lounge, in any event.

But Royd, secretly, silently, lived everywhere, and ferreted out
all of their little secrets.

The cyberneticist talked to her computers, and seemed to prefer their company to that of humans.

The xenobiologist was surly, argumentative, and a solitary drinker.

The two linguists, lovers in public, seldom had sex and snapped bitterly at each other in private.

The psipsych was a hypochondriac given to black depressions, which worsened in the close confines of the *Nightflyer.*

Royd watched them work, eat, sleep, copulate; he listened untiringly to their talk. Within a week, the nine of them no longer seemed the same to him at all. Each of them was strange and unique, he had concluded.

By the time the *Nightflyer* had been under drive for two weeks, two of the passengers had come to engage even more of his attention. He neglected none of them, watched all, but now, specially, he focused on Karoly d'Branin and Melantha Jhirl.

"Most of all, I want to know the *why* of them," Karoly d'Branin told him one false night the second week out from Avalon. Royd's luminescent ghost sat close to d'Branin in the darkened lounge, watching him drink bittersweet chocolate. The others were all asleep. Night and day are meaningless on a starship, but the *Nightflyer* kept the usual cycles, and most of the passengers followed them. Only Karoly d'Branin, administrator and generalist, kept his own solitary time.

"The *if* of them is important as well, Karoly," Royd replied, his soft voice coming from the communicator panels in the walls. "Can you be truly certain if these aliens of yours exist?"

"*I* can be certain," Karoly d'Branin replied. "That is enough. If everyone else were certain as well, we would have a fleet of research ships instead of your little *Nightflyer.*" He sipped at his chocolate, and gave a satisfied sigh. "Do you know the Nor T'alush, Royd?"

The name was strange to him, but it took Royd only a moment to consult his library computer. "An alien race on the other side of human space, past the Fyndii worlds and the Damoosh. Possibly legendary."

D'Branin chuckled. "Your library is out-of-date. You must supplement it the next time you are on Avalon. Not legends, no, real enough, though far away. We have little information about the Nor T'alush, but we are sure they exist, though you and I may never meet one. They were the start of it all.

"I was coding some information into the computers, a packet newly arrived from Dam Tullian after twenty standard years in transit. Part of it was Nor T'alush folklore. I had no idea how long that had taken to get to Dam Tullian, or by what route it had come, but it was fascinating material. Did you know that my first degree was in xenomythology?"

"I did not," Royd said. "Please continue."

"The *volcryn* story was among the Nor T'alush myths. It awed me; a race of sentients moving out from some mysterious origin in the core of the galaxy, sailing towards the galactic edge and, it was alleged, eventually bound for intergalactic space itself, meanwhile keeping always to the interstellar depths, no planetfalls, seldom coming within a light-year of a star. And doing it all *without a stardrive,* in ships moving only a fraction of the speed of light! That was the detail that obsessed me! Think how *old* they must be, those ships!"

"Old," Royd agreed. "Karoly, you said *ships.* More than one?"

"Oh, yes, there are," d'Branin said. "According to the Nor T'alush, one or two appeared first, on the innermost edges of their trading sphere, but others followed. Hundreds of them, each solitary, moving by itself, bound outward, always the same. For fifteen thousand standard years they moved between the Nor T'alush stars, and then they began to pass out from among them. The myth said that the last *volcryn* ship was gone three thousand years ago."

"Eighteen thousand years," Royd said, adding, "are your Nor T'alush that old?"

D'Branin smiled. "Not as star-travelers, no. According to their own histories, the Nor T'alush have only been civilized for about half that long. That stopped me for a while. It seemed to make the *volcryn* story clearly a legend. A wonderful legend, true, but nothing more.

"Ultimately, however, I could not let it alone. In my spare time, I investigated, cross-checking with other alien cosmologies to see whether this particular myth was shared by any races other than the Nor T'alush. I thought perhaps I would get a thesis out of it. It was a fruitful line of inquiry.

"I was startled by what I found. Nothing from the Hrangans, or the Hrangan slaveraces, but that made sense, you see. They were *out* from human space, the *volcryn* would not reach them until after they had passed through our own sphere. When I looked *in*, however, the *volcryn* story was everywhere. The Fyndii had it, the Damoosh appeared to accept it as literal truth—and the Damoosh, you know, are the oldest race we have ever encountered—and there was a remarkably similar story told among the gethsoids of Aath. I checked what little was known about the races said to flourish further in still, beyond even the Nor T'alush, and they had the *volcryn* story too."

"The legend of the legends," Royd suggested. The specter's wide mouth turned up in a smile.

"Exactly, exactly," d'Branin agreed. "At that point, I called in the experts, specialists from the Institute for the Study of Non-human Intelligence. We researched for two years. It was all there, in the files and the libraries at the Academy. No one had ever looked before, or bothered to put it together.

"The *volcryn* have been moving through the manrealm for most of human history, since before the dawn of spaceflight. While we twist the fabric of space itself to cheat relativity, they have been sailing their great ships right through the heart of our alleged civilization, past our most populous worlds, at stately slow sublight speeds, bound for the Fringe and the dark between the galaxies. Marvelous, Royd, marvelous!"

"Marvelous," Royd agreed.

Karoly d'Branin set down his chocolate cup and leaned forward eagerly towards Royd's projection, but his hand passed through empty light when he tried to grasp his companion by the forearm. He seemed disconcerted for a moment, before he began to laugh at himself. "Ah, my *volcryn*. I grow overenthused, Royd. I am so close now. They have preyed on my mind for a dozen years, and within a month I will have them. Then, *then,* if only I can open communication, if only my people can reach them, then at last I will know the *why* of it!"

The ghost of Royd Eris, master of the *Nightflyer,* smiled for him and looked on through calm unseeing eyes.

Passengers soon grow restless on a starship under drive, sooner on one as small and spare as the *Nightflyer.* Late in the second week, the speculation began. Royd heard it all.

"Who is this Royd Eris, really?" the xenobiologist complained one night when four of them were playing cards. "Why doesn't he come out? What's the purpose of keeping himself sealed off from the rest of us?"

"Ask him," the linguist suggested.

No one did.

When he was not talking to Karoly d'Branin, Royd watched Melantha Jhirl. She was good to watch. Young, healthy, active, Melantha Jhirl had a vibrancy about her that the others could not touch. She was big in every way; a head taller than anyone else on board, large-framed, large-breasted, long-legged, strong, muscles moving fluidly beneath shiny coal-black skin. Her appetites were big as well. She ate twice as much as any of her colleagues, drank heavily without ever seeming drunk, exercised for hours every day on equipment she had brought with her and set up in one of the cargo holds. By the third week out she had sexed with all four of the men on board and two of the other women. Even in bed she was always active, exhausting most of her partners. Royd watched her with consuming interest.

"I am an improved model," she told him once as she worked out on her parallel bars, sweat glistening on her bare skin, her long black hair confined in a net.

"Improved?" Royd said. He could not send his holographic ghost down to the holds, but Melantha had summoned him with the communicator to talk while she exercised, not knowing he would have been there anyway.

She paused in her routine, holding her body aloft with the strength of her arms. "Altered, Captain," she said. She had taken to calling him that. "Born on Prometheus among the elite, child of two genetic wizards. Improved, Captain. I require twice the energy you do, but I use it all. A more efficient metabolism, a stronger and more durable body, an expected lifespan half again the normal human's. My people have made some terrible mistakes when they try to radically redesign the lessers, but the small improvements they do well."

She resumed her exercises, moving quickly and easily, silent until she had finished. Then, breathing heavily, she crossed her arms and cocked her head and grinned. "Now you know my life story, Captain, unless you care to hear the part about my defection to Avalon, my extraordinary work in nonhuman anthropology, and my tumultuous and passionate lovelife. Do you?"

"Perhaps some other time," Royd said, politely.

"Good," Melantha Jhirl replied. She snatched up a towel and began to dry the sweat from her body. "I'd rather hear your life story, anyway. Among my modest attributes is an insatiable curiosity. Who are you, Captain? Really?"

"One as improved as you," Royd replied, "should certainly be able to guess."

Melantha laughed, and tossed her towel at the communicator grill.

By that time all of them were guessing, when they did not think Royd was listening. He enjoyed the rumors.

"He talks to us, but he can't be seen," the cyberneticist said. "This ship is uncrewed, seemingly all automated except for him. Why not entirely automated, then? I'd wager Royd Eris is a fairly sophisticated computer system, perhaps an Artificial Intelligence. Even a modest program can carry on a blind conversation indistinguishable from a human's."

The telepath was a frail young thing, nervous, sensitive, with limp flaxen hair and watery blue eyes. He sought out Karoly d'Branin in his cabin, the cramped single, for a private conversation. "I feel it," he said excitedly. "Something is wrong, Karoly, something is very wrong. I'm beginning to get frightened."

D'Branin was startled. "Frightened? I don't understand, my friend. What is there for you to fear?"

The young man shook his head. "I don't know, I don't know. Yet it's there, I feel it. Karoly, I'm picking up something. You know I'm good, I am, that's why you picked me. Class one, tested, and I tell you I'm afraid. I sense it. Something dangerous. Something volatile—and alien."

"My *volcryn?*" D'Branin said.

"No, no, impossible. We're in drive, they're light-years away." The telepath's laugh was desperate. "I'm not *that* good, Karoly. I've heard your Crey story, but I'm only a human. No, this is close. On the ship."

"One of us?"

"Maybe," the telepath said. "I can't sort it out."

D'Branin sighed and put a fatherly hand on the young man's

shoulder. "I thank you for coming to me, but I cannot act unless you have something more definite. This feeling of yours—could it be that you are just tired? We have all of us been under strain. Inactivity can be taxing."

"This is real," the telepath insisted, but he left peacefully.

Afterward d'Branin went to the psipsych, who was lying in her sleepweb surrounded by medicines, complaining bitterly of aches. "Interesting," she said when d'Branin told her. "I've felt something too, a sense of threat, very vague, diffuse. I thought it was me, the confinement, the boredom, the way I feel. My moods betray me at times. Did he say anything more specific?"

"No."

"I'll make an effort to move around, read him, read the others, see what I can pick up. Although, if this is real, he should know it first. He's a one, I'm only a three."

D'Branin nodded, reassured. Later, when the rest had gone to sleep, he made some chocolate and talked to Royd through the false night. But he never mentioned the telepath once.

"Have you noticed the clothes on that holograph he sends us?" the xenobiologist said to the others. "A decade out of style, at least. I don't think he really looks like that. What if he's deformed, sick, ashamed to be seen the way he really looks? Perhaps he has some disease. The Slow Plague can waste a person terribly, but it takes decades to kill, and there are other contagions, manthrax and new leprosy and Langamen's Disease. Could it be that Royd's self-imposed quarantine is just that. A quarantine. Think about it."

In the fifth week out, Melantha Jhirl pushed her pawn to the sixth rank and Royd saw it was unstoppable and resigned. It was his eighth straight defeat at her hands in as many days. She was sitting cross-legged on the floor of the lounge, the chessmen spread out before her on a viewscreen, its receiver dark. Laughing, she swept them away. "Don't feel bad, Royd," she told him. "I'm an improved model. Always three moves ahead."

"I should tie in my computer," he replied. "You'd never know." His holographic ghost materialized suddenly, standing in front of the viewscreen, and smiled at her.

"I'd know within three moves," Melantha Jhirl said. "Try it." She stood up and walked right through his projection on her way to the kitchen, where she found herself a bulb of beer. "When are you going to break down and let me behind your wall for a visit, Captain?" she asked, talking up to a communicator grill. She refused to treat his ghost as real. "Don't you get lonely there? Sexually frustrated? Claustrophobic?"

"I've flown the *Nightflyer* all my life, Melantha," Royd said. His projection ignored, winked out. "If I were subject to claustrophobia, sexual frustration, or loneliness, such a life would have been impossible. Surely that should be obvious to you, being as improved a model as you are?"

She took a squeeze of her beer and laughed her mellow, musical laugh at him. "I'll solve you yet, Captain," she warned.

"Fine," he said. "Meanwhile, tell me some more lies about your life."

"Have you ever heard of Jupiter?" the xenotech demanded of the others. She was drunk, lolling in her sleepweb in the cargo hold.

"Something to do with Earth," one of the linguists said. "The same myth system originated both names, I believe."

"Jupiter," the xenotech announced loudly, "is a gas giant in the same solar system as Old Earth. Didn't know that, did you? They were on the verge of exploring it when the stardrive was discovered, oh, way back. After that, nobody bothered with gas giants. Just slip into drive and find the habitable worlds, settle them, ignore the comets and the rocks and the gas giants—there's another star just a few light-years away, and it has more habitable planets. But there were people who thought those Jupiters might have life, you know. Do you see?"

The xenobiologist looked annoyed. "If there is intelligent life on the gas giants, it shows no interest in leaving them," he snapped. "All of the sentient species we have met up to now have originated on worlds similar to Earth, and most of them are oxygen breathers. Unless you suggest that the *volcryn* are from a gas giant?"

The xenotech pushed herself up to a sitting position and smiled conspiratorially. "Not the *volcryn*," she said. "Royd Eris. Crack that forward bulkhead in the lounge, and watch the methane and ammonia come smoking out." Her hand made a sensuous waving motion through the air, and she convulsed with giddy laughter.

"I dampened him," the psipsych reported to Karoly d'Branin

during the sixth week. "Psionine-4. It will blunt his receptivity for several days, and I have more if he needs it."

D'Branin wore a stricken look. "We talked several times, he and I. I could see that he was becoming ever more fearful, but he could never tell me the why of it. Did you absolutely have to shut him off?"

The psipsych shrugged. "He was edging into the irrational. You should never have taken a class one telepath, d'Branin. Too unstable."

"We must communicate with an alien race. I remind you that is no easy task. The *volcryn* are perhaps more alien than any sentients we have yet encountered. Because of that we needed class one skills."

"Glib," she said, "but you might have no working skills at all, given the condition of your class one. Half the time he's catatonic and half the time crazy with fear. He insists that we're all in real physical danger, but he doesn't know why or from what. The worst of it is I can't tell if he's really sensing something or simply having an acute attack of paranoia. He certainly displays some classic paranoid symptoms. Among other things, he believes he's being watched. Perhaps his condition is completely unrelated to us, the *volcryn*, and his talent. I can't be sure at this point in time."

"What of your own talent?" d'Branin said. "You are an empath, are you not?"

"Don't tell me my job," she said sharply. "I sexed with him last week. You don't get more proximity or better rapport for esping than that. Even under those conditions, I couldn't be sure of anything. His mind is a chaos, and his fear is so rank it stank up the sheets. I don't read anything from the others either, besides the ordinary tensions and frustrations. But I'm only a three, so that doesn't mean much. My abilities are limited. You know I haven't been feeling well, d'Branin. I can barely breathe on this ship. My head throbs. Ought to stay in bed."

"Yes, of course," d'Branin said hastily. "I did not mean to criticize. You have been doing all you can under difficult circumstances. Yet, I must ask, is it vital he be dampened? Is there no other way? Royd will take us out of drive soon, and we will make contact with the *volcryn*. We will need him."

The psipsych rubbed her temple wearily. "My other option was an injection of esperon. It would have opened him up completely, tripled his psionic receptivity for a few hours. Then, hopefully, he could home in this danger he's feeling. Exorcise it if it's false, deal with it if it's real. But psionine-4 is a lot safer. The physical side effects of esperon are debilitating, and emotionally I don't think he's stable enough to deal with that kind of power. The psionine should tell us something. If his paranoia continues to persist, I'll know it has nothing to do with his telepathy."

"And if it does not persist?" Karoly d'Branin said.

She smiled wickedly. "Then we'll know that he really was picking up some sort of threat, won't we?"

False night came, and Royd's wraith materialized while Karoly d'Branin sat brooding over his chocolate. "Karoly," the apparition said, "would it be possible to tie in the computer your team brought on board with my shipboard system? Those *volcryn* stories fascinate me, and I'd like to be able to study them at my leisure."

"Certainly," d'Branin replied in an offhand, distracted manner. "It is time we got our system up and running in any case. Soon, now, we will be dropping out of drive."

"Soon," Royd agreed. "Approximately seventy hours from now."

At dinner the following day, Royd's projection did not appear. The academicians ate uneasily, expecting their host to materialize at any moment, take his accustomed place, and join in the mealtime conversation. Their expectations were still unfulfilled when the afterdinner pots of chocolate and spiced tea and coffee were set on the table before them.

"Our captain seems to be occupied," Melantha Jhirl observed, leaning back in her chair and swirling a snifter of brandy.

"We will be shifting out of drive soon," Karoly d'Branin said. "There are preparations to make."

Some of the others looked at one another. All nine of them were present, although the young telepath seemed lost in his own head. The xenobiologist broke the silence. "He doesn't eat. He's a damned holograph. What does it matter if he misses a meal? Maybe it's just as well. Karoly, a lot of us have been getting uneasy about Royd. What do you know about this mystery man anyway?"

D'Branin looked at him with wide, puzzled eyes. "Know, my

friend?" he said, leaning forward to refill his cup with the thick, bittersweet chocolate. "What is there to know?"

"Surely you've noticed that he never comes out to play with us," the female linguist said drily. "Before you engaged his ship, did anyone remark on this quirk of his?"

"I'd like to know the answer to that too," her partner said. "A lot of traffic comes and goes through Avalon. How did you come to choose Eris? What were you told about him?"

D'Branin hesitated. "Told about him? Very little, I must admit. I spoke to a few port officials and charter companies, but none of them were acquainted with Royd. He had not traded out of Avalon originally, you see."

"Where *is* he from?" the linguists demanded in unison. They looked at each other, and the woman continued. "We've listened to him. He has no discernible accent, no idiosyncrasies of speech to betray his origins. Tell us, where did this *Nightflyer* come from?"

"I—I don't know, actually," d'Branin admitted, hesitating. "I never thought to ask him about it."

The members of his research team glanced at each other incredulously. "You never thought to *ask?*" the xenotech said. "How did you select this ship, then?"

"It was available. The administrative council approved my project and assigned me personnel, but they could not spare an Academy ship. There were budgetary constraints as well." All eyes were on him.

"What d'Branin is saying," the psipsych interrupted, "is that the Academy was pleased with his studies in xenomyth, with the discovery of the *volcryn* legend, but less than enthusiastic about his plan to prove the *volcryn* real. So they gave him a small budget to keep him happy and productive, assuming that this little mission would be fruitless, and they assigned him workers who wouldn't be missed back on Avalon." She looked around at each person. "Except for d'Branin," she said, "not a one of us is a first-rate scholar."

"Well, you can speak for yourself," Melantha Jhirl said. "I volunteered for this mission."

"I won't argue the point," the psipsych said. "The crux is that the choice of the *Nightflyer* is no large enigma. You engaged the cheapest charter you could find, didn't you, d'Branin?"

"Some of the available ships would not even consider my proposition," d'Branin said. "The sound of it is odd, we must admit. And many ship masters seemed to have a superstitious fear of dropping out of drive in interstellar space, without a planet near. Of those who agreed to the conditions, Royd Eris offered the best terms, and he was able to leave at once."

"And we *had* to leave at once," said the female linguist. "Otherwise the *volcryn* might get away. They've only been passing through this region for ten thousand years, give or take a few thousand," she said sarcastically.

Someone laughed. D'Branin was nonplussed. "Friends, no doubt I could have postponed departure. I admit I was eager to meet my *volcryn,* to ask them the questions that have haunted me, to discover the why of them, but I must also admit that a delay would have been no great hardship. But *why?* Royd is a gracious host, a skilled pilot, he has treated us well."

"He has made himself a cipher," someone said.

"What is he hiding?" another voice demanded.

Melantha Jhirl laughed. When all eyes had moved to her, she grinned and shook her head. "Captain Royd is perfect, a strange man for a strange mission. Don't any of you love a mystery? Here we are flying light-years to intercept a hypothetical alien starship from the core of the galaxy that has been outward bound for longer than humanity has been having wars, and all of you are upset because you can't count the warts on Royd's nose." She leaned across the table to refill her brandy snifter. "My mother was right," she said lightly. "Normals are subnormal."

"Melantha is correct," Karoly d'Branin said quietly. "Royd's foibles and neuroses are his business, if he does not impose them on us."

"It makes me uncomfortable," someone complained weakly.

"For all we know, Karoly," said the xenotech, "we might be traveling with a criminal or an alien."

"*Jupiter,*" someone muttered. The xenotech flushed red, and there was sniggering around the long table.

But the young, pale-haired telepath looked up suddenly and stared at them all with wild, nervous eyes. "An *alien,*" he said.

The psipsych swore. "The drug is wearing off," she said quickly to d'Branin. "I'll have to go back to my room to get some more."

All of the others looked baffled; d'Branin had kept his telepath's condition a careful secret. "What drug?" the xenotech demanded. "What's going on here?"

"Danger," the telepath muttered. He turned to the cyberneticist sitting next to him, and grasped her forearm in a trembling hand. "We're in danger, I tell you, I'm reading it. Something *alien.* And it means us ill."

The psipsych rose. "He's not well," she announced to the others. "I've been dampening him with psionine, trying to hold his delusions in check. I'll get some more." She started towards the door.

"Wait," Melantha Jhirl said. "Not psionine. Try esperon."

"Don't tell me my job, woman."

"Sorry," Melantha said. She gave a modest shrug. "I'm one step ahead of you, though. Esperon might exorcise his delusions, no?"

"Yes, but—"

"And it might let him focus on this threat he claims to detect, correct?"

"I know the characteristics of esperon," the psipsych said testily.

Melantha smiled over the rim of her brandy glass. "I'm sure you do," she said. "Now listen to me. All of you are anxious about Royd, it seems. You can't stand not knowing what he's concealing about himself. You suspect him of being a criminal. Fears like that won't help us work together as a team. Let's end them. Easy enough." She pointed. "Here sits a class one telepath. Boost his power with esperon and he'll be able to recite our captain's life history to us, until we're all suitably bored with it. Meanwhile he'll also be vanquishing his personal demons."

"He's watching us," the telepath said in a low, urgent voice.

"Karoly," the xenobiologist said, "this has gone too far. Several of us are nervous, and this boy is terrified. I think we all need an end to the mystery of Royd Eris. Melantha is right."

D'Branin was troubled. "We have no right—"

"We have the *need,*" the cyberneticist said.

D'Branin's eyes met those of the psipsych, and he sighed. "Do it," he said. "Get him the esperon."

"He's going to kill me," the telepath screamed and leapt to his feet. When the cyberneticist tried to calm him with a hand on his arm, he seized a cup of coffee and threw it square in her face.

It took three of them to hold him down. "Hurry," one commanded, as the youth struggled.

The psipsych shuddered and quickly left the lounge.

Royd was watching.

When the psipsych returned, they lifted the telepath to the table and forced him down, pulling aside his hair to bare the arteries in his neck.

Royd's ghost materialized in its empty chair at the foot of the long dinner table. "Stop that," it said calmly. "There is no need."

The psipsych froze in the act of slipping an ampule of esperon into her injection gun, and the xenotech startled visibly and released one of the telepath's arms. But the captive did not pull free. He lay on the table, breathing heavily, too frightened to move, his pale blue eyes fixed glassily on Royd's projection.

Melantha Jhirl lifted her brandy glass in salute. "Boo," she said. "You've missed dinner, Captain."

"Royd," said Karoly d'Branin, "I am sorry."

The ghost stared unseeing at the far wall. "Release him," said the voice from the communicators. "I will tell you my great secret, if my privacy intimidates you so."

He *has* been watching us," the male linguist said.

"Tell, then," the xenotech said suspiciously. "What are you?"

"I liked your guess about the gas giants," Royd said. "Sadly, the truth is less dramatic. I am an ordinary *Homo sapien* in late middle-age. Sixty-eight standard, if you require precision. The holograph you see before you was the real Royd Eris, although some years ago. I am older now."

"Oh?" The cyberneticist's face was red where the coffee had scalded her. "Then why the secrecy?"

"I will begin with my mother," Royd replied. "The *Nightflyer* was her ship originally, custom-built to her design in the Newholme spaceyards. My mother was a freetrader, a notably successful one. She made a fortune through a willingness to accept the unusual consignment, fly off the major trade routes, take her cargo a month or a year or two years beyond where it was customarily transferred. Such practices are riskier but more profitable than flying the mail runs. My mother did not worry about how often she and her crews returned home. Her ships were her home. She seldom visited the same world twice if she could avoid it."

"Adventurous," Melantha said.

"No," said Royd. "Sociopathic. My mother did not like people, you see. Not at all. Her one great dream was to free herself from the necessity of crew. When she grew rich enough, she had it done. The *Nightflyer* was the result. After she boarded it at Newholme, she never touched a human being again, or walked a planet's surface. She did all her business from the compartments that are now mine. She was insane, but she did have an interesting life, even after that. The worlds she saw, Karoly! The things she might have told you! Your heart would break. She destroyed most of her records, however, for fear that other people might get some use or pleasure from her experience after her death. She was like that."

"And you?" the xenotech said.

"I should not call her my mother," Royd continued. "I am her cross-sex clone. After thirty years of flying this ship alone, she was bored. I was to be her companion and lover. She could shape me to be a perfect diversion. She had no patience with children, however, and no desire to raise me herself. As an embryo, I was placed in a nurturant tank. The computer was my teacher. I was to be released when I had attained the age of puberty, at which time she guessed I would be fit company.

"Her death, a few months after the cloning, ruined the plan. She had programmed the ship for such an eventuality, however. It dropped out of drive and shut down, drifted in interstellar space for eleven years while the computer made a human being out of me. That was how I inherited the *Nightflyer*. When I was freed, it took me some years to puzzle out the operation of the ship and my own origins."

"Fascinating," said d'Branin.

"Yes," said the female linguist, "but it doesn't explain why you keep yourself in isolation."

"Ah, but it does," Melantha Jhirl said. "Captain, perhaps you should explain further for the less improved models?"

"My mother hated planets," Royd said. "She hated stinks and dirt and bacteria, the irregularity of the weather, the sight of other people. She engineered for us a flawless environment, as sterile as she could possibly make it. She disliked gravity as well. She was accustomed to weightlessness, and preferred it. These were the conditions under which I was born and raised.

"My body has no natural immunities to anything. Contact with any of you would probably kill me, and would certainly make me very sick. My muscles are feeble, atrophied. The gravity the *Nightflyer* is now generating is for your comfort, not mine. To me it is agony. At the moment I am seated in a floating chair that supports my weight. I still hurt, and my internal organs may be suffering damage. It is one reason why I do not often take on passengers."

"You share your mother's opinion of the run of humanity, then?" the psipsych said.

"I do not. I like people. I accept what I am, but I did not choose it. I experience human life in the only way I can, vicariously, through the infrequent passengers I dare to carry. At those times, I drink in as much of their lives as I can."

"If you kept your ship under weightlessness at all times, you could take on more riders, could you not?" suggested the xeno-biologist.

"True," Royd said politely. "I have found, however, that most people choose not to travel with a captain who does not use his gravity grid. Prolonged free-fall makes them ill and uncomfortable. I could also mingle with my guests, I know, if I kept to my chair and wore a sealed environment suit. I have done so. I find it lessens my participation instead of increasing it. I become a freak, a maimed thing, one who must be treated differently and kept at a distance. I prefer isolation. As often as I dare, I study the aliens I take on as riders."

"Aliens?" the xenotech said, in a confused voice.

"You are all aliens to me," Royd answered.

Silence then filled the *Nightflyer's* lounge.

"I am sorry this had to happen, my friend," Karoly d'Branin said to the ghost.

"Sorry," the psipsych said. She frowned and pushed the ampule of esperon into the injection chamber. "Well, it's glib enough, but is it the truth? We still have no proof, just a new bedtime story. The holograph could have claimed it was a creature from Jupiter, a computer, or a diseased war criminal just as easily." She took two quick steps forward to where the young telepath still lay on the table. "He still needs treatment, and we still need confirmation. I don't care to live with all this anxiety, when we can end it all now." Her hand pushed the unresisting head to one side, she found the artery, and pressed the gun to it.

"No," the voice from the communicator said sternly. "Stop. I order it. This is my ship. Stop."

The gun hissed loudly, and there was a red mark when she lifted it from the telepath's neck.

He raised himself to a half-sitting position, supported by his elbows, and the psipsych moved close to him. "Now," she said in her best professional tones, "focus on Royd. You can do it, we all know how good you are. Wait just a moment, the esperon will open it all up for you."

His pale blue eyes were clouded. "Not close enough," he muttered. "One, I'm one, tested. Good, you know I'm good, but I got to be *close.*" He trembled.

She put an arm around him, stroked him, coaxed him. "The esperon will give you range," she said. "Feel it, feel yourself grow stronger. Can you feel it? Everything's getting clear, isn't it?" Her voice was a reassuring drone. "Remember the danger now, remember, go find it. Look beyond the wall, tell us about it. Tell us about Royd. Was he telling the truth? Tell us. You're good, we all know that, you can tell us." The phrases were almost an incantation.

He shrugged off her support and sat upright by himself. "I can feel it," he said. His eyes were suddenly clearer. "Something— my head hurts—I'm *afraid!*"

"Don't be afraid," the psipsych said. "The esperon won't make your head hurt, it just makes you better. Nothing to fear." She stroked his brow. "Tell us what you see."

The telepath looked at Royd's ghost with terrified little-boy eyes, and his tongue flicked across his lower lip. "He's—"

Then his skull exploded.

It was three hours later when the survivors met again to talk.

In the hysteria and confusion of the aftermath, Melantha Jhirl had taken charge. She gave orders, pushing her brandy aside and snapping out commands with the ease of one born to it, and the others seemed to find a numbing solace in doing as they were told. Three of them fetched a sheet, and wrapped the headless body of the young telepath within, and shoved it through the driveroom airlock at the end of the ship. Two others, on Melantha's order, found water and cloth and began to clean up the lounge. They did not get far. Mopping the blood from the tabletop, the cyberneticist suddenly began to retch violently. Karoly d'Branin, who had sat still and shocked since it happened, woke and took the blood-soaked rag from her hand and led her away, back to his cabin.

Melantha Jhirl was helping the psipsych, who had been standing very close to the telepath when he died. A sliver of bone had penetrated her cheek just below her right eye, she was covered with blood and pieces of flesh and bone and brain, and she had gone into shock. Melantha removed the bone splinter, led her below, cleaned her, and put her to sleep with a shot of one of her own drugs.

And at length, she got the rest of them together in the largest of the cargo holds, where three of them slept. Seven of the surviving eight attended. The psipsych was still asleep, but the cyberneticist seemed to have recovered. She sat cross-legged on the floor, her features pale and drawn, waiting for Melantha to begin.

It was Karoly d'Branin who spoke first, however, "I do not understand," he said. "I do not understand what has happened. What could. . . ."

"Royd killed him, is all," the xenotech said bitterly. "His secret was endangered, so he just—just blew him apart."

"I cannot believe that," Karoly d'Branin said, anguished. "I cannot. Royd and I, we have talked, talked many a night when the rest of you were sleeping. He is gentle, inquisitive, sensitive. A dreamer. He understands about the *volcryn*. He would not do such a thing."

"His holograph certainly winked out quick enough when it happened," the female linguist said. "And you'll notice he hasn't had much to say since."

"The rest of you haven't been usually talkative either," Melantha Jhirl said. "I don't know what to think, but my impulse is to side with Karoly. We have no proof that the captain was responsible for what happened."

The xenotech make a loud rude noise. "Proof."

"In fact," Melantha continued unperturbed, "I'm not even sure anyone is responsible. Nothing happened until he was given the esperon. Could the drug be at fault?"

"Hell of a side effect," the female linguist muttered.

The xenobiologist frowned. "This is not my field, but I know esperon is an extremely potent drug, with severe physical effects as well as psionic. The instrument of death was probably his own talent, augmented by the drug. Besides boosting his principal power, his telepathic sensitivity, esperon would also tend to bring out other psi-talents that might have been latent in him."

"Such as?" someone demanded.

"Biocontrol. Telekinesis."

Melantha Jhirl was way ahead of him. "Increase the pressure inside his skull sharply, by rushing all the blood in his body to his brain. Decrease the air pressure around his head simultaneously, using teke to induce a short-lived vacuum. Think about it."

They thought about it, and none of them liked it.

"It could have been self-induced," Karoly d'Branin said.

"Or a stronger talent could have turned his power against him," the xenotech said stubbornly.

"No human telepath has talent on that order, to seize control of someone else, body and mind and soul, even for an instant."

"Exactly," the xenotech said. "No *human* telepath."

"Gas giant people?" The cyberneticist's tone was mocking.

The xenotech stared her down. "I could talk about Crey sensitives or *githyanki* soulsucks, name a half-dozen others off the top of my head, but I don't need to. I'll only name one. A Hrangan Mind."

That was a disquieting thought. All of them fell silent and moved uneasily, thinking of the vast, inimicable power of a Hrangan Mind hidden in the command chambers of the *Nightflyer,* until Melantha Jhirl broke the spell. "That is ridiculous," she said. "Think of what you're saying, if that isn't much to ask. You're supposed to be xenologists, the lot of you, experts in alien languages, psychology, biology, technology. You don't act the part. We warred with Old Hranga for a thousand years, but we *never* communicated successfully with a Hrangan Mind. If Royd Eris is a Hrangan, they've certainly improved their conversational skills in the centuries since the Collapse."

The xenotech flushed. "You're right," she mumbled. "I'm jumpy."

"Friends," Karoly d'Branin said, "we must not panic or grow hysterical. A terrible thing has happened. One of our colleagues is dead, and we do not know why. Until we do, we can only go on. This is no time for rash actions against the innocent. Perhaps, when we return to Avalon, an investigation will tell us what happened. The body is safe, is it not?"

"We cycled it through the airlock into the driveroom," said the male linguist. "Vacuum in there. It'll keep."

"And it can be examined on our return," d'Branin said, satisfied.

"That return should be immediate," the xenotech said. "Tell Eris to turn this ship around."

D'Branin looked stricken. "But the *volcryn!* A week more, and we will know them, if my figures are correct. To return would take us six weeks. Surely it is worth one week additional to know that they exist?"

The xenotech was stubborn. "A man is dead. Before he died, he talked about aliens and danger. Maybe we're in danger too. Maybe these *volcryn* are the cause, maybe they're more potent than even a Hrangan Mind. Do you care to risk it? And for what? Your sources may be fictional or exaggerated or wrong, your interpretations and computations may be incorrect, or they may have changed course—the *volcryn* may not even be within light-years of where we'll drop out!"

"Ah," Melantha Jhirl said, "I understand. Then we shouldn't go on because they won't be there, and besides, they might be dangerous."

D'Branin smiled and the female linguist laughed. "Not funny," said the xenotech, but she argued no more.

"No," Melantha continued, "any danger we are in will not increase significantly in the time it will take us to drop out of drive and look about for *volcryn*. We would have to drop out anyway, to reprogram. Besides, we have come a long way for these *volcryn,* and I admit to being curious." She looked at each of them in turn, but none of them disagreed. "We continue, then."

"And what do we do with Royd?" D'Branin asked.

"Treat the captain as before, if we can," Melantha said decisively. "Open lines to him and talk. He's probably as shocked and dismayed by what happened as we are, and possibly fearful that we might blame him, try to hurt him, something like that. Se we reassure him. I'll do it, if no one else wants to talk to him." There were no volunteers. "All right. But the rest of you had better try to act normally."

"Also," said d'Branin, "we must continue with our preparations.

Our sensory instruments must be ready for deployment as soon as we shift out of drive and reenter normal space, our computer must be functioning."

"It's up and running," the cyberneticist said quietly. "I finished this morning, as you requested." She had a thoughtful look in her eyes, but d'Branin did not notice. He turned to the linguists and began discussing some of the preliminaries he expected from them, and in a short time the talk had turned to the *volcryn,* and little by little the fear drained out of the group.

Royd, listening, was glad.

She returned to the lounge alone.

Someone had turned out the lights. "Captain?" she said, and he appeared to her, pale, glowing softly, with eyes that did not really see. His clothes, filmy and out-of-date, were all shades of white and faded blue. "Did you hear, Captain?"

His voice over the communicator betrayed a faint hint of surprise. "Yes. I hear and I see everything on my *Nightflyer,* Melantha. Not only in the lounge. Not only when the communicators and viewscreens are on. How long have you known?"

"Known?" She laughed. "Since you praised the gas giant solution to the Roydian mystery."

"I was under stress. I have never made a mistake before."

"I believe you, Captain," she said. "No matter. I'm the improved model, remember? I'd guessed weeks ago."

For a time Royd said nothing. Then: "When do you begin to reassure me?"

"I'm doing so right now. Don't you feel reassured yet?"

The apparition gave a ghostly shrug. "I am pleased that you and Karoly do not think I murdered that man."

She smiled. Her eyes were growing accustomed to the room. By the faint light of the holograph, she could see the table where it had happened, dark stains across its top. Blood. She heard a faint dripping, and shivered. "I don't like it in here."

"If you would like to leave, I can be with you wherever you go."

"No," she said. "I'll stay. Royd, if I asked you to, would you shut off your eyes and ears throughout the ship? Except for the lounge? It would make the others feel better, I'm sure."

"They don't know."

"They will. You made that remark about gas giants in everyone's hearing. Some of them have probably figured it out by now."

"If I told you I had cut myself off, you would have no way of knowing whether it was the truth."

"I could trust you," Melantha said.

Silence. The specter looked thoughtful. "As you wish," Royd's voice said finally. "Everything off. Now I see and hear only in here."

"I believe you."

"Did you believe my story?" Royd asked.

"Ah," she said. "A strange and wondrous story, Captain. If it's a lie, I'll swap lies with you any time. You do it well. If it's true, then you are a strange and wondrous man."

"It's true," the ghost said quietly. "Melantha—" His voice hesitated.

"Yes."

"I watched you copulating."

She smiled. "Ah," she said. "I'm good at it."

"I wouldn't know," Royd said. "You're good to watch."

Silence. She tried not to hear the dripping. "Yes," she said after a long hesitation.

"Yes? What?"

"Yes, Royd, I would probably sex with you if it were possible."

"How did you know what I was thinking?"

"I'm an improved model," she said. "And no, I'm not a telepath. It wasn't so difficult to figure out. I told you, I'm three moves ahead of you."

Royd considered that for a long time. "I believe I'm reassured," he said at last.

"Good," said Melantha Jhirl. "Now reassure me."

"Of what?"

"What happened in here? Really?"

Royd said nothing.

"I think you know something," Melantha said. "You gave up your secret to stop us from injecting him with esperon. Even after your secret was forfeit, you ordered us not to go ahead. Why?"

"Esperon is a dangerous drug," Royd said.

"More than that, Captain," Melantha said. "What killed him?"

"I didn't."

"One of us? The *volcryn?*"

Royd said nothing.

"Is there an alien aboard your ship, Captain?" she asked. "Is that it?"

Silence.

"Are we in danger? Am *I* in danger, Captain? I'm not afraid. Does that make me a fool?"

"I like people," Royd said at last. "When I can stand it, I like to have passengers. I watch them, yes. It's not so terrible. I like you and Karoly especially. You have nothing to fear. I won't let anything happen to you."

"What might happen?" she asked.

Royd said nothing.

"And what about the others, Royd? Are you taking care of them, too? Or only Karoly and me?"

No reply.

"You're not very talkative tonight," Melantha observed.

"I'm under strain," his voice replied. "Go to bed, Melantha Jhirl. We've talked long enough."

"All right, Captain," she said. She smiled at his ghost and lifted her hand. His own rose to meet it. Warm dark flesh and pale radiance brushed, melded, were one. Melantha Jhirl turned to go. It was not until she was out in the corridor, safe in the light once more, that she began to tremble.

False midnight. The talks had broken up, the nightmares had faded, and the academicians were lost in sleep. Even Karoly d'Branin slept, his appetite for chocolate quelled by his memories of the lounge.

In the darkness of the largest cargo hold, three sleepwebs hung, sleepers snoring softly in two. The cyberneticist lay awake, thinking, in the third. Finally, she rose, dropped lightly to the floor, pulled on her jumpsuit and boots, and shook the xenotech from her slumber. "Come," she whispered, beckoning. They stole off into the corridor, leaving Melantha Jhirl to her dreams.

"What the hell," the xenotech muttered when they were safely beyond the door. She was half-dressed, disarrayed, unhappy.

"There's a way to find out if Royd's story was true," the cyberneticist said carefully. "Melantha won't like it, though. Are you game to try?"

"What?" the other asked. Her face betrayed her interest.

"Come," the cyberneticst said.

One of the three lesser cargo holds had been converted into a computer room. They entered quietly; all empty. The system was up, but dormant. Currents of light ran silkily down crystalline channels in the data grids, meeting, joining, splitting apart again; rivers of wan multihued radiance crisscrossing a black landscape. The chamber was dim, the only noise a low buzz at the edge of human hearing, until the cyberneticist moved through it, touching keys, tripping switches, directing the silent luminescent currents. Slowly the machine woke.

"What are you *doing?*" the xenotech said.

"Karoly told me to tie in our system with the ship," the cyberneticist replied as she worked. "I was told Royd wanted to study the *volcryn* data. Fine, I did it. Do you understand what that means?"

Now the xenotech was eager. "The two systems are tied together!"

"Exactly. So Royd can find out about the *volcryn,* and we can find out about Royd." She frowned. "I wish I knew more about the *Nightflyer's* hardware, but I think I can feel my way through. This is a pretty sophisticated system d'Branin requisitioned."

"Can you take over?" the xenotech asked excitedly.

"Take over?" The cyberneticist sounded puzzled. "You been drinking again?"

"No, I'm serious. Use your system to break into the ship's control, overwhelm Eris, countermand his orders, make the *Nightflyer* respond to us, down here."

"Maybe," the cyberneticist said doubtfully, slowly. "I could try, but why do that?"

"Just in case. We don't have to use the capacity. Just so we have it, if an emergency arises."

The cyberneticist shrugged. "Emergencies and gas giants. I only want to put my mind at rest about Royd." She moved over to a readout panel, where a half-dozen meter-square viewscreens curved around a console, and brought one of them to life. Long fingers brushed across holographic keys that appeared and disappeared as she touched them, the keyboard changing shape even as she used it. Characters began to flow across the viewscreen, red flickerings encased in glassy black depths. The cyberneticist watched, and finally froze them. "Here," she said, "here's my answer about the hardware. You can dismiss your takeover idea, unless those gas giant people of yours are going to help. The *Nightflyer's* bigger and smarter than our little system here. Makes sense, when you stop to think about it. Ship's all automated, except for Royd." She whistled and coaxed her search program with soft words of encouragement. "It looks as though there *is* a Royd, though. Configurations are all wrong for a robot ship. Damn, I would have bet anything." The characters began to flow again, the cyberneticist watching the figures as they drifted by. "Here's life support specs, might tell us something." A finger jabbed, and the screen froze once more.

"Nothing unusual," the xenotech said in disappointment.

"Standard waste disposal. Water recycling. Food processor, with protein and vitamin supplements in stores." She began to whistle. "Tanks of Renny's moss and neograss to eat up the CO_2. Oxygen cycle, then. No methane or ammonia. Sorry about that."

"Go sex with a computer."

The cyberneticist smiled. "Ever tried it?" Her fingers moved again. "What else should I look for? Give me some ideas."

"Check the specs for nurturant tanks, cloning equipment, that sort of thing. Find Royd's life history. His mother's. Get a readout on the business they've done, all this alleged trading." Her voice grew excited, and she took the cyberneticist by her shoulder. "A log, a ship's log! There's got to be a log. Find it! You must!"

"All right." She whistled, happy, one with her systems, riding the data winds, in control, curious. The readout screen turned a bright red and began to blink at her, but she only smiled. "Security," she said, her fingers a blur. As suddenly as it had come, the blinking red field was gone. "Nothing like slipping past another system's security. Like slipping onto a man."

Down the corridor, an alarm sounded a whooping call. "Damn," the cyberneticist said, "that'll wake everyone." She glanced up when the xenotech's fingers dug painfully into her shoulder, squeezing, hurting.

A gray steel panel slid almost silently across the access to the corridor. "Wha—?" the cyberneticist said.

"That's an emergency airseal," the xenotech said in a dead voice. She knew starships. "It closes when they're about to load or unload cargo in vacuum."

Their eyes went to the huge curving outer airlock above their heads. The inner lock was almost completely open, and as they watched it clicked into place, and the seal on the outer door cracked, and now it was open half a meter, sliding, and beyond was twisted nothingness so bright it burned the eyes.

"Oh," the cyberneticist said. She had stopped whistling.

Alarms were hooting everywhere. The passengers began to stir. Melantha Jhirl leapt from her sleepweb and darted into the corridor, nude, concerned, alert. Karoly d'Branin sat up drowsily. The psipsych muttered fitfully in her drug-induced sleep. The xenobiologist cried out in alarm.

Far away metal crunched and tore, and a violent shudder ran through the ship, throwing the linguists out of their sleepwebs, knocking Melantha from her feet.

In the command quarters of the *Nightflyer* was a spherical room with featureless white walls, a lesser sphere—control console—suspended in its center. The walls were always blank when the ship was in drive; the warped and glaring underside of spacetime was painful to behold.

But now darkness woke in the room, a holoscape coming to life, cold black and stars everywhere, points of icy unwinking brilliance, no up and no down and no direction, the floating control sphere the only feature in the simulated sea of night.

The *Nightflyer* had shifted out of drive.

Melantha Jhirl found her feet again and thumbed on a communicator. The alarms were still hooting, and it was hard to hear. "Captain," she shouted, "what's happening?"

"I don't know," Royd's voice replied. "I'm trying to find out. Wait here. Gather the others to you."

She did as he had said and only when they were all together in the corridor did she slip back to her web to don some clothing. She found only six of them. The psipsych was still unconscious and could not be roused, and they had to carry her. And the xenotech and cyberneticist were missing. The rest looked uneasily at the seal that blocked cargo hold three.

The communicator came back to life as the alarm died. "We have returned to normal space," Royd's voice said, "but the ship is damaged. Hold three, your computer room, was breached while we were under drive. It was ripped apart by the flux. The computer automatically dropped us out of drive, or the drive forces might have torn my entire ship apart."

"Royd," d'Branin said, "two of my team are . . ."

"It appears that your computer was in use when the hold was breached," Royd said carefully. "We can only assume that they are dead. I cannot be sure. At Melantha's request, I have deactivated most of my eyes and ears, retaining only the lounge inputs. I do not know what happened. But this is a small ship, Karoly, and if they are not with you, we must assume the worst." He paused briefly. "If it is any consolation, they died quickly and painlessly."

The two linguists exchanged a long, meaningful look. The xenobiologist's face was red and angry, and he started to say something. Melantha Jhirl slipped her hand over his mouth firmly. "Do we know how it happened, Captain?" she asked.

"Yes," he said, reluctantly.

The xenobiologist had taken the hint, and Melantha took away her hand to let him breathe. "Royd?" she prompted.

"It sounds insane, Melantha," his voice replied, "but it appears your colleagues opened the hold's loading lock. I doubt that they did so deliberately, of course. They were apparently using the system interface to gain entry to the the *Nightflyer's* data storage and controls."

"I see," Melantha said. "A terrible tragedy."

"Yes," Royd agreed. "Perhaps more terrible than you think. I have yet to assess the damage to my ship."

"We should not keep you, Captain, if you have duties to perform," Melantha said. "All of us are shocked, and it is difficult to talk now. Investigate the condition of your ship, and we'll continue our discussion in the morning. All right?"

"Yes," Royd said.

Melantha thumbed the communicator plate. Now officially, the device was off. Royd could not hear them.

Karoly d'Branin shook his large, grizzled head. The linguists sat close to one another, hands touching. The psipsych slept. Only the xenobiologist met her gaze. "Do you believe him?" he snapped abruptly.

"I don't know," Melantha Jhirl said, "but I do know that the other three cargo holds can all be flushed just as hold three was.

I'm moving my sleepweb into a cabin. I suggest those who are living in hold two do the same."

"Good idea," the female linguist said. "We can crowd in. It won't be comfortable, but I don't think I'd sleep the sleep of angels in the holds anymore."

"We should also take our suits out of storage in four and keep them close at hand," her partner suggested.

"If you wish," Melantha said. "It's possible that all the locks might pop open simultaneously. Royd can't fault us for taking precautions." She flashed a grim smile. "After today, we've earned the right to act irrationally."

"This is no time for your damned jokes, Melantha," the xenobiologist said, fury in his voice. "Three dead, a fourth maybe deranged or comatose, the rest of us endangered—"

"We still have no idea what is happening," she pointed out.

"Royd Eris is killing us!" he shouted, pounding his fist into an open palm to emphasize his point. "I don't know who or what he is and I don't know if that story he gave us is true, and I don't *care.* Maybe he's a Hrangan Mind or the avenging angel of the *volcryn* or the second coming of Jesus Christ. What the hell difference does it make? *He's killing us!"*

"You realize," Melantha said gently, "that we cannot actually know whether the good captain has turned off his inputs down here. He could be watching and listening to us right now. He isn't, of course. He told me he wouldn't and I believe him. But we have only his word on that. Now, *you* don't appear to trust Royd. If that's so, you can hardly put any faith in his promises. It follows that from your point of view it might not be wise to say the things that you're saying." She smiled slyly.

The xenobiologist was silent.

"The computer is gone, then," Karoly d'Branin said in a low voice before Melantha could resume.

She nodded. "I'm afraid so."

He rose unsteadily to his feet. "I have a small unit in my cabin," he said. "A wrist model, perhaps it will suffice. I must get the figures from Royd, learn where we have dropped out. The *volcryn*—" He shuffled off down the corridor and disappeared into his cabin.

"Think how distraught he'd be if *all* of us were dead," the female linguist said bitterly. "Then he'd have no one to help him look for *volcryn*."

"Let him go," Melantha said. "He is as hurt as any of us, maybe more so. He wears it differently. His obsessions are his defense."

"What's *our* defense?"

"Ah," said Melantha. "Patience, maybe. All of the dead were trying to breach Royd's secret when they died. We haven't tried. Here we sit discussing their deaths."

"You don't find that suspicious?"

"Very," Melantha Jhirl said. "I even have a method of testing my suspicions. One of us can make yet another attempt to find out whether our captain told us the truth. If he or she dies, we'll know." She stood up abruptly. "Forgive me, however, if I'm not the one who tries. But don't let me stop you if you have the urge. I'll note the results with interest. Until then, I'm going to move out of the cargo area and get some sleep."

"Arrogant bitch," the male linguist observed almost conversationally after Melantha had left.

"Do you think he can hear us?" the xenobiologist whispered quietly.

"Every pithy word," the female linguist said, rising. They all stood up. "Let's move our things and put her"—she jerked a thumb at the psipsych—"back to bed." Her partner nodded.

"Aren't we going to *do* anything?" the xenobiologist said. "Make plans. Defenses."

The linguist gave him a withering look, and pulled her companion off in the other direction.

"Melantha? Karoly?"

She woke quickly, alert at the mere whisper of her name, and sat up in the narrow bunk. Next to her, Karoly d'Branin moaned softly and rolled over, yawning.

"Royd?" she asked. "Is it morning now?"

"Yes," replied the voice from the walls. "We are drifting in interstellar space three light-years from the nearest star, however. In such a context, does morning have meaning?"

Melantha laughed. "Debate it with Karoly, when he wakes up enough to listen. Royd, you said *drifting*? How bad . . . ?"

"Serious," he said, "but not dangerous. Hold three is a complete ruin, hanging from my ship like a broken metal eggshell, but the damage was confined. The drives themselves are intact, and the *Nightflyer's* computers did not seem to suffer from your machine's destruction. I feared they might. Electronic death trauma."

D'Branin said, "Eh? Royd?"

Melantha patted him. "I'll tell you later, Karoly," she said. "Royd, you sound serious. Is there more?"

"I am worried about our return flight, Melantha," he said. "When I take the *Nightflyer* back into drive, the flux will be playing directly on portions of the ship that were never engineered to withstand it. The airseal across hold three is a particular concern. I've run some projections, and I don't know if it can take the stress. If it bursts, my whole ship will split apart in the middle. My engines will go shunting off by themselves, and the rest . . ."

"I see. Is there anything we can do?"

"Yes. The exposed areas would be easy enough to reinforce. The outer hull is armored to withstand the warping forces, of course. We could mount it in place, a crude shield, but it would suffice. Large portions of the hull were torn loose when the locks opened, but they are still out there, floating within a kilometer or two, and could be used."

At some point, Karoly d'Branin had come awake. "My team has four vacuum sleds. We can retrieve these pieces for you."

"Fine, Karoly, but that is not my primary concern. My ship is self-repairing within certain limits, but this exceeds those limits. I will have to do this myself."

"You?" d'Branin said. "Friend, you said—that is, your muscles, your weakness—cannot we help with this?"

"I am only a cripple in a gravity field, Karoly," Royd said. "Weightless, I am in my element, and I will be killing our gravity grid momentarily, to try to gather my own strength for the repair work. No, you misunderstand. I am capable of the work. I have the tools, and my own heavy-duty sled."

"I think I know what you are concerned about," Melantha said.

"I'm glad," Royd said. "Perhaps, then, you can answer my question. If I emerge from the safety of my chambers, can you keep your friends from killing me?"

Karoly d'Branin was shocked. "Royd, Royd, we are scholars, we are not soldiers or criminals, we do not—we are human, how can you think that we would threaten you?"

"Human," Royd repeated, "but alien to me, suspicious of me. Give me no false assurances, Karoly."

The administrator sputtered. Melantha took his hand and bid him quiet. "Royd," she said, "I won't lie to you. You'd be in some danger. But I'd hoped that, by coming out, you'd make the rest of them joyously happy. They'd be able to see that you told the truth, wouldn't they?"

"They would," Royd said, "but would it be enough to offset their suspicions? They believe I killed your friends, do they not?"

"Some, perhaps. Half believe it, half fear it. They are frightened, Captain. *I* am frightened."

"No more than I."

"I would be less frightened if I knew what *did* happen. Do you know?"

Silence.

"Royd, if . . ."

"I tried to stop the esperon injection," he said. "I might have saved the other two, if I had seen them, heard them, known what they were about. But you made me turn off my monitors, Melantha. I cannot help what I cannot see." Hesitation. "I would feel safer if I could turn them back on. I am blind and deaf. It is frustrating. I cannot help if I am blind and deaf."

"Turn them on, then," Melantha said suddenly. "I was wrong. I did not understand. Now I do, though."

"Understand what?" Karoly said.

"You do not understand," Royd said. "You do *not*. Don't pretend that you do, Melantha Jhirl. *Don't!*" The calm voice from the communicator was shrill with emotion.

"What?" Karoly said. "Melantha, I do not understand."

Her eyes were thoughtful. "Neither do I," she said. "Neither do I, Karoly." She kissed him lightly. "Royd," she resumed, "it seems to me you must make this repair, regardless of what promises we can give you. You won't risk your ship by slipping back into drive in your present condition. The only other option is to drift here until we all die. What choice do we have?"

"I have a choice," Royd said with deadly seriousness. "I could kill all of you, if that were the only way to save my ship."

"You could try," Melantha said.

"Let us have no more talk of death," d'Branin said.

"You are right, Karoly," Royd said. "I do not wish to kill any of you. But I must be protected."

"You will be," Melantha said. "Karoly can set the others to chasing your hull fragments. I'll never leave your side. I'll assist you; the work will be done three times as fast."

Royd was polite. "In my experience, most planet-bound are clumsy and easily tired in weightlessness. It would be more efficient if I worked alone."

"It would not," she replied. "I remind you that I'm the improved model, Captain. Good in free-fall as well as in bed. I'll help."

"As you will. In a few moments, I shall depower the gravity grid. Karoly, go and prepare your people. Unship your sled and suit up. I will exit *Nightflyer* in three hours after I have recovered from the pains of your gravity. I want all of you outside the ship when I leave."

It was as though some vast animal had taken a bite out of the universe.

Melantha Jhirl waited on her sled close by the *Nightflyer,* and looked at stars. It was not so very different out here, in the depths of interstellar space. The stars were cold, frozen points of light; unwinking, austere, more chill and uncaring somehow than the same suns made to dance and twinkle by an atmosphere. Only the absence of a landmark primary reminded her of where she was: in the places between, where men do not stop, where the *volcryn* sail ships impossibly ancient. She tried to pick out Avalon's sun, but she did not know where to search. The configurations were strange to her, and she had no idea of how she was oriented. Behind her, before her, above, all around, the starfields stretched endlessly. She glanced down, beneath her sled and the *Nightflyer,* expecting still more alien stars, and the bite hit her with an almost physical force.

Melantha fought off a wave of vertigo. She was suspended above a pit, a yawning chasm in the universe, black, starless, vast.

Empty.

She remembered then: the Tempter's Veil. Just a cloud of dark gas, nothing really, galactic pollution that obscured the light from the stars of the Fringe. But this close at hand, it looked immense, terrifying. She had to break her gaze when she began to feel as if she were falling. It was a gulf beneath her and the frail silver-white shell of the *Nightflyer,* a gulf about to swallow them.

Melantha touched one of the controls on the sled's forked handle, swinging around so the Veil was to her side instead of beneath her. That seemed to help somehow. She concentrated on the *Nightflyer.* It was the largest object in her universe, brightly lit, ungainly; three small eggs side-by-side, two larger spheres beneath and at right angles, lengths of tube connecting it all. One of the eggs was shattered now, giving the craft an unbalanced cast.

She could see the other sleds as they angled through the black, tracking the missing pieces of eggshell, grappling with them, bringing them back. The linguistic team worked together, as always, sharing a sled. The xenobiologist was alone. Karoly d'Branin had a silent passenger; the psipsych, freshly drugged, asleep in the suit they had dressed her in. Royd had insisted that the ship be cleared completely, and it would have taken time and care to rouse the psipsych to consciousness; this was the safer course.

While her colleagues labored, Melantha Jhirl waited for Royd Eris, talking to the others occasionally over the comm link. The two linguists, unaccustomed to weightlessness, were complaining a lot. Karoly tried to soothe them. The xenobiologist worked in silence, argued out. He had been vehement earlier in his opposition to going outside, but Melantha and Karoly had finally worn him down and it seemed as if he had nothing more to say. Melantha now watched him flit across her field of vision, a stick figure in form-fitting black armor standing stiff and erect at the controls of his sled.

At last the circular airlock atop the foremost of the *Nightflyer's* major spheres dilated, and Royd Eris emerged. She watched him approach, wondering what he would look like. She had so many different pictures. His genteel, cultured, too-formal voice sometimes reminded her of the dark aristocrats of her native Prometheus, the wizards who toyed with human genes. At other times his naïvete made her think of him as an inexperienced youth. His ghost was a tired looking thin young man, and he was supposed to be considerably older than that pale shadow, but Melantha found it difficult to hear an old man talking when he spoke.

Royd's sled was larger than theirs and of a different design; a long oval plate with eight jointed grappling arms bristling from its underside like the legs of a metal spider, and the snout of a heavy-duty cutting laser mounted above. His suit was odd too, more massive than the Academy worksuits, with a bulge between its shoulder blades that was probably a powerpack, and rakish radiant fins atop shoulders and helmet.

But when he was finally near enough for Melantha to see his face, it was just a face. White, very white, that was the predominant impression she got; white hair cropped very short, a white stubble around the sharply chiseled lines of his jaw, almost invisible eyebrows beneath which blue eyes moved restlessly. His skin was pale and unlined, scarcely touched by time.

He looked wary, she thought. And perhaps a bit frightened.

He stopped his sled close to hers, amid the twisted ruin that had been cargo hold three, and surveyed the damage, the pieces of floating wreckage that once had been flesh and blood, glass, metal, plastic. Hard to distinguish now, all of them fused and burned and frozen together. "We have a good deal of work to do, Melantha," he said.

"First let's talk," she replied. She shifted her sled closer and reached out to him, but the distance was still too great, the width of the two vacuum sleds keeping them apart. Melantha backed off, and turned herself over completely, so that Royd hung upside down in her world and she upside down in his. Then she moved toward him again, positioning her sled directly over/under his. Their gloved hands met, brushed, parted. Melantha adjusted her altitude. Their helmets touched.

"I don't—" Royd began to say uncertainly.

"Turn off your comm," she commanded. "The sound will carry through the helmets."

He blinked and used his tongue controls and it was done.

"Now we can talk," she said.

"I do not like this, Melantha," he said. "This is too obvious. This is dangerous."

"There's no other way," she said. "Royd, I *do* know."

"Yes," he said. "I knew you did. Three moves ahead, Melantha. I remember the way you play chess. You are safer if you feign ignorance, however."

"I understand that, Captain. Other things I'm less sure about. Can we talk about it?"

"No. Don't ask me to. Just do as I tell you. You are in danger, all of you, but I can protect you. The less you know, the better

I can protect you." Through the transparent faceplates, his expression was grim.

She stared into his upside-down eyes. "Your ship is killing us, Captain. That's my suspicion, anyway. Not you. It. Only that doesn't make sense. You command the *Nightflyer*. How can it act independently? And why? What motive? How was that psionic murder accomplished? It can't be the ship. Yet it can't be anything else. Help me, Captain."

He blinked; there was anguish behind his eyes. "I should never have accepted Karoly's charter. Not with a telepath among you. It was risky. But I wanted to see the *volcryn*.

"You understand too much already, Melantha," Royd continued. "I can't tell you more. The ship is malfunctioning, that is all you need know. It is not safe to push too hard. As long as I am at the controls, however, you and your colleagues are in small danger. Trust me."

"Trust is a two-way bond," Melantha said steadily.

Royd lifted his hand and pushed her away, then tongued his comm back to life. "Enough gossip," he briskly announced. "We have repairs to make. Come. I want to see just how improved you are."

In the solitude of her helmet, Melantha Jhirl swore softly.

The xenobiologist watched Royd Eris emerge on his oversized work sled, watched Melantha Jhirl move to him, watched as she turned over and pressed her faceplate to his. He could scarcely contain his rage. Somehow they were all in it together, Royd and Melantha and possibly old d'Branin as well, he thought sourly. She had protected him from the first, when they might have taken action together, stopped him, found out who or what he was. And now three were dead, killed by the cipher in the misshapen spacesuit, and Melantha hung upside down, her face pressed to his like lovers kissing.

He tongued off his comm and cursed. The others were out of sight, off chasing spinning wedges of half-slagged metal. Royd and Melantha were engrossed in each other, the ship abandoned and vulnerable. This was his chance. No wonder Eris had insisted that all of them precede him into the void; outside, isolated from the controls of the *Nightflyer*, he was only a man. A weak one at that.

Smiling a thin hard smile, the xenobiologist brought his sled around in a wide circle and vanished into the gaping maw of the driveroom. His lights flickered past the ring of nukes and sent long bright streaks along the sides of the closed cylinders of the stardrives, the huge engines that bent the stuff of spacetime, encased in webs of metal and crystal. Everything was open to the vacuum. It was better that way; atmosphere corroded and destroyed.

He set the sled down, dismounted, moved to the airlock. This was the hardest part, he thought. The headless body of the young telepath was tethered loosely to a massive support strut, a grisly guardian by the door. The xenobiologist had to stare at it while he waited for the lock to cycle. Whenever he glanced away, somehow he would find his eyes creeping back to it. The body looked almost natural, as if it had never had a head. The xenobiologist tried to remember the young man's face, and failed, but then the lock door slid open and he gratefully pushed the thought away and entered.

He was alone in the *Nightflyer*.

A cautious man, he kept his suit on, though he collapsed the helmet and yanked loose the suddenly limp metallic fabric so it fell behind his back like a hood. He could snap it in place quickly enough if the need arose. In cargo hold four, where they had stored their equipment, the xenobiologist found what he was looking for; a portable cutting laser, charged and ready. Low power, but it would do.

Slow and clumsy in weightlessness, he pulled himself through the corridor into the darkened lounge.

It was chilly inside, the air cold on his cheeks. He tried not to notice. He braced himself at the door and pushed off across the width of the room, sailing above the furniture, which was all safely bolted into place.

As he drifted toward his objective, something wet and cold touched his face. It startled him, but it was gone before he could make out what it was.

When it happened again, he snatched at it, caught it, and felt briefly sick. He had forgotten. No one had cleaned the lounge yet. The—*remains* were still there, floating now, blood and flesh and bits of bone and brain. All around him.

He reached the far wall, stopped himself with his arms, pulled himself down to where he wanted to go. The bulkhead. The wall.

No doorway was visible, but the metal couldn't be very thick. Beyond was the control room, the computer access, safety, power. The xenobiologist did not think of himself as a vindictive man. He did not intend to harm Royd Eris, that judgment was not his to make. He would take control of the *Nightflyer,* warn Eris away, make certain the man stayed sealed in his suit. He would take them all back without any more mysteries, any more killings. The Academy arbiters could listen to the story, and probe Eris, and decide the right and wrong of it, guilt and innocence, what should be done.

The cutting laser emitted a thin pencil of scarlet light. The xenobiologist smiled and applied it to the bulkhead. It was slow work, but he had patience. They would not have missed him, quiet as he'd been, and if they did they would assume he was off sledding after some hunk of salvage. Eris' repairs would take hours, maybe days, to finish. The bright blade of the laser smoked where it touched the metal. He applied himself diligently.

Something moved on the periphery of his vision, just a little flicker, barely seen. A floating bit of brain, he thought. A sliver of bone. A bloody piece of flesh, hair still hanging from it. Horrible things, but nothing to worry about. He was a biologist, he was used to blood and brains and flesh. And worse, and worse; he had dissected many an alien in his day.

Again the motion caught his eye, teased at it. Not wanting to, he found himself drawn to look. He could not *not* look, somehow, just as he had been unable to ignore the headless telepath in the airlock. He looked.

It was an eye.

The xenobiologist trembled and the laser slipped sharply off to one side, so he had to wrestle with it to bring it back to the channel he was cutting. His heart raced. He tried to calm himself. Nothing to be frightened of. No one was home, and if Royd should return, well, he had the laser as a weapon and he had his suit on if an airlock blew.

He looked at the eye again, willing away his fear. It was just an eye, the eye of the young telepath, intact, bloody but intact, the same watery blue eye the boy had when alive, nothing supernatural. A piece of dead flesh, floating in the lounge amid other pieces of dead flesh. Someone should have cleaned up the lounge, he thought angrily. It was indecent to leave it like this, it was uncivilized.

The eye did not move. The other grisly bits were drifting on the air currents that flowed across the room, but the eye was still. Fixed on him. Staring.

He cursed himself and concentrated on the laser, on his cutting. He had burned an almost straight line up the bulkhead for about a meter. He began another at right angles.

The eye watched dispassionately. The xenobiologist suddenly found he could not stand it. One hand released its grip on the laser, reached out, caught the eye, flung it across the room. The action made him lose balance. He tumbled backward, the laser slipping from his grasp, his arms flapping like the wings on some absurd heavy bird. Finally he caught an edge of the table and stopped himself.

The laser hung in the center of the room, still firing, turning slowly where it floated. That did not make sense. It should have ceased fire when he released it. A malfunction, he thought. Smoke rose from where the thin line of the laser traced a path across the carpet.

With a shiver of fear, the xenobiologist realized that the laser was turning towards him.

He raised himself, put both hands flat against the table, pushed off out of the way.

The laser was turning more swiftly now.

He slammed into a wall, grunted in pain, bounced off the floor, kicked. The laser was spinning quickly, chasing him. He soared, braced himself for a ricochet off the ceiling. The beam swung around, but not fast enough. He'd get it while it was still firing off in the other direction.

He moved close, reached, and saw the eye.

It hung just above the laser. Staring.

The xenobiologist made a small whimpering sound low in his throat, and his hand hesitated—not long, but long enough—and the scarlet beam came up and around.

Its touch was a light, hot caress across his neck.

It was more than an hour later before they missed him. Karoly d'Branin noticed his absence first, called for him over the comm net, and got no answer. He discussed it with the others.

Royd Eris moved his sled back from the armor plate he had just mounted, and through his helmet Melantha Jhirl could see the lines around his mouth grow hard. His eyes were sharply alert.

It was just then that the screaming began.

A shrill bleat of pain and fear, followed by choked, anguished sobbing. They all heard it. It came over the comm net and filled their helmets.

"It's him," a woman's voice said. The linguist.

"He's hurt," her partner added. "He's crying for help. Can't you hear it?"

"Where?" someone started.

"The ship," the female linguist said. "He must have returned to the ship."

Royd Eris said, "No. I warned—"

"We're going to go check," the linguist said. Her partner cut free the hull fragment they had been towing, and it spun away, tumbling. Their sled angled down towards the *Nightflyer*.

"Stop," Royd said. "I'll return to my chambers and check from there, if you wish. Stay outside until I give you clearance."

"Go to hell," the linguist snapped at him over the open circuit.

"Royd, my friend, what can you mean?" Karoly d'Branin said. His sled was in motion too, hastening after the linguists, but he had been further out and it was a long way back to the ship. "He is hurt, perhaps seriously. We must help."

"No," Royd said. "Karoly, *stop.* If your colleague went back to the ship alone he is dead.

"How do you know that?" the male linguist demanded. "Did you arrange it? Set traps?"

"Listen to me," Royd continued. "You can't help him now. Only I could have helped him, and he did not listen to me. Trust me. Stop."

In the distance, d'Branin's sled slowed. The linguists did not. "We've already listened to you too damn much, I'd say," the woman said. She almost had to shout to be heard above the sobs and whimpers, the agonized sounds that filled their universe. "Melantha," she said, "keep Eris right where he is. We'll go carefully, find out what is happening inside, but I don't want him getting back to his controls. Understood?"

Melantha Jhirl hesitated. Sounds of terror and agony beat against her ears; it was hard to think.

Royd swung his sled around to face her, and she could feel the weight of his stare. "Stop them," he said. "Melantha, Karoly, order it. They do not know what they are doing." His voice was edged with despair.

In his face, Melantha found decision. "Go back inside quickly, Royd. Do what you can, I'm going to try to intercept them."

He nodded to her across the gulf, but Melantha was already in motion. Her sled backed clear of the work area, congested with hull fragments and other debris, then accelerated briskly as she raced toward the rear of the *Nightflyer*.

But even as she approached, she knew it was too late. The linguists were too close, and already moving much faster than she was.

"Don't," she said, authority in her tone. "The ship isn't safe, damn it."

"Bitch," was all the answer she got.

Karoly's sled pursued vainly. "Friends, you must stop, please, I beg it of you, let us talk this out together."

The unending whimpers were his only reply.

"I am your superior," he said. "I order you to wait outside. Do you hear me? I order it, I invoke the authority of the Academy. Please, my friends, please listen to me."

Melantha watched as the linguists vanished down the long tunnel of the driveroom.

A moment later she halted her sled near the waiting black mouth, debating whether she should follow them into the *Nightflyer*. She might be able to catch them before the airlock opened.

Royd's voice, hoarse counterpoint to the crying, answered her unvoiced question. "Stay, Melantha. Proceed no further."

She looked behind her. Royd's sled was approaching.

"What are you doing?" she demanded. "Royd, use your own lock. You have to get back inside!"

"Melantha," he said calmly, "I cannot. The ship will not respond to me. The control lock will not dilate. I don't want you or Karoly inside the ship until I can return to my controls."

Melantha Jhirl looked down the shadowed barrel of the drive-room, where the linguists had vanished.

"What will—?"

"Beg them to come back, Melantha. Plead with them. Perhaps there is still time, if they will listen to you."

She tried. Karoly d'Branin tried too. The crying, the moaning, the twisted symphony went on and on. But they could not raise the two linguists at all.

"They've cut out their comm," Melantha said furiously. "They don't want to listen to us. Or that . . . that *sound.*"

Royd's sled and Karoly d'Branin's reached her at the same time. "I do not understand," Karoly said. "What is happening?"

"It is simple, Karoly," Royd replied. "I am being kept outside until—until Mother is done with them."

The linguists left their vacuum sled next to the one the xenobiologist had abandoned and cycled through the airlock in unseemly haste, with hardly a glance for the grim doorman.

Inside they paused briefly to collapse their helmets. "I can still hear him," the man said.

The woman nodded. "The sound is coming from the lounge. Hurry."

They kicked and pulled their way down the corridor in less than a minute. The sounds grew steadily louder, nearer. "He's in there," the woman said when they reached the chamber door.

"Yes," her partner said, "but is he alone? We need a weapon. What if . . . Royd had to be lying. There *is* someone else on board. We need to defend ourselves."

The woman would not wait. "There are two of us," she said. "Come *on!"* With that she launched herself through the doorway and into the lounge.

It was dark inside. What little light there was spilled through the door from the corridor. Her eyes took a long moment to adjust. "Where are you?" she cried in confusion. The lounge seemed empty, but maybe it was only the light.

"Follow the sound," the man suggested. He stood in the door, glancing warily about for a minute, before he began to feel his way down a wall groping with his hands.

The woman, impatient, propelled herself across the room, searching. She brushed against a wall in the kitchen area, and that made her think of weapons. She knew where the utensils were stored. "Here," she said, "here, I've got a knife, that should thrill you." She waved it, and brushed against a floating bubble of blood as big as her fist. It burst and reformed into a hundred smaller globules.

"Oh, merciful God," the man said in a voice thick with fear. "What?" she demanded. "Did you find him? Is he—?"

He was fumbling his way back towards the door, creeping along the wall the way he had come. "Get out of here," he warned. "Oh, *hurry.*"

"Why?" She trembled despite herself.

"I found the source," he said. "The screams, the crying. Come *on!*"

"Wha—"

He whimpered, "It was the grill. Oh, don't you see? It's coming from the communicator!" He reached the door, and sighed audibly, and he did not wait for her. He bolted down the corridor and was gone.

She braced herself and positioned herself in order to follow him. The sounds stopped. Just like that: turned off.

She kicked, floated towards the door, knife in hand.

Something dark crawled from beneath the dinner table and rose to block her path. She saw it clearly for a moment, outlined in the light from the corridor. The xenobiologist, still in his vacuum suit, but with his helmet pulled off. He had something in his hands that he raised to point at her. It was a laser, she saw, a simple cutting laser.

She was moving straight towards him. She flailed and tried to stop herself, but she could not.

When she got quite close, she saw that he had a second mouth below his chin, and it was grinning at her, and little droplets of blood flew from it, wetly, as he moved.

The man rushed down the corridor in a frenzy of fear, bruising himself as he smashed into walls. Panic and weightlessness made him clumsy. He kept glancing over his shoulder as he fled, hoping to see his lover coming after him, but terrified of what he might see in her stead.

It took a long, *long* time for the airlock to open. As he waited, trembling, his pulse began to slow. He steadied himself with an effort. Once inside the chamber, with the inner door sealed between him and the lounge, he began to feel safe.

Suddenly he could barely remember why he had been so terrified.

And he was ashamed; he had run, abandoned her. And for what? What had frightened him so? An empty lounge? Noises from a communicator? Why, that only meant the xenobiologist was alive somewhere else in the ship, in pain, spilling his agony into a comm unit.

Resolute, he reached out and killed the cycle on the airlock, then reversed it. The air that had been partially sucked out came gusting back into the chamber.

The man shook his head ruefully. He'd hear no end of this, he knew. She would never let him forget it. But at least he would return, and apologize. That would count for something.

As the inner door rolled back, he felt a brief flash of fear again, an instant of stark terror when he wondered what might have emerged from the lounge to wait for him in the corridors of the *Nightflyer*. He willed it away.

When he stepped out, she was waiting for him.

He could see neither anger nor disdain in her curiously calm features, but he pushed himself toward her and tried to frame a plea for forgiveness anyway. "I don't know why I—"

With languid grace, her hand came out from behind her back. The knife was in it. That was when he finally noticed the hole burned in her suit, just between her breasts.

"Your *mother?*" Melantha Jhirl said incredulously as they hung helpless in the emptiness beyond the ship.

"She can hear everything we say," Royd replied. "But at this point, it no longer makes any difference. Your friend must have done something very foolish, very threatening. Now she is determined to kill you all."

"She, she, what do you mean?" D'Branin's voice was puzzled. "Royd, surely you do not tell us that your mother is still alive. You said she died even before you were born."

"She did, Karoly," Royd said. "I did not lie to you."

"No," Melantha said. "I didn't think so. But you did not tell us the whole truth either."

Royd nodded. "Mother is dead, but her—ghost still lives, and animates my *Nightflyer*. My control is tenuous at best."

"Royd," d'Branin said, "My *volcryn* are more real than any ghosts." His voice chided gently.

"I don't believe in ghosts either," Melantha Jhirl said with a frown.

"Call it what you will, then," Royd said. "My term is as good as any. The reality is unchanged. My mother, or some part of my mother, lives in the *Nightflyer,* and she is killing you all as she has killed others before."

"Royd, you do not make sense," d'Branin said. "I—"

"Karoly, let the captain explain."

"Yes," Royd said. "The *Nightflyer* is very—very *advanced,* you know. Automated, self-repairing, large. It had to be, if Mother were to be freed from the necessity of crew. It was built on Newholme, you will recall. I have never been there, but I understand that Newholme's technology is quite sophisticated. Avalon could not duplicate this ship, I suspect. There are few worlds that could."

"The point, Captain?"

"The point—the point is the computers, Melantha. They had to be extraordinary. They are, believe me, they are. Crystal-matrix cores, lasergrid data retrieval, and other—other features."

"Are you telling us that the *Nightflyer* is an Artificial Intelligence?"

"No," Royd said, "not as I understand it. But it is something close. Mother had a capacity for personality impress built in. She filled the central crystal with her own memories, desires, quirks, her loves and her—hates. That was why she trusted the computer with my education, you see? She knew it would raise me as she herself would, had she the patience. She programmed it in certain other ways as well."

"And you cannot deprogram, my friend?" Karoly asked.

Royd's voice was despairing. "I have *tried,* Karoly. But I am a weak hand at systems work, and the programs are very complicated, the machines very sophisticated. At least three times I have eradicated her, only to have her surface once again. She is a phantom program, and I cannot track her. She comes and goes as she will. A ghost, do you see? Her memories and her personality are so intertwined with the programs that run the *Nightflyer* that I cannot get rid of her without wiping the entire system. But that would leave me helpless. I could never reprogram, and with the computers down the entire ship would fail, drives, life support, everything. I would have to leave the *Nightflyer,* and that would kill me."

"You should have told us, my friend," Karoly d'Branin said. "On Avalon, we have many cyberneticists, some very great minds. We might have aided you. We could have provided expert help."

"Karoly, I have *had* expert help. Twice I have brought systems specialists on board. The first one told me what I have just told you; that it was impossible without wiping the programs completely. The second had trained on Newholme. She thought she could help me. Mother killed her."

"You are still omitting something," Melantha Jhirl said. "I understand how your cybernetic ghost can open and close airlocks at will and arrange other accidents of that nature. But that first death, our telepath, how do you explain that?"

"Ultimately I must bear the guilt," Royd replied. "My loneliness led me to a grievous error. I thought I could safeguard you, even with a telepath among you. I have carried other riders safely. I watch them constantly, warn them away from dangerous acts. If Mother attempts to interfere, I countermand her directly from the control room. That usually works. Not always. Usually. Before you she had killed only five times, and the first three died when I was quite young. That was how I learned about her. That party included a telepath too.

"I should have known better, Karoly. My hunger for life has doomed you all to death. I overestimated my own abilities, and underestimated her fear of exposure. She strikes out when she is threatened, and telepaths are always a threat. They sense her, you see. A malign, looming presence, they tell me, something cool and hostile and inhuman."

"Yes," Karoly d'Branin said, "yes, that was what he said. An alien, he was certain of it."

"No doubt she feels alien to a telepath used to the familiar contours of organic minds. Hers is not a human brain, after all. What it is I cannot say—a complex of crystalline memories, a hellish network of interlocking programs, a meld of circuitry and spirit. Yes, I can understand why she might feel alien."

"You still haven't explained how a computer program could explode a man's skull," Melantha said patiently.

"Have you ever held a whisper-jewel?" Royd Eris asked her.

"Yes," she replied. She had even owned one once; a dark blue crystal, packed with the memories of a particularly satisfying bout of lovemaking. It had been esperetched on Avalon, her feelings impressed onto the jewel, and for more than a year she had only to touch it to grow randy. It had finally faded, though, and afterwards she had lost it.

"Then you know that psionic power can be stored," Royd said. "The central core of my computer system is resonant crystal. I think Mother impressed it as she lay dying."

"Only an esper can etch a whisper-jewel," Melantha said.

"You never asked me the *why* of it, Karoly," Royd said. "Nor you, Melantha. You never asked why Mother hated people so. She was born gifted, you see. On Avalon, she might have been a class one, tested and trained and honored, her talent nurtured and rewarded. I think she might have been very famous. She might have been stronger than a class one, but perhaps it is only after death that she acquired such power, linked as she is to the *Nightflyer.*

"The point is moot. She was not born on Avalon. On her birth world, her ability was seen as a curse, something alien and fearful. So they cured her of it. They used drugs and electroshock and hypnotraining that made her violently ill whenever she tried to use her talent. She never lost her power, of course, only the ability to use it effectively, to control it with her conscious mind. It remained part of her, suppressed, erratic, a source of shame and pain. And half a decade of institutional cure almost drove her insane. No wonder she hated people."

"What was her talent? Telepathy?"

"No. Oh, some rudimentary ability perhaps. I have read that all psi talents have several latent abilities in addition to their one developed strength. But Mother could not read minds. She had some empathy, although her cure had twisted it curiously, so that the emotions she felt literally sickened her. But her major strength, the talent they took five years to shatter and destroy, was teke."

Melantha Jhirl swore. "No wonder she hated gravity. Telekinesis under weightlessness is—"

"Yes," Royd finished. "Keeping the *Nightflyer* under gravity tortures me, but it limits Mother."

In the silence that followed that comment, each of them looked down the dark cylinder of the driveroom. Karoly d'Branin moved awkwardly on his sled. "They have not returned," he said finally.

"They are probably dead," Royd said dispassionately.

"What will we do, friend Royd? We must plan. We cannot wait here indefinitely."

"The first question is what can *I* do," Royd Eris replied. "I have talked freely, you'll note. You deserved to know. We have passed the point where ignorance was a protection. Obviously things have gone too far. There have been too many deaths and you have been witness to all of them. Mother cannot allow you to return to Avalon alive."

"Ah," said Melantha, "true. But what shall she do with *you?* Is your own status in doubt, Captain?"

"The crux of the problem," Royd admitted. "You are still three moves ahead, Melantha. I wonder if it will suffice. Your opponent is four ahead this game, and most of your pawns are already captured. I fear checkmate is imminent."

"Unless I can persuade my opponent's king to desert, no?"

She could see Royd smile at her wanly. "She would probably kill me too if I choose to side with you."

Karoly d'Branin was slow to grasp the point. "But—but what else could you—"

"My sled has a laser. Yours do not. I could kill you both, right now, and thereby earn my way into the *Nightflyer*'s good graces."

Across the three meters that lay between their sleds, Melantha's eyes met Royd's. Her hands rested easily on the thruster controls. "You could try, Captain. Remember, the improved model isn't easy to kill."

"I would not kill you, Melantha Jhirl," Royd said seriously. "I have lived sixty-eight standard years and I have never lived at all. I am tired, and you tell grand gorgeous lies. If we lose, we will all die together. If we win, well, I shall die anyway, when they destroy the *Nightflyer*—either that or live as a freak in an orbital hospital, and I would prefer death—"

"We will build you a new ship, Captain," Melantha said.

"Liar," Royd replied. But his tone was cheerful. "No matter. I have not had much of a life anyway. Death does not frighten me. If we win, you must tell me about your *volcryn* once again, Karoly. And you, Melantha, you must play chess with me once more, and . . ." His voice trailed off.

"And sex with you?" she finished, smiling.

"If you would," he said quietly. "I have never—*touched,* you know. Mother died before I was born." He shrugged. "Well, Mother has heard all of this. Doubtless she will listen carefully to any plans we might make, so there is no sense making them. There is no chance now that the control lock will admit me, since it is keyed directly into the ship's computer. So we must follow your colleagues through the driveroom, and enter through the manual lock, and take what chances we are given. If I can reach consoles and restore gravity, perhaps we—"

He was interrupted by a low groan.

For an instant Melantha thought the *Nightflyer* was wailing at them again, and she was surprised that it was so stupid as to try the same tactic twice. Then the groan sounded a second time, and in the back of Karoly d'Branin's sled the forgotten fourth survivor struggled against the bonds that held her down. D'Branin hastened to free her, and the psipsych tried to rise to her feet and almost floated off the sled, until he caught her hand and pulled her back. "Are you well?" he asked. "Can you hear me? Have you pain?"

Imprisoned beneath a transparent faceplate, wide frightened eyes flicked rapidly from Karoly to Melantha to Royd, and then to the broken *Nightflyer*. Melantha wondered whether the woman was insane, and started to caution d'Branin, when the psipsych spoke suddenly.

"The *volcryn*," was all she said, "the *volcryn*. Oh, oh, the *volcryn!*"

Around the mouth of the driveroom, the ring of nuclear engines took on a faint glow. Melantha Jhirl heard Royd suck in his breath sharply. She gave the thruster controls of her sled a violent twist. "Hurry," she said, "the *Nightflyer* is preparing to move."

A third of the way down the long barrel of the driveroom, Royd pulled abreast of her, stiff and menacing in his black, bulky armor. Side by side they sailed past the cylindrical stardrives and the cyberwebs; ahead, dimly lit, was the main airlock and its ghastly sentinel.

"When we reach the lock, jump over to my sled," Royd said. "I want to stay armed and mounted, and the chamber is not large enough for two sleds."

Melantha Jhirl risked a quick glance behind her. "Karoly," she called. "Where are you?"

"I am outside, Melantha," the answer came. "I cannot come, my friend. Forgive me."

"But we have to stay together," she said.

"No," d'Branin's voice replied, "no, I could not risk it, not when we are so close. It would be so tragic, so futile, Melantha, to come so close and fail. Death I do not mind, but I must see them first, finally, after all these years." His voice was firm and calm.

Royd Eris cut in. "Karoly, my mother is going to move the ship. Don't you understand? You will be left behind, lost."

"I will wait," d'Branin replied. "My *volcryn* are coming, and I will wait for them."

Then there was no more time for conversation, for the airlock was almost upon them. Both sleds slowed and stopped, and Royd Eris reached out and began the cycle while Melantha moved to the rear of the huge oval worksled. When the outer door moved aside, they glided through into the lock chamber.

"When the inner door opens, it will begin," Royd told her evenly. "Most of the permanent furnishings are either built in or welded or bolted into place, but the things that your team brought on board are not. Mother will use those things as weapons. And beware of doors, airlocks, any equipment tied in to the *Nightflyer*'s computer. Need I warn you not to unseal your suit?"

"Hardly," she replied.

Royd lowered the sled a little, and its grapplers made a metallic sound as they touched against the chamber floor.

The inner door opened, and Royd applied his thrusters.

Inside the linguists were waiting, swimming in a haze of blood. The man had been slit from crotch to throat and his intestines moved like a nest of pale, angry snakes. The woman still held the knife. They swam closer with a grace they had never possessed in life.

Royd lifted his foremost grapplers and smashed them to the side. The man caromed off a bulkhead, leaving a wide wet mark where he struck, and more of his guts came sliding out. The woman lost control of the knife. Royd accelerated past them, driving up the corridor, through the cloud of blood.

"I'll watch behind," Melantha said, and she turned and put her back to his. Already the two corpses were safely behind them. The knife was floating uselessly in the air. She started to tell Royd that they were all right when the blade abruptly shifted and came after them, as if some invisible force had taken hold of it.

"Swerve!" she shouted.

The sled shot widly to one side. The knife missed by a full meter, and glanced ringingly off a bulkhead.

But it did not drop. It came at them again.

The lounge loomed ahead. Dark.

"The door is too narrow," Royd said. "We will have to abandon the sled, Melantha." Even as he spoke, they hit: he wedged the sled squarely into the doorframe, and the sudden impact jarred them loose.

For a moment Melantha floated clumsily in the corridor, trying to get her balance. The knife slashed at her, opening her suit and her shoulder. She felt sharp pain and the warm flush of bleeding. *"Damn,"* she shrieked. The knife came around again, spraying droplets of blood.

Melantha's hand darted out and caught it.

She muttered something under her breath, and wrenched the blade free of the force that had been gripping it.

Royd had regained the controls of his sled and seemed intent on some manipulation. Beyond, in the dimness of the lounge, Melantha saw a dark semi-human shape float into view.

"Royd!" she warned, but as she did the thing activated its laser. The pencil beam caught Royd square in the chest.

He touched his own firing stud. The sled's heavy-duty laser cindered the xenobiologist's weapon and burned off his right arm and part of his chest. Its pulsing shaft hung in the air, and smoked against the far bulkhead.

Royd made some adjustments and began cutting a hole. "We'll be through in five minutes or less," he said curtly, without stopping or looking up.

"Are you all right?" Melantha asked.

"I'm uninjured," he replied. "My suit is better armored than yours, and his laser was a low-powered toy."

Melantha turned her attention back to the corridor.

The linguists were pulling themselves toward her, one on each side of the passage, to come at her from two directions at once. She flexed her muscles. Her shoulder throbbed where she had been cut. Otherwise she felt strong, almost reckless. "The corpses are coming after us again," she told Royd. "I'm going to take them."

"Is that wise?" he asked. "There are two of them."

"I'm an improved model," Melantha said, "and they're dead." She kicked herself free of the sled and sailed toward the man. He raised his hands to block her. She slapped them aside, bent one arm back and heard it snap, and drove her knife deep into his throat before she realized what a useless gesture that was. The man continued to flail at her. His teeth snapped grotesquely.

Melantha withdrew her blade, seized him, and with all her considerable strength threw him bodily down the corridor. He tumbled, spinning wildly, and vanished into the haze of his own blood.

Melantha then flew in the opposite direction.

The woman's hands went around her from behind.

Nails scrabbled against her faceplate until they began to bleed, leaving red streaks on the plastic.

Melantha spun to face her attacker, grabbed a thrashing arm, and flung the woman down the passageway to crash into her struggling companion.

"I'm through," Royd announced.

She turned to see. A smoking meter-square opening had been cut through one wall of the lounge. Royd killed the laser, gripped both sides of the doorframe, and pushed himself towards it.

A piercing blast of sound drilled through her head. She doubled over in agony. Her tongue flicked out and clicked off the comm; then there was blessed silence.

In the lounge it was raining. Kitchen utensils, glasses and plates, pieces of human bodies all lashed violently across the room, and glanced harmlessly off Royd's armored form. Melantha—eager to follow—drew back helplessly. That rain of death would cut her up to pieces in her lighter, thinner vacuum suit. Royd reached the far wall and vanished into the secret control section of the ship. She was alone.

The *Nightflyer* lurched, and sudden acceleration provided a brief semblance of gravity. She was thrown to one side. Her injured shoulder smashed painfully against the sled.

All up and down the corridor doors were opening.

The linguists were moving toward her once again.

The *Nightflyer* was a distant star sparked by its nuclear engines. Blackness and cold enveloped them, and below was the unending emptiness of the Tempter's Veil, but Karoly d'Branin did not feel afraid. He felt strangely transformed.

The void was alive with promise.

"They *are* coming," he whispered. "Even I, who have no psi

at all, even I can feel it. The Crey story must be so, even from light-years off they can be sensed. Marvelous!"

The psipsych seemed very small. "The *volcryn*," she muttered. "What good can they do us. I hurt. The ship is gone. D'Branin, my head aches." She made a small frightened noise. "The boy said that, just after I injected him, before . . . before . . . you know. He said that his head hurt."

"Quiet, my friend. Do not be afraid. I am here with you. Wait. Think only of what we shall witness, think only of that!"

"I can sense them," the psipsych said.

D'Branin was eager. "Tell me, then. We have the sled. We shall go to them. Direct me."

"Yes," she agreed. "Yes. Oh, yes."

Gravity returned: in a flicker, the universe became almost normal.

Melantha fell to the deck, landed easily and rolled, and was on her feet cat-quick.

The objects that had been floating ominously through the open doors along the corridor all came clattering down.

The blood was transformed from a fine mist to a slick covering on the corridor floor.

The two corpses dropped heavily from the air, and lay still.

Royd spoke to her. His voice came from the communicator grills built into the walls, not over her suit comm. "I made it," he said.

"I noticed," she replied.

"I'm at the main control console," he continued. "I have restored the gravity with a manual override, and I'm cutting off as many computer functions as possible. We're still not safe, though. She will try to find a way around me. I'm countermanding her by sheer force, as it were. I cannot afford to overlook anything, and if my attention should lapse for even a moment . . . Melantha, was your suit breached?"

"Yes. Cut at the shoulder."

"Change into another one. *Immediately*. I think the counter programming I'm doing will keep the locks sealed, but I can't take any chances."

Melantha was already running down the corridor, towards the cargo hold where the suits and equipment were stored.

"When you have changed," Royd continued, "dump the corpses into the mass conversion unit. You'll find the appropriate hatch near the driveroom, just to the left of the main lock. Convert any other loose objects that are not indispensable as well; scientific instruments, books, tapes, tableware—"

"Knives," suggested Melantha.

"By all means."

"Is teke still a threat, Captain?"

"Mother is vastly weaker in a gravity field," Royd said. "She has to fight it. Even boosted by the *Nightflyer*'s power, she can only move one object at a time, and she has only a fraction of the lifting force she wields under weightless conditions. But the power is still there, remember. Also, it is possible she will find a way to circumvent me and cut out the gravity again. From here I can restore it in an instant, but I don't want any weapons lying around even for that brief period of time."

Melantha had reached the cargo area. She stripped off her vacuum suit and slipped into another one in record time. Then she gathered up the discarded suit and a double armful of instruments and dumped them into the conversion chamber. Afterwards she turned her attention to the bodies. The man was no problem. The woman crawled down the hall after her as she pushed him through, and thrashed weakly when it was her own turn, a grim reminder that the *Nightflyer*'s powers were not all gone. Melantha easily overcame her feeble struggles and forced her through.

The corpse of the xenobiologist was less trouble, but while she was cleaning out the lounge a kitchen knife came spinning at her head. It came slowly, though, and Melantha just batted it aside, then picked it up and added it to the pile for conversion.

She was working through the second cabin, carrying the psi-psych's abandoned drugs and injection gun under her arm, when she heard Royd cry out.

A moment later, a force like a giant invisible hand wrapped itself around her chest and squeezed and pulled her, struggling, to the floor.

Something was moving across the stars.

Dimly and far off, d'Branin could see it, though he could not yet make out details. But it was there, that was unmistakable, some vast shape that blocked off a section of the starscape. It was coming at them dead on.

How he wished he had his team with him now, his telepath, his experts, his instruments.

He pressed harder on the thrusters.

Pinned to the floor, hurting, Melantha Jhirl risked opening her suit's comm. She had to talk to Royd. "Are you there?" she asked. "What's happening?" The pressure was awful, and it was growing steadily worse. She could barely move.

The answer was pained and slow in responding. ". . . outwitted . . . me," Royd's voice managed. ". . . hurts . . . to . . . talk."

"Royd—"

". . . she . . . teked . . . dial . . . up . . . two . . . gees . . . three . . . higher . . . right . . . here . . . on . . . the . . . board . . . all . . . I . . . have to . . . to do . . . turn it . . . back . . . back . . . let me. . . ."

Silence. Then, finally, when Melantha was near despair, Royd's voice again. One word: ". . . can't . . ."

Melantha's chest felt as if it were supporting ten times her own weight. She could imagine the agony Royd must be in; Royd, for whom even one gravity was painful and dangerous. Even if the dial was an arm's length away she knew his feeble musculature would never let him reach it. "Why," she started, having somewhat less trouble talking than Royd, "why would she turn *up* the . . . gravity . . . it . . . weakens her too, yes?"

". . . yes . . . but . . . in a . . . a . . . time . . . hour . . . minute . . . my . . . my heart . . . will burst . . . and . . . and then . . . you alone . . . she . . . will . . . kill gravity . . . kill you . . ."

Painfully, Melantha reached out her arm and dragged herself half a length down the corridor. "Royd . . . hold on . . . I'm coming . . ." She dragged herself forward again. The psipsych's drug kit was still under her arm, impossibly heavy. She eased it down and started to shove it aside, then reconsidered. Instead she opened its lid.

The ampules were all neatly labeled. She glanced over them quickly, searching for adrenaline or synthastim, anything that might give her the strength she needed to reach Royd. She found several stimulants, selected the strongest, and was loading it into the injection gun with awkward, agonized slowness when her eyes chanced on the supply of esperon.

Melantha did not know why she hesitated. Esperon was only one of a half-dozen psionic drugs in the kit, but something about seeing it bothered her, reminded her of something she could not quite lay her finger on. She was trying to sort it out when she heard the noise.

"Royd," she said, "your mother . . . could she move . . . she couldn't move anything . . . teke it . . . in this high a gravity . . . could she?"

"Maybe," he answered, ". . . if . . . concentrate . . . all her . . . power . . . hard . . . maybe possible . . . why?"

"Because," Melantha Jhirl said grimly, "because something . . . someone . . . is cycling through the airlock."

The *volcryn* ship filled the universe.

"It is not truly a ship, not as I thought it would be," Karoly d'Branin was saying. His suit, Academy-designed, had a built-in encoding device, and he was recording his comments for posterity, strangely secure in the certainty of his impending death. "The scale of it is difficult to imagine, difficult to estimate. Vast, vast. I have nothing but my wrist computer, no instruments, I cannot make accurate measurements, but I would say, oh, a hundred kilometers, perhaps as much as three hundred, across. No solid mass, of course, not at all. It is delicate, airy, no ship as we know ships. It is—oh, beautiful—it is crystal and gossamer, alive with its own dim lights, a vast intricate kind of spiderwebby craft—it reminds me a bit of the old starsail ships they used once, in the days before drive, but this great construct, it is not solid, it cannot be driven by light. It is no ship at all, really. It is all open to vacuum, it has no sealed cabins or life-support spheres, none visible to me, unless blocked from my line of sight in some fashion, and no, I cannot believe that, it is too open, too fragile. It moves quite rapidly. I would wish for the instrumentation to measure its speed, but it is enough to be here. I am taking our sled at right angles to it, to get clear of its path, but I cannot say that I will make it. It moves so much faster than we. Not at light speed, no, far below it, but still faster than the *Nightflyer* and its nuclear engines, I would guess. Only a guess.

"The *volcryn* craft has no visible means of propulsion. In fact,

I wonder how—perhaps it *is* a light-sail, laser-launched millennia ago, now torn and rotted by some unimaginable catastrophe—but no, it is too symmetrical, too beautiful, the webbings, the great shimmering veils near the nexus, the beauty of it.

"I must describe it, I must be more accurate, I know. It is difficult, I grow too excited. It is large, as I have said, kilometers across. Roughly—let me count—yes, roughly octagonal in shape. The nexus, the center, is a bright area, a small darkness surrounded by a much greater area of light, but only the dark portion seems entirely solid—the lighted areas are translucent, I can see stars through them, discolored, shifted towards the purple. Veils, I call those the veils. From the nexus and the veils eight long—oh, vastly long—spurs project, not quite spaced evenly, so it is not a true geometric octagon—ah, I see better now, one of the spurs is shifted, oh, very slowly, the veils are rippling—they are mobile then, those projections, and the webbing runs from one spur to the next, around and around, but there are—patterns, odd patterns, it is not at all the simple webbing of a spider. I cannot quite see order in the patterns, in the traceries of the webs, but I feel sure that the order is there, the meaning is waiting to be found.

"There are lights. Have I mentioned the lights? The lights are the brightest around the center nexus, but they are nowhere very bright, a dim violet. Some visible radiation, then, but not much. I would like to take an ultraviolet reading of this craft, but I do not have the instrumentation. The lights move. The veils seem to ripple, and lights run constantly up and down the length of the spurs, at differing rates of speed, and sometimes other lights can be seen traversing the webbing, moving across the patterns. I do not know what the lights are or whether they emanate from inside the craft or outside.

"The *volcryn* myths, this is really not much like the legends, not truly. Though, as I think, now I recall a Nor T'alush report that the *volcryn* ships were impossibly large, but I took that for exaggeration. And lights, the *volcryn* have often been linked to lights, but those reports were so vague, they might have meant anything, described anything from a laser propulsion system to simple exterior lighting, I could not know it meant this. Ah, what mysteries! The ship is still too far away for me to see the finer detail. I think perhaps the darker area in the center *is* a craft, a life capsule. The *volcryn* must be inside it. I wish my team was with me, my telepath. He was a class one, we might have made contact, might have communicated with them. The things we would learn! The things they have seen! To think how old this craft is, how ancient this race, how long they have been outbound! It fills me with awe. Communication would be such a gift, such an impossible gift, but they are so alien."

"D'Branin," the psipsych said in a low, urgent voice. "Can't you feel?"

Karoly d'Branin looked at his companion as if seeing her for the first time. "Can *you* feel them? You are a three, can you sense them now, strongly?"

"Long ago," the psipsych said. "Long ago."

"Can you project? Talk to them. Where are they? In the center area?"

"Yes," she replied, and she laughed. Her laugh was shrill and hysterical, and d'Branin had to recall that she was a very sick woman. "Yes, in the center, d'Branin, that's where the pulses come from. Only you're wrong about them. It's not a *them* at all, your legends are all lies, lies, I wouldn't be surprised if we were the first to ever see your *volcryn,* to ever come this close. The others, those aliens of yours, they merely *felt,* deep and distantly, sensed a bit of the nature of the *volcryn* in their dreams and visions, and fashioned the rest to suit themselves. Ships, and wars, and a race of eternal travelers, it is all—all—"

"What do you mean, my friend?" Karoly said, baffled. "You do not make sense. I do not understand."

"No," the psipsych said, her voice suddenly gentle. "You do not, do you? You cannot feel it, as I can. So clear now. This must be how a one feels, all the time. A one full of esperon."

"What do you feel? *What?"*

"It's not a *them,* Karoly," the psipsych said. "It's an *it.* Alive, Karoly, and quite mindless, I assure you."

"Mindless?" d'Branin said. "No, you must be wrong, you are not reading correctly. I will accept that it is a single creature if you say so, a single great marvelous star-traveler, but how can it be mindless? You sensed it, its mind, its telepathic emanations. You and the whole of the Crey sensitives and all the others. Perhaps its thoughts are too alien for you to read."

"Perhaps," the psipsych admitted, "but what I do read is not so terribly alien at all. Only animal. Its thoughts are slow and dark and strange, hardly thoughts at all, faint. The brain must be huge, I grant you that, but it can't be devoted to conscious thought."

"What do you mean?"

"The propulsion system, d'Branin. Don't you *feel?* The pulses? They are threatening to rip off the top of my skull. Can't you guess what is driving your damned *volcryn* across the galaxy? Why they avoid gravity wells? Can't you guess how it is moving?"

"No," d'Branin said, but even as he denied it a dawn of comprehension broke across his face, and he looked away from his companion, back at the swelling immensity of the *volcryn,* its lights moving, its veils a-ripple, as it came on and on, across light-years, light centuries, across eons.

When he looked back to her, he mouthed only a single word: "Teke," he said. Silence filled their world.

She nodded.

Melantha Jhirl struggled to lift the injection gun and press it against an artery. It gave a single loud hiss, and the drug flooded her system. She lay back and gathered her strength, tried to think. Esperon, esperon, why was that important? It had killed the telepath, made him a victim of his own abilities, tripled his power and his vulnerability. Psi. It all came back to psi.

The inner door of the airlock opened. The headless corpse came through.

It moved with jerks, unnatural shufflings, never lifting its legs from the floor. It sagged as it moved, half-crushed by the weight upon it. Each shuffle was crude and sudden; some grim force was literally yanking one leg forward, then the next. It moved in slow motion, arms stiff by its sides.

But it moved.

Melantha summoned her own reserves and began to crawl away from it, never taking her eyes off its advance.

Her thoughts went round and round, searching for the piece out of place, the solution to the chess problem, finding nothing.

The corpse was moving faster than she was. Clearly, visibly it was gaining.

Melantha tried to stand. She got to her knees, her heart pounding. Then one knee. She tried to force herself up, to lift the impossible burden on her shoulders. She was strong, she told herself. She was the improved model.

But when she put all her weight on one leg, her muscles would not hold her. She collapsed, awkwardly, and when she smashed against the floor it was as if she had fallen from a building. She heard a sharp *snap,* and a stab of agony flashed up the arm she had tried to use to break her fall. She blinked back tears and choked on her own scream.

The corpse was halfway up the corridor. It must be walking on two broken legs, she realized. It didn't care.

"Melantha . . . heard you . . . are . . . you . . . Melantha?"

"Quiet," she snapped at Royd. She had no breath to waste on talk.

Now she had only one arm. She used the disciplines she had taught herself, willed away the pain. She kicked feebly, her boots scraping for purchase, and she pulled herself forward with her good arm.

The corpse came on and on.

She dragged herself across the threshold of the lounge, worming her way under the crashed sled, hoping it would delay the cadaver.

It was a meter behind her.

In the darkness, in the lounge, there where it had all begun, Melantha Jhirl ran out of strength.

Her body shuddered, and she collapsed on the damp carpet, and she knew that she could go not further.

On the far side of the door, the corpse stood stiffly. The sled began to shake. Then, with the scrape of metal against metal, it slid backwards, moving in tiny sudden increments, jerking itself free and out of the way.

Psi. Melantha wanted to curse it, and cry. Vainly she wished for a psi power of her own, a weapon to blast apart the teke-driven corpse that stalked her. She was improved, she thought angrily, but not improved enough. Her parents had given her all the genetic gifts they could arrange, but psi was beyond them. The gene was astronomically rare, recessive, and—

—and suddenly it came to her.

"Royd!" she yelled, put all of her remaining will into her words. "The dial . . . *teke it.* Royd, teke it!"

His reply was very faint, troubled. ". . . can't . . . I don't . . . Mother . . . only . . . her . . . not me . . . no . . ."

"Not mother," she said, desperate. "You always . . . say . . .
mother. I forgot . . . forgot. Not your mother . . . listen . . .
you're a *clone* . . . same genes . . . you have it, too. The power."

"Don't," he said. "Never . . . must be . . . sex-linked."

"No! It *isn't.* I know . . . Promethean, Royd . . . don't tell a
Promethean . . . about genes . . . turn it!"

The sled jumped a third of a meter, and listed to the side. A
path was clear.

The corpse came forward.

". . . trying," Royd said. "Nothing . . . I *can't!"*

"She *cured* you," Melantha said bitterly. "Better than . . . she
was . . . cured . . . pre-natal . . . but it's only . . . suppressed
. . . you *can!"*

"I . . . don't . . . know . . . how."

The corpse now stood above her. Stopped. Pale-fleshed hands
trembled spasticly. Began to rise.

Melantha swore, and wept, and made a futile fist.

And all at once the gravity was gone. Far, far away, she heard
Royd cry out and then fall silent.

The corpse bobbed awkwardly into the air, its hands hanging
limply before it. Melantha, reeling in the weightlessness, tried to
ready herself for its furious assault.

But the body did not move again. It floated dead and still.
Melantha moved to it, pushed it, and it sailed across the room.

"Royd?" she said uncertainly.

There was no answer.

She pulled herself through the hole into the control chamber.

And found Royd Eris, master of the *Nightflyer,* prone on his
back in his armored suit, dead. His heart had given out.

But the dial on the gravity grid was set at zero.

I have held the *Nightflyer*'s crystalline soul within my hands.

It is deep and red and multifaceted, large as my head, and icy
to the touch. In its scarlet depths, two small sparks of light burn
fiercely and sometimes seem to whirl.

I have crawled through the consoles, wound my way carefully
past safeguards and cybernets, taking care to damage nothing, and
I have laid rough hands on that great crystal, knowing that it is
where *she* lives.

And I cannot bring myself to wipe it.

Royd's ghost has asked me not to.

Last night we talked about it once again, over brandy and chess in the lounge. Royd cannot drink of course, but he sends his specter to smile at me, and he tells me where he wants his pieces moved.

For the thousandth time he offered to take me back to Avalon, or any world of my choice, if only I would go outside and complete the repairs we abandoned so many years ago, so that the *Nightflyer* might safely slip into stardrive.

For the thousandth time I refused.

He is stronger now, no doubt. Their genes are the same, after all. Their power is the same. Dying, he too found the strength to impress himself upon the great crystal. The ship is alive with both of them, and frequently they fight. Sometimes she outwits him for a moment, and the *Nightflyer* does odd, erratic things. The gravity goes up or down or off completely. Blankets wrap themselves around my throat when I sleep. Objects come hurtling out of dark corners.

Those times have come less frequently of late, though. When they do come, Royd stops her, Or I do. Together, the *Nightflyer* is ours.

Royd claims he is strong enough alone, that he does not really need me, that he can keep her under check. I wonder. Over the chessboard, I still beat him nine games out of ten.

And there are other considerations. Our work, for one. Karoly would be proud of us.

The *volcryn* will soon enter the mists of the Tempter's Veil, and we follow close behind. Studying, recording, doing all that old d'Branin would have wanted us to do. It is all in the computer. It is also on tape and on paper, should the computer ever be wiped. It will be interesting to see how the *volcryn* thrives in the Veil. Matter is so thick there, compared to the thin diet of interstellar hydrogen on which the creature has fed for endless eons.

We have tried to communicate with it, with no success. I do not believe it is sentient at all.

And lately Royd has tried to imitate its ways, gathering all his energies in an attempt to move the *Nighflyer* by teke. Sometimes, oddly, his mother even joins him in those efforts. So far they have failed, but we will keep trying.

So the work goes on, and it *is* important work, though not the field I trained for, back on Avalon. We know that our results will reach humanity. Royd and I have discussed it. Before I die, I will destroy the central crystal and clear the computers, and afterwards I will set course manually for the close vicinity of an inhabited world. I know I can do it. I have all the time I need, and I am an improved model.

I will not consider the other option, though it means much to me that Royd suggests it again and again. No doubt I could finish the repairs. Perhaps Royd could control the ship without me, and continue the work. But that is not important.

When I finally touched him, for the first and last and only time, his body was still warm. But *he* was gone already. He never felt my touch. I could not keep that promise.

But I can keep my other.

I will not leave him alone with her.

Ever.

FRITZ LEIBER
Horrible Imaginings

"Present fears are less than horrible imaginings."
—MACBETH

OLD RAMSEY RYKER only commenced thinking about going to see (through one-way glass) the young women fingering their genitals *after* he started having the low-ceilinged dreams without light—the muttering dull black nightmares—but *before* he began catching glimpses of the vanishing young-old mystery girl, who wore black that twinkled, lurking in the first-floor ground-level corridors, or disappearing into the elevator, and once or twice slipping along the upstairs halls of the apartment tree (or skeleton) that is, with one exception, the sole scene of the action in this story, which does not venture farther, disturb the privacy of the apartments themselves, or take one step out into the noisy metropolitan street. Here all is hushed.

I mean by the *apartment tree* all the public or at least tenant-shared space within the thirteen-floor building where Ryker lived alone. With a small effort you can visualize that volume of connected space as a rather repetitious tree (color it red or green if it helps, as they do in "You are *here*" diagrammatic maps; I see it as pale gray myself, for that is the color of the wallpaper in the outer halls, pale gray faintly patterned with dingy silver): its roots the basement garage where some tenants with cars rented space along with a few neighborhood shopkeepers and businessmen; its trunk the central elevator shaft with open stairway beside it (the owner of the building had periodic difficulties with the fire inspectors about the latter—they wanted it walled off with heavy self-closing doors at each floor; certainly a building permit would never have been granted today—or in the last three decades, for that matter—for such a lofty structure with an open stairwell); its

branches the three halls, two long, one short, radiating out from
the shaft-stairwell trunk and identical at each level except for
minor features; from the top floor a sort of slanted, final thick
branch of stairs led, through a stout door (locked on the outside
but open on the inside—another fire regulation), to the roof and
the strong, floored weatherproof shed holding the elevator's motor
and old-fashioned mechanical relays. But we won't stir through
that door either to survey the besmogged but nonetheless impressive
cityscape and hunt for the odd star or (rarer still) an interesting
window.

At ground level one of the long corridors led to the street door;
on the floors above, to the front fire escape. The other long ones
led to the alley fire escape. The short hall was blind (the fire
inspector would shake his head at that feature too, and frown).

And then of course we should mention, if only for the sake of
completists, the apartment tree's micro-world, its tiniest twigs and
leaflets, in a sense: all the cracks and crevices (and mouse- and
rat-holes, if any) going off into the walls, ceilings, and floors, with
perhaps some leading to more spacious though still cramped
volumes of space.

But it would be discourteous of us to wander—and so frivo-
lously—through the strange labyrinthine apartment tree with its
angular one- and two-bedroom forbidden fruit, when all the time
Ramsey Ryker, a lofty, gaunt old man somewhat resembling a
neatly dressed scarecrow, is waiting impatiently for us with his
equally strange and tortuous problems and concerns. Of these,
the black nightmares were the worst by far and also in a way the
cause of, or at least the prelude to, all the others.

Actually they were the worst nightmares in a restrained sort of
way that Ramsey ever remembered having in the seven decades
of his life and the only ones, the only dreams of any sort for that
matter, without any visual element at all (hence the "black"), but
only sound, touch, intramuscular feelings, and smell. And the
black was really inky, midnight, moonless and starless, sooty,
utter—all those words. It didn't even have any of those faint
churning points of light we see, some of them tinted, when we
shut our eyes in absolute darkness and when supposedly we're
seeing rods and cones of our retina fire off without any photons
of outside light hitting them. No, the only light in his nightmares,
if any, was of the phantom sort in which *memories* are painted—
a swift, sometimes extensive-seeming flash which starts to fade the

instant it appears and never seems to be in the retina at all, something far more ghostly even than the nebular churnings that occur under the eyelids in the inkiest dark.

He'd been having these nightmares every two or three nights, regular almost as clockwork, for at least a month now, so that they were beginning to seriously worry and oppress him. I've said "nightmares" up to now, but really there was only *one,* repeated with just enough changes in its details to convince him that he was experiencing new nightmares rather than just remembering the first. This made them more ominously terrifying; he'd know what was coming—up to a point—and suffer the more because of that.

Each "performance" of his frightening lightless dream, on those nights when his unconscious decided to put on a show, would begin the same way. He would gradually become aware, as though his mind were rising with difficulty from unimaginable depths of sleep, that he was lying stretched out naked on his back with his arms extended neatly down his sides, but that he was *not* in his bed—the surface beneath him was too ridged and hard for that. He was breathing shallowly and with difficulty—or rather he discovered that if he tried to investigate his breathing, speed or slow it, expand his chest more fully, he ran the danger of bringing on a strangling spasm or coughing fit. This prospect frightened him; he tried never to let it happen.

To check on this, explore the space around him, he would next in his dream try to lift up a hand and arm, stretch a leg sideways— and find out that he could *not,* that so far as any gross movement of limbs went he was paralyzed. This naturally would terrify him and push him toward panic. It was all he could do not to strain, thrash (that is, try to), gasp, or cry out.

Then as his panic slowly subsided, as he schooled himself to quietly endure this limitation on his actions, he would discover that his paralysis was not complete, that if he went about it slowly he could move a bit, wag his head about an inch from side to side, writhe a little the superficial muscles and skin under his shoulders and down his back and buttocks and legs, stir his heels and fingertips slightly. It was in this way that he discovered that the hard surface under him consisted of rough laths set close together, which were very dusty—no, *gritty.*

Next in his dream came an awareness of sound. At first it would seem the normal muttering hum of any big city, but then he'd begin to distinguish in it a faint rustling and an infinitesimal rapid clicking that was very much closer and seemed to get nearer each moment and he'd think of insects and spiders and he'd feel new terror gusting through him and there'd be another struggle to stave off hysteria. At this point in his dream he'd usually think of cockroaches, armies of them, as normal to big cities as the latter's muttering sounds, and his terror would fade though his revulsion would mount. Filthy creatures! but who could be frightened of them? True, his dear wife, now dead five years, had had a dread of stepping on one in the dark and hearing it crunch. (That reaction he found rather hard to understand. He was, well, if not exactly pleasured, then well satisfied to step on cockroaches, or mash them in the sink.)

His attention would then likely return to the muttering, growling, faintly buzzing, somehow *nasal* component of the general sound, and he'd begin to hear voices in it, though he could seldom identify the words or phrases—it was like the voices of a crowd coming out of a theater or baseball park or meeting hall and commenting and arguing droningly and wearily about what they'd just seen or heard. *Male* voices chiefly, cynical, sarcastic, deprecating, mean, sleepily savage, and ignorant, very ignorant, he'd feel sure. And never as loud or big as they ought to be; there was always a *littleness* about them. (Was his hearing impaired in his nightmares? Was he dreaming of growing deaf?) Were they the voices of depraved children? No, they were much too low—deep throat tones. Once he'd asked himself, "Midgets?" and had the thought, rich in dream wisdom, "A man lying down is not even as tall as a midget."

After sound, odor would follow, as his senses were assaulted cumulatively. First dry, stale, long-confined—somehow so natural seeming he would be unaware of the scents. But then he would smell smoke and know a special pang of fright—was he to be burned alive, unable to move? And the fire sirens when the engines came, tinied by distance and by muffling walls, no larger than those of toys?

But then he would identify it more precisely as tobacco smoke, the reeking smoke of cigars chiefly. He remembered how his dead wife had hated that, though smoking cigarettes herself.

After that, a whole host of supporting odors: toilet smells and the cheap sharp perfumes used to balance those out, stinking old flesh, the fishy reek of unwashed sex, locker rooms, beer, disinfectants, wine-laden vomit—all fitting very nicely, too, with the ignorant low growling.

After sound and odor, touch, living touch. Behind the lobe of his right ear, in his jaw's recessed angle, where a branch of the carotid pulses close to the surface, there'd come an exploring prod from the tip of something about as big as a baby's thumb, a pencil's eraserhead, snout of a mouse or of a garter snake, an embryo's fist, an unlit cigarette, a suppository, the phallus of a virile mannequin—a probing and a thrusting that did not stop and did not go away.

At that point his dream, if it hadn't already, would turn into full nightmare. He'd try to jerk his head sideways, throw himself over away from it, thrash his arms and legs, yell out unmindful of what it did to his breathing—and find that the paralysis still gripped him, its bonds growing tighter the more he struggled, his vocal cords as numb as if these were his life's last gaspings.

And then—more touches of the same puppet sort: his side, his thigh, between two fingers, up and down his body. The sounds and odors would get darker still as a general suffocating oppression closed in. He'd visualize grotesquely in imagination's lightless lightning flashes, which like those of memory are so utterly different from sight, a crowd of squatty, groping male Lilliputians, a press of dark-jowled, thickset, lowbrowed, unlovely living dolls standing or leaning in locker-room attitudes, each one nursing with one hand beneath his paunch a half-erect prick with a casual lasciviousness and with the other gripping a beer can or cigar or both, while all the while they gargled out unceasingly a thick oozy stream of shitty talk about crime and sports and sex, about power and profit. He envisioned their tiny prick nubs pressing in on him everywhere, as if he were being wrapped tighter and tighter in a rubber blanket that was all miniscule elastic knobs.

At this moment he would make a supreme effort to lift his head, reckless of heart attack, fighting for each fraction of an inch of upward movement, and find himself grinding his forehead and nose into a rough gritty wooden surface that had been there, not three inches above him, all the while, like the lid of a shallow coffin.

Then, and only then, in that moment of intensest horror, he'd wake at last, stretched out tidily in his own bed, gasping just a little, and with a totally unjoyous hard-on that seemed more like the symptom of some mortal disease than any prelude to pleasure.

The reader may at this point object that by entering Ramsey's bedroom we have strayed beyond the apartment-tree limits set for the actions of this story. Not so, for we have been examining only his *memories* of his nightmares, which never have the force of the real thing. In this fashion we peered into his dream, perhaps into his bedroom, but we never turned on the light. The same applies to his thoughts about and reactions to those erections which troubled his nightmare wakings and which seemed to him so much more like tumorous morbid growths—almost, cancers— than any swellings of joy.

Now Ramsey was sufficiently sophisticated to wonder whether his nightmares were an expression, albeit an unusual and most unpleasant one, of a gathering sexual arousal in himself, which his invariable waking hard-ons would seem to indicate, and whether the discharge of that growing sexual pressure would not result in the nightmares ceasing or at least becoming fewer in number and of a lesser intensity. On the one hand, his living alone was very thoroughgoing; he had formed no new intimacies since his wife's death five years earlier and his coincidental retirement and moving here. On the other, he had a deep personal prejudice against masturbation, not on moral or religious grounds, but from the conviction that such acts demanded a living accomplice or companion to make them effectively real, no matter how distant and tenuous the relation between the two parties, an adventuring-out into the real world and some achievement there, however slight.

Undoubtedly there were guilty shadows here—his life went back far enough for him to have absorbed in childhood mistaken notions of the unhealthiness of auto-eroticism that still influenced his feelings if not his intellect. And also something of the work-ethic of Protestantism, whereby everything had its price, had to be worked and sweated and suffered for.

With perhaps—who knows?—a touch of the romantic feeling that sex wasn't worth it without the spice of danger, which also required a venturing out beyond one's private self.

Now on the last occasion—about eight months ago—when Ramsey had noted signs of growing sexual tension in himself (signs far less grotesquely inappropriate, frightening, oppressive, and depressing than his current nightmares—which appeared to end with a strong hint of premature burial), he had set his imagination in a direction leading toward that tension's relief by venturing some four blocks into the outer world (the world beyond the apartment tree's street door) to a small theater called Ultrabooth, where for a modest price (in these inflated times) he could make contact with three living girls (albeit a voiceless one through heavy one-way glass), who would strip and display themselves intimately to him in a way calculated to promote arousal.

(A pause to note we've once more gone outside the apartment tree, but only by way of a remembered venturing—and memory is less real even than dream, as we have seen.)

The reason Ramsey had not at once again had recourse to these young ladies as soon as his nightmares began with their telltale terminal hard-ons, providing evidence of growing sexual pressure even if the peculiar nightmare contents did not, was that he had found their original performance, though sufficient for his purpose as it turned out, rather morally troubling and aesthetically unsatisfying in some respects and giving rise to various sad and wistful reflections in his mind as he repeated their performance in memory.

Ducking through a small, brightly lit marquee into the dim lobby of Ultrabooth, he'd laid a $10 bill on the counter before the bearded young man without looking at him, taken up the $2 returned with the considerate explanation that this was a reduction for senior citizens, and joined the half-dozen or so silent waiting men who mostly edged about restlessly yet slowly, not looking at each other.

After a moderate wait and some small augmentation of their number, there came a stirring from beyond the red velvet ropes as the previous audience was guided out a separate exit door. Ryker gravitated forward with the rest of the new audience. After a two-minute pause, a section of red rope was hooked aside, and they surged gently ahead into a shallow inner foyer from which two narrow dark doorways about fifteen feet apart led onward.

Ryker was the fourth man through the left-hand doorway. He found himself in a dim, curving corridor. On his left, wall. On his right, heavy curtains partly drawn aside from what looked like large closets, each with a gloomy window at the back. He entered the first that was unoccupied (the second), fumbled the curtains shut behind him, and clumsily seated himself facing the window on the cubicle's sole piece of furniture, a rather low barstool.

Actually, his booth wasn't crampingly small. Ryker estimated its floor space as at least one half that of the apartment tree's elevator, which had a six-person capacity.

As his eyes became accommodated to the darkness of his booth
and the dimness of the sizable room beyond, he saw that the
latter was roughly circular and walled by rectangular mirrors, each
of which, he realized, must be the window of a booth such as his
own—except one window space was just a narrow curtain going
to the floor. A wailing bluesy jazz from an unseen speaker gently
filled his ears, very muted.

The windows were framed with rows of frosted light bulbs barely
turned on—must have them on a rheostat, he thought. The floor
was palely and thickly carpeted, and there were a few big pale
pillows set about. From the ceiling hung four velvet-covered ropes
thinner than those in the lobby. Each ended in a padded leather
cuff. He also noted uneasily two velvet-covered paddles, no larger
than Ping-Pong ones, lying on one of the big pillows. The dimness
made everything seem grimy, as though fine soot were falling
continuously from the ceiling like snow.

He sensed a stirring in the other booths, and he saw that a girl
had entered the room of mirrors while he'd been intent on the
paddles. At first he couldn't tell whether she was naked or not,
but then as she slowly walked out, hardly glancing at the mirrors,
face straight ahead like a sleepwalker's, the music began to come
up and the lights too, brighter and brighter. He saw she was a
blonde, age anywhere from nineteen to twenty-nine—how could
you know for sure? He hoped nineteen. And she was wearing a
net brassiere bordered by what looked like strips of white rabbit's
fur. A tiny apron of the same kind of fur hung down over her
crotch, attached to some sort of G-string, and she wore short white
rabbit's fur boots.

She yawned and stretched, looked around, and then swiftly
removed these items of apparel, but instead of letting them fall
or laying them down on one of the pillows, she carried them over
to the curtained doorway which interrupted the wall of mirrors
and handed them through to someone. They were taking no
chances on the fur getting dirty—how many performances a day
was it the girls gave? He also realized that the right- and left-hand
passages to the booths didn't join behind, as he'd imagined at
first—there had to be an entry passage for the performer. Good
thing he hadn't tried to go all the way around and check on all
the booths before picking one—and maybe lost his.

The vertical slit in the curtain widened, and the now naked
blonde was joined by a naked brunette of the same undetermined

youth. They embraced tenderly yet perfunctorily, as if in a dream, swaying with the music's wails, then leaned apart, brushing each other's small breasts, fingers lingering at the erecting nipples, then trailing down to touch each other's clefts. They separated then and began to work their way around the booths, facing each mirror in turn, swaying and writhing, bumping and grinding, arching back, bellying toward. The brunette was across from him, the blonde off to his left and coming closer. His mouth was dry, his breaths came faster. He was getting a hard-on, he told himself, or about to. He was jealous about the time the blonde spent at each other window and yet somehow dreaded her coming.

And then she was writhing in front of him, poker-faced, looking down toward him. Could she see him? Of course not!—he could see the windows across from him, and they just reflected his blank window. But suppose she bent down and pressed her face and flattening nose-tip against the glass, cupping her hands to either side to shut out light? Involuntarily he flinched backward, caught himself and almost as swiftly stretched his face forward to admire her breasts as she preened, trailing her fingers across them. Yes, yes, he thought desperately, dutifully, they were small, firm, not at all pendulous, big nippled with large aureoles, splendid, yes splendid, yes splendid. . . .

And then he was forcing his gaze to follow her hands down her slender waist past her belly button and pale pubic hair and stretch open the lips of her cleft.

It was all so very confusing, those flaps and those ribbons of membrane, of glistening pinkish-red membrane. Really, a man's genitals were much neater, more like a good and clear diagram, a much more sensible layout. And when you were young you were always in too much of a hurry to study the female ones, too damn excited, keyed up, overwhelmed by the importance of keeping a hard-on. That, and the stubborn old feeling that you mustn't look, that was against the rules, this was dirty. With his wife he'd always done it in the dark, or almost. And now when you were old and your eyesight wasn't so good anymore. . . . One slender finger moved out from the bent stretching ones to point up, then down, to indicate clitoris and cunt. Whyn't she point out her urethra too? It was somewhere there, in between. The clitoris was hard to make out in the midst of all that red squirming. . . .

And then without warning she had spun around, bent over,

and was looking at him from between her spread legs, and her
hand came back around her side to jab a finger twice at the
shadowed sallow pucker of her anus, as if she were saying, "And
here's my asshole, see? My God, how long does it take you dumb
bastards to get things straight?"

Really, it was more like an anatomy lesson taught by a bored,
clown-white cadaver than any sort of spicy erotic cocktail. Where
was the faintest hint of the flirtatious teasing that in old times,
Ryker recalled, gave such performances a point? Why, this girl
had come in almost naked and divested herself of the scant
remainder with all the romance of someone taking out dental
plates before retiring. My God, was that how they got ready for
the full act in private? Where was the slow unbuttoning, the
sudden change of mind and buttoning up again? Where was the
enthusiastic self-peek down her pulled-forward bodice followed by
the smile and knowing wink that said, "Oh, boy, what I got down
there! Don't you wish . . . ?" Where was the teasing that over-
reached itself, the accidental exposure of a goody, pretended embarrassment, and the overhasty hiding of it, leading to further
revelations, as one who covering her knees bares her rear end?
Where the feigned innocence, prudish or naive? the sense of wicked
play, precocious evil? Above all, where was the illusion that her
body's treasures were just that? her choicest possessions and her
chiefest pride, secret 'tween her and you, hoarded like miser's
gold, though shared out joyously and generously at the end?

The girl, instead of graciously overhearing his racing thoughts
(they must be audible!) and at least attempting to make some
corrections for them in her behavior, last of all seized handholds
at the corners of the window and set the soles of her feet against
the sides and dangled there spread open and bent for a short
while, rocking back and forth, like a poker-faced slender ape, so
he could see it all at once after a fashion: asshole, cunt, and
clitoris—and urethra—wherever that was.

That was the show's highpoint of excitement, or shock at any
rate, for Ryker. Although a third girl appeared and the other two
got her undressed and strung up by the padded straps on the
velvet ropes, and did some things to her with their lips and tongues
and the lightly brushing velvet paddles, that was the high point—
or whatever.

Afterward he slipped out into the street feeling very conspicuous,
but even more relieved. He swore he'd never visit the ignorant

place again. But that night he had awakened ejaculating in a wet dream. Afterward he couldn't be quite sure whether his hand mightn't have helped and what sort of dream it had been otherwise, if any—certainly not one of his troll-haunted, buried-alive nightmares.

No, they were gone forever, or at any rate for the next five months.

And then when they did come back, against all his hopes, and when they continued on, and when he found himself balanced between the nightmares and Ultrabooth, and the days seemed dry as dust, there had come the welcome interruption of the Vanishing Lady.

The first time Ryker had seen her, so far as he could recall, they'd been at opposite ends of the long, low entry hall, a good forty feet apart. He had been fumbling for his key outside the street door, which was thick oak framing a large glass panel backed by metal tracery. She'd been standing in profile before the gray elevator door, the small window of which was lit, indicating the cage was at this floor. His gaze approved her instantly (for some men life is an unceasing beauty contest); he liked the way her dark knee-length coat was belted in trimly and the neat look of her head, either dark hair drawn in rather closely or a cloche hat. Automatically he wondered whether she was young and slender or old and skinny.

And then as he continued to look at her, key poised before the lock, she turned her head in his direction and his heart did a little fillip and shiver. *She looked at me,* was what he felt, although the corridor was dimly lit and from this far away a face was little more than a pale oval with eye-smudges—and now her hair or hat made it a shadowed oval. It told you no more about her age than her profile had. Just the same, it was now turned toward him.

All this happened quite swiftly.

But then he had to look down at the lock in order to fit his key into it (a fussy business that seemed to take longer with each passing year) and turn it (he sometimes forgot which way) and shove the door open with his other hand, and by that time she'd moved out of sight.

She couldn't have taken the elevator up or down, he told himself as he strode the corridor a little more briskly than was his wont, for the small glass window in its door still shone brightly. She must have just drifted out of sight to the right, where the stairs were and the brass-fronted mailboxes and the window and door to the manager's office and, past those, the long and short back corridors of the ground floor.

But when he reached that foyer, it was empty and the manager's window unoccupied, though not yet dark and shuttered for the night. She must have gone up the stairs or to a back apartment on this floor, though he'd heard no receding footsteps or shutting door confirm that theory.

Just as he opened the elevator door he got the funniest hunch that he'd find her waiting for him there—that she'd entered the cage while he'd been unlocking the front door, but then not pushed a button for a floor. But the cage was as empty as the foyer. So much for hunches! He pushed the 14 button at the top of the narrow brass panel, and by the time he got there, he'd put the incident out of his mind, though a certain wistfulness clung to his general mood.

And he probably would have forgotten it altogether except that late the next afternoon, when he was returning from a rather long walk, the same thing happened to him all over again, the whole incident repeating itself with only rather minor variations. For instance, this time her eyes seemed barely to stray in his direction; there wasn't the same sense of a full look. And something flashed faintly at her chest level, as if she were wearing jewelry of some sort, a gemmed pendant—or brooch more likely, since her coat was tightly shut. He was sure it was the same person, and there was the same sense of instant approval or attraction on his part, only stronger this time (which was natural enough, he told himself later). And he went down the hall faster this time and hurried on without pausing to check the stairs and the back corridor, though his chance of hearing footsteps or a closing door was spoiled by the siren of an ambulance rushing by outside. Returning thoughtfully to the foyer, he found the cage gone, but it came down almost immediately, debarking a tenant he recognized—third or fourth floor, he thought—who said rather puzzledly in answer to a question by Ryker that he thought he'd summoned the elevator directly from One and it had been empty when it had reached his floor.

Ryker thanked him and boarded the elevator.

The cage's silvered gray paper and polished fittings made it seem quite modern. Another nice touch was the little window in its door, which matched those in the floor doors when both were shut, so that you got a slow winking glimpse of each floor as you rose past—as Ryker now glimpsed the second floor go down. But actually it was an ancient vehicle smartened up, and so was the system that ran it. You had to hold down a button for an appreciable time to make the cage respond, because it worked by mechanical relays in the elevator room on the roof, not by the instant response to a touch of electronic modern systems. Also, it couldn't remember several instructions and obey them in order as the modern ones could; it obeyed one order only and then waited to be given the next one manually.

Ryker was very conscious of that difference between automatic and manual. For the past five years he had been shifting his own bodily activities from automatic to manual: running (hell, trotting was the most you could call it!—a clumping trot), going down stairs, climbing them, walking outside, even getting dressed and—almost—writing. Used to be he could switch on automatic for those and think about something else. But now he had to do more and more things a step at a time, and watching and thinking about each step too, like a baby learning (only you never did learn; it never got automatic again). And it took a lot more time, everything did. Sometimes you had to stand very still even to think.

Another floor slowly winked by. Ryker caught the number painted on the shaft side of its elevator door just below that door's little window—5. What a slow trip it was!

Ryker did a lot of his real thinking in this elevator part of the apartment tree. It wasn't full of loneliness and ambushing memories the way his apartment was, or crawling with the small dangers and hostilities that occupied most of his mind when he was in the street world outside. It was a world between those, a restful pause between two kinds of oppression, inhabited only by the mostly anonymous people with whom he shared his present half-life, his epilogue life, and quite unlike the realer folk from whom he had been rather purposefully disengaging himself ever since his wife's and his job's deaths.

They were an odd lot, truly, his present fellow-inhabitants of the apartment tree. At least half of them were as old as he, and many of them engaged in the same epilogue living as he was, so far as he could judge. Perhaps a quarter were middle-aged; Ryker liked them least of all—they carried tension with them, things he was trying to forget. While rather fewer than a quarter were young. These always hurried through the apartment tree on full automatic, as if it were a place of no interest whatever, a complete waste of time.

He himself did not find it so, but rather the only place where he could think and observe closely at the same time, a quiet realm of pause. He saw nothing strange in the notion of ghosts (if he'd believed in such) haunting the neighborhood where they'd died—most of them had spent their last few years studying that area in greatest detail, impressing their spirits into its very atoms, while that area steadily grew smaller, as if they were beetles circling a nail to which they were tethered by a thread that slowly wound up, growing shorter and shorter with every circumambulation they made.

Another floor numeral with its little window slid into and out of view—8 only. God, what snaillike, well-frog pace!

The only denizen of the apartment tree with whom Ryker had more than a recognition acquaintance (you could hardly call the one he had with the others nodding, let alone speaking) was Clancy, rough-cut manager-janitor of the building, guardian of the gates of the apartment tree and its historian, a retired fireman who managed to make himself available and helpful without becoming oppressive or officious. Mrs. Clancy was an altogether more respectable and concierge-like character who made Ryker feel uncomfortable. He preferred always to deal with her husband, and over the years a genuine though strictly limited friendship (it never got beyond "Clancy" and "Mr. Ryker") had sprung up between them.

The figure 12 appeared and disappeared in the window. He kept his eyes on the empty rectangle and gave an accustomed chuckle when the next figure was 14, with none intervening. Superstition, how mighty, how undying! (Though somehow the travel between the last two floors, Twelve and Fourteen, always seemed to take longest, by a fraction. There was food for thought there. Did elevators get tired?—perhaps because the air grew more rarified with increased altitude?)

The window above the 14 steadied. There was a clicking; the gray door slid open sideways, he pushed through the outer door, and as he did so, he uttered another chuckle that was both cheerful and sardonic. He'd just realized that after all his journeying in the apartment tree, he'd at last become interested in one of his nameless traveling companions. The elevator-tree world also held the Vanishing Lady.

It was surprising how lighthearted he felt.

As if in rebuke for this and for his springing hopes not clearly defined, he didn't see the Vanishing Lady for the next three days, although he devised one or two errands for himself that would bring him back to the apartment tree at dusk, and when he did spot her again on the fourth day, the circumstances were altered from those of their first two encounters.

Returning from another of his little twilight outings and unlocking the heavy street door, he noted that the hall and distant foyer were a little bit dimmer than usual, as if some small, normal light source were gone, with the effect of a black hole appearing suddenly in the fabric of reality.

As he started forward warily, he discerned the explanation. The doors to the elevator were wide open, but the ceiling light in the cage had been switched (or gone) off, so that where a gray door gleaming by reflection should have been, there was an ominous dark upright rectangle.

And then, as he continued to advance, he saw that the cage wasn't empty. Light angling down into it from the foyer's ceiling fixture revealed the slender figure of the Vanishing Lady leaning with her back against the cage's wall just behind the column of buttons. The light missed her head, but showed the rest of her figure well enough, her dejected posture, her motionless passivity.

As he imperceptibly quickened his stride straight toward her, the slanting light went on, picking up bits of detail here and there in the gloom, almost as if summoning them: the glossy gleam of black oxfords, the muted one of black stockings, and the in-between sheen of her sleek coat. The nearest black-gloved hand appeared to be clutching that together snugly, and from the closure there seemed to come faint diamond glimmers like the faintest ghost of a sparkler shower, so faint he couldn't be sure whether it was really there, or just his own eyes making the churning points of light there are in darkness. The farthest jetty hand held forward a small brass object which he first took for an apartment door key got out well in advance (as some nervous people will) but then saw to be a little too narrow and too long for that.

He was aware of a mounting tension and breathlessness—and sense of strangeness too. And then without warning, just as he was about to enter the cage and simultaneously switch its light on, he heard himself mutter apologetically, "Sorry, I've got to check my mailbox first," and his footsteps veered sharply but smoothly to the right with never a hesitation.

For the next few seconds his mind was so occupied with shock at this sudden rush of timidity, this flinching away from what he'd thought he wanted to do, that he actually had his keys out, was advancing the tiny flat one toward the brass-fronted narrow box he'd checked this noon as always, before he reversed his steps with a small growl of impatience and self-rebuke and hurried back past the manager's shuttered window and around the stairs.

The elevator doors were closed and the small window glowed bright. But just as he snatched at the door to open it, the bright rectangle narrowed from the bottom and winked out, the elevator growled softly as the cage ascended, and the door resisted his yank. Damn! He pressed his hand against it, listening intently. Soon—after no more than five or six seconds, he thought—he heard the cage stop and its door *clump* open. Instantly he was thumbing the button. After a bit he heard the door *clump* shut and the growling recommence. Was it growing louder or softer— coming down or going away? Louder! Soon it had arrived, and he was opening the door—rather to the surprise of its emerging occupant, a plump lady in a green coat.

Her eyebrows rose at his questions, rather as had happened on the previous such occasion. She'd been on Three when she'd buzzed for the elevator, she said. No, there'd been no one in it when it arrived, no one had got off, it had been empty. Yes, the light *had* been off in the elevator when it had come up, but she hadn't missed anyone on account of that—and she'd turned it on again. And then she'd just gotten in and come down. Had he been buzzing for it? Well, she'd been pushing the button for One, too. What did it matter?

She made for the street door, glancing back at Ryker dubiously, as if she were thinking that, whatever he was up to, she didn't ever want that excited old man tracking *her* down.

Then for a while Ryker was so busy trying to explain that to himself (Had there been time for her to emerge and shut the doors silently and hurry down the long hall or tiptoe up the stairs before the cage went up to Three? Well, just possibly, but it would have had to be done with almost incredible rapidity. Could he have *imagined* her—projected her onto the gloom inside the cage, so to speak? Or had the lady in green been lying? Were she and the Vanishing Lady confederates? And so on . . .) that it was some time before he began to try to analyze the reasons for his self-betrayal.

Well, for one thing, he told himself, he'd been so gripped by his desire to see her close up that he'd neglected to ask himself what he'd do once he'd achieved that, how he'd make conversation if they were alone together in the cage—and that these questions popping up in his mind all at once had made him falter. And then there was his lifelong habit, he had to admit, of automatically shrinking from all close contact with women save his mother and wife, especially if the occasion for it came upon him suddenly. Or had he without knowing it become just a little frightened of this mysterious person who had stirred him erotically—the apartment tree was always dimly lit, there'd never been anyone else around when she'd appeared, there'd been something so woeful-melancholy about her attitude (though that was probably part of her attraction), and finally she *had* vanished three times unaccountably—so that it was no wonder he had veered aside from entering the elevator, its very lightlessness suggesting a trap. (And that made him recall another odd point. Not only had the light inside the elevator been switched off but the door, which always automatically swung shut unless someone held it open or set a fairly heavy object, such as a packed suitcase or a laden-large shopping bag, against it, had been standing open. And he couldn't recall having seen any such object or other evidence of propping or wedging. Mysterious. In fact, as mysterious as his suffocation dreams, which at least had lessened in number and intensity since the Vanishing Lady had turned up.)

Well, he told himself with another effort at being philosophical, now that he'd thought all these things through, at least he'd behave more courageously if a similar situation arose another time.

But when the Vanishing Lady next appeared to Ramsey, it was under conditions that did not call for that sort of courage. There were others present.

He'd come in from outside and found the empty cage ready and waiting, but he could hear another party just close enough behind him that he didn't feel justified in taking off without them—though there'd been enough times, God knows, when he'd been left behind under the same circumstances. He dutifully waited, holding the door open. There had been times, too, when this politeness of his had been unavailing—when the people had been

bound for a ground-floor apartment, or when it had been a lone
woman and she'd found an excuse for not making her journey
alone with him.

The party finally came into view—two middle-aged women and
a man—and the latter insisted on holding the door himself. Ryker
relinquished it without argument and went to the back of the
cage, the two women following. But the man didn't come inside;
he held the door for yet a third party he'd evidently heard coming
behind *them.*

The third party arrived, an elderly couple, but that man insisted
on holding the door in his turn for the second man and his own
ancient lady. They were six, a full load, Ryker counted. But then,
just as the floor door was swinging shut, someone caught it from
the outside, and the one who skipped in last was the Vanishing
Lady.

Ramsey mightn't have seen her if he hadn't been tall, for the
cage was now almost uncomfortably crowded, although none of
them were conspicuous heavyweights. He glimpsed a triangle of
pale face under dark gleaming eyes, which fixed for an instant on
his, and he felt a jolt of excitement, or something. Then she had
whipped around and was facing front, like the rest. His heart was
thudding and his throat was choked up. He knew the sheen of
her black hair and coat, the dull felt of her close-fitting hat, and
watched them raptly. He decided from the flash of face that she
was young or very smoothly powdered.

The cage stopped at the seventh floor. She darted out without
a backward glance and the elderly couple followed her. He wanted
to do something but he couldn't think what, and someone pressed
another button.

As soon as the cage had resumed its ascent, he realized that he
too could have gotten out on Seven and at least seen where she
went in, discovered her apartment number. But he hadn't acted
quickly enough and some of these people probably knew he lived
on Fourteen and would have wondered.

The rest got out on Twelve and so he did the last floor alone—
the floor that numerically was two floors, actually only one, yet
always seemed to take a bit too long, the elevator growing tired,
ha-ha-ha.

Next day he examined the names on the seventh-floor mailboxes,
but that wasn't much help. Last names only, with at most an
initial or two, was the rule. No indication of sex or marital status.

And, as always, fully a third were marked only as OCCUPIED. It was safer that way, he remembered being told (something about anonymous phone calls or confidence games), even if it somehow always looked suspicious, vaguely criminal.

Late the next afternoon, when he was coming in from the street, he saw a man holding the elevator door open for two elderly women to enter. He hurried his stride, but the man didn't look his way before following them.

But just at that moment, the Vanishing Lady darted into view from the foyer, deftly caught the closing door, and with one pale glance over her shoulder at Ryker, let herself in on the heels of the man. Although he was too far away to see her eyes as more than twin gleams, he felt the same transfixing jolt as he had the previous day. His heart beat faster too.

And then as he hurried on, the light in the little window in the gray door winked out as the elevator rose up and away from him. A few seconds later he was standing in front of the electrically locked door with its dark little window and staring ruefully at the button and the tiny circular telltale just above it, which now glowed angry red to indicate the elevator was in use and unresponsive to any summons.

He reproached himself for not having thought to call out, "Please wait for me," but there'd hardly been time to think, and besides it would have been such a departure from his normal, habitually silent behavior. Still, another self-defeat, another self-frustration, in his pursuit of the Vanishing Lady! He wished this elevator had, like those in office buildings or hotels, a more extensive telltale beside or over its door that told which floor it was on or passing, so you could trace its course. It would be helpful to know whether it stopped at Seven again this time—it was hard to hear it stop when it got that far away. Of course you could run up the stairs, racing it, if you were young enough and in shape. He'd once observed two young men who were sixth-floor residents do just that, pitting the one's strong legs and two-or-three-steps-at-a-time against the other's slow elevator—and never learned who won. For that matter, the young tenants, who were mostly residents of the lower floors, where the turnover of apartments was brisker, quite often went charging blithely up the stairs even when the elevator was waiting and ready, as if to advertise (along with their youth) their contempt for its tedious *elderly* pace. If *he* were young again now, he asked himself, would he have raced up after a vanished girl?

The telltale went black. He jabbed the button, saw it turn red again as the cage obediently obeyed his summons.

Next afternoon found him staring rather impatiently at the red telltale on the fourteenth floor, this time while waiting to travel to the ground floor and so out. And this time it had been red for quite some while, something that happened not infrequently, since the cage's slow speed and low capacity made it barely adequate to service a building of this size. And while it stayed red it was hard to tell how many trips it was making and how long people were holding the door at one floor. He'd listened to numerous speculative conversations about "what the elevator was doing," as if it had a mind and volition of its own, which one humorist had indeed suggested. And there were supposed to be certain people (sometimes named and sometimes not) who did outrageous and forbidden things, such as jamming the floor door open while they went back to get things they'd forgotten, or picked up friends on other floors as they went down (or up), organizing an outing or party or having secret discussions and arguments before reaching the less private street. There were even said to be cases of people "pulling the elevator away" from other people who were their enemies, just to spite them.

The most colorful theory, perhaps, was that held by two elderly ladies, both old buffs of elevator travel, whom Ramsey had happened to overhear on two occasions. The cornerstone of their theory was that all the building's troubles were caused by its younger tenants and the teenage sons and daughters of tenants. "Mrs. Clancy told me," one of them had whispered loudly once, "that they know a way of stopping the thing between floors so they can smooch together and shoot dope and do all sorts of other nasty things—even, if you can believe, go the whole way with each other." Ryker had been amused; it gave the cage a certain erotic aura.

And every once in a while the elevator did get stuck between floors, sometimes with people in it and sometimes not, especially between the twelfth and fourteenth floors, Clancy had once told him, "like it was trying to stop at the thirteenth!"

But now the elevator's vagaries weren't all that amusing to Ramsey standing alone on the top floor, so after one more session of pettish button-pushing—the telltale had gone briefly black, but evidently someone else had beat him to the punch—he decided to "walk down for exercise," something he'd actually done intentionally upon occasion.

As he descended the apartment tree (he thought of himself as an old squirrel sedately scampering zigzag down the barky outside of the trunk the elevator shaft made), he found himself wondering how the elevator could be so busy when all the corridors were so silent and empty. (But maybe things were happening just before his footstep-heralded arrivals and after his departures—they heard him coming and hid themselves until he was by. Or maybe there was some sort of basement crisis.) The floors were all the same, or almost so: the two long corridors ending in doors of wire-reinforced glass which led to the front and alley fire escapes; these were also lit midway by frosted glass spheres like full moons hanging in space; in either wall beside these handsome globes were set two narrow full-length mirrors in which you could see yourself paced along by two companions.

The apartment tree boasted many mirrors, a luxury note like its silver-arabesqued gray wallpaper. There was a large one opposite each elevator door and there were three in the lobby.

As he ended each flight, Ramsey would look down the long alley corridor, make a U-turn, and walk back to the landing (glancing into the short corridor and the elevator landing, which were lit by a central third moon and one large window), all this while facing the long front corridor, then make another U-turn and start down the next flight.

(He did discover one difference between the floors. He counted steps going down, and while there were nineteen between the fourteenth and the twelfth floors, there were only seventeen between all the other pairs. So the cage had to travel a foot and a bit farther to make that Fourteen-Twelve journey; it didn't just *seem* to take longer, it *did*. So much for tired elevators!)

So it went for nine floors.

But when he made his U-turn onto the third floor he saw that the front corridor's full moon had been extinguished, throwing a gloom on the whole passageway, while silhouetted against the wired glass at the far end was a swayed, slender figure looking very much like that of the Vanishing Lady. He couldn't make out her pale triangle of face or gleaming eyes because there was no front light on her; she was only shaped darkness, yet he was sure it was she.

In walking the length of the landing, however, there was time
to think that if he continued on beyond the stairs, it would be
an undeniable declaration of his intention to meet her, he'd have
to keep going, he had no other excuse; also, there'd be the
unpleasant impression of him closing in ominously, relentlessly,
on a lone trapped female.

As he advanced she waited at the tunnel's end, silent and
unmoving, a shaped darkness.

He made his customary turn, keeping on down the stairs. He
felt so wrenched by what was happening that he hardly knew
what he was thinking or even feeling, except his heart was thudding
and his lungs were gasping as if he'd just walked ten stories upstairs
instead of down.

It wasn't until he had turned into the second floor and seen
through the stairwell, cut off by ceiling, the workshoes and twill
pants of Clancy, the manager, faced away from him in the lobby,
that he got himself in hand. He instantly turned and retraced his
steps with frantic haste. He'd flinched away again, just when he'd
sworn he wouldn't! Why, there were a dozen questions he could
politely ask her to justify his close approach. Could he be of
assistance? Was she looking for one of the tenants? some apartment
number? Etcetera.

But even as he rehearsed these phrases, he had a sinking feeling
of what he was going to find on Three.

He was right. There was no longer a figure among the shadows
filling the dark front corridor.

And then, even as he was straining his eyes to make sure, with
a flicker and a flash the full moon came on again and shone
steadily.

Showing no one at all.

Ramsey didn't look any further but hurried back down the
stairs. He wanted to be with people, anyone, just people in the
street.

But Mr. Clancy was still in the lobby, communing with himself.
Ramsey suddenly felt he simply had to share at least part of the
story of the Vanishing Lady with someone.

So he told Clancy about the defective light bulb inside the front
globe on Three, how it had started to act like a globe that's near
the end of its lifetime, arcing and going off and on by itself,
unreliable. Only then did he, as if idly, an afterthought, mention
the woman he'd seen and then got to wondering about and gone

back and not seen, adding that he thought he'd also seen her in the lobby once or twice before.

He hadn't anticipated the swift seriousness of the manager's reaction. Ramsey'd hardly more than mentioned the woman when the ex-fireman asked sharply, "Did she look like a bum? I mean, for a woman—"

Ramsey told him that no, she didn't, but he hadn't more than sketched his story when the other said, "Look, Mr. Ryker, I'd like to go up and check this out right away. You said she was all in black, didn't you? Yeah. Well, look, you stay here, would you do that? And just take notice if anybody comes down. I won't be long."

And he got in the elevator, which had been waiting there, and went up. To Four or Five, or maybe Six, Ramsey judged from the cage's noises and the medium-short time the telltale flared before winking out. He imagined that Clancy would leave it there and then hunt down the floors one by one, using the stairs.

Pretty soon Clancy did reappear by way of the stairs, looking thoughtful. "No," he said, "she's not there anymore, at least not in the bottom half of the building—and I don't see her doing a lot of climbing. Maybe she got somebody to take her in, or maybe it *was* just one of the tenants. Or . . . ?" He looked a question at Ramsey, who shook his head and said, "No, nobody came down the stairs or elevator."

The manager nodded and then shook his own head slowly. "I don't know, maybe I'm getting too suspicious," he said. "I don't know how much you've noticed, Mr. Ryker, living way on top, but from time to time this building is troubled by bums—winos and street people from south of here—trying to get inside and shelter here, especially in winter, maybe go to sleep in a corner. Most of them are men, of course, but there's an occasional woman bum." He paused and chuckled reflectively. "Once we had an invasion of women bums, though they weren't that exactly."

Ramsey looked at him expectantly.

Clancy hesitated, glanced at Ramsey, and after another pause said, "That's why we turn the buzzer system off at eleven at night and keep it off until eight in the morning. If we left it on, why, any time in the night a drunken wino would start buzzing apartments until he got one who'd buzz the door open (or he might push a dozen at once, so somebody'd be sure to buzz the door), and once he was inside, he'd hunt himself up an out-of-the-way spot where he could sleep it off and be warm. And if he had cigarettes, he'd start smoking them to put him to sleep, dropping the matches anywhere, but mostly under things. There's where your biggest danger is—fire. Or he'd get an idea and start bothering tenants, ringing their bells and knocking on their doors, and then anything could happen. Even with the buzzer system off, some of them get in. They'll stand beside the street door and then follow a couple that's late getting home, or the same with the newsboy delivering the morning paper before it's light. Not following them directly, you see, but using a foot (sometimes a cane or crutch) to block the door just before it locks itself, and then coming in soon as the coast's clear."

Ramsey nodded several times appreciatively, but then pressed the other with "But you were going to tell me something about an invasion of female bums?"

"Oh, that," Clancy said doubtfully. A look at Ramsey seemed to reassure him. "That was before your time—you came here about five years ago, didn't you? Yeah. Well, this happened . . . let's see . . . about two years before that. The Mrs. and I generally don't talk about it much to tenants, because it gives . . . gave the building a bad name. Not really any more now, though. Seven years and all's forgotten, eh?"

He broke off to greet respectfully a couple who passed by on their way upstairs. He turned back to Ramsey. "Well, anyway," he continued more comfortably, "at this time I'm talking about, the Mrs. and I had been here ourselves only a year. Just about long enough to learn the ropes, at least some of them.

"Now there's one thing about a building like this I got to explain," he interjected. "You never, or almost never, get any disappearances—you know, tenants sneaking their things out when they're behind on the rent, or just walking out one day, leaving their things, and never coming back (maybe getting mugged to death, who knows?)—like happens all the time in those fleabag hotels and rooming houses south of us. Why, half of *their* renters are on dope or heavy medication to begin with, and come from prisons or from mental hospitals. Here you get a steadier sort of tenant, or at least the Mrs. and I try to make it be like that.

"Well, back then, just about the steadiest tenant we had, though not the oldest by any means, was a tall, thin, very handsome and distinguished-looking youngish chap, name of Arthur J. Stensor, third floor front. Very polite and soft-spoken, never raised his voice. Dark complected, but with blonde hair which he wore in a natural—not so common then; once I heard him referred to by another tenant as 'that frizzy bleached Negro,' and I thought they were being disrespectful. A sharp dresser but never flashy—he had class. He always wore a hat. Rent paid the first of the month in cash with never a miss. Rent for the garage space too—he kept a black Lincoln Continental in the basement that was always polished like glass; never used the front door much but went and came in that car. And his apartment was furnished to match: oil paintings in gold frames, silver statues, hi-fi, *big*-screen TV and the stuff to record programs and films off it when that *cost,* all sorts of fancy clocks and vases, silks and velvets, more stuff like that than you'd ever believe.

"And when there was people with him, which wasn't too often, they were as classy as he and his car and his apartment, especially the women—high society and always young. I remember once being in the third-floor hall one night when one of those stunners swept by me and he let her in, and thinking, 'Well, if that filly was a call girl, she sure came from the best stable in town.' Only I remember thinking at the same time that *I* was being disrespectful, because A. J. Stensor was just a little too respectable for even the classiest call girl. Which was a big joke on me considering what happened next."

"Which was?" Ramsey prompted, after they'd waited for a couple more tenants to go by.

"Well, at first I didn't connect it at all with Stensor," Clancy responded, "though it's true I hadn't happened to see him for the last five or six days, which was sort of unusual, though not all that much so. Well, what happened was this invasion—no, goddammit! this *epidemic*—of good-looking hookers, mostly tall and skinny, or at least skinny, through the lower halls and lobby of this building. Some of them were dressed too respectable for hookers, but most of them wore the street uniform of the day— which was high heels, skintight blue jeans, long lace blouses worn outside the pants, and lots of bangles—and when you saw them talking together palsy-walsy, the respectable-looking and the not, you knew they all had to be."

"How did it first come to you?" Ramsey asked. "Tenants complain?"

"A couple," Clancy admitted. "Those old biddies who'll report a young and good-looking woman on the principle that if she's

young and good-looking she can't be up to any good purpose.
But the really funny thing was that most of the reports of them
came in just by way of gossip—either to me direct, or by way of
the Mrs., which is how it usually works—like it was something
strange and remarkable—which it was, all right! Questions too,
such as what the hell they were all up to, which was a good one
to ask, by the way. You see, they weren't any of them *doing*
anything to complain of. It was broad day and they certainly
weren't trying to pick anyone up, they weren't plying their trade
at all, you might say, they weren't even smiling at anybody,
especially men. No, they were just walking up and down and
talking together, looking critical and angry more than anything,
and very serious—like they'd picked our apartment building for
a hookers' convention, complete with debates, some sort of feminist
or union thing, except they hadn't bothered to inform the man-
agement. Oh, when I'd cough and ask a couple of them what
they were doing, they'd throw me some excuse without looking
at me—that they had a lunch date with a lady here but she didn't
seem to be in and they couldn't wait, or that they were shopping
for apartments but these weren't suitable—and at the same time
they'd start walking toward the street door, or toward the stairs
if they were on the third or second floor, still gabbing together
in private voices about whatever it was they were debating, and
then they'd sweep out, still not noticing me even if I held the
door for them.

"And, then, you know, in twenty minutes they'd be back inside!
or at least I'd spot one of them that was. Some of them *must*
have had front door keys, I remember thinking—and as it turned
out later, some of them did."

By this time Mr. Clancy had warmed to his story and was giving
out little chuckles with every other sentence, and he almost forgot
to lower his voice next time a tenant passed.

"There was one man they took notice of. I forgot about that.
It could have given me a clue to what was happening, but I didn't
get it. We had a tenant then on one of the top floors who was
tall and slim and rather good-looking—young-looking too, although he wasn't—and always wore a hat. Well, I was in the
lobby and four or five of the hookers had just come in the front
door, debating of course, when this guy stepped out of the elevator
and they all spotted him and made a rush for him. But when
they got about a dozen feet away from him and he took off his

hat—maybe to be polite, he looked a little scared, I don't know what he thought—showing his wavy black hair which he kept dyed, the hookers all lost interest in him—as if he'd looked like someone they knew, but closer up turned out not to be (which *was* the case, though I still didn't catch on then)—and they swept past him and on up the stairs as if that was where they'd been rushing in the first place.

"I tell you, that was some weird day. Hookers dressed all ways—classy-respectable, the tight-jeans and lacy-blouse uniform, mini-skirts, one in what looked like a kid's sailor suit cut for a woman, a sad one all in black looking like something special for funerals . . . you know, maybe to give first aid to a newly bereaved husband or something." He gave Ryker a quick look, continuing, "And although almost all of them were skinny, I recall there was a fat one wearing a mumu and swinging gracefully like a belly dancer.

"The Mrs. was after me to call the police, but our owner sort of discourages that, and I couldn't get him on the phone.

"In the evening the hookers tapered off and I dropped into bed, all worn out from the action, the wife still after me to call the police, but I just conked out cold, and so the only one to see the last of the business was the newsboy when he came to deliver at four-thirty about. Later on he dropped back to see me, couldn't wait to tell me about it.

"Well, he was coming up to the building, it seems, pushing his shopping cart of morning papers, when he sees this crowd of good-looking women (he wasn't wise to the hookers' convention the day before) around the doorway, most of them young and all of them carrying expensive-looking objects—paintings, vases, silver statues of naked girls, copper kitchenware, gold clocks, that sort of stuff—like they were helping a wealthy friend move. Only there is a jam-up, two or three of them are trying to maneuver an oversize dolly through the door, and on that dolly is the biggest television set the kid ever saw and also the biggest record player.

"A woman at the curb outside, who seems a leader, sort of very cool, is calling directions to them how to move it, and close beside her is another woman, like her assistant or gopher maybe. The leader's calling out directions, like I say, in a hushed voice, and the other women are watching, but they're all very quiet, like you'd expect people to be at that hour of the morning, sober people at any rate, not wanting to wake the neighbors.

"Well, the kid's looking all around, every which way, trying to take in everything—there was a lot of interesting stuff to see, I gather, and more inside—when the gopher lady comes over and hunkers down beside him—he was a runt, that newsboy was, and ugly too—and wants to buy a morning paper. He hauls it out for her and she gives him a five-dollar bill and tells him to keep the change. He's sort of embarrassed by that and drops his eyes, but she tells him not to mind, he's a handsome boy and a good hard-working one, she wished she had one like him, and he deserves everything he gets, and she puts an arm around him and draws him close and all of a sudden his downcast eyes are looking inside her blouse front and he's getting the most amazing anatomy lesson you could imagine.

"He has some idea that they're getting the dolly clear by now and that the other women are moving, but she's going on whispering in his ear, her breath's like steam, what a good boy he is and how grateful his parents must be, and *his* only worry, she'll hug him so tight he won't be able to look down her blouse.

"After a bit she ends his anatomy lesson with a kiss that almost smothers him and then stands up. The women are all gone and the dolly's vanishing around the next corner. Before she hurries after it, she says, 'So long, kid. You got your bonus. Now deliver your papers.'

"Which, after he got over his daze, is what he did, he said.

"Well, of course, as soon as he mentioned the big television and player, I flashed on what I'd been missing all yesterday, though it was right in front of my eyes if I'd just looked. Why they'd been swarming on Three, why they rushed the guy from Seven and then lost interest in him when he took off his hat and they saw his hair was black dyed (instead of frizzy blonde), and why the hookers' convention wasn't still going on today. All that loot could have only come from one place—Stensor's. In spite of him being so respectable, he'd been running a string of call girls all the time, so that when he ran out on them owing them all money (I flashed on that at the same time), they'd collected the best way they knew how.

"I ran to his apartment, and you know the door wasn't even locked—one of them must have had a key to it too. Of course the place was stripped and of course no sign of Stensor.

"Then I did call the police of course but not until I'd checked the basement. His black Continental was gone, but there was no way of telling for sure whether he'd taken it or the gals had got that too.

"It surprised me how fast the police came and how many of them there were, but it showed they must have had an eye on him already, which maybe explained why he left so sudden without taking his things. They asked a lot of questions and came back more than once, were in and out for a few days. I got to know one of the detectives, he lived locally, we had a drink together once or twice, and he told me they were really after Stensor for drug dealing, he was handling cocaine back in those days when it was first getting to be the classy thing, they weren't interested in his call girls except as he might have used them as pushers. They never did turn him up though, far as I know, and there wasn't even a line in the papers about the whole business."

"So that was the end of your one-day hooker invasion?" Ryker commented, chuckling rather dutifully.

"Not quite," Clancy said, and hesitated. Then with a "What-difference-can-it-make?" shrug, he went on, "Well, yes, there was a sort of funny follow-up but it didn't amount to much. You see, the story of Stensor and the hookers eventually got around to most of the tenants in the building, as such things will, though some of them got it garbled, as you can imagine happens, that he was a patron and maybe somehow victim of call girls instead of running them. Well, anyhow, after a bit, we (the Mrs. mostly) began to get these tenant reports of a girl—a young woman—seen waiting outside the door to Stensor's apartment, or wandering around in other parts of the building, but mostly waiting at Stensor's door. And this was after there were other tenants in that apartment. A sad-looking girl."

"Like, out of all those hookers," Ryker said, "she was the only one who really loved him and waited for him. A sort of leftover."

"Yeah, or the only one who hadn't got her split of the loot," Clancy said. "Or maybe he owed her more than the others. I never saw her myself, although I went chasing after her a couple of times when tenants reported her. I wouldn't have taken any stock in her except the descriptions did seem to hang together. A college-type girl, they'd say, and mostly wearing black. And sort of sad. I told the detective I knew, but he didn't seem to make anything out of it. They never did pick up any of the women, he said, far as he knew. Well, that's all there is to the follow-up—like I said, nothing much. And after two or three months tenants stopped seeing her."

He broke off, eyeing Ryker just a little doubtfully.

"But it stuck in your mind," that one observed, "for all these years, so that when I told you about seeing a woman in black near the same door, you rushed off to check up on her, just on the chance? Though you'd never seen her yourself, even once?"

Clancy's expression became a shade unhappy. "Well, no," he admitted, glancing up and down the hall, as though hoping someone would come along and save him from answering. "There was a little more than that," he continued uneasily, "though I wouldn't want anyone making too much of it, or telling the Mrs. I told them.

"But then, Mr. Ryker, you're not the one to be gossipping or getting the wind up, are you?" he continued more easily, giving his tenant a hopeful look.

"No, of course I'm not," Ryker responded, a little more casually than he felt. "What was it?"

"Well, about four years ago we had another disappearance here, a single man living alone and getting on in years but still active. He didn't own any of the furniture, his possessions were few, nothing at all fancy like Stensor's, no friends or relations we knew of, and he came to us from a building that knew no more; in fact we didn't realize he was gone until the time for paying the rent came round. And it wasn't until then that I recalled that the last time or two I spoke to him he'd mentioned something about a woman in an upstairs hall, wondering if she'd found the people or the apartment number she seemed to be looking for. Not making a complaint, you see, just mentioning, just idly wondering, so that it wasn't until he disappeared that I thought of connecting it up with Stensor's girl at all."

"He say if she was young?" Ryker asked.

"He wasn't sure. She was wearing a black outside coat and hat or scarf of something that hid her face, and she made a point of not noticing him when he looked at her and thought of asking if she needed help. He did say she was thin, though, I remember."

Ryker nodded.

Clancy continued, "And then a few years ago there was this couple on Nine that had a son living with them, a big fat lug who looked older than he was and was always being complained about whether he did anything or not. One of the old ladies in the apartment next to their bathroom used to kick to us about him running water for baths at two or three in the morning. And he had the nerve to complain to us about *them,* claiming they pulled the elevator away from him when he wanted to get it, or made it go in the opposite direction to what he wanted when he was in it. I laughed in his pimply face at that. Not that those two old biddies wouldn't have done it to him if they'd figured a way and they'd got the chance.

"His mother was a sad soul who used to fuss at him and worry about him a lot. She'd bring her troubles to the Mrs. and talk and talk—but I think really she'd have been relieved to have him off her mind.

"His father was a prize crab, an ex-army officer forever registering complaints—he had a little notebook for them. But half the time he was feuding with me and the Mrs., wouldn't give us the time of day—or of course ask it. I know *he'd* have been happy to see his loud-mouthed dumb son drop out of sight.

"Well, one day the kid comes down to me here with a smart-ass grin and says, 'Mr. Clancy, you're the one who's so great, aren't you, on chasing winos and hookers out of here, not letting them freeload in the halls for a minute? Then how come you let—'

" 'Go on,' I tell him, 'what do you know about hookers?'

"But that doesn't faze him, he just goes on (he was copying his father, I think, actually), 'Then how come you let this skinny little hooker in a black fur coat wander around the halls all the time, trying to pick guys up?'

" 'You're making this up,' I tell him flat, 'or you're imagining things, or else one of our lady tenants is going to be awful sore at you if she ever hears you've been calling her a hooker.'

" 'She's nobody from this building,' the kid insists, 'she's got more class. That fur coat cost money. It's hard to check out her face, though, because she never looks at you straight on and she's got this black hat she hides behind. I figure she's an old bag— maybe thirty, even—and wears the hat so you can't see her wrinkles, but that she's got a young bod, young and wiry. I bet she takes karate lessons so she can bust the balls of any guy that gets out of line, or maybe if he just doesn't satisfy her—'

" 'You're pipe-dreaming, kid,' I tell him.

" 'And you know what?' he goes on. 'I bet you she's got nothing on but black stockings and a garter belt under that black fur coat she keeps wrapped so tight around her, so when she's facing a guy she can give him a quick flash of her bod, to lead him on—'

" 'And you got a dirty mind,' I say. 'You're making this up.'

" 'I am not,' he says. 'She was just now up on Ten before I came down and leering at me sideways, giving me the come on.'

" 'What were you doing up on Ten?' I ask him loud.

" 'I always go up a floor before I buzz the elevator,' he answers me quick, 'so's those old dames won't know it's me and buzz it away from me.'

" 'All right, quiet down, kid,' I tell him. 'I'm going up to Ten right now, to check this out, and you're coming with me.'

"So we go on up to Ten and there's nobody there and right away the kid starts yammering, 'I bet you she picked up a trick in this building and they're behind one of these doors screwing, right now. Old Mr. Lucas—'

"I was really going to give him a piece of my mind then, tell him off, but on the way up I'd been remembering that girl of Stensor's who lingered behind, maybe for a long time, if there was anything to what the other guy told me. And somehow it gave me a sort of funny feeling, so all I said was something like 'Look here, kid, maybe you're making this up and maybe not. Either way, I still think you got a dirty mind. But if you did see this hooker and you ever see her again, don't you have anything to do with her—and don't go off with her if she should ask you. You just come straight to me and tell me, and if I'm not here, you find a cop and tell him. Hear me?'

"You know, that sort of shut him up. 'All right, all right!' he said and went off, taking the stairs going down."

"And did *he* disappear?" Ryker asked after a bit. He seemed vaguely to remember the youth in question, a pallid and lumbering lout who tended to brush against people and bump into doorways when he passed them.

"Well, you know, in a way that's a matter for argument," Clancy answered slowly. "It was the last time I saw him—that's a fact. And the Mrs. never saw him again either. But when she asked his mother about him, *she* just said he was off visiting friends for a while, but then a month or so later she admitted to the Mrs. that he *had* gone off without telling them a word—to join a commune, she thought, from some of the things he'd been saying, and that was all right with her, because his father just couldn't get along with him, they had such fights, only she wished he'd have the consideration to send her a card or something."

"And that was the last of it?" Ryker asked.

Clancy nodded slowly, almost absently. "That was damn all of it," he said softly. "About ten months later the parents moved. The kid hadn't turned up. There was nothing more."

"Until now," Ryker said, "when I came to you with my questions about a woman in black—and on Three at that, where this Stensor had lived. It wasn't a fur coat, of course, and I didn't think of her being a hooker—" (Was that true? he wondered) "—and it brought it all back to you, which now included what the young man had told you, and so you checked out the floors and then very kindly told me the whole story so as to give me the same warning you gave him?"

"But you're an altogether different sort of person, Mr. Ryker," Clancy protested. "I'd never think—But yes, allowing for that, that about describes it. You can't be too careful."

"No, you can't. It's a strange business," Ryker commented, shaking his head, and then added, making it sound much more casual, even comical, than he felt it, "You know, if this had happened fifty years ago, we'd be thinking maybe we had a ghost."

Clancy chuckled uneasily and said, "Yeah, I guess that's so."

Ryker said, "But the trouble with that idea would have been that there's nothing in the story about a woman disappearing, but three men—Stensor, and the man who lived alone, and the young man who lived with his parents."

"That's so," Mr. Clancy said.

Ryker stirred himself. "Well, thanks for telling me all about it," he said as they shook hands. "And if I should run into the lady again, I won't take any chances. I'll report it to you, Clancy. But not to the Mrs."

"I know you will, Mr. Ryker," Clancy affirmed.

Ryker himself wasn't nearly so sure of that. But he felt he had to get away to sort out his impressions. The dingy silvery walls were becoming oppressive.

Ryker made his walk a long one, brisk and thoughtful to begin with, dawdling and mind-wandering to finish, so that it was almost sunset by the time he reentered the apartment tree (and our story), but he had his impressions sorted. Clancy had—possibly—given the Vanishing Lady a history, funny to start with (that "hookers' convention"!) but then by stages silly, sad, sinister. Melancholy, moody, and still mysterious.

The chief retroactive effect of Clancy's story on his memories of his own encounters with the Vanishing Lady had been to intensify their sexual color, give them a sharper, coarser erotic note—an Ultrabooth note, you could say. In particular Ryker was troubled that ever since hearing Clancy narrate the loutish youth's steamy adolescent imagining that his "little hooker" had worn nothing but black stockings and a garter belt under her black fur coat, he was unable to be sure whether he himself had had similar simmering fantasy flashes during his encounters with her.

Could he be guilty, at his age, he asked himself, of such callow and lurid fantasies? The answer to that was, of course, "Of course." And then wasn't the whole romantic business of the Vanishing Lady just a retailoring of Ultrabooth to his own taste, something that made an Ultrabooth girl his alone? Somehow, he hoped not. But had he any real plan for making contact with her if she ever did stop vanishing? His unenterprising behavior when he'd had the chance to get into the elevator with her alone, and later the chance to get off the elevator at the same floor as she, and today the opportunity to meet her face to face on the third floor, indicated clearly that the answer to that question was "No." Which depressed him.

To what extent did Clancy believe in his story and in the reality of the girl who'd reportedly lingered on? He obviously had enjoyed telling it, and likely (from his glibness) had done so more than once, to suitable appreciative listeners. But did he believe she was one continuing real entity, or just a mixture of suggestion, chance, and mistaken resemblances, gossip, and outright lies? He'd never seen her himself—had this made Clancy doubt her reality, or contrariwise given him a stubborn hankering to catch sight of her himself for once at least? On the whole, Ryker thought Clancy was a believer—if only judging by his haste to search for her.

And as for the ghost idea, which you couldn't get around because it fitted her appearing and disappearing behavior so well, no matter how silly and unfashionable such a suggestion might be—Clancy's reaction to that had seemed uneasy; skepticism rather than outright "Nonsense!" rejection.

Which was very much like Ryker's own reaction to it, he realized. He knew there'd been some feelings of fear mixed in with the excitement during all his later encounters with her, before he'd heard Clancy's story. How would he feel now, after hearing it, if he should see her again, he wondered uncomfortably. More fear? Or would he now spot clues to her unreality? Would she begin to melt into mist? Would she look different simply because of what he'd heard about her?

Most likely, reality being the frustrating thing it was, he thought with an unamused inward guffaw, he'd simply never glimpse her again and never know. The stage having been set, all manifestations would cease.

But then, as he let the front door slip from his hand and swing toward its click-solemnized self-locking, he saw the Vanishing Lady forty feet away exactly as he had the first two times, real, no ghostliness anywhere (the name for the material of her coat came to his mind—velour), her shadowed face swung his way, or almost so, and modestly reaverted itself, and she moved out of sight on her black oxfords.

He reached the foyer fast as he could manage, its emptiness neither startling nor relieving him, nor the emptiness of the long back hall. He looked at the Clancys' door and the shuttered office window and shook his head and smiled. (Report this adventure? Whyever?) He started toward the stairs, but shook his head again and smiled more ruefully—he was already breathing very hard. He entered the elevator, and as he firmly pressed the Fourteen button with his thumb and heard the cage respond, he saw the dark gleaming eyes of the Vanishing Lady looking in at him anxiously, imploringly—they were open very wide—through the narrowing small window in the doors.

The next thing he was aware of, the cage was passing Three and he had just croaked out a harsh "Good evening"—the chalky aftertaste of these words was in his throat. The rest of the trip seemed interminable.

When the cage reached Fourteen, his thumb was already pressing the One button—and that trip seemed interminable too.

No sign of anyone anywhere, on One. He looked up the stairs, but he was breathing harder than even before. Finally he got back into the elevator and hovered his thumb over the 14 button. He could touch but not press it down. He brought his face close to the empty little window and waited and waited—and waited.

His thumb did not press down then, but the cage responded. The little window slipped shut. "It's out of my hands," he told himself fatalistically; "I'm being pulled somewhere." And from somewhere the thought came to him: What if a person were confined to this apartment tree forever, never leaving it, just going up and down and back and forth, and down and up and forth and back?

The cage didn't stop until Twelve, where the door was opened by a white-haired couple. Responding to their apologies with a reassuring head-shake and a signed "It's all right," Ryker pressed past them and, gasping gently and rapidly, mounted the last flight of stairs very slowly, very slowly. The two extra steps brought on a fit of swirling dizziness, but it passed and he slowly continued on toward his room. He felt frustrated, confused and very tired. He clung to the thoughts that he had reversed the elevator's course as soon as he could, despite his fright, and returned downstairs to hunt for her, and that in his last glimpse of them, her eyes had looked frightened too.

That night he had the muttering black nightmare again, all of it for the first time in weeks, and stronger, he judged afterward, than he'd ever before experienced it. The darkness seemed more impenetrable, solid, an ocean of black concrete congealing about him. The paralysis more complete, black canvas mummy wrappings drawn with numbing tightness, a spiral black cocoon tourniquet-tight. The dry and smoky odors more intense, as though he were baking and strangling in volcanic ash, while the sewerstenches vied in disgustingness with fruity-flowery reeks meant to hide them. The sullen ghost-light of his imagination showed the micro-males grosser and more cockroachlike in their hordes. And when finally under the goad of intensest horror he managed to stir himself and strain upward, feeling his heart and veins tearing with the effort, he encountered within a fraction of an inch his tomb's coarsely lined ceiling, which showered gritty ash into his gasping mouth and sightless eyes.

When he finally fought his way awake it was day, but his long sleep had in no way rested him. He felt tired still and good for nothing. Yesterday's story and walk had been too long, he told himself, yesterday's elevator encounter too emotionally exhausting. "Prisoners of the apartment tree," he murmured.

The Vanishing Lady was in very truth an eternal prisoner of the apartment tree, knowing no other life than there and no sleep anywhere except for lapsings that were as sudden as a drunkard's blackouts into an unconsciousness as black as Ryker's nightmares,

but of which she retained no memory whatever save for a general
horror and repulsion which colored all her waking thoughts.

She'd come awake walking down a hall, or on the stairs or in
the moving elevator, or merely waiting somewhere in the tall and
extensive apartment tree, but mostly near its roots and generally
alone. Then she'd simply continue whatever she was doing for a
while, sensing around her (if the episode lasted long enough, she
might begin to wander independently), thinking and feeling and
imagining and wondering as she moved or stood, always feeling
a horror, until something would happen to swoop her back into
black unconsciousness again. The something might be a sudden
sound or thought, a fire siren, say, sight of a mirror or another
person, encounter with a doorknob, or with the impulse to take
off her gloves, the chilling sense that someone had noticed her or
was about to notice her, the fear that she might inadvertently
walk through a silver-gray, faintly grimy wall, or slowly be absorbed
into the carpet, sink through the floor. She couldn't recall those
last things ever happening, and yet she dreaded them. Surely she
went *somewhere,* she told herself, when she blacked out. She
couldn't just collapse down on the floor, else there'd be some clue
to that next time she came awake—and she was always on her
feet when that happened. Besides, not often, but from time to
time, she noticed she was wearing different clothes—*similar* clothes,
in fact always black or some very dark shade close to it, but of
a definitely different cut or material (leather, for instance, instead
of cloth). And she couldn't possibly change her clothes or, worse,
have them changed for her, in a semi-public place like the apartment tree—it would be unthinkable, too horribly embarrassing.
Or rather—since we all know that the unthinkable and the horribly
embarrassing (and the plain horrible too, for that matter) *can*
happen—it would be too *grotesque.*

That was her chief trouble about everything, of course, she knew
so little about her situation—in fact, knew so little about herself
and the general scheme of things that held sway in this area,
period. That she suffered from almost total amnesia, that much
was clear to her. Usually she assumed that she lived (alone?) in
one of the apartments hanging on the tree, or else was forever
visiting someone who did, but then why couldn't she remember
the number or somehow get inside that apartment, or come awake
inside, or else get out the door into the street if she were headed
that way? Why, oh why, couldn't she once ever wake in a hospital

bed?—that would be pure heaven! except for the thought of what *kind* of a hospital and what things they had passing as doctors and nurses.

But just as she realized her amnesia, she knew she must have some way of taking care of herself during her unconscious times, or be the beneficiary of another's or others' system of taking care of her, for she somehow got her rest and other necessary physical reliefs, she must somehow get enough food and drink to keep her functioning, for she never felt terribly tired or seriously sick or weak and dizzy—except just before her topplings into unconsciousness, though sometimes those came without any warning at all, as sudden as the strike of Pentothal.

She remembered knowing drunks (but not their names—her memory was utterly worthless on names) who lived hours and days of their lives in states of total blackout, safely crossing busy streets, eating meals, even driving cars, without a single blink of remembered awareness, as if they had a guardian angel guiding them, to the point of coming awake in distant cities, not having the ghost of an idea as to how they'd got there. (Well, she could hardly be a drunk; she didn't stagger and there was never a bottle in her purse, the times she came awake clutching a purse.)

But those were all deductions and surmises, unanchored and unlabeled memories that bobbed up in her mind and floated there awhile. What did she really know about herself?

Pitifully little. She didn't know her name or that of any friend or relative. Address and occupation, too, were blanks. Ditto education, race, religion, and marital status. Oh Christ! she didn't even know what city she was in or how *old* she was! and whether she was good-looking, ugly, or merely nondescript. Sometimes one of those last questions would hit her so hard that she would forget and start to look into one of the many mirrors in the apartment tree, or else begin to take off her gloves, so she could check it that way—hey! maybe find a tag with her name on it sewed inside her coat! But any of these actions would, of course, plunge her back into the black unconsciousness from which *this time* there might be no awakening.

And what about the general scheme of things that held sway in this area? What did she know about that? Precious little, too. There was this world of the apartment tree which she knew very well although she didn't permit herself to look at every part of it equally. Mirrors were taboo, unless you were so placed you couldn't

see your own reflection in them; so mostly were people's faces.
People meant danger. Don't look at them, they might look at
you.

Then there was the outside world, a mysterious and wonderful
place, a heaven of delights where there was everything desirable
you could think or imagine, where there was freedom and repose.
She took this on faith and on the evidence of most of her memories.
(Though, sad to say, those memories' bright colors seemed to fade
with time. Having lost names, they tended to lose other details,
she suspected. Besides, it was hard to keep them vivid and bright
when your only conscious life was a series of same-seeming, frantic,
frightened little rushes and hidings and waits in the apartment
tree, glued together at the ends like stretches of film—and the
glue was black.)

But between those two worlds, the outside and the inside,
separating them, there was a black layer (who knows how thick?)
of unspeakable horrors and infinite terrors. What its outer surface
was, facing the outside world, she could only guess, but its inside
surface was clearly the walls, ceilings, and floors of the apartment
tree. That was why she worried so much that she might become
forgetful and step through them without intending to—she didn't
know if she were insubstantial enough to do that (though she
sometimes felt so), but she *might* be, or become so, and in any
case she didn't intend to try! And why she had a dread of cracks
and crevices and small holes anywhere and *things which could go
through such cracks and holes,* leading logically enough to a fear
of rats and mice and cockroaches and water bugs and similar
vermin.

Deep down inside herself she felt quite sure, most of the time,
that she spent all her unconscious life in the black layer, and that
it was her experiences there, or her dreams there, that infected
all her times awake with fear. But it didn't do to think of that,
it was too terrible, and so she tried to occupy her mind fully with
her normal worries and dreads, and with observing permitted
things in the apartment tree, and with all sorts of little notions
and fantasies.

One of her favorite fantasies, conceived and enjoyed in patches
of clear thinking and feeling in the mostly on-guard, frantic stretches
of her ragtag waking life, was that she really lived in a lovely
modern hospital, occupied a whole wing of it, in fact, the favorite
daughter of a billionaire no doubt, where she was cared for by

stunningly handsome, sympathetic doctors and bevies of warm-
hearted merry nurses who simply cosseted her to swooning with
tender loving care, fed her the most delicious foods and drinks,
massaged her endlessly, stole kisses sometimes (it was a rather
naughty place), and the only drawback was that she was asleep
throughout all these delightful operations.

Ah, but (she fantasized) you could tell just by looking at the
girl—her eyes closed, to be sure, but her lips smiling—that somewhere deep within she knew all that was happening, *somewhere
she enjoyed.* She was a sly one!

And then, when all the hospital was asleep, she would rise
silently from her bed, put on her clothes, and still in a profound
sleep sneak out of the hospital without waking a soul, hurry to
this place, dive in an instant through the horror layer, and come
awake!

But then, unfortunately, because of her amnesia, she would
forget the snow white hospital and all her specific night-to-night
memories of its delights and her wonderfully clever escapes from
it.

But she could daydream of the hospital to her heart's content,
almost! That alone was a matchless reward, worth everything, if
only you looked at it the right way.

And then after a while, of course, she'd realize it was time to
hurry back to the hospital before anyone there woke up and
discovered she was gone. So she would, generally without letting
on to herself what she was doing, seek or provoke an incident
which would hurtle her back into unconsciousness again, transform
her into her incredibly clever blacked-out other self who could
travel anywhere in the universe unerringly, do almost anything—
and with her eyes closed! (It wouldn't do to let the doctors and
nurses ever suspect she'd been out of bed. Despite their inex-
haustible loving-kindness they'd be sure to do something about
it, maybe even come here and get her, and bar her from the
apartment tree forever.)

So even the nicest daydreams had their dark sides.

As for the worst of her daydreams, the nastiest of her imaginings,
it didn't do to think of them at all—they were pure black-layer,
through and through. There was the fantasy of the eraser-worms
for instance—squirmy, crawling, sleek, horny-armored things about
an inch long and of the thickness and semi-rigidity of a pencil
eraser or a black telephone cord; once they were loose they could

go anywhere, and there were hordes of them.

She would imagine them. . . . Well, wasn't it better to imagine them outright than to pretend she'd had a dream about them? for that would be admitting that she might have dreamed about them in the black layer, which would mean she might actually have *experienced* them in the black layer, wasn't that so? Well, anyway, she would start by imagining herself in utter darkness. It was strange, wasn't it, how, not often, but sometimes, you couldn't keep yourself from imagining the worst things? For a moment they became irresistible, a sort of nasty reverse delight.

Anyhow, she would imagine she was lying in utter darkness— sometimes she'd close her eyes and cup her hands over them to increase the illusion, and once, alone in the elevator, greatly daring, she had switched off the light—and then she'd feel the first worm touch her toe, then crawl inquisitively, peremptorily between her big toe and the next, as if it owned her. Soon they'd be swarming all over her, investigating every crevice and orifice they reached, finally assaulting her head and face. She'd press her lips tightly together, but then they'd block her nostrils (it took about two of them, thrusting together, to do each of those) and she'd be forced to part her lips to gasp and then they'd writhe inside. She'd squeeze her eyes tight shut, but nevertheless . . . and she had no way to guard her ears and other entries.

It was only bearable because you knew you were doing it to yourself and could stop any time you wanted. And maybe it was a sort of test to prove that, in a pinch, you *could* stand it—she wasn't sure. And although you told yourself it was nothing but imagination, it did give you ideas about the black layer.

She'd rouse from such a session shaking her head and with a little indrawn shudder, as if to say, "Who would believe the things she's capable of?" and "You're brooding, you're getting into yourself too much, child. Talk to others. Get out of yourself!" (And perhaps it was just as well there was seldom opportunity— long enough lulls—to indulge in such experimenting in the nervous, unpredictable, and sometimes breathless-paced existence of the apartment tree.)

There were any number of reasons why she couldn't follow her own advice and speak to others in the apartment tree, strike up conversations, even look at them much, do more than steal in- frequent glances at their faces, but the overriding one was the deep conviction that *she had no right to be in the apartment tree* and that she'd get into serious trouble if she drew attention to herself. She might even be barred from the tree forever, sentenced to the black layer. (And if that last were the ridiculous nonsense idea it sounded like—where was the court and who would pronounce sentence?—why did it give her the cold shivers and a sick depression just to mention it to herself?)

No, she *didn't* have an apartment here, she'd tell herself, or any friend in the building. That was why she never had any keys— or any money either, or any little notebooks in which she could find out things about herself, or letters from others or even bills! No, she was a homeless waif and she had nothing. (The only thing she always or almost always carried was a complete riddle to her: a brass tube slim as a soda straw about four inches long which at one end went through a smooth cork not much bigger around than an eraser-worm—don't think of those!)

At other times she'd tell herself she needn't have any fear of being spotted, caught, unmasked, shown to be an illegal intruder by the other passers-through of the apartment tree, because she was *invisible* to them, or almost all of them. The proof of this (which was so obvious, right before your eyes, that you missed it) was simply that none of them noticed her, or spoke to her, or did her the little courtesies which they did each other, such as holding the elevator door for her. She had to move aside for them, not they for her!

This speculation about being invisible led to another special horror for her. Suppose, in her efforts to discover how old she was, she ever did manage to take off her gloves and found, not the moist hands of a young woman, nor yet the dry vein-crawling ones of a skinny old hag, but simply emptiness? What if she managed to open her coat and found herself, chin tucked in, staring down at lining? What if she looked into a mirror and saw nothing, except the wall behind her, or else only another mirror with reflections of reflections going back to infinity?

What if she were a ghost? Although it was long ago, or seemed long ago, she could recall, she thought, the dizzying chill *that* thought had given her the first time she'd had it. It fitted. Ghosts were supposed to haunt one place and to appear and disappear by fits and starts, and even then to be visible only to the sensitive few. None of the ghost stories she knew told it from the ghosts' side—what they thought and felt, how much they understood, and whether they ever knew what they were (ghosts) and what they were doing (haunting).

(And there even had been the "sensitive few" who had seemed to see her—and she looked back at them flirtatiously—though she didn't like to remember those episodes because they frightened her and made her feel foolish—whyever had she flirted? taken that risk?—and in the end made her mind go blurry. There'd been that big fat boy—whatever had she seen in him?—and before him a gentle old man, and before *him*—no, she certainly didn't have to push her memory back that far, no one could make her!)

But now that thought—that she might be a ghost—had become only one more of her familiar fancies, coming back into her mind every once in a while as regular as clockwork and with a little but not much of the original shock the idea had once given her. "Part of my repertoire," she told herself drolly. (God knows how she'd managed to stand her existence if things didn't seem funny to her once in a while.)

But most times weren't so funny. She kept coming back and coming back to what seemed after all the chief question: How *long* had her conscious life, *this* conscious life, lasted? And the only final answer she could get to this, in moments of unpanic, was that she couldn't tell.

It might be months or years. Long enough so that although not looking at their faces, she'd gotten to know the tenants of the apartment tree by their clothes and movements, the little things they said to each other, their gaits and favorite expressions. Gotten to know them well enough so that she could recognize them when they'd changed their clothes, put on new shoes, slowed down their gait, begun to use a cane. Sometimes completely new ones would appear and then slowly become old familiars—new tenants moving in. And then these old familiars might in their turn disappear—moved away, or died. My God, had she been here for decades? She remembered a horror story in which a beautiful young woman woke from a coma to find herself dying of old age. Would it be like that for her when she at last faced the mirror?

And if she *were* a ghost, would not the greatest horror for such a being be to die as a ghost?—to feel you had one tiny corner of existence securely yours, from which you could from time to time glimpse the passing show, and then be mercilessly swept out of that?

Or it might, on the other hand, be only minutes, hours, days at most—of strangely clear-headed fever dreaming, or of eternity-seeming withdrawal from a drug. Memory's fallible. Mind's capable of endless tricks. How could you be sure?

Well, whatever the truth was about the "How long?" business, she needn't worry about it for a while. The last few days (and weeks, or hours and minutes, who cared?) she'd been having a brand-new adventure. Yes, you could call it a flirtation if you wanted, but whatever you called it and in spite of the fact that it had its bad and scary parts, it had made her feel happier, gayer, braver, even more devil-may-care than she had in ages. Why, already it had revealed to her what she'd seen in the big fat boy and in the old man before him. My goodness, she'd simply *seen* them, felt interest in them, felt concern for them, yes, loved them. For that was the way it was now.

But that was then and this was now.

From the first time she'd happened to see Ryker (she didn't know his name then, of course) gazing so admiringly and wonderstruck at her from the front door, she'd known he couldn't possibly mean her harm, be one of the dangerous ones who'd send her back to the hospital or the black layer, or whatever. What had surprised her was the extent of her own inward reaction. She had a friend!—someone who thought she amounted to something, who *cared*. It made her dizzy, delirious. She managed to walk only a few steps, breasting the emotional tide, before she collapsed happily into the arms of darkness.

The second time it happened almost exactly the same way, only this time she was anticipating and needed only the barest glimpse—a flicker of her eyes his way—to assure herself that there hadn't been any mistake the first time, that he did feel that way about her, that he loved her.

By the time of their third meeting, she'd worked herself up into a really daring mood—she'd prepared a surprise for him and was waiting for him in the elevator. She'd even mischievously switched off the light (when she had the strength to do things like that, she knew she was in fine fettle), and was managing somehow to hold the door open (that surprised even her) so that she'd gradually be revealed to him as he came down the hall—a sort of hide-and-seek game. As to what happened after that, she'd take her chances!

Then when he'd walked past her, making a feeble excuse about his mailbox—that was one of the bad parts. What was the matter with him? Was he, a tenant, actually scared of her, a trespasser, a waif? And if so, how was he scared of her?—as a woman or as a possible criminal who'd try to rob or rape him, or maybe as a ghost? Was he shy, or had his smiles and admiration meant nothing, been just politeness? She almost lost her hold on the door then, but she managed not to. "Hurry up, hurry up, you old scaredy cat!" she muttered perkily under her breath. "I can't hold this door forever!"

And then someone on an upper floor buzzed the elevator, startling her, and she did lose her hold on the doors and they closed and the cage moved upward. She felt a sudden surge of hopelessness at being thwarted by mere chance, and she blacked out.

But next time she came awake her spirits were soon soaring again. In fact, that was the time when on sheerest impulse, she'd darted into a crowded elevator after him, which was something she never did—too much chance of being forced against someone and revealing your presence that way even if invisible.

Well, *that* didn't happen, but only because she kept herself pressed as flat against the door as possible and had some luck. At the first stop she hopped out thankfully, and changing her plans simply flew up the stairs, outdistancing the creaking cage, and when he didn't get out at Twelve, went on to Fourteen, and changing her plans again (she had the feeling it was almost time to black out), she simply followed him as he plodded to his room and noted its number before she lost consciousness. That was how she learned his name—by going to the mailboxes next time and checking his number, which said: R. RYKER. Oh, she might be a stupid little orphan of the apartment tree, but she had her tricks!

That time his arrival down on the ground floor front hall caught her unawares. Another man was holding the elevator door for two older ladies and with an encouraging glance at Ryker (he smiled back!) she darted in after them (she didn't mind a *few* fellow passengers, she could dodge them), thinking the man would go on holding the door open for Ryker. But he didn't, and she hesitated to hold it open from where she was standing (it would have looked too much like magic to the others) and so that chance of a shared ride and meeting was botched.

But that one failure didn't break her general mood of self-confidence and being on top of the situation. If fact, her mind seemed to be getting sharper and her memories to be opening.

She got a hunch that something had once happened on the third floor in the front hall that was important to her, and it was while brooding there about it that she had her second unexpected encounter with Ryker. He came walking down the stairs and saw her and for a moment she thought he was going to march straight up to her, but once again his courage or whatever seemed to fail him and he kept on down and in her disappointment she blacked out.

These unanticipated meetings wouldn't do, she told herself, they didn't work, so the next time Ryker arrived by the front door she was waiting for him in the lobby. Then, just as things appeared to be working out, *her* courage failed, she got a sudden terrible fit of stage fright and fled up the stairs, though managing to turn at the top of the first flight and watch. She saw him pass the elevator after a hurried inspection of it and move toward the mailboxes and back hall. But he returned from there almost at once and entered the elevator. She realized that he'd gone to the back hall to look for her and, her courage restored, she flew down the stairs, but there was only time to peer once through the little elevator window at him (and he peered back) before the cage's ascent blocked the window. She waited dejectedly by the shaft, heard faintly the elevator stop at the top—and then immediately start down again. Was he coming back on her account? she asked herself, feeling dizzy, her mind wavering on the edge of blackness. She managed to hold onto her consciousness just long enough for it to tell her that, indeed, he was!—and looking anxious and expectant as he came out of the elevator—before it blacked out entirely.

Ramsey Ryker did not reenter the apartment tree from his own apartment until the next evening. Any attentive and thoughtful observer, had there been one to accompany him down in the elevator and match his measured footsteps to the front door, would have deduced two things about him.

First, from cologne-whiff overlying a faintly soapy fragrance and from gleaming jowl, spotless white collar, faintly pink scalp between strands of combed white hair, and small even tie-knot, that he had recently bathed, shaved very closely, and arrayed himself with equal care, so that except for his age you might have been sure he was going out on a romantic date.

Second, from his almost corpselike pallor, his abstracted expression, and "slow march" ritualistic movements, that the evening's business was a not altogether pleasurable or at least a very serious one.

And if the observer had in addition been an *imaginative* or perhaps merely suggestible person, he might have added these two impressions together and got the sinister total of "If ever a man could be said to have dressed himself for his own funeral. . . ."

And if that same hypothetical observer had been on hand twenty minutes later to witness Ryker's return to the apartment tree, he would have got an additional funereal shudder from the circumstance that Ryker's lapel now sported a white carnation while his left hand carefully held a small floral spray, the chief feature of which was a white orchid.

But even this observer would have been surprised at the expression of excited delight that suffused and faintly colored Ryker's pale forward-straining countenance as he entered the hall. Of course sometimes merely getting cleaned up and dressed and venturing outdoors will cheer an elderly person amazingly, but this mood change seemed to and indeed did have a more specific outside stimulus.

For Ryker saw that the circumstances of his third encounter with the Vanishing Lady had been reproduced. There was that same impression of additional gloom, a black hole opening, swiftly seen to be due to the elevator doors standing open and that cage dark, and the dim-gleaming slender figure of the Vanishing Lady in profile just inside and just beyond the column of control buttons.

But this time her posture did not seem dejected but relaxedly alive: her head was bent, it's true, but it also seemed turned a little in his direction, as if she were scanning his approach coquettishly, there was more if anything of an elusive shimmering dim sparkle about her shoulders and her front, she held again (left hand this time, the nearer one) that mysterious little brass object he'd mistaken for a key, the total effect being surprisingly erotic, as if it were a black-and-silver drawing, "Assignation in the Shadows"; while all the while he hurried on eagerly, faster and faster, fiercely arming himself against any last-minute cringings aside, determined to let only a premature closing of its doors bar him from that elevator tonight.

Without the slightest hesitation he strode into the dark cage, bowing slightly to her as he did so, reaching his right hand toward the top of the buttons column, where the light switch was, to turn

it on, and said in a low and respectful voice, "Good evening."
This last came out deeper and more resonant than he'd intended,
so that it had a rather sepulchral sound. And his third movement
was not completed, for just as he entered, she raised her head
and simultaneously reached her black-gloved right hand and that
arm across her body and the lower half of her face, apparently
anticipating his intention to switch on the light, so that his own
hand drew back.

He turned facing her as he stepped past her and settled his back
against that of the elevator. Her outstretched arm concealed her
lips, so he couldn't tell if she smiled or not, but her gleaming
eyes followed him as he moved across the cage, and at least they
didn't frown. The effect was provocative, alluring.

But her outreached hand did not turn on the light. Instead its
black forefinger seemed to lay itself against the flat brass between
the 12 and 14 buttons. But she must have pressed one or the
other of those in so doing, for the doors growled shut and the
cage moved upward.

That plunged the cage in gloom, but not quite as deeply as he
would have expected, for the strange pale glimmering around her
neck and her black coat's closure seemed to strengthen a little,
almost sparkle (real or imagined? her body's aura, could it be? or
only his old eyes dazzling?) and a twinkle of other light came in
by the little window as they passed the second floor. In his state
of heightened awareness he dimly yet distinctly saw her right hand
drop away from the button panel and her other hand join it,
creep a little way into its sleeve and then in one swift backward
motion strip the glove from her right hand, which then uncurled
gracefully toward him palm upward through the dark between
them like a slender white sash ending in five slim white ribbons
of unequal length. Advancing a step and bowing his head toward
it, he gently received its cool weightless length upon his own
fingers, touched his lips to the smooth slim palm, and withdrawing
laid across it the white orchid he'd been carrying. Another little
window winked by.

She pressed the slender spray against her throat and with her
yet-gloved hand touched his as if in thanks. *She* wondered why
she had pressed *between* the buttons and why the cage had responded, why she had not blacked out while drawing off her glove.
Dark memories threatened opening, not without fear. She tugged
a little at Ryker's hand in drawing her own away.

Emboldened, he advanced another step, bringing him almost against her. Her cat-triangular small face tilted up toward his, half of it pale, the other half dark mouth, gray gleaming eyes, their shadowed orbits under slim black brows. His left hand brushed her side and slid behind her, pressed her slim back. His right sought out the fingers at her throat holding his orchid and caressed them, playing with them gently. He felt her suede-soft gloved fingers creeping at the back of his neck.

She slid the orchid with its insubstantial spray inside her coat and her ungloved moist hand stroked his dry cheek. His hand felt out two large round buttons at her neck, tilted them through their thread-bordered slits, and the collar of her coat fell open. The diamond sparkling that had long puzzled him intensified, gushed up and poured out fountainlike, as if he had uncovered her aura's nest—or was his old heart blowing up a diamond hurricane? or his old eyes jaggedly spinning out a diamond migraine pattern? He gazed down through this ghostly scintillation, these microscopic stars, at a landscape pearly gray and cool as the moon's, the smooth valley where the orchid lodged between her small jutting breasts with their dark silver nipples, a scene that was not lost, though it swung and narrowed a little, when her small hands drew his head down to hers and their lips met in a leisurely kiss that dizzied him unalarmingly.

It occurred to him whimsically that although the pearly landscape he continued to admire might seem to stretch on and on, it had an exceedingly low black sky, an extremely low ceiling, air people would say. Now why should that fantasy carry overtones which were more sinister than amusing? he wondered idly.

It was at that moment that he became aware that he was smelling cigar smoke. The discovery did not particularly startle or alarm him, but it did awaken his other senses a little from their present great dreamy preoccupation, though not entirely. Indeed, in one sense that preoccupation deepened, for at that moment the tip of her tongue drew a very narrow line into their kiss. But at the same time, as he noted that the elevator had come to rest, that its creaking groan had been replaced by a growling mutter which he liked still less, while a wavering ruddy glow, a shadowed reddish flickering, was mounting the walls of the cage from some unknown source below, and that the thin reek of cigar smoke was becoming more acrid.

Unwillingly, wearily (he was anything but tired, yet this cost an effort), he lifted his gaze without breaking their kiss, without thinking of breaking it, and continuing to fondle her back and neck, until he was looking across her shoulder.

He saw, by the red glow, that the door of the cage had opened without his having noticed it and that the elevator was at the fourteenth floor.

But not *quite* at the fourteenth floor, for the outer door was closed tight and the little window in it that had the numeral 14 painted under it stood about eighteen inches higher than it should.

So the floor of the cage must be the same distance below the floor of Fourteen.

Still unalarmed, grudging each effort, he advanced his head across her shoulder until he could look down over it. As he did so, she leaned her head back and turned it a little sideways, accommodating, so that their kiss was still unbroken, meanwhile hugging him more tightly and making muffled and inarticulate crooning sounds as if to say "It is all right."

The space between the two floors (which was also the space between the ceiling of Twelve and the floor of Fourteen) was wide open, a doorway five feet wide and scarcely one foot high in the raw wall of the shaft, and through that doorway there was pouring into the bottom of the cage from the very low-ceilinged thirteenth floor a pulsing crimson glow which nevertheless seemed more steady in hue, more regular in its variations of intensity than that of any fire.

This furnace-light revealed, clustered around their ankles but spreading out more scatteredly to fill the elevator's carpeted floor, a horde of dark squat forms, a milling host of what appeared to be (allowing for the extreme foreshortening) stocky Lilliputian human beings, some lifting their white faces to peer up, others bent entirely to the business at hand. For instance, two pairs of them struggled with dull metal hooks almost as large as they were and to which stout cords were attached, others carried long prybars, one jauntily balanced on his shoulder what looked like a white paper packet about as big (relative to him) as an unfolded Sunday newspaper, while more than half of them held between two fingers tiny black cylinders from one end of which interweaving tiny tendrils of smoke arose, forming a thin cloud, and which when they applied the other ends to their tiny mugs, glowed winkingly red in the red light, as if they were a swarm of hellish lightless fireflies.

It may seem most implausible to assert that Ramsey Ryker did not feel terror and panic at this extremely grotesque sight (for he realized also that he had somehow penetrated the realm of his nightmares) and highly unlikely to record that his kiss and the Vanishing Lady's continued unbroken (save for the hurried puffings and inhalations normal in such a contact), yet both were so. True, as he wormed his head back across her shoulder to its first vantage point, his heart pounded alarmingly, there was a roaring in his ears, and waves of blackness threatened to overwhelm his vision and forced their way up into his skull, while the simple shifting movement he intended proved unexpectedly difficult to execute (his head felt heavy, not so much looking over her shoulder as slumped on it)—but these were physical reactions with many causes. His chief mental reactions to the beings he'd seen clustered around their feet were that they would have been interesting at another time and that they presumably had their own place, business, and concerns in the great scheme of things, and that just now he had his own great business and concerns he must return to, as hopefully they to theirs. Also, the Vanishing Lady's caresses and murmurings of reassurance and encouragement had their helpful and soothing effects.

But when he was once more gazing down into what we may call without any sarcasm his steep and narrow valley of delights, he could no longer tell whether the ghostly silver sparks that fountained from it were inside or outside his eyes and skull, the exquisite outlines wavered and were lost in mists, his fingers fondling her neck and her low back grew numb and powerless, all power save that of vision drained from his every part, he grew lax, and with her hands solicitously supporting and guiding him, he sank by degrees, his heavy head brushing her black coat entirely open and resting successively against her naked breasts, belly, and thighs, until he was laid out upon his back corner-to-corner in the small cage, head to the front of it, feet to the back, level with the hitherto unsuspected thirteenth floor, while the Vanishing Lady in assisting him had stooped until she now sat upon her heels, her upper body erect, her chin high, having never once looked down.

With a slow effortless movement she regained her full stature, her hands trailing limply down, one of them still gripping the brass tube. The jaunty homunculus lifted his white paper packet to the other, and she clipped it securely between thumb and forefinger, still without the slightest downward glance, raised it until it was before her eyes, and eagerly but carefully unfolded it.

Ryker watched her attentively from the floor. His entire consciousness, almost, had focused in on her until he saw only her face and shoulders, her busy hands and matchless breasts. They looked very clear but very far away, like something seen through the wrong end of a telescope. He was only most dimly aware of the movements closer to him, of the way the two large dull hooks were being effortfully fitted under his shoulders and beneath his armpits. He watched with great interest but no comprehension, aware only of the beauty of the sight, as she fitted the cork-protected end of the brass tube into one nostril, delicately applied the other end to the flat unfolded square of white paper, and slowly but deeply inhaled. He did not hear the distant windlass creaking nor feel the hooks tighten against his armpits as he was dragged out of the elevator into the thirteenth floor and his consciousness irised in toward nothingness.

Nor did the Vanishing Lady honor either his disappearance or his captors' with even one last glance as she impatiently shifted the brass tube to her other nostril and applied it to an edge of the diminished pile of crystals outspread on the white packet paper, the sight of which had instantly recalled to her mind the use of that tube and much more besides, not all of which she was tickled to relearn: the sullen waitings for Artie Stensor, her own entrapment by the thirteenth floor, the finding of Artie there in his new and degenerate imprisoned form, the sessions that reduced her also to such a form, her deal with the reigning homunculi, the three services (or was it four?) she'd promised them, the luring and entrapment of the other two tenants. She put all that out of her mind as she inhaled slowly, very evenly, and deeply, the mouth of the brass tube like that of some tiny reaping machine eating its way up and down the edge of the coke or "snow" or whatever else you might call the sovereign diamond sparkling dream drug, until the paper was empty.

She felt the atoms of her body loosening their hold on each other and those of her awareness and memory tightening theirs as with a fantastic feeling of liberation she slowly floated up through the ceiling of the cage into the stale air of the dark and cavernous shaft and then rose more and more swiftly along the black central cables until she shot through the shaft's ceiling, winked through the small lightless room in which were the elevator's black motor and relays, and burst out of the apartment tree into the huge dizzying night.

South shone the green coronet of the Hilton, west the winking red light that outlined the tripod TV tower atop Sutro Crest, northeast the topaz-sparkling upward-pointing arrow of the Transamerican Pyramid. Farther east, north, and west, all lapped in low fog, were the two great bridges, Bay and Golden Gate, and the unlimited Pacific Ocean. She felt she could see, go anywhere.

She spared one last look and sorrow pang for the souls entombed—or, more precisely, *immured*—in San Francisco and then, awareness sharpening and consciousness expanding, sped on up and out, straight toward that misty, nebula-swathed multiple star in Orion called the Trapezium.

CORNELL WOOLRICH
Jane Brown's Body

1

THREE O'CLOCK in the morning. The highway is empty, under a malignant moon. The oil drippings make the roadway gleam like a blue-satin ribbon. The night is still but for a humming noise coming up somewhere behind a rise of ground.

Two other, fiercer, whiter moons, set close together, suddenly top the rise, shoot a fan of blinding platinum far down ahead of them. Headlights. The humming burgeons into a roar. The touring car is going so fast it sways from side to side. The road is straight. The way is long. The night is short.

The man hunched at the wheel is tense; his eyes are fixed unblinkingly on the hem of the black curtain that the headlights roll up before him. His eyes are like two little lumps of coal. His face is brown; his hair is white. His figure is gaunt, but there is power in the bony wrists that grip the wheel, and power in the locked jaws that show white with their own tension.

The speedometer needle flickers a little above eighty. . . .

The rear-view mirror shows a very tired young woman napping on the back seat. Her legs are tucked up under her, and the laprobe has been swathed around her from the waist down. One black-gloved hand is twisted in the looped cord dangling from the side of the car; it hangs there even as she sleeps, of its own weight. She sways with a limpness, a lack of reflex-resistance, that almost suggests an absence of life.

She has on a tiny pillbox hat with a fine-meshed veil flaring out all around below it. The wind keeps pushing it back like a film across her face. The contact of her nose makes a funny little knob on it. It should billow out at that point with her breathing,

311

at such close contact. It doesn't, just caves in as though she were
sucking it through parted lips. She sleeps with her mouth slightly
open.

The moon is the only thing that keeps up with this careening
car, grinning down derisively on it all the way, mile after mile,
as though to say, "I'm on to you!"

A scattering of pinpoint lights shows up in the blackness ahead.
A town or village straddling the highway. The indicator on the
speedometer begins to lose ground. The man glances in his mirror
at the girl, a little anxiously as if this oncoming town were some
kind of test to be met.

An illuminated road sign flashes by.

CAUTION!
MAIN STREET AHEAD—SLOW UP

The man nods grimly, as if agreeing with that first word. But
not in the way it is meant.

The lights grow bigger, spread out on either side. Street lights
peer out here and there among the trees. The highway suddenly
sprouts a plank sidewalk on each side of it. Dark store-windows
glide by.

With an instinctive gesture, the man dims his lights from blinding
platinum to just a pale wash. A lunch-room window drifts by.

The lights of a big bus going his way wink just ahead. He makes
ready to swerve out and get past it. And then there is an unlooked-
for complication. A railroad right-of-way bisects the main street
here. Perhaps no train has passed all night until now. Perhaps no
other will pass until morning. Five minutes sooner, five minutes
later, and he could have avoided the delay. But just as car and
lighted bus approach, side by side, a bell starts ringing, zebra-
striped barriers weighted with red lanterns are slowly lowered, and
the road is blocked off. The two cars are forced to halt abreast
while a slow procession of freight cars files endlessly by. Almost
simultaneously, a large milk-truck has turned in behind him from
the side road, sealing him in.

The lights of the bus shine into the car and fall on the sleeping
woman. There is only one passenger in the bus, but he is on the
near side, and he looks idly out the window into the neighboring
machine. His eye drops to the sleeping woman and remains there,
as any man's would.

There is a terrible rigidity about the man at the wheel now. White shows over his knuckles. His eyes are glued on the mirror, in which he can see the bus passenger gazing casually into the rear of his car. A shiny thread starts down his face, catches in one of its leathery furrows. Sweat. A second one follows. His chest is rising and falling under his coat and he breathes as if he has been running.

The man at the bus window keeps looking at the woman, looking at her. He doesn't mean anything by it, probably. There's nothing else for him to look at. Why shouldn't he look at a woman, even a sleeping one? She must be beautiful under that veil. Some men are born starers-at-women, anyway.

But as the endless freight cars click by ahead, as the long scrutiny keeps up, one of the white-knuckled hands on the wheel is moving. It leaves the polished wooden rim, drops to its owner's lap. The whiteness goes out of it. It starts crawling up under his coat, buries itself between the buttoned halves, comes out again, white over the knuckles again, gripping an automatic.

His eyes have never once left the rear-view mirror, never once left the reflection of the bus-passenger's face. He acts as if he is waiting for some expression to come into it. Some certain, telltale expression. He acts as if, then, he will do something with that gun on his lap.

But the caboose has finally terminated the endless chain of freight cars, the bell stops ringing, the barriers slowly rise. The bus driver unlumbers his clutch, the line of lighted windows start to edge forward. The gun vanishes, the hand that held it returns to the wheel empty. A moment later bus, and passenger, and face have all spurted ahead. The touring car hangs back a moment, to give it a good start. The milk truck signals impatiently for clearance, then cuts out around the obstacle, lurches ahead.

The leathery-faced man at the wheel has his under lip thrust out, expelling hot breath of relief up past his own face. He touches the two liquid threads the drops of sweat left on his face, blots them.

He goes on into the night, along the arrow-straight highway, under the peering moon. The lady sways and dreams, and puckers her veil in.

A long slow rise begins, and now the car starts to buck when he gives it the accelerator. He looks at the gauge; his gas is dwindling fast. The tan washes out of his face for a moment. He's on a main road, after all. All he has to do is pull over, wait for a tow-line, if he runs out of gas. Why that fleeting panic on his face?

He nurses the car forward on the dregs of gas remaining. Zigzags it from side to side of the highway, to lessen the incline that might defeat it. It goes by fits and starts, slower all the time, but he's near the crest now. If he can only reach it, he can coast down the dip on the other side without an engine.

The car creeps up over the rise, hesitates, about to stall. Before him the road dips downward under the moon for miles. In the distance a white glow marks a filling station. He maneuvers the wheel desperately in and out, the momentum of the descent catches at the machine, and a moment later it's coasting along at increasing speed.

The filling station blazes nearer, an aurora borealis in the middle of the dark countryside. He dare not go past, yet he's very tense as the car rolls within the all-revealing light. He glances anxiously in the mirror. He wonders about the window shades, but leaves them the way they are. There's nothing that draws the human eye quicker than a suggestively lowered shade.

He turns aside, inches up the runway, brakes to a stop. An attendant jumps over.

"Five," he says, and sits there watching the man hook up the pipeline. Watching him with utter absorption. The gun is in his lap again, bedded under the hem of his coat.

The grease monkey approaches the front window. "Wash your windows, chief?"

The driver stretches his lips into a grin. "Leave 'em."

The monkey grins back, and his eyes wander on past the driver to the girl in the back of the car, rest there for a minute.

"Dead tired," the man at the wheel says. "Here's your money; keep the change." The car moves out of the yellow radiance into the sheltering gloom again. Secrecy wells up into its interior once more, like India ink.

The flabbergasted attendant is shouting something after him. "Hey, mister, that's a twenty-dollar bill you—"

The car is racing along again now. The man at the wheel tenses. What's that peppering sound coming up behind him? A small, single beam of light is seesawing after him. If the man was frightened by the bus and by the filling station, what word can describe the look on his face now, as his mirror shows him a

state policeman on his tail? Teeth bared in a skull-like flash, he
fights down an impulse to open up, to try to race for it. He pulls
over to the side, slows, stops. Again the gun comes out, and again
it is bedded under his thigh with the butt protruding in readiness
on the side away from the window. Then he sits grinding his fist
into the hollow of his other hand.

The motorcycle flashes by, loops awkwardly around, comes back.
The rider gets off, walks over, planks his foot down heavily on
the runningboard. He ducks his head, leers in at him, beetle-
browed.

"What's your hurry, fellow? I clocked you at eighty."

"Eighty-four," corrects the leathery-faced man, with a dangerous
quietness that cannot be mistaken for humility.

"Well, fifty's the limit around here. Lemme see your license."

The driver takes out his license with his left hand; the right is
lying idly beside his right thigh, on cold black metal.

The state cop reads by the dashboard-light, leaning even further
in to do so. His own weapon is way out behind at his hip; the
window frame would block his elbow in a sudden reach. "Anton
Denholt. Doctor, eh? I'm surprised at you, all the more reason
you oughta have more sense! Next state, too, huh? You people
are the ones give us the most trouble. Well, you're in my state
now, get that; you didn't quite make that state-line marker down
there—"

Denholt glances along the road as if he hadn't seen the marker
before. "I didn't try to," he says in that same toneless voice.

The cop nods thoughtfully. "I guess you could have at that,"
he admits. "What were you doing eighty-four for—?"

Perhaps Denholt can't stand waiting for the man to discover
the girl sleeper in back, perhaps his nerves are so frayed by now
that he'd rather call attention to her himself and get it over with.
He jerks his head toward the back seat. "On her account," he
says. "Every minute counts."

The cop peers back. "She sick, Doc?" he asks, a little more
considerately.

Denholt says, "It's a matter of life and death." And again he
is speaking the absolute truth, far more than the trooper can guess.

The cop begins to look apologetic. "Why didn't you say so?
There's a good hospital at Rawling. You must have passed by
there an hour ago. Why didn't you take her there?"

"No. I can make it where I'm going, if you'll only let me be on my way. I want to get her home before the baby—"

The cop gives a low whistle. "No wonder you were burning up the road!" He slaps his book closed, hands Denholt back his license. "You want an escort? You'll make better time. My beat ends at that marker down there, but I can put in a call for you—"

"No thanks," says Denholt blandly. "I haven't much further to go."

The touring car glides off. There is a sort of fatalism in Denholt's attitude now, as he urges the car back to high speed. What else can happen to him, after what just did? What else is there to be afraid of—now?

Less than forty miles past the state line, he leaves the great transcontinental highway and turns off into a side road, a "feeder." Presently it begins to take a steady upgrade, into the foothills of a chain of mountains. The countryside changes, becomes wilder, lonelier. Trees multiply to the thickness of woodlands. The handiwork of man, all but the roadway itself, slowly disappears.

He changes his course a second time, leaves the feeder for what is little better than an earth-packed trail, sharply tilted, seldom used. The climb is steady. Through occasional breaks in the trees of the thickly wooded slopes that support the trail, he can see the low country he has left below, the ribbon of the trunkroad he was on, an occasional winking light like a glowworm toiling slowly along it. There are hairpin turns; overhanging branches sway back with a hiss as he forces his way through. He has to go much slower here, but he seems to know the way.

A barbed-wire fence leaps suddenly out from nowhere, begins to parallel the miserable road. Four rungs high, each rung three strands in thickness, viciously spined, defying penetration by anything but the smallest animals. Strange, to want privacy that badly in such an out-of-the-way place. A double gate sidles along in it, double-padlocked, and stops abreast of him as his car comes to a halt. A placard beside it reads in the diamond-brightness of the headlights: "Private Property. Keep Out." A common-enough warning, but strange to find it here in this mountain fastness. Even, somehow, sinister.

He gets out, opens both padlocks, edges the freed halves of the gate inward with his shoe. Instantly a jarring, jangling sound explodes from one of the trees nearby. An alarm bell, wired to the gate. Its clang is frightening in this dark silence. It too spells lack of normality, seems the precaution of a fanatic.

The car drives through, stops while the man closes and fastens the prickly gate behind it. The bell shuts off; the stillness is deafening by contrast. The car goes on until the outline of a house suddenly uptilts the searching headlight-beams, logbuilt, sprawling, resembling a hunting-lodge. But there's no friendliness to it. There is something ominous and forbidding about its look, so dark, so forgotten, so secretive-looking. The kind of a house that has a maw to swallow with—a one-way house, that you feel will never disgorge any living thing that enters it. Leprous in the moonlight festering on its roof. And the two round sworls of light played by the heads of the car against its side, intersecting, form a pear-shaped oval that resembles a gleaming skull.

The man leaves the car again, jumps up under a sort of a shed arrangement sheltering the main entrance. Metal clashes and a black opening yawns. He vanishes through it, while pulsing bright-beamed car and sleeping lady wait obediently outside.

Light springs up within—the yellow-green wanness of coal-oil, shining out through the door to make the coal-black treetrunks outside seem even blacker. The place looks eerier than ever now.

Homecoming?

The man's shadow lengthens, blacks out of the doorway, and he's ready to receive the patient lady. He kills the engine, opens the rear door and reaches in for her with outstretched arms. He disengages her dangling wrist from the interwined support-strap, brushes off the laprobe, cradles her body in upturned arms, and waddles inside with her, like someone carrying something very precious. The door bangs shut behind him at a backward thrust of his heel, and darkness swallows up the world outside.

2

HE CARRIES her through the building into an extension hidden from view from the outside. There is a distinct difference between it and the rest of the rambling structure. Its walls are not log, but brick, covered with plaster, that must have been hauled to this inaccessible place at great trouble and expense. It's wired for electricity, current supplied by a homemade generator. Dazzling, clinical-white light beats down from above in here. And there are no chairs here, no rough-hewn tables, anything like that. Instead, retorts and bunsen-burners. A zinc operating table. Solution pans. A glass case of instruments. And across one entire side of the room, a double tier of mesh cages, each containing a rabbit.

He comes in swiftly with his burden, puts her down on the zinc table. She never stirs. He turns back and closes the door, bolts it both at top and at bottom. He strips off coat and shirt and undershirt, slips into a surgeon's white jacket. He takes a hypodermic needle out of the instrument case, drops it into a pan of antiseptic solution, lights a flame under it. Then he goes back to the table.

The girl's figure has retained the double-up position it held all during the long ride; it lies on her side, legs tucked-up under her as they were on the car seat, arm thrust out, wrist dangling just as the strap held it. Denholt seems to have expected this, yet he frowns just a little. He tries to straighten out the stiffened limbs; they resist him. Not all his strength can force them into a straight line with the torso. He begins to do what he has to do with frantic haste, as if every moment was both an obstacle and a challenge.

This is so. For rigor is setting in; the sleeping lady has been dead the better part of the night. . . .

Denholt tears her things off arm over arm, with motions like an overhand swimmer. Hat and veil, black dress, shoes, hosiery, fall about the floor.

The girl was evidently pretty; she must have been quite young too. The rouge she put on in life still frames her parted lips. Her figure is slim and shapely, unmarred by wounds. There is no blood on her at all. That is important. Denholt races up with a jar of alcohol, douses it all over her with a great slapping splash.

He seizes the hypo from the scalding pan, hurriedly fills the barrel at a retort of colorless liquid, turns the huddled dripping figure over on its face, sweeps the nape-hair out of the way with one hand. He poises the needle at the base of the skull, looks briefly at the whitewashed ceiling as though in prayer, presses the plunger home.

He stands back, lets the hypo fall with a clash. It breaks, but that doesn't matter; if it has failed, he never wants to use one again.

The needle's tiny puncture doesn't close up as it would in living tissue; it remains a visible, tiny, black pore. He takes a wad of cotton, holds it pressed there, to keep the substance just injected from trickling out again. He is trembling all over. And the seconds tick into minutes.

Outside it must be dawn, but no light penetrates the sealed-up laboratory. It must be dawn, and the last breath went out of this body on the table—how long before? Irretrievably gone from this world, as dead as though she had lived a thousand years ago. Men have cut the Isthmus of Panama and joined the two oceans; they have bored tunnels that run below rivers; built aluminum planes that fly from Frisco to Manila; sent music over the air and photographs over wires; but never, when the heart-beat of their own kind has once stopped, never when the spark of life has fled, have they been able to reanimate the mortal clay with that commonest yet most mysterious of all processes; the vital force. And this man thinks he can—this man alone, out of all the world's teeming billions!

Five minutes that are centuries have gone by. There has been no change in her face or body. He lifts the wad of cotton now because his thumb and forefinger ache from holding it so steadily. And then—

The black puncture has vanished. The indented skin has closed up to erase it. Denholt tries to tell himself that this is due to the moisture of the serum itself or to the pressure of his fingers; but he knows that only life can do that—neither moisture nor pressure if there isn't life. Shrinking from facing disappointment, he whispers aloud: "It's still there; I don't see it, that's all. My eyes aren't sharp enough."

Tottering, he moves around the zinc table, picks up a small mirror, comes back with it. He turns her head slightly, holds the glass to the rigid mouth. Something wavers across it, too nebulous for the eye to discern at first. It comes again, stronger. Like a flurry. The glass mists, then clears. Then it mists once more, unmistakably now.

"The nervous exudation of my own fingers, holding it," he whispers. But he knows better. He drops the mirror as he did the needle. It clashes and shivers into pieces. But it has told him all it could.

There remains the heart to go by. If breath has done that to the glass, the heart will show it. Without the heart, no breath.

He turns her over completely, now, on her back once more. His hand slowly descends to her chest, like a frightened bird spiraling to rest. It leaps up again spasmodically, as though it has received a galvanic shock at what it felt. Not alone a vibration, but warmth. Warmth slowly diffusing around the region of the heart; a lessening of the stone coldness that grips the body elsewhere. The whole chest cavern is slowly rising and falling. The heart is alive, has come back to life, in a dead body. And life is spreading, catching on!

Awed almost beyond endurance—even though he has given up his whole life for this, believing he *could* accomplish it, believing some day it *would* happen—he collapses to his knees, buries his head against the side of the table, sobs broken-heartedly. For extreme joy and extreme sorrow are indistinguishable beyond a certain point. Denholt is a very humble, a very terrified man, at the moment, almost regretting what he had done—he has set God's law at bay, and he knows it. Pride, triumph, the overweening egotism that spells complete insanity will come later.

He rouses himself presently. She still needs help, attention, or he may lose her again. How often that happened with the rabbits until he learned what to do. The warm radiations from the heart have spread all over the body now, and it is a greater warmth than that of his own body. A ruddy flush, a fever-redness, has replaced the dead-white hue, especially over the heart and on the face and throat. It needs a furnace-temperature like this to cause the once-stagnant blood to circulate anew. He snatches up a thermometer, applies it. One hundred and five degrees, high enough to kill her all over again a second time. But death must be burned out and new life infused at a molten heat, for this is not biological birth—but pure chemistry.

He must work fast.

He opens the door of the electric refrigerator, removes a pail of finely chopped ice he had prepared. The fearful heat of almost-boiling blood must be offset or it will destroy her before she has begun again to live. He wraps a rubber sheet around her, packs her body with the chopped ice, rolls her tightly up in it. He tests her temperature repeatedly. Within five minutes it has gone down considerably. The ice has all melted, as if placed on a hot stove. As he opens the sheet streams of water trickle out of the four corners. But the heart and the lungs are still going, the first danger has been met and overcome, the process of revivification has not in itself destroyed her. A delirious groan escaping her lips is the first sound she makes in this second life of hers; a feverish tossing from side to side the first movement. She is in full delirium. But delirium is the antithesis of death; it is the body's struggle to survive.

The laboratory has done all it can for her; from now on it is a matter of routine medical care, nursing, as in an ordinary illness. He wraps her in a thick blanket, unbolts the door, removes her from the cold zinc table and carries her to a bed in a room in another part of the house.

All through the long hours of the day he sits by her, as a mother sits by her only child in mortal illness, counting each breath she takes, feeling her pulse, helping her heart-action with a little digitalis, pouring a little warm milk and brandy down her parched throat from time to time. Watching, waiting, for the second great mystery to unfold itself. A mystery as great or greater than the one he has already witnessed. Will reason return full-panoplied, or will the brain remain dead or crippled in an otherwise living body? Will she be some inarticulate, idiot thing better left unrevived? Or will she remember who she was, what went before— be the first human to bridge the gap of death, to tell the living what awaits them on the other side of the shadowy border?

All through the day the fever-reaction induced by the serum continues—and unconsciousness with it—but she lives. Undeniably she lives! At nightfall the fever increases a little, but then all fevers do; any doctor knows that. At midnight of the second night, a full twenty-four hours after she died, there is a sudden, unexpected break in her heavy breathing, and before the watcher has quite realized it, her eyes are wide open for the first time. She has regained consciousness! For the first time he sees the color of her eyes—blue—as the lids go up. Blue eyes, that have seen death, now looking into his. Calmly, undilated, unfrightened, peaceful.

He hastily takes her temperature. Normal. The serum has at last been accepted by her system. All that remains now is the answer to the second mystery. In medieval terms, has he saved her soul as well as her body? In modern scientific ones, have the accumulated memories of the past existence been carried over into this one, or were her brain cells damaged beyond repair?

The blue eyes fix themselves on him, stare unblinkingly. He says softly, almost afraid of the sound of his own voice, "Good evening." The blue eyes continue to stare. He waits, trembling. He knows that she was an American, knew the language. He whispers it over again, "Good evening, young lady."

A change is coming over her face. The staring blue eyes fill with tears that presently overflow and stream down her face. The eyes themselves narrow in a squint. The lips that knew rouge, cigarettes, and men's kisses, pucker into infant's whimper. A feeble bleating cry, the wail of a new-born child, escapes from her. The wordless, pitiful sound that any nursery knows.

The shock, the disappointment, is terrific; his gaunt face pales, he clutches his chair to keep from slumping off it, lets out a long sighing breath. Then presently, somewhat recovered, he takes out a shiny gold watch from his pocket, dangles it before her eyes. The light flashes from it. The tears stop, the wailing breaks off short. Her eyes sparkle with interest. She reaches toward it with ten fingers whose nails still bear adult nail lacquer; her mouth wreathes in an infantile grin. She says, "Da!" and crows with pleasure. Reason is back—at least in its primary stages. For if she were a new-born infant, this would be a highly precocious reaction. Her faculties are intact. It is not as bad as he thought.

He will have to teach her to speak, to walk all over again, as one does any child, that is all. Intelligence has returned, but not memory. Her memory went into the grave. He murmurs to himself, "Her body is twenty-two, but she is in the infancy of a second life. I will call her Nova, the New One." He rubs his hand over his eyes.

Exhausted by his long vigil he slumps to the floor beside the bed, goes to sleep with his head resting against its edge. Above him the resurrected woman's hands stray gropingly to his thick white hair, clutch playfully at it like a child in its crib. . . .

3

THE PLANE is a hopeless wreck, and even in the act of crawling out into the blinding rain, Penny O'Shaughnessy wonders dazedly why he's still alive. Dazedly, but briefly. O'Shaughnessy is not the kind to waste time wondering. Just one more lucky break, he supposes. His whole adult life has been an unbroken succession of them. His given nickname itself is a token of this, dating from the time he was sighted flying in from the open Caribbean after a particularly devastating hurricane had turned half the Lesser Antilles upside down.

"I just went up over it and waited till it went by below," he explained, alighting midst the splinters of the airport hangar.

"A bad penny always turns up," someone muttered incredulously.

Who else had ever met the business-end of a bolt of lightning in midflight, as he had just now, flying blind through a storm, lost a wing, managed to come down still alive even if it is on a wooded mountainside, to cut the contact at the moment of crashing so that he wasn't roasted alive, and crawl out with just a wrenched shoulder and a lot of cuts and bruises? He couldn't bail out because he was flying too low, hoping for a break through the clouds through which to spot something flat enough to come down on; he doesn't like bailing out anyway, hates to throw away a good plane.

This one lying all over the side of the mountain around him is not so good any more, he has to admit. The first thing he does is feel in his pocket, haul out a rabbit's foot, and stroke it twice. Then he straightens up, hobbles a short distance further from the wreck, turns to survey it. Almost instantly the lightning, which already stunned him once in the air, strikes a nearby tree with a bang and a shower of sparks. It cracks, comes down with a propeller-like whirr of foliage, and flattens what's left of his engine into the ground.

"All right, you don't like my crate," O'Shaughnessy grumbles, with a back-arm swing at the elements in general. "I believed you the first time!"

He trudges off, neck bowed against the rain, which forms a solid curtain around him. He hasn't the faintest idea where he is, because he was flying blind a full forty minutes before the crash. There is no visibility to speak of, just a pall of rain and mist, with the black silhouettes of trees peering through all around. The sharp slant of the ground tells him he's on the mountainside. He takes the downgrade; people, houses, are more often to be found in valleys than on mountains.

The ground is muddy soup around him; he doesn't walk as much as skid on his heels from tree trunk to tree trunk, using them as brakes to prevent a headlong fall. Rain water gets in between clothes and skin; the cuts and welts tingle; the wrenched shoulder pounds, and the thickening of the gloom around him tells him it is night.

"All set," he mutters, "to spend a quiet evening at home!"

The tree trunks blend into the surrounding darkness, and it gets harder to aim for them each time; he has to ski-jump blindly and coast with outspread arms, hoping one will stop him before he lands flat on his face. He misses one altogether—or else it isn't there in the first place—goes skittering down in axle-grease mud, wildly spiraling with his arms to keep his balance, and finally flattens into something that rasps and stings. A barbed-wire fence.

All the air has been knocked out of his stomach, and one of the wicked spines just missed his left eye, taking a gouge at his brow instead. But more than that, the jar he has thrown into the thing has set off an electric alarm bell somewhere up in one of the trees nearby. Its clamor blasts through the steady whine and slap of the rain.

His clothing has caught in ten different places, and skin with it in half of them. As he pulls himself free, swearing, and the vibrations of the obstacle lessen, the alarm breaks off. He kicks the fence vengefully with his foot, and this elicits an added spasm or two from the bell-battery, then once more it stops.

He is too preoccupied for a minute rubbing his gashes with his bare hands and wincing, to proceed with an investigation of this inhospitable barrier. Suddenly a rain-washed glow of murky light is wavering toward him on the other side of the fence, zigzagging uncertainly as though its bearer were picking his way.

"What the—" Somebody living up here in this forsaken place?

The light stops flush against the fence directly opposite where he is standing and behind it he can made out a hooded, cloaked figure. O'Shaughnessy must be practically invisible behind the rain-mist and darkness.

"That yours?" he growls, balling a fist at the fence. "Look what it did to me! Come out here and I'll—!"

A musical voice from below the hood speaks softly: "Who are you? Why are you here?"

"A girl!" O'Shaughnessy gasps, and the anger leaves his voice. "Sorry, I couldn't make you out. Didn't mean to tear loose that way, but I'm clawed up." He stares at her for a long minute. Twenty-three, pretty, he can see that much. Blue eyes gaze levelly back at him from under the hood she is wearing as he steps up closer to the fence. "I cracked up further back along the mountain, the plane came down—"

"What's a plane?" she asks, round-eyed.

His jaw drops slightly and he stares at her with disapproval, thinks she is trying to be cute or something. He keeps waiting for the invitation to shelter that a dog would be given, in such weather, at such an out-of-the-way place as this. It isn't forthcoming.

"Got a house back there?" he says finally.

She nods, and drops of rain fly off her hood. "Yes, straight back there." Just that, answered as asked.

He says with growing impatience, "Well, won't you let me in a few minutes? I won't bite you!" The reason he thinks she's playing a part, knows better, is that her voice is city bred, not like a mountain girl's.

She says helplessly, "It's locked and *he* has the keys. No one ever came here before, so I don't know what to do. I can't ask him because he's in the laboratory, and I'm not allowed to disturb him when he's in there."

"Well, haven't you got a telephone I can use at least?"

"What's a telephone?" she wants to know, without a trace of mockery.

This time O'Shaughnessy flares up. Enough is enough. "What kind of a person are you anyway? All right, keep your shelter. I'm not going to stand here begging. Would it be too much to tell me which direction the nearest road or farmhouse is from here, or would you rather not do that either?"

"I don't know," she answers. "I've never been outside this"— indicating the fence—"never been out there where you're standing."

It's beginning to dawn on him that she's not trying to make fun of him. He senses some mystery about her, and this whole place, but what it is he can't imagine. "Who lives here with you?" he asks curiously.

"Papa," she answers simply.

She's already been missed, for a voice shouts alarmedly: "Nova! Nova, where are you?" And a second lantern looms toward them, zigzagging hurriedly through the mist. A blurred figure emerges, stops short in fright at sight of the man outside the barrier, nearly drops the lantern. "Who's that? Who are you? How'd you get here?" The questions are almost panic-stricken.

"Papa," thinks O'Shaughnessy, "doesn't like company. Wonder

why?" He explains his situation in a few brief words.

The man comes closer, motions the girl back as though O'Shaughnessy were some dangerous animal in a zoo-cage. "Are you alone?" he asks, peering furtively around.

O'Shaughnessy has never lacked self-assertiveness with other men, quite the reverse. "Who'd you think I had with me, the Lafayette Escadrille?" he says bluntly. "Why so cagy, mister? Got a guilty conscience about something? Or are you making mash back there? Did you ever hear of giving a stranger shelter?" He swipes accumulated raindrops off his jaw and flicks them disgustedly down.

The hooded girl is hovering there in the background, looking uncertainly from one to the other. The man with the lantern gives a forced laugh. "We're not trying to hide anything. We're not afraid of anything. You're mistaken," he protests. A protest that rings about as true as a lead quarter to O'Shaughnessy's experienced ears. "I wouldn't for the world want you to—er, go away from here spreading stories that there's anything strange about this place—you know how folks talk, first thing you know they'll be coming around snooping—"

"So that's it," says O'Shaughnessy within his chest.

The man on the other side of the fence has taken a key out, is jabbing it hurriedly at the padlocks. So hurriedly that now he almost seems afraid O'Shaughnessy will get away before he can get the gate open. "Er—won't they send out and look for you, when they find out you're overdue at the airport?"

O'Shaughnessy snaps briefly, "I wasn't expected anywhere. I was flying my own time; the crate belonged to me. What d'ye think, I'm somebody's errand-boy, or one of these passenger-plane pilots?" He expectorates to show his contempt, his independence.

The black shoe-button eyes opposite him gleam, as though this is an eminently satisfactory situation, as though he couldn't ask for a better one. He swings the gate-halves apart. "Come in," he urges with belated insistence. "Come in by all means! Get back in the house, Nova, you'll get soaked—and see that you close *that* door! I'm Doctor Denholt, sir, and please don't think there's anything strange about us here."

"I do already," says O'Shaughnessy, bluntly, as he steps through the enclosure. He cocks his head at the renewed blare of the alarm bell.

Denholt hastily closes and refastens the gate, shutting off the clangor. "Just an ordinary precaution, we're so cut off here," he explains.

O'Shaughnessy refrains from further comment; he is on this man's domain now. He has one iron-clad rule, like an Arab: Never abuse hospitality. "I'm O'Shaughnessy," he says. They shake hands briefly. The doctor's hand is slender and flexible, that of a skilled surgeon. But it is soft, too, and there is a warning of treachery in that pliability.

He leads his uninvited guest into the lamp-lighted house, which looks mighty good to O'Shaughnessy, warm and dry and cheerful in spite of its ugly, rustic furniture. The girl has discarded her cape and hood; O'Shaughnessy glimpses her in the main room, crouched before the clay-brick fireplace readying a fire, as Denholt ushers him into his own bedroom. Her hair, he sees now, is long and golden; her feet are stockingless in home-made deerskin moccasins, her figure slim and childlike in a cheap little calico dress.

At the rear of the room is a door tightly closed. The flyer's trained eyes, as they flicker past it, notice two things. It is metal, specially constructed, unlike the crude plank-panels of the rest of the house. A thread of platinum-bright light outlines it on three sides, too intense to be anything but high-voltage electricity. Electricity in there, coal-oil out here.

He hears the girl: "He's in the laboratory, I'm not allowed to disturb him when he's in there."

He hears the man: "See that you close *that* door."

He says to himself: "I wonder what's in back of there."

In Denholt's sleeping-quarters he peels off his drenched things, reveals a bodyful of livid welts, barbed-wire lacerations, and black grease smudges. His host purses his lips in long-forgotten professional inspection. "You *are* pretty badly scraped up! Better let me fix up some of those cuts for you, that barbed-wire's liable to be rusty. Just stand there where you are a minute." He takes the water-logged clothing outside to the girl.

O'Shaughnessy crooks a knowing eyebrow at himself, waiting there. "Why not in the laboratory, where he keeps all his stuff and the light's better? See no evil, think no evil, I guess."

Denholt hurries back with hot water, dressings, antiseptic. O'Shaughnessy flinches at the searing touch of it, grins shamefacedly even as he does so, "Can't take it any more, I guess. In Shanghai once I had to have a bad tooth pulled by a local dentist;

his idea of an anaesthetic was to have his daughter wave a fan at me while he hit it out with a mallet and steel bar."

"Did you yell?"

"Naw. Ashamed to in front of a girl."

He catches Denholt staring with a peculiar intentness at his bared torso and muscular shoulders. "Pretty husky, aren't you?" the doctor remarks, offhandedly. But something chilly passes down the flyer's back at the look that goes with the words. O'Shaughnessy wonders what it means. Or do all doctors look at you that way, sort of calculatingly, as though you'd do nicely for some experiment they had in mind?

"Yep," he answers almost challengingly, "I guess I can take care of myself all right if I have to."

Denholt just looks at him with veiled guile.

4

OUTSIDE AFTERWARD, at the rough pine-board table set in the cheerful glow of the blazing hearth, Denholt's borrowed clothes on him, he has a better chance to study the girl at closer range. There is nothing strange about her in the least; she is all youthful animation, her face flushed with the excitement of having a stranger at their board; sits there devouring him with her eyes, as if she never saw an outsider before. But in her talk and in her movements there is perfect rhythm, harmony, coordination, balance, call it what you will; she is an utterly normal young girl.

The old man on the other hand—O'Shaughnessy characterizes him mentally thus—the old man has this brooding light in his eyes, is spasmodic and disconnected in his talk and gestures. The isolation, the years of loneliness, have done that to him perhaps, O'Shaughnessy thinks.

"All right," he says to himself, "that's his own business. But why does he keep a lovely kid like that cooped up here? Never heard of a plane, a telephone. What's he trying to do to her? Darned shame!"

Denholt catches him watching the girl. "Eat," he urges, "eat up, man. You need strength after what you went through."

The flyer grins, obeys. Yet something about the way it was said, the appraising look that went with it, makes him feel like a fowl being fattened for slaughter. He shakes his head baffledly.

Lightning keeps flaring like flashlight-powder outside the windowpanes every half-minute or so; there is an incessant roll of celestial drums all up and down the mountainside, so deep that O'Shaughnessy can feel it in his chest at times; the rain on the roof sounds like a steak frying.

Denholt is staring abstractedly into his plate, fingers drumming soundlessly on the table. O'Shaughnessy turns to the girl, to break the silence. "Have you lived here long?"

"Two years."

His eyebrows move a little, upward. She doesn't know what a plane is, a phone? "Where'd you live before then?"

"I was born here," she answers shyly.

He thinks she's misunderstood. "You look older than two to me," he says with a laugh.

The point seems to baffle her too, as if it has never occurred to her before. "That's as far back as I can remember," she says slowly. "Last spring, and the spring before, when I was learning to talk and walk—that's two years, isn't it? How long ago did you learn to talk?"

He can't answer; a chunk of rabbit has gone down whole; he's lucky he doesn't choke. But it isn't the bolted rabbit that stiffens the hairs on the back of his neck, puts a needle of fear through his heart.

"That'll do, Nova," says Denholt sharply. There's a strain around the eyes. His fork drops with a clash, as if he has just had a fright. "You'll find—er, some cigarettes in a drawer in my bedroom for Mr. O'Shaughnessy." And as soon as she's left the table, he leans forward confidentially toward the flyer. "I'd better give you a word of explanation. She's not quite—right." He touches his own head. "That's why—the fence and all that. I keep her secluded up here with me, it's more humane you know. Don't take anything she says too seriously."

O'Shaughnessy won't commit himself on this point, not even by a monosyllable. Just looks at his host, keeps his own counsel. It sounds reasonable enough, Lord knows, but he can't forget the girl's clear, sane eyes, nor Denholt's hungry, probing, almost gloating, stare. If anyone is crazy in this house—the little chill plays on his spine once more, and his flesh crawls under the borrowed clothes.

They have very little to say to one another, after that, while they sit there puffing away and the fire in the hearth slowly dies down into itself. The girl is in the adjoining room, washing the dishes. The waning fire throws the two men's shadows on the walls, long and wavering. Denholt's in particular, looks like that of a monster breathing smoke out of its nostrils. O'Shaughnessy grins a little at the idea.

He crushes out his cigarette. "Well," he says, "looks like the storm'll keep up all night. Guess I better make a break for it."

Denholt stiffens, then smiles. "You're not thinking of leaving *now?* You'll spend the rest of the night wandering around in circles out there in the dark! Wait till daylight at least, maybe it'll let up by then. There's an extra room back there, you won't be any trouble at all."

The girl says from the doorway, almost frightenedly, "Oh, please, don't go yet, Mr. O'Shaughnessy! It's so nice having you."

She waits for his answer.

O'Shaughnessy gives them both a long look in turn. Then he uncrosses his long legs, recrosses them the other way around. "I'm staying, then," he says quietly.

Denholt gets up. "I've a little work to finish—something I was in the midst of when—er, your arrival interrupted me. If you'll excuse me for a few minutes—you can go to bed any time you feel like it." And then, with a covert glance toward the kitchen doorway, "Just bear in mind what I said. Don't take anything she says too seriously."

The girl comes in after the doctor has gone, sits shyly down on the opposite side of the cleared table. That strange hungry look of hers rests steadily on his face, as if she never had seen anyone like him before.

"I'm glad you're staying," she murmurs finally. "I wanted you to because—well, maybe if you're here, I won't have to take my injection."

O'Shaughnessy droops his lids a little. "What kind of an injection?" he says with almost somnolent slowness.

She turns her hand up, down again. "I don't know, I only know I have to take them. About once a month. He says it's bad for me if I miss any. Tomorrow would be the day, if you hadn't come." She screws up her eyes at him pathetically. "I don't like them, because they hurt so, and they make me feel so ill afterward. Once I tried to run away, but I couldn't get through the fence."

There's something a little flinty in O'Shaughnessy's eyes that wasn't there before. "And what'd he do when he caught you?" His own hand on the table flexes a little.

"Oh nothing. Just talked to me, told me I had to have them whether I liked it or not. He said it was for my own sake he gives them to me. He said if I went too long without getting one—"

"What would happen?"

"He didn't say. Just said something pretty awful."

O'Shaughnessy growls to himself deep in his throat. Drugging, eh? Maybe that's why she can't remember further back than two years, and why she says such weird things from time to time. But on second thought, it can't be that, either. The infrequency of the injections argue against it. There wouldn't be pain, if it were some kind of a drug. And if it were something able to affect her memory of the far past, why not the recent past as well? O'Shaughnessy's no medical man, but he's knocked around enough to know a little something; in the Orient and South America he's seen the telltale traces of almost every known narcotic under the sun. There is absolutely no sign of it about Nova. She is as fresh as that rain falling from the sky outside.

He only asks her one question, to make sure. "Do you dream—dream about pretty things—after you've had one of these shots?"

"No," she shudders, "I feel like I'm all on fire. I woke up once and there was all ice around me—"

Not a drug, then. Maybe he has Denholt all wrong; maybe she really does need these treatments—vaccine or serum it sounds like—maybe she had some ghastly illness that robbed her of her memory, the use of her limbs, two years ago, and these injections are to speed her recovery, guard her against a relapse. Still, Denholt did try to pass her off as mentally unbalanced, when she isn't at all. No, there's something the man is up to—something secret and—and ugly. The barbed-wire fence, the alarm-bell show that too. Why bring her way up here when she could have far better care and attention—*if* she needs any—at a hospital in one of the big cities?

"Did you really mean what you said about only learning to walk and talk the spring before last?"

"Yes," she says. "I'll show you one of the copy-books he taught me out of." She comes back with a dog-eared primer.

He thumbs through it. "C is for Cat. Does-the-Cat-see-the-Rat?" He closes it, more at sea than ever.

"Were you as big as now when he taught you to walk?"

"Yes. I wore this same dress I have on now, that's how I can tell. I learned by myself, mostly. He used to put me down on the floor over there by the wall, and then put a lump of sugar on a chair all the way across the room, and coax me to walk over to get it. If I crawled on my hands and knees, he wouldn't let me have the sugar. After awhile I got so I could stand up straight—"

"Stop!" he says, with a sudden sharp intake of breath. "It's enough to make a person go crazy just trying to figure out! There's—there's craziness in it somewhere! And I know on whose part. Not yours! God knows what he did to you the first twenty years of your life to make you forget everything you should have known—"

She doesn't answer. She can't seem to understand what he means. But her eyes show fright at the force of his speech. He sees he may do more harm than good by telling her other people aren't like she is. She's grown up, and she's been held here in some kind of mental thralldom—that's the closest he can get to the answer. And the man that would do that to another human being is a monster and a maniac.

His voice hoarse with pity and anger, he says, "Tell me now, did you ever see any other man but me and the doctor before in your life?"

"No," she breathes, "that's why I like you so much."

"Didn't you even ever see another girl—have someone like yourself around you to talk with?"

"No," she murmurs again. "Only him. No one else at all."

He rises as if he can't stand any more of it, takes three quick turns around his chair, raises it, bangs it down again.

She watches him timidly, not speaking, with just that fright in her eyes. He slumps down in his chair again, looks at her broodingly. Somehow he knows he's going to take her with him when he leaves, and he wonders if he has any right to. What'll he do with her afterward—turn her loose like a lamb among wolves? Drag her around with him from bar to cantina to bistro, when he's not up in the air risking his neck for some Chinese war lord or Nicaraguan outlaw? His kind of a life—At least she has peace here, and a sort of security.

The bolts shoot back behind the laboratory door. He sees her glance past him, but doesn't turn his head to look. On the wall opposite Denholt's long wavering silhouette appears more ominous now than before. Madman, criminal, samaritan—which? Playing the role of God to this girl—in some obscure way that O'Shaughnessy cannot fathom even yet—which he has no right to do. Better the cantinas and the tropical hell-holes of his own life. If she has anything in her, she'll rise above them; this way she hasn't even a chance to do that.

Her quick whisper reaches him while Denholt is in the act of closing the door after him. "Don't let him give me another injection. Maybe if *you* ask him not to he'll listen to you!"

"You've had your last!" O'Shaughnessy says, decisively.

Denholt approaches the table, looks suspiciously from one to the other. Then a smile crosses his face. "Still up, eh? How about a nice hot toddy for both of us before we turn in?" Nova makes a move to leave her chair and he quickly forestalls her. "I'll fix it myself."

O'Shaughnessy doesn't miss that. He stares up into the other's face, takes his time about answering. "Why not?" he says, finally, jutting out his chin.

Denholt goes into the kitchen. O'Shaughnessy can see him pouring whiskey into two tumblers, spooning sugar, from where he is. The doctor keeps looking obliquely out at him from time to time, with a sort of smirk of satisfaction on his face.

O'Shaughnessy says quietly to the girl, sitting there feasting her eyes on him with a doglike devotion: "Go over there to my coat, hanging up over the fireplace. You'll find an oil-silk packet in the inside pocket, full of papers and things. Take the papers out and just bring me the folder. Don't let him see you."

He thrusts the moisture-proof oblong down just under the collar of his shirt, buttons the neck over it, stretches the collarband out as far as it will go, to create a gap. Then he bends forward a little, sticks his elbows on the table, rests his chin on his hands. His upthrust arms obscure his chest and neck. He drawls something she doesn't understand—one more of the many incomprehensible things he is always saying: "I can smell a Mickey a mile away."

Denholt comes in with the two toddies, says to her, "You'd better go to your room now, Nova, it's getting late, and you're going to need all your strength. *Tomorrow,* you know."

She shivers when she hears that, slowly withdraws under the

compulsion of Denholt's stare, sending appealing looks at
O'Shaughnessy. A door closes after her somewhere in the back.

Denholt has noticed the telegraphic communication between
them. "I don't know what my ward has been telling you—" he
begins.

O'Shaughnessy is not showing his cards yet. "Not a thing, Doc,"
he says. "Not a thing. Why? Is there something she *could* tell?"

"No, no, of course not," Denholt covers up hastily. "Only—
er, she gets delusions about injections and things. That's why I
don't allow her in the laboratory any more. She caught me giving
a rabbit an injection one day, and she'd be perfectly capable of
telling you that it was *she* I gave it to, and what's more, believing
it herself. Let's drink up, shall we?"

He hands his guest one of the two glasses. O'Shaughnessy takes
it with one hand, keeps the other cupped along the line of his
jaw. He hoists it an eighth of an inch. "Here's to *tomorrow.*"

Denholt's piercing gaze transfixes him for a minute. Then he
relaxes into a slow, derisive smile. "Here's to *tonight,*" he con-
tradicts, "tomorrow will take care of itself."

O'Shaughnessy thrusts the rim of his glass up under his lower
lip, slowly levels it until it is horizontal—and empty. The forked
hand supporting his chin is between it and Denholt. He's a sloppy
drinker, the collar of his shirt gets a little wet. . . .

The yellow-green of the doctor's oil lamp recedes waveringly
from the doorway of the bedroom O'Shaughnessy is to occupy.
Pitch blackness wells up all around, cut by an occasional calcium-
flare of lightning outside the high, small window. The flashes are
less frequent now and the rain has let up.

O'Shaughnessy is lying flat on his back, on the rickety cot. He
has left on his trousers and shirt. Denholt said, perhaps with
ghastly double meaning, "I'm sure you'll be dead to the world in
no time at all!" as he went out just now. The first thing the flyer
does, as the waning lamp glow finally snuffs out altogether and
a door closes somewhere in the distance, is to take out the bulging
waterlogged oil-silk envelope from his shirt and let its contents
trickle silently onto the floor.

The rustle of the slackening rain outside begins to lull his senses
before he knows it. The ache of his wrenched shoulder lessens, is
erased by oncoming sleep. The lids of his eyes droop closed. He
catches them the first time, holds them open by sheer willpower.

Not a sound, not a whisper comes to help him keep awake. The lonely mountain house is deathly still; only the rain and the far-off thunder sound outside. The girl's story begins to take on a dream-like quality, unreal, remote, fantastic—

The muffled creak of a pinewood floor-board, somewhere just beyond the open door of his room, jerks his senses awake. At first he thinks he's still at the stick of his plane, makes vague motions to keep from going into a tailspin. . . . Then he remembers where he is.

Twenty minutes, half an hour, an hour maybe, since Denholt's murky lamp-glow flickered away from the door. Maybe even more than that. O'Shaughnessy swears at himself mentally for fading out like this. But it's all right; if this is it now—

It must be deep in the night. There's no rain now any more, just the plink of loose drops as they detach themselves one by one from the eaves. A pale silver radiance, little more than a phantom glint, is coming through the window up over him. Dawn? No, a late moon, veiled by the last of the storm clouds.

The creak is repeated, closer at hand, a little more distinct this time. He can hear breathing with it. Outstretched there on the cot, he begins drawing up his knees closer to his body, tensing himself for the spring. What'll *he* have—a knife, a gun, some viciously-keen surgical instrument? O'Shaughnessy widens his arms, into a sort of simulation of a welcoming embrace. The dark hides the great fists, the menacing grin at his mouth.

Something comes over the threshold. O'Shaughnessy can *sense* the stirring of air at its furtive passage, rather than see or hear anything. There's a whispered footfall within the room itself. A blur of motion glides momentarily through the wan silvery light, which isn't strong enough to focus it clearly, into the concealing dark on his side of it.

There's a clang from the bucked cot-frame, the upward fling of a body, a choked sound of fright as a pair of arms lash out in a bear-hug. In the soft purring tones of a tea-kettle O'Shaughnessy's voice pours out unprintable maledictions.

Her softness warns him just in time, before he's done more than pinion her arms fast and drive all the breath out of her body. "Don't," she pants, "it's me." His arms drop away, he blows out breath like a steam-valve, the reaction staggers him back a step to the wall, off balance. "You! Why didn't you whisper a warning? I was—"

"I was afraid he'd hear me. He's in the laboratory. He left the door open behind him and I've been watching him from outside in the dark—"

"What's he think he's going to do, give you one of them shots again?"

"No, it's you—he's going to do something to you, I don't know what! He took your coat in there, and took all the papers in it and burned them. Then he—he lit flames under all those big glass things, and put a needle in a pan to soak, like he does with me. But this time he has a silk cord in there with him, and he made a big loop in it and measured it round his own neck first, then took it off again and practiced throwing it and pulling it tight. He's got a big black thing in there too, you hold it this way and point it—"

"A gun," says O'Shaughnessy softly, mockingly. "He's not missing any bets, is he? Knockout drops, a noose, a positive. How's he fixed for hand grenades?"

She puts the flats of her hands against his chest. "Don't stay, please! I don't want—things like that to happen to you! Go before he gets through! He's awfully quick and strong, you ought to see how he ran after me that time when I tried to get to the fence! Maybe you can sneak by outside the door without his seeing you, or get out one of the windows—Don't stand there without moving like that! Please don't wait. That's why I came in here to you. There's steam coming from the pan the needle's in already. I saw it!" And then, in a low heartbroken wail, "Aren't you going to go?"

Instead he sits down on the edge of the cot, leisurely puts on the soiled canvas shoes Denholt has lent him. Reaches toward her, draws her over, and stands her before him.

"Nova, d'you like me?" he says.

"I like you very much."

He rubs his hair awry with one hand, as though at his wits' end. "Don't be givin' me any blarney now. D'you want to marry me?"

"What's marry?"

"I ought to be shot," he says softly to himself. "Well—d'you want to be with me always, go wherever I go, tell me how good I am when I'm good, buck me up when I'm down in the dumps— and one of these days, pretty soon, wear black for me?"

"Yes," she says softly, "I want to be near you. If that's to marry, then that's what I want."

He puts out his hand at her. "Shake, Mrs. O'Shaughnessy! Now let's get out of here." He goes over to the door, looks out at the distant bar of light escaping across their path from the open laboratory-door. "Got anything you want to bring with you? You're standing in the middle of your wardrobe right now, I guess. Got any idea where he keeps that key?"

"The one to the padlock on the gate outside? In the pockets of his coat, I guess; he always seems to reach in there for it. He hasn't got it on, though; he's got on that white thing he wears in the laboratory. It must be in the room where he sleeps."

"Okay, we'll try lifting it. I wouldn't mind roughing that bird up, only I don't want anything to happen to you. He's probably got an aim, with that gun of his, like a cockeyed nervewreck with palsy. Stick close behind me."

5

THEY GLIDE through the velvety dark, O'Shaughnessy in the lead, the girl behind him, keeping contact with her fingers resting lightly against the back of his shoulder. The vague outline of the room doorway seems to move toward them, not they toward it, to come abreast, to slip past. Ahead there is just that bar sinister of bleaching whiteness, falling across the floor of the main room and leaping up one wall.

"Gotta watch these boards," he breathes across his shoulder, "you woke me up getting in here, and you don't weigh what I do." The touch of her fingers against his back tells him she's shaking all over. "It's all right. You're with me now."

A board whimpers a little, and he gets off it with catlike litheness before it goes into a full-bodied creak. The gash of laboratory whiteness comes slowly nearer, outlining the angles of things even beyond its own radius. This house, he thinks, is as black physically as it is in spirit. Little tinkering, puttering sounds become audible from the still-distant laboratory, magnified in the stillness. Mania at its preparations.

She signals with her fingertips, abreast of an open door. "In here?" he whispers. They turn aside and glide through. "Stand here right beside the door where I can find you again. I'll see if I can locate his coat."

He does after a lot of cautious circling and navigation; it is hanging from a peg in the wall. He finds the key very quickly, though to her it must seem forever that he's standing there fumbling with the coat. He slips back to her, jaunty with his own peculiar jauntiness even in this eerie situation. "Got it. Now here we go."

Outside again. Step by step through the silence and the blackness, the triangular wedge of white ahead the only visible thing. A board barks treacherously under him, this time before he can withdraw his foot. They stand rigid, while the echoes move into the night. The tinkering has stopped abruptly. Questioning silence from the laboratory now. O'Shaughnessy nudges her with his elbow, and they draw in against the wall.

Not a sound from the laboratory. The bar of escaping light, narrow as a candlestick until now, slowly, insinuatingly, broadens out fan-shaped as the door behind it silently widens. A silhouette bisects it, Denholt's outline thrown before him over the floor and up the wall, rigid, standing just within the opening, listening.

The grin has come back to O'Shaughnessy's face; he reaches behind him and squeezes her throbbing wrist reassuringly. It seems so long ago that he was last afraid of anything. Seventeen, was he then? Eighteen? Sometimes he thinks he's missing a lot by being like this—fear gives life a fillip. He wonders how it is he lost it all, and what there is—if anything—ever to bring it back.

One thing's sure, she's being afraid for the both of them, and plenty left over; her pulse is a whipcord under the thumb that is holding her wrist.

The silhouette moves at last, begins to recede within the lighted room. The noise that conjured it up, like a genie out of a bottle, hasn't been repeated. The tinkerings and drippings resume where they left off. Only the path of light remains wider than before, a ticklish gap to bridge undiscovered. When they are almost abreast of it and can hear Denholt's breathing inside. O'Shaughnessy stops, gropes behind him, draws Nova around in front of him. He transfers the padlock key to her palm, closes her fingers over it. "I want to be sure you make that gate, no matter what. Take a deep breath and get across that lighted place. Don't be afraid, I'm right here backing you up."

She edges forward, cranes her neck toward the open door.

Apparently Denholt's back is toward it. She takes a quick soundless sidestep, with instinctive feminine deftness, and is on the other side of the luminous barrier. He can see her there anxiously waiting for him to join her.

A moment later he is beside her again, bringing with him a quick bird's-eye glimpse of white-coated form bent over, laboriously pouring something from a retort into a hypodermic-barrel. In the background a pair of operating tables, not just one. One an improvised one—planks bridging two chairs, with a rubber sheet draped over them. "Doubleheader coming up," thinks O'Shaughnessy. "Rain—no game."

She is tugging insistently at his arm, but he is suddenly resistant, immobile. She turns her face up toward his. "O'Shaughnessy, come on! Any minute he's—"

"My rabbit's foot. He's got it in there with him, in my coat. I couldn't go without it—"

"O'Shaughnessy, he'll kill you."

"Him and what sextet? Get over there to the door, kid, and start working on it. I want you in the clear in case that gun of his starts going boom. I've got to go in after my lucky paw, no two ways about it." He has to jog her, push her slightly, to get her to tear herself away from him. Finally she slips off in the dark with a little whimper of protest. He waits there until a faint clicking comes from the main door. Then a bolt grates miserably as she clears it, and there is sudden, startled silence from within the gleaming laboratory.

O'Shaughnessy, muscles taut as wires, rounds the angle of the doorframe, unhurried, casual. Digs a thumb at the man in the white jacket who has just whirled to face the door. "My coat, Doc. I'm leaving."

Denholt has just finished putting down the loaded needle he was preparing. The gun the girl mentioned is on the table, but under his hand already.

"So you think you're leaving? You're very foolish, my friend. It would have been easier to sleep, the way I meant you to. No fright, no last-minute agony. You would not have seen your own death."

"No fright, no agony this way either." O'Shaughnessy calmly reaches for his coat, extracts the charm, stuffs it into his trouser pocket. "Don't be so handy burning my identification papers next time," he says, "or I'll slap your head all the way around your neck—"

The gun is up now, level with his chest.

Behind them in the darkness the heavy outer door swings open with a grinding whirr. Denholt takes a quick step forward. O'Shaughnessy doesn't move from before him, blocking his way. He's flexing his wrists slightly, in and out.

A patter of quick, light footsteps recedes outside in the open, flying over the clayey rain-wet ground.

"Who's that?"

"Who should it be? That's the girl. I'm taking her with me."

Denholt's face is a sudden mask of dismay. "You can't!" he cries shrilly. "You don't know what it means, you fool! You can't take her out into the world with you! She's got to stay here, she needs *me!*" He raises his voice to a frenzied shout. "Nova! Come back here!"

"That's your story and you're stuck with it." O'Shaughnessy raises his own voice, in a bull rumble. He shifts dead-center in front of the leveled gun, to keep Denholt from snaking past around him.

"Get out of my way, or I'll shoot you dead. I didn't want to puncture your skin, damage any vital organ, but if I have to, you're the loser! Nothing can bring you back then, do you hear me, nothing can bring you back! You'll *stay* dead!"

O'Shaughnessy just stands, crouched a little, measuring him with his eyes. O'Shaughnessy is a gambler; he senses a reluctance on Denholt's part to shoot him, and he plays on it for what it's worth. Instead of giving ground before the weapon, he takes a sidling step in, and another.

The alarm-bell begins ringing somewhere off in the dripping trees. . . . She's got the last barrier open, she's made it.

A sudden taut cord down the side of Denholt's neck reveals to O'Shaughnessy the muscular signal sent down to his unseen trigger finger. He swerves like a drunk. A foreshortened bar of orange, like a tube-light, seems to solder the two of them together for a second. Noise and smoke come later. O'Shaughnessy isn't aware of pain, only knows that he's been hit somewhere and mustn't be hit any more. He has the gun hand in his own now, ten fingers obeying two different brains, clutching a single weapon. It goes off again, and again, and again—four, five, six times.

O'Shaughnessy is hitting Denholt on the side of his head with his free arm, great, walloping, pile-driver blows. The two of them stagger together, like partners in a crazy dance. Glass is breaking all around them. Gray smoke from the six shots, pink-and-white dust from the chipped brick-and-plaster walls, swirl around them in a rainbow haze. Something vividly green flares up from one of the overturned retorts, goes right out again. O'Shaughnessy tears the emptied gun away, flings it off somewhere. More breaking glass, and this time a tart pungent smell that makes the nostrils sting. The crunch of pulverized tube glass underfoot makes it sound as if they were scuffling in sand or hard-packed snow.

O'Shaughnessy can't hit with his left arm, he notices; the shoulder blocks off the brain-message each time. He just uses that arm to hold Denholt where his right-hand blows can find him. He has lost track of the other's left hand for a moment, it comes back again around his body from somewhere, with a warning flash to it. Scalpel or something.

O'Shaughnessy dives, breaks, puts space between them. A downward hiss misses his chest barrel, he pounces, traps the arm before it can come up again, vises it between his own arm and upthrust thigh, starts forcing it out of joint. The thing drops with a musical ting! He scuffs it aside, takes a quick step back to get driving-force, sends a shattering haymaker in. Denholt topples, skids through broken tube-glass, lies there stunned, tilted on one elbow.

O'Shaughnessy, his shoulder throbbing with pain like a bass drum, pants grimly: "Now—got it through your head I'm taking her?" He turns and shuffles unsteadily toward the door.

Denholt is trying to struggle up, gabbling: "You're taking her to her death!"

The alarm bell keeps pealing, waiting. O'Shaughnessy stumbles out of the laboratory, on through the darkness toward the front door. Cool, dank, before-dawn air swirls about him. He turns and sees Denholt outlined there behind him in the lighted doorway, where he has dragged himself, hanging weakly onto the frame, holding up one arm in imprecation—or in warning.

"Remember what I'm saying. You're dooming her. This is the thirtieth of June—remember this date, remember it well! You'll know, you'll know soon enough! You'll come crawling back to me—with her—begging me to help you! You'll get down on your bended knees to me, you'll grovel at my feet—that'll be my hour!"

"Have another shot—on me," O'Shaughnessy growls back from the darkness under the trees.

"You're not taking her out to life, you're taking her out to her death—the most awful death a human being ever experienced!"

The shrieking, maddened voice dwindles away behind him in the house, and he can make out Nova waiting tremblingly for him at the opened barbed-wire barrier. He stumbles to her through the mud of the storm-wrack, holding his bullet-seared shoulder. He grins and drawls in that quiet way of his above the slackening noise of the exhausted alarm-bell: "H'lo, Mrs. O'Shaughnessy. Shall we go now?"

He takes her arm.

6

O'SHAUGHNESSY, DICKERING with a man named Tereshko at the bar of the Palmer House, Chicago, excuses himself, steps into a booth to call his North Side flat.

"Why not have your wife join us for dinner?" Tereshko says. "Say, at the Chez Paree. We can talk business to music just as well as here."

"Great," says O'Shaughnessy. Business after all is a form of warfare; you bring all your available weapons to bear. If you don't you're a fool. You could call Nova O'Shaughnessy's illuminating beauty that of a star-shell. If he uses it to help dazzle this wary gentleman he is trying to dent, it doesn't mean he values it any the less himself.

So he says into the phone: "Nova, I want you to meet me at Chez Paree. I've got a man with me. He's looking for a pilot, and he's talking big money, so be as beautiful as you can. Take a cab, honey." Nova is still new to the city streets. "Just one thing. Any offer under seventy-five hundred and you give me a look, much as to say, 'Isn't he funny?' Get it? And not a word about—that place on the mountain, of course."

At the Paree they order a table for three. They've been drinking a good deal, and Tereshko is beginning to show it. He isn't drunk but he loses some of his caginess. Loosens up, so to speak.

"You had much experience locating mining claims from the air?" he resumes.

"No, just flying. But as I understand it, all you want is to be piloted up there, so you can look them over yourself. I can guarantee to do that for you. All I need's the general direction and plenty of gas."

It's obvious that money isn't the hitch. This Tereshko has that written all over him, in a flashy uncouth sort of way. His hesitancy—and O'Shaughnessy is a good judge of men's motives—seems to stem from caution, as though he wants to make sure whom he's dealing with first before he puts all his cards on the table. He can't doubt by now that O'Shaughnessy's an experienced enough flier to get him anywhere he wants to go, after the clippings and documents he's been showing him all afternoon long.

"Of course," Tereshko feels his way, offering the applicant a cigarette out of a platinum case with an emerald catch, "what I'm mainly interested in is to see that the whole undertaking is kept strictly between ourselves. I don't want known to anyone what its object or destination is. No one at all, is that clear? Not even after it's been wound up."

"I can give you a guarantee on that too. I'm no loudspeaker."

"No, you seem like the sort that minds his own business—that's why I approached you in the first place." He—very unwisely—signals for another drink.

Tereshko relaxes still further. "I don't mind telling you," he admits, "that the whole mine-location business was just camouflage. What I'm looking for is already mined and minted, only it was put back in the ground. And it's all the way around the compass from where I said. Not British Columbia at all, but in one of the Florida keys, we think. Maybe one of the Bahamas. I suppose that gives you the clue. Well, it looks like you're our man, so there's no harm in your knowing."

"Pirate stuff, eh?"

"Yes and no," says Tereshko. "Certainly was a pirate all right, but he dates from prohibition days and not Captain Kidd's time. Guess you know who I mean now."

O'Shaughnessy doesn't, but it doesn't cost anything to let the other think so.

"He won't get out until, let's see—" A pecan-sized diamond flames as he figures on his fingers. "1948, or is it '50? Hell, he was a great guy and all that," he goes on by way of self-excuse, "but you can't blame the rest of us. After all, we're getting older every day. He got his, why shouldn't we get ours? He's served two years of his sentence—why should we wait?"

"Then you have no right to it?"

"Any more than he had!" snaps the other. "It's nobody's money. It don't even belong to the saps he got it from, because he gave 'em needle-beer for it at four bits a throw."

"One way of looking at it," says O'Shaughnessy non-commitally.

"What other way of looking at it is there? Is it doing anybody any good lying where it is in the ground? We wouldn't have to go to all this trouble only—you see banks were no good, nor safe-deposit boxes nor anything else, because his trouble was—Government trouble. He musta seen it coming up. We didn't, but he musta, because we all remember how just before it happened he went off on a cruise down Florida waters in his motor yacht. Just him and a small crew to run the thing for him and, oh yes, some girl he was playing around with at the time. None of *us,* not one of us. We all thought that was funny, too, because he was a guy loved company. Until then he'da caught cold without the bunch of us being around him all the time. Well funnier still, just before turning back they touch at Havana. Him and this dame go ashore and nobody else's allowed to leave the boat. Then, on very sudden orders from him, the yacht leaves Havana—without him and the girl coming back to it. It's supposed to pick them up later at Bimini or something. It was never seen in one piece again. A piece of charred wood was picked up later with its name on it. Must have been destroyed at sea by an explosion, and not a soul aboard escaped alive. Funny, huh, to send it on ahead like that, when it could have waited right in the harbor for them? They were the only two it had to cater to."

"Funny is right, but not for laughing," O'Shaughnessy agrees.

"Just when we were getting out our black neckties and armbands, a cable comes from him. 'Hope you're not worried, I'm okay, taking the next plane north, and wasn't that a terrible accident?' Thirty days later to the hour, Uncle Sam jumps on his neck and—" He pinches his fingers together, kisses them, flies them apart. "How much turned up, when the smoke had cleared away? Five grand. Why, he used to carry as much as that around in his pocket for change! Does it look like I'm right, or does it look like I'm right? Every other lead we've had since then has petered out. It took us long enough to tumble, but now I think we've got it added up right. Now, d'you think you can help us swing it?"

O'Shaughnessy shrugs. "What's hard about it? I can taxi you around for a month, two months, as long as it takes you to locate it. An amphibian is the answer, of course. Now there's this: you'll have to stake me to the plane. I banged my own up week before last—that's when I got this busted shoulder. Don't get the idea I can't fly—lightning butted in, that was all."

"We'll provide you with the plane," Tereshko assures him. "You shop around and pick up what you think you'll need, and you can keep it, as an extra bonus, when we get back."

"Just how long will I last after that to enjoy the use of it?" wonders O'Shaughnessy knowingly. But that isn't really a deterrent—people have thought they'd get rid of him, once he's served his purpose, before now—and haven't made a go of it. These fellows'll find that out too.

"The wren would come in handy for a guide—did you ever think of contacting her?" he says thoughtfully.

"Did we think?" scoffs the other. "His cell door wasn't closed behind him yet before we started to put on the pressure. Well we put it on too heavy. We had her figured all wrong. It just happens she was one of those innocent babes, hadn't known what it was all about until the lid blew off—musta thought he made his dough in stocks and bonds or something."

O'Shaughnessy makes that derisive sound with his lips commonly known as the raspberry.

"No, that's what we thought too," Tereshko assures him, "but it was on the level. He used to tell us everything was on the up-and-up between them—you know what I mean, and she wasn't really his moll. . . . He called her his madonna—"

"Machine-gun madonna," chuckles O'Shaughnessy.

"He was going to marry her. She was only a kid, seventeen or something like that. Well, between the shock of finding out who she'd been mixed up with, and us putting the pressure on her, the poor dame never had a chance. She claimed she didn't know anything that went on during that cruise. So then we lock her up in a dark garage overnight, to frighten her into talking. We frightened her all right, but not into talking. Just our luck—he'd never let her cut her hair, said she looked like an angel with it long. So she has a hairpin to unlock the engines of all the cars in there—and there was about six of them—and starts them all turning over and breathes the monoxide until she's gone. With a kitten he gave her still in her arms."

"Fine note." O'Shaughnessy scowls sympathetically. Not with them, but with the harried, friendless girl in the garage.

Tereshko grins.

"Yeah, ain't it? Of all the dirty tricks! We hadda leave her lie in there all next day. Then we sneaked her out after dark, carried her miles away, and planted her somewhere else. I never even read about them finding her. If they did, they never tumbled to who she was, not a word about it came out in the pa—"

"Here's my wife," O'Shaughnessy interrupts, standing up. He's sighted her across Tereshko's shoulder as she comes in from the street just then, stands there a second, looks around. She's something to look at, as she locates them, starts over toward them, with a smile for him on her face.

Tereshko, whose chair is facing the other way, follows him to his feet, turning around to greet her as he does so.

O'Shaughnessy is saying, "Nova, meet Mr. Vincent Tereshko."

There's a tinkle as Tereshko's cocktail glass hits the floor. There's a peculiar hiss at the same time, like an overheated radiator, or an inner tube deflating. Tereshko sort of reels back, the low top of the chair he has just risen from catches him across the spine, he goes over it, dumping the back of his head onto the soft padded seat, and then he and chair alike roll over sideward to the floor. Instantly he scrambles up again, gives a hoarse cry that sounds like, "No! Get away from me! You're not real."

He makes flailing motions with both arms, buffeting the air before him, then turns and runs through the foyer and out into the street.

They come out of their trance after awhile, not right away. "Well, I'll be a—Did you see that? What bit him? A minute ago he's sitting here chatting with me, then all at once he goes haywire."

"It was—me," she says wonderingly, still staring after Tereshko.

He flips his head impatiently at such an idea. "Nah, how could it have been you? Talk sense. You're not used to crowds yet, every time anyone looks at you you think something's the matter." He can't, after all, really tell who or what Tereshko saw.

"It was, O'Shaughnessy," she insists troubledly. "He was looking right at me, right into my face. Something must be the matter with me! Is there anything wrong with the way I look? Because that's the second time tonight that's happened—"

He turns to her, startled. "Second! What d'you mean?"

"Just now, outside the door. There was a man sitting waiting in a limousine for someone, and as I got out of my cab, he turned around and looked at me, and then he—he gave a yell like this

one did, and started off, tearing down the street a mile a minute
as if he'd seen a ghost—"

O'Shaughnessy looks puzzled.

"Turn around a minute. Lemme see," he says. Then as she
slowly revolves before him: "You're okay from every angle. I
don't see anything about you to scare grown men out of their
wits. He musta seen somebody or something in back of you that
did that to him. The heck with it. Let's go home. It looks like
the deal's off, and I'm just as satisfied. It had a bad smell to it
from the beginning."

Seventy-two hours go by, the lull before the storm. Then, the
third night after that, he happens to come back to the flat earlier
than usual. He's down to his last few dollars, and he's been
tramping around all day trying to make connections. But free-
lance pilots, flying soldiers of fortune, don't seem to be in great
demand at the moment. He has her to look after now. . . .

He spots her standing at the curb in front of their house, as
he rounds the corner. She's looking for a taxi. She signals one,
and just as she's on the point of getting in, he shouts: "Hey Nova!
What's the idea?" and comes running up just in time.

She seems astonished to see him. Not confused, just astonished.

"I'm sorry it took me so long. I didn't mean to keep you waiting
like that. Is that why you changed your mind and came back
here instead? You're not sore, are you, O'Shaughnessy?"

He says: "What're you talking about? Sore about what?"

"Why, because I'm half an hour late in meeting you."

"Who told you to meet me?"

She's more astonished than ever. "Why, you did! You telephoned
me over an hour ago and said to take a taxi and come out and
meet you at—"

He takes a look around him up and down the street. "Come
on upstairs," he says crisply. "Never mind, driver, we don't want
you." And upstairs: "What else did I say?"

"You told me to come as quickly as I could, that's all."

"Don't you know my voice on the wire?"

"I've never heard anybody else's but yours, so I thought it was
you again. You sounded a little far-off, that's all."

"Well it wasn't me. And I'm wondering who it was. Listen,
Nova, honey, don't go out any more by yourself after this. I'll
give you a password over the phone from now on. Barbed wire,

how'll that be? If you don't hear me say barbed wire, you'll know
it isn't me."

"Yes, O'Shaughnessy."

The following evening, when he comes back, he has trouble
getting in. His latchkey works, but she has something shoved up
against the door on the inside, a chair inserted under the knob,
maybe. It doesn't hold him very long, and she's standing there
in the middle of the room shaking like a leaf.

"What'd you do that for?" he asks. "And how'd that hole get
in the door, over the lock?"

She runs over and hangs on tight. "They called again. They
said it was you, but I knew it wasn't because they didn't say
barbed wire."

"They try to get you to come out again?"

"No, they didn't. They said, 'We've got a message for you from
Benny.' Who's Benny?"

O'Shaughnessy just looks at her, eyes narrowing.

"Then they said, 'Oh, so your torch went out?' Then they
laughed and they said, 'Where'd you get hold of the mick?' What's
a mick?"

"Me," he says slowly, wondering. "Anything else?"

She shakes her head dazedly. "I couldn't make head or tail out
of it. They said, 'You sure put one over on us, didn't you? It
was a good gag while it lasted, but it's run out now. We'll be
seeing you.' "

"Then what?"

"Oh, O'Shaughnessy, I was so scared. I didn't know where to
get hold of you, except you were downtown in the Loop somewhere. I locked the door and I hid in the closet, just left it open
on a crack. In about half an hour, all of a sudden I could see
the doorknob slowly turning, as if someone was out there trying
it. Then when that wouldn't work the bell started to ring, and a
voice said thickly, 'It's me, babe. Let me in, I forgot my key.'
But I knew it wasn't you. I got way in the far corner of the closet
and pulled all the clothes over me—"

Meanwhile he's taken his gun out of the valise where he keeps
it and is checking it over, his wrists trembling a little with rage.
That's a man's vital spot, the helpless thing he loves.

She goes on:

"Then something went *pokk* right into the door and came
through on this side. I couldn't stand it any more, I was afraid

they'd come in and get me. I ran out of the closet and climbed
out that window there onto the fire escape and got into the flat
next door and begged the lady to hide me. I told her someone was trying to break into our flat, and she started to call the
police, but by that time they'd gone. I could hear feet scuttling
down the stairs, a whole lot of them, and a big car driving off
outside—"

Walking back and forth, trying to dope it out, tapping the
muzzle of his gun against his palm, he says, "Listen kid, I don't
know what we're up against, it may be just a false alarm, but—
Shooting a bullet-hole through your door in broad daylight makes
it look like the McCoy. If I could only figure what it was all
about! It's no one in *my* life. I've made enough enemies, heaven
knows, but not in this country. Nova, tell me the truth—were
you ever in Chicago before?" He stands still and looks at her.

"Never, O'Shaughnessy, never, until we came here two weeks
ago. I don't know anyone here but you. I've never spoken to
anyone but you the whole time we've been here. You've got to
believe me!"

He does, how could he help it?

But then, what is it? What would you call it anyway? If he had
anything, he'd say it had the earmarks of an attempted snatch,
for ransom. Mistaken identity? Yes, but who do they take her to
be? The whole thing's a maze. He wonders if he ought to give it
to the police to handle for him. But then, what can he tell them?
Somebody impersonated me on the phone to my wife, somebody
tried to break into my flat while I was out. It doesn't stack up
to much when you put it that way. And he's an individualist,
anyway, used to being on his own. When it comes to anything
threatening Nova, he'd rather take care of her himself.

Tereshko rings up unexpectedly that night. "This is Tereshko,
O'Shaughnessy," he says. "I'm down on lower State Street. I'd
like to conclude that transaction we were talking over. Can you
run down and meet me for ten minutes or so?"

"What happened to you the other night? Something seemed to
frighten you."

A phony laugh. "Me? Not at all. I got kinda sick all of a
sudden, and beat it for the street."

O'Shaughnessy motions Nova over, puts the receiver to her ear
and whispers: "This the same voice you heard the other times?"
She listens, shakes her head.

So he says into the phone: "Frankly, the deal's off, count me out."

Tereshko doesn't seem very perturbed, perhaps he doesn't realize how much he revealed that night. "Sorry you feel that way, but you know best. Come down anyway for a drink, to show there's no hard feeling. Come alone."

O'Shaughnessy decides then and there that he will, to see what this is all about. That first night Tereshko was all for having Nova join them. Tonight he wanted O'Shaughnessy to come down alone. Does Tereshko want Nova left alone in the flat? Is *he* the one behind all this? Nothing like finding out. He says, "Get your hat." And on the street, a couple of blocks away: "You've never been to a movie, have you? Well, you're going to one now."

He buys two seats, takes her in, finds a place for her. "Now don't move from there till I come back and get you!" As if she were a child.

"Yes, O'Shaughnessy."

There is no sign of Tereshko at the taproom where they were supposed to meet. O'Shaughnessy waits ten minutes, leaves, goes back and gets Nova. He fingers the gun in his pocket as they near their flat. "So now," he says to himself grimly, "I think I know *who* I'm up against—if not why."

The flat door falls back unfastened before them. They give one another a look. "I thought—I saw you lock it after us when we left," she whispers.

"You thought right," he says grimly. He goes in first, gun bared.

No one there. "Must have blown open," he says. "Maybe sneak thieves."

This alarms her. "My clothes! All the pretty things you gave me!" He grins a little at the woman of it, while she runs to the closet to find out. She comes out again as puzzled as ever.

"Anything missing?"

"No, but—I don't remember *this* being on here before." She's holding one up to show him. A large lily is pinned to the front of it!

"Maybe it came that way and you've forgotten it."

She strokes it with her fingers. "But it's alive. They don't put *live* ones on them."

Even he knows that. He also knows what lilies stand for as a rule. He softly starts to whistle a bar or two. "Chicago, Chicago, I'll show you around—"

SOME CHURCH belfry on the other side of the river bongs twelve times. "Got everything in?" he says quietly. "I'll carry the bags down. You put out the lights."

She tiptoes submissively down the stairs after him. "I don't know how far we can get on five bucks," he remarks, "but it's a cinch I can't leave you up there by yourself any more in the daytime, and I can't drag you all over town with me either. Maybe we can get a room on the other side of the city—"

Just inside the doorway he puts down the bags, motions her to stand by them a minute. He saunters out ahead, carefully casual. Peers up one way, down the other. Nothing. The street's dead to the world.

Then suddenly, from nowhere, *ping!* Something flicks off the wall just behind him, flops at his feet like a dead bug. He doesn't bend down to look closer, he can tell what kind of a bug it is all right. He's seen that kind of bug before, plenty of times. No flash, no report, to show which direction it came from. Silencer, of course.

He hasn't moved. *Fsssh!* and a bee or wasp in a hurry strokes by his cheek, tingles, draws a drop of slow blood. Another *pokk!* from the wall, another bug rolling over. The insect-world seems very streamlined, very self-destructive, tonight.

He takes a wary step back, slips inside the doorway again, still facing front. If he could only spot the flash, see where it was coming from, he could send them a few back. Meanwhile, he's half-in, half-out of the iron-grilled, thick, glass street door.

There's an anvil-like sound, and the warped spokes of a wheel show up in the glass, centering in a neat, round hole. Powdery stuff like dandruff dusts his shoulder. Another bug has dropped inside the hallway.

Hands are gripping at his coat, pulling at him from behind. "O'Shaughnessy, don't—you'll kill yourself standing there like that! Think of *me!*"

"Douse that bulb back there, swat it with your handbag—I want to see if I can catch the flashes."

But she won't do it, and that traps him into going back and doing it himself. Then her arms wind around him when she gets him back there at the far end of the hallway, and she clings for dear life.

"No! No! I won't let you—What good'll you be to me dead? What'll become of me?" He gives in at last—it's either that or drag her bodily after him back to the entrance clinging like a barnacle.

"All right, all right. There must be a back way out of here."

But, at the outlet to the electric-lighted basement passageway, as he emerges in advance of her—there are again winged insects on the loose, spitting off the wall. "Wait a minute!" he says, cutting short her plaintive remonstrances. "I think I caught the flash that time! Along the edge of the roof on that next house. Wait'll it comes again." And cuts his hand at her backhand. "The bulb. The bulb." This time she obeys, blackness inks the passage behind him.

He draws and slowly raises his gun, standing perfectly still, face tilted to the sky. Gambler's odds: his life against the chances of hitting a powder-flash six stories up. His left thumbnail scrapes past the rabbit foot imbedded in his vest-pocket, half absent-mindedly.

A winking gleam just over the cornice up there, a flare from his own gun as fire draws fire. A chipping of the stonework just over and behind his head, and then something black and gangling falling clumsily down six stories, a blur against the gray gloom of the walls. A sickening thud against cement, just out of sight behind the eight-foot dividing fence.

More flashes up there, six in a row, and a sound like hail or gravel down where they are. But O'Shaughnessy's already back inside the sheltering passageway. "It won't work. There's still a second one up there, and we could never get over that eight-foot fence alive. They seem to be doing this up in style. Come on back up to the flat."

She goes up the inner stairs with her hands shielding her face. "That fall. I hope he was dead before—he landed."

"That evens the score a little," he says unsentimentally. "They that live by the sword—"

Night in a Chicago flat. He says: "The door's locked, and I'm here with Buster. You try to get a little sleep, honey, your old man'll look after you."

"But promise me you'll stay up here with me, you won't go down there again."

"I promise."

So, fully dressed, she lies there on the bed, and after a while she sleeps, while he stands guard at the shade-drawn window, gun in hand, the spark of his cigarette held carefully behind his back.

A milkman comes and never dreams the muzzle of a gun is four inches away from his head on the other side of the door as he stoops to set down a bottle of milk. Nova sleeps on, like a child. Night in a Chicago flat.

Three hours after daylight they're ready to leave. There are enough people on the streets now to give them a chance. If they don't get out now, they never will. This net that's been meshed loosely around them all night will be pulled tight by the time darkness comes a second time. They want him out of the way, but they want her alive. That much he's sure of.

Just before they go, he murmurs, "There's a cab been standing there ever since dawn, probably all night, just past the next corner. There's no public hack-stand at that spot, either."

"Do you think that's—them?"

"I don't give a hoot whether it is or not, I can't breathe in here any more, I've got to get out in the open! Stick close behind me, and if I tumble, you keep going. I've been shot at before. I'm a bad penny that always turns up again."

But then, as he puts his hand out to the doorknob, a sudden rigidity, as though some indefinable sound has reached him from outside it. "There's someone out there," he breathes.

She winces. "We're too late."

He motions her behind him, shielding her; reaches out and does something to the lock, levels his gun. "It's open," he calls out. "Come in at your own risk."

Nothing for a minute. Then very slowly it starts to fall back toward them.

"Quicker than that or I'll shoot!" He kicks it the rest of the way with the edge of his foot.

The tremblingly upraised arms are the first things they see. And the empty background behind the solitary figure. O'Shaughnessy takes a step backward, propelling her with him, not in retreat but to give himself elbow-room.

The face is Oriental, Chinese. Spectacles and close-cropped hair. Hat fallen off just now at the unexpected welcome.

O'Shaughnessy: "This is the place you wanted?"

"Yes, if you will permit me to mop my forehead—"

"You warm?"

"No, but my reception was."

"All right, close the door behind you. We've been a little draughty here all night."

The visitor bows nervously. "Allow me to introduce myself—"

"You're on the air."

"I am Lawrence Lee, American name. I have come to offer you interesting proposition—"

"I just had one, thanks, a couple days ago."

"I had great trouble finding you—"

"You're going to have even greater losing me, if this is a come-on."

"I represent the illustrious Benevolent-Wisdom Yang. His recruiting-agent in United States. He has ordered a shipment of lovely planes, and needs someone who will know how to make them work. Your reputation has reached our ears. Can I offer you post on generalissimo's staff?"

O'Shaughnessy, gun still bared, sticks his left hand in his pocket, pulls it out again, lets the lining trail after it. "You make it sound interesting—up to a point."

"Five hundred dollars American, a week."

"I'm no greenhorn, I've been in China before. I'm O'Shaughnessy of Winnipeg, he can't get another like me. The coolies used to bow down and worship in their rice-paddies whenever I passed overhead." That he can stand and bargain like this, when both their lives are hanging by a thread, is—well, just part of his being O'Shaughnessy.

"Two thousand, p'aps?"

"More like it." He turns to her, still huddled behind him. "Shall we do it, just for the fun of it?" Then, with a grin to the emissary, "Yang would not, I take it, be interested in a dead pilot?"

The agent, with Oriental lack of humor: "Dead pilot could not handle planes satisfactory."

"Well, I may have a little trouble getting through alive from here to the Northwest Station. I can't promise you I will." She shudders at this point, clings closer. "However, that's my lookout. You leave two through tickets for Frisco on tap for us at the ticket office, and if I don't show up to claim them, you can always get a refund from the railroad—and another pilot."

"Today-train agreeable? Shall do. Boat-tickets will be waiting in

Frisco at N.Y.K. Line office. And for binder, one thousand advance suitable?"

O'Shaughnessy says in Chinese, "I could not wound your generosity by refusing." Then in English, "Carry your hat in your hand leaving here, so your face can be seen clearly."

The envoy bows himself out. "Happy comings-down."

When they're alone once more, he says to her: "Shanghai-ho. The Coast Limited leaves at eleven, so we've got just one hour to make it."

"But how are we going to get out of here?"

"I don't know yet, but we are." He goes back to the window, peers narrowly down through the gap of the drawn shade. "There goes Confucius without anyone stopping him; I guess they didn't tie him up with me." Then, "Who's that fat woman walking up and down out there with a poodle?"

"Oh, that's the lady in the rear flat I climbed into yesterday. She always airs her dogs like that regularly every morning."

"Dogs?" She's only got the one."

"She's got two in the flat. She has to take them down in relays because they fight."

"I've got it now!" he says. "Wait'll she comes upstairs again."

"What are you going to do?"

"You're going to take the next one down. I'm going to see that you get to the station and safely aboard that train first of all. I'll stall them off here; you call me back as soon as you get there. Then I'll make a break for it myself—"

"Leave you—?" she wails.

"I'm giving the orders in this ground crew. Here she comes now." He goes to the door, stops her, brings her in with him. She's globular and baby-faced, with carefully gilded hair under a large cartwheel hat that flops around her face.

"Do you want to do something for us? I've got to get my wife out of the building and I can't do it openly—we're being watched. Will you lend her your hat and coat and dog? Your other dog."

"I'll gladly lend my hat and coat but Fifi—my little Fifi—who'll bring her back?"

"She'll turn her over to the station master for you, you can call for her later. I tell you her life is in danger. Do this, won't you?"

"Yes," she says, looking at Nova. "I think I understand. I was sure I'd seen your face somewhere before—in the paper, you know. Tell me, what was he like? Was he as bad as they said? I heard he used to make people stand with their feet in buckets of cement—"

"Skip it," says O'Shaughnessy, "you've got your wires crossed."

It only takes a couple of minutes for the change. The wide-brimmed concealing hat hides everything but Nova's chin. He ties a couple of pillows around her with cord, one in front and one in back, under the coat, apologizing, "No offense," to the woman as he does so.

"That's all right," she sighs. "I know I've filled out."

The fat lady stays up in their flat; she thinks it will be a good idea to give them a glimpse of her passing back and forth behind the windows. Make them think Nova's there. For this purpose they raise the shades once more. He goes down to the lower hall with Nova and the dog. Their parting is a mixture of comedy and tension. "I'll be standing here behind the door covering you with my gun. Don't be frightened. Imitate her waddle. Walk slow and keep your eye on the dog, like she does. Give yourself a good two blocks before you jump for it. And don't drop those pillows to the sidewalk, whatever you do!"

"Oh, O'Shaughnessy, if you don't show up, I'm going to die."

"I'll be there with bells on."

The bulky, padded figure eases out through the door, minces after the dog, straining at its leash. He edges up slantwise against the door, screened by an abutment of the hall wall, peering out after her, gun ready, until she passes from his radius of vision. Then quickly chases upstairs where the window will give him a wider perspective.

The dog stops. The figure under the concealing hat brim stands patiently by. They go on again a few yards. They stop again. "Darn dog!" he chafes, sweating with impatience in the hollows of his hands. Finally, almost imperceptibly, by fits and starts, she's progressed around the corner and out of sight.

He glues his eyes on the motionless taxi now. That street she just went up is a continuation of the one it's on. If it makes a move, starts out after her suddenly, he'll know—

Slow tense minutes. She must be a block away now. The cab's still standing. She ought to be off the streets by this time, safely installed in a cab, whirling toward the station. They've put it over!

He takes a deep breath of released tension, steps back into the room away from the window. The worst's over, she's made it.

All that's left now is to sit tight until she calls him to let him know she's reached the station. Fifteen minutes ought to do the trick, making every allowance for traffic-hitches and lights.

He sits there smoking calmly, waiting. The fat lady is still there in the flat. This, to her, is romance with a capital R. She's enjoying it more than a box of marshmallows. She's eating it up.

And then in a flash, before he quite knows how it's happened, seventeen minutes have passed, and the call is two minutes overdue, and the calmness is going out with every noseful of smoke he's expelling.

Twenty minutes. He throws down his cigarette, and takes three or four quick turns around the room. "She should have called by now," he says.

"Yes, she should have," agrees the fat lady. "It doesn't take that long to get from here to the Northwest Station."

Twenty-five minutes, half an hour. "Maybe the phone's out of order—" But he's afraid to get on and test it, afraid to block her call. He shakes his fist at it helplessly.

He's prowling back and forth like a lion with distemper now. There's a shiny streak down one side of his face. "I shouldn't have let her go ahead—I ought to be hung! Something's gone wrong. I can't stand this any more!" he says with a choked sound. "I'm starting now—"

"But how are you—"

"Spring for it and fire as I go if they try to stop me." And then as he barges out, the fat lady waddling solicitously after him, "Stay there; take it if she calls—tell her I'm on the way—"

He plunges straight at the street-door from all the way back in the hall, like a fullback headed for a touchdown. That's the best way. Gun bedded in his pocket, but hand gripping it ready to let it fly through lining and all. He slaps the door out of his way without slowing and skitters out along the building, head and shoulders defensively lowered.

It *was* the taxi, you bet. No sound from it, at least not at this distance, just a thin bluish haze slowly spreading out around it that might be gas-fumes if its engine were turning; and at his end a long row of dun-colored spurts—of dust and stone-splinters— following him along the wall of the flat he's tearing away from. Each succeeding one a half yard too far behind him, smacking into where he was a second ago. And they never catch up.

He rounds the corner unscathed, spins like a dervish on one

leg, brakes with the other, snaps a shot back at the cab, mist-haloed now, which is just getting into gear; and slipping out away from the curb. Glass tinkles faintly back there—he got the wind-shield maybe—and he sees the cab lurch crazily for a minute, as though more than glass got the bullet.

Then he sprints up the street without waiting to see any more. His own shots make plenty of noise, and the vicinity is coming to shocked life around him. Nothing in sight though that's any good to him—a slow-moving truck, a laundry-wagon. But music somewhere ahead—a cab radio—and he steers toward the sound, locates it just around the next corner, is in and on the way almost between two notes of a single bar. At the wheel himself.

The driver rears up in consternation in the back, holding a handful of pinochle cards, shrieks, "Hey! what's the—"

"All right, climb around here and take it—I'm in a hurry, got no time to lower the gangplank!"

"What about these other guys?" The back of the cab is alive with shanghaied card-playing cab drivers.

"They'll have to come along for the ride." Two blocks behind the other cab has showed up, is putting on a burst of speed. O'Shaughnessy warns, as the driver crawls over his lap: "I want you to keep that cab back there where it belongs—zigzag, I don't care what you do—but lose it. It means your back-tires if you don't!"

The rear-view mirror suddenly spatters into crystal confetti.

"See, what'd I tell you? Left, left, get offa here, don't stay in a straight line with 'em!"

The driver says, "What *you* done? I don't like this!" He takes a turn that nearly lands them axle-shafts in air.

A series of two-wheel turns, and a combination of lights in their favor—the rabbit's foot must be working again—closing down after them like portcullises each time. They shake them off.

It's twelve-and-a-half minutes before train time when he jumps down at the Northwest Station, slaps one of Lawrence Lee's sawbucks in through the cab-window and dives inside.

At the barrier: "Tickets, please!"

"Wasn't one left here for me with you?"

"Nope."

"My wife must have taken them through to the train with her, then. Didn't you see her—pretty blonde, big floppy hat—?"

"All blondes are pretty to me, haven't seen a bad-looking one so far today—"

"Buddy, I'm not interested in your love life, I wanna get through here to see if I can find her—"

"Hey, come back here!"

The agony of that wild, headlong plunge into car after car, calling: "Nova! Nova!" from the vestibule of each one. No sign of her. Upstairs again at a mile a minute, nearly knocking over the gateman a second time—eight minutes to train-time now.

At the ticket-window. "Two for the Coast—O'Shaughnessy— were they picked up?"

"Nope, here they are waiting for you."

Uncalled for! She never got here, then! Seven minutes to find her, in a city of four million people! Outside again, and looking around him dazed. Dazed—and dangerous—and yet helpless. Ready to give this town something to be tough about, but not knowing where to start in—Instinctively touching the rabbit's foot, that habit of his. And then—like a genie at the summons of Aladdin's lamp—a redcap, haphazardly accosting him in line of duty. One out of the dozens swarming all over the place, but the right one, the right one out of all of them!

"Cab, boss?"

"No. Wait, George—blonde lady, big droopy hat, did you see anyone like that drive up here at all the past half-hour or so?"

"Li'l dog with a haircut 'cepting on its ankles?"

"Yes! Yes!" He grabs the guy by both shoulders. "Hurry up and tell me, for Pete's sake!"

The redcap shows his teeth.

"That sho' was a dirty trick that lady have played on her. She done come away without bringin' no change fo' her cab fare, and the driver he wouldn't listen to her no-how, he turn around and take her to the police station."

"Which?"

"Neares' one, I reckon."

And there she is when he tears in a couple minutes later, sitting on a bench under the desk-sergeant's eye, dog and all. Driver, too.

"We've been trying to reach you, young fellow." The sergeant clears his throat meaningly, winks at O'Shaughnessy to show he won't give him away. Wife starting on a vacation, somebody else answering the phone; *he* understands. "Couldn't seem to get you."

"How much is it? We've got a train to make."

"Two dollas and twenny cents," says the driver.

"Here it is. And here's a little something extra—" Wham! and the driver nearly brings down the rear wall of the room as he lands into it.

Then he's outside with her again, minus dog and pillows now, in another machine, tearing back to the station. Three minutes to spare. He doesn't notice as he jumps down that the cab ahead of theirs, the one that's just pulled into the driveway before them, has a shattered windshield.

They don't have to be mind-readers, these others, to figure out where he and she will head for. If they're on their way out of town, that means one of the stations. They've cased the La Salle Street Station first, now this one.

He starts her through the big vaulted place at a quick trot. Then suddenly a shout somewhere behind them, "There they are!" and five men are streaming in after them, one with a bloody bandage over his head.

O'Shaughnessy daren't shoot; the station's alive with people crisscrossing the line of fire. His pursuers can't either; not that the risk of hitting somebody else would deter them, but they're sprinting after him too fast to stop for aim. A redcap goes keeling over, and one of the rodmen topples over a piece of hand-luggage the porter dropped, goes sliding across the smooth floor on his stomach. And above it all the amplifier blaring out remorselessly, "Coast Limited—Kansas City—Denver—Salt Lake City—San Francisco! 'Board!"

He wedges her through the closing barrier, throws the tickets at the gateman. A shot, and looking back he can see the uniformed figure at the gate toppling, even while the gateman still tries to wedge it closed. A young riot is taking place back there, shouts, scuffling, station-guards' clubs swinging. But one figure squeezes through, detaches itself, comes darting after him, gun out. Tereshko.

O'Shaughnessy shoves her into a car vestibule. "Get on, kid. Be right with you." The train is already giving its first few preliminary hitches—forward.

Tereshko's gun flames out as he comes on; the shot hits the L of El Dorado, the Pullman's gold-lettered name, slowly slipping past behind O'Shaughnessy's back. Tereshko never had a chance for another shot. O'Shaughnessy closes in bare-handed; his fist swings out, meets Tereshko half way as he crashes into it, lands him spread-eagled on the platform. The gun goes flying up in a foreshortened arc, comes down again with a clank, and fires innocuously.

O'Shaughnessy flicks him a derisive salute from over one ear. "I gotta make a train, or I'd stay and do it right!" He turns and catches the hand-rail of the next-to-the-last vestibule as it glides by, swings himself aboard. Tereshko stands staring blurredly down his own nose at the dwindling observation-platform of the Coast Limited.

O'Shaughnessy sinks wearily down in the seat beside Nova, and as she shrinks into the protective angle of his outstretched arm, he tells her grimly: "You're O'Shaughnessy's girl for keeps. Let 'em try to take you away from me now!"

8

O'SHAUGHNESSY, MINUTES after his Bellanca has kissed the hard-packed earth of the Shanghai municipal airport, is already on one of the airport phones asking for the Broadway Mansions. Seven weeks out of Shanghai, seven weeks back in the red mountains of Szechuan, China's "wild west," piloting the great General Yang around, dropping a few well-placed bombs for him, and trans-shipping machine-gun parts inland from below Ichang, which is as far as the river boats can go. No commission in Yang's fighting-forces, nothing like that—just his own crate, his own neck, payment in American gold dollars, and a leave of absence whenever he feels like it, which happens to be right now. Seven weeks is a plenty long time.

He's still in the crumpled slacks and greasy khaki shirt he left the interior in, but under them a triple-tiered money-belt, twice around the chest and once across the waist, packed with good solid chunky gold eagles, outlawed at home now but as good as ever over here. Fifteen-thousand dollars' worth; two thousand a week salary, and a thousand bonus for obliterating a caterpillar tank that General Yank didn't like the looks of. Not bad, two thousand a week. But seven weeks is still a long time, any way you look at it.

Her voice comes over the wire throbbing with expectancy; every time it's rung she's hoped it was he—and now at last it is.

"O'Shaughnessy." A love song in one word. She's never called him by anything but that.

"Just grounded. I've brought back fifteen-thousand-worth of red paint with me. Turn the shower on, lay out my dude-clothes, and get ready for a celebration!"

He just lingers long enough to see his plane put to bed properly, then grabs a cab at the airport-gate. "The Settlement," and forgetting that he's not inland any more, that Shanghai's snappier than Chicago, "Chop-chop."

"Sure, Mike," grins the slant-eyed driver. "Hop in."

A change has come over the city since he went away, he can feel that the minute they hit the outskirts, clear the congested native sections, and cross the bridge into the Settlement. Shanghai is already tuning-up for its oncoming doom, without knowing it. A city dancing on the brink of the grave. There's an electric tension in the air, the place never seemed so gay, so hectic, as tonight; the roads opening off the Bund a welter of blinking, flashing neon lights, in ideographs and Latin letters alike, as far as the eye can see. Traffic hopelessly snarled at every crossing, cops piping on their whistles, packed sidewalks, the blare of saxophones coming from taxi-dance mills, and overhead the feverish Oriental stars competing with intercrossed searchlight beams from some warships or other on the Whang-poo. Just about the right town and the right night to have fifteen thousand bucks in, all at one time.

He says: "Hold it, Sam," in front of a jewelry store in Bubbling Well Road, lopes in, comes out again with a diamond solitaire in his pocket.

The skyscraper Mansions shows up, he vaults out, counts windows up to the tenth floor, three over from the corner. Brightly lighted, waiting for him. Shies a five-dollar bill at the driver.

The elevator seems to crawl up; he feels like getting out and pushing. A pair of Englishmen stare down their noses at his waste rag outfit. The rush of her footsteps on one side of the door matches his long stride on the other.

"I'd recognize your step with cotton in my ears!"

"Watch it, you'll get fusel-oil all over you!"

They go in together in a welter of disjointed expressions, such as any pair might utter. "I thought you were never coming back this time!"

"Boy, you certainly made time getting dressed. All set to go, aren't you?"

As a matter of fact she isn't, it's her gloves that mislead him. She has on a shimmery silver dress, but no shoes. Her hair is still down too.

He laughs. "What do you do, put on your gloves before your shoes?"

A shadow of something passes over her face. Instantly she's smiling again. "Just knowing you were back got me so rattled—"

He takes a quick shower, jumps into his best suit. Comes in on her just as she is struggling into a pair of silver dancing-shoes—just in time to catch the expression of livid agony on her pretty face. She quickly banishes it.

"Matter—too tight? Wear another pair—"

"No, no, it isn't that. They're right for me—my feet got a little swollen wearing those Chinese things all day."

He lets it go. "Come on, where'll it be? Astor House, American Club, Jockey Club?" He laughs again as she drenches herself with expensive perfume, literally empties the bottle over herself. "Incidentally, I think we'll move out of here. Something seems to be the matter with the drains in this apartment, you can notice a peculiar musty odor inside there—decay—"

The haunted look of a doomed thing flickers in her eyes. She takes his arm with desperate urgency. "Let's—let's go. Let's get out into the open, O'Shaughnessy. It's such a lovely night, and you're back, and—life is so short!"

That air of electric tension, of a great city on the edge of an abyss, is more noticeable than ever at the White Russian cabaret called, not inappropriately, "New York." You wouldn't know you were in China. An almond-eyed platinum-blonde has just finished wailing, with a Mott Street accent, "You're gonna lose your gal."

O'Shaughnessy leads Nova back to the table apologizing. "I knew I wasn't cut out for dancing, but I didn't know how bad I was until I got a look at your face just now. All screwed up like you were on the rack. Kid, why didn't you speak up—"

"It wasn't you, O'Shaughnessy," she gasps faintly. "My—my feet are killing me—"

"Well, I've got something here that'll cure that. We don't get together often, Mrs. O'Shaughnessy, but when we do—the sky's the limit." He takes the three-thousand-dollar ring out of his pocket, blows on it, shows it to her. "Take off your glove, honey, and lemme see how this headlight looks on your finger—"

Her face is a white, anguished mask. He reaches toward her right hand. "Go ahead, take the glove off."

The tense, frightened way she snatches it back out of his reach gives her away. He tumbles. The smile slowly leaves his face. "What's the matter—don't you want my ring? You trying to cover up something with those gloves? You fixed your hair with them on, you powdered your nose with them on—What's under them? Take 'em off, let me see."

"No, O'Shaughnessy. No!"

His voice changes. "I'm your husband, Nova. Take off those gloves and let me see your hands!"

She looks around her agonized. "Not here, O'Shaughnessy! Oh, not here!"

She sobs deep in her throat, even as she struggles with one glove. Her eyes are wet, pleading. "One more night, give me one more night," she whispers brokenly. "You're leaving Shanghai again in such a little while. Don't ask to see my hands. O'Shaughnessy, if you love me. . . ."

The glove comes off, flops loosely over, and there's suddenly horror beating into his brain, smashing, pounding, battering. He reels a little in his chair, has to hold onto the edge of the table with both hands, at the impact of it.

A clawlike thing—two of the finger extremities already bare of flesh as far as the second joint; two more with only shriveled, bloodless, rotting remnants of it adhering, only the thumb intact, and that already unhealthy-looking, flabby. A dead hand—the hand of a skeleton—on a still-living body. A body he was dancing with only a few minutes ago.

A rank odor, a smell of decay, of the grave and of the tomb, hovers about the two of them now.

A woman points from the next table, screams. She's seen it, too. She hides her face, cowers against her companion's shoulder, shudders. Then he sees it too. His collar's suddenly too tight for him.

Others see it, one by one. A wave of impalpable horror spreads centrifugally from that thing lying there in the blazing electric light on O'Shaughnessy's table. The skeleton at the feast!

She says forlornly, in the stunned stillness: "You wanted me to wear your ring, O'Shaughnessy—" and slips it over that denuded bone protruding like a knobby spine from her hand. Loosely, like a loop, it falls down to the base of the thing, hangs there, flashing prismatically, in an inconceivable horror. Diamonds for the dead.

The spell breaks; the glitter of the diamond perhaps does it, shattering his hypnosis, freeing him. So lifelike there, so out of place. Not a word has passed between them, but for that one lament of hers. He seizes her to him suddenly, their two chairs go over, their champagne glasses crash to the floor. He pulls out a wing of his coat, wraps it concealing around the thing that was once her hand, clutches it to him, hurries her out of the place, his arm protectively about her. The flash of a silver dress, a whiff of gardenia, a hint of moldy, overturned earth, as they go by, and the dead has been removed from among the living. The ring drops off the insufficient bone-sliver that carries it, rolls unheeded across the floor.

"Not so fast, O'Shaughnessy," she pleads brokenly. "My feet too—they're that way. My knees. My side, where the ribs are. It's coming out all over me."

And then, in the cab hurtling them through the mocking constellations that were the Bund an hour ago, she says: "Life was swell, though, while it lasted. Just knowing you has made—well, everything."

He says again what he said before: "No one is going to take you away from me!"

The English doctor says, "Looks rather bad, y'know, old man."

O'Shaughnessy, white-lipped, growls out something. . . .

The German doctor says, "Neffer before haff I such a thing seen. This case will become zenzational—"

"The case will, but what about her, that's what I want to know?"

"My *gut* man—"

"I get it. Send the bill around—!"

The American doctor says, "There's just a slim chance—what you might call a thousand-to-one shot, that chaulmoogra oil might benefit her."

"I thought you said it wasn't leprosy?"

"It isn't. It may be some Chinese disease none of us have ever heard of before. She seems to be *dying alive.* Her bodily functions are unimpaired, the X-rays show; whatever it is seems to be striking on the surface. If it continues unchecked—and there doesn't seem to be anything we can do to stop it—the whole skeletal structure will be revealed—you'll have an animated corpse on your hands! And then of course . . . death."

The French doctor—the French, they are a very logical race and make good doctors—says: "M'sieu, they have all been on the wrong track—"

O'Shaughnessy's wan face lights up. "What can you tell me?"

"I can tell you only this: there is no hope. Your wife is lost to you. If you are a merciful man—I do not give you this advice as doctor, I give it to you as one husband to another—you will go to one of the opium houses of Chapei, buy a quantity sufficient for *two* at least—"

O'Shaughnessy says in a muffled voice, "I'm no quitter. I'll beat this rap."

There's pity in the Frenchman's face. "Go to Chapei, *mon ami*. Go tonight. I say this for the sake of your own sanity. Your mind will crumble at the sight of what it will have to behold in a few more weeks."

O'Shaughnessy says the name of his Maker twice, puts his arm up swiftly over his face. The doctor's hand comes to rest on his shoulder. "I can see what led them astray, the others. They sought for disease. There is no disease there. No malady. No infection. It is not that; it is the state of death, itself, that has her. How shall I say? This flesh that rots, drops away, is, paradoxically, healthy tissue. My microscopes do not lie. Just as, let us say, a person who has been shot dead by a bullet is otherwise a healthy person. But he lies in his grave and nature dissolves his flesh. That is what we have here. The effect without the cause—"

O'Shaughnessy raises his head after a while, gets up, moves slowly toward the door. "You, at least," he says, "are a square shooter. All right, medical science tells me she's as good as dead. I'm not licked yet. There's a way."

The doctor shrugs gloomily. "How? What way is there? Lourdes, you are thinking of?"

"An awful way," O'Shaughnessy says, "but a way."

He stumbles out into the bright sunlight of the Concession, roams around hopelessly. Along the Avenue of the Two Republics, bordering the French Concession, he finds himself beginning to tremble all over, suddenly.

Fear! Fear again, for the first time since his 'teens. Fear, that he thought he would never know any more. Fear that no weapon, no jeopardy, no natural cataclysm, has ever been able to inspire until now. And now here it is running icily through him in the hot Chinese noon. Fear for the thing he loves, the only fear that can ever wholly cow the reckless and the brave.

Fear of the Way, the Way that he mentioned to the doctor. Fear of the implication involved in it. A mad voice howling in the darkness sounds in his ears again: "You'll come crawling back to me, begging me to help! *That'll be my hour!*" Oh, not that his own life will assuredly be forfeit as part of the bargain, that isn't what makes him tremble. Nor any amount of pain and horror that vindictive mania can devise. He can stand it with a smile, to give her an hour, a day, or a week of added life. It's what will come after, what she must face alone without him, once he's out of the way. The barbed-wire fence—cooped up with a madman; kept trapped like an animal in a cage, after having known the world. Better if he'd left her as he'd found her. . . .

But that's the Way, and there is no other. And once his mind's made up, the trembling and aimless walking stops, and he can look doom in the face without flinching.

He has their boat-tickets in his pocket when he goes back to the Mansions. All down the corridor, from the elevator-shaft to their door, there's that cloying odor of perfumery—to conceal another, different one.

She's propped up in bed, a native *amuh* sitting by her fanning her. He stops short in surprise. The screwy clock of this bedevilment seems to have spun backward again to that awful night, when he first came out of the interior—and didn't know yet. For she's beautiful there, composed, placid again, expressionless as a wax doll, the stigma of the knowledge of approaching doom erased from her face.

"The mask came," she says through it, in a slightly resonant voice. Her own features, reproduced by a clever Chinese craftsman, at her terrified request—before anything happens to them. Not for herself, this, for the man who stands there looking at her— the man whom life and love have laughed at, the man to whom life and love and laughter, too, have been denied.

He gestures the Chinese woman out of the room.

When they're alone Nova asks, as tonelessly as though she were asking what the weather was like, "Any hope?"

"Not here." It's not the first time it's been asked and answered that way, so there's no shock to it any more.

He sees a small canvas bag upon the table beside her bed. "What's that?"

"Another agent of Yang was here while you were out. He left this bag of gold, and a thinly veiled threat that your tea will be bitter if you don't report back soon. They think you've run out on them. Better go back, O'Shaughnessy."

"Not a chance, darling. I've sold my plane. We're taking the early morning back to the States. I'm taking you back to Denholt."

She is silent for a long minute. He can see her shivering through the thick, brocaded, Chinese jacket, pretty much the way he was, out in the sun-baked streets.

He sits down close beside her. "You've knocked around with me now for almost a year. You've talked to lots of other girls your age. You must have found out by now that none of them learned to walk and talk as late as you did. Something happened to you, and there's only one man alive knows what it was and what's to be done about it. Those injections—can't you see that he was keeping you alive in some way? It's our only chance, we've got to go back there, we've got to get more of his stuff." And bitterly, as he hauls out a valise and tosses up the lid, "O'Shaughnessy wasn't so smart. O'Shaughnessy knows when he's licked . . ."

Down the Whangpoo to the Yangtse, and out into the China Sea. A race against time now. A race against death. And the odds are so tall against them. The widest body of water in the world to cross. Then a whole continent afterward from west to east. Three weeks at the very least. Can she hold out that long by sheer will-power? Or have they waited too long, like fools? Then too, how can he be sure there is help waiting at the end of the long journey, even the help that they both dread so? Suppose Denholt is gone. How to locate him again in time? He may be in a strait jacket at this very moment, unable to tell a serum from a split of White Rock. The odds are pretty steep. But—at least there *are* odds.

She sits in a deck chair covered up to her chin in a steamer rug; her beautiful masked face above it never smiles, never frowns, never changes—just the eyes alive and the voice. He haunts the chart that marks their daily progress. Comes back to it a hundred times a day, says prayers before it while it lengthens a pitiful notch at a time, in red ink across the graph.

Kobe. Bad news. A Japanese English-language paper has picked

up the story from something that must have come out in Shanghai
after they left. Fright sounds through the mask. "It's—it's leaked
out already. Here. 'Beautiful girl stricken with living death. First
case of its kind on record. Being rushed home by husband'—"

She makes a small, plaintive sound. "Don't you see? The papers
in America will pick it up, follow it through, play it up. And
your name's here. *They,* whoever they were, they'll know it means
us, they'll find out we're coming back. They'll be waiting for us
to land, they'll—we'll never make it. Oh, let's turn back,
O'Shaughnessy! Let me die in China—what's the difference where
it is? I've brought you enough grief, don't let me be the cause
of—"

He takes her in his arms and holds her tight. "You don't seem
to think much of my ability to take care of us."

She makes a thoughtless gesture to reach out and clasp his hand
understandingly; but she remembers and draws the gloved claw
back again.

Days pass. The story has circulated now, and turned the ship
into a buzzing beehive of curiosity. People find excuses to go by
her on the deck, just so they can turn and stare. O'Shaughnessy
overhears two men bet that she won't reach Frisco alive. She tries
to smoke a cigarette through the lips of the mask one afternoon,
to buoy up his spirits a little. Smoke comes out of her hair-line,
under her chin, before her ears. A steward drops a loaded bouillon-
tray at the sight of her. Nova stays in her cabin after that.

9

THREE THOUSAND years later they're at Honolulu. Leis and steel
guitars above deck; and below, something that scarcely stirs, that
lies still now, saturated with cologne, smothered with fresh-cut
flowers as though she were already on her bier. It's too painful
to force the fleshless footbones to support her tottering body any
more, even swathed in bandages, except for a few moments at a
time. Reporters try to get in to see her; O'Shaughnessy has to
swing his fists to get them to keep their distance.

Out to sea again, on the last leg of the trip. Sometimes he
bends down, whispers low, like a prizefighter's second in his corner

when the bout's going against him. "You can make it. Just a little longer, honey. Do it for O'Shaughnessy." Sometimes, in the depths of night, he goes up on the boatdeck, shakes his fist—at what? The ship, the limitless ocean, the elusive horizon that never comes any nearer, the stars overhead that don't give a rap?

The rabbit's paw has hardly been out of his palm the whole way over. All the pelt's worn off it with his stroking. His thumb has developed an ineradicable habit of turning inward on itself, circling his palm. "You and me," he says to it grimly. "We'll do the trick."

Frisco at last. And the anchor plunges into the waters of the bay—they've made it—! The three of them, he and she and the rabbit's foot. There's still a voice behind that mask—faltering, weak, but alive. Still living eyes behind those immobile eyeholes with their double tier of lashes—real and artificial.

He's wirelessed ahead from the Islands for a cabin plane, and it's tuned up and waiting at the airport over in Oakland. He gets Nova through the gang of reporters clogging the deck, has her carried down the gangplank on a stretcher while flashlights go off around her like a constellation. Into a car outside the Customs House, while the newsmen like a pack of hounds in full cry swarm around them, yapping. But there's one man who doesn't pepper him with questions, doesn't say a word—just takes a good look at the beautiful graven face being transferred from stretcher to car, and then dives into the nearest phone-booth. O'Shaughnessy isn't near enough to overhear him ask for long-distance. . . .

And then the plane, with a relief pilot to spell O'Shaughnessy. Up and due east. "And we don't come down again for snow or rain or fog or engine-trouble until you hit Louisville," says O'Shaughnessy.

All through the day they hurl through space. "You got that Kentucky map I asked you to get hold of?"

He locates the mountain on it finally, draws a big ring around it. "Here's where we come down, inside that circle."

"But on what? How do we know what's there? It'll be dark long before we make it," the relief pilot protests.

"Here's where we come down," is O'Shaughnessy's remorseless answer. "if we splinter into match wood. Here, right on the perimeter, where this feeder branches off from the trunk-highway on the west and climbs up. That's as close as we can get."

"Radio ahead, contact one of the towns near there to have

something waiting for you at that point, otherwise you may be held up for hours."

"Yeah, that's it," nods O'Shaughnessy. He starts calling the county seat.

Nova shakes her head. He bends down close to hear what she wants to say. "That may bring *them* down on us, if you mention the place—tip them off where we're going to land."

"How can they beat our time in, unless they're already somewhere around there?"

"But that's it, they may be. You wirelessed him from Honolulu and mentioned a chart of this one county. They may have intercepted that message. They're likely to be within reach of your set, and this'll bring them right to the exact spot."

"Then that'll bring them grief!" is all he says. He fiddles with the dials "Hello, Wellsville? This is a private chartered plane coming your way, with a desperately ill passenger on board. We need ground transport badly. . . ."

"Hello, this is Wellsville. This is Wellsville. There are no facilities here."

"I'm not asking for hospitalization. All I want is ground transport. I want a car where Route 19 bisects the highway."

"Well—I dunno—"

"Have you been reading the papers lately?" O'Shaughnessy barks. "This is Penny O'Shaughnessy—Yes, yes, the 'Dying-Alive Girl,' if you insist! Now do I get a car at that particular spot?"

"I'll start out now."

"We don't want any publicity. Come alone. We should be there by ten. Tilt your headlights upward to guide us, keep snapping them off and on at two-minute intervals, we're going to have to land in pitch-darkness. If we live through it, be ready to start off at a moment's notice. Don't let us down, there's a human life at stake. This is her last chance."

Louisville, an hour after dark, is a carpet of gilt thumbtacks below them, with straight, twinkling lines like strings of beads leading out from it. Southeastward now, toward the Tennessee state-line.

At nine a continuous line of little pinpoints, stretched straight as an arrow, shows up below. They follow it, flying so low now the twinkling lights of an occasional car crawling along it seems to be right under them. Then, in thirty, forty minutes, a firefly down there in the dark fields, going off, on, off, on.

O'Shaughnessy clutches his pilot jubilantly by the shoulder. "See it? Here, gimme the controls—I *couldn't* go wrong, not this late in the game!"

Around and around in a narrowing spiral. Then way out, and around, and in again in a straight swoop that barely seems to skim the roof of the waiting car. "Hold on!" he warns, and slaps the pocket holding the rabbit's foot. The earth comes up flat like a blackboard. A jolt, a rise, a dip, another bump, a short stretch of wobbly taxiing, a shudder, and he cuts off his engine.

The car, waiting off across the field, has lowered its headlights to guide them. Carrying her between them they waver toward it up a thinly-talcumed path of light-motes. A rail fence shows up. "All right, driver! You in the car!" shouts O'Shaughnessy. "Come out here and give us a hand over this!"

A figure jumps out, hurries to meet them on the outside of the fence.

They ease her over the top rail, the newcomer holding her in both arms until O'Shaughnessy can scramble over and relieve him.

They pass her into the back of the car. Then suddenly, a dark motionless outline shows up a little way up the sideroad, under shadowing trees that all but blot it out—materializes into a second car, unlighted, stalled, apparently deserted.

The plane pilot, who has been standing off to one side, looking on, cries out: "Hey, there's a guy lying here at the side of the road, out—"

"Take it easy, pal," an unseen voice purrs. An orange hyphen flicks toward the pilot from somewhere just behind the car. A report shatters the crossroads' stillness, and the pilot leans over toward the road, as though he saw a coin lying there and was languidly about to pick it up.

O'Shaughnessy doesn't wait for him to complete the fall. He whirls back toward Nova, flings out his arms to keep her from going into this car that is a trap. The blurred oval of a second face, not that of the man who helped to carry her to it, looms at him in the dark, above her body.

"No you don't," a voice says blandly, "she's coming with us—we're taking up where we left off that night—and she ain't fooling us this time!"

A second red-orange spearhead leaps straight at O'Shaughnessy. The whole world seems to stand still. Then the gun behind it crashes, and there's a cataclysm of pain all over him, and a shock goes through him as if he ran head-on into a stone wall.

A voice from the car says blurredly, while the ground rushes up to meet him, "Finish him up, you guys! I'm getting so I don't trust their looks no more, no matter how stiff they act!"

Three comets seem to dart down at him as he lies there on the ground. Asphalt-grits fly up beside his skull. A hot wire creases his side while something that feels like a mallet pounds his shoulder. He can feel his mouth opening; he must be trying to say something.

Far away, from some low-flying soundless plane in the skies, a pair of voices reach him. "Did you hear where they were headed for?"

"Yeah, and it sounds like a swell idea—"

High up over him the chattering motor swells into a roar, the air he is trying to breathe is sucked away from him along the ground, grit and road-dust swirl over him. God, they're flying low! What're they trying to do—? Looking down his own body he can see a red light poised momentarily on the toe of his shoe. Then it dips below it, and it's gone. And he's alone there, with the unconscious pilot lying a little way off for company, and some other guy he's never even seen, only spoken to over the radio.

He wants to sleep so badly—dying they call it—and he can't. Something's bothering him to keep him awake. Something that won't let him alone. Not about Nova, not about the still pilot either. Something about this other, strange guy.

And then he remembers. The guy has a car, that's what it is. The guy brought a car here. The guy is dead now, but the car is still standing there, back a little ways under some trees. He saw it himself.

He's got to get into that car. He may be half dead, but cars don't die; it'll get him wherever he wants to go, good as ever. And where he wants to go is just where Nova is, no matter where.

He rolls over on his face first. And a lot of hot wet stuff comes out on his shoulder and his chest and hip. That makes everything come alive again and hurt like blazes. He starts pulling himself around the other way, with his good arm and shoulder for a propeller, like something maimed that ought to be put out of its misery with a big stick.

Then when he gets all the way around in a half circle, there's the car, with the pilot and the other guy for milestones leading to it. He starts dragging himself toward it. He can tell it's no use trying to get up on his feet.

He comes up to the pilot first, rests full length beside him a minute, reaches out, shakes him a little.

Frazier moans a little—almost a bleat—stirs a little.

O'Shaughnessy inches on toward the car. Like a caterpillar goes, contracting in the middle, expanding again, contracting, expanding. Like a caterpillar someone's stepped on, though. He leaves a moist trail behind him along the asphalt roadbed.

It's easy to rear up as high as the running-board, but above that there's a long unbroken stretch of glossy tonneau up to the door handle. He makes it, on the heels of his hands and the points of his elbows, using them for grips, like vacuum cups. The window's down, luckily, and a hand on the sill of the frame keeps him up. He falls, sprawling, into the seat.

Light funnels out of the dead headlights again, across the two men on the ground. He jockeys slowly around, then straightens out.

The rush of air through the open windows clears some of the cobwebs from his bullet-stunned mind. He knows where they went and where to follow. "Did you hear where they were heading for?" the first voice had said. And the second answered, "Sounds like a swell idea."

The dirt-packed mountain-detour branches off at last, and the new-made treads of the car ahead are plainly visible along it. It's a hard trail to tackle, with just one good arm to steady the wheel by, and a grade like a loose plank tilted before your face, and obscuring branches and foliage whistling in at you through the windows.

The barbed-wire fence starts up beside him after awhile. He wonders if Denholt still lives behind it. The scooped-out hollows of their ruts are still before him, plain as day, and broken branches hanging down at right-angles. The fence suddenly crumples into the ground, and a big gap torn in it where the gate used to be, where he remembers it, shows him how they got in.

He turns in after them, brakes only when their own car, broad side to him, blocks further progress. Beyond, the house shows palely against his partly-deflected headlights. He gets out, bangs the car door after him out of habit, lurches over to their car, steadies himself against it for a moment. Caution is for the healthy. He laughs sort of crazily and stamps onto the wooden porch. He hangs onto the door-frame for a minute, then goes on through the unguarded opening.

They haven't even closed the door after them, they're so sure they've left all opposition dead behind them where the highway crosses Route 19. That white light from the laboratory is streaming out to guide him. They're in there, all of them; he can hear their voices as he comes draggingly nearer. One voice, raised above the others, strident, threatening.

"Don't tell us you don't know what we mean! Why the barbed-wire fence and all the trimmings, if it ain't around here somewhere? Why was the Brown girl, here, heading this way so fast with that guy she calls her husband? And a nifty place, if there ever was one! Here we was thinking it was somewhere down in the Florida keys all the time! That's just like the Boss, goes off on a cruise in one direction to cover up, sends the do-re-mi in another. He was always smart that way, always doing things like that. Now *you* be smart."

"There's no money here. I don't know who you are, what brings you here, but there's no money here. Only the—the results of a lifetime of—For God's sake, be careful!"

That's Denholt's voice. Already O'Shaughnessy has reached the threshold by now and stands there looking in at them like an apparition, unnoticed. Their backs are all to him, even Nova's, gripped cruelly between two of them, held upright. Only Denholt is facing his way, at bay against the far wall.

Even from behind, O'Shaughnessy can spot one of those backs, Tereshko.

10

HE IS standing near a retort filled with colorless fluid; as Denholt's frantic warning singles it out, his elbow has just grazed it, caused it to teeter. The plea has exactly the opposite effect it was intended to; it is something precious to that old crank standing there before him, so his impulse is to destroy it forthwith. He deliberately completes the shove, sweeps it off the trestle it rests on. "Nuts with all this junk y'got here! This is a phony front. Who y'think y'kidding?"

The retort shivers into pieces on the floor. Its contents flood out, spread, dissipate beyond recovery.

Denholt lets out a hoarse, anguished cry. And leaps at the wanton destroyer of his whole life's work. Tereshko's gun raps out almost perfunctorily; smoke blooms between them; Denholt staggers, turns around the other way, then goes down to his knees slowly like a penitent in prayer.

They hear him say, in the brief silence: "Yes, it's better this way—now." Then he falls forward on his face.

O'Shaughnessy's leap for Tereshko crashes through the rear-guard, sends the four behind Tereshko lurching off-balance. Nova released, totters aside, keeps herself from falling against the edge of the operating table. They whirl, see who faces them and forget, in their utter disbelief, to use their guns. Tereshko goes down backward, his neck caught in the grip of O'Shaughnessy's arm, while the Irishman's other fist is pounding, flailing, slashing, into the side of Tereshko's head and ribs.

The struggle doesn't last long; it's too unequal. Their momentary surprise overcome, they close in on him. The well-directed slice of a gun-butt slackens the good arm; it's easy to pry the disabled one from around the racketeer's collar.

Tereshko is trembling with his anger. "Now *him* again!" he protests, as though at an injustice. "All they do is die and then get up and walk around again! What'sa matter, you guys using spitballs for slugs? No, don't kick at him, that'll never do it—I think the guy has nine lives!"

"Wait!" The mask has spoken, and they turn in awe at the impassive face looking at them. Face that lies now if it never did before—so calm, so untroubled, so serene, at the scene before it. "What is it you want of us—of me? Why do you hound us like this? What have we ever done to you?"

Tereshko sneers, "You're Benedetto's girl, ain't you? You're Jane Brown, ain't you? You oughta know what we want of you. We did his dirty work for seven long years, you just come in on the pay-off at the end. Where's the profits of those seven years, when two bits out of every fifty-cent glass of beer drunk east of the Mississippi went into his pockets? Where's the million and a quarter dollars in gold and Federal Reserve notes that dropped from sight when he was arrested?"

"I never saw or knew Benedetto," says the mask slowly.

"You lying tomato! I'm looking right at the face he used to kiss in front of all of us. I'm looking right at the face that stood in a diamond frame on his bureau, every time I went in there to make a report. I'm hearing the voice that used to call him Benny-boy, I'm seeing the eyes that cried when he got sent away—Oh, no! You're Jane Brown, all right."

Gloved hands rise from the enfolding cloak, undo tiny straps behind the ears, below the golden hair on top of the head. "Look closer still—and tell me if I'm Benedetto's girl—if I'm Jane Brown!" The face drops off—a shell—and yet repeats itself, identical, still unravaged, only paler, beneath.

They gasp in surprise. And then in the midst of a deep silence, Tereshko says: "All right, that's a mask—so what?" but his voice trembles a little.

Her hands flutter up and down the cloak fastenings, seize it to throw it open. "Look closer," she says, "and tell me if you know me!"

"No, Nova—don't!" O'Shaughnessy cries from the floor.

She says softly: "Close your eyes, O'Shaughnessy, and keep them closed, if you love me. For no love could survive this—no love in all the world."

Dumbly obedient, he holds his hands there in front of his eyes. A rustle of Nova's cloak, a swirl of air as it flies back. A choking sound from someone near him. A gun thudding to the floor. Then a wild, terrible scream—a sudden rush of feet, five pairs of them, around and past him and toward the door. A stampede of mortal terror.

"Get away from me! What—are you?"

Above it all, her voice, serene, sepulchral. "Now—am I Bene-detto's girl—am I anyone's girl any more?"

Across the wooden floor of the front of the house rushes the retreat of scuffling shoe-leather. A door bangs. The motor of their car comes to life—gears clash and scream. The car sound dies away—then suddenly comes a far-off crash carried thinly on the still night. One dim, final cry of pain and death—and dead silence drops at last like a curtain on a play. Within the room, for long minutes, there is no movement.

"They must have gone off the road," O'Shaughnessy says tautly. His hands fall from before his eyes, and Nova's cloak is closed again. How close to death she must be, he thinks, to drive the living to their own deaths in wild flight just from the look of her.

A gun, dropped there on the laboratory floor, is all that's left of them. O'Shaughnessy toes it aside and it skitters across the room. Painfully, inch by inch, he hauls himself over beside Denholt, lifts the scientist's head and shoulders in his arms. Denholt's eyes, still alive, turn toward him.

O'Shaughnessy's voice rasps like a file. "You've got to save her. Got to! Kill me if I've wronged you—but I've brought her back to you—you're the only one who can do anything. . . . Denholt, can you hear me?"

The dying man nods, points helplessly to the shattered retort, the evaporating stain on the floor.

"Was that it—?" O'Shaughnessy shakes him wildly in his fright. "There must be more. That can't be all! Can't you tell me how to make more?"

A sigh filters through the parted lips. "No time."

"Haven't you got it written down?"

A feeble shake of the head. "Afraid to—Jealous someone else would steal it from me—"

O'Shaughnessy's bony hands claw at Denholt's shoulders. "But you can't mean—that she's got to die. That there isn't anything you with your knowledge or I with my love can do for her—anything at all—?" Something, like a cold hand, closes his throat. Something else, like little needles, pricks his eyes until the lashes are moistened. Nova, standing there motionless, slowly droops her head.

A thin tensile hand grips O'Shaughnessy's arm to arrest his attention. A hand that must have been very strong once. "Wait. Lean down closer, so you can hear me—I was filling a hypo—for one of the rabbits—when they broke in. I don't remember what became—Look around, see if you can find it—Enough for one injection, if it's intact—hurry, it's getting dark, I'm going fast."

But before he does look for it, before he makes a move, he remembers to touch that mascot in his pocket, the rabbit's foot. "Help me," he says to her then, "you know what it looks like, you used to see enough of them—"

She raises her head, steps aside—and there it is behind her, lying on the operating table. A previous liquid glinting within its transparent eyes.

"Yes, that's it. All there is left now. It'll be lost forever in a few more minutes when I go. I'm taking it with me—after what I've seen tonight of human nature, too much power for evil in it—it's better, for our own sakes, the way Nature ordered it—"

"Shall I lift you up, do you think you can stand long enough to—"

"No time." He motions to Nova, weakly. She draws near. "Recline on the floor here, where I can reach you—" Then to O'Shaughnessy, "Sweep the hair from the base of her head. Hold my arm at the elbow, steady it—"

The needle falls, emptied.

O'Shaughnessy murmurs, staring dully at the floor: "A month more—this'll give her. Maybe I'm a fool to have done it. What torture that month is going to be—knowing now our only chance is gone. Well, maybe that French doctor was right. . . ."

Again that hand on his arm. "Listen—She will be ill, very ill, for twenty-four hours. The reaction. Keep ice packed around her until the temperature goes down. Then—after that—the injection will arrest it for a while. It can't mend what's already happened—but it will give you that one month. Maybe a little—longer. I am sorry that I can't give you more—or any real hope at all."

Then whatever was human and compassionate in Denholt dies out, and the scientist replaces the man. "I want you to know why I failed. I must tell someone. I brought everything in her to life—but the blood. That was dead, stayed dead. As it circulated in her veins it carried death through her body. The injections I gave her held that flowing decay at bay—no more.

"I didn't realize that—I do now. The chemical composition of the blood changed in death—nothing I have done restored it. It would always defeat the serum—eventually. She was not really alive in her own right; she was being kept alive by a sort of artificial combustion introduced into her system at periodic intervals."

O'Shaughnessy's eyes glare dully. "You had no right," he says. "You had no right to do it. It wasn't fair to her or to me—or"—and he smiles ruefully—"even to those fear-crazy gunmen who are smeared all over your mountainside right now. You tried to bring life, Denholt—and you've got nothing but death on your hands."

The pale, almost lifeless lips flicker in a ghastly smile. "My death, too," he whispers. He struggles to rise in O'Shaughnessy's arms. And there is a pitiful attempt at self-justification. "If you hadn't come along, O'Shaughnessy—who can say? None of this—would have been. And yet, you represented the human element—the thing I didn't reckon on. Yes. It was the blood that defeated me—the passionate warm blood of men and women, hungry and greedy and alive—the blood I couldn't put into Jane Brown's body. . . ."

O'Shaughnessy's shoulder still throbs with pain and there is blood trickling down the arm inside the sleeve, coming out below the cuff, oozing over his wrist and his hands. O'Shaughnessy stares at it dully and remembers Denholt's last words; and then suddenly strength comes to him to do the thing he must do. There is a car outside and down below a plane waiting. And there is Nova, her pale face flushed and hectic with the fever, her eyes flickering closed, her breathing labored. And here—here, you crazy gods of Fate, is O'Shaughnessy, the man who hasn't been afraid, not for himself anyway, since he was eighteen. Yes, all the pieces of the mosaic are here to hand, and the pattern has just fallen into place in O'Shaughnessy's mind.

He is a little light-headed, and giddy, but there is a hard core of will in his brain. He can stand now, where before he could only crawl like a snake with its spine crushed. He scoops Nova up in his arms, totters for one step with her, before his walk is firm and steady.

Nova's head stirs against his shoulder. Her eyes are open. "What are we to do now?" she murmurs, with the fever heat thickening her tones.

"What does it matter?" O'Shaughnessy says. He doesn't want to tell her, doesn't want her to know. "I'm with you, Jane."

He says that to show her that he can call her by her right name without feeling, that he doesn't hold Jane Brown against her. But she won't let him. That name isn't hers.

"My name," she says, childlike, "is Nova. Nova—O'Shaughnessy."

She doesn't speak again all the time he is putting her into the car, where she slumps against the cushions like a rag doll, no more than half conscious, or while they are driving down the mountainside, or even while he carries her to the plane that is still standing there.

He goes, a little more unsteadily now, to kneel beside the wounded pilot.

"How you feeling?" O'Shaughnessy's words are jerky.

The pilot nods. "I'm okay, I guess. Feels like just a nick."

"That's all right, then," O'Shaughnessy says. He pushes a wad of bills into Frazier's hand, helps the man to sit up. "I'm going to take your plane. I'm glad you're feeling okay, because I'd have to take the plane anyway—only it's nice that I don't have to leave you here dying. You can use the car there."

Wrinkles of worry blossom at the corners of the relief pilot's eyes. "You sound kinda crazy to me—what happened up there? What's this money for?"

"That's to square you for the plane—in case. . . . Well, just in case."

Then he is gone, weaving across the uneven ground. Frazier gets up and wobbles after him. "Hi, wait a minute. The propeller—"

In a few minutes, his hands are on the blades and from inside the plane-cabin O'Shaughnessy's voice is calling, "Contact," and Frazier yanks, the propeller spins. Frazier falls back and the plane taxis jerkily with a sputtering roar of the engine.

O'Shaughnessy somehow negotiates a take-off from an impossibly tip-tilted angle, and Frazier stands there watching, jaw dropped, until the black of the sky and the distance have inked out the tiny plane lights.

"Screwball," he mutters and paws the sweat from his face.

O'Shaughnessy's hard-knuckled hands grasp the stick hard. Thunder rumbles above the roar of the motor; lightning stabs the darkness. Rain begins to slash down around the plane.

O'Shaughnessy remembers another storm, another plane, another night; and he glances at the girl beside him. She seems to sense his gaze upon her, her eyes open; her lips would speak but the fever that is burning through her won't let the words come. They are in her eyes, though, as plain as any words could be, and her whole heart is with them. No question there at all, just courage and confidence.

"I brought you into this," he says—to those eyes. "Now I'm taking you out of it. There's no place in it for us any longer."

Her fingers inside the glove tighten on his hand convulsively as if to say: "Alone, O'Shaughnessy? Must I go alone?"

At least that's the way he figures it, for he says quickly: "With me, honey. Together."

The pressure of the fingers relaxes, then tightens, but more steadily this time, reassured and reassuring. That's her way of saying:

"All right, O'Shaughnessy. It's all right with me."

Her face blurs in O'Shaughnessy's eyes; he begins to whistle a silly tune that even he can't hear, and somehow it is comforting. Lightning again and a louder crash of thunder. A gust of wind rocks the plane. The black bulk of a granite ridge that looks like a giant comber whipped up by a typhoon and frozen by the hands of God shows up ahead and a little below.

O'Shaughnessy's hand blunders out to take Nova's gloved one in his own. She whimpers a little, and stirs. O'Shaughnessy slides the stick forward, the plane tilts sharply down; the mountainside, rocky and desolate, seems to be reaching up for them, but in these seconds they are alone, the two of them, with the sky and the storm.

It takes will power and nerve to hold the stick that way, to keep his eyes open and watch the rocky face of the cliff, pine-bearded, rush up at them. O'Shaughnessy's mouth flattens, his face goes white. And then in that final fraction of a moment, he laughs, a little crazily—a laugh of defiance, of mocking farewell, and, somehow, of conquest.

"Here we go, baby!" he shouts, teeth bared. "Now I'm going to find out what it really feels like to fly into the side of a mountain! . . ."

There is only the storm to hear the smash of the plane as it splinters itself against the rock—and the storm drowns the sound out with thunder, just as the lightning turns pale the flame that rises, like a hungry tongue, from the wreckage.

THEODORE STURGEON
Killdozer

Before the race was the deluge, and before the deluge another race, whose nature it is not for mankind to understand. Not unearthly, not alien, for this was their earth and their home.

There was a war between this race, which was a great one, and another. The other was truly alien, a sentient cloudform, an intelligent grouping of tangible electrons. It was spawned in mighty machines by some accident of a science before our aboriginal conception of its complexities. And the machines, servants of the people, became the people's masters, and great were the battles that followed. The electron-beings had the power to warp the delicate balances of atom-structure, and their life-medium was metal, which they permeated and used to their own ends. Each weapon the people developed was possessed and turned against them, until a time when the remnants of that vast civilization found a defense—

An insulator. The terminal product or by-product of all energy research—neutronium.

In its shelter they developed a weapon. What it was we shall never know, and our race will live—or we shall know, and our race will perish as theirs perished. For, to destroy the enemy, it got out of hand and its measureless power destroyed them with it, and their cities, and their possessed machines. The very earth dissolved in flame, the crust writhed and shook and the oceans boiled. Nothing escaped it, nothing that we know as life, and nothing of the pseudolife that had evolved within the mysterious force-fields of their incomprehensible machines, save one hardy mutant.

Mutant it was, and ironically this one alone could have been

385

*killed by the first simple measures used against its kind—but it
was past time for simple expediences. It was an organized electron-
field possessing intelligence and mobility and a will to destroy,
and little else. Stunned by the holocaust, it drifted over the grumbling globe, and in a lull in the violence of the forces gone wild on
Earth, sank to the steaming ground in its half-conscious exhaustion.
There it found shelter—shelter built by and for its dead enemies.
An envelope of neutronium. It drifted in, and its consciousness at
last fell to its lowest ebb. And there it lay while the neutronium,
with its strange constant flux, its interminable striving for perfect
balance, extended itself and closed the opening. And thereafter in
the turbulent eons that followed, the envelope tossed like a gray
bubble on the surface of the rolling sphere, for no substance on
Earth would have it or combine with it.*

*The ages came and went, and chemical action and reaction did
their mysterious work, and once again there was life and evolution.
And a tribe found the mass of neutronium, which is not a substance
but a static force, and were awed by its aura of indescribable chill,
and they worshiped it and built a temple around it and made
sacrifices to it. And ice and fire and the seas came and went, and
the land rose and fell as the years went by, until the ruined temple
was on a knoll, and the knoll was an island. Islanders came and
went, lived and built and died, and races forgot. So now, somewhere
in the Pacific to the west of the archipelago called Islas Revilla-
gigeda, there was an uninhabited island. And one day—*

CHUB HORTON and Tom Jaeger stood watching the *Sprite* and
her squat tow of three cargo lighters dwindle over the glassy sea.
The big ocean-going towboat and her charges seemed to be moving
out of focus rather than traveling away. Chub spat cleanly around
the cigar that grew out of the corner of his mouth.

"That's that for three weeks. How's it feel to be a guinea pig?"

"We'll get it done." Tom had little crinkles all around the outer
ends of his eyes. He was a head taller than Chub and rangy, and
not so tough, and he was a real operator. Choosing him as a
foreman for the experiment had been wise, for he was competent
and he commanded respect. The theory of airfield construction
that they were testing appealed vastly to him, for here were no
officers-in-charge, no government inspectors, no time-keeping or
reports. The government had allowed the company a temporary

land grant, and the idea was to put production-line techniques into the layout and grading of the project. There were six operators and two mechanics and more than a million dollars' worth of the best equipment that money could buy. Government acceptance was to be on a partially completed basis, and contingent on government standards. The theory obviated both gold-bricking and graft, and neatly sidestepped the man-power shortage. "When that black-topping crew gets here, I reckon we'll be ready for 'em," said Tom.

He turned and scanned the island with an operator's vision and saw it as it was, and in all the stages it would pass through, and as it would look when they had finished, with four thousand feet of clean-draining runway, hard-packed shoulders, four acres of plane-park, the access road and the short taxiway. He saw the lay of each lift that the power shovel would cut as it brought down the marl bluff, and the ruins on top of it that would give them stone to haul down the salt-flat to the little swamp at the other end, there to be walked in by the dozers.

"We got time to walk the shovel up there to the bluff before dark."

They walked down the beach toward the outcropping where the equipment stood surrounded by crates and drums of supplies. The three tractors were ticking over quietly, the two-cycle Diesel chuckling through their mufflers and the big D-7 whacking away its metronomic compression knock on every easy revolution. The Dumptors were lined up and silent, for they would not be ready to work until the shovel was ready to load them. They looked like a mechanical interpretation of Dr. Doolittle's "Pushme-pullyou," the fantastic animal with two front ends. They had two large driving wheels and two small steerable wheels. The motor and the driver's seat were side by side over the front—or smaller—wheels; but the driver faced the dump body between the big rear wheels, exactly the opposite of the way he would sit in a dump truck. Hence, in traveling from shovel to dumping-ground, the operator drove backwards, looking over his shoulder, and in dumping he backed the machine up but he himself traveled forward—quite a trick for fourteen hours a day! The shovel squatted in the midst of all the others, its great hulk looming over them, humped there with its boom low and its iron chin on the ground, like some great tired dinosaur.

Rivera, the Puerto Rican mechanic, looked up grinning as Tom and Chub approached, and stuck a bleeder wrench into the top pocket of his coveralls.

"She says 'Sigalo,' " he said, his white teeth flashlighting out of the smear of grease across his mouth. "She says she wan' to get dirt on dis paint." He kicked the blade of the Seven with his heel.

Tom sent the grin back—always a surprising thing in his grave face.

"That Seven'll do that, and she'll take a good deal off her bitin' edge along with the paint before we're through. Get in the saddle, Goony. Build a ramp off the rocks down to the flat there, and blade us off some humps from here to the bluff yonder. We're walking the dipper up there."

The Puerto Rican was in the seat before Tom had finished, and with a roar the Seven spun in its length and moved back along the outcropping to the inland edge. Rivera dropped his blade and the sandy marl curled and piled up in front of the dozer, loading the blade and running off in two even rolls at the ends. He shoved the load toward the rocky edge, the Seven revving down as it took the load, *blat blat blatting* and pulling like a supercharged ox as it fired slowly enough for them to count the revolutions.

"She's a hunk of machine," said Tom.

"A hunk of operator, too," gruffed Chub, and added, "for a mechanic."

"The boy's all right," said Kelly. He was standing there with them, watching the Puerto Rican operate the dozer, as if he had been there all along, which was the way Kelly always arrived places. He was tall, slim, with green eyes too long and an easy stretch to the way he moved, like an attenuated cat. He said, "Never thought I'd see the day when equipment was shipped set up ready to run like this. Guess no one ever thought of it before."

"There's times when heavy equipment has to be unloaded in a hurry these days," Tom said. "If they can do it with tanks, they can do it with construction equipment. We're doin' it to build something instead, is all. Kelly, crank up the shovel. It's oiled. We're walking it over to the bluff."

Kelly swung up into the cab of the big dipper-stick and, diddling the governor control, pulled up the starting handle. The Murphy Diesel snorted and settled down into a thudding idle. Kelly got into the saddle, set up the throttle a little, and began to boom up.

"I still can't get over it," said Chub. "Not more'n a year ago we'd a had two hundred men on a job like this."

Tom smiled. "Yeah, and the first thing we'd have done would be to build an office building, and then quarters. Me, I'll take this way. No timekeepers, no equipment-use reports, no progress and yardage summaries, no nothin' but eight men, a million bucks worth of equipment, an' three weeks. A shovel an' a mess of tool crates'll keep the rain off us, an' army field rations'll keep our bellies full. We'll get it done, we'll get out and we'll get paid."

Rivera finished the ramp, turned the Seven around and climbed it, walking the new fill down. At the top he dropped his blade, floated it, and backed down the ramp, smoothing out the rolls. At a wave from Tom he started out across the shore, angling up toward the bluff, beating out the humps and carrying fill into the hollows. As he worked, he sang, feeling the beat of the mighty motor, the micrometric obedience of that vast implacable machine.

"Why doesn't that monkey stick to his grease guns?"

Tom turned and took the chewed end of a match stick out of his mouth. He said nothing, because he had for some time been trying to make a habit of saying nothing to Joe Dennis. Dennis was an ex-accountant, drafted out of an office at the last gasp of a defunct project in the West Indies. He had become an operator because they needed operators badly. He had been released with alacrity from the office because of his propensity for small office politics. It was a game he still played, and completely aside from his boiled-looking red face and his slightly womanish walk, he was out of place in the field; for boot-licking and back-stabbing accomplish even less out on the field than they do in an office. Tom, trying so hard to keep his mind on his work, had to admit to himself that of all Dennis' annoying traits the worst was that he was as good a pan operator as could be found anywhere, and no one could deny it.

Dennis certainly didn't.

"I've seen the day when anyone catching one of those goonies so much as sitting on a machine during lunch, would kick his fanny," Dennis groused. "Now they give 'em a man's work and a man's pay."

"Doin' a man's work, ain't he?" Tom said.

"He's a Puerto Rican!"

Tom turned and looked at him levelly. "Where was it you said *you* come from," he mused. "Oh yeah. Georgia."

"What do you mean by that?"

Tom was already striding away. "Tell you as soon as I have to," he flung back over his shoulder. Dennis went back to watching the Seven.

Tom glanced at the ramp and then waved Kelly on. Kelly set his housebrake so the shovel could not swing, put her into travel gear, and shoved the swing lever forward. With a crackling of drive chains and a massive scrunching of compacting coral sand, the shovel's great flat pads carried her over and down the ramp. As she tipped over the peak of the ramp the heavy manganese steel bucket-door gaped open and closed, like a hungry mouth, slamming up against the bucket until suddenly it latched shut and was quiet. The big Murphy Diesel crooned hollowly under compression as the machine ran downgrade and then the sensitive governor took hold and it took up its belly-beating thud.

Peebles was standing by one of the door-pan combines, sucking on his pipe and looking out to sea. He was grizzled and heavy, and from under the bushiest gray brows looked the calmest gray eyes Tom had ever seen. Peebles had never gotten angry at a machine—a rare trait in a born mechanic—and in fifty-odd years he had learned it was even less use getting angry at a man. Because no matter what, you could always fix what was wrong with a machine. He said around his pipestem:

"Hope you'll give me back my boy, there."

Tom's lips quirked in a little grin. There had been an understanding between old Peebles and himself ever since they had met. It was one of those things which exists unspoken—they knew little about each other because they had never found it necessary to make small talk to keep their friendship extant. It was enough to know that each could expect the best from the other, without persuasion.

"Rivera?" Tom asked. "I'll chase him back as soon as he finishes that service road for the dipper-stick. Why—got anything on?"

"Not much. Want to get that arc welder drained and flushed and set up a grounded table in case you guys tear anything up." He paused. "Besides, the kid's filling his head up with too many things at once. Mechanicing is one thing; operating is something else."

"Hasn't got in his way much so far, has it?"

"Nope. Don't aim t' let it, either. 'Less you need him."

Tom swung up on the pan tractor. "I don't need him that bad, Peeby. If you want some help in the meantime, get Dennis."

Peebles said nothing. He spat. He didn't say anything at all.

"What's the matter with Dennis?" Tom wanted to know.

"Look yonder," said Peebles, waving his pipestem. Out on the beach Dennis was talking to Chub, in Dennis' indefatigable style, standing beside Chub, one hand on Chub's shoulder. As they watched they saw Dennis call his side-kick, Al Knowles.

"Dennis talks too much," said Peebles. "That most generally don't amount to much, but that Dennis, he sometimes *says* too much. Ain't got what it takes to run a show, and knows it. Makes up for it by messin' in between folks."

"He's harmless," said Tom.

Still looking up the beach, Peebles said slowly:

"Is, so far."

Tom started to say something, then shrugged. "I'll send you Rivera," he said, and opened the throttle. Like a huge electric dynamo, the two-cycle motor whined to a crescendo. Tom lifted the dozer with a small lever by his right thigh and raised the pan with the long control sprouting out from behind his shoulder. He moved off, setting the rear gate of the scraper so that anything the blade bit would run off to the side instead of loading into the pan. He slapped the tractor into sixth gear and whined up to and around the crawling shovel, cutting neatly in under the boom and running on ahead with his scraper blade just touching the ground, dragging to a fine grade the service road Rivera had cut.

Dennis was saying, "It's that little Hitler stuff. Why should I take that kind of talk? 'You come from Georgia,' he says. What is he—a Yankee or something?"

"A crackah f'm Macon," chortled Al Knowles, who came from Georgia, too. He was tall and stringy and round-shouldered. All of his skill was in his hands and feet, brains being a commodity he had lived without all his life until he had met Dennis and used him as a reasonable facsimile thereof.

"Tom didn't mean nothing by it," said Chub.

"No, he didn't mean nothin'. Only that we do what he says the way he says it, specially if he finds a way we don't like it. *You* wouldn't do like that, Chub. Al, think Chub would carry on thataway?"

"Sure wouldn't," said Al, feeling it expected of him.

"Nuts," said Chub, pleased and uncomfortable, and thinking, what have I got against Tom?—not knowing, not liking Tom as well as he had. "Tom's the man here, Dennis. We got a job to do—let's skit and git. Man can take anything for a lousy six weeks."

"Oh, sho'," said Al.

"Man can take just so much," Dennis said. "What they put a man like that on top for, Chub? What's the matter with you? Don't you know grading and drainage as good as Tom? Can Tom stake out a side hill like you can?"

"Sure, sure, but what's the difference, long as we get a field built? An' anyhow, hell with bein' the boss-man. Who gets the blame if things don't run right, anyway?"

Dennis stepped back, taking his hand off Chub's shoulder, and stuck an elbow in Al's ribs.

"You see that, Al? Now there's a smart man. That's the thing Uncle Tom didn't bargain for. Chub, you can count on Al and me to do just that little thing."

"Do just what little thing?" asked Chub, genuinely puzzled.

"Like you said. If the job goes wrong, the boss gets blamed. So if the boss don't behave, the job goes wrong."

"Uh-huh," agreed Al with the conviction of mental simplicity.

Chub double-took this extraordinary logical process and grasped wildly at anger as the conversation slid out from under him. "I didn't say any such thing! This job is goin' to get done, no matter what! Hitler ain't hangin' no iron cross on me or anybody else around here if I can help it."

"Tha's the ol' fight," feinted Dennis. "We'll show that guy what we think of his kind of sabotage."

"You talk too much," said Chub and escaped with the remnants of coherence. Every time he talked with Dennis he walked away feeling as if he had an unwanted membership card stuck in his pocket that he couldn't throw away with a clear conscience.

Rivera ran his road up under the bluff, swung the Seven around, punched out the master clutch and throttled down, idling. Tom was making his pass with the pan, and as he approached, Rivera slipped out of the seat and behind the tractor, laying a sensitive hand on the final drive casing and sprocket bushings, checking for overheating. Tom pulled alongside and beckoned him up on the pan tractor.

"*Que pase*, Goony? Anything wrong?"

Rivera shook his head and grinned. "Nothing wrong. She is perfect, that '*De Siete.*' She—"

"That what? 'Daisy Etta'?"

"*De siete.* In Spanish, D-7. It means something in English?"

"Got you wrong," smiled Tom. "But Daisy Etta is a girl's name in English, all the same."

He shifted the pan tractor into neutral and engaged the clutch, and jumped off the machine. Rivera followed. They climbed aboard the Seven, Tom at the controls.

Rivera said "Daisy Etta," and grinned so widely that a soft little chuckling noise came from behind his back teeth. He reached out his hand, crooked his little finger around one of the tall steering clutch levers, and pulled it all the way back. Tom laughed outright.

"You got something there," he said. "The easiest runnin' cat ever built. Hydraulic steerin' clutches and brakes that'll bring you to a dead stop if you spit on 'em. Forward an' reverse lever so's you got all your speeds front and backwards. A little different from the old jobs. They had no booster springs, eight-ten years ago; took a sixty-pound pull to get a steerin' clutch back. Cuttin' a side-hill with an angle-dozer really was a job in them days. You try it sometime, dozin' with one hand, holdin' her nose out o' the bank with the other, ten hours a day. And what'd it get you? Eighty cents an hour an' ' "—Tom took his cigarette and butted the fiery end out against the horny palm of his hand—"these."

"*Santa Maria!*"

"Want to talk to you, Goony. Want to look over the bluff, too, at that stone up there. It'll take Kelly pret' near an hour to get this far and sumped in, anyhow."

They started up the slope, Tom feeling the ground under the four-foot brush, taking her up in a zigzag course like a hairpin road on a mountainside. Though the Seven carried a muffler on the exhaust stack that stuck up out of the hood before them, the blat of four big cylinders hauling fourteen tons of steel upgrade could outshout any man's conversation, so they sat without talking, Tom driving, Rivera watching his hands flick over the controls.

The bluff started in a low ridge running almost the length of the little island, like a lopsided backbone. Toward the center it rose abruptly, sent a wing out toward the rocky outcropping at the beach where their equipment had been unloaded, and then rose again to a small, almost square plateau area, half a mile square. It was humpy and rough until they could see all of it,

when they realized how incredibly level it was, under the brush
and ruins that covered it. In the center—and exactly in the center
they realized suddenly—was a low, overgrown mound. Tom threw
out the clutch and revved her down.

"Survey report said there was stone up here," Tom said, vaulting
out of the seat. "Let's walk around some."

They walked toward the knoll, Tom's eyes casting about as he
went. He stooped down into the heavy, short grass and scooped
up a piece of stone, blue-gray, hard and brittle.

"Rivera—look at this. This is what the report was talking about.
See—more of it. All in small pieces, though. We need big stuff
for the bog if we can get it."

"Good stone?" asked Rivera.

"Yes, boy—but it don't belong here. Th' whole island's sand
and marl and sandstone on the outcrop down yonder. This here's
a bluestone, like diamond clay. Harder'n blazes. I never saw this
stuff on a marl hill before. Or near one. Anyhow, root around
and see if there is any big stuff."

They walked on. Rivera suddenly dipped down and pulled grass
aside.

"Tom—here's a beeg one."

Tom came over and looked down at the corner of stone sticking
up out of the topsoil. "Yeh. Goony, get your girl-friend over here
and we'll root it out."

Rivera sprinted back to the idling dozer and climbed aboard.
He brought the machine over to where Tom waited, stopped,
stood up and peered over the front of the machine to locate the
stone, then sat down and shifted gears. Before he could move the
machine Tom was on the fender beside him, checking him with
a hand on his arm.

"No, boy—no. Not third. First. And half throttle. That's it.
Don't try to bash a rock out of the ground. Go on up to it easy;
set your blade against it, lift it out, don't boot it out. Take it
with the middle of your blade, not the corner—get the load on
both hydraulic cylinders. Who told you to do like that?"

"No one tol' me, Tom. I see a man do it, I do it."

"Yeah? Who was it?"

"Dennis, but—"

"Listen, Goony, if you want to learn anything from Dennis,
watch him while he's on a pan. He dozes like he talks. That

reminds me—what I wanted to talk to you about. You ever have any trouble with him?"

Rivera spread his hands. "How I have trouble when he never talk to me?"

"Well, that's all right then. You keep it that way. Dennis is O.K., I guess, but you better keep away from him."

He went on to tell the boy then about what Peebles had said concerning being an operator and a mechanic at the same time. Rivera's lean dark face fell, and his hand strayed to the blade control, touching it lightly, feeling the composition grip and the machined locknuts that held it. When Tom had quite finished he said:

"O.K., Tom—if you want, you break 'em, I feex 'em. But if you wan' help some time, I run *Daisy Etta* for you, no?"

"Sure, kid, sure. But don't forget, no man can do everything."

"You can do everything," said the boy.

Tom leaped off the machine and Rivera shifted into first and crept up to the stone, setting the blade gently against it. Taking the load, the mighty engine audibly bunched its muscles; Rivera opened the throttle a little and the machine set solidly against the stone, the tracks slipping, digging into the ground, piling loose earth up behind. Tom raised a fist, thumb up, and the boy began lifting his blade. The Seven lowered her snout like an ox pulling through mud; the front of the tracks buried themselves deeper and the blade slipped upward an inch on the rock, as if it were on a ratchet. The stone shifted, and suddenly heaved itself up out of the earth that covered it, bulging the sod aside like a ship's slow bow-wave. And the blade lost its grip and slipped over the stone. Rivera slapped out the master clutch within an ace of letting the mass of it poke through his radiator core. Reversing, he set the blade against it again and rolled it at last into daylight.

Tom stood staring at it, scratching the back of his neck. Rivera got off the machine and stood beside him. For a long time they said nothing.

The stone was roughly rectangular, shaped like a brick with one end cut at about a thirty-degree angle. And on the angled face was a square-cut ridge, like the tongue on a piece of milled lumber. The stone was about $3 \times 2 \times 2$ feet, and must have weighed six or seven hundred pounds.

"Now that," said Tom, bug-eyed, "didn't grow *here,* and if it did it never grew that way."

"Una piedra de una casa," said Rivera softly. "Tom, there was a building here, no?"

Tom turned suddenly to look at the knoll.

"There is a building here—or what's left of it. Lord on'y knows how old—"

They stood there in the slowly dwindling light, staring at the knoll; and there came upon them a feeling of oppression, as if there were no wind and no sound anywhere. And yet there was wind, and behind them *Daisy Etta* whacked away with her muttering idle, and nothing had changed and—was that it? That nothing had changed? That nothing would change, or could, here?

Tom opened his mouth twice to speak, and couldn't, or didn't want to—he didn't know which. Rivera slumped down suddenly on his hunkers, back erect, and his eyes wide.

It grew very cold. "It's cold," Tom said, and his voice sounded harsh to him. And the wind blew warm on them, the earth was warm under Rivera's knees. The cold was not a lack of heat, but a lack of something else—warmth, but the specific warmth of life-force, perhaps. The feeling of oppression grew, as if their recognition of the strangeness of the place had started it, and their increasing sensitivity to it made it grow.

Rivera said something, quietly, in Spanish.

"What are you looking at?" asked Tom.

Rivera started violently, threw up an arm, as if to ward off the crash of Tom's voice.

"I . . . there is nothin' to see, Tom. I feel this way wance before. I dunno—" He shook his head, his eyes wide and blank. "An' after, there was being wan hell of a thunderstorm—" His voice petered out.

Tom took his shoulder and hauled him roughly to his feet. "Goony! You slap-happy?"

The boy smiled, almost gently. The down on his upper lip held little spheres of sweat. "I ain' nothin', Tom. I'm jus' scare like hell."

"You scare yourself right back up there on that cat and git to work," Tom roared. More quietly then, he said, "I know there's something—wrong—here, Goony, but that ain't goin' to get us a runway built. Anyhow, I know what to do about a dawg 'at gits gunshy. Ought to be able to do as much fer you. Git along to th' mound now and see if it ain't a cache o' big stone for us. We got a swamp down there to fill."

Rivera hesitated, started to speak, swallowed and then walked slowly over to the Seven. Tom stood watching him, closing his mind to the impalpable pressure of something, somewhere near, making his guts cold.

The bulldozer nosed over to the mound, grunting, reminding Tom suddenly that the machine's Spanish slang name was *puerco*— pig, boar. Rivera angled into the edge of the mound with the cutting corner of the blade. Dirt and brush curled up, fell away from the mound and loaded from the bank side, out along the moldboard. The boy finished his pass along the mound, carried the load past it and wasted it out on the flat, turned around and started back again.

Ten minutes later Rivera struck stone, the manganese steel screaming along it, a puff of gray dust spouting from the cutting corner. Tom knelt and examined it after the machine had passed. It was the same kind of stone they had found out on the flat— and shaped the same way. But here it was a wall, the angled faces of the block ends obviously tongued and grooved together.

Cold, cold as—

Tom took one deep breath and wiped sweat out of his eyes.

"I don't care," he whispered, "I got to have that stone. I got to fill me a swamp." He stood back and motioned to Rivera to blade into a chipped crevice in the buried wall.

The Seven swung into the wall and stopped while Rivera shifted into first, throttled down and lowered his blade. Tom looked up into his face. The boy's lips were white. He eased in the master clutch, the blade dipped and the corner swung neatly into the crevice.

The dozer blatted protestingly and began to crab sideways, pivoting on the end of the blade. Tom jumped out of the way, ran around behind the machine, which was almost parallel with the wall now, and stood in the clear, one hand raised ready to signal, his eyes on the straining blade. And then everything happened at once.

With a toothy snap the block started and came free, pivoting outward from its square end, bringing with it its neighbor. The block above them dropped, and the whole mound seemed to settle. And *something* whooshed out of the black hole where the rocks had been. Something like a fog, but not a fog that could be seen, something huge that could not be measured. With it came a gust of that cold which was not cold, and the smell of ozone, and the prickling crackle of a mighty static discharge.

Tom was fifty feet from the wall before he knew he had moved. He stopped and saw the Seven suddenly buck like a wild stallion, once, and Rivera turning over twice in the air. Tom shouted some meaningless syllable and tore over to the boy, where he sprawled in the rough grass, lifted him in his arms, and ran. Only then did he realize that he was running from the machine.

It was like a mad thing. Its moldboard rose and fell. It curved away from the mound, howling governor gone wild, controls flailing. The blade dug repeatedly into the earth, gouging it up in great dips through which the tractor plunged, clanking and bellowing furiously. It raced away in a great irregular arc, turned and came snorting back to the mound, where it beat at the buried wall, slewed and scraped and roared.

Tom reached the edge of the plateau sobbing for breath, and kneeling, laid the boy gently down on the grass.

"Goony, boy . . . hey—"

The long silken eyelashes fluttered, lifted. Something wrenched in Tom as he saw the eyes, rolled right back so that only the whites showed. Rivera drew a long quivering breath which caught suddenly. He coughed twice, threw his head from side to side so violently that Tom took it between his hands and steadied it.

"*Ay . . . Maria madre . . . que me pasado,* Tom—w'at has happen to me?"

"Fell off the Seven, stupid. You . . . how you feel?"

Rivera scrabbled at the ground, got his elbows half under him, then sank back weakly. "Feel O.K. Headache like hell. W-w'at happen to my feets?"

"Feet? They hurt?"

"No hurt—" The young face went gray, the lips tightened with effort. "No nothin', Tom."

"You can't move 'em?"

Rivera shook his head, still trying. Tom stood up. "You take it easy. I'll go get Kelly. Be right back."

He walked away quickly and when Rivera called to him he did not turn around. Tom had seen a man with a broken back before.

At the edge of the little plateau Tom stopped, listening. In the deepening twilight he could see the bulldozer standing by the mound. The motor was running; she had not stalled herself. But what stopped Tom was that she wasn't idling, but revving up and down as if an impatient hand were on the throttle—*hroom hrooom,* running up and up far faster than even a broken governor should permit, then coasting down to near silence, broken by the explosive punctuation of sharp and irregular firing. Then it would run up and up again, almost screaming, sustaining a r.p.m. that threatened every moving part, shaking the great machine like some deadly ague.

Tom walked swiftly toward the Seven, a puzzled and grim frown on his weather-beaten face. Governors break down occasionally, and once in a while you will have a motor tear itself to pieces, revving up out of control. But it will either do that or it will rev down and quit. If an operator is fool enough to leave his machine with the master clutch engaged, the machine will take off and run the way Seven had—but it will not turn unless the blade corner catches in something unresisting, and then the chances are very strong that it will stall. But in any case, it was past reason for any machine to act this way, revving up and down, running, turning, lifting and dropping the blade.

The motor slowed as he approached, and at last settled down into something like a steady and regular idle. Tom had the sudden crazy impression that it was watching him. He shrugged off the feeling, walked up and laid a hand on the fender.

The Seven reacted like a wild stallion. The big Diesel roared, and Tom distinctly saw the master clutch lever snap back over center. He leaped clear, expecting the machine to jolt forward, but apparently it was in a reverse gear, for it shot backwards, one track locked, and the near end of the blade swung in a swift vicious arc, breezing a bare fraction of an inch past his hip as he danced back out of the way.

And as if it had bounced off a wall, the tractor had shifted and was bearing down on him, the twelve-foot blade rising, the two big headlights looming over him on their bow-legged supports, looking like the protruding eyes of some mighty toad. Tom had no choice but to leap straight up and grasp the top of the blade in his two hands, leaning back hard to brace his feet against the curved moldboard. The blade dropped and sank into the soft topsoil, digging a deep little swale in the ground. The earth loading on the moldboard rose and churned around Tom's legs; he stepped wildly, keeping them clear of the rolling drag of it. Up came the blade then, leaving a four-foot pile at the edge of the pit; down and up the tractor raced as the tracks went into it; up and up as they climbed the pile of dirt. A quick balance and overbalance as the machine lurched up and over like a motorcycle taking a jump off a ramp, and then a spine-shaking crash as fourteen tons of metal smashed blade-first into the ground.

Part of the leather from Tom's tough palms stayed with the blade as he was flung off. He went head over heels backwards, but had his feet gathered and sprang as they touched the ground; for he knew that no machine could bury its blade like that and get out easily. He leaped to the top of the blade, got one hand on the radiator cap, vaulted. Perversely, the cap broke from its hinge and came away in his hand, in that split instant when only that hand rested on anything. Off balance, he landed on his shoulder with his legs flailing the air, his body sliding off the hood's smooth shoulder toward the track now churning the earth beneath. He made a wild grab at the air intake pipe, barely had it in his fingers when the dozer freed itself and shot backwards up and over the hump. Again that breathless flight pivoting over the top, and the clanking crash as the machine landed, this time almost flat on its tracks.

The jolt tore Tom's hand away, and as he slid back over the hood the crook of his elbow caught the exhaust stack, the dull red metal biting into his flesh. He grunted and clamped the arm around it. His momentum carried him around it, and his feet crashed into the steering clutch levers. Hooking one with his instep, he doubled his legs and whipped himself back, scrabbling at the smooth warm metal, crawling frantically backward until he finally fell heavily into the seat.

"Now," he gritted through a red wall of pain, "you're gonna git operated." And he kicked out the master clutch.

The motor wailed, with the load taken off so suddenly. Tom grasped the throttle, his thumb clamped down on the ratchet release, and he shoved the lever forward to shut off the fuel.

It wouldn't shut off; it went down to a slow idle, but it wouldn't shut off.

"There's one thing you can't do without," he muttered, "compression."

He stood up and leaned around the dash, reaching for the compression-release lever. As he came up out of the seat, the engine revved up again. He turned to the throttle, which had snapped back into the "open" position. As his hand touched it the master clutch lever snapped in and the howling machine lurched forward with a jerk that snapped his head on his shoulders and threw him heavily back into the seat. He snatched at the hydraulic blade control and threw it to "float" position; and then as the falling moldboard touched the ground, into "power down." The cutting edge bit into the ground and the engine began to labor. Holding the blade control, he pushed the throttle forward with his other hand. One of the steering clutch levers whipped back and struck him agonizingly on the kneecap. He involuntarily let go of the blade control and the moldboard began to rise. The engine began to turn faster and he realized that it was not responding to the throttle. Cursing, he leaped to his feet; the suddenly flailing steering clutch levers struck him three times in the groin before he could get between them.

Blind with pain, Tom clung gasping to the dash. The oil-pressure gauge fell off the dash to his right, with a tinkling of broken glass, and from its broken quarter-inch line scalding oil drenched him. The shock of it snapped back his wavering consciousness. Ignoring the blows of the left steering clutch and the master clutch which had started the same mad punching, he bent over the left end of the dash and grasped the compression lever. The tractor rushed forward and spun sickeningly, and Tom knew he was thrown. But as he felt himself leave the decking his hand punched the compression lever down. The great valves at the cylinder heads opened and locked open; atomized fuel and superheated air chattered out, and as Tom's head and shoulders struck the ground the great wild machine rolled to a stop, stood silently except for the grumble of water boiling in the cooling system.

Minutes later Tom raised his head and groaned. He rolled over and sat up, his chin on his knees, washed by wave after wave of pain. As they gradually subsided, he crawled to the machine and pulled himself to his feet, hand over hand on the track. And groggily he began to cripple the tractor, at least for the night.

He opened the cock under the fuel tank, left the warm yellow fluid gushing out on the ground. He opened the drain on the reservoir by the injection pump. He found a piece of wire in the crank box and with it tied down the compression release lever. He crawled up on the machine, wrenched the hood and ball jar off the air intake precleaner, pulled off his shirt and stuffed it down the pipe. He pushed the throttle all the way forward and locked it with the locking pin. And he shut off the fuel on the main line from the tank to the pump.

Then he climbed heavily to the ground and slogged back to the edge of the plateau where he had left Rivera.

They didn't know Tom was hurt until an hour and a half later—there had been too much to do—rigging a stretcher for the Puerto Rican, building him a shelter, an engine crate with an Army pup tent for a roof. They brought out the first-aid kit and the medical books and did what they could—tied and splinted and dosed with an opiate. Tom was a mass of bruises, and his right arm, where it had hooked the exhaust stack, was a flayed mass. They fixed him up then, old Peebles handling the sulfa powder and bandages like a trained nurse. And only then was there talk.

"I've seen a man thrown off a pan," said Dennis, as they sat around the coffee urn munching C rations. "Sittin' up on the arm rest on a cat, looking backwards. Cat hit a rock and bucked. Threw him off on the track. Stretched him out ten feet long." He in-whistled some coffee to dilute the mouthful of food he had been talking around, and masticated noisily. "Man's a fool to set up there on one side of his butt even on a pan. Can't see why the' goony was doin' it on a dozer."

"He wasn't," said Tom.

Kelly rubbed his pointed jaw. "He set flat on th' seat an' was th'owed?"

"That's right."

After an unbelieving silence Dennis said, "What was he doin'—drivin' over sixty?"

Tom looked around the circle of faces lit up by the over-artificial brilliance of a pressure lantern, and wondered what the reaction would be if he told it all just as it was. He had to say something, and it didn't look as if it could be the truth.

"He was workin'," he said finally. "Bucking stone out of the wall of an old building up on the mesa there. One turned loose an' as it did the governor must've gone haywire. She bucked like a loco hoss and run off."

"Run off?"

Tom opened his mouth and closed it again, and just nodded.

Dennis said, "Well, reckon that's what happens when you put a mechanic to operatin'."

"That had nothin' to do with it," Tom snapped.

Peebles spoke up quickly. "Tom—what about the Seven? Broke up any?"

"Some," said Tom. "Better look at the steering clutches. An' she was hot."

"Head's cracked," said Harris, a burly young man with shoulders like a buffalo and a famous thirst.

"How do you know?"

"Saw it when Al and me went up with the stretcher to get the kid while you all were building the shelter. Hot water runnin' down the side of the block."

"You mean you walked all the way out to the mound to look at that tractor while the kid was lyin' there? I told you where he was!"

"Out to the mound!" Al Knowles' pop eyes teetered out of their sockets. "We found that cat stalled twenty feet away from where the kid was!"

"What!"

"That's right, Tom," said Harris. "What's eatin' you? Where'd you leave it?"

"I told you . . . by the mound . . . the ol' building we cut into."

"Leave the startin' motor runnin'?"

"Starting motor?" Tom's mind caught the picture of the small, two-cylinder gasoline engine bolted to the side of the big Diesel's crankcase, coupled through a Bendix gear and clutch to the flywheel of the Diesel to crank it. He remembered his last glance at the still machine, silent but for the sound of water boiling. "Hell no!"

Al and Harris exchanged a glance. "I guess you were sort of slap-happy at the time, Tom," Harris said, not unkindly. "When we were halfway up the hill we heard it, and you know you can't mistake that racket. Sounded like it was under a load."

Tom beat softly at his temples with his clenched fists. "I left that machine dead," he said quietly. "I got compression off her and tied down the lever. I even stuffed my shirt in the intake. I drained the tank. But—I didn't touch the starting motor."

Peebles wanted to know why he had gone to all that trouble. Tom just looked vaguely at him and shook his head. "I shoulda pulled the wires. I never thought about the starting motor," he whispered. Then, "Harris—you say you found the starting motor running when you got to the top?"

"No—she was stalled. And hot—awmighty hot. I'd say the startin' motor was seized up tight. That must be it, Tom. You left the startin' motor runnin' and somehow engaged the clutch an'

Bendix." His voice lost conviction as he said it—it takes seventeen separate motions to start a tractor of this type. "Anyhow, she was in gear an' crawled along on the little motor."

"I done that once," said Chub. "Broke a con rod on an Eight, on a highway job. Walked her about three-quarters of a mile on the startin' motor that way. Only I had to stop every hundred yards and let her cool down some."

Not without sarcasm, Dennis said, "Seems to me like the Seven was out to get th' goony. Made one pass at him and then went back to finish the job."

Al Knowles haw-hawed extravagantly.

Tom stood up, shaking his head, and went off among the crates to the hospital they had jury-rigged for the kid.

A dim light was burning inside, and Rivera lay very still, with his eyes closed. Tom leaned in the doorway—the open end of the engine crate—and watched him for a moment. Behind him he could hear the murmur of the crew's voices; the night was otherwise windless and still. Rivera's face was the peculiar color that olive skin takes when drained of blood. Tom looked at his chest and for a panicky moment thought he could discern no movement there. He entered and put a hand over the boy's heart. Rivera shivered, his eyes flew open, and he drew a sudden breath which caught raggedly at the back of his throat. "Tom . . . Tom!" he cried weakly.

"O.K., Goony . . . *que pase?*"

"She comeen back . . . Tom!"

"Who?"

"El de siete."

Daisy Etta—"She ain't comin' back, kiddo. You're off the mesa now. Keep your chin up, fella."

Rivera's dark, doped eyes stared up at him without expression. Tom moved back and the eyes continued to stare. They weren't seeing anything. "Go to sleep," he whispered. The eyes closed instantly.

Kelly was saying that nobody ever got hurt on a construction job unless somebody was dumb. "An' most times you don't realize how dumb what you're doin' is until somebody does get hurt."

"The dumb part was gettin' a kid, an' not even an operator at that, up on a machine," said Dennis in his smuggest voice.

"I heard you try to sing that song before," said old Peebles quietly. "I hate to have to point out anything like this to a man because it don't do any good to make comparisons. But I've worked with that fella Rivera for a long time now, an' I've seen 'em as good but doggone few better. As far as you're concerned, you're O.K. on a pan, but the kid could give you cards and spades and still make you look like a cost accountant on a dozer."

Dennis half rose and mouthed something filthy. He looked at Al Knowles for backing and got it. He looked around the circle and got none. Peebles lounged back, sucking on his pipe, watching from under those bristling brows. Dennis subsided, running now on another tack.

"So what does that prove? The better you say he is, the less reason he had to fall off a cat and get himself hurt."

"I haven't got the thing straight yet," said Chub, in a voice whose tone indicated "I hate to admit it, but—"

About this time Tom returned, like a sleepwalker, standing with the brilliant pressure lantern between him and Dennis. Dennis rambled right on, not knowing he was anywhere near: "That's something you never will find out. That Puerto Rican is a pretty husky kid. Could be Tom said somethin' he didn't like an' he tried to put a knife in Tom's back. They all do, y'know. Tom didn't get all that bashin' around just stoppin' a machine. They must of went round an' round for a while an' the goony wound up with a busted back. Tom sets the dozer to walk him down while he lies there and comes on down here and tries to tell us—" His voice fluttered to a stop as Tom loomed over him.

Tom grabbed the pan operator up by the slack of his shirt front with his uninjured arm and shook him like an empty burlap bag.

"Skunk," he growled, "I oughta lower th' boom on you." He set Dennis on his feet and backhanded his face with the edge of his forearm. Dennis went down—cowered down, rather than fell. "Aw, Tom, I was just talkin'. Just a joke, Tom, I was just—"

"Yellow, too," snarled Tom, stepping forward, raising a solid Texan boot. Peebles barked "Tom!" and the foot came back to the ground.

"Out o' my sight," rumbled the foreman. "Git!"

Dennis got. Al Knowles said vaguely, "Naow, Tom, y'all cain't—"

"You, y'wall-eyed string-bean!" Tom raved, his voice harsh and strained. "Go 'long with yer Siamese twin!"

"O.K., O.K.," said Al, white-faced, and disappeared into the dark after Dennis.

"Nuts to this," said Chub. "I'm turnin' in." He went to a crate and hauled out a mosquito-hooded sleeping bag and went off without another word. Harris and Kelly, who were both on their feet, sat down again. Old Peebles hadn't moved.

Tom stood staring out into the dark, his arms straight at his sides, his fists knotted.

"Sit down," said Peebles gently. Tom turned and stared at him.

"Sit down. I can't change that dressing 'less you do." He pointed at the bandage around Tom's elbow. It was red, a widening stain, the tattered tissues having parted as the big Georgian bunched his infuriated muscles. He sat down.

"Talkin' about dumbness," said Harris calmly, as Peebles went to work, "I was about to say that I got the record. I done the dumbest thing anybody ever did on a machine. You can't top it."

"I could," said Kelly. "Runnin' a crane dragline once. Put her in boom gear and started to boom her up. Had an eighty-five-foot stick on her. Machine was standing on wooden mats in th' middle of a swamp. Heard the motor miss and got out of the saddle to look at the filter-glass. Messed around back there longer than I figured, and the boom went straight up in the air and fell backwards over the cab. Th' jolt tilted my mats an' she slid backwards slow and stately as you please, butt-first into the mud. Buried up to the eyeballs, she was." He laughed quietly. "Looked like a ditching machine!"

"I still say I done the dumbest thing ever, bar none," said Harris. "It was on a river job, widening a channel. I come back to work from a three-day binge, still rum-dumb. Got up on a dozer an' was workin' around on the edge of a twenty-foot cliff. Down at the foot of the cliff was a big hickory tree, an' growin' right along the edge was a great big limb. I got the dopey idea I should break it off. I put one track on the limb and the other on the cliff edge and run out away from the trunk. I was about halfway out, an' the branch saggin' some, before I thought what would happen if it broke. Just about then it did break. You know hickory—if it breaks at all it breaks altogether. So down we go into thirty feet of water—me an' the cat. I got out from under somehow. When all them bubbles stopped comin' up I swum around lookin' down at it. I was still paddlin' around when the superintendent came rushin' up. He wants to know what's up. I yell at him, 'Look down there, the way that water is movin' an' shiftin', looks like the cat is workin' down there.' He pursed his lips and *tsk tsked*. My, that man said some nasty things to me."

"Where'd you get your next job?" Kelly exploded.

"Oh, he didn't fire me," said Harris soberly. "Said he couldn't afford to fire a man as dumb as that. Said he wanted me around to look at whenever he felt bad."

Tom said, "Thanks, you guys. That's as good a way as any of sayin' that everybody makes mistakes." He stood up, examining the new dressing, turning his arm in front of the lantern. "You all can think what you please, but I don't recollect there was any dumbness went on on that mesa this evenin'. That's finished with, anyway. Do I have to say that Dennis' idea about it is all wet?"

Harris said one foul word that completely disposed of Dennis and anything he might say.

Peebles said, "It'll be all right. Dennis an' his popeyed friend'll hang together, but they don't amount to anything. Chub'll do whatever he's argued into."

"So you got 'em all lined up, hey?" Tom shrugged. "In the meantime, are we going to get an airfield built?"

"We'll get it built," Peebles said. "Only—Tom, I got no right to give you any advice, but go easy on the rough stuff after this. It does a lot of harm."

"I will if I can," said Tom gruffly. They broke up and turned in.

Peebles was right. It did do harm. It made Dennis use the word "murder" when they found, in the morning, that Rivera had died during the night.

The work progressed in spite of everything that had happened. With equipment like that, it's hard to slow things down. Kelly bit two cubic yards out of the bluff with every swing of the big shovel, and Dumptors are the fastest short-haul earth movers yet devised. Dennis kept the service road clean for them with his pan, and Tom and Chub spelled each other on the bulldozer they had detached from its pan to make up for the lack of the Seven, spending their alternate periods with transit and stakes. Peebles was rod-man for the surveys, and in between times worked on setting up his field shop, keeping the water cooler and battery chargers running, and lining up his forge and welding tables. The operators fueled and serviced their own equipment, and there was little delay. Rocks and marl came out of the growing cavity in the side of the central mesa—a whole third of it had to come out—were spun down to the edge of the swamp, which lay across the lower end of the projected runway, in the hornet-howling dump-tractors, their big driving wheels churned up vast clouds of dust, and were dumped and spread and walked in by the whining two-cycle dozer. When muck began to pile up in front of the fill, it was blasted out of the way with carefully placed charges of sixty percent dynamite and the craters filled with rocks, stone from the ruins, and surfaced with easily compacting marl, run out of a clean deposit by the pan.

And when he had his shop set up, Peebles went up the hill to get the Seven. When he got to it he just stood there for a moment scratching his head, and then, shaking his head, he ambled back down the hill and went for Tom.

"Been looking at the Seven," he said, when he had flagged the moaning two-cycle and Tom had climbed off.

"What'd you find?"

Peebles held out an arm. "A list as long as that." He shook his head. "Tom, what really happened up there?"

"Governor went haywire and she run away," Tom said promptly, deadpan.

"Yeah, but—" For a long moment he held Tom's eyes. Then he sighed. "O.K., Tom. Anyhow, I can't do a thing up there. We'll have to bring her back and I'll have to have this tractor to tow her down. And first I have to have some help—the track idler adjustment bolt's busted and the right track is off the track rollers."

"Oh-h-h. So that's why she couldn't get to the kid, running on the starting motor. Track would hardly turn, hey?"

"It's a miracle she ran as far as she did. That track is really jammed up. Riding right up on the roller flanges. And that ain't the half of it. The head's gone, like Harris said, and Lord only knows what I'll find when I open her up."

"Why bother?"

"What?"

"We can get along without that dozer," said Tom suddenly. "Leave her where she is. There's lots more for you to do."

"But what for?"

"Well, there's no call to go to all that trouble."

Peebles scratched the side of his nose and said, "I got a new head, track master pins—even a spare starting motor. I got tools to make what I don't stock." He pointed at the long row of dumps left by the hurtling dump-tractors while they had been talking. "You got a pan tied up because you're using this machine to doze with, and you can't tell me you can't use another one. You're gonna have to shut down one or two o' those Dumptors if you go on like this."

"I had all that figured out as soon as I opened my mouth," Tom said sullenly. "Let's go."

They climbed on the tractor and took off, stopping for a moment at the beach outcropping to pick up a cable and some tools.

Daisy Etta sat at the edge of the mesa, glowering out of her stilted headlights at the soft sward which still bore the impression of a young body and the tramplings of the stretcher-bearers. Her general aspect was woebegone—there were scratches on her olive-drab paint and the bright metal of the scratches was already dulled red by the earliest powder-rust. And though the ground was level, she was not, for her right track was off its lower rollers, and she stood slightly canted, like a man who has had a broken hip. And whatever passed for consciousness within her mulled over that paradox of the bulldozer that every operator must go through while he is learning his own machine.

It is the most difficult thing of all for the beginner to understand, that paradox. A bulldozer is a crawling powerhouse, a behemoth of noise and toughness, the nearest thing to the famous irresistible force. The beginner, awed and with the pictures of unconquerable Army tanks printed on his mind from the newsreels, takes all in his stride and with a sense of limitless power treats all obstacles alike, not knowing the fragility of a cast-iron radiator core, the mortality of tempered manganese, the friability of over-heated babbitt, and most of all, the ease with which a tractor can bury itself in mud. Climbing off to stare at a machine which he has reduced in twenty seconds to a useless hulk, or which was running a half-minute before on ground where it now has its tracks out of sight, he has that sense of guilty disappointment which overcomes any man on having made an error in judgment.

So, as she stood, *Daisy Etta* was broken and useless. These soft persistent bipeds had built her, and if they were like any other race that built machines, they could care for them. The ability to reverse the tension of a spring, or twist a control rod, or reduce to zero the friction in a nut and lock-washer, was not enough to repair the crack in a cylinder head nor bearings welded to a crankshaft in an overheated starting motor. There had been a lesson to learn. It had been learned. *Daisy Etta* would be repaired, and the next time—well, at least she would know her own weaknesses.

Tom swung the two-cycle machine and edged in next to the Seven, with the edge of his blade all but touching *Daisy Etta's* push-beam. They got off and Peebles bent over the drum-tight right track.

"Watch yourself," said Tom.

"Watch what?"

"Oh—nothin', I guess." He circled the machine, trained eyes probing over frame and fittings. He stepped forward suddenly and grasped the fuel-tank drain cock. It was closed. He opened it; golden oil gushed out. He shut it off, climbed up on the machine and opened the fuel cap on top of the tank. He pulled out the bayonet gauge, wiped it in the crook of his knee, dipped and withdrew it.

The tank was more than three quarters full.

"What's the matter?" asked Peebles, staring curiously at Tom's drawn face.

"Peeby, I opened the cock to drain this tank. I left it with oil runnin' out on the ground. She shut herself off."

"Now, Tom, you're lettin' this thing get you down. You just thought you did. I've seen a main-line valve shut itself off when it's worn bad, but only 'cause the fuel pump pulls it shut when the motor's runnin'. But not a gravity drain."

"Main-line valve?" Tom pulled the seat up and looked. One glance was enough to show him that this one was open.

"She opened this one, too."

"O.K.—O.K. Don't look at me like that!" Peebles was as near to exasperation as he could possibly get. "What difference does it make?"

Tom did not answer. He was not the type of man who, when faced with something beyond his understanding, would begin to doubt his own sanity. His was a dogged insistence that what he saw and sensed was what had actually happened. In him was none of the fainting fear of madness that another, more sensitive, man might feel. He doubted neither himself nor his evidence, and so could free his mind for searching out the consuming "why" of a problem. He knew instinctively that to share "unbelievable" happenings with anyone else, even if they had really occurred, was to put even further obstacles in his way. So he kept his clamlike silence and stubbornly, watchfully, investigated.

The slipped track was so tightly drawn up on the roller flanges that there could be no question of pulling the master pin and opening the track up. It would have to be worked back in place— a very delicate operation, for a little force applied in the wrong direction would be enough to run the track off altogether. To complicate things, the blade of the Seven was down on the ground and would have to be lifted before the machine could be maneuvered, and its hydraulic hoist was useless without the motor.

Peebles unhooked twenty feet of half-inch cable from the rear of the smaller dozer, scratched a hole in the ground under the Seven's blade, and pushed the eye of the cable through. Climbing over the moldboard, he slipped the eye on to the big towing hook bolted to the underside of the belly-guard. The other end of the cable he threw out on the ground in front of the machine. Tom mounted the other dozer and swung into place, ready to tow. Peebles hooked the cable onto Tom's drawbar, hopped up on the Seven. He put her in neutral, disengaged the master clutch, and put the blade control over into "float" position, then raised an arm.

Tom perched upon the arm rest of his machine, looking backwards, moved slowly, taking up the slack in the cable. It straightened and grew taut, and as it did it forced the Seven's blade upward. Peebles waved for slack and put the blade control into "hold." The cable bellied downward away from the blade.

"Hydraulic system's O.K., anyhow," called Peebles, as Tom throttled down. "Move over and take a strain to the right, sharp as you can without fouling the cable on the track. We'll see if we can walk this track back on."

Tom backed up, cut sharply to the right, and drew the cable out almost at right angles to the other machine. Peebles held the right track of the Seven with the brake and released both steering clutches. The left track now could turn free, the right not at all. Tom was running at a quarter throttle in his lowest gear, so that his machine barely crept along, taking the strain. The Seven shook gently and began to pivot on the taut right track, unbelievable foot-pounds of energy coming to bear on the front of the track where it rode high up on the idler wheel. Peebles released the right brake with his foot and applied it again in a series of skilled, deft jerks. The track would move a few inches and stop again, force being applied forward and sideward alternately, urging the track persuasively back in place. Then, a little jolt and she was in, riding true on the five truck rollers, the two track carrier rollers, the driving sprocket and the idler.

Peebles got off and stuck his head in between the sprocket and the rear carrier, squinting down and sideways to see if there were any broken flanges or roller bushes. Tom came over and pulled him out by the seat of his trousers. "Time enough for that when you get her in the shop," he said, masking his nervousness. "Reckon she'll roll?"

"She'll roll. I never saw a track in that condition come back that easy. By gosh, it's as if she was tryin' to help!"

"They'll do it sometimes," said Tom, stiffly. "You better take the tow-tractor, Peeby. I'll stay with this'n."

"Anything you say."

And cautiously they took the steep slope down, Tom barely holding the brakes, giving the other machine a straight pull all the way. And so they brought *Daisy Etta* down to Peebles' outdoor shop, where they pulled her cylinder head off, took off her starting motor, pulled out a burned clutch facing, had her quite helpless—

And put her together again.

"I tell you it was outright, cold-blooded murder," said Dennis hotly. "An' here we are takin' orders from a guy like that. What are we goin' to do about it?" They were standing by the cooler—Dennis had run his machine there to waylay Chub.

Chub Horton's cigar went down and up like a semaphore with a short circuit. "We'll skip it. The blacktopping crew will be here in another two weeks or so, an' we can make a report. Besides, I don't know what happened up there any more than you do. In the meantime we got a runway to build."

"You don't know what happened up there? Chub, you're a smart man. Smart enough to run this job better than Tom Jaeger even if he wasn't crazy. And you're surely smart enough not to believe all that cock and bull about that tractor runnin' out from under that grease-monkey. Listen—" he leaned forward and tapped Chub's chest. "He said it was the governor. I saw that governor myself an' heard ol' Peebles say there wasn't a thing wrong with it. Th' throttle control rod had slipped off its yoke, yeah—but you know what a tractor will do when the throttle control goes out. It'll idle or stall. It won't run away, whatever."

"Well, maybe so, but—"

"But nothin'! A guy that'll commit murder ain't sane. If he did it once, he can do it again and I ain't fixin' to let that happen to me."

Two things crossed Chub's steady but not too bright mind at this. One was that Dennis, whom he did not like but could not shake, was trying to force him into something that he did not want to do. The other was that under all of his swift talk Dennis was scared spitless.

"What do you want to do—call up the sheriff?"

Dennis ha-ha-ed appreciatively—one of the reasons he was so hard to shake. "I'll tell you what we can do. As long as we have you here, he isn't the only man who knows the work. If we stop takin' orders from him, you can give 'em as good or better. An' there won't be anything he can do about it."

"Doggone it, Dennis," said Chub, with sudden exasperation. "What do you think you're doin'—handin' me over the keys to the kingdom or something? What do you want to see me bossin' around here for?" He stood up. "Suppose we did what you said? Would it get the field built any quicker? Would it get me any more money in my pay envelope? What do you think I want—glory? I passed up a chance to run for councilman once. You think I'd raise a finger to get a bunch of mugs to do what I say—when they do it anyway?"

"Aw, Chub—I wouldn't cause trouble just for the fun of it. That's not what I mean at all. But unless we do something about that guy we ain't safe. Can't you get that through your head?"

"Listen, windy. If a man keeps busy enough he can't get into no trouble. That goes for Tom—you might keep that in mind. But it goes for you, too. Get back up on that rig an' get back to the marl pit." Dennis, completely taken by surprise, turned to his machine.

"It's a pity you can't move earth with your mouth," said Chub as he walked off. "They could have left you to do this job singlehanded."

Chub walked slowly toward the outcropping, switching at beach pebbles with a grade stake and swearing to himself. He was essentially a simple man and believed in the simplest possible

approach to everything. He liked a job where he could do everything required and where nothing turned up to complicate things.
He had been in the grading business for a long time as an operator
and survey party boss, and he was remarkable for one thing—he
had always held aloof from the cliques and internecine politics
that are the breath of life to most construction men. He was
disturbed and troubled at the back-stabbing that went on around
him on various jobs. If it was blunt, he was disgusted, and subtlety
simply left him floundering and bewildered. He was stupid enough
so that his basic honesty manifested itself in his speech and actions,
and he had learned that complete honesty in dealing with men
above and below him was almost invariably painful to all concerned, but he had not the wit to act otherwise, and did not try
to. If he had a bad tooth, he had it pulled out as soon as he
could. If he got a raw deal from a superintendent over him, that
superintendent would get told exactly what the trouble was, and
if he didn't like it, there were other jobs. And if the pulling and
hauling of cliques got in his hair, he had always said so and left.
Or he had sounded off and stayed; his completely selfish reaction
to things that got in the way of his work had earned him a lot
of regard from men he had worked under. And so, in this instance,
he had no hesitation about choosing a course of action. Only—
how did you go about asking a man if he was a murderer?

He found the foreman with an enormous wrench in his hand,
tightening up the new track adjustment bolt they had installed in
the Seven.

"Hey, Chub! Glad you turned up. Let's get a piece of pipe over
the end of this thing and really bear down." Chub went for the
pipe, and they fitted it over the handle of the four-foot wrench
and hauled until the sweat ran down their backs, Tom checking
the track clearance occasionally with a crowbar. He finally called
it good enough and they stood there in the sun gasping for breath.

"Tom," panted Chub, "did you kill that Puerto Rican?"

Tom's head came up as if someone had burned the back of
his neck with a cigarette.

"Because," said Chub, "if you did you can't go on runnin' this
job."

Tom said, "That's a lousy thing to kid about."

"You know I ain't kiddin'. Well, did you?"

"No!" Tom sat down on a keg, wiped his face with a bandanna.
"What's got into you?"

"I just wanted to know. Some of the boys are worried about it."

Tom's eyes narrowed. "Some of the boys, huh? I think I get it. Listen to me, Chub. Rivera was killed by that thing there." He thumbed over his shoulder at the Seven, which was standing ready now, awaiting only the building of a broken cutting corner on the blade. Peebles was winding up the welding machine as he spoke. "If you mean, did I put him up on the machine before he was thrown, the answer is yes. That much I killed him, and don't think I don't feel it. I had a hunch something was wrong up there, but I couldn't put my finger on it and I certainly didn't think anybody was going to get hurt."

"Well, what was wrong?"

"I still don't know." Tom stood up. "I'm tired of beatin' around the bush, Chub, and I don't much care any more what anybody thinks. There's somethin' wrong with that Seven, something that wasn't built into her. They don't make tractors better'n that one, but whatever it was happened up there on the mesa has queered this one. Now go ahead and think what you like, and dream up any story you want to tell the boys. In the meantime you can pass the word—nobody runs that machine but me, understand? Nobody!"

"Tom—"

Tom's patience broke. "That's all I'm going to say about it! If anybody else gets hurt, it's going to be me, understand? What more do you want?"

He strode off, boiling. Chub stared after him, and after a long moment reached up and took the cigar from his lips. Only then did he realize that he had bitten it in two; half the butt was still inside his mouth. He spat and stood there, shaking his head.

"How's she going, Peeby?"

Peebles looked up from the welding machine. "Hi, Chub, have her ready for you in twenty minutes." He gauged the distance between the welding machine and the big tractor. "I should have forty feet of cable," he said, looking at the festoons of arc and ground cables that hung from the storage hooks in the back of the welder. "Don't want to get a tractor over here to move the thing, and don't feel like cranking up the Seven just to get it close enough." He separated the arc cable and threw it aside, walked to the tractor, paying the ground cable off his arm. He threw out the last of his slack and grasped the ground clamp when he was eight feet from the machine. Taking it in his left hand, he pulled hard, reaching out with his right to grasp the moldboard of the Seven, trying to get it far enough to clamp on to the machine.

Chub stood there watching him, chewing on his cigar, absent-mindedly diddling with the controls on the arc-welder. He pressed the starter-button, and the six-cylinder motor responded with a purr. He spun the work-selector dials idly, threw the arc generator switch—

A bolt of incredible energy, thin, searing, blue-white, left the rod-holder at his feet, stretched itself *fifty feet* across to Peebles, whose fingers had just touched the moldboard of the tractor. Peebles' head and shoulders were surrounded for a second by a violet nimbus, and then he folded over and dropped. A circuit breaker clacked behind the control board of the welder, but too late. The Seven rolled slowly backward, without firing, on level ground, until it brought up against a road-roller.

Chub's cigar was gone, and he didn't notice it. He had the knuckles of his right hand in his mouth, and his teeth sunk into the pudgy flesh. His eyes protruded; he crouched there and quivered, literally frightened out of his mind. For old Peebles was almost burned in two.

They buried him next to Rivera. There wasn't much talk afterwards; the old man had been a lot closer to all of them than they had realized until now. Harris, for once in his rum-dumb, lighthearted life, was quiet and serious, and Kelly's walk seemed to lose some of its litheness. Hour after hour Dennis' flabby mouth worked, and he bit at his lower lip until it was swollen and tender. Al Knowles seemed more or less unaffected, as was to be expected from a man who had something less than the brains of a chicken. Chub Horton had snapped out of it after a couple of hours and was very nearly himself again. And in Tom Jaeger swirled a black, furious anger at this unknowable curse that had struck the camp.

And they kept working. There was nothing else to do. The shovel kept up its rhythmic swing and dig, swing and dump, and the Dumptors screamed back and forth between it and the little that there was left of the swamp. The upper end of the runway was grassed off; Chub and Tom set grade stakes and Dennis began the long job of cutting and filling the humpy surface with his pan. Harris manned the other and followed him, a cut behind. The shape of the runway emerged from the land, and then that of the paralleling taxiway; and three days went by. The horror of Peebles' death wore off enough so that they could talk about it, and very little of the talk helped anybody. Tom took his spells at everything, changing over with Kelly to give him a rest from the shovel, making a few rounds with a pan, putting in hours on a Dumptor. His arm was healing slowly but clean, and he worked grimly in spite of it, taking a perverse sort of pleasure from the pain of it. Every man on the job watched his machine with the solicitude of a mother with her first-born; a serious breakdown would have been disastrous without a highly skilled mechanic.

The only concession that Tom allowed himself in regard to Peebles' death was to corner Kelly one afternoon and ask him about the welding machine. Part of Kelly's rather patchy past had been spent in a technical college, where he had studied electrical engineering and women. He had learned a little of the former and enough of the latter to get him thrown out on his ear. So, on the off-chance that he might know something about the freak arc, Tom put it to him.

Kelly pulled off his high-gauntlet gloves and batted sandflies with them. "What sort of an arc was that? Boy, you got me there. Did you ever hear of a welding machine doing like that before?"

"I did not. A welding machine just don't have that sort o' push. I saw a man get a full jolt from a 400-amp welder once, an' although it sat him down it didn't hurt him any."

"It's not amperage that kills people," said Kelly, "it's voltage. Voltage is the pressure behind a current, you know. Take an amount of water, call it amperage. If I throw it in your face, it won't hurt you. If I put it through a small hose you'll feel it. But if I pump it through the tiny holes on a Diesel injector nozzle at about twelve hundred pounds, it'll draw blood. But a welding arc generator just is not wound to build up that kind of voltage. I can't see where any short circuit anywhere through the armature or field windings could do such a thing."

"From what Chub said, he had been foolin' around with the work selector. I don't think anyone touched the dials after it happened. The selector dial was run all the way over to the low current application segment, and the current control was around the halfway mark. That's not enough juice to get you a good bead with a quarter-inch rod, let alone kill somebody—or roll a tractor back thirty feet on level ground."

"Or jump fifty feet," said Kelly. "It would take thousands of volts to generate an arc like that."

"Is it possible that something in the Seven could have pulled that arc? I mean, suppose the arc wasn't driven over, but was drawn over? I tell you, she was hot for four hours after that."

Kelly shook his head. "Never heard of any such thing. Look, just to have something to call them, we call direct current terminals positive and negative, and just because it works in theory we say that current flows from negative to positive. There couldn't be any more positive attraction in one electrode than there is negative drive in the other; see what I mean?"

"There couldn't be some freak condition that would cause a sort of oversize positive field? I mean one that would suck out the negative flow all in a heap, make it smash through under a lot of pressure like the water you were talking about through an injector nozzle?"

"No, Tom. It just don't work that way, far as anyone knows. I dunno, though—there are some things about static electricity that nobody understands. All I can say is that what happened couldn't happen and if it did it couldn't have killed Peebles. And you know the answer to that."

Tom glanced away at the upper end of the runway, where the two graves were. There was bitterness and turbulent anger naked there for a moment, and he turned and walked away without another word. And when he went back to have another look at the welding machine, *Daisy Etta* was gone.

Al Knowles and Harris squatted together near the water cooler. "Bad," said Harris.

"Nevah saw anythin' like it," said Al. "Ol' Tom come back f'm the shop theah jus' *raisin'* Cain. 'Weah's 'at Seven gone? Weah's 'at Seven?' I never heered sech cah'ins on."

"Dennis did take it, huh?"

"Sho' did."

Harris said, "He came spoutin' around to me a while back, Dennis did. Chub'd told him Tom said for everybody to stay off that machine. Dennis was mad as a wet hen. Said Tom was carryin' that kind o' business too far. Said there was probably somethin' about the Seven Tom didn't want us to find out. Might incriminate him. Dennis is ready to say Tom killed the kid."

"Reckon he did, Harris?"

Harris shook his head. "I've known Tom too long to think that. If he won't tell us what really happened up on the mesa, he has a reason for it. How'd Dennis come to take the dozer?"

"Blew a front tire on his pan. Came back heah to git anothah rig—maybe a Dumptor. Saw th' Seven standin' theah ready to go. Stood theah lookin' at it and cussin' Tom. Said he was tired of bashin' his kidneys t'pieces on them othah rigs an' bedamned if he wouldn't take suthin' that rode good fo' a change. I tol' him ol' Tom'd raise th' roof when he found him on it. He had a couple mo' things t'say 'bout Tom then."

"I didn't think he had the guts to take the rig."

"Aw, he talked hisself blind mad."

They looked up as Chub Horton trotted up, panting. "Hey, you guys, come on. We better get up there to Dennis."

"What's wrong?" asked Harris, climbing to his feet.

"Tom passed me a minute ago lookin' like the wrath o' God and hightailin' it for the swamp fill. I asked him what was the matter and he hollered that Dennis had took the Seven. Said he was always talkin' about murder, and he'd get his fill of it foolin' around that machine." Chub went wall-eyed, licked his lips beside his cigar.

"Oh-oh," said Harris quietly. "That's the wrong kind o' talk for just now."

"You don't suppose he—"

"Come on!"

They saw Tom before they were halfway there. He was walking slowly, with his head down. Harris shouted. Tom raised his face, stopped, stood there waiting with a peculiarly slumped stance.

"Where's Dennis?" barked Chub.

Tom waited until they were almost up to him and then weakly raised an arm and thumbed over his shoulder. His face was green.

"Tom—is he—"

Tom nodded, and swayed a little. His granite jaw was slack.

"Al, stay with him. He's sick. Harris, let's go."

Tom was sick, then and there. Very. Al stood gaping at him, fascinated.

Chub and Harris found Dennis. All of twelve square feet of him, ground and churned and rolled out into a torn-up patch of earth. *Daisy Etta* was gone.

Back at the outcropping, they sat with Tom while Al Knowles

took a Dumptor and roared away to get Kelly.

"You saw him?" he said dully after a time.

Harris said, "Yeh."

The screaming Dumptor and a mountainous cloud of dust arrived, Kelly driving, Al holding on with a death-grip to the dump-bed guards. Kelly flung himself off, ran to Tom. "Tom—what is all this? Dennis dead? And you . . . you—"

Tom's head came up slowly, the slackness going out of his long face, a light suddenly coming into his eyes. Until this moment it had not crossed his mind what these men might think.

"I—what?"

"Al says you killed him."

Tom's eyes flicked at Al Knowles, and Al winced as if the glance had been a quirt.

Harris said, "What about it, Tom?"

"Nothing about it. He was killed by that Seven. You saw that for yourself."

"I stuck with you all along," said Harris slowly. "I took everything you said and believed it."

"This is too strong for you?" Tom asked.

Harris nodded. "Too strong, Tom."

Tom looked at the grim circle of faces and laughed suddenly. He stood up, put his back against a tall crate. "What do you plan to do about it?"

There was a silence. "You think I went up there and knocked that windbag off the machine and ran over him?" More silence. "Listen. I went up there and saw what you saw. He was dead before I got there. That's not good enough either?" He paused and licked his lips. "So after I killed him I got up on the tractor and drove it far enough away so you couldn't see or hear it when you got there. And then I sprouted wings and flew back so's I was halfway here when you met me—*ten minutes* after I spoke to Chub on my way up!"

Kelly said vaguely, "Tractor?"

"Well," said Tom harshly to Harris, "was the tractor there when you and Chub went up and saw Dennis?"

"No—"

Chub smacked his thigh suddenly. "You could of drove it into the swamp, Tom."

Tom said angrily, "I'm wastin' my time. You guys got it all figured out. Why ask me anything at all?"

"Aw, take it easy," said Kelly. "We just want the facts. Just what did happen? You met Chub and told him that Dennis would get all the murderin' he could take if he messed around that machine. That right?"

"That's right."

"Then what?"

"Then the machine murdered him."

Chub, with remarkable patience, asked, "What did you mean the day Peebles was killed when you said that something had queered the Seven up there on the mesa?"

Tom said furiously, "I meant what I said. You guys are set to crucify me for this and I can't stop you. Well, listen. Something's got into that Seven. I don't know what it is and I don't think I ever will know. I thought that after she smashed herself up that it was finished with. I had an idea that when we had her torn down and helpless we should have left her that way. I was dead right but it's too late now. She's killed Rivera and she's killed Dennis and she sure had something to do with killing Peebles. And my idea is that she won't stop as long as there's a human being alive on this island."

"Whaddaya know!" said Chub.

"Sure, Tom, sure," said Kelly quietly. "That tractor is out to get us. But don't worry; we'll catch it and tear it down. Just don't you worry about it any more; it'll be all right."

"That's right, Tom," said Harris. "You just take it easy around camp for a couple of days till you feel better. Chub and the rest of us will handle things for you. You had too much sun."

"You're a swell bunch of fellows," gritted Tom, with the deepest sarcasm. "You want to live," he shouted, "git out there and throw that maverick bulldozer!"

"That maverick bulldozer is at the bottom of the swamp where you put it," growled Chub. His head lowered and he started to move in. "Sure we want to live. The best way to do that is to put you where you can't kill anybody else. *Get him!*"

He leaped. Tom straightened him with his left and crossed with his right. Chub went down, tripping Harris. Al Knowles scuttled to a toolbox and dipped out a fourteen-inch crescent wrench. He circled around, keeping out of trouble, trying to look useful. Tom loosened a haymaker at Kelly, whose head seemed to withdraw like a turtle's; it whistled over, throwing Tom badly off balance. Harris, still on his knees, tackled Tom's legs; Chub hit him in the small of the back with a meaty shoulder, and Tom went flat on his face. Al Knowles, holding the wrench in both hands, swept it up and back like a baseball bat; at the top of its swing Kelly reached over, snatched it out of his hands and tapped Tom delicately behind the ear with it. Tom went limp.

It was late, but nobody seemed to feel like sleeping. They sat around the pressure lantern, talking idly. Chub and Kelly played an inconsequential game of casino, forgetting to pick up their points; Harris paced up and down like a man in a cell, and Al Knowles was squinched up close to the light, his eyes wide and watching, watching—

"I need a drink," said Harris.

"Tens," said one of the casino players.

Al Knowles said, "We shoulda killed him. We oughta kill him now."

"There's been too much killin' already," said Chub. "Shut up, you." And to Kelly, "With big casino," sweeping up cards.

Kelly caught his wrist and grinned. "Big casino's the ten of diamonds, not the ten of hearts. Remember?"

"Oh."

"How long before the blacktopping crew will be here?" quavered Al Knowles.

"Twelve days," said Harris. "And they better bring some likker."

"Hey, you guys."

They fell silent.

"Hey!"

"It's Tom," said Kelly. "Building sixes, Chub."

"I'm gonna go kick his ribs in," said Knowles, not moving.

"I heard that," said the voice from the darkness. "If I wasn't hog-tied—"

"We know what you'd do," said Chub. "How much proof do you think we need?"

"Chub, you don't have to do any more to him!" It was Kelly, flinging his cards down and getting up. "Tom, you want water?"

"Yes."

"Siddown, siddown," said Chub.

"Let him lie there and bleed," Al Knowles said.

"Nuts!" Kelly went and filled a cup and brought it to Tom. The big Georgian was tied thoroughly, wrists together, taut rope between elbows and elbows behind his back, so that his hands were immovable over his solar plexus. His knees and ankles were bound as well, although Knowles' little idea of a short rope between ankles and throat hadn't been used.

"Thanks, Kelly." Tom drank greedily, Kelly holding his head. "Goes good." He drank more. "What hit me?"

"One of the boys. 'Bout the time you said the cat was haunted."

"Oh, yeah." Tom rolled his head and blinked with pain.

"Any sense asking you if you blame us?"

"Kelly, does somebody else have to get killed before you guys wake up?"

"None of us figure there will be any more killin'—now."

The rest of the men drifted up. "He willing to talk sense?" Chub wanted to know.

Al Knowles laughed, "Hyuk! hyuk! Don't he look dangerous now!"

Harris said suddenly, "Al, I'm gonna hafta tape your mouth with the skin off your neck."

"Am I the kind of guy that makes up ghost stories?"

"Never have that I know of, Tom." Harris kneeled down beside him. "Never killed anyone before, either."

"Oh, get away from me. Get away," said Tom tiredly.

"Get up and make us," jeered Al.

Harris got up and backhanded him across the mouth. Al squeaked, took three steps backward and tripped over a drum of grease. "I told you," said Harris almost plaintively. "I *told* you, Al."

Tom stopped the bumble of comment. "Shut up!" he hissed. "SHUT UP!" he roared.

They shut.

"Chub," said Tom, rapidly, evenly. "What did you say I did with that Seven?"

"Buried it in the swamp."

"Yeh. Listen."

"Listen at what?"

"Be quiet and listen!"

So they listened. It was another still, windless night, with a thin crescent of moon showing nothing true in the black and muffled silver landscape. The smallest whisper of surf drifted up from the beach, and from far off to the right, where the swamp was, a scandalized frog croaked protest at the manhandling of his mudhole. But the sound that crept down, freezing their bones, came from the bluff behind their camp.

It was the unmistakable staccato of a starting engine.

"The Seven!"

" 'At's right, Chub," said Tom.

"Wh-who's crankin' her up?"

"Are we all here?"

"All but Peebles and Dennis and Rivera," said Tom.

"It's Dennis' ghost," moaned Al.

Chub snapped, "Shut up, lamebrain."

"She's shifted to Diesel," said Kelly, listening.

"She'll be here in a minute," said Tom. "Y'know, fellas, we can't all be crazy, but you're about to have a time convincin' yourself of it."

"You like this, doncha?"

"Some ways. Rivera used to call that machine *Daisy Etta,* 'cause she's *de siete* in Spig. *Daisy Etta,* she wants her a man."

"Tom," said Harris, "I wish you'd stop that chatterin'. You make me nervous."

"I got to do somethin'. I can't run," Tom drawled.

"We're going to have a look," said Chub. "If there's nobody on that cat, we'll turn you loose."

"Mighty white of you. Reckon you'll get back before she does?"

"We'll get back, Harris, come with me. We'll get one of the pan tractors. They can outrun a Seven. Kelly, take Al and get the other one."

"Dennis' machine has a flat tire on the pan," said Al's quivering voice.

"Pull the pin and cut the cables, then! Git!" Kelly and Al Knowles ran off.

"Good huntin', Chub."

Chub went to him, bent over. "I think I'm goin' to have to apologize to you, Tom."

"No you ain't. I'd a done the same. Get along now, if you think you got to. But hurry back."

"I got to. An' I'll hurry back."

Harris said, "Don't go 'way boy." Tom returned the grin, and they were gone. But they didn't hurry back. They didn't come back at all.

It was Kelly who came pounding back, with Al Knowles on his heels, a half hour later. "Al—gimme your knife."

He went to work on the ropes. His face was drawn.

"I could see some of it," whispered Tom. "Chub and Harris?"

Kelly nodded. "There wasn't nobody on the Seven like you said." He said it as if there were nothing else in his mind, as if the most rigid self-control was keeping him from saying it over and over.

"I could see the lights," said Tom. "A tractor angling up the hill. Pretty soon another, crossing it, lighting up the whole slope."

"We heard it idling up there somewhere," Kelly said. "Olive-drab paint—couldn't see it."

"I saw the pan tractor turn over—oh, four, five times down the hill. It stopped, lights still burning. Then something hit it and rolled it again. That sure blacked it out. What turned it over first?"

"The Seven. Hanging up there just at the brow of the bluff. Waited until Chub and Harris were about to pass, sixty, seventy feet below. Tipped over the edge and rolled down on them with her clutches out. Must've been going thirty miles an hour when she hit. Broadside. They never had a chance. Followed the pan as it rolled down the hill and when it stopped booted it again."

"Want me to rub yo' ankles?" asked Al.

"You! Get outa my sight!"

"Aw, Tom—" whimpered Al.

"Skip it, Tom," said Kelly. "There ain't enough of us left to carry on that way. Al, you mind your manners from here on out, hear?"

"Ah jes' wanted to tell y'all. I knew you weren't lyin' 'bout Dennis, Tom, if only I'd stopped to think. I recollect when Dennis said he'd take that tractuh out . . . 'membah, Kelly? . . . He went an' got the crank and walked around to th' side of th' machine and stuck it in th' hole. It was barely in theah befo' the startin' engine kicked off. 'Whadda ya know!' he says t'me. 'She started by here'f! I nevah pulled that handle!' And I said, 'She sho' rarin' t'go!' "

"You pick a fine time to 'recollec' ' something," gritted Tom. "C'mon—let's get out of here."

"Where to?"

"What do you know that a Seven can't move or get up on?"

"That's a large order. A big rock, maybe."

"Ain't nothing that big around here," said Tom.

Kelly thought a minute, then snapped his fingers. "Up on the top of my last cut with the shovel," he said. "It's fourteen feet if it's an inch. I was pullin' out small rock an' topsoil, and Chub told me to drop back and dip out marl from a pocket there. I sumped in back of the original cut and took out a whole mess o' marl. That left a big neck of earth sticking thirty feet or so out of the cliff. The narrowest part is only about four feet wide. If *Daisy Etta* tries to get us from the top, she'll straddle the neck and hang herself. If she tries to get us from below, she can't get traction to climb; it's too loose and too steep."

"And what happens if she builds herself a ramp?"

"We'll be gone from there."

"Let's go."

Al agitated for the choice of a Dumptor because of its speed, but was howled down. Tom wanted something that could not get a flat tire and that would need something really powerful to turn it over. They took the two-cycle pan tractor with the bulldozer blade that had been Dennis' machine and crept out into the darkness.

It was nearly six hours later that *Daisy Etta* came and woke them up. Night was receding before a paleness in the east, and a fresh ocean breeze had sprung up. Kelly had taken the first lookout and Al the second, letting Tom rest the night out. And Tom was far too tired to argue the arrangement. Al had immediately fallen asleep on his watch, but fear had such a sure, cold hold on his vitals that the first faint growl of the big Diesel engine snapped him erect. He tottered on the edge of the tall neck of earth that they slept on and squeaked as he scrabbled to get his balance.

"What's giving?" asked Kelly, instantly wide awake.

"It's coming," blubbered Al. "Oh my, oh my—"

Kelly stood up and stared into the fresh, dark dawn. The motor boomed hollowly, in a peculiar way heard twice at the same time as it was thrown to them and echoed back by the bluffs under and around them.

"It's coming and what are we goin' to do?" chanted Al. "What is going to happen?"

"My head is going to fall off," said Tom sleepily. He rolled to a sitting position, holding the brutalized member between his hands. "If that egg behind my ear hatches, it'll come out a full-sized jack-hammer." He looked at Kelly. "Where is she?"

"Don't rightly know," said Kelly. "Somewhere down around the camp."

"Probably pickin' up our scent."

"Figure it can do that?"

"I figure it can do anything," said Tom. "Al, stop your moanin'."

The sun slipped its scarlet edge into the thin slot between sea and sky, and rosy light gave each rock and tree a shape and a shadow. Kelly's gaze swept back and forth, back and forth, until, minutes later, he saw movement.

"There she is!"

"Where?"

"Down by the grease rack."

Tom rose and stared. "What's she doin'?"

After an interval Kelly said, "She's workin'. Diggin' a swale in front of the fuel drums."

"You don't say. Don't tell me she's goin' to give herself a grease job."

"She don't need it. She was completely greased and new oil put in the crankcase after we set her up. But she might need fuel."

"Not more'n half a tank."

"Well, maybe she figures she's got a lot of work to do today." As Kelly said this Al began to blubber. They ignored him.

The fuel drums were piled in a pyramid at the edge of the camp, in forty-four-gallon drums piled on their sides. The Seven was moving back and forth in front of them, close up, making pass after pass, gouging earth up and wasting it out past the pile. She soon had a huge pit scooped out, about fourteen feet wide, six feet deep and thirty feet long, right at the very edge of the pile of drums.

"What you reckon she's playin' at?"

"Search me. She seems to want fuel, but I don't . . . look at that? She's stopped in the hole; she's pivoting, smashing the top corner of the moldboard into one of the drums on the bottom!"

Tom scraped the stubble on his jaw with his nails. "An' you wonder how much that critter can do! Why, she's got the whole thing figured out. She knows if she tried to punch a hole in a fuel drum that she'd only kick it around. If she did knock a hole in it, how's she going to lift it? She's not equipped to handle hose, so . . . see? Look at her now! She just gets herself lower than the bottom drum on the pile, and punches a hole. She can do that then, with the whole weight of the pile holding it down. Then she backs her tank under the stream of fuel runnin' out!"

"How'd she get the cap off?"

Tom snorted and told them how the radiator cap had come off

its hinges as he vaulted over the hood the day Rivera was hurt.

"You know," he said after a moment's thought, "if she knew as much then as she does now, I'd be snoozin' beside Rivera and Peebles. She just didn't know her way around then. She run herself like she'd never run before. She's learned plenty since."

"She has," said Kelly, "and here's where she uses it on us. She's headed this way."

She was. Straight out across the roughed-out runway she came, grinding along over the dew-sprinkled earth, yesterday's dust swirling up from under her tracks. Crossing the shoulder line, she took the rougher ground skillfully, angling up over the occasional swags in the earth, by-passing stones, riding free and fast and easily. It was the first time Tom had actually seen her clearly running without an operator, and his flesh crept as he watched. The machine was unnatural, her outline somehow unreal and dreamlike purely through the lack of the small silhouette of a man in the saddle. She looked hulked, compact, dangerous.

"What are we gonna do?" wailed Al Knowles.

"We're gonna sit and wait," said Kelly, "and you're gonna shut your trap. We won't know for five minutes yet whether she's going to go after us from down below or from up here."

"If you want to leave," said Tom gently, "go right ahead." Al sat down.

Kelly looked ruminatively down at his beloved power shovel, sitting squat and unlovely in the cut below them and away to their right. "How do you reckon she'd stand up against the dipper stick?"

"If it ever came to a rough-and-tumble," said Tom, "I'd say it would be just too bad for *Daisy Etta*. But she wouldn't fight. There's no way you could get the shovel within punchin' range; *Daisy*'d just stand there and laugh at you."

"I can't see her now," whined Al.

Tom looked. "She's taken the bluff. She's going to try it from up here. I move we sit tight and see if she's foolish enough to try to walk out here over that narrow neck. If she does, she'll drop on her belly with one truck on each side. Probably turn herself over trying to dig out."

The wait then was interminable. Back over the hill they could hear the laboring motor; twice they heard the machine stop momentarily to shift gears. Once they looked at each other hopefully as the sound rose to a series of bellowing roars, as if she were backing and filling; then they realized that she was trying to take some particularly steep part of the bank and having trouble getting traction. But she made it; the motor revved up as she made the brow of the hill, and she shifted into fourth gear and came lumbering out into the open. She lurched up to the edge of the cut, stopped, throttled down, dropped her blade on the ground and stood there idling. Al Knowles backed away to the very edge of the tongue of earth they stood on, his eyes practically on stalks.

"O.K.—put up or shut up," Kelly called across harshly.

"She's looking the situation over," said Tom. "That narrow pathway don't fool her a bit."

Daisy Etta's blade began to rise, and stopped just clear of the ground. She shifted without clashing her gears, began to back slowly, still at little more than an idle.

"She's gonna jump!" screamed Al. "I'm gettin' out of here!"

"Stay here, you fool," shouted Kelly. "She can't get us as long as we're up here! If you go down, she'll hunt you down like a rabbit."

The blast of the Seven's motor was the last straw for Al. He squeaked and hopped over the edge, scrambling and sliding down the almost sheer face of the cut. He hit the bottom running.

Daisy Etta lowered her blade and raised her snout and growled forward, the blade loading. Six, seven, seven and a half cubic yards of dirt piled up in front of her as she neared the edge. The loaded blade bit into the narrow pathway that led out to their perch. It was almost all soft, white, crumbly marl, and the great machine sank nose down into it, the monstrous overload of topsoil spilling down on each side.

"She's going to bury herself!" shouted Kelly.

"No—wait." Tom caught his arm. "She's trying to turn—she made it! She made it! She's ramping herself down to the flat!"

"She is—and she's cut us off from the bluff!"

The bulldozer, blade raised as high as it could possibly go, the hydraulic rod gleaming clean in the early light, freed herself of the last of her tremendous load, spun around and headed back upward, sinking her blade again. She made one more pass between them and the bluff, making a cut now far too wide for them to jump, particularly to the crumbly footing at the bluff's edge. Once down again, she turned to face their haven, now an isolated pillar of marl, and revved down, waiting.

"I never thought of this," said Kelly guiltily. "I knew we'd be safe from her ramping up, and I never thought she'd try it the other way!"

"Skip it. In the meantime, here we sit. What happens—do we wait up here until she idles out of fuel, or do we starve to death?"

"Oh, this won't be a siege, Tom. That thing's too much of a killer. Where's Al? I wonder if he's got guts enough to make a pass near here with our tractor and draw her off?"

"He had just guts enough to take our tractor and head out," said Tom. "Didn't you know?"

"He took our—*what?*" Kelly looked out toward where they had left their machine the night before. It was gone. "Why the dirty little yellow rat!"

"No sense cussin'," said Tom steadily, interrupting what he knew was the beginning of some really flowery language. "What else could you expect?"

Daisy Etta decided, apparently, how to go about removing their splendid isolation. She uttered the snort of too-quick throttle, and moved into their peak with a corner of her blade, cutting out a huge swipe, undercutting the material over it so that it fell on her side and track as she passed. Eight inches disappeared from that side of their little plateau.

"Oh-oh. That won't do a-tall," said Tom.

"Fixin' to dig us down," said Kelly grimly. "Take her about twenty minutes. Tom, I say leave."

"It won't be healthy. You just got no idea how fast that thing can move now. Don't forget, she's a good deal more than she was when she had a man runnin' her. She can shift from high to reverse to fifth speed forward like that"—he snapped his fingers—"and she can pivot faster'n you can blink and throw that blade just where she wants it."

The tractor passed under them, bellowing, and their little table was suddenly a foot shorter.

"Awright," said Kelly. "So what do you want to do? Stay here and let her dig the ground out from under our feet?"

"I'm just warning you," said Tom. "Now listen. We'll wait until she's taking a load. It'll take her a second to get rid of it when she knows we're gone. We'll split—she can't get both of us. You head out in the open, try to circle the curve of the bluff and get where you can climb it. Then come back over here to the cut. A man can scramble off a fourteen-foot cut faster'n any tractor ever built. I'll cut in close to the cut, down at the bottom. If she takes after you, I'll get clear all right. If she takes after me, I'll try to make the shovel and at least give her a run for her money. I can play hide an' seek in an' around and under that dipper-stick all day is she wants to play."

"Why me out in the open?"

"Don't you think those long laigs o' yours can outrun her in that distance?"

"Reckon they got to," grinned Kelly. "O.K., Tom."

They waited tensely. *Daisy Etta* backed close by, started another pass. As the motor blatted under the load, Tom said, "Now!" and they jumped. Kelly, catlike as always, landed on his feet. Tom, whose knees and ankles were black and blue with rope bruises, took two staggering steps and fell. Kelly scooped him to his feet as the dozer's steel prow came around the bank. Instantly she was in fifth gear and howling down at them. Kelly flung himself to the left and Tom to the right, and they pounded away, Kelly out toward the runway, Tom straight for the shovel. *Daisy Etta* let them diverge for a moment, keeping her course, trying to pursue both; then she evidently sized Tom up as the slower, for she swung toward him. The instant's hesitation was all Tom needed to get the little lead necessary. He tore up to the shovel, his legs going like pistons, and dived down between the shovel's tracks.

As he hit the ground, the big manganese-steel moldboard hit the right track of the shovel, and the impact set all forty-seven tons of the great machine quivering. But Tom did not stop. He scrabbled his way under the rig, stood up behind it, leaped and caught the sill of the rear window, clapped his other hand on it, drew himself up and tumbled inside. Here he was safe for the moment; the huge tracks themselves were higher than the Seven's blade could rise, and the floor of the cab was a good sixteen inches higher than the top of the track. Tom went to the cab door and peeped outside. The tractor had drawn off and was idling.

"Study away," gritted Tom, and went to the big Murphy Diesel. He unhurriedly checked the oil with the bayonet gauge, replaced it, took the governor cut-out rod from its rack and inserted it in the governor casing. He set the master throttle at the halfway mark, pulled up the starter-handle, twitched the cut-out. The motor spit a wad of blue smoke out of its hooded exhaust and caught. Tom put the rod back, studied the fuel-flow glass and pressure gauges, and then went to the door and looked out again. The

Seven had not moved, but it was revving up and down in that uneven fashion it had shown up on the mesa. Tom had the extraordinary idea that it was gathering itself to spring. He slipped into the saddle, threw the master clutch. The big gears that half-filled the cab obediently began to turn. He kicked the brake-locks loose with his heels, let his feet rest lightly on the pedals as they rose.

Then he reached over his head and snapped back the throttle. As the Murphy picked up he grasped both hoist and swing levers and pulled them back. The engine howled; the two-yard bucket came up off the ground with a sudden jolt as the cold friction grabbed it. The big machine swung hard to the right; Tom snapped his hoist lever forward and checked the bucket's rise with his foot on the brake. He shoved the crowd lever forward; the bucket ran out to the end of its reach, and the heel of the bucket wiped across the Seven's hood, taking with it the exhaust stack, muffler and all, and the pre-cleaner on the air intake. Tom cursed. He had figured on the machine's leaping backward. If it had, he would have smashed the cast-iron radiator core. But she had stood still, making a split-second decision.

Now she moved, though, and quickly. With that incredibly fast shifting, she leaped backwards and pivoted out of range before Tom could check the shovel's mad swing. The heavy swing-friction blocks smoked acridly as the machine slowed, stopped and swung back. Tom checked her as he was facing the Seven, hoisted his bucket a few feet, and rehauled, bringing it about halfway back, ready for anything. The four great dipper-teeth gleamed in the sun. Tom ran a practiced eye over cables, boom and dipper-stick, liking the black polish of crater compound on the sliding parts, the easy tension of well-greased cables and links. The huge machine stood strong, ready and profoundly subservient for all its brute power.

Tom looked searchingly at the Seven's ruined engine hood. The gaping end of the broken air-intake pipe stared back at him. "Aha!" he said. "A few cupfuls of nice dry marl down there'll give you something to chew on."

Keeping a wary eye on the tractor, he swung into the bank, dropped his bucket and plunged it into the marl. He crowded it deep, and the Murphy yelled for help but kept on pushing. At the peak of the load a terrific jar rocked him in the saddle. He looked back over his shoulder through the door and saw the Seven backing off again. She had run up and delivered a terrific punch to the counterweight at the back of the cab. Tom grinned tightly. She'd have to do better than that. There was nothing back there but eight or ten tons of solid steel. And he didn't much care at the moment whether or not she scratched his paint.

He swung back again, white marl running away on both sides of the heaped bucket. The shovel rode perfectly now, for a shovel is counterweighted to balance true when standing level with the bucket loaded. The hoist and swing frictions and the brake linings had heated and dried themselves of the night's condensation moisture, and she answered the controls in a way that delighted the operator in him. He handled the swing lever lightly, back to swing to the right, forward to swing to the left, following the slow dance the Seven had started to do, stepping warily back and forth like a fighter looking for an opening. Tom kept the bucket between himself and the tractor, knowing that she could not hurl a tool that was built to smash hard rock for twenty hours a day and like it.

Daisy Etta bellowed and rushed in. Tom snapped the hoist lever back hard, and the bucket rose, letting the tractor run underneath. Tom punched the bucket trip, and the great steel jaw opened, cascading marl down on the broken hood. The tractor's fan blew it back in a huge billowing cloud. The instant that it took Tom to check and dump was enough, however, for the tractor to dance back out of the way, for when he tried to drop it on the machine to smash the coiled injector tubes on top of the engine block, she was gone.

The dust cleared away, and the tractor moved in again, feinted to the left, then swung her blade at the bucket, which was just clear of the ground. Tom swung to meet her, her feint having gotten her in a little closer than he liked, and bucket met blade with a shower of sparks and a clank that could be heard for half a mile. She had come in with her blade high, and Tom let out a wordless shout as he saw that the A-frame brace behind the blade had caught between two of his dipper-teeth. He snatched at his hoist lever and the bucket came up, lifting with it the whole front end of the bulldozer.

Daisy Etta plunged up and down and her tracks dug violently into the earth as she raised and lowered her blade, trying to shake herself free. Tom rehauled, trying to bring the tractor in closer, for the boom was set too low to attempt to lift such a dead weight.

As it was, the shovel's off track was trying its best to get off the ground. But the crowd and rehaul frictions could not handle her alone; they began to heat and slip.

Tom hoisted a little; the shovel's off track came up a foot off the ground. Tom cursed and let the bucket drop, and in an instant the dozer was free and running clear. Tom swung wildly at her, missed. The dozer came in on a long curve; Tom swung to meet her again, took a vicious swipe at her which she took on her blade. But this time she did not withdraw after being hit, but bored right in, carrying the bucket before her. Before Tom realized what she was doing, his bucket was around in front of the tracks and between them, on the ground. It was as swift and skillful a maneuver as could be imagined, and it left the shovel without the ability to swing as long as *Daisy Etta* could hold the bucket trapped between the tracks.

Tom crowded furiously, but that succeeded only in lifting the boom higher in the air, since there is nothing to hold a boom down but its own weight. Hoisting did nothing but make his frictions smoke and rev the engine down dangerously close to the stalling point.

Tom swore again and reached down to the cluster of small levers at his left. These were the gears. On this type of shovel, the swing lever controls everything except crowd and hoist. With the swing lever, the operator, having selected his gear, controls the travel—that is, power to the tracks—in forward and reverse; booming up and booming down; and swinging. The machine can do only one of these things at a time. If she is in travel gear, she cannot swing. If she is in swing gear, she cannot boom up or down. Not once in years of operating would this inability bother an operator; now, however, nothing was normal.

Tom pushed the swing gear control down and pulled up on the travel. The clutches involved were jaw clutches, not frictions, so that he had to throttle down to an idle before he could make the castellations mesh. As the Murphy revved down, *Daisy Etta* took it as a signal that something could be done about it, and she shoved furiously into the bucket. But Tom had all controls in neutral and all she succeeded in doing was to dig herself in, her sharp new cleats spinning deep into the dirt.

Tom set his throttle up again and shoved the swing lever forward. There was a vast crackling of drive chains; and the big tracks started to turn.

Daisy Etta had sharp cleats; her pads were twenty inches wide and her tracks were fourteen feet long, and there were fourteen tons of steel on them. The shovel's big flat pads were three feet wide and twenty feet long, and forty-seven tons aboard. There was simply no comparison. The Murphy bellowed the fact that the work was hard, but gave no indications of stalling. *Daisy Etta* performed the incredible feat of shifting into a forward gear while she was moving backwards, but it did her no good. Round and round her tracks went, trying to drive her forward, gouging deep; and slowly and surely she was forced backward toward the cut wall by the shovel.

Tom heard a sound that was not part of a straining machine; he looked out and saw Kelly up on top of the cut, smoking, swinging his feet over the edge, making punching motions with his hands as if he had a ringside seat at a big fight—which he certainly had.

Tom now offered the dozer little choice. If she did not turn aside before him, she would be borne back against the bank and her fuel tank crushed. There was every possibility that, having her pinned there, Tom would have time to raise his bucket over her and smash her to pieces. And if she turned before she was forced against the bank, she would have to free Tom's bucket. This she had to do.

The Murphy gave him warning, but not enough. It crooned as the load came off, and Tom knew then that the dozer was shifting into a reverse gear. He whipped the hoist lever back, and the bucket rose as the dozer backed away from him. He crowded it out and let it come smashing down—and missed. For the tractor danced aside—and while he was in travel gear he could not swing to follow it. *Daisy Etta* charged then, put one track on the bank and went over almost on her beam-ends, throwing one end of her blade high in the air. So totally unexpected was it that Tom was quite unprepared. The tractor flung itself on the bucket, and the cutting edge of the blade dropped between the dipper teeth. This time there was the whole weight of the tractor to hold it there. There would be no way for her to free herself—but at the same time she had trapped the bucket so far out from the center pin of the shovel that Tom couldn't hoist without overbalancing and turning the monster over.

Daisy Etta ground away in reverse, dragging the bucket out until it was checked by the bumper-blocks. Then she began to crab sideways, up against the bank and when Tom tried tentatively to rehaul, she shifted and came right with him, burying one whole end of her blade deep into the bank.

Stalemate. She had hung herself up on the bucket, and she had immobilized it. Tom tried to rehaul, but the tractor's anchorage in the bank was too solid. He tried to swing, to hoist. All the overworked frictions could possibly give out was smoke. Tom grunted and throttled to an idle, leaned out the window. *Daisy Etta* was idling too, loudly without her muffler, the stackless exhaust giving out an ugly flat sound. But after the roar of the two great motors the partial silence was deafening.

Kelly called down, "Double knockout, hey?"

"Looks like it. What say we see if we can't get close enough to her to quiet her down some?"

Kelly shrugged. "I dunno. If she's really stopped herself, it's the first time. I respect that rig, Tom. She wouldn't have got herself into that spot if she didn't have an ace up her sleeve."

"Look at her, man! Suppose she was a civilized bulldozer and you had to get her out of there. She can't raise her blade high enough to free it from those dipper-teeth, y'know. Think you'd be able to do it?"

"It might take several seconds," Kelly drawled. "She's sure high and dry."

"O.K., let's spike her guns."

"Like what?"

"Like taking a bar and prying out her tubing." He referred to the coiled brass tubing that carried the fuel, under pressure, from the pump to the injectors. There were many feet of it, running from the pump reservoir, stacked in expansion coils over the cylinder head.

As he spoke *Daisy Etta*'s idle burst into that maniac revving up and down characteristic of her.

"What do you know!" Tom called above the racket. "Eavesdropping!"

Kelly slid down the cut, stood up on the track of the shovel and poked his head in the window. "Well, you want to get a bar and try?"

"Let's go!"

Tom went to the toolbox and pulled out the pinch bar that Kelly used to replace cables on his machine, and swung to the ground. They approached the tractor warily. She revved up as they came near, began to shudder. The front end rose and dropped and the tracks began to turn as she tried to twist out of the vise her blade had dropped into.

"Take it easy, sister," said Tom. "You'll just bury yourself. Set still and take it, now, like a good girl. You got it comin'."

"Be careful," said Kelly. Tom hefted the bar and laid a hand on the fender.

The tractor literally shivered, and from the rubber hose connection at the top of the radiator, a blinding stream of hot water shot out. It fanned and caught them both full in the face. They staggered back, cursing.

"You O.K., Tom?" Kelly gasped a moment later. He had got most of it across the mouth and cheek. Tom was on his knees, his shirt tail out, blotting at his face.

"My eyes . . . oh, my eyes—"

"Let's see!" Kelly dropped down beside him and took him by the wrists, gently removing Tom's hands from his face. He whistled. "Come on," he gritted. He helped Tom up and led him away a few feet. "Stay here," he said hoarsely. He turned, walked back toward the dozer, picking up the pinchbar. "You dirty——!" he yelled, and flung it like a javelin at the tube coils. It was a little high. It struck the ruined hood, made a deep dent in the metal. The dent promptly inverted with a loud *thung-g-g!* and flung the bar back at him. He ducked; it whistled over his head and caught Tom in the calves of his legs. He went down like a poled ox, but staggered to his feet again.

"Come on!" Kelly snarled, and taking Tom's arm, hustled him around the turn of the cut. "Sit down! I'll be right back."

"Where you going? Kelly—be careful!"

"Careful and how!"

Kelly's long legs ate up the distance back to the shovel. He swung into the cab, reached back over the motor and set up the master throttle all the way. Stepping up behind the saddle, he opened the running throttle and the Murphy howled. Then he hauled back on the hoist lever until it knuckled in, turned and leaped off the machine in one supple motion.

The hoist drum turned and took up slack; the cable straightened as it took the strain. The bucket stirred under the dead weight of the bulldozer that rested on it; and slowly, then, the great flat tracks began to lift their rear ends off the ground. The great obedient mass of machinery teetered forward on the tips of her tracks, the

Murphy revved down and under the incredible load, but it kept the strain. A strand of the two-part hoist cable broke and whipped around, singing; and then she was balanced—overbalanced—

And the shovel had hauled herself right over and had fallen with an earth-shaking crash. The boom, eight tons of solid steel, clanged down onto the blade of the bulldozer, and lay there, crushing it down tightly onto the imprisoning row of dipper-teeth.

Daisy Etta sat there, not trying to move now, racing her motor impotently. Kelly strutted past her, thumbing his nose, and went back to Tom.

"Kelly! I thought you were never coming back! What happened?"

"Shovel pulled herself over on her nose."

"Good boy! Fall on the tractor?"

"Nup. But the boom's laying across the top of her blade. Caught like a rat in a trap."

"Better watch out the rat don't chew its leg off to get out," said Tom, drily. "Still runnin', is she?"

"Yep. But we'll fix that in a hurry."

"Sure. Sure. How?"

"How? I dunno. Dynamite, maybe. How's the optics?"

Tom opened one a trifle and grunted. "Rough. I can see a little, though. My eyelids are parboiled, mostly. Dynamite, you say? Well—"

Tom sat back against the bank and stretched out his legs. "I tell you, Kelly, I been too blessed busy these last few hours to think much, but there's one thing that keeps comin' back to me— somethin' I was mullin' over long before the rest of you guys knew anything was up at all, except that Rivera had got hurt in some way I wouldn't tell you all about. But I don't reckon you'll call me crazy if I open my mouth now and let it all run out?"

"From now on," Kelly said fervently, "nobody's crazy. After this I'll believe anything."

"O.K. Well, about that tractor. What do you suppose has got into her?"

"Search me. I dunno."

"No—don't say that. I just got an idea we can't stop at 'I dunno.' We got to figure all the angles on this thing before we know just what to do about it. Let's just get this thing lined up. When did it start? On the mesa. How? Rivera was opening an old building with the Seven. This thing came out of there. Now here's what I'm getting at. We can dope these things out about it: It's intelligent. It can only get into a machine and not into a man. It—"

"What about that? How do you know it can't?"

"Because it had the chance to and didn't. I was standing right by the opening when it kited out. Rivera was upon the machine at the time. It didn't directly harm either of us. It got into the tractor, and the tractor did. By the same token, it can't hurt a man when it's out of a machine, but that's all it wants to do when it's in one. O.K.?

"To get on: once it's in one machine it can't get out again. We know that because it had plenty of chances and didn't take them. That scuffle with the dipper-stick, f'r instance. My face woulda been plenty red if it had taken over the shovel—and you can bet it would have if it could."

"I got you so far. But what are we going to do about it?"

"That's the thing. You see, I don't think it's enough to wreck the tractor. We might burn it, blast it, take whatever it was that got into it up on the mesa."

"That makes sense. But I don't see what else we can do than just break up the dozer. We haven't got a line on actually what the thing is."

"I think we have. Remember I asked you all those screwy questions about the arc that killed Peebles. Well, when that happened, I recollected a flock of other things. One—when it got out of that hole up there, I smelled that smell that you notice when you're welding; sometimes when lightning strikes real close."

"Ozone," said Kelly.

"Yeah—ozone. Then, it likes metal, not flesh. But most of all, there was that arc. Now, that was absolutely screwy. You know as well as I do—better—that an arc generator simply don't have the push to do a thing like that. It can't kill a man, and it can't throw an arc no fifty feet. But it did. An' that's why I asked you if there could be something—a field, or some such—that could *suck* current out of a generator, all at once, faster than it could flow. Because this thing's electrical; it fits all around."

"Electronic," said Kelly doubtfully, thoughtfully.

"I wouldn't know. Now then. When Peebles was killed, a funny thing happened. Remember what Chub said? The Seven moved back—straight back, about thirty feet, until it bumped into a roadroller that was standing behind it. It did that with no fuel in the starting engine—without even using the starting engine, for that matter—and with the compression valves locked open!

"Kelly, that thing in the dozer can't do much, when you come right down to it. It couldn't fix itself up after that joy-ride on the mesa. It can't make the machine do too much more than the machine can do ordinarily. What it actually can do, seems to me, is to make a spring push instead of pull, like the control levers, and make a fitting slip when it's supposed to hold, like the ratchet on the throttle lever. It can turn a shaft, like the way it cranks its own starting motor. But if it was so all-fired high-powered, it wouldn't have to use the starting motor! The absolute biggest job it's done so far, seems to me, was when it walked back from that welding machine when Peebles got his. Now, why did it do that just then?"

"Reckon it didn't like the brimstone smell, like it says in the Good Book," said Kelly sourly.

"That's pretty close, seems to me. Look, Kelly—this thing *feels* things. I mean, it can get sore. If it couldn't it never woulda kept driving in at the shovel like that. It can think. But if it can do all those things, then it can be *scared!*"

"Scared? Why should it be scared?"

"Listen. Something went on in that thing when the arc hit it. What's that I read in a magazine once about heat—something about molecules runnin' around with their heads cut off when they got hot?"

"Molecules do. They go into rapid motion when heat is applied. But—"

"But nothin'. That machine was hot for four hours after that. But she was hot in a funny way. Not just around the place where the arc hit, like as if it was a welding arc. But hot all over—from the moldboard to the fuel-tank cap. Hot everywhere. And just as hot behind the final drive housings as she was at the top of the blade where the poor guy put his hand.

"And look at this." Tom was getting excited, as his words crystallized his ideas. "She was scared—scared enough to back off from that welder, putting everything she could into it, to get back from that welding machine. And after that, she was sick. I say that because in the whole time she's had that whatever-ya-call-it in her, she's never been near men without trying to kill them, except for those two days after the arc hit her. She had juice enough to start herself when Dennis came around with the crank, but she still needed someone to run her till she got her strength back."

"But why didn't she turn and smash up the welder when Dennis took her?"

"One of two things. She didn't have the strength, or she didn't have the guts. She was scared, maybe, and wanted out of there, away from that thing."

"But she had all night to go back for it!"

"Still scared. Or . . . oh, *that's* it! She had other things to do first. Her main idea is to kill men—there's no other way you can figure it. It's what she was built to do. Not the tractor—they don't build 'em sweeter'n that machine; but the thing that's runnin' it."

"What *is* that thing?" Kelly mused. "Coming out of that old building—temple—what have you—how old is it? How long was it there? What kept it in there?"

"What kept it in there was some funny gray stuff that lined the inside of the buildin'," said Tom. "It was like rock, an' it was like smoke.

"It was a color that scared you to look at it, and it gave Rivera and me the creeps when we got near it. Don't ask me what it was. I went up there to look at it, and it's gone. Gone from the building, anyhow. There was a little lump of it on the ground. I don't know whether that was a hunk of it, or all of it rolled up into a ball. I get the creeps again thinkin' about it."

Kelly stood up. "Well, the heck with it. We been beatin' our gums up here too long anyhow. There's just enough sense in what you say to make me want to try something nonsensical, if you see what I mean. If that welder can sweat the Ol' Nick out of that tractor, I'm on. Especially from fifty feet away. There should be a Dumptor around here somewhere; let's move from here. Can you navigate now?"

"Reckon so, a little." Tom rose and together they followed the cut until they came on the Dumptor. They climbed on, cranked it up and headed toward camp.

About halfway there Kelly looked back, gasped, and putting his mouth close to Tom's ear, bellowed against the scream of the motor, "Tom! 'Member what you said about the rat in the trap biting off a leg?"

Tom nodded.

"Well, *Daisy* did too! She's left her blade an' pushbeams an' she's followin' us in!"

They howled into the camp, gasping against the dust that followed when they pulled up by the welder.

Kelly said, "You cast around and see if you can find a drawpin to hook that rig up to the Dumptor with. I'm goin' after some water an' chow!"

Tom grinned. Imagine old Kelly forgetting that a Dumptor had no drawbar! He groped around to a toolbox, peering out of the narrow slit beneath swollen lids, felt behind it and located a shackle. He climbed up on the Dumptor, turned it around and backed up to the welding machine. He passed the shackle through the ring at the end of the steering tongue of the welder, screwed in the pin and dropped the shackle over the front towing hook of the Dumptor. A dumptor being what it is, having no real front and no real rear, and direct reversing gears in all speeds, it was no trouble to drive it "backwards" for a change.

Kelly came pounding back, out of breath. "Fix it? Good. Shackle? No drawbar! *Daisy*'s closin' up fast; I say let's take the beach. We'll be concealed until we have a good lead out o' this pocket, and the going's pretty fair, long as we don't bury this jalopy in the sand."

"Good," said Tom as they climbed on and he accepted an open tin of K. "Only go easy; bump around too much and the welder'll slip off the hook. An' I somehow don't want to lose it just now."

They took off, zooming up the beach. A quarter of a mile up, they sighted the Seven across the flat. It immediately turned and took a course that would intercept them.

"Here she comes," shouted Kelly, and stepped down hard on the accelerator. Tom leaned over the back of the seat, keeping his eye on their tow. "Hey! Take it easy! Watch it! *Hey!*"

But it was too late. The tongue of the welding machine responded to that one bump too many. The shackle jumped up off the hook, the welder lurched wildly, slewed hard to the left. The tongue dropped to the sand and dug in; the machine rolled up on it and snapped it off, finally stopped, leaning crazily askew. By a miracle it did not quite turn over.

Kelly tramped on the brakes and both their heads did their utmost to snap off their shoulders. They leaped off and ran back to the welder. It was intact, but towing it was now out of the question.

"If there's going to be a showdown, it's gotta be here."

The beach here was about thirty yards wide, the sand almost level, and undercut banks of sawgrass forming the landward edge in a series of little hummocks and headlands. While Tom stayed with the machine, testing starter and generator contacts, Kelly walked up one of the little mounds, stood up on it and scanned the beach back the way he had come. Suddenly he began to shout and wave his arms.

"What's got into you?"

"It's Al!" Kelly called back. "With the pan tractor!"

Tom dropped what he was doing, and came to stand beside Kelly. "Where's the Seven? I can't see."

"Turned on the beach and followin' our track. Al! You little skunk, c'mere!"

Tom could now dimly make out the pan tractor cutting across directly toward them and the beach.

"He don't see *Daisy Etta*," remarked Kelly disgustedly, "or he'd sure be headin' the other way."

Fifty yards away Al pulled up and throttled down. Kelly shouted and waved to him. Al stood up on the machine, cupped his hands around his mouth. "Where's the Seven?"

"Never mind that! Come here with that tractor!"

Al stayed where he was. Kelly cursed and started out after him. "You stay away from me," he said when Kelly was closer.

"I ain't got time for you now," said Kelly. "Bring that tractor down to the beach."

"Where's that *Daisy Etta*?" Al's voice was oddly strained.

"Right behind us." Kely tossed a thumb over his shoulder. "On the beach."

Al's pop eyes clicked wide almost audibly. He turned on his heel and jumped off the machine and started to run. Kelly uttered a wordless syllable that was somehow more obscene than anything else he had ever uttered, and vaulted into the seat of the machine. "Hey!" he bellowed after Al's rapidly diminishing figure. "You're runnin' right into her." Al appeared not to hear, but went pelting down the beach.

Kelly put her into fifth gear and poured on the throttle. As the tractor began to move he whacked out the master clutch, snatched the overdrive lever back to put her into sixth, rammed the clutch in again, all so fast that she did not have time to stop rolling. Bucking and jumping over the rough ground the fast machine whined for the beach.

Tom was fumbling back to the welder, his ears telling him better than his eyes how close the Seven was—for she was certainly no nightingale, particularly without her exhaust stack. Kelly reached the machine as he did.

"Get behind it," snapped Tom. "I'll jamb the tierod with the shackle, and you see if you can't bunt her up into that pocket between those two hummocks. Only take it easy—you don't want to tear up that generator. Where's Al?"

"Don't ask me. He run down the beach to meet *Daisy*."

"He *what?*"

The whine of the two-cycle drowned out Kelly's answer, if any. He got behind the welder and set his blade against it. Then in a low gear, slipping his clutch in a little, he slowly nudged the machine toward the place Tom had indicated. It was a little hollow in between two projecting banks. The surf and the high-tide mark dipped inland here to match it; the water was only a few feet away.

Tom raised his arm and Kelly stopped. From the other side of the projecting shelf, out of their sight now, came the flat roar of the Seven's exhaust. Kelly sprang off the tractor and went to help Tom, who was furiously throwing out coils of cable from the rack back of the welder. "What's the game?"

"We got to ground that Seven some way," panted Tom. He threw the last bit of cable out to clear it of kinks and turned to the panel. "How was it—about sixty volts and the amperage on 'special application'?" He spun the dials, pressed the starter button. The motor responded instantly. Kelly scooped up ground clamp and rod holder and tapped them together. The solenoid governor picked up the load and the motor hummed as a good live spark took the jump.

"Good," said Tom, switching off the generator. "Come on, Lieutenant General Electric, figure me out a way to ground that maverick."

Kelly tightened his lips, shook his head. "I dunno—unless somebody actually clamps this thing on her."

"No, boy, can't do that. If one of us gets killed—"

Kelly tossed the ground clamp idly, his lithe body taut. "Don't give me that, Tom. You know I'm elected because you can't see good enough yet to handle it. You know you'd do it if you could. You—"

He stopped short, for the steadily increasing roar of the approaching Seven had stopped, was blatting away now in that extraordinary irregular throttling that *Daisy Etta* affected.

"Now, what's got into her?"

Kelly broke away and scrambled up the bank. "Tom!" he gasped. "Tom—come up here!"

Tom followed, and they lay side by side, peering out over the top of the escarpment at the remarkable tableau.

Daisy Etta was standing on the beach, near the water, not moving. Before her, twenty or thirty feet away, stood Al Knowles, his arms out in front of him, talking a blue steak. *Daisy* made far too much racket for them to hear what he was saying.

"Do you reckon he's got guts enough to stall her off for us?" said Tom.

"If he has, it's the queerest thing that's happened yet on this old island," Kelly breathed, "an' that's saying something."

The Seven revved up till she shook, and then throttled back. She ran down so low then that they thought she had shut herself down, but she caught on the last two revolutions and began to idle quietly. And then they could hear.

Al's voice was high, hysterical. "—I come t' he'p you, I come t' he'p you, don't kill me, I'll he'p you—" He took a step forward; the dozer snorted and he fell to his knees. "I'll wash you an' grease you and change yo' ile," he said in a high singsong.

"The guy's not human," said Kelly wonderingly.

"He ain't housebroke either," Tom chuckled.

"—lemme he'p you. I'll fix you when you break down. I'll he'p you kill those other guys—"

"She don't need any help!" said Tom.

"The louse," growled Kelly. "The rotten little double-crossing polecat!" He stood up. "Hey, you Al! Come out o' that. I mean now! If she don't get you I will, if you don't move."

Al was crying now. "Shut up!" he screamed. "I know who's bawss hereabouts, an' so do you!" He pointed at the tractor. "She'll kill us all off'n we don't do what she wants!" He turned back to the machine. "I'll k-kill 'em fo' you. I'll wash you and shine you up and f-fix yo' hood. I'll put yo' blade back on. . . ."

Tom reached out and caught Kelly's leg as the tall man started out, blind mad. "Git back here," he barked. "What you want to do—get killed for the privilege of pinnin' his ears back?"

Kelly subsided and came back, threw himself down beside Tom, put his face in his hands. He was quivering with rage.

"Don't take on so," Tom said. "The man's plumb loco. You

can't argue with him any more'n you can with *Daisy,* there. If he's got to get his, *Daisy*'ll give it to him."

"Aw, Tom, it ain't that. I know he ain't worth it, but I can't sit up here and watch him get himself killed. I can't, Tom."

Tom thumped him on the shoulder, because there were simply no words to be said. Suddenly he stiffened, snapped his fingers. "There's our ground," he said urgently, pointing seaward. "The water—the wet beach where the surf runs. If we can get our ground clamp out there and her somewhere near it—"

"Ground the pan tractor. Run it out into the water. It ought to reach—partway, anyhow."

"That's it—c'mon."

They slid down the bank, snatched up the ground clamp, attached it to the frame of the pan tractor.

"I'll take it," said Tom, and as Kelly opened his mouth, Tom shoved him back against the welding machine. "No time to argue," he snapped, swung on to the machine, slapped her in gear and was off. Kelly took a step toward the tractor, and then his quick eye saw a bight of the ground cable about to foul a wheel of the welder. He stooped and threw it off, spread out the rest of it so it would pay off clear. Tom, with the incredible single-mindedness of the trained operator, watched only the block line of the trailing cable on the sand behind him. When it straightened, he stopped. The front of the tracks were sloshing in the gentle surf. He climbed off the side away from the Seven and tried to see. There was movement, and the growl of her motor now running at a bit more than idle, but he could not distinguish much.

Kelly picked up the rod-holder and went to peer around the head of the protruding bank. Al was on his feet, still crooning hysterically, sidling over toward *Daisy Etta.* Kelly ducked back, threw the switch on the arc generator, climbed the bank and crawled along through the sawgrass paralleling the beach until the holder in his hand tugged and he knew he had reached the end of the cable. He looked out at the beach; measured carefully with his eye the arc he would travel if he left his position and, keeping the cable taut, went out on the beach. At no point would he come within seventy feet of the possessed machine, let alone fifty. She had to be drawn in closer. And she had to be maneuvered out to the wet sand, or in the water—

Al Knowles, encouraged by the machine's apparent decision not to move, approached, though warily, and still running off at the mouth. "—we'll kill 'em off an' then we'll keep it a secret and the' bahges'll come an' take us offen th' island and we'll go to anothah job an' kill us lots mo' . . . an' when yo' tracks git dry an' squeak we'll wet 'em up with blood, and you'll be rightly king o' th' hill . . . look yondah, look yondah, *Daisy Etta,* see them theah, by the otheh tractuh, theah they are, kill 'em, *Daisy,* kill 'em, *Daisy,* an' lemme he'p . . . heah me. *Daisy,* heah me, say you heah me—" and the motor roared in response. Al laid a timid hand on the radiator guard, leaning far over to do it, and the tractor still stood there grumbling but not moving. Al stepped back, motioned with his arm, began to walk off slowly toward the pan tractor, looking backwards as he did so like a man training a dog. "C'mon, c'mon, theah's one theah, le's *kill'm, kill'm, kill'm. . . .*"

And with a snort the tractor revved up and followed.

Kelly licked his lips without effect because his tongue was dry, too. The madman passed him, walking straight up the center of the beach, and the tractor, now no longer a bulldozer, followed him; and there the sand was bone dry, sun-dried, dried to powder. As the tractor passed him, Kelly got up on all fours, went over the edge of the bank onto the beach, crouched there.

Al crooned, "I love ya, honey, I love ya, 'deed I do—"

Kelly ran crouching, like a man under machine-gun fire, making himself as small as possible and feeling as big as a barn door. The torn-up sand where the tractor had passed was under his feet now; he stopped, afraid to get too much closer, afraid that a weakened, badly grounded arc might leap from the holder in his hand and serve only to alarm and infuriate the thing in the tractor. And just then Al saw him.

"There!" he screamed; and the tractor pulled up short. "Behind you! Get'm *Daisy! Kill'm, kill'm, kill'm.*"

Kelly stood up almost wearily, fury and frustration too much to be borne. "In the water," he yelled, because it was what his whole being wanted. "Get'er in the water! Wet her tracks, Al!"

"Kill'm, kill'm—"

As the tractor started to turn, there was a commotion over by the pan tractor. It was Tom, jumping, shouting, waving his arms, swearing. He ran out from behind his machine, straight at the Seven. *Daisy Etta's* motor roared and she swung to meet him, Al barely dancing back out of the way. Tom cut sharply, sand spouting under his pumping feet, and ran straight into the water. He went out to about waist deep, suddenly disappeared. He surfaced, spluttering, still trying to shout. Kelly took a better grip on his rod holder and rushed.

Daisy Etta, in following Tom's crazy rush, had swung in beside the pan tractor, not fifteen feet away; and she, too, was now in the surf. Kelly closed up the distance as fast as his long legs would let him; and as he approached to within that crucial fifty feet, Al Knowles hit him.

Al was frothing at the mouth, gibbering. The two men hit full tilt; Al's head caught Kelly in the midriff as he missed a straightarm, and the breath went out of him in one great *whoosh!* Kelly went down like tall timber, the whole world turned to one swirling red-gray haze. Al flung himself on the bigger man, clawing, smacking, too berserk to ball his fists.

"Ah'm go' to kill you," he gurgled. "She'll git one, I'll git t'other, an' then she'll know—"

Kelly covered his face with his arms, and as some wind was sucked at last into his laboring lungs, he flung them upward and sat up in one mighty surge. Al was hurled upward and to one side, and as he hit the ground Kelly reached out a long arm, and twisted his fingers into the man's coarse hair, raised him up, and came across with his other fist in a punch that would have killed him had it landed square. But Al managed to jerk to one side enough so that it only amputated a cheek. He fell and lay still. Kelly scrambled madly around in the sand for his welding-rod holder, found it and began to run again. He couldn't see Tom at all now, and the Seven was standing in the surf, moving slowly from side to side, backing out, ravening. Kelly held the rod-clamp and its trailing cable blindly before him and ran straight at the machine. And then it came—that thin, soundless bolt of energy. But this time it had its full force, for poor old Peebles' body had not been the ground that this swirling water offered. *Daisy Etta* literally leaped backwards toward him, and the water around her tracks spouted upward in hot steam. The sound of her engine ran up and up, broke, took on the rhythmic, uneven beat of a swing drummer. She threw herself from side to side like a cat with a bag over its head. Kelly stepped a little closer, hoping for another bolt to come from the clamp in his hand, but there was none, for—

"The circuit breaker!" cried Kelly.

He threw the holder up on the deck plate of the Seven in front of the seat, and ran across the little beach to the welder. He reached behind the switchboard, got his thumb on the contact hinge and jammed it down.

Daisy Etta leaped again, and then again, and suddenly her motor stopped. Heat in turbulent waves blurred the air over her. The little gas tank for the starting motor went out with a cannon's roar, and the big fuel tank, still holding thirty-odd gallons of Diesel oil followed. It puffed itself open rather than exploded, and threw a great curtain of flame over the ground behind the machine. Motor or no motor, then, Kelly distinctly saw the tractor shudder convulsively. There was a crawling movement of the whole frame, a slight wave of motion away from the fuel tank, approaching the front of the machine, and moving upward from the tracks. It culminated in the crown of the radiator core, just in front of the radiator cap; and suddenly an area of six or seven square inches literally *blurred* around the edges. For a second, then, it was normal, and finally it slumped molten, and liquid metal ran down the sides, throwing out little sparks as it encountered what was left of the charred paint. And only then was Kelly conscious of agony in his left hand. He looked down. The welding machine's generator had stopped, though the motor was still turning, having smashed the friable coupling on its drive shaft. Smoke poured from the generator, which had become little more than a heap of slag. Kelly did not scream, though, until he looked and saw what had happened to his hand—

When he could see straight again, he called for Tom, and there was no answer. At last he saw something out in the water, and plunged in after it. The splash of cold salt water on his left hand he hardly felt, for the numbness of shock had set in. He grabbed at Tom's shirt with his good hand, and then the ground seemed to pull itself out from under his feet. That was it, then—a deep hole right off the beach. The Seven had run right to the edge of it, had kept Tom there out of his depth and—

He flailed wildly, struck out for the beach, so near and so hard to get to. He gulped a stinging lungful of brine, and only the lovely shock of his knee striking solid beach kept him from giving up to the luxury of choking to death. Sobbing with effort, he dragged Tom's dead weight inshore and clear of the surf. It was then that he became conscious of a child's shrill weeping; for a mad moment he thought it was he himself, and then he looked and saw that it was Al Knowles. He left Tom and went over to the broken creature.

"Get up, you," he snarled. The weeping only got louder. Kelly rolled him over on his back—he was quite unresisting—and belted him back and forth across the mouth until Al began to choke. Then he hauled him to his feet and led him over to Tom.

"Kneel down, scum. Put one of your knees between his knees." Al stood still. Kelly hit him again and he did as he was told.

"Put your hands on his lower ribs. There. O.K. Lean, you rat. Now sit back." He sat down, holding his left wrist in his right hand, letting the blood drop from the ruined hand. "Lean. Hold it—sit back. Lean. Sit. Lean. Sit."

Soon Tom sighed and began to vomit weakly, and after that he was all right.

This is the story of *Daisy Etta,* the bulldozer that went mad and had a life of its own, and not the story of the flat-top *Marokuru* of the Imperial Japanese Navy, which has been told elsewhere. But there is a connection. You will remember how the *Marokuru* was cut off from its base by the concentrated attack on Truk, how it slipped far to the south and east and was sunk nearer to our shores than any other Jap warship in the whole course of the war. And you will remember how a squadron of five planes, having been separated by three vertical miles of water from their flight deck, turned east with their bombloads and droned away for a suicide mission. You read that they bombed a minor airfield in the outside of Panama's far-flung defenses, and all hands crashed in the best sacrificial fashion.

Well, that was no airfield, no matter what it might have looked like from the air. It was simply a roughly graded runway, white marl against brown scrub-grass.

The planes came two days after the death of *Daisy Etta,* as Tom and Kelly sat in the shadow of the pile of fuel drums, down in the coolth of the swag that *Daisy* had dug there to fuel herself. They were poring over paper and pencil, trying to complete the impossible task of making a written statement of what had happened on the island, and why they and their company had failed to complete their contract. They had found Chub and Harris, and had buried them next to the other three. Al Knowles was tied up in the camp, because they had heard him raving in his sleep, and it seemed he could not believe that *Daisy* was dead and he still wanted to go around killing operators for her. They knew that there must be an investigation, and they knew just how far their story would go; and having escaped a monster like *Daisy Etta,* life was far too sweet for them to want to be shot for sabotage. And murder.

The first stick of bombs struck three hundred yards behind them at the edge of the camp, and at the same instant a plane whistled low over their heads, and that was the first they knew about it. They ran to Al Knowles and untied his feet and the three of them headed for the bush. They found refuge, strangely enough, inside the mound where *Daisy Etta* had first met her possessor.

"Bless their black little hearts," said Kelly as he and Tom stood on the bluff and looked at the flaming wreckage of a camp and five medium bombers below them. And he took the statement they had been sweating out and tore it across.

"But what about him?" said Tom, pointing at Al Knowles, who was sitting on the ground, playing with his fingers. "He'll still spill the whole thing, no matter if we do try to blame it all on the bombing."

"What's the matter with that?" said Kelly.

Tom thought a minute, then grinned. "Why, nothing! That's just the sort of thing they'll expect from him!"

H. P. LOVECRAFT
The Shadow Out of Time

1

AFTER TWENTY-TWO years of nightmare and terror, saved only by a desperate conviction of the mythical source of certain impressions, I am unwilling to vouch for the truth of that which I think I found in Western Australia on the night of July 17–18, 1935. There is reason to hope that my experience was wholly or partly an hallucination—for which, indeed, abundant causes existed. And yet, its realism was so hideous that I sometimes find hope impossible.

If the thing did happen, then man must be prepared to accept notice of the cosmos, and of his own place in the seething vortex of time, whose merest mention is paralyzing. He must, too, be placed on guard against a specific, lurking peril which, though it will never engulf the whole race, may impose monstrous and unguessable horrors upon certain venturesome members of it.

It is for this latter reason that I urge, with all the force of my being, a final abandonment of all the attempts at unearthing those fragments of unknown, primordial masonry which my expedition set out to investigate.

Assuming that I was sane and awake, my experience on that night was such as has befallen no man before. It was, moreover, a frightful confirmation of all I had sought to dismiss as myth and dream. Mercifully there is no proof, for in my fright I lost the awesome object which would—if real and brought out of that noxious abyss—have formed irrefutable evidence.

When I came upon the horror I was alone—and I have up to now told no one about it. I could not stop the others from digging in its direction, but chance and the shifting sand have so far saved them from finding it. Now I must formulate some definite statement—not only for the sake of my own mental balance, but to warn such others as may read it seriously.

These pages—much in whose earlier parts will be familiar to close readers of the general and scientific press—are written in the cabin of the ship that is bringing me home. I shall give them to my son, Professor Wingate Peaslee of Miskatonic University— the only member of my family who stuck to me after my queer amnesia of long ago, and the man best informed on the inner facts of my case. Of all living persons, he is least likely to ridicule what I shall tell of that fateful night.

I did not enlighten him orally before sailing, because I think he had better have the revelation in written form. Reading and rereading at leisure will leave with him a more convincing picture than my confused tongue could hope to convey.

He can do anything that he thinks best with this account— showing it, with suitable comment, in any quarters where it will be likely to accomplish good. It is for the sake of such readers as are unfamiliar with the earlier phases of my case that I am prefacing the revelation itself with a fairly ample summary of its background.

My name is Nathaniel Wingate Peaslee, and those who recall the newspaper tales of a generation back—or the letters and articles in psychological journals six or seven years ago—will know who and what I am. The press was filled with the details of my strange amnesia in 1908–13, and much was made of the traditions of horror, madness, and witchcraft which lurked behind the ancient Massachusetts town then and now forming my place of residence. Yet I would have it known that there is nothing whatever of the mad or sinister in my heredity and early life. This is a highly important fact in view of the shadow which fell so suddenly upon me from *outside* sources.

It may be that centuries of dark brooding had given to crumbling, whisper-haunted Arkham a peculiar vulnerability as regards such shadows—though even this seems doubtful in the light of those other cases which I later came to study. But the chief point is that my own ancestry and background are altogether normal. What came, came from *somewhere else*—where, I even now hesitate to assert in plain words.

I am the son of Jonathan and Hannah (Wingate) Peaslee, both of wholesome old Haverhill stock. I was born and reared in Haverhill—at the old homestead in Boardman Street near Golden

Hill—and did not go to Arkham till I entered Miskatonic University as instructor of political economy in 1895.

For thirteen years more my life ran smoothly and happily. I married Alice Keezar of Haverhill in 1896, and my three children, Robert, Wingate and Hannah were born in 1898, 1900, and 1903, respectively. In 1898 I became an associate professor, and in 1902 a full professor. At no time had I the least interest in either occultism or abnormal psychology.

It was on Thursday, May 14, 1908, that the queer amnesia came. The thing was quite sudden, though later I realized that certain brief, glimmering visions of several hours previous—chaotic visions which disturbed me greatly because they were so unprecedented—must have formed premonitory symptoms. My head was aching, and I had a singular feeling—altogether new to me—that someone else was trying to get possession of my thoughts.

The collapse occurred about 10:20 A.M., while I was conducting a class in Political Economy VI—history and present tendencies of economics—for juniors and a few sophomores. I began to see strange shapes before my eyes, and to feel that I was in a grotesque room other than the classroom.

My thoughts and speech wandered from my subject, and the students saw that something was gravely amiss. Then I slumped down, unconscious, in my chair, in a stupor from which no one could arouse me. Nor did my rightful faculties again look out upon the daylight of our normal world for five years, four months, and thirteen days.

It is, of course, from others that I have learned what followed. I showed no sign of consciousness for sixteen and a half hours, though removed to my home at 27 Crane Street, and given the best of medical attention.

At 3 A.M. May 15th my eyes opened and I began to speak, but before long the doctors and my family were thoroughly frightened by the trend of my expression and language. It was clear that I had no remembrance of my identity and my past, though for some reason I seemed anxious to conceal this lack of knowledge. My eyes gazed strangely at the persons around me, and the flections of my facial muscles were altogether unfamiliar.

Even my speech seemed awkward and foreign. I used my vocal organs clumsily and gropingly, and my diction had a curiously stilted quality, as if I had laboriously learned the English language from books. The pronunciation was barbarously alien, whilst the idiom seemed to include both scraps of curious archaism and expressions of a wholly incomprehensible cast.

Of the latter, one in particular was very potently—even terrifiedly—recalled by the youngest of the physicians twenty years afterward. For at that late period such a phrase began to have an actual currency—first in England and then in the United States—and though of much complexity and indisputable newness, it reproduced in every least particular the mystifying words of the strange Arkham patient of 1908.

Physical strength returned at once, although I required an odd amount of reeducation in the use of my hands, legs, and bodily apparatus in general. Because of this and other handicaps inherent in the mnemonic lapse, I was for some time kept under strict medical care.

When I saw that my attempts to conceal the lapse had failed, I admitted it openly, and became eager for information of all sorts. Indeed, it seemed to the doctors that I lost interest in my proper personality as soon as I found the case of amnesia accepted as a natural thing.

They noticed that my chief efforts were to master certain points in history, science, art, language, and folklore—some of them tremendously abstruse, and some childishly simple—which remained, very oddly in many cases, outside my consciousness.

At the same time they noticed that I had an inexplicable command of many almost unknown sorts of knowledge—a command which I seemed to wish to hide rather than display. I would inadvertently refer, with casual assurance, to specific events in dim ages outside of the range of accepted history—passing off such references as a jest when I saw the surprise they created. And I had a way of speaking of the future which two or three times caused actual fright.

These uncanny flashes soon ceased to appear, though some observers laid their vanishment more to a certain furtive caution on my part than to any waning of the strange knowledge behind them. Indeed, I seemed anomalously avid to absorb the speech, customs, and perspectives of the age around me; as if I were a studious traveler from a far, foreign land.

As soon as permitted, I haunted the college library at all hours; and shortly began to arrange for those odd travels, and special courses at American and European Universities, which evoked so much comment during the next few years.

I did not at any time suffer from a lack of learned contacts, for my case had a mild celebrity among the psychologists of the period. I was lectured upon as a typical example of secondary personality—even though I seemed to puzzle the lecturers now and then with some bizarre symptoms or some queer trace of carefully veiled mockery.

Of real friendliness, however, I encountered little. Something in my aspect and speech seemed to excite vague fears and aversions in everyone I met, as if I were a being infinitely removed from all that is normal and healthful. This idea of a black, hidden horror connected with incalculable gulfs of some sort of *distance* was oddly widespread and persistent.

My own family formed no exception. From the moment of my strange waking my wife had regarded me with extreme horror and loathing, vowing that I was some utter alien usurping the body of her husband. In 1910 she obtained a legal divorce, nor would she ever consent to see me even after my return to normality in 1913. These feelings were shared by my elder son and my small daughter, neither of whom I have ever seen since.

Only my second son, Wingate, seemed able to conquer the terror and repulsion which my change aroused. He indeed felt that I was a stranger, but though only eight years old held fast to a faith that my proper self would return. When it did return he sought me out, and the courts gave me his custody. In succeeding years he helped me with the studies to which I was driven, and today, at thirty-five, he is a professor of psychology at Miskatonic.

But I do not wonder at the horror I caused—for certainly, the mind, voice, and facial expression of the being that awakened on May 15, 1908, were not those of Nathaniel Wingate Peaslee.

I will not attempt to tell much of my life from 1908 to 1913, since readers may glean all the outward essentials—as I largely had to do—from files of old newspapers and scientific journals.

I was given charge of my funds, and spent them slowly and on the whole wisely, in travel and in study at various centers of learning. My travels, however, were singular in extreme, involving long visits to remote and desolate places.

In 1909 I spent a month in the Himalayas, and in 1911 aroused much attention through a camel trip into the unknown deserts of Arabia. What happened on those journeys I have never been able to learn.

During the summer of 1912 I chartered a ship and sailed in
the Arctic, north of Spitzbergen, afterward showing signs of disappointment.

Later in that year I spent weeks alone beyond the limits of
previous or subsequent exploration in the vast limestone cavern
systems of western Virginia—black labyrinths so complex that no
retracing of my steps could even be considered.

My sojourns at the universities were marked by abnormally
rapid assimilation, as if the secondary personality had an intelligence enormously superior to my own. I have found, also, that
my rate of reading and solitary study was phenomenal. I could
master every detail of a book merely by glancing over it as fast
as I could turn the leaves; while my skill at interpreting complex
figures in an instant was veritably awesome.

At times there appeared almost ugly reports of my power to
influence the thoughts and acts of others, though I seemed to
have taken care to minimize displays of this faculty.

Other ugly reports concerned my intimacy with leaders of oc-
cultist groups, and scholars suspected of connection with nameless
bands of abhorrent elder-world hierophants. These rumors, though
never proved at the time, were doubtless stimulated by the known
tenor of some of my reading—for the consultation of rare books
at libraries cannot be effected secretly.

There is tangible proof—in the form of marginal notes—that I
went minutely through such things as the Comte d'Erlette's *Cultes
des Goules,* Ludvig Prinn's *De Vermis Mysteriis,* the *Unaussprechlichen Kulten* of von Junzt, the surviving fragments of the
puzzling *Book of Eibon,* and the dreaded *Necronomicon* of the
mad Arab Abdul Alhazred. Then, too, it is undeniable that a fresh
and evil wave of underground cult activity set in about the time
of my odd mutation.

In the summer of 1913 I began to display signs of ennui and
flagging interest, and to hint to various associates that a change
might soon be expected in me. I spoke of returning memories of
my earlier life—though most auditors judged me insincere, since
all the recollections I gave were casual, and such as might have
been learned from my old private papers.

About the middle of August I returned to Arkham and reopened
my long-closed house in Crane Street. Here I installed a mechanism
of the curious aspect, constructed piecemeal by different makers
of scientific apparatus in Europe and America, and guarded care-

fully from the sight of any one intelligent enough to analyze it.

Those who did see it—a workman, a servant, and the new housekeeper—say that it was a queer mixture of rods, wheels, and mirrors, though only about two feet tall, one foot wide, and one foot thick. The central mirror was circular and convex. All this is borne out by such makers of parts as can be located.

On the evening of Friday, September 26, I dismissed the housekeeper and the maid until noon of the next day. Lights burned in the house till late, and a lean, dark, curiously foreign-looking man called in an automobile.

It was about one A.M. that the lights were last seen. At 2:15 A.M. a policeman observed the place in darkness, but the stranger's motor still at the curb. By 4 o'clock the motor was certainly gone.

It was 6 o'clock that a hesitant, foreign voice on the telephone asked Dr. Wilson to call at my house and bring me out of a peculiar faint. This call—a long-distance one—was later traced to a public booth in the North Station in Boston, but no sign of the lean foreigner was ever unearthed.

When the doctor reached my house he found me unconscious in the sitting room—in an easy-chair with a table drawn up before it. On the polished top were scratches showing where some heavy object had rested. The queer machine was gone, nor was anything afterward heard of it. Undoubtedly the dark, lean foreigner had taken it away.

In the library grate were abundant ashes, evidently left from the burning of every remaining scrap of paper on which I had written since the advent of the amnesia. Dr. Wilson found my breathing very peculiar, but after a hypodermic injection it became more regular.

At 11:15 A.M., September 27th, I stirred vigorously, and my hitherto masklike face began to show signs of expression. Dr. Wilson remarked that the expression was not that of my secondary personality, but seemed much like that of my normal self. About 11:30 I muttered some very curious syllables—syllables which seemed unrelated to any human speech. I appeared, too, to struggle against something. Then, just after noon—the housekeeper and the maid having meanwhile returned—I began to mutter in English:

"—of the orthodox economists of that period, Jevons typifies the prevailing trend toward scientific correlation. His attempt to link the commercial cycle of prosperity and depression with the physical cycle of the solar spots forms perhaps the apex of—"

Nathaniel Wingate Peaslee had come back—a spirit in whose time scale it was still Thursday morning in 1908, with the economics class gazing up at the battered desk on the platform.

2

MY REABSORPTION into normal life was a painful and difficult process. The loss of over five years creates more complications than can be imagined, and in my case there were countless matters to be adjusted.

What I heard of my actions since 1908 astonished and disturbed me, but I tried to view the matter as philosophically as I could. At last, regaining custody of my second son, Wingate, I settled down with him in the Crane Street house and endeavored to resume my teaching—my old professorship having been kindly offered me by the college.

I began work with the February, 1914, term, and kept at it just a year. By that time I realized how badly my experience had shaken me. Though perfectly sane—I hoped—and with no flaw in my original personality, I had not the nervous energy of the old days. Vague dreams and queer ideas continually haunted me, and when the outbreak of the World War turned my mind to history I found myself thinking of periods and events in the oddest possible fashion.

My conception of *time*—my ability to distinguish between consecutiveness and simultaneousness—seemed subtly disordered; so that I formed chimaerical notions about living in one age and casting one's mind all over eternity for knowledge of past and future ages.

The War gave me strange impressions of remembering some of its far-off consequences—as if I knew how it was coming out and could look *back* upon it in the light of future information. All such quasi-memories were attended with much pain, and with a feeling that some artificial psychological barrier was set against them.

When I diffidently hinted to others about my impressions, I met with varied responses. Some persons looked uncomfortably at me, but men in the mathematics department spoke of new developments in those theories of relativity—then discussed only in learned circles—which were later to become so famous. Dr. Albert Einstein, they said, was rapidly reducing time to the status of a mere dimension.

But the dreams and disturbed feelings gained on me, so that I had to drop my regular work in 1915. Certain of the impressions were taking an annoying shape—giving me the persistent notion that my amnesia had formed some unholy sort of exchange; that the secondary personality had indeed been an intruding force from unknown regions, and that my own personality had suffered displacement.

Thus I was driven to vague and frightful speculations concerning the whereabouts of my true self during the years that another had held my body. The curious knowledge and strange conduct of my body's late tenant troubled me more and more as I learned further details from persons, papers, and magazines.

Queernesses that had baffled others seemed to harmonize terribly with some background of black knowledge which festered in the chasms of my subconsciousness. I began to search feverishly for every scrap of information bearing on the studies and travels of that other one during the dark years.

Not all of my troubles were as semi-abstract as this. There were the dreams—and these seemed to grow in vividness and concreteness. Knowing how most would regard them, I seldom mentioned them to any one but my son or certain trusted psychologists, but eventually I commenced a scientific study of other cases in order to see how typical or nontypical such visions might be among amnesia victims.

My results, aided by psychologists, historians, anthropologists, and mental specialists of wide experience, and by a study that included all records of split personalities from the days of demoniac-possession legends to the medically realistic present, at first bothered me more than they consoled me.

I soon found that my dreams had, indeed, no counterpart in the overwhelming bulk of true amnesia cases. There remained, however, a tiny residue of accounts which for years baffled and shocked me with their parallelism to my own experience. Some of them were bits of ancient folklore; others were case histories in the annals of medicine; one or two were anecdotes obscurely buried in standard histories.

It thus appeared that, while my special kind of affliction was prodigiously rare, instances of it had occurred at long intervals ever since the beginning of men's annals. Some centuries might contain one, two, or three cases, others none—or at least none whose record survived.

The essence was always the same—a person of keen thoughtfulness seized with a strange secondary life and leading for a greater or lesser period an utterly alien existence typified at first by vocal and bodily awkwardness, and later by a wholesale acquisition of scientific, historic, artistic, and anthropological knowledge; an acquisition carried on with feverish zest and with a wholly abnormal absorptive power. Then a sudden return of the rightful consciousness, intermittently plagued ever after with vague unplaceable dreams suggesting fragments of some hideous memory elaborately blotted out.

And the close resemblance of those nightmares to my own—even in some of the smallest particulars—left no doubt in my mind of their significantly typical nature. One or two of the cases had an added ring of faint, blasphemous familiarity, as if I had heard of them before through some cosmic channel too morbid and frightful to contemplate. In three instances there was specific mention of such an unknown machine as had been in my house before the second change.

Another thing that worried me during my investigation was the somewhat greater frequency of cases where a brief, elusive glimpse of the typical nightmares was afforded to persons not visited with well-defined amnesia.

These persons were largely of mediocre mind or less—some so primitive that they could scarcely be thought of as vehicles for abnormal scholarship and preternatural mental acquisitions. For a second they would be fired with alien force—then a backward lapse, and a thin, swift-fading memory of unhuman horrors.

There had been at least three such cases during the past half century—one only fifteen years before. Had something been groping blindly through time from some unsuspected abyss in nature? Were these faint cases monstrous, sinister experiments of a kind and authorship utterly beyond sane belief?

Such were a few of the formless speculations of my weaker hours—fancies abetted by myths which my studies uncovered. For I could not doubt but that certain persistent legends of immemorial antiquity apparently unknown to the victims and physicians connected with recent amnesia cases, formed a striking and awesome elaboration of memory lapses such as mine.

Of the nature of the dreams and impressions which were growing so clamorous I still almost fear to speak. They seemed to savor of madness, and at times I believed I was indeed going mad. Was there a special type of delusion afflicting those who had suffered lapses of memory? Conceivably, the efforts of the subconscious mind to fill up a perplexing blank with pseudomemories might give rise to strange imaginative vagaries.

This, indeed—though an alternative folklore theory finally seemed to me more plausible—was the belief of many of the alienists who helped me in my search for parallel cases, and who shared my puzzlement at the exact resemblances sometimes discovered.

They did not call the condition pure insanity, but classed it rather among neurotic disorders. My course in trying to track down and analyze it, instead of vainly seeking to dismiss or forget it, they heartily endorsed as correct according to the best psychological principles. I especially valued the advice of such physicians as had studied me during my possession by the other personality.

My first disturbances were not visual at all, but concerned the more abstract matters which I have mentioned. There was, too, a feeling of profound and inexplicable horror concerning myself. I developed a queer fear of seeing my own form, as if my eyes would find it something utterly alien and inconceivably abhorrent.

When I did glance down and behold the familiar human shape in quiet gray or blue clothing, I always felt a curious relief, though in order to gain this relief I had to conquer an infinite dread. I shunned mirrors as much as possible, and was always shaved at the barber's.

It was a long time before I correlated any of these disappointed feelings with the fleeting visual impressions which began to develop. The first such correlation had to do with the odd sensation of an external, artificial restraint on my memory.

I felt that the snatches of sight I experienced had a profound and terrible meaning, and a frightful connection with myself, but that some purposeful influence held me from grasping that meaning and that connection. Then came that queerness about the element of time, and with it desperate efforts to place the fragmentary dream glimpses in the chronological and spatial pattern.

The glimpses themselves were at first merely strange rather than horrible. I would seem to be in an enormous vaulted chamber whose lofty stone groinings were well nigh lost in the shadows overhead. In whatever time or place the scene might be, the principle of the arch was known as fully and used as extensively as by the Romans.

There were colossal, round windows and high, arched doors, and pedestals or tables each as tall as the height of an ordinary room. Vast shelves of dark wood lined the walls, holding what seemed to be volumes of immense size with strange hieroglyphs on their backs.

The exposed stonework held curious carvings, always in curvilinear mathematical designs, and there were chiseled inscriptions in the same characters that the huge books bore. The dark granite masonry was a monstrous megalithic type, with lines of convex-topped blocks fitting the concave-bottomed courses which rested upon them.

There were no chairs, but the tops of the vast pedestals were littered with books, papers, and what seemed to be writing materials—oddly figured jars of a purplish metal, and rods with stained tips. Tall as the pedestals were, I seemed at times able to view them from above. On some of them were great globes of luminous crystal serving as lamps, and inexplicable machines formed of vitreous tubes and metal rods.

The windows were glazed, and latticed with stout-looking bars. Though I dared not approach and peer out them, I could see from where I was the waving tops of singular fernlike growths. The floor was of massive octagonal flagstones, while rugs and hangings were entirely lacking.

Later, I had visions of sweeping through Cyclopean corridors of stone, and up and down gigantic inclined planes of the same monstrous masonry. There were no stairs anywhere, nor was any passageway less than thirty feet wide. Some of the structures through which I floated must have towered in the sky for thousands of feet.

There were multiple levels of black vaults below, and never-opened trapdoors, sealed down with metal bands and holding dim suggestions of some special peril.

I seemed to be a prisoner, and horror hung broodingly over everything I saw. I felt that the mocking curvilinear hieroglyphs on the walls would blast my soul with their message were I not guarded by a merciful ignorance.

Still later my dreams included vistas from the great round

windows, and from the titanic flat roof, with its curious gardens, wide barren area, and high, scalloped parapet of stone, to which the topmost of the inclined planes led.

There were almost endless leagues of giant buildings, each in its garden, and ranged along paved roads fully two hundred feet wide. They differed greatly in aspect, but few were less than five hundred feet square or a thousand feet high. Many seemed so limitless that they must have had a frontage of several thousand feet, while some shot up to mountainous altitudes in the gray, steamy heavens.

They seemed to be mainly of stone or concrete, and most of them embodied the oddly curvilinear type of masonry noticeable in the building that held me. Roofs were flat and garden-covered, and tended to have scalloped parapets. Sometimes there were terraces and higher levels, and wide, cleared spaces amidst the gardens. The great roads held hints of motion, but in the earlier visions I could not resolve this impression into details.

In certain places I beheld enormous dark cylindrical towers which climbed far above any of the other structures. These appeared to be of a totally unique nature and showed signs of prodigious age and dilapidation. They were built of a bizarre type of square-cut basalt masonry, and tapered slightly toward their rounded tops. Nowhere in any of them could the least traces of windows or other apertures save huge doors be found. I noticed also some lower buildings—all crumbling with the weathering of aeons—which resembled these dark, cylindrical towers in basic architecture. Around all these aberrant piles of square-cut masonry there hovered an inexplicable aura of menace and concentrated fear, like that bred by the sealed trapdoors.

The omnipresent gardens were almost terrifying in their strangeness, with bizarre and unfamiliar forms of vegetation nodding over broad paths lined with curiously carven monoliths. Abnormally vast fern-like growths predominated—some green, and some of gastly, fungoid pallor.

Among them rose great spectral things resembling calamites, whose bamboo-like trunks towered to fabulous heights. Then there were tufted forms like fabulous cycads, and grotesque dark-green shrubs and trees of coniferous aspect.

Flowers were small, colorless, and unrecognizable, blooming in geometrical beds and at large among the greenery.

In a few of the terrace and roof-top gardens were larger and more vivid blossoms of almost offensive contours and seeming to suggest artificial breeding. Fungi of inconceivable size, outlines, and colors speckled the scene in patterns bespeaking some unknown but well-established horticultural tradition. In larger gardens on the ground there seemed to be some attempt to preserve the irregularities of nature, but on the roofs there was more selectiveness, and more evidences of the topiary art.

The skies were almost always moist and cloudy, and sometimes I would seem to witness tremendous rains. Once in a while, though, there would be glimpses of the Sun—which looked abnormally large—and of the Moon, whose markings held a touch of difference from the normal that I could never quite fathom. When—very rarely—the night sky was clear to any extent, I beheld constellations which were nearly beyond recognition. Known outlines were sometimes approximated, but seldom duplicated; and from the position of the few groups I could recognize, I felt I must be in the Earth's southern hemisphere, near the Tropic of Capricorn.

The far horizon was always steamy and indistinct, but I could see that great jungles of unknown tree ferns, Calamites, Lepidodendro, and sigillaria lay outside the city, their fantastic frondage waving mockingly in the shifting vapors. Now and then there would be suggestions of motion in the sky, but these my early visions never resolved.

By the autumn of 1914 I began to have infrequent dreams of strange floatings over the city and through the regions around it. I saw interminable roads through forests of fearsome growths with mottled, fluted, and banded trunks, and past other cities as strange as the one which persistently haunted me.

I saw monstrous constructions of black or iridescent stone in glades and clearings where perpetual twilight reigned, and traversed long causeways over swamps so dark that I could tell but little of their moist, towering vegetation.

Once I saw an area of countless miles strewn with age-blasted basaltic ruins whose architecture had been like that of the few windowless, round-topped towers in the haunting city.

And once I saw the sea—a boundless, steamy expanse beyond the colossal stone piers of an enormous town of domes and arches.

As I have said, it was not immediately that these wild visions began to hold their terrifying quality. Certainly, many persons have dreamed intrinsically stranger things—things compounded of unrelated scraps of daily life, pictures, and reading, and arranged in fantastically novel forms by the unchecked caprices of sleep.

For some time I accepted the visions as natural, even though I had never before been an extravagant dreamer. Many of the vague anomalies, I argued, must have come from trivial sources too numerous to track down; while others seemed to reflect a common textbook knowledge of the plants and other conditions of the primitive world of a hundred and fifty million years ago— the world of the Permian or Triassic Age.

In the course of some months, however, the element of terror did figure with accumulating force. This was when the dreams began so unfailingly to have the aspect of memories, and when my mind began to link them with my growing abstract disturbances—the feeling of mnemonic restraint, the curious impressions regarding time, the sense of a loathsome exchange with my secondary personality of 1908–13, and, considerably later, the inexplicable loathing of my own person.

As certain definite details began to enter the dreams, their horror increased a thousandfold—until by October, 1915, I felt I must do something. It was then that I began an intensive study of other cases of amnesia and visions, feeling that I might thereby objectivize my trouble and shake clear of its emotional grip.

However, as before mentioned, the result was at first almost exactly opposite. It disturbed me vastly to find that my dreams had been so closely duplicated; especially since some of the accounts were too early to admit of any geological knowledge—and therefore of any idea of primitive landscapes—on the subjects' part.

What is more, many of these accounts supplied very horrible details and explanations in connection with the visions of great buildings and jungle gardens—and other things. The actual sights and vague impressions were bad enough, but what was hinted or asserted by some of the other dreamers savored of madness and blasphemy. Worst of all, my own pseudomemory was aroused to wilder dreams and hints of coming revelations. And yet most doctors deemed my course, on the whole, an advisable one.

I studied psychology systematically, and under the prevailing stimulus my son Wingate did the same—his studies leading eventually to his present professorship. In 1917 and 1918 I took special courses at Miskatonic. Meanwhile, my examination of medical, historical, and anthropological records became indefatigable, involving travels to distant libraries, and finally including even a reading of the hideous books of forbidden lore in which my secondary personality had been so disturbingly interested.

Some of the latter were the actual copies I had consulted in my altered state, and I was greatly disturbed by certain marginal notations and ostensible *corrections* of the hideous text in a script and idiom which somehow seemed oddly unhuman.

These markings were mostly in the respective languages of the various books, all of which the writer seemed to know with equal, though obviously, academic facility. One note appended to von Junzt's *Unaussprechlichen Kulten,* however, was alarmingly otherwise. It consisted of certain curvilinear hieroglyphs in the same ink as that of the German corrections, but following no recognized human pattern. And these hieroglyphs were closely and unmistakably akin to the characters constantly met with in my dreams—characters whose meaning I would sometimes momentarily fancy I knew, or was just on the brink of recalling.

To complete my black confusion, many libarians assured me that, in view of previous examinations and records of consultation of the volumes in question, all of these notations must have been made by myself in my secondary state. This despite the fact that I was and still am ignorant of three of the languages involved. Piecing together the scattered records, ancient and modern, anthropological and medical, I found a fairly consistent mixture of myth and hallucination whose scope and wildness left me utterly dazed. Only one thing consoled me: the fact that the myths were of such early existence. What lost knowledge could have brought pictures of the Paleozoic or Mesozoic landscape into these primitive fables, I could not even guess; but the pictures had been there. Thus, a basis existed for the formation of a fixed type of delusion.

Cases of amnesia no doubt created the general myth pattern—but afterward the fanciful accretions of the myths must have reacted on amnesia sufferers and colored their pseudomemories. I myself had read and heard all the early tales during my memory lapse—my quest had amply proved that. Was it not natural, then, for my subsequent dreams and emotional impressions to become

colored and molded by what my memory subtly held over from
my secondary state?

A few of the myths had significant connections with other cloudy
legends of the prehuman world, especially those Hindu tales involving stupefying gulfs of time and forming part of the lore of
modern theosophists.

Primal myth and modern delusion joined in their assumption
that mankind is only one—perhaps the least—of the highly evolved
and dominant races of this planet's long and largely unknown
career. Things of inconceivable shape, they implied, had reared
towers to the sky and delved into every secret of nature before
the first amphibian forbear of man had crawled out of the hot
sea three hundred million years ago.

Some had come down from the stars; a few were as old as the
cosmos itself; others had arisen swiftly from terrane germs as far
behind the first germs of our life cycle as those germs are behind
ourselves. Spans of thousands of millions of years, and linkages
of other galaxies and universes, were spoken of. Indeed, there was
no such thing as time in its humanly accepted sense.

But most of the tales and impressions concerned a relatively
late race, of a queer and intricate shape, resembling no life form
unknown to science, which had lived till only fifty million years
before the advent of man. This, they indicated, was the greatest
race of all because it alone had conquered the secret of time.

It had learned all things that ever were known or ever would
be known on the Earth, through the power of its keener minds
to project themselves into the past and future, even through gulfs
of millions of years, and study the lore of every age. From the
accomplishments of this race arose all legends of prophets, including those in human mythology.

In its vast libraries were volumes of texts and pictures holding
the whole of Earth's annals—histories and descriptions of every
species that had ever been or that ever would be, with full records
of their arts, their achievements, their languages, and their psy-
chologies.

With this aeon-embracing knowledge, the Great Race chose
from every era and life form such thoughts, arts, and processes
as might suit its own nature and situation. Knowledge of the past,
secured through a kind of mind-casting outside the recognized
senses, was harder to glean than knowledge of the future.

In the latter case the course was easier and more material. With suitable mechanical aid a mind would project itself forward in time, feeling its dim, extrasensory way till it approached the desired period. Then, after preliminary trials, it would seize on the best discoverable representative of the highest of that period's life forms. It would enter the organism's brain and set up therein its own vibrations, while the displaced mind would strike back to the period of the displacer, remaining in the latter's body till a reverse process was set up.

The projected mind, in the body of the organism of the future, would then pose as a member of the race whose outward form it wore, learning as quickly as possible all that could be learned of the chosen age and its massed information and techniques.

Meanwhile the displaced mind, thrown back to the displacer's age and body, would be carefully guarded. It would be kept from harming the body it occupied, and would be drained of all its knowledge by trained questioners. Often it could be questioned in its own language, when previous quests into the future had brought back records of that language.

If the mind came from a body whose language the Great Race could not physically reproduce, clever machines would be made, on which the alien speech could be played as on a musical instrument.

The Great Race's members were immense rugose cones ten feet high, and with head and other organs attached to foot-thick distensible limbs spreading from the apexes. They spoke by the clicking or scraping of huge paws or claws attached to the end of two of their four limbs, and walked by the expansion and contraction of a viscous layer attached to their vast, ten-foot bases.

When the captive mind's amazement and resentment had worn off, and when—assuming that it came from a body vastly different from the Great Race's—it had lost its horror at its unfamiliar, temporary form, it was permitted to study its new environment and experience a wonder and wisdom approximating that of its displacer.

With suitable precautions, and in exchange for suitable services, it was allowed to rove all over the habitable world in titan airships or on the huge boat-like, atomic-engined vehicles which traversed the great roads, and to delve freely into the libraries containing the records of the planet's past and future.

This reconciled many captive minds to their lot; since none were other than keen, and to such minds the unveiling of hidden mysteries of Earth—closed chapters of inconceivable pasts and dizzying vortices of future time which include the years ahead of their own natural ages—forms always, despite the abysmal horrors often unveiled, the supreme experience of life.

Now and then certain captives were permitted to meet other captive minds seized from the future—to exchange thoughts with consciousnesses living a hundred or a thousand or a million years before or after their own ages. And all were urged to write copiously in their own languages of themselves and their respective periods such documents to be filed in the great central archives.

It may be added that there was one special type of captive whose privileges were far greater than those of the majority. These were the dying *permanent* exiles, whose bodies in the future had been seized by keen-minded members of the Great Race who, faced with death, sought to escape mental extinction.

Such melancholy exiles were not as common as might be expected, since the longevity of the Great Race lessened its love of life—especially among those superior minds capable of projection. From cases of the permanent projection of elder minds arose many of those lasting changes of personality noticed in later history—including mankind's.

As for the ordinary cases of exploration—when the displacing mind had learned what it wished in the future, it would build an apparatus like that which had started its flight and reverse the process of projection. Once more it would be in its own body in its own age while the lately captive mind would return to that body of the future to which it properly belonged.

Only when one or the other of the bodies had died during the exchange was this restoration impossible. In such cases, of course, the exploring mind had—like those of the death escapers—to live out an alien-bodied life in the future; or else the captive mind—like the dying permanent exiles—had to end it days in the form and past age of the Great Race.

This fate was less horrible when the captive mind was also of the Great Race—a not infrequent occurrence, since in all its periods that race was intensely concerned with its own future. The number of dying permanent exiles of the Great Race was very slight—largely because of the tremendous penalties attached to displacements of future Great Race minds by the moribund.

Through projection, arrangements were made to inflict these

penalties on the offending minds in their new future bodies—and sometimes forced reexchanges were effected.

Complex cases of the displacement of exploring or already captive minds by minds in various regions of the past had been known and carefully rectified. In every age since the discovery of mind projection, a minute but well-recognized element of the population consisted of Great Race minds from past ages, sojourning for a longer or shorter while.

When a captive mind of alien origin was returned to its own body in the future, it was purged by an intricate mechanical hypnosis of all it had learned in the Great Race's Age—this because of certain troublesome consequences inherent in the general carrying forward of knowledge in large quantities.

The few existing instances of clear transmission had caused, and would cause at known future times, great disasters. And it was largely in consequence of two cases of the kind—said the old myths—that mankind had learned what it had concerning the Great Race.

Of all things surviving physically and directly from that aeon-distant world, there remained only certain ruins of great stones in far places and under the sea, and parts of the text of the frightful Pnakotic Manuscripts.

Thus the returning mind reached its own age with only the faintest and most fragmentary vision of what it had undergone since its seizure. All memories that could be eradicated were eradicated, so that in most cases only a dream-shadowed blank stretched back to the time of the first exchange. Some minds recalled more than others, and the chance joining of memories had at rare times brought hints of the forbidden past to future ages.

There probably never was a time when groups or cults did not secretly cherish certain of these hints. In the *Necronomicon* the presence of such a cult among human beings was suggested—a cult that sometimes gave aid to minds voyaging down the aeons from the days of the Great Race.

And, meanwhile, the Great Race itself waxed well-nigh omniscient, and turned to the task of setting up exchanges with the minds of other planets, and of exploring their pasts and futures. It sought likewise to fathom the past years and origin of that black, aeon-dead orb in far space whence its own mental heritage had come—for the mind of the Great Race was older than its bodily form.

The beings of a dying elder world, wise with the ultimate secrets, had looked ahead for a new world and species wherein they might have long life, and had sent their minds *en masse* into that future race best adapted to house them—the cone-shaped things that peopled our Earth a billion years ago.

Thus the Great Race came to be, while the myriad minds sent backward were left to die in the horror of strange shapes. Later the race would again face death, yet would live through another forward migration of its best minds into the bodies of others who had a longer physical span ahead of them.

Such was the background of intertwined legend and hallucination. When, around 1920, I had my researches in coherent shape, I felt a slight lessening of the tension which their earlier stages had increased. After all, and in spite of the fancies prompted by blind emotions, were not most of my phenomena readily explainable? Any chance might have turned my mind to dark studies during the amnesia—and then I read the forbidden legends and met the members of ancient and ill-regarded cults. That, plainly, supplied the material for the dreams and disturbed feelings which came after the return of memory.

As for the marginal notes in dream hieroglyphs and languages unknown to me, but laid at my door by librarians—I might easily have picked up a smattering of the tongues during my secondary state, while the hieroglyphs were doubtless coined by my fancy from descriptions in old legends, and afterward woven into my dreams. I tried to verify certain points through conversations with known cult leaders, but never succeeded in establishing the right connections.

At times the parallelism of so many cases in so many distant ages continued to worry me as it had at first, but on the other hand I reflected that the excitant folklore was undoubtedly more universal in the past than in the present.

Probably all the other victims whose cases were like mine had had a long and familiar knowledge of the tales I had learned only when in my secondary state. When these victims had lost their memory, they had associated themselves with the creatures of their household myths—the fabulous invaders supposed to displace men's minds—and had thus embarked upon quests for knowledge which they thought they could take back to a fancied, nonhuman past.

Then, when their memory returned, they reversed the associative process and thought of themselves as the former captive minds instead of as the displacers. Hence the dreams and pseudomemories following the conventional myth pattern.

Despite the seeming cumbrousness of these explanations, they came finally to supersede all others in my mind—largely because of the greater weakness of any rival theory. And a substantial number of eminent psychologists and anthropologists gradually agreed with me.

The more I reflected, the more convincing did my reasoning seem; till in the end I had a really effective bulwark against the visions and impressions which still assailed me. Suppose I did see strange things at night? These were only what I had heard and read of. Suppose I did have odd loathings and perspectives and pseudomemories? These, too, were only echoes of myths absorbed in my secondary state. Nothing that I might dream, nothing that I might feel, could be of any actual significance.

Fortified by this philosophy, I greatly improved in nervous equilibrium, even though the visions—rather than the abstract impressions—steadily became more frequent and more disturbingly detailed. In 1922 I felt able to undertake regular work again, and put my newly gained knowledge to practical use by accepting an instructorship in psychology at the university.

My old chair of political economy had long been adequately filled—besides which, methods of teaching economics had changed greatly since my heyday. My son was at this time just entering on the post-graduate studies leading to his present professorship, and we worked together a great deal.

4

I CONTINUED, however, to keep a careful record of the *outré* dreams which crowded upon me so thickly and vividly. Such a record, I argued, was of genuine value as a psychological document. The glimpses still seemed damnably like memories, though I fought off this impression with a goodly measure of success.

In writing, I treated the phantasmata as things seen; but at all other times I brushed them aside like any gossamer illusions of the night. I had never mentioned such matters in common conversation; though reports of them, filtering out as such things will, had aroused sundry rumors regarding my mental health. It is amusing to reflect that these rumors were confined wholly to laymen, without a single champion among physicians or psychologists.

Of my visions after 1914 I will here mention only a few, since fuller accounts and records are at the disposal of the serious student. It is evident that with time the curious inhibitions somewhat waned, for the scope of my visions vastly increased. They have never, though, become other than disjointed fragments seemingly without clear motivation.

Within the dreams I seemed gradually to acquire a greater and greater freedom of wandering. I floated through many strange buildings of stone, going from one to the other along mammoth underground passages which seemed to form the common avenues of transit. Sometimes I encountered those gigantic sealed trapdoors in the lowest level, around which such an aura of fear and forbiddenness clung.

I saw tremendous tessellated pools, and rooms of curious and inexplicable utensils of myriad sort. Then there were colossal caverns of intricate machinery whose outlines and purpose were wholly strange to me, and whose sound manifested itself only after many years of dreaming. I may here remark that sight and sound are the only senses I have ever exercised in the visionary world.

The real horror began in May, 1915, when I first saw the living things. This was before my studies had taught me what, in view of the myths and case histories, to expect. As mental barriers wore down, I beheld great masses of thin vapor in various parts of the building and in the streets below.

These steadily grew more solid and distinct, till at last I could trace their monstrous outlines with uncomfortable ease. They seemed to be enormous, iridescent cones, about ten feet high and ten feet wide at the base, and made up of some ridgy, scaly, semi-elastic matter. From their apexes projected four flexible, cylindrical members, each a foot thick, and of a ridgy substance like that of the cones themselves.

These members were sometimes contracted almost to nothing, and sometimes extended to any distance up to about ten feet. Terminating two of them were enormous claws or nippers. At the end of a third were four red, trumpetlike appendages. The fourth terminated in an irregular yellowish globe some two feet in diameter and having three great dark eyes ranged along its central circumference.

Surmounting this head were four slender gray stalks bearing flowerlike appendages, whilst from its nether side dangled eight greenish antennae or tentacles. The great base of the central cone was fringed with a rubbery, gray substance which moved the whole entity through expansion and contraction.

Their action, though harmless, horrified me even more than their appearance—for it is not wholesome to watch monstrous objects doing what one had known only human beings to do. These objects moved intelligently about the great rooms, getting books from the shelves and taking them to the great tables, or *vice versa,* and sometimes writing diligently with a peculiar rod gripped in the greenish head tentacles. The huge nippers were used in carrying books and in conversation—speech consisting of a kind of clicking.

The objects had no clothing, but wore satchels or knapsacks suspended from the top of the conical trunk. They commonly carried their head and its supporting member at the level of the cone top, though it was frequently raised or lowered.

The other three great members tended to rest downward at the sides of the cone, contracted to about five feet each, when not in use. From their rate of reading, writing, and operating their machines—those on the tables seemed somehow connected with thought—I concluded that their intelligence was enormously greater than man's.

Afterward I saw them everywhere; swarming in all the great chambers and corridors, tending monstrous machines in vaulted crypts, and racing along the vast roads in gigantic, boat-shaped cars. I ceased to be afraid of them, for they seemed to form supremely natural parts of their environment.

Individual difference amongst them began to be manifest, and a few appeared to be under some kind of restraint. These latter, though showing no physical variation, had a diversity of gestures and habits which marked them off not only from the majority, but very largely from one another.

They wrote a great deal in what seemed to my cloudy vision a vast variety of characters—never the typical curvilinear hieroglyphs of the majority. A few, I fancied, used our own familiar alphabet. Most of them worked much more slowly than the general mass of the entities.

All this time my own part in the dreams seemed to be that of a disembodied consciousness with a range of vision wider than the normal, floating freely about, yet confined to the ordinary avenues and speeds of travel. Not until August, 1915, did any suggestions of bodily existence begin to harass me. I say harass, because the first phase was purely abstract, though infinitely terrible, association of my previously noted body-loathing with the scenes of my visions.

For a while my chief concern during dreams was to avoid looking down at myself, and I recall how grateful I was for the total absence of large mirrors in the strange rooms. I was mightily troubled by the fact that I always saw the great tables—whose height could not be under ten feet—from a level not below that of their surfaces.

And then the morbid temptation to look down at myself became greater and greater, till one night I could not resist it. At first my downward glance revealed nothing whatever. A moment later I perceived that this was because my head lay at the end of a flexible neck of enormous length. Retracting this neck and gazing down very sharply, I saw the scaly, rugose, iridescent bulk of a vast cone ten feet tall and ten feet wide at the base. That was when I waked half of Arkham with my screaming as I plunged madly up from the abyss of sleep.

Only after weeks of hideous repetition did I grow half reconciled to these visions of myself in monstrous form. In the dreams I now moved bodily among the other unknown entities, reading terrible books from the endless shelves and writing for hours at the great tables with a stylus managed by the green tentacles that hung down from my head.

Snatches of what I read and wrote would linger in my memory. There were horrible annals of other worlds and other universes, and of stirrings of formless life outside of all universes. There were records of strange orders of beings which had peopled the world in forgotten pasts, and frightful chronicles of grotesque-bodied intelligences which would people it millions of years after the death of the last human being.

I learned of chapters in human history whose existence no scholar of today has ever suspected. Most of these writings were in the language of the hieroglyphs; which I studied in a queer

way with the aid of droning machines, and which was evidently
an agglutinative speech with root systems utterly unlike any found
in human languages.

Other volumes were in other unknown tongues learned in the
same queer way. A very few were in languages I knew. Extremely
clever pictures, both inserted in the records and forming separate
collections, aided me immensely. And all the time I seemed to
be setting down a history of my own age in English. On waking,
I could recall only minute and meaningless scraps of the unknown
tongues which my dream self had mastered, though whole phrases
of the history stayed with me.

I learned—even before my waking self had studied the parallel
cases or the old myths from which the dreams doubtless sprang—
that the entities around me were of the world's greatest race, which
had conquered time and had sent exploring minds into every age.
I knew, too, that I had been snatched from my age, while another
used my body in that age, and that a few of the other strange
forms housed similarly captured minds. I seemed to talk, in some
odd language of claw clickings, with exiled intellects from every
corner of the solar system.

There was a mind from the planet we know as Venus, which
would live incalculable epochs to come, and one from an outer
moon of Jupiter six million years in the past. Of Earthly minds
there were some from the winged, star-headed, half-vegetable race
of paleogean Antarctica; one from the reptile people of fabled
Valusia; three from the furry prehuman Hyperborean worshippers
of Tsathoggua; one from the wholly abominable Tcho-Tchos; two
from the Arachnid denizens of Earth's last age; five from the
hardy Coleopterous species immediately following mankind, to
which the Great Race was someday to transfer its keenest minds
en masse in the face of horrible peril; and several from different
branches of humanity.

I talked with the mind of Yiang-Li, a philosopher from the
cruel empire of Tsan-Chan, which is to come in 5,000 A.D.; with
that of a general of the great-headed brown people who held South
Africa in 50,000 B.C.; with that of a twelfth-century Florentine
monk named Bartolomeo Corsi; with that of a king of Lomar
who ruled that terrible polar land one hundred thousand years
before the squat, yellow Inutos came from the west to engulf it.

I talked with the mind of Nug-Soth, a magician of the dark
conquerors of 16,000 A.D.; with that of a Roman named Titus

Cempronius Blaesus, who had been a quaestor in Sulla's time; with that of Khephnes, an Egyptian of the 14th Dynasty, who told me the hideous secret of Nyarlathotep; with that of a priest of Atlantis' middle kingdom; with that of a Suffolk gentleman of Cromwell's day, James Woodville; with that of a court astronomer of pre-Inca Peru; with that of the Australian physicist Nevel Kingston-Brown, who will die in 2,518 A.D.; with that of an archimage of vanished Yhe in the Pacific; with that of Theodotides, a Graeco-Bactrian official of 200 B.C.; with that of an aged Frenchman of Louis XIII's time named Pierre-Louis Montagny; with that of Crom-Ya, a Cimmerian chieftain of 15,000 B.C.; and with so many others that my brain cannot hold the shocking secrets and dizzying marvels I learned from them.

I awakened each morning in a fever, sometimes frantically trying to verify or discredit such information as fell within the range of modern human knowledge. Traditional facts took on new and doubtful aspects, and I marveled at the dream fancy which could invent such surprising addenda to history and science.

I shivered at the mysteries the past may conceal, and trembled at the menaces the future may bring forth. What was hinted in the speech of post-human entities of the fate of mankind produced such an effect on me that I will not set it down here.

After man there would be the mighty beetle civilization, the bodies of whose members the cream of the Great Race would seize when the monstrous doom overtook the elder world. Later, as the Earth's span closed, the transferred minds would again migrate through time and space—to another stopping place in the bodies of the bulbous vegetable entities of Mercury. But there would be races after them, clinging pathetically to the cold planet and burrowing to its horror-filled core, before the utter end.

Meanwhile, in my dreams, I wrote endlessly in that history of my own age which I was preparing—half voluntarily and half through promises of increased library and travel opportunities—for the Great Race's central archives. The archives were in a colossal subterranean structure near the city's center, which I came to know well through frequent labors and consultations. Meant to last as long as the race, and to withstand the fiercest of Earth's convulsions, this titan repository surpassed all other buildings in the massive, mountainlike firmness of its construction.

The records, written or printed on great sheets of a curiously tenacious cellulose fabric were bound into books that opened from the top, and were kept in individual cases of a strange, extremely light rustless metal of grayish hue, decorated with mathematical designs and bearing the title in the Great Race's curvilinear hieroglyphs.

These cases were stored in tiers of rectangular vaults—like closed, locked shelves—wrought of the same rustless metal and fastened by knobs with intricate turnings. My own history was assigned a specific place in the vaults of the lowest or vertebrate level—the section devoted to the cultures of mankind and of the furry and reptilian races immediately preceding it in Terrestrial dominance.

But none of the dreams ever gave me a full picture of daily life. All were the merest misty, disconnected fragments, and it is certain that these fragments were not unfolded in their rightful sequence. I have, for example, a very imperfect idea of my own living arrangements in the dream world; though I seem to have possessed a great stone room of my own. My restrictions as a prisoner gradually disappeared, so that some of the visions included vivid travels over the mighty jungle roads, sojourns in strange cities, and explorations of some of the vast, dark, windowless ruins from which the Great Race shrank in curious fear. There were also long sea voyages in enormous, many-decked boats of incredible swiftness, and trips over wild regions in closed, projectilelike airships lifted and moved by electrical repulsion.

Beyond the wide, warm ocean were other cities of the Great Race, and on one far continent I saw the crude villages of the black-snouted, winged creatures who would evolve as a dominant stock after the Great Race had sent its foremost minds into the future to escape the creeping horror. Flatness and exuberant green life were always the keynote of the scene. Hills were low and sparse, and usually displayed signs of volcanic forces.

Of the animals I saw, I could write volumes. All were wild; for the Great Race's mechanized culture had long since done away with domestic beasts, while food was wholly vegetable or synthetic. Clumsy reptiles of great bulk floundered in steaming morasses, fluttered in the heavy air, or spouted in the seas and lakes; and among these I fancied I could vaguely recognize lesser, archaic prototypes of many forms—Dinosaurs, Pterodactyls, Itchthyosaurs, Labyrinthodonts, Plesiosaurs, and the like—made familiar through paleontology. Of birds or mammals there were none that I could discover.

The ground and swamps were constantly alive with snakes,

lizards, and crocodiles, while insects buzzed incessantly among the lush vegetation. And far out at sea, unspied and unknown monsters spouted mountainous columns of foam into the vaporous sky. Once I was taken under the ocean in a gigantic submarine vessel with searchlights, and glimpsed some living horrors of awesome magnitude. I saw also the ruins of incredible sunken cities, and the wealth of crinoid, brachiopod, coral, and ichthyic life which everywhere abounded.

Of the physiology, psychology, folkways, and detailed history of the Great Race my visions preserved but little information, and many of the scattered points I here set down were gleaned from my study of old legends and other cases rather than from my own dreaming.

For in time, of course, my reading and research caught up with and passed the dreams in many phases, so that certain dream fragments were explained in advance and formed verifications of what I had learned. This consolingly established my belief that similar reading and research, accomplished by my secondary self, had formed the source of the whole terrible fabric of pseudo-memories.

The period of my dreams, apparently, was one somewhat less than 150,000,000 years ago, when the Paleozoic Age was giving place to the Mesozoic. The bodies occupied by the Great Race represented no surviving—or even scientifically known—line of Terrestrial evolution, but were of a peculiar, closely homogeneous, and highly specialized organic type inclining as much to the vegetable as to the animal state.

Cell action was of an unique sort almost precluding fatigue, and wholly eliminating the need of sleep. Nourishment, assimilated through the red trumpetlike appendages on one of the great flexible limbs, was always semifluid and in many aspects wholly unlike the food of existing animals.

The beings had but two of the senses which we recognize—sight and hearing, the latter accomplished through the flowerlike appendages on the gray stalks above their head. Of other and incomprehensible senses—not, however, well utilizable by alien captive minds inhabitating their bodies—they possessed many. Their three eyes were so situated as to give them a range of vision wider than the normal. Their blood was a sort of deep-greenish ichor of great thickness.

They had no sex, but reproduced through seeds or spores which clustered on their bases and could be developed only under water. Great, shallow tanks were used for the growth of their young— which were, however, reared only in small numbers on account of the longevity of individuals—four or five thousand years being the common life span.

Markedly defective individuals were quickly disposed of as soon as their defects were noticed. Disease and the approach of death were, in the absence of a sense of touch or of physical pain, recognized by purely visual symptoms.

The dead were incinerated with dignified ceremonies. Once in a while, as before mentioned, a keen mind would escape death by forward projection in time; but such cases were not numerous. When one did occur, the exiled mind from the future was treated with the utmost kindness till the dissolution of its unfamiliar tenement.

The Great Race seemed to form a single, loosely knit nation or league, with major institutions in common, though there were four definite divisions. The political and economic system of each unit was a sort of fascistic socialism, with major resources rationally distributed, and power delegated to a small governing board elected by the votes of all able to pass certain educational and psychological tests. Family organization was not overstressed, though ties among persons of common descent were recognized, and the young were generally reared by their parents.

Resemblances to human attitudes and institutions were, of course, most marked in those fields where on the one hand highly abstract elements were concerned, or, where on the other hand there was a dominance of the basic, unspecialized urges common to all organic life. A few added likenesses came through conscious adoption as the Great Race probed the future and copied what it liked.

Industry, highly mechanized, demanded but little time from each citizen; and the abundant leisure was filled with intellectual and aesthetic activities of various sorts.

The sciences were carried to an unbelievable height of development, and art was a vital part of life, though at the period of my dreams it had passed its crest and meridian. Technology was enormously stimulated through the constant struggle to survive, and to keep in existence the physical fabric of great cities, imposed by the prodigious geologic upheavals of those primal days.

Crime was surprisingly scant, and was dealt with through highly efficient policing. Punishments ranged from privilege deprivation and imprisonment to death or major emotion wrenching, and were never administered without a careful study of the criminal's motivations.

Warfare, largely civil for the last few millennia though sometimes waged against reptilian and octopodic invaders, or against the winged, star-headed Old Ones who centered in the antarctic, was infrequent though infinitely devastating. An enormous army, using cameralike weapons which produced tremendous electrical effects, was kept on hand for purposes seldom mentioned, but obviously connected with the ceaseless fear of the dark, windowless elder ruins and of the great sealed trapdoors in the lowest subterranean levels.

This fear of the basalt ruins and trapdoors was largely a matter of unspoken suggestion—or, at most, of furtive quasi-whispers. Everything specific which bore on it was significantly absent from such books as were on the common shelves. It was the one subject lying altogether under a taboo among the Great Race, and seemed to be connected alike with horrible bygone struggles, and with that future peril which would someday force the race to send its keener minds ahead *en masse* in time.

Imperfect and fragmentary as were the other things presented by dreams and legends, this matter was still more bafflingly shrouded. The vague old myths avoided it—or perhaps all allusions had for some reason been excised. And in the dreams of myself and others, the hints were peculiarly few. Members of the Great Race never intentionally referred to the matter, and what could be gleaned came only from some of the more sharply observant captive minds.

According to these scraps of information, the basis of the fear was a horrible elder race of half polypous, utterly alien entities which had come through space from immeasurably distant universes and had dominated the Earth and three other solar planets about six hundred million years ago. They were only partly material—as we understand matter—and their type of consciousness and media of perception differed widely from those of Terrestrial organisms. For example, their senses did not include that of sight; their mental world being a strange, nonvisual pattern of impressions.

They were, however, sufficiently material to use implements of normal matter when in cosmic areas containing it; and they required housing—albeit of a peculiar kind. Though their senses could penetrate all material barriers, their substance could not; and certain forms of electrical energy could wholly destroy them.

They had the power of aerial motion, despite the absence of wings or any other visible means of levitation. Their minds were of such texture that no exchange with them could be effected by the Great Race.

When these things had come to the Earth they had built mighty basalt cities of windowless towers, and had preyed horribly upon the beings they found. Thus it was when the minds of the Great Race sped across the void from that obscure, transgalactic world known in the disturbing and debatable Eltdown Shards as Yith.

The newcomers, with the instruments they created, had found it easy to subdue the predatory entities and drive them down to those caverns of inner earth which they had already joined to their abodes and begun to inhabit.

Then they had sealed the entrances and left them to their fate, afterward occupying most of their great cities and preserving certain important buildings for reasons connected more with superstition than with indifference, boldness, or scientific and historical zeal.

But as the aeons passed, there came vague, evil signs that the elder things were growing strong and numerous in the inner world. There were sporadic irruptions of a particularly hideous character in certain small and remote cities of the Great Race, and in some of the deserted elder cities which the Great Race had not peopled—places where the paths to the gulfs below had not been properly sealed or guarded.

After that greater precautions were taken, and many of the paths were closed forever—though a few were left with sealed trapdoors for strategic use in fighting the elder things if ever they broke forth in unexpected places.

The irruptions of the elder things must have been shocking beyond all description, since they had permanently colored the psychology of the Great Race. Such was the fixed mood of horror that the very aspect of the creatures was left unmentioned. At no time was I able to gain a clear hint of what they looked like.

There were veiled suggestions of a monstrous plasticity, and of temporary lapses of visibility, while other fragmentary whispers referred to their control and military use of great winds. Singular whistling noises, and colossal footprints made up of five circular toe marks, seemed also to be associated with them.

It was evident that the coming doom so desperately feared by the Great Race—the doom that was one day to send millions of keen minds across the chasm of time to strange bodies in the safer future—had to do with a final successful irruption of the elder beings.

Mental projections down the ages had clearly foretold such a horror, and the Great Race had resolved that none who could escape should face it. That the foray would be a matter of vengeance, rather than an attempt to reoccupy the outer world, they knew from the planet's later history—for their projections showed the coming and going of subsequent races untroubled by the monstrous entities.

Perhaps these entities had come to prefer Earth's inner abysses to the variable, storm-ravaged surface, since light meant nothing to them. Perhaps, too, they were slowly weakening with the aeons. Indeed, it was known that they would be quite dead in the time of the post-human beetle race which the fleeing minds would tenant.

Meanwhile, the Great Race maintained its cautious vigilance, with potent weapons ceaselessly ready despite the horrified banishing of the subject from common speech and visible records. And always the shadow of nameless fear hung about the sealed trapdoors and the dark, windowless elder towers.

5

THAT IS the world of which my dreams brought me dim, scattered echoes every night. I cannot hope to give any true idea of the horror and dread contained in such echoes, for it was upon a wholly intangible quality—the sharp sense of pseudomemory—that such feelings mainly depended.

As I have said, my studies gradually gave me a defense against these feelings in the form of rational psychological explanations; and this saving influence was augmented by the subtle touch of accustomedness which comes with the passage of time. Yet in spite of everything the vague, creeping terror would return momentarily now and then. It did not, however, engulf me as it had before; and after 1922 I lived a very normal life of work and recreation.

In the course of years I began to feel that my experience—together with the kindred cases and the related folklore—ought to be definitely summarized and published for the benefit of serious students; hence, I prepared a series of articles briefly covering the whole ground and illustrated with crude sketches of some of the shapes, scenes, decorative motifs, and hieroglyphs remembered from the dreams.

These appeared at various times during 1928 and 1929 in the *Journal of the American Psychological Society,* but did not attract much attention. Meanwhile, I continued to record my dreams with the minutest care, even though the growing stack of reports attained troublesomely vast proportions.

On July 10, 1934, there was forwarded to me by the Psychological Society the letter which opened the culminating and most horrible phase of the whole mad ordeal. It was postmarked Pilbarra, Western Australia, and bore the signature of one whom I found, upon inquiry, to be a mining engineer of considerable prominence. Enclosed were some very curious snapshots. I will reproduce the text in its entirety, and no reader can fail to understand how tremendous an effect it and the photographs had upon me.

I was, for a time, almost stunned and incredulous; for, although I had often thought that some basis of fact must underlie certain phases of the legends which had colored my dreams, I was none the less unprepared for anything like a tangible survival from a lost world remote beyond all imagination. Most devastating of all were the photographs—for here, in cold, incontrovertible realism, there stood out against a background of sand certain worn-down, water-ridged, storm-weathered blocks of stone whose slightly convex tops and slightly concave bottoms told their own story.

And when I studied them with a magnifying glass I could see all too plainly, amidst the betterings and pittings, the traces of those vast curvilinear designs and occasional hieroglyphs whose significance had become so hideous to me. But here is the letter, which speaks for itself:

49 Dampier St.,
Pilbarra, W. Australia,
May 18, 1934.

Prof. N. W. Peaslee,
c/o Am. Psychological Society,
30 E. 41st St.,
New York City, U.S.A.

MY DEAR SIR:
A recent conversation with Dr. E. M. Boyle of Perth, and some papers with your articles which he has just sent me,

make it advisable for me to tell you about certain things I
have seen in the Great Sandy Desert east of our gold field
here. It would seem, in view of the peculiar legends about
old cities with huge stonework and strange designs and hieroglyphs which you describe, that I have come upon something
very important.

The blackfellows have always been full of talk about "great
stones with marks on them," and seem to have a terrible
fear of such things. They connect them in some way with
their common racial legends about Buddai, the gigantic old
man who lies asleep for ages underground with his head on
his arm, and who will someday awake and eat up the world.

There are some very old and half-forgotten tales of enormous underground huts of great stones, where passages lead
down and down, and where horrible things have happened.
The blackfellows claim that once some warriors, fleeing in
battle, went down into one and never came back, but that
frightful winds began to blow from the place soon after they
went down. However, there usually isn't much in what these
natives say.

But what I have to tell is more than this. Two years ago,
when I was prospecting about five hundred miles east in the
desert, I came on a lot of queer pieces of dressed stone
perhaps 3 × 2 × 2 feet in size, and weathered and pitted
to the very limit.

At first I couldn't find any of the marks the blackfellows
told about, but when I looked close enough I could make
out some deeply carved lines in spite of the weathering. There
were peculiar curves, just like what the blackfellows had tried
to describe. I imagine there must have been thirty or forty
blocks, some nearly buried in the sand, and all within a circle
perhaps a quarter of a mile in diameter.

When I saw some, I looked around closely for more, and
made a careful reckoning of the place with my instruments.
I also took pictures of ten or twelve of the most typical
blocks, and will enclose the prints for you to see.

I turned my information and pictures over to the government at Perth, but they have done nothing about them.

Then I met Dr. Boyle, who had read your articles in the
Journal of the American Psychological Society, and, in time,
happened to mention the stones. He was enormously interested and became quite excited when I showed him my

snapshots, saying that the stones and the markings were just like those of the masonry you had dreamed about and seen described in legends.

He meant to write you, but was delayed. Meanwhile, he sent me most of the magazines with your articles and I saw at once, from your drawings and descriptions, that my stones are certainly the kind you mean. You can appreciate this from the enclosed prints. Later on you will hear directly from Dr. Boyle.

Now I can understand how important all this will be to you. Without question we are faced with the remains of an unknown civilization older than any dreamed of before, and forming a basis for your legends.

As a mining engineer I have some knowledge of geology, and can tell you that these blocks are so ancient they frighten me. They are mostly sandstone and granite, though one is almost certainly made of a queer sort of cement or concrete.

They bear evidence of water action, as if this part of the world had been submerged and come up again after long ages—all since those blocks were made and used. It is a matter of hundreds of thousands of years—or Heaven knows how much more. I don't like to think about it.

In view of your previous diligent work in tracking down the legends and everything connected with them, I cannot doubt but that you will want to lead an expedition to the desert and make some archaeological excavations. Both Dr. Boyle and I are prepared to cooperate in such work if you— or organizations known to you—can furnish the funds.

I can get together a dozen miners for the heavy digging— the blackfellows would be of no use, for I've found that they have an almost maniacal fear of this particular spot. Boyle and I are saying nothing to others, for you very obviously ought to have precedence in any discoveries or credit.

The place can be reached from Pilbarra in about four days by motor tractor—which we'd need for our apparatus. It is somewhat west and south of Warburton's path of 1873, and one hundred miles southeast of Joanna Spring. We could float things up the De Grey River instead of starting from Pilbarra—but all that can be talked over later.

Roughly the stones lie at a point about 22° 3' 14" South

Latitude, 125° 0′ 39″ East Longitude. The climate is tropical, and the desert conditions are trying.

I shall welcome further correspondence upon this subject, and am indeed keenly eager to assist in any plan you may devise. After studying your articles I am deeply impressed with the profound significance of the whole matter. Dr. Boyle will write later. When rapid communication is needed, a cable to Perth can be relayed by wireless.

Hoping profoundly for an early message,
Believe me,
Most faithfully yours,
ROBERT B. F. MACKENZIE

Of the immediate aftermath of this letter, much can be learned from the press. My good fortune in securing the backing of Miskatonic University was great, and both Mr. Mackenzie and Dr. Boyle proved invaluable in arranging matters at the Australian end. We were not too specific with the public about our objects, since the whole matter would have lent itself unpleasantly to sensational and jocose treatment by the cheaper newspapers. As a result, printed reports were sparing; but enough appeared to tell of our quest for reported Australian ruins and to chronicle our various preparatory steps.

Professor William Dyer of the college's geology department—leader of the Miskatonic Antarctic Expedition of 1930–31—Ferdinand C. Ashley of the department of ancient history, and Tyler M. Freeborn of the department of anthropology—together with my son Wingate—accompanied me.

My correspondent, Mackenzie, came to Arkham early in 1935 and assisted in our final preparations. He proved to be a tremendously competent and affable man of about fifty, admirably well-read, and deeply familiar with all the conditions of Australian travel.

He had tractors waiting at Pilbarra, and we chartered a tramp steamer sufficiently small to get up the river to that point. We were prepared to excavate in the most careful and scientific fashion, sifting every particle of sand, and disturbing nothing which might seem to be in or near its original situation.

Sailing from Boston aboard the wheezy *Lexington* on March 28, 1935, we had a leisurely trip across the Atlantic and Mediterranean, through the Suez Canal, down the Red Sea, and across the Indian Ocean to our goal. I need not tell how the sight of the low, sandy West Australian coast depressed me, and how I detested the crude mining town and dreary gold fields where the tractors were given their last loads.

Dr. Boyle, who met us, proved to be elderly, pleasant and intelligent—and his knowledge of psychology led him into many long discussions with my son and me.

Discomfort and expectancy were oddly mingled in most of us when at length our party of eighteen rattled forth over the arid leagues of sand and rock. On Friday, May 31, we forded a branch of the De Grey and entered the realm of utter desolation. A certain positive terror grew on me as we advanced to this actual site of the elder world behind the legends—a terror, of course, abetted by the fact that my disturbing dreams and pseudomemories still beset me with unabated force.

It was on Monday, June 3, that we saw the first of the half-buried blocks. I cannot describe the emotions with which I actually touched—in objective reality—a fragment of Cyclopean masonry in every respect like the blocks in the walls of my dream buildings. There was a distinct trace of carving—and my hands trembled as I recognized part of a curvilinear decorative scheme made hellish to me through years of tormenting nightmare and baffling research.

A month of digging brought a total of some 1250 blocks in varying stages of wear and disintegration. Most of these were carven megaliths with curved tops and bottoms. A minority were smaller, flatter, plain-surfaced and square or octagonally cut—like those of the floors and pavements in my dreams—while a few were singularly massive and curved or slanted in such a manner as to suggest use in vaulting or groining, or as parts of arches or round window casings.

The deeper—and farther north and east—we dug, the more blocks we found—though we still failed to discover any trace of arrangement among them. Professor Dyer was appalled at the measureless age of the fragments, and Freeborn found traces of symbols which fitted darkly into certain Papuan and Polynesian legends of infinite antiquity. The condition and scattering of the blocks told mutely of vertiginous cycles of time and geologic upheavals of cosmic savagery.

We had an airplane with us, and my son Wingate would often go up to different heights and scan the sand-and-rock waste for signs of dim, large-scale outlines—either differences of level or trails of scattered blocks. His results were virtually negative; for whenever he would one day think he had glimpsed some significant trend, he would on his next trip find the impression replaced by another equally insubstantial—a result of the shifting, wind-blown sand.

One or two of these ephemeral suggestions, affected me queerly and disagreeably. They seemed, after a fashion, to dovetail horribly with something I had dreamed or read, but which I could no longer remember. There was a terrible familiarity about them— which somehow made me look furtively and apprehensively over the abominable, sterile terrain.

Around the first week in July I developed an unaccountable set of mixed emotions about that general northeasterly region. There was horror, and there was curiosity—but more than that, there was a persistent and perplexing illusion of memory.

I tried all sorts of psychological expedients to get these notions out of my head, but met with no success. Sleeplessness also gained upon me, but I almost welcomed this because of the resultant shortening of my dream periods. I acquired the habit of taking long, lone walks in the desert late at night—usually to the north or northeast, whither the sum of my strange new impulses seemed subtly to pull me.

Sometimes, on these walks, I would stumble over nearly buried fragments of the ancient masonry. Though there were fewer visible blocks here than where we had started, I felt sure that there must be a vast abundance beneath the surface. The ground was less level than at our camp, and the prevailing high winds now and then piled the sand into fantastic temporary hillocks—exposing low traces of the elder stones while it covered other traces.

I was queerly anxious to have the excavations extend to this territory, yet at the same time dreaded what might be revealed. Obviously, I was getting into a rather bad state—all the worse because I could not account for it.

An indication of my poor nervous health can be gained from my response to an odd discovery which I made on one of my nocturnal rambles. It was on the evening of July 11, when the Moon flooded the mysterious hillocks with a curious pallor.

Wandering somewhat beyond my usual limits, I came upon a great stone which seemed to differ markedly from any we had yet encountered. It was almost wholly covered, but I stooped and cleared away the sand with my hands, later studying the object carefully and supplementing the Moonlight with my electric torch.

Unlike the other very large rocks, this one was perfectly square-cut, with no convex or concave surface. It seemed, too, to be of a dark basaltic substance, wholly dissimilar to the granite and sandstone and occasional concrete of the now familiar fragments.

Suddenly I rose, turned, and ran for the camp at top speed. It was a wholly unconscious and irrational flight, and only when I was close to my tent did I fully realize why I had run. Then it came to me. The queer dark stone was something which I had dreamed and read about, and which was linked with the uttermost horrors of the aeon-old legendry.

It was one of the blocks of that basaltic elder masonry which the fabled Great Race held in such fear—the tall, windowless ruins left by those brooding, half-material, alien things that festered in Earth's nether abysses and against whose windlike, invisible forces the trapdoors were sealed and the sleepless sentinels posted.

I remained awake all night, but by dawn realized how silly I had been to let the shadow of a myth upset me. Instead of being frightened, I should have had a discoverer's enthusiasm.

The next forenoon I told the others about my find, and Dyer, Freeborn, Boyle, my son, and I set out to view the anomalous block. Failure, however, confronted us. I had formed no clear idea of the stone's location and a late wind had wholly altered the hillocks of shifting sand.

6

I COME now to the crucial and most difficult part of my narrative—all the more difficult because I cannot be quite certain of its reality. At times I feel uncomfortably sure that I was not dreaming or deluded; and it is this feeling—in view of the stupendous implications which the objective truth of my experience would raise—which impels me to make this record.

My son—a trained psychologist with the fullest and most sympathetic knowledge of my whole case—shall be the primary judge of what I have to tell.

First let me outline the externals of the matter, as those at the camp know them: On the night of July 17–18, after a windy day,

I retired early but could not sleep. Rising shortly before eleven and afflicted as usual with that strange feeling regarding the northeastward terrain, I set out on one of my typical nocturnal walks, seeing and greeting only one person—an Australian miner named Tupper—as I left our precincts.

The Moon, slightly past full, shone from a clear sky, and drenched the ancient sands with a white, leprous radiance which seemed to me somehow infinitely evil. There was no longer any wind, nor did any return for nearly five hours, as amply attested by Tupper and others who saw me walking rapidly across the pallid, secret-guarding hillocks toward the northeast.

About 3:30 A.M., a violent wind blew up, waking everyone in camp and felling three of the tents. The sky was unclouded, and the desert still blazed with that leprous Moonlight. As the party saw to the tents my absence was noted, but in view of my previous walks this circumstance gave no one alarm. And yet, as many as three men—all Australians—seemed to feel something sinister in the air.

Mackenzie explained to Professor Freeborn that this was a fear picked up from blackfellow folklore—the natives having woven a curious fabric of malignant myth about the high winds which at long intervals sweep across the sands under a clear sky. Such winds, it is whispered, blow out of the great stone huts under the ground, where terrible things have happened—and are never felt except near places where the big marked stones are scattered. Close to four the gale subsided as suddenly as it had begun, leaving the sand hills in new and unfamiliar shapes.

It was just past five, with the bloated, fungoid Moon sinking in the west, when I staggered into camp—hatless, tattered, features scratched and ensanguined, and without my electric torch. Most of the men had returned to bed, but Professor Dyer was smoking a pipe in front of his tent. Seeing my winded and almost frenzied state, he called Dr. Boyle, and the two of them got me on my cot and made me comfortable. My son, roused by the stir, soon joined them, and they all tried to force me to lie still and attempt sleep.

But there was no sleep for me. My psychological state was very extraordinary—different from anything I had previously suffered. After a time I insisted upon talking—nervously and elaborately explaining my condition.

I told them I had become fatigued, and had lain down in the

sand for a nap. There had, I said, been dreams even more frightful than usual—and when I was awakened by the sudden high wind my overwrought nerves had snapped. I had fled in panic, frequently falling over half-buried stones and thus gaining my tattered and bedraggled aspect. I must have slept long—hence the hours of my absence.

Of anything strange either seen or experienced I hinted absolutely nothing—exercising the greatest self-control in that respect. But I spoke of a change of mind regarding the whole work of the expedition, and urged a halt in all digging toward the northeast.

My reasoning was patently weak—for I mentioned a dearth of blocks, a wish not to offend the superstitious miners, a possible shortage of funds from the college, and other things either untrue or irrelevant. Naturally, no one paid the least attention to my new wishes—not even my son, whose concern for my health was very obvious.

The next day I was up and around the camp, but took no part in the excavations. I decided to return home as soon as possible for the sake of my nerves, and made my son promise to fly me in the plane to Perth—a thousand miles to the southwest—as soon as he had surveyed the region I wished let alone.

If, I reflected, the thing I had seen was still visible, I might decide to attempt a specific warning even at the cost of ridicule. It was just conceivable that the miners who knew the local folklore might back me up. Humoring me, my son made the survey that very afternoon, flying over all the terrain my walk could possibly have covered. Yet nothing of what I had found remained in sight.

It was the case of the anomalous basalt block all over again—the shifting sand had wiped out every trace. For an instant I half regretted having lost a certain awesome object in my stark fright—but now I know that the loss was merciful. I can still believe my whole experience an illusion—especially if, as I devoutly hope, that hellish abyss is never found.

Wingate took me to Perth on July 20, though declining to abandon the expedition and return home. He stayed with me until the 25th, when the steamer for Liverpool sailed. Now, in the cabin of the *Empress,* I am pondering long and frantically upon the entire matter, and have decided that my son, at least, must be informed. It shall rest with him whether to diffuse the matter more widely.

In order to meet any eventuality I have prepared this summary of my background—as already known in a scattered way to others—and will now tell as briefly as possible what seemed to happen during my absence from the camp that hideous night.

Nerves on edge, and whipped into a kind of perverse eagerness by that inexplicable, dread-mingled, mnemonic urge toward the northeast, I plodded on beneath the evil, burning Moon. Here and there I saw, half shrouded by the sand, those primal Cyclopean blocks left from nameless and forgotten aeons.

The incalculable age and brooding horror of this monstrous waste began to oppress me as never before, and I could not keep from thinking of my maddening dreams, of the frightful legends which lay behind them, and of the present fears of natives and miners concerning the desert and its carven stones.

And yet I plodded on as if to some eldritch rendezvous—more and more assailed by bewildering fancies, compulsions, and pseudomemories. I thought of some of the possible contours of the lines of stones as seen by my son from the air, and wondered why they seemed at once so ominous and so familiar. Something was fumbling and rattling at the latch of my recollection, while another unknown force sought to keep the portal barred.

The night was windless, and the pallid sand curved upward and downward like frozen waves of the sea. I had no goal, but somehow plowed along as if with fate-bound assurance. My dreams welled up into the waking world, so that each sand-embedded megalith seemed part of endless rooms and corridors of prehuman masonry, carved and hieroglyphed with symbols that I knew too well from years of custom as a captive mind of the Great Race.

At moments I fancied I saw those omniscient, conical horrors moving about at their accustomed tasks, and I feared to look down lest I find myself one with them in aspect. Yet all the while I saw the sand-covered blocks as well as the rooms and corridors; evil, burning Moon as well as the lamps of luminous crystal; the endless desert as well as the waving ferns beyond the windows. I was awake and dreaming at the same time.

I do not know how long or how far—or indeed, in just what direction—I had walked when I first spied the heap of blocks bared by the day's wind. It was the largest group in one place that I had seen so far, and so sharply did it impress me that the visions of fabulous aeons faded suddenly away.

Again there were only the desert and the evil Moon and the shards of an unguessed past. I drew close and paused, and cast the added light of my electric torch over the tumbled pile. A hillock had blown away, leaving a low, irregularly round mass of megaliths and smaller fragments some forty feet across and from two to eight feet high.

From the very outset I realized that there was some utterly unprecedented quality about those stones. Not only was the mere number of them quite without parallel, but something in the sandworn traces of design arrested me as I scanned them under the mingled beams of the Moon and my torch.

Not that any one differed essentially from the earlier specimens we had found. It was something subtler than that. The impression did not come when I looked at one block alone, but only when I ran my eye over several almost simultaneously.

Then, at last, the truth dawned upon me. The curvilinear patterns on many of those blocks were closely related—parts of one vast decorative conception. For the first time in this aeon-shaken waste I had come upon a mass of masonry in its old position—tumbled and fragmentary, it is true, but nonetheless existing in a very definite sense.

Mounting at a low place, I clambered laboriously over the heap; here and there clearing away the sand with my fingers, and constantly striving to interpret varieties of size, shape, and style and relationships of design.

After a while I could vaguely guess at the nature of the bygone structure, and at the designs which had once stretched over the vast surfaces of the primal masonry. The perfect identity of the whole with some of my dream glimpses appalled and unnerved me.

This was once a Cyclopean corridor thirty feet wide and thirty feet tall, paved with octagonal blocks and solidly vaulted overhead. There would have been rooms opening off on the right, and at the farther end one of those strange inclined planes would have wound down to still lower depths.

I started violently as these conceptions occurred to me, for there was more in them than the blocks themselves had supplied. How did I know that this level should have been far underground? How did I know that the plane leading upward should have been behind me? How did I know that the long subterrane passage to the Square of Pillars ought to lie on the left one level above me?

How did I know that the room of machines and the rightward-leading tunnel to the central archives ought to lie two levels below?

How did I know that there would be one of those horrible metal-banded trapdoors at the very bottom four levels down? Bewildered by this intrusion from the dream world, I found myself shaking and bathed in a cold perspiration.

Then, as a last, intolerable touch, I felt that faint, insidious stream of cool air trickling upward from a depressed place near the center of the hugh heap. Instantly, as once before, my visions faded, and I saw again only the evil Moonlight, the brooding desert, and the spreading tumulus of paleogean masonry. Something real and tangible, yet fraught with infinite suggestions of nighted mystery, now confronted me. For that stream of air could argue but one thing—a hidden gulf of great size beneath the disordered blocks on the surface.

My first thought was of the sinister blackfellow legend of vast underground huts among the megaliths where horrors happened and great winds are born. Then thoughts of my own dreams came back, and I felt dim pseudomemories tugging at my mind. What manner of place lay below me? What primal, inconceivable source of age-old myth cycles and haunting nightmares might I be on the brink of uncovering?

It was only for a moment that I hesitated, for more than curiosity and scientific zeal was driving me on and working against my growing fear.

I seemed to move almost automatically, as if in the clutch of some compelling fate. Pocketing my torch, and struggling with a strength that I had not thought I possessed, I wrenched aside first one titan fragment of stone and then another, till there welled up a strong draft whose dampness contrasted oddly with the desert's dry air. A black rift began to yawn, and at length—when I had pushed away every fragment small enough to budge—the leprous Moonlight blazed on an aperture of ample width to admit me.

I drew out my torch and cast a brilliant beam into the opening. Below me was a chaos of tumbled masonry, sloping roughly down toward the north at an angle of about forty-five degrees, and evidently the result of some bygone collapse from above.

Between its surface and the ground level was a gulf of impenetrable blackness at whose upper edge were signs of gigantic, stress-heaved vaulting. At this point, it appeared, the desert's sands lay directly upon a floor of some titan structure of Earth's youth—how preserved through aeons of geologic convulsion I could not then and cannot now even attempt to guess.

In retrospect, the barest idea of a sudden lone descent into such a doubtful abyss—and at a time when one's whereabouts were unknown to any living soul—seems like the utter apex of insanity. Perhaps it was—yet that night I embarked without hesitancy upon such a descent.

Again there was manifest that lure and driving of fatality which had all along seemed to direct my course. With torch flashing intermittently to save the battery, I commenced a mad scramble down the sinister, Cyclopean incline below the opening—sometimes facing forward as I found good hand and foot holds, and at other times turning to face the heap of megaliths as I clung and fumbled more precariously.

In two directions beside me, distant walls of carven, crumbling masonry loomed dimly under the direct beams of my torch. Ahead, however, was darkness.

I kept no track of time during my downward scramble. So seething with baffling hints and images was my mind that all objective matters seemed withdrawn to incalculable distances. Physical sensation was dead, and even fear remained as a wraith-like, inactive gargoyle leering impotently at me.

Eventually I reached a level floor strewn with fallen blocks, shapeless fragments of stone, and sand and detritus of every kind. On either side—perhaps thirty feet apart—rose massive walls culminating in huge groinings. That they were carved I could just discern, but the nature of the carvings was beyond my perception.

What held me most was the vaulting overhead. The beam from my torch could not reach the roof, but the lower parts of monstrous arches stood out distinctly. And so perfect was their identity with what I had seen in countless dreams of the elder world, that I trembled actively for the first time.

Behind and high above, a faint luminous blur told of the distant Moonlight world outside. Some vague shred of caution warned me that I should not let it out of my sight, lest I have no guide for my return.

I now advanced toward the wall at my left, where the traces of carving were plainest. The littered floor was nearly as hard to traverse as the downward heap had been, but I managed to pick my difficult way.

At one place I heaved aside some blocks and kicked away the detritus to see what the pavement was like, and shuddered at the utter, fateful familiarity of the great octagonal stones whose buckled surface still held roughly together.

Reaching a convenient distance from the wall, I cast the search-light slowly and carefully over its worn remnants of carving. Some bygone influx of water seemed to have acted on the sandstone surface, while there were curious incrustations which I could not explain.

In places the masonry was very loose and distorted, and I wondered how many aeons more this primal, hidden edifice could keep its remaining traces of form amidst Earth's heavings.

But it was the carvings themselves that excited me most. Despite their time-crumbled state, they were relatively easy to trace at close range; and the complete, intimate familiarity of every detail almost stunned my imagination. That the major attributes of this hoary masonry should be familiar, was not beyond normal cred-ibility.

Powerfully impressing the weavers of certain myths, they had become embodied in a stream of cryptic lore which, somehow, coming to my notice during the amnesic period, had evoked vivid images in my subconscious mind.

But how could I explain the exact and minute fashion in which each line and spiral of these strange designs tallied with what I had dreamed for more than a score of years? What obscure, forgotten inconography could have reproduced each subtle shading and nuance which so persistently, exactly, and unvaryingly besieged my sleeping vision night after night?

For this was no chance of remote resemblance. Definitely and absolutely, the millennially ancient, aeon-hidden corridor in which I stood was the original of something I knew in sleep as intimately as I knew my own house in Crane Street. Arkham. True, my dreams showed the place in its undecayed prime; but the identity was no less real on that account. I was wholly and horribly oriented.

The particular structure I was in was known to me. Known, too, was its place in that terrible elder city of dream. That I could visit unerringly any point in that structure or in that city which had escaped the changes and devastations of uncounted ages, I realized with hideous and instinctive certainty. What in Heaven's name could all this mean? How had I come to know what I knew? And what awful reality could lie behind those antique tales of the beings who had dwelt in this labyrinth of primordial stone?

Words can convey only fractionally the welter of dread and

bewilderment which ate at my spirit. I knew this place. I knew what lay below me, and what had lain overhead before the myriad towering stories had fallen to dust and debris and the desert. No need now, I thought with a shudder, to keep that faint blur of Moonlight in view.

I was torn betwixt a longing to flee and a feverish mixture of burning curiosity and driving fatality. What had happened to this monstrous megalopolis of old in the millions of years since the time of my dreams? Of the subterrene mazes which had underlain the city and linked all the titan towers, how much had still survived the writhings of Earth's crust?

Had I come upon a whole buried world of unholy archaism? Could I still find the house of the writing master, and the tower where S'gg'ha, the captive mind from the star-headed vegetable carnivores of Antarctica, had chiseled certain pictures on the blank spaces of the walls?

Would the passage at the second level down to the hall of the alien minds, be still unchoked and traversable? In that hall the captive mind of an incredible entity—a half-plastic denizen of the hollow interior of an unknown trans-Plutonian planet eighteen million years in the future—had kept a certain thing which it had modeled from clay.

I shut my eyes and put my hand to my head in a vain, pitiful effort to drive these insane dream fragments from my consciousness. Then, for the first time I felt acutely the coolness, motion, and dampness of the surrounding air. Shuddering, I realized that a vast chain of aeon-dead black gulfs must indeed be yawning somewhere beyond and below me.

I thought of the frightful chambers and corridors and inclines as I recalled them from my dreams. Would the way to the central archives still be open? Again that driving fatality tugged insistently at my brain as I recalled the awesome records that once lay cased in those rectangular vaults of rustless metal.

There, said the dreams and legends, had reposed the whole history, past and future, of the cosmic space-time continuum—written by captive minds from every orb and every age in the solar system. Madness, of course—but had I not now stumbled into a nighted world as mad as I?

I thought of the locked metal shelves, and of the curious knob twistings needed to open each one. My own came vividly into my consciousness. How often had I gone through that intricate routine of varied turns and pressures in the Terrestrial vertebrate section on the lowest level! Every detail was fresh and familiar.

If there was such a vault as I had dreamed of, I could open it in a moment. It was then that madness took me utterly. An instant later, and I was leaping and stumbling over the rocky debris toward the well-remembered incline to the depths below.

7

FROM THAT point forward my impressions are scarcely to be relied on—indeed, I still possess a final, desperate hope that they all form parts of some demoniac dream or illusion born of delirium. A fever raged in my brain, and everything came to me through a kind of haze—sometimes only intermittently.

The rays of my torch shot feebly into the engulfing blackness, bringing phantasmal flashes of hideously familiar walls and carvings, all blighted with the decay of ages. In one place a tremendous mass of vaulting had fallen, so that I had to clamber over a mighty mound of stones reaching almost to the ragged grotesquely stalactited roof.

It was all the ultimate apex of nightmare, made worse by the blasphemous tug of pseudomemory. One thing only was unfamiliar, and that was my own size in relation to the monstrous masonry. I felt oppressed by a sense of unwonted smallness, as if the sight of these towering walls from a mere human body was something wholly new and abnormal. Again and again I looked nervously down at myself, vaguely disturbed by the human form I possessed.

Onward through the blackness of the abyss I leaped, plunged and staggered—often falling and bruising myself, and once nearly shattering my torch. Every stone and corner of that demoniac gulf was known to me, and at many points I stopped to cast beams of light through choked and crumbling, yet familiar, archways.

Some rooms had totally collapsed; others were bare, or debris-filled. In a few I saw masses of metal—some fairly intact, some broken, and some crushed or battered—which I recognized as the colossal pedestals or tables of my dreams. What they could in truth have been, I dared not guess.

I found the downward incline and began its descent—though after a time halted by a gaping, ragged chasm whose narrowest point could not be much less than four feet across. Here the stonework had fallen through, revealing incalculable inky depths beneath.

I knew there were two more cellar levels in this titan edifice, and trembled with fresh panic as I recalled the metal-clamped trapdoor on the lowest one. There could be no guards now—for what had lurked beneath had long since done its hideous work and sunk into its long decline. By the time of the posthuman beetle race it would be quite dead. And yet, as I thought of the native legends, I trembled anew.

It cost me a terrible effort to vault that yawning chasm, since the littered floor prevented a running start—but madness drove me on. I chose a place close to the left-hand wall—where the rift was least wide and the landing spot reasonably clear of dangerous debris—and after one frantic moment reached the other side in safety.

At last, gaining the lower level, I stumbled on past the archway of the room of machines, within which were fantastic ruins of metal, half buried beneath fallen vaulting. Everything was where I knew it would be, and I climbed confidently over the heaps which barred the entrance of a vast transverse corridor. This, I realized, would take me under the city to the central archives.

Endless ages seemed to unroll as I stumbled, leaped, and crawled along that debris-cluttered corridor. Now and then I could make out carvings on the age-stained walls—some familiar, others seemingly added since the period of my dreams. Since this was a subterrene house-connecting highway, there were no archways save when the route led through the lower levels of various buildings.

At some of these intersections I turned aside long enough to look down well-remembered corridors and into well-remembered rooms. Twice only did I find any radical changes from what I had dreamed of—and in one of these cases I could trace the sealed-up outlines of the archway I remembered.

I shook violently, and felt a curious surge of retarding weakness as I steered a hurried and reluctant course through the crypt of one of those great windowless, ruined towers whose alien, basalt masonry bespoke a whispered and horrible origin.

This primal vault was round and fully two hundred feet across, with nothing carved upon the dark-hued stonework. The floor was here free from anything save dust and sand, and I could see the apertures leading upward and downward. There were no stairs nor inclines—indeed, my dreams had pictured those elder towers as wholly untouched by the fabulous Great Race. Those who had built them had not needed stairs or inclines.

In the dreams, the downward aperture had been tightly sealed and nervously guarded. Now it lay open—black and yawning, and giving forth a current of cool, damp air. Of what limitless caverns of eternal light might brood below, I would not permit myself to think.

Later, clawing my way along a badly heaped section of the corridor, I reached a place where the roof had wholly caved in. The debris rose like a mountain, and I climbed up over it, passing through a vast, empty space where my torchlight could reveal neither walls nor vaulting. This, I reflected, must be the cellar of the house of the metal purveyors, fronting on the third square not far from the archives. What had happened to it I could not conjecture.

I found the corridor again beyond the mountain of detritus and stone, but after a short distance encountered a wholly choked place where the fallen vaulting almost touched the perilously sagging ceiling. How I managed to wrench and tear aside enough blocks to afford a passage, and how I dared disturb the tightly packed fragments when the least shift of equilibrium might have brought down all the tons of superincumbent masonry to crush me to nothingness, I do not know.

It was sheer madness that impelled and guided me—if, indeed, my whole underground adventure was not—as I hope—a hellish delusion or phase of dreaming. But I did make—or dream that I made—a passage that I could squirm through. As I wriggled over the mound of debris—my torch, switched continuously on, thrust deeply in my mouth—I felt myself torn by the fantastic stalactites of the jagged floor above me.

I was now close to the great underground archival structure which seemed to form my goal. Sliding and clambering down the farther side of the barrier, and picking my way along the remaining stretch of corridor with handheld, intermittently flashing torch, I came at last to a low, circular crypt with arches—still in a marvelous state of preservation—opening off on every side.

The walls, or such parts of them as lay within reach of my torchlight, were densely hieroglyphed and chiseled with typical curvilinear symbols—some added since the period of my dreams.

This, I realized, was my fated destination, and I turned at once through a familiar archway on my left. That I could find a clear passage up and down the incline to all the surviving levels, I had, oddly, little doubt. This vast, Earth-protected pile, housing the annals of all the solar system, had been built with supernal skill and strength to last as long as the system itself.

Blocks of stupendous size poised with mathematical genius and bound with cements of incredible toughness had combined to form a mass as firm as the planet's rocky core. Here, after ages more prodigious than I could sanely grasp, its buried bulk stood in all its essential contours, the vast, dust-drifted floors scarce sprinkled with the litter elsewhere so dominant.

The relatively easy walking from this point onward went curiously to my head. All the frantic eagerness hitherto frustrated by obstacles now took itself out in a kind of febrile speed, and I literally raced along the low-roofed, monstrously well-remembered aisles beyond the archway.

I was past being astonished by the familiarity of what I saw. On every hand the great hieroglyphed metal shelf doors loomed monstrously; some yet in place, others sprung open, and still others bent and buckled under bygone geological stresses not quite strong enough to shatter the titan masonry.

Here and there a dust-covered heap beneath a gaping, empty shelf seemed to indicate where cases had been shaken down by the Earth tremors. On occasional pillars were great symbols and letters proclaiming classes and subclasses of volumes.

Once I paused before an open vault where I saw some of the accustomed metal cases still in position amidst the omnipresent gritty dust. Reaching up, I dislodged one of the thinner specimens with some difficulty, and rested it on the floor for inspection. It was titled in the prevailing curvilinear hieroglyphs, though something in the arrangement of the characters seemed subtly unusual.

The odd mechanism of the hooked fastener was perfectly well known to me, and I snapped up the still rustless and workable lid and drew out the book within. The latter, as expected, was some twenty by fifteen inches in area, and two inches thick; the thin metal covers opening at the top.

Its tough cellulose pages seemed unaffected by the myriad cycles of time they had lived through, and I studied the queerly pigmented, brush-drawn letters of the text—symbols unlike either the usual curved hieroglyphs or any alphabet known to human scholarship—with a haunting, half-aroused memory.

It came to me that this was the language used by a captive mind I had known slightly in my dreams—a mind from a large asteroid on which had survived much of the archaic life and lore of the primal planet whereof it formed a fragment. At the same time I recalled that this level of the archives was devoted to volumes dealing with the non-Terrestrial planets.

As I ceased poring over this incredible document, I saw that the light of my torch was beginning to fail, hence quickly inserted the extra battery I always had with me. Then, armed with the stronger radiance, I resumed my feverish racing through unending tangles of aisles and corridors—recognizing now and then some familiar shelf, and vaguely annoyed by the acoustic conditions which made my footfalls echo incongruously in these catacombs.

The very prints of my shoes behind me in the millennially untrodden dust made me shudder. Never before, if my mad dreams held anything of truth, had human feet pressed upon those immemorial pavements.

Of the particular goal of my insane racing, my conscious mind held no hint. There was, however, some force of evil potency pulling at my dazed will and buried recollection, so that I vaguely felt I was not running at random.

I came to a downward incline and followed it to profound depths. Floors flashed by me as I raced, but I did not pause to explore them. In my whirling brain there had begun to beat a certain rhythm which set my right hand twitching in unison. I wanted to unlock something, and felt that I knew all the intricate twists and pressures needed to do it. It would be like a modern safe with a combination lock.

Dream or not, I had once known and still knew. How any dream—or any scrap of unconsciously absorbed legend—could have taught me a detail so minute, so intricate, and so complex, I did not attempt to explain to myself. I was beyond all coherent thought. For was not this whole experience—this shocking familiarity with a set of unknown ruins, and this monstrously exact identity of everything before me with what only dreams and scraps of myth could have suggested—a horror beyond all reason?

Probably it was my basic conviction then—as it is now during my saner moments—that I was not awake at all, and that the entire buried city was a fragment of febrile hallucination.

Eventually, I reached the lowest level and struck off to the right of the incline. For some shadowy reason I tried to soften my steps, even though I lost speed thereby. There was a space I was afraid to cross on this last, deeply buried floor.

As I drew near it I recalled what thing in that space I feared. It was merely one of the metal-barred and closely guarded trapdoors. There would be no guards now, and on that account I trembled and tiptoed as I had done in passing through that black basalt vault where a similar trapdoor had yawned.

I felt a current of cold damp air, as I had felt there, and wished that my course led in another direction. Why I had to take the particular course I was taking, I did not know.

When I came to the space I saw that the trapdoor yawned wildly open. Ahead, the shelves began again, and I glimpsed on the floor before one of them a heap very thinly covered with dust, where a number of cases had recently fallen. At the same moment a fresh wave of panic clutched me, though for some time I could not discover why.

Heaps of fallen cases were not uncommon, for all through the aeons this lightless labyrinth had been racked by the heavings of Earth and had echoed at intervals to the deafening clatter of toppling objects. It was only when I was nearly across the space that I realized why I shook so violently.

Not the heap, but something about the dust of the level floor, was troubling me. In the light of my torch it seemed as if that dust were not as even as it ought to be—there were places where it looked thinner, as if it had been disturbed not many months before. I could not be sure, for even the apparently thinner places were dusty enough; yet a certain suspicion of regularity in the fancied unevenness was highly disquieting.

When I brought the torchlight close to one of the queer places I did not like what I saw—for the illusion of regularity became very great. It was as if there were regular lines of composite impressions—impressions that went in threes, each slightly over a foot square, and consisting of five nearly circular three-inch prints, one in advance of the other four.

These possible lines of foot-square impression appeared to lead in two directions, as if something had gone somewhere and returned. They were, of course, very faint, and may have been illusions or accidents; but there was an element of dim, fumbling terror about the way I thought they ran. For at one end of them was the heap of cases which must have clattered down not long before, while at the other end was the ominous trapdoor with the cool, damp wind, yawning unguarded down to abysses past imagination.

8

THAT MY strange sense of compulsion was deep and overwhelming is shown by its conquest of my fear. No rational motive could have drawn me on after that hideous suspicion of prints and the creeping dream memories it excited. Yet my right hand, even as it shook with fright, still twitched rhythmically in its eagerness to turn a lock it hoped to find. Before I knew it I was past the heap of lately fallen cases and running on tiptoe through aisles of utterly unbroken dust toward a point which I seemed to know morbidly, horribly well.

My mind was asking itself questions whose origin and relevancy I was only beginning to guess. Would the shelf be reachable by a human body? Could my human hand master all the aeon-remembered motions of the lock? Would the lock be undamaged and workable? And what would I do—what dare I do—with what— as I now commenced to realize—I both hoped and feared to find? Would it prove the awesome, brain-shattering truth of something past normal conception, or show only that I was dreaming?

The next I knew I had ceased my tiptoed racing and was standing still, staring at a row of maddeningly familiar hieroglyphed shelves. They were in a state of almost perfect preservation, and only three of the doors in this vicinity had sprung open.

My feelings toward these shelves cannot be described—so utter and insistent was the sense of old acquaintance. I was looking high up a row near the top and wholly out of my reach, and wondering how I could climb to best advantage. An open door four rows from the bottom would help, and the locks of the closed doors formed possible holds for hands and feet. I would grip the torch between my teeth, as I had in other places where both hands were needed. Above all I must make no noise.

How to get down what I wished to remove would be difficult, but I could probably hook its movable fastener in my coat collar and carry it like a knapsack. Again I wondered whether the lock would be undamaged. That I could repeat each familiar motion I had not the least doubt. But I hoped the thing would not scrape or creak—and that my hand could work it properly.

Even as I thought these things I had taken the torch in my mouth and begun to climb. The projecting locks were poor supports; but as I had expected, the opened shelf helped greatly. I used both the swinging door and the edge of the aperture itself in my ascent, and managed to avoid any loud creaking.

Balanced on the upper edge of the door, and leaning far to my right, I could just reach the lock I sought. My fingers, half numb from climbing, were very clumsy at first; but I soon saw that they were anatomically adequate. And the memory rhythm was strong in them.

Out of unknown gulfs of time the intricate, secret motions had somehow reached my brain correctly in every detail—for after less than five minutes of trying there came a click whose familiarity was all the more startling because I had not consciously anticipated it. In another instant the metal door was slowly swinging open with only the faintest grating sound.

Dazedly I looked over the row of grayish case ends thus exposed, and felt a tremendous surge of some wholly inexplicable emotion. Just within reach of my right hand was a case whose curving hieroglyphs made me shake with a pang infinitely more complex than one of mere fright. Still shaking, I managed to dislodge it amidst a shower of gritty flakes, and ease it over toward myself without any violent noise.

Like the other case I had handled, it was slightly more than twenty by fifteen inches in size, with curved mathematical designs in low relief. In thickness it just exceeded three inches.

Crudely wedging it between myself and the surface I was climbing, I fumbled with the fastener and finally got the hook free. Lifting the cover, I shifted the heavy object to my back, and let the hook catch hold of my collar. Hands now free, I awkwardly clambered down to the dusty floor and prepared to inspect my prize.

Kneeling in the gritty dust, I swung the case around and rested it in front of me. My hands shook, and I dreaded to draw out the book within almost as much as I longed—and felt compelled—to do so. It had very gradually become clear to me what I ought to find, and this realization nearly paralyzed my faculties.

If the thing were there—and if I were not dreaming—the implications would be quite beyond the power of the human spirit to bear. What tormented me most was my momentary inability to feel that my surroundings were a dream. The sense of reality was hideous—and again becomes so as I recall the scene.

At length I tremblingly pulled the book from its container and stared fascinatedly at the well-known hieroglyphs on the cover. It seemed to be in prime condition, and the curvilinear letters of the title held me in almost as hypnotized a state as if I could read them. Indeed, I cannot swear that I did not actually read them in some transient and terrible access of abnormal memory.

I do not know how long it was before I dared to lift that thin metal cover. I temporized and made excuses to myself. I took the torch from my mouth and shut it off to save the battery. Then, in the dark, I collected my courage—finally lifting the cover without turning on the light. Last of all, I did indeed flash the torch upon the exposed page—steeling myself in advance to suppress any sound no matter what I should find.

I looked for an instant, then collapsed. Clenching my teeth, however, I kept silent. I sank wholly to the floor and put a hand to my forehead amidst the engulfing blackness. What I dreaded and expected was there. Either I was dreaming, or time and space had become a mockery.

I must be dreaming—but I would test the horror by carrying this thing back and showing it to my son if it were indeed a reality. My head swam frightfully, even though there were no visible objects in the unbroken gloom to swirl about me. Ideas and images of the starkest terror—excited by the vistas which my glimpse had opened up—began to throng in upon me and cloud my senses.

I thought of those possible prints in the dust, and trembled at the sound of my own breathing as I did so. Once again I flashed on the light and looked at the page as a serpent's victim may look at his destroyer's eyes and fangs.

Then, with clumsy fingers, in the dark, I closed the book, put it in its container, and snapped the lid and the curious, hooked fastener. This was what I must carry back to the outer world if it truly existed—if the whole abyss truly existed—if I, and the world itself, truly existed.

Just when I tottered to my feet and commenced my return I cannot be certain. It comes to me oddly—as a measure of my sense of separation from the normal world—that I did not even once look at my watch during those hideous hours underground.

Torch in hand, and with the ominous case under one arm, I eventually found myself tiptoeing in a kind of silent panic past the draft-giving abyss and those lurking suggestions of prints. I lessened my precautions as I climbed up the endless inclines, but could not shake off a shadow of apprehension which I had not felt on the downward journey.

I dreaded having to repass through that black basalt crypt that was older than the city itself, where cold drafts welled up from unguarded depths. I thought of that which the Great Race had feared, and of what might still be lurking—be it ever so weak and dying—down there. I thought of those five-circle prints and of what my dreams had told me of such prints—and of strange winds and whistling noises associated with them. And I thought of the tales of the modern blackfellows, wherein the horror of great winds and nameless ruins was dwelt upon.

I knew from a carven wall symbol the right floor to enter, and came at last—after passing that other book I had examined—to the great circular space with the branching archways. On my right, and at once recognizable, was the arch through which I had arrived. This I now entered, conscious that the rest of my course would be harder because of the tumbled state of the masonry outside the archive building. My new metal-cased burden weighed upon me, and I found it harder and harder to be quiet as I stumbled among debris and fragments of every sort.

Then I came to the ceiling-high mound of debris through which I had wrenched a scanty passage. My dread at wriggling through again was infinite, for my first passage had made some noise, and I now—after seeing those possible prints—dreaded sound above all things. The case, too, doubled the problem of traversing the narrow crevice.

But I clambered up the barrier as best I could, and pushed the case through the aperture ahead of me. Then, torch in mouth, I scrambled through myself—my back torn as before by stalactites.

As I tried to grasp the case again, it fell some distance ahead of me down the slope of the debris, making a disturbing clatter and arousing echoes which sent me into a cold perspiration. I lunged for it at once, and regained it without further noise—but a moment afterward the slipping of blocks under my feet raised a sudden and unprecedented din.

That din was my undoing. For, falsely or not, I thought I heard it answered in a terrible way from spaces far behind me. I thought I heard a shrill, whistling sound, like nothing else on Earth, and beyond any adequate verbal description. If so, what followed has a grim irony—save for the panic of this thing, the second thing might never have happened.

As it was, my frenzy was absolute and unrelieved. Taking my torch in my hand and clutching feebly at the case, I leaped and bounded wildly ahead with no idea in my brain beyond a mad desire to race out of these nightmare ruins to the waking world of desert and Moonlight which lay so far above.

I hardly knew it when I reached the mountain of debris which towered into the vast blackness beyond the caved-in roof, and bruised and cut myself repeatedly in scrambling up its steep slope of jagged blocks and fragments.

Then came the great disaster. Just as I blindly crossed the summit, unprepared for the sudden dip ahead, my feet slipped utterly and I found myself involved in a mangling avalanche of sliding masonry whose cannon-loud uproar split the black, cavern air in a deafening series of Earth-shaking reverberations.

I have no recollection of emerging from this chaos, but a momentary fragment of consciousness shows me as plunging and tripping and scrambling along the corridor amidst the clangor—case and torch still with me.

Then, just as I approached that primal basalt crypt I had so dreaded, utter madness came. For as the echoes of the avalanche died down, there became audible a repetition of that frightful alien whistling I thought I had heard before. This time there was no doubt about it—and what was worse, it came from a point not behind but *ahead of me.*

Probably I shrieked aloud then. I have a dim picture of myself as flying through the hellish basalt vault of the elder things, and hearing that damnable alien sound piping up from the open, unguarded door of limitless nether blacknesses. There was a wind, too—not merely a cool, damp draft, but a violent, purposeful blast belching savagely and frigidly from that abominable gulf whence the obscene whistling came.

There are memories of leaping and lurching over obstacles of every sort, with that torrent of wind and shrieking sound growing moment by moment, and seeming to curl and twist purposefully around me as it struck out wickedly from the spaces behind and beneath.

Though in my rear, that wind had the odd effect of hindering instead of aiding my progress; as if it acted like a noose or lasso thrown around me. Heedless of the noise I made, I clattered over a great barrier of blocks and was again in the structure that led to the surface.

I recall glimpsing the archway to the room of machines and almost crying out as I saw the incline leading down to where one of those blasphemous trapdoors must be yawning two levels below. But instead of crying out I muttered over and over to myself that this was all a dream from which I must soon awake. Perhaps I was in camp—perhaps I was at home in Arkham. As these hopes bolstered up my sanity I began to mount the incline to the higher level.

I knew, of course, that I had the four-foot cleft to recross, yet was too racked by other fears to realize the full horror until I came almost upon it. On my descent, the leap across had been easy—but could I clear the gap as readily when going uphill, and hampered by fright exhaustion, the weight of the metal case, and the anomalous backward tug of that demon wind? I thought of these things at the last moment, and thought also of the nameless entities which might be lurking in the black abysses below the chasm.

My wavering torch was growing feeble, but I could tell by some obscure memory when I neared the cleft. The chill blasts of wind and the nauseous whistling shrieks behind me were for the moment like a merciful opiate, dulling my imagination to the horror of the yawning gulf ahead. And then I became aware of the added blasts and whistling in front of me—tides of abomination surging up through the cleft itself from depths unimagined and unimaginable.

Now, indeed, the essence of pure nightmare was upon me. Sanity departed—and, ignoring everything except the animal impulse of flight, I merely struggled and plunged upward over the incline's debris as if no gulf had existed. Then I saw the chasm's edge, leaped frenziedly with every ounce of strength I possessed, and was instantly engulfed in a pandemoniac vortex of loathsome sound and utter, materially tangible blackness.

That is the end of my experience, so far as I can recall. Any further impressions belong wholly to the domain of phantasmagoric delirium. Dream, madness, and memory merged wildly together in a series of fantastic, fragmentary delusions which can have no relation to anything real.

There was a hideous fall through incalculable leagues of viscous, sentient darkness, and a babel of noises utterly alien to all that we know of the Earth and its organic life. Dormant, rudimentary senses seemed to start into vitality within me, telling of pits and voids peopled by floating horrors and leading to sunless crags and oceans and teeming cities of windowless, basalt towers upon which no light ever shone.

Secrets of the primal planet and its immemorial aeons flashed through my brain without the aid of sight or sound, and there were known to me things which not even the wildest of former dreams had ever suggested. And all the while cold fingers of damp vapor clutched and picked at me, and that eldritch, damnable whistling shrieked fiendishly above all the alternations of babel and silence in the whirlpools of darkness around.

Afterward there were visions of the Cyclopean city of my dreams—not in ruins, but just as I had dreamed of it. I was in my conical, nonhuman body again, and mingled with crowds of the Great Race and the captive minds who carried books up and down the lofty corridors and vast inclines.

Then, superimposed upon these pictures, were frightful, momentary flashes of a nonvisual consciousness involving desperate struggles, a writhing free from clutching tentacles of whistling wind, an insane, batlike flight through half-solid air, a feverish burrowing through the cyclone-whipped dark, and a wild stumbling and scrambling over fallen masonry.

Once there was a curious, intrusive flash of half sight—a faint, diffuse suspicion of bluish radiance far overhead. Then there came a dream of wind-pursued climbing and crawling—of wriggling into a blaze of sardonic moonlight through a jumble of debris which slid and collapsed after me amidst a morbid hurricane. It was the evil, monotonous beating of that maddening moonlight which at last told me of the return of what I had once known as the objective, waking world.

I was clawing prone through the sands of the Australian desert, and around me shrieked such a tumult of wind as I had never before known on our planet's surface. My clothing was in rags, and my whole body was a mass of bruises and scratches.

Full consciousness returned very slowly, and at no time could

I tell just where delirious dream left off and true memory began. There had seemed to be a mound of titan blocks, an abyss beneath it, a monstrous revelation from the past, and a nightmare horror at the end—but how much of this was real?

My flashlight was gone, and likewise my metal case I may have discovered. Had there been such a case—or any abyss—or any mound? Raising my head, I looked behind me, and saw only the sterile, undulant sands of the desert.

The demon wind died down, and the bloated, fungoid moon sank reddeningly in the west. I lurched to my feet and began to stagger southwestward toward the camp. What in truth had happened to me? Had I merely collapsed in the desert and dragged a dream-racked body over miles of sand and buried blocks? If not, how could I bear to live any longer?

For, in this new doubt, all my faith in the myth-born unreality of my visions dissolved once more into the hellish older doubting. If that abyss was real, then the Great Race was real—and its blasphemous reachings and seizures in the cosmos-wide vortex of time were no myths or nightmares, but a terrible, soul-shattering actuality.

Had I, in full, hideous fact, been drawn back to a prehuman world of a hundred and fifty million years ago in those dark, baffling days of the amnesia? Had my present body been the vehicle of a frightful alien consciousness from paleogean gulfs of time?

Had I, as the captive mind of those shambling horrors, indeed known that accursed city of stone in its primordial heyday, and wriggled down those familiar corridors in the loathsome shape of my captor? Were those tormenting dreams of more than twenty years the offspring of stark, monstrous memories?

Had I once veritably talked with minds from reachless corners of time and space, learned the universe's secrets, past and to come, and written the annals of my own world for the metal cases of those titan archives? And were those others—those shocking elder things of the mad winds and demon pipings—in truth a lingering, lurking menace, waiting and slowly weakening in black abysses while varied shapes of life drag out their multimillennial courses on the planet's age-racked surface?

I do not know. If that abyss and what it held were real, there is no hope. Then, all too truly, there lies upon this world of man a mocking and incredible shadow out of time. But, mercifully there is no proof that these things are other than fresh phases of my myth-born dreams. I did not bring back the metal case that would have been a proof, and so far those subterranean corridors have not been found.

If the laws of the universe are kind, they will never be found. But I must tell my son what I saw or thought I saw, and let him use his judgment as a psychologist in gauging the reality of my experience, and communicating this account to others.

I have said that the awful truth behind my tortured years of dreaming hinges absolutely upon the actuality of what I thought I saw in those Cyclopean, buried ruins. It has been hard for me, literally, to set down that crucial revelation, though no reader can have failed to guess it. Of course, it lay in that book within the metal case—the case which I pried out of its lair amidst the dust of a million centuries.

No eye had seen, no hand had touched that book since the advent of man to this planet. And yet, when I flashed my torch upon it in that frightful abyss, I saw that the queerly pigmented letters on the brittle, aeon-browned cellulose pages were not indeed any nameless hieroglyphs of Earth's youth. They were, instead, words of the English language in my own handwriting.

ROBERT AICKMAN
The Stains

AFTER ELIZABETH ultimately died, it was inevitable that many people should come forward with counsel, and doubtless equally inevitable that the counsel be so totally diverse.

There were two broad and opposed schools.

The first considered that Stephen should "treasure the memory" (though it was not always put like that) for an indefinite period, which, it was implied, might conveniently last him out to the end of his own life. These people attached great importance to Stephen "not rushing anything." The second school urged that Stephen marry again as soon as he possibly could. They said that, above all, he must not just fall into apathy and let his life slide. They said he was a man made for marriage and all it meant.

Of course, both parties were absolutely right in every way. Stephen could see that perfectly well.

It made little difference. Planning, he considered, would be absurd in any case. Until further notice, the matter would have to be left to fate. The trouble was, of course, that fate's possible options were narrowing and dissolving almost weekly, as they had already been doing throughout Elizabeth's lengthy illness. For example (the obvious and most pressing example): how many women would want to marry Stephen now? A number, perhaps; but not a number that he would want to marry. Not after Elizabeth. That in particular.

They told him he should take a holiday, and he took one. They told him he should see his doctor, and he saw him. The man who had looked after Elizabeth had wanted to emigrate, had

521

generously held back while Elizabeth had remained alive, and had then shot off at once. The new man was half-Sudanese, and Stephen found him difficult to communicate with, at least upon a first encounter, at least on immediate topics.

In the end, Stephen applied for and obtained a spell of compassionate leave, and went, as he usually did, to stay with his elder brother, Harewood, in the north. Harewood was in orders: the Reverend Harewood Hooper BD, MA. Their father and grandfather had been in orders too, and had been incumbents of that same small church in that same small parish for thirty-nine years and forty-two years respectively. So far, Harewood had served for only twenty-three years. The patron of the living, a private individual, conscientious and very long lived, was relieved to be able to rely upon a succession of such dedicated men. Unfortunately, Harewood's own son, his one child, had dropped out, and was now believed to have disappeared into Nepal. Harewood himself cared more for rock growths than for controversies about South Africa or for other such fashionable church preoccupations. He had published two important books on lichens. People often came to see him on the subject. He was modestly famous.

He fostered lichens on the flagstones leading up to the rectory front door; on the splendidly living stone walls, here gray stone, there yellow; even in the seldom used larders and pantries; assuredly on the roof, which, happily, was of stone slabs also.

As always when he visited his brother, Stephen found that he was spending much of his time out of doors; mainly, being the man he was, in long, solitary walks across the heathered uplands. This had nothing to do with Harewood's speciality. Harewood suffered badly from bronchitis and catarrh, and nowadays went out as little as possible. The domestic lichens, once introduced, required little attention—only observation.

Rather it was on account of Harewood's wife, Harriet, that Stephen roamed; a lady in whose company Stephen had never been at ease. She had always seemed to him a restless woman; jumpy and puzzling; the very reverse of all that had seemed best about Elizabeth. A doubtful asset, Stephen would have thought, in a diminishing rural parish; but Stephen himself, in a quiet and unobtruding way, had long been something of a skeptic. Be that as it might, he always found that Harriet seemed to be baiting and fussing him, not least when her husband was present; even, unforgivably, when Elizabeth, down in London, had been battling through her last dreadful years. On every visit, therefore, Stephen wandered about for long hours in the open, even when ice was in the air and snow on the tenuous tracks.

But Stephen did not see it as a particular hardship. Elizabeth, who might have done—though, for his sake, she could have been depended upon to conceal the fact—had seldom come on these visits at any time. She had never been a country girl, though fond of the sea. Stephen positively liked wandering unaccompanied on the moors, though he had little detailed knowledge of their flora and fauna, or even of their archeology, largely industrial and fragmentary. By now he was familiar with most of the moorland routes from the rectory and the village; and, as commonly happens, there was one that he preferred to all the others, and nowadays found himself taking almost without having to make a decision. Sometimes even, asleep in his London flat that until just now had been *their* London flat, he found himself actually dreaming of that particular soaring trail, though he would have found it difficult to define what properties of beauty or poetry or convenience it had of which the other tracks had less. According to the map, it led to a spot named Burton's Clough.

There was a vague valley or extended hollow more or less in the place which the map indicated, but to Stephen it seemed every time too indefinite to be marked out for record. Every time he wondered whether this was indeed the place; whether there was not some more decisive declivity that he had never discovered. Or possibly the name derived from some event in local history. It was the upwards walk to the place that appealed to Stephen, and, to an only slightly lesser extent, the first part of the slow descent homewards, supposing that the rectory could in any sense be called home: never the easily attainable but inconclusive supposed goal, the Clough. Of course there was always R. L. Stevenson's traveling hopefully to be inwardly quoted; and on most occasions hitherto Stephen had inwardly quoted it.

Never had there been any human being at, near, or visible from the terrain around Burton's Clough, let alone in the presumptive clough itself. There was no apparent reason why there should be. Stephen seldom met anyone at all on the moors. Only organizations go any distance afoot nowadays, and this was not an approved didactic district. All the work of agriculture is for a period being done by machines. Most of the cottages are peopled by transients. Everyone is supposed to have a car.

But that morning, Stephen's first in the field since his bereavement six weeks before, there *was* someone, and down at the bottom of the shallow clough itself. The person was dressed so as to be almost lost in the hues of autumn, plainly neither tripper nor trifler. The person was engaged in some task.

Stephen was in no state for company, but that very condition, and a certain particular reluctance that morning to return to the rectory before he had to, led him to advance further, not descending into the clough but skirting along the ridge to the west of it, where, indeed, his track continued.

If he had been in the Alps, his shadow might have fallen in the early autumn sun across the figure below, but in the circumstances that idea would have been fanciful, because, at the moment, the sun was no more than a misty bag of gleams in a confused sky. None the less, as Stephen's figure passed, comparatively high above, the figure below glanced up at him. Stephen could see that it was the figure of a girl. She was wearing a fawn shirt and pale green trousers, but the nature of her activity remained uncertain.

Stephen glanced away, then glanced back.

She seemed still to be looking up at him, and suddenly he waved to her, though it was not altogether the kind of thing he normally did. She waved back at him. Stephen even fancied she smiled at him. It seemed quite likely. She resumed her task.

He waited for an instant, but she looked up no more. He continued on his way more slowly, and feeling more alive, even if only for moments. For those moments, it had been as if he still belonged to the human race, to the mass of mankind.

Only once or twice previously had he continued beyond the top of Burton's Clough, and never for any great distance. On the map (it had been his father's map), the track wavered on across vast area of nothing very much, merely contour lines and occasional habitations with odd, possibly evocative, names: habitations which, as Stephen knew from experience, regularly proved, when approached, to be littered ruins or not to be detectable at all. He would not necessarily have been averse from the twelve or fourteen miles solitary walk involved, at least while Elizabeth had been secure and alive, and at home in London; but conditions at the rectory had never permitted so long an absence. Harriet often

made clear that she expected her guests to be present punctually
at all meals and punctually at such other particular turning points
of a particular day as the day itself might define.

On the present occasion, and at the slow pace into which he
had subsided, Stephen knew that he should turn back within the
next ten to fifteen minutes; but he half-understood that what he
was really doing was calculating the best time for a second possible
communication with the girl he had seen in the clough. If he
reappeared too soon, he might be thought, at such a spot, to be
pestering, even menacing; if too late, the girl might be gone. In
any case, there was an obvious limit to the time he could give
to such approach as might be possible.

As the whole matter crystallized within him, he turned on the
instant. There was a stone beside the track at the point where he
did it; perhaps aforetime a milepost, at the least a waymark. Its
location seemed to justify his action. He noticed that it too was
patched with lichen. When staying with Harewood, he always
noticed; and more and more at other times too.

One might almost have thought that the girl had been waiting
for him. She was standing at much the same spot, and looking
upwards abstractedly. Stephen saw that beside her on the ground
was a gray receptacle. He had not noticed it before, because its
vague color sank into the landscape, as did the girl herself, cos-
tumed as she was. The receptacle seemed to be half-filled with
gray contents of some kind.

As soon as he came into her line of sight, and sometime before
he stood immediately above her, the girl spoke.

"Are you lost? Are you looking for someone?"

She must have had a remarkably clear voice, because her words
came floating up to Stephen like bubbles in water.

He continued along the ridge towards her while she watched
him. Only when he was directly above her did he trust his own
words to reach her.

"No. I'm really just filling in time. Thank you very much."

"If you go on to the top, there's a spring."

"I should think you have to have it pointed out to you. With
all this heather."

She looked down for a moment, then up again. "Do you live
here?"

"No. I'm staying with my brother. He's the rector. Perhaps you go to his church?"

She shook her head. "No. We don't go to any church."

That could not be followed up, Stephen felt, at his present distance and altitude. "What are you doing?" he asked.

"Collecting stones for my father."

"What does he do with them?"

"He wants the mosses and lichens."

"Then," cried Stephen, "you *must* know my brother. Or your father must know him. My brother is one of the great authorities on lichens." This unexpected link seemed to open a door; and, at least for a second, to open it surprisingly wide.

Stephen found himself bustling down the rough but not particularly steep slope towards her.

"My father's not an *authority,*" said the girl, gazing seriously at the descending figure. "He's not an authority on anything."

"Oh, you misunderstand," said Stephen. "My brother is only an amateur too. I didn't mean he was a professor or anything like that. Still, I think your father must have heard of him."

"I don't think so," said the girl. "I'm almost sure not."

Stephen had nearly reached the bottom of the shallow vale. It was completely out of the wind down there, and surprisingly torrid.

"Let me see," he said, looking into the girl's basket, before he looked at the girl.

She lifted the basket off the ground. Her hand and forearm were brown.

"Some of the specimens are very small," he said, smiling. It was essential to keep the conversation going, and it was initially more difficult now that he was alone with her in the valley, and close to her.

"It's been a bad year," she said. "Some days I've found almost nothing. Nothing that could be taken home."

"All the same, the basket must be heavy. Please put it down." He saw that it was reinforced with stout metal strips, mostly rusty.

"Take a piece for yourself, if you like," said the girl. She spoke as if they were portions of iced cake, or home-made coconut fudge.

Stephen gazed full at the girl. She had a sensitive face with gray-green eyes and short reddish hair—no, auburn. The *démodé* word came to Stephen on the instant. Both her shirt and her trousers were worn and faded: familiar, Stephen felt. She was wearing serious shoes, but little cared for. She was a part of nature.

"I'll take this piece," Stephen said. "It's conglomerate."

"Is it?" said the girl. Stephen was surpirsed that after so much ingathering, she did not know a fact so elementary.

"I might take this piece too, and show the stuff on it to my brother."

"Help yourself," said the girl. "But don't take them all."

Feeling had been building up in Stephen while he had been walking solitarily on the ridge above. For so long he had been isolated, insulated, incarcerated. Elizabeth had been everything to him, and no one could ever be like her, but "attractive" was not a word that he had used to himself about her, not for a long time; not attractive as this girl was attractive. Elizabeth had been a part of him, perhaps the greater part of him; but not mysterious, not fascinating.

"Well, I don't know," said Stephen. "How far do you have to carry that burden?"

"The basket isn't full yet. I must go on searching for a bit."

"I am sorry to say I can't offer to help. I have to go back."

All the same, Stephen had reached a decision.

The girl simply nodded. She had not yet picked up the basket again.

"Where do you live?"

"Quite near."

That seemed to Stephen to be almost impossible, but it was not the main point.

Stephen felt like a schoolboy; though not like himself as a schoolboy. "If I were to be here after lunch tomorrow, say at half past two, would you show me the spring? The spring you were talking about."

"Of course," she said. "If you like."

Stephen could not manage the response so obviously needed, gently confident; if possible, even gently witty. For a moment, in fact, he could say nothing. Then—"Look," he said. He brought an envelope out of his pocket and in pencil on the back of it he wrote: "Tomorrow. Here. 2:30 P.M. To visit the spring."

He said, "It's too big," and tore one end off the envelope, aware that the remaining section bore his name, and that the envelope had been addressed to him care of his brother. As a matter of fact, it had contained the final communication from the undertaking firm. He wished they had omitted his equivocal and rather ridiculous OBE.

He held the envelope out. She took it and inserted it, without a word, into a pocket of her shirt, buttoning down the flap. Stephen's heart beat at the gesture.

He was not exactly sure what to make of the situation or whether the appointment was to be depended upon. But at such moments in life, one is often sure of neither thing, nor of anything much else.

He looked at her. "What's your name?" he asked, as casually as he could.

"Nell," she answered.

He had not quite expected that, but then he had not particularly expected anything else either.

"I look forward to our walk, Nell," he said. He could not help adding, "I look forward to it very much."

She nodded and smiled.

He fancied that they had really looked at one another for a moment.

"I must go on searching," she said.

She picked up the heavy basket, seemingly without particular effort, and walked away from him, up the valley.

Insanely, he wondered about *her* lunch. Surely she must have some? She seemed so exceptionally healthy and strong.

His own meal was all scarlet runners, but he had lost his appetite in any case, something that had never previously happened since the funeral, as he had noticed with surprise on several occasions.

Luncheon was called lunch, but the evening meal was none the less called supper, perhaps from humility. At supper that evening, Harriet referred forcefully to Stephen's earlier abstemiousness.

"I trust you're not sickening, Stephen. It would be a bad moment. Dr. Gopalachari's on holiday. Perhaps I ought to warn you."

"Dr. Who?"

"No, not Dr. Who. Dr. Gopalachari. He's a West Bengali. We are lucky to have him."

Stephen's brother, Harewood, coughed forlornly.

* * *

For luncheon, the next day, Stephen had even less appetite, even though it was mashed turnip, cooked, or at least served, with mixed peppers. Harriet loved all things oriental.

On an almost empty stomach, he hastened up the long but not steep ascent. He had not known he could still walk so fast uphill, but for some reason the knowledge did not make him particularly happy, as doubtless it should have done.

The girl, dressed as on the day before, was seated upon a low rock at the spot from which he had first spoken to her. It was not yet twenty past. He had discerned her seated shape from afar, but she had proved to be sitting with her back to the ascending track and to him. On the whole, he was glad that she had not been watching his exertions, inevitably comical, albeit triumphant.

She did not even look up until he actually stood before her. Of course this time she had no basket.

"Oh, hullo," she said.

He stood looking at her. "We're both punctual."

She nodded. He was panting quite strenuously, and glad to gain a little time.

He spoke. "Did you find many more suitable stones?"

She shook her head, then rose to her feet.

He found it difficult not to stretch out his arms and draw her to him.

"Why is this called Burton's Clough, I wonder? It seems altogether too wide and shallow for a clough."

"I didn't know it was," said the girl.

"The map says it is. At least I think this is the place. Shall we go? Lead me to the magic spring."

She smiled at him. "Why do you call it *that?*"

"I'm sure it *is* magic. It must be."

"It's just clear water," said the girl, "and very, very deep."

Happily, the track was still wide enough for them to walk side by side, though Stephen realized that, further on, where he had not been, this might cease to be the case.

"How long are you staying here?" asked the girl.

"Perhaps for another fortnight. It depends."

"Are you married?"

"I *was* married, Nell, but my wife unfortunately died." It seemed unnecessary to put any date to it, and calculated only to cause stress.

"I'm sorry," said the girl.

"She was a wonderful woman and a very good wife."

To that the girl said nothing. What could she say?

"I am taking a period of leave from the civil service," Stephen volunteered. "Nothing very glamorous."

"What's the civil service?" asked the girl.

"You ought to know *that*," said Stephen in mock reproof: more or less mock. After all, she was not a child, or not exactly. All the same, he produced a childlike explanation. "The civil service is what looks after the country. The country would hardly carry on without us. Not nowadays. Nothing would run properly."

"Really not?"

"No. Not run *properly*." With her it was practicable to be lightly profane.

"Father says that all politicians are evil. I don't know anything about it."

"Civil servants are not politicians, Nell. But perhaps this is not the best moment to go into it all." He said that partly because he suspected she had no wish to learn.

There was a pause.

"Do you like walking?" she asked.

"Very much. I could easily walk all day. Would you come with me?"

"I *do* walk all day, or most of it. Of course I have to sleep at night. I lie in front of the fire."

"But it's too warm for a fire at this time of year." He said it to keep the conversation going, but, in fact, he was far from certain. He himself was not particularly warm at that very moment. He had no doubt cooled off after speeding up the ascent, but the two of them were, nonetheless, walking reasonably fast, and still he felt chilly, perhaps perilously so.

"Father always likes a fire," said the girl. "He's a cold mortal."

They had reached the decayed milestone or waymark at which Stephen had turned on the previous day. The girl had stopped and was fingering the lichens with which it was spattered. She knelt against the stone with her left arm round the back of it.

"Can you put a name to them?" asked Stephen.

"Yes, to some of them."

"I am sure your father has one of my brother's books on his shelf."

"I don't think so," said the girl. "We have no shelves. Father can't read."

She straightened up and glanced at Stephen.

"Oh, but surely—"

For example, and among other things, the girl herself was perfectly well spoken. As a matter of fact, hers was a noticeably beautiful voice. Stephen had noticed it, and even thrilled to it, when first he had heard it, floating up from the bottom of the so-called clough. He had thrilled to it ever since, despite the curious things the girl sometimes said.

They resumed their way.

"Father has no eyes," said the girl.

"That is terrible," said Stephen. "I hadn't realized."

The girl said nothing.

Stephen felt his first real qualm, as distinct from mere habitual self-doubt. "Am I taking you away from him? Should you go back to him?"

"I'm never with him by day," said the girl. "He finds his way about."

"I know that does happen," said Stephen guardedly. "All the same—"

"Father doesn't need a civil service to run him," said the girl. The way she spoke convinced Stephen that she had known all along what the civil service was and did. He had from the first supposed that to be so. Everyone knew.

"You said your dead wife was a wonderful woman," said the girl.

"Yes, she was."

"My father is a wonderful man."

"Yes," said Stephen. "I am only sorry about his affliction."

"It's not an affliction," said the girl.

Stephen did not know what to say to that. The last thing to be desired was an argument of any kind whatever, other perhaps that a fun argument.

"Father doesn't need to get things out of books," said the girl.

"There are certainly other ways of learning," said Stephen. "I expect that was one of the things you yourself learned at school."

He suspected she would say she had never been to school. His had been a half-fishing remark.

But all she replied was, "Yes."

Stephen looked around him for a moment. Already, he had gone considerably further along the track than ever before. "It really is beautiful up here." It seemed a complete wilderness. The track had wound among the wide folds of the hill, so that nothing but wilderness was visible in any direction.

"I should like to live here," said Stephen. "I should like it *now*." He knew that he partly meant "now that Elizabeth was dead."

"There are empty houses everywhere," said the girl. "You can just move into one. It's what Father and I did, and now it's our home."

Stephen supposed that that at least explained something. It possibly elucidated one of the earliest of her odd remarks.

"I'll help you to find one, if you like," said the girl. "Father says that none of them have been lived in for hundreds of years. I know where all the best ones are."

"I'll have to think about that," said Stephen. "I have my job, you must remember." He wanted her to be rude about his job.

But she only said, "We'll look now, if you like."

"Tomorrow, perhaps. We're looking for the spring now."

"Are you tired?" asked the girl, with apparently genuine concern, and presumably forgetting altogether what he had told her about his longing to walk all day.

"Not at all tired," said Stephen, smiling at her.

"Then why were you looking at your watch?"

"A bad habit picked up in the civil service. We all do it."

He had observed long before that she had no watch on her lovely brown forearm, no bracelet; only the marks of thorn scratches and the incisions of sharp stones. The light golden bloom on her arms filled him with delight and with desire.

In fact, he had omitted to time their progression, though he timed most things, so that the habit had wrecked his natural faculty. Perhaps another twenty or thirty minutes passed, while they continued to walk side by side, the track having as yet shown no particular sign of narrowing, so that one might think it still led somewhere, and that people still went there. As they advanced, they said little more of consequence for the moment; or so it seemed to Stephen. He surmised that there was now what is termed an understanding between them, even though in a sense he himself understood very little. It was more a phase for pleasant nothings, he deemed, always supposing that he could evolve a sufficient supply of them, than for meaningful questions and reasonable responses.

Suddenly, the track seemed not to narrow, but to stop, even to vanish. Hereunto it had been surprisingly well trodden. Now he could see nothing but knee-high heather.

"The spring's over there," said the girl in a matter of fact way, and pointing. Such simple and natural gestures are often the most beautiful.

"How right I was in saying that I could never find it alone!" remarked Stephen.

He could not see why the main track should not lead to the spring—if there really was a spring. Why else should the track be beaten to this spot? The mystery was akin to the Burton's Clough mystery. The uplands had been settled under other conditions than ours. Stephen, on his perambulations, had always felt that, everywhere.

But the girl was standing among the heather a few yards away, and Stephen saw that there was a curious serpentine rabbit run that he had failed to notice—except that rabbits do not run like serpents. There were several fair-sized birds flying overhead in silence. Stephen fancied they were kites.

He wriggled his way down the rabbit path, with little dignity.

There was the most beautiful small pool imaginable: clear, deep, lustrous, gently heaving at its center, or near its center. It stood in a small clearing.

All the rivers in Britain might be taken as rising here, and thus flowing until the first moment of their pollution.

Stephen became aware that now the sun really *was* shining. He had not noticed before. The girl stood on the far side of the pool in her faded shirt and trousers, smiling seraphically. The pool pleased her, so that suddenly everything pleased her.

"Have you kept the note I gave you?" asked Stephen.

She put her hand lightly on her breast pocket, and therefore on her breast.

"I'm glad," said Stephen.

If the pool had not been between them, he would have seized her, whatever the consequences.

"Just clear water," said the girl.

The sun brought out new colors in her hair. The shape of her head was absolutely perfect.

"The track," said Stephen, "seems to be quite well used. Is this where the people come?"

"No," said the girl. "They come to and from the places where they live."

"I thought you said all the houses were empty."

"What I said was there are many empty houses."

"That *is* what you said. I'm sorry. But the track seems to come to an end. What do the people do then?"

"They find their way," said the girl. "Stop worrying about them."

The water was still between them. Stephen was no longer in doubt that there was indeed something else between them. Really there was. The pool was intermittently throwing up tiny golden waves in the pure breeze, then losing them again.

"We haven't seen anybody," said Stephen. "I never do see anyone."

The girl looked puzzled.

Stephen realized that the way he had put it, the statement that he never saw anyone, might have been tactless. "When I go for my long walks alone," he added.

"Not only then," said the girl.

Stephen's heart turned over slightly.

"Possibly," he said. "I daresay you are very right."

The kites were still flapping like torn pieces of charred pasteboard in the high air, though in the lower part of it.

"You haven't even looked to the bottom of the pool yet," said the girl.

"I suppose not." Stephen fell on his knees, as the girl had done at the milestone or waymark, and gazed downwards through the pellucid near-nothingness beneath the shifting golden rods. There were a few polished stones round the sides, but little else that he could see, and nothing that seemed of significance. How should there be, of course? Unless the girl had put it there, as Stephen realized might have been possible.

Stephen looked up. "It's a splendid pool," he said.

But now his eye caught something else; something other than the girl and the pool. On the edge of the rising ground behind the girl stood a small stone house. It was something else that Stephen had not previously noticed. Indeed, he had been reasonably sure that there had been nothing and no one, not so much as a hint of mankind, not for a quite long way, a quite long time.

"Is that where one of the people lives?" he asked, and in his turn pointed. "Or perhaps more than one?"

"It's empty," said the girl.

"Should we go and look?"

"If you like," said the girl. Stephen quite saw that his expressed response to the glorious little spring had been inadequate. He had lost the trick of feeling, years and years ago.

"It's a splendid pool," he said again, a little self-consciously.

Despite what the girl had said, Stephen had thought that to reach the house above them, they would have to scramble through the high heather. But he realized at once that there was a path, which was one further thing he had not previously noticed.

The girl went before, weaving backwards and forwards up the hillside. Following her, with his thoughts more free to wander, as the exertion made talking difficult, Stephen suddenly apprehended that the need to return for Harriet's teatime had for a season passed completely from his mind.

Apprehending it now, he did not even look at his watch. Apart from anything else, the struggle upwards was too intense for even the smallest distraction or secondary effort. The best thing might be for his watch simply to stop.

They were at the summit, with a wider horizon, but still Stephen could see no other structure than the one before him, though this time he gazed around with a certain care. From here, the pool below them seemed to catch the full sun all over its surface. It gleamed among the heathered rocks like a vast luminous sea anemone among weeds.

Stephen could see at once that the house appeared basically habitable. He had expected jagged holes in the walls, broken panes in the windows, less than half a roof, ubiquitous litter.

The door simply stood open, but it was a door, not a mere gap; a door in faded green, like the girl's trousers. Inside, the floorboards were present and there was even a certain amount of simple furniture, though, as an estate agent would at once have pointed out with apologies, no curtains and no carpets.

"Nell. Somebody lives here already," Stephen said sharply, before they had even gone upstairs.

"Already?" queried the girl.

Stephen made the necessary correction. "Somebody lives here."

"No," said the girl. "No one. Not for centuries."

Of course that was particularly absurd and childish. Much of this furniture, Stephen thought, was of the kind offered by the furnishing department of a good Co-op. Stephen had sometimes come upon such articles on visits paid in the course of his work. He had to admit, however, that he had little idea when such houses as this actually were built at these odd spots on the moors. Possibly as long ago as in the seventeenth century? Possibly only sixty or eighty years ago? Possibly—?

They went upstairs. There were two very low rooms, hardly as much as half lighted from one small and dirty window in each. One room was totally unfurnished. The sole content of the other was a double bed which absorbed much of the cubic capacity available. It was a quite handsome country object, with a carved head and foot. It even offered a seemingly intact mattress, badly in need of a wash.

"Someone *must* be living here," said Stephen. "At least sometimes. Perhaps the owners come here for the weekend. Or perhaps they're just moving in."

As soon as he spoke, it occurred to him that the evidence was equally consistent with their moving out, but he did not continue.

"Lots of the houses are like this," said the girl. "No one lives in them."

Stephen wondered vaguely whether the clear air or some factor of that kind might preserve things as if they were still in use. It was a familiar enough notion, though, in his case, somewhat unspecific. It would be simpler to disbelieve the girl, who was young and without experience, though perfectly eager, at least when others were eager. They returned downstairs.

"Shall we see some more houses?" asked the girl.

"I don't think I have the time."

"You said you had a fortnight. I know what a fortnight is."

"Yes." He simply could not tell her that he had to report for Harriet's astringent teatime; nor, even now, was that in the forefront of his mind. The truth was that whereas hitherto he had been trying to paddle in deep waters, he was now floundering in them.

The girl had a suggestion. "Why not live *here* for a fortnight?"

"I am committed to staying with my brother. He's not very fit. I should worry about him if I broke my word." He realized that he was speaking to her in a more adult way than before. It had really begun with her speaking similarly to him.

"Does your worrying about him do him any good?"

"Not much, I'm afraid."

"Does your worrying about everything do *you* any good?"

"None whatever, Nell. None at all."

He turned aside and looked out of the window; the parlor window might not be too grand a term, for all its need of cleaning.

He addressed her firmly. "Would you give me a hand with all the things that need to be done? Even for a tenancy of a fortnight?"

"If you like."

"We should have to do a lot of shopping."

The girl, standing behind him, remained silent. It was an unusual non-response.

"I should have to cook on a primus stove," said Stephen. "I wonder if we can buy one? I used to be quite good with them." Rapture was beginning.

The girl said nothing.

"We might need new locks on the doors."

The girl spoke. "There is only one door."

"So there is," said Stephen. "In towns, houses have two, a front door and a back door. When trouble comes in at one, you can do a bolt through the other."

"People don't need a lock," said the girl. "Why should they?"

He turned away from the filthy window and gazed straight at her. "Suppose I was to fall in love with you?" he said.

"Then you would not have to go back after a fortnight."

It could hardly have been a straighter reply.

He put one arm round her shoulders, one hand on her breast, so that the note he had written her lay between them. He remembered that the first letter written to a woman is always a love letter. "Would you promise to visit me every day?"

"I might be unable to do that."

"I don't want to seem unkind, but you did say that your father could manage."

"If he discovers, he will keep me at home and send my sister out instead. He has powers. He's very frightening."

Stephen relaxed his hold a little. He had been all along well aware how sadly impracticable was the entire idea.

For example: he could hardly even drive up to this place with supplies; even had his car not been in the course of an opportune overhaul in London, a very complete overhaul after all this anxious time. And that was only one thing; one among very many.

"Well, what's the answer?" Stephen said, smiling at her in the wrong way, longing for her in a very different way.

"I can't come and go the whole time," said the girl.

"I see," said Stephen.

He who had missed so many opportunities, always for excellent reasons, and for one excellent reason in particular, clearly saw that this might be his last opportunity, and almost certainly was.

"How should we live?" he asked. "I mean how should we eat and manage?"

"As the birds do," said the girl.

Stephen did not inquire of her how she came to know Shakespeare, as people put it. He might ask her that later. In the meantime, he could see that the flat, floating birds he had taken to be kites, were indeed drifting past the dirty window, and round and round the house, as it seemed. Of course his questions had been mere routine in any case. He could well have killed himself if she had made a merely routine response.

"Let's see," he said. He gently took her hand. He kissed her softly on the lips. He returned with her upstairs.

It would perhaps have been more suitable if he had been leading the party, but that might be a trifle. Even the damp discoloration of the mattress might be a trifle. Harriet's teatime could not, in truth, be forced from the mind, but it was provisionally overruled. One learned the trick in the course of one's work, or one would break altogether.

There were of course only the bed and the mattress; no sheets or blankets; no Spanish or Kashmiri rugs; no entangling silkiness, no singing save that of the moor. Elizabeth had never wished to make love like that. She had liked to turn on the record player, almost always Brahms or Schumann (the Rhenish Symphony was her particular favorite), and to ascend slowly into a deep fully made bed. But the matter had not seriously arisen for years. Stephen had often wondered why not.

Nell was lying on her front. Seemingly expectant and resistant at the same time, she clung like a clam. Her body was as brown as a pale chestnut, but it was a strong and well-made body. Her short hair was wavy rather than curly. Stephen was ravished by the line of it on her strong neck. He was ravished by her relaxed shoulder blade. He was ravished by her perfect waist and thighs. He was ravished by her youth and youthful smell.

"Please turn over," he said, after tugging at her intermittently, and not very effectively.

Fortunately, he was not too displeased by his own appearance. The hair on his body was bleaching and fading, but otherwise he could, quite sincerely, see little difference from when he had been twenty-four, and had married Elizabeth. He knew, however, that at these times sincerity is not enough; nor objectivity either. When are they?

"Please," he said softly in Nell's ear. Her ears were a slightly unusual shape, and the most beautiful he had ever beheld, or beheld so intently.

He put his hand lightly on her neck. "Please," he said.

She wriggled over in a single swift movement, like a light stab from an invisible knife. He saw that her eyes were neither closed nor open, neither looking at him, nor looking at anything but him.

On the skin between her right shoulder and her right breast was a curious, brownish, grayish, bluish, irregular mark or patch, which had been hidden by her shirt, though Stephen could not quite see how. It was more demanding of attention than it might have been, partly because of its position, and partly, where Stephen was concerned, because of something vaguely else. In any case, it would mean that the poor girl could not reposefully wear a low-cut dress, should the need arise. Though it was by no means a birthmark in the usual sense, Nell had probably been lying on her front through chagrin about it. Upon Stephen, however, the effect was to make him love her more deeply; perhaps love her for the first time. He did not want her or her body to be quite perfect. In a real person, it would be almost vulgar. At this point, Harriet and Harriet's teatime came more prominently into view for a few seconds.

Nell might say something about the mark sooner or later. He would never take an initiative.

At the moment, she said nothing at all. He simply could not make out whether she was watching him or not. Her mouth was long and generous; but had not her whole proceeding been generous in a marvelous degree? He could not even make out whether she

was taut or relaxed. No small mystery was Nell after years and
years of a perfect, but always slow-moving, relationship with
Elizabeth!

He kissed her intimately. When she made no particular response,
not even a grunt, he began to caress her, more or less as he had
caressed his wife. He took care not to touch the peculiar blemish,
or even to enter its area. There was no need to do so. It occurred
to Stephen that the mark might be the consequence of an injury;
and so might in due course disappear, or largely so. In the end
that happened even to many of the strangest human markings.
One day, as the nannies used to say.

Suddenly she made a wild plunge at him that took away his
breath. The surprise was directly physical, but moral also. He had
found it a little difficult to assess Nell's likely age, and inquiry
was out of the question; but he had supposed it probable that she
was a virgin, and had quite deliberately resolved to accept the
implication. Or so he had believed of himself.

Now she was behaving as a maenad.

As an oread, rather; Stephen thought at a later hour. For surely
these moors were mountains, often above the thousand-foot contour; boundless uplands peopled solely by unwedded nymphs and
their monstrous progenitors? Stephen had received a proper education at a proper place: in Stephen's first days, one had not
made the grade, Stephen's grade, otherwise. Stephen's parents had
undertaken sacrifices so immense that no one had fully recovered
from them.

The last vestige of initiative had passed from Stephen like a
limb. And yet, he fancied, it was not because Nell was what
Elizabeth would have called unfeminine, but merely because she
was young, and perhaps because she lived without contamination,
merging into the aspect and mutability of remote places. So, at
least, he could only suppose.

Soon he ceased to suppose anything. He knew bliss unequalled,
unprecedented, assuredly unimagined. Moreover, the wonder lasted
for longer than he would have conceived of as possible. That
particularly struck him.

Nell's flawed body was celestial. Nell herself was more wonderful
than the dream of death. Nell could not possibly exist.

*   *   *

He was fondling her and feeling a trifle cold; much as Elizabeth would have felt. Not that it mattered in the very least. Nell was no maenad or oread. She was a half-frightened child, sweetly soft, responsive to his every thought, sometimes before he had fully given birth to it. She was a waif, a foundling. And it was he who had found her. And only yesterday.

"Tell me about your sister," said Stephen. He realized that it was growing dark as well as chilly.

"She's not like *me.* You wouldn't like her."

Stephen knew that ordinary, normal girls always responded much like that.

He smiled at Nell. "But what *is* she like?"

"She's made quite differently. You wouldn't care for her."

"Has she a name?"

"Of a sort."

"What do you and your father call her?"

"We call her different things at different times. You're cold."

So she was human, after all, Stephen thought.

She herself had very little to put on. Two fairly light garments, a pair of stout socks, her solid shoes.

They went downstairs.

"Would you care to borrow my sweater?" asked Stephen. "Until tomorrow?"

She made no reply, but simply stared at him through the dusk in the downstairs room, the living place, the parlor, the *salon.*

"Take it," said Stephen. It was a heavy garment. Elizabeth had spent nearly four months knitting it continuously, while slowly recovering from her very first disintegration. It was in thick complex stitches and meant to last for ever. When staying with Harewood, Stephen wore it constantly.

Nell took the sweater but did not put it on. She was still staring at him. At such a moment her gray-green eyes were almost luminous.

"We'll meet again tomorrow," said Stephen firmly. "We'll settle down here tomorrow. I must say something to my brother and sister-in-law, and I don't care what happens after that. Not now. At least I *do* care. I care very much. As you well know."

"It's risky," she said.

"Yes," he replied, because it was necessary to evade all discussion. "Yes, but it can't be helped. You come as early as you can, and I'll arrive with some provisions for us. We really need some blankets too, and some candles. I'll see if I can borrow a Land-Rover from one of the farms." He trusted that his confidence and his firm, practical actions would override all doubts.

"I may be stopped," she said. "My father can't read books but he can read minds. He does it all the time."

"You must run away from him," said Stephen firmly. "We'll stay here for a little, and then you can come back to London with me."

She made no comment on that, but simply repeated, "My father can read *my* mind. I only have to be in the same room with him. He's frightening."

Her attitude to her father seemed to have changed considerably. It was the experience of love, Stephen supposed; first love.

"Obviously, you must try to be in a *different* room as much as possible. It's only for one more night. We've known each other now for two days."

"There's only one room."

Stephen had known that such would be her rejoinder.

He well knew also that his behavior might seem unromantic and even cold-hearted. But the compulsion upon him could not be plainer: if he did not return to the rectory tonight, Harriet, weakly aided by Harewood, would have the police after him; dogs would be scurrying across the moors, as if after Hercules, and perhaps searchlights sweeping also. Nothing could more fatally upset any hope of a quiet and enduring compact with such a one as Nell. He was bound for a rough scene with Harriet and Harewood as it was. It being now long past teatime, he would be lucky if Harriet had not taken action before he could reappear. Speed was vital and, furthermore, little of the situation could be explained with any candor to Nell. First, she would simply not understand what he said (even though within her range she was shrewd enough, often shrewder than he). Second, in so far as she did understand, she would panic and vanish. And he had no means of tracking her down at all. She was as shy about her abode as about the mark on her body; though doubtless with as little reason, or so Stephen hoped. He recognized that parting from her at all might be as unwise as it would be painful, but it was the lesser peril. He could not take her to London tonight, or to anywhere, because there was no accessible transport. Not nowadays. He could not take her to the rectory, where Harriet might make Harewood lay an anathema upon her. They could not stay in the moorland house without food or warmth.

"I'll walk with you to the top of the clough," he said.

She shook her head. "It's not there I live."

"Where then?" he asked at once.

"Not that way at all."

"Will you get there?"

She nodded: in exactly what spirit it was hard to say.

He refrained from inquiring how she would explain the absence of specimens for her father. Two or three stones dragged from the walls of the house they were in, might serve the purpose in any case, he thought: outside and inside were almost equally mossed, lichened, adorned, encumbered.

"Goodnight, Nell. We'll meet tomorrow morning. Here." He really had to go. Harriet was made anxious by the slightest irregularity, and when she became anxious, she became frenzied. His present irregularity was by no means slight already; assuredly not slight by Harriet's standards.

To his great relief, Nell nodded again. She had still not put on his sweater.

"In a few days' time, we'll go to London. We'll be together always." He could hardly believe his own ears listening to his own voice saying such things. After all this time! After Elizabeth! After so much inner peace and convinced adoration and asking for nothing more! After the fearful illness!

They parted with kisses but with little drama. Nell sped off into what the map depicted as virtual void.

"All the same," Stephen reflected, "I must look at the map again. I'll try to borrow Harewood's dividers."

He pushed back through the heather, rejoicing in his sense of direction, among so many other things to rejoice about, and began lumbering down the track homewards. The light was now so poor that he walked faster and faster; faster even than he had ascended. In the end, he was running uncontrollably.

Therefore, his heart was already pounding when he discovered that the rectory was in confusion; though, at the rectory, even confusion had a slightly wan quality.

During the afternoon, Harriet had had a seizure of some kind, and during the evening had been taken off in a public ambulance.

"What time did it happen?" asked Stephen. He knew from all too much experience that it was the kind of thing that people did ask.

"I don't really know, Stephen," replied Harewood. "I was in my specimens room reading the *Journal,* and I fear that a considerable time may have passed before I came upon her. I was too distressed to look at my watch even then. Besides, between ourselves, my watch loses rather badly."

Though Stephen tried to help in some way, the improvised evening meal was upsetting. Harriet had planned rissoles sautéd in ghee, but neither of the men really knew how to cook with ghee. The home-made Congress Pudding was nothing less than nauseous. Very probably, some decisive final touches had been omitted.

"You see how it is, young Stephen," said Harewood, after they had munched miserably but briefly. "The prognosis cannot be described as hopeful. I may have to give up the living."

"You can't possibly do that, Harewood, whatever happens. There is Father's memory to think about. I'm sure I should think about him more often myself." Stephen's thoughts were, in fact, upon quite specially different topics.

"I don't wish to go, I assure you, Stephen. I've been very happy here."

The statement surprised Stephen, but was of course thorougly welcome and appropriate.

"There is always prayer, Harewood."

"Yes, Stephen, indeed. I may well have been remiss. That might explain much."

They had been unable to discover where Harriet hid the coffee, so sat for moments in reverent and reflective silence, one on either side of the bleak table: a gift from the nearest branch of the Free India League.

Stephen embarked upon a tentative *démarche.* "I need hardly say that I don't want to leave you in the lurch."

"It speaks for itself that there can be no question of that."

Stephen drew in a quantity of air. "To put it absolutely plainly. I feel that for a spell you would be better off at this time without me around to clutter up the place and make endless demands."

For a second time within hours, Stephen recognized quite clearly that his line of procedure could well be seen as cold-blooded; but, for a second time, he was acting under extreme compulsion—compulsion more extreme than he had expected ever again to encounter, at least on the hither side of the Styx.

"I should never deem you to be doing that, young Stephen. Blood is at all times, even the most embarrassing times, thicker than water. It was Cardinal Newman, by the way, who first said that; a prelate of a different soteriology."

Stephen simply did not believe it, but he said nothing. Harewood often came forward with such assertions, but they were almost invariably erroneous. Stephen sometimes doubted whether Harewood could be completely relied upon even in the context of his private speciality, the lichens.

"I think I had better leave tomorrow morning and so reduce the load for a span. I am sure Doreen will appreciate it." Doreen was the intermittent help; a little brash, where in former days no doubt she would have been a little simple. Stephen had always supposed that brashness might make it more possible to serve Harriet. Doreen had been deserted, childless, by her young husband; but there had been a proper divorce. Harewood was supposed to be taking a keen interest in Doreen, who was no longer in her absolutely first youth.

"You will be rather more dependent upon Doreen for a time," added Stephen.

"I suppose that may well be," said Harewood. Stephen fancied that his brother almost smiled. He quite saw that he might have thought so because of the ideas in his own mind, at which he himself was smiling continuously.

"You must do whatever you think best for all concerned, Stephen," said Harewood. "Including, of course, your sister-in-law, dear Harriet."

"I think I should go now and perhaps come back a little later."

"As you will, Stephen. I have always recognized that you have a mind trained both academically and by your work. I am a much less coordinated spirit. Oh yes, I know it well. I should rely very much upon your judgement in almost any serious matter."

Circumstanced as at the moment he was, Stephen almost blushed.

But Harewood made things all right by adding, "Except perhaps in certain matters of the spirit which, in the nature of things, lie quite particularly between my Maker and myself alone."

"Oh, naturally," said Stephen.

"Otherwise," continued Harewood, "and now that Harriet is unavailable—for a very short time only, we must hope—it is upon you, Stephen, that I propose to rely foremost, in many pressing concerns of this world."

Beyond doubt, Harewood now was not all but smiling. He was smiling nearly at full strength. He explained this immediately.

"My catarrh seems very much better," he said. "I might consider setting forth in splendor one of these days. Seeking specimens, I mean."

Stephen plunged upon impulse.

"It may seem a bit odd in the circumstances, but I should be glad to have the use of a Land-Rover. There's a building up on the moors I should like to look at again before I go, and it's too far to walk in the time. There's a perfectly good track to quite near it. Is there anyone you know of in the parish who would lend me such a thing? Just for an hour or two, of course."

Harewood responded at once. "You might try Tom Jarrold. I regret to say that he's usually too drunk to drive. Indeed, one could never guarantee that his vehicle will even leave the ground."

Possibly it was not exactly the right reference, but what an excellent and informed parish priest Harewood was suddenly proving to be!

Harewood had reopened the latest number of the *Journal,* which he had been sitting on in the chair all the time. His perusal had of course been interrupted by the afternoon's events.

"Don't feel called upon to stop talking," said Harewood. "I can read and listen at the same time perfectly well."

Stephen reflected that the attempt had not often been made when Harriet had been in the room.

"I don't think there's anything more to say at the moment. We seem to have settled everything that *can* be settled."

"I shall be depending upon you in many different matters, remember," said Harewood, but without looking up from the speckled diagrams.

As soon as Stephen turned on the hanging light in his bedroom, he noticed the new patch on the wallpaper; if only because it was immediately above his bed. The wallpaper had always been lowering anyway. He was the more certain that the particular patch was new because, naturally, he made his own bed each morning, which involved daily confrontation with that particular surface. Of course there had always been the other such patches among the marks on the walls.

Still, the new arrival was undoubtedly among the reasons why Stephen slept very little that night, even though, in his own estimation, he needed sleep so badly. There again, however, few do sleep in the first phase of what is felt to be a reciprocated relationship: equally fulfilling and perilous, always deceptive, and always somewhere known to be. The mixed ingredients of the last two days churned within Stephen, as in Harriet's battered cookpot; one rising as another fell. He was treating Harewood as he himself would not wish to be treated; and who could tell what had really led to Harriet's collapse?

In the end, bliss drove out bewilderment, and seemed the one thing sure, as perhaps it was.

Later still, when daylight was all too visible through the frail curtains, Stephen half dreamed that he was lying inert on some surface he could not define and that Nell was administering water to him from a chalice. But the chalice, doubtless a consecrated object to begin with, and certainly of fairest silver from the Spanish mines, was blotched and blemished. Stephen wanted to turn away, to close his eyes properly, to expostulate, but could do none of these things. As Nell gently kissed his brow, he awoke fully with a compelling thirst. He had heard of people waking thirsty in the night, but to himself he could not remember it ever before happening. He had never lived like that.

There was no water in the room, because the house was just sufficiently advanced to make visitors go to the bathroom. Stephen walked quietly down the passage, then hesitated. He recollected that nowadays the bathroom door opened with an appalling wrench and scream.

It would be very wrong indeed to take the risk of waking poor Harewood, in his new isolation. Stephen crept on down the stairs towards the scullery, and there *was* Harewood, sleeping like the dead, not in the least sprawling, but, on the contrary, touchingly compressed and compact in the worn chair. For a moment, he looked like a schoolboy, though of course in that curtained light.

Harewood was murmuring contentedly. "Turn over. No, right over. You can trust me"; then, almost ecstatically, almost like a juvenile, "It's beautiful. Oh, it's beautiful."

Stephen stole away to the back quarters, where both the luncheon and the supper washing-up, even the washing-up after tea, all awaited the touch of a vanished hand.

The cold tap jerked and jarred as it always did, but when Stephen went back, Harewood was slumbering still. His self-converse was now so ideal that it had fallen into incoherence. The cheap figure on the mantel of Shiva or somebody, which Stephen had always detested, sneered animatedly.

But there Nell really was; really, really was.

In his soul, Stephen was astonished. Things do not go like that in real life, least of all in the dreaded demesne of the heart.

However, they unloaded the Land-Rover together, as if everything were perfectly real; toiling up the heather paths with heavy loads, Nell always ahead, always as strong as he: which was really rather necessary.

"I must take the Rover back. Come with me."

He had not for a moment supposed that she would, but she did, and with no demur.

"It's rough going," he said. But she merely put her brown hand on his thigh, as she sat and bumped beside him.

They were a pair now.

"It won't take a moment while I settle with the man."

He was determined that it should not. It must be undesirable that the two of them be seen together in the village. Probably it was undesirable that he himself, even alone, be seen there before a long time had passed. He might perhaps steal back one distant day like Enoch Arden, and take Harewood completely by surprise, both of them now bearded, shaggily or skimpily. What by then would have become of Nell?

They walked upwards hand in hand. Every now and then he said something amorous or amusing to her, but not very often because, as he had foreseen, the words did not come to him readily. He was bound to become more fluent as his heart reopened. She was now speaking more often than he was: not merely more shrewd, but more explicit.

"I'm as close to you as that," she said, pointing with her free hand to a patch of rocky ground with something growing on it—growing quite profusely, almost exuberantly. She had spoken in reply to one of his questions.

He returned the squeeze of the hand he was holding.

"We'll be like the holly and the ivy," she volunteered later, "and then we'll be like the pebble and the shard."

He thought that both comparisons were, like Harewood's comparisons, somewhat inexact, but, in her case, all the more adorable by reason of it. He kissed her.

At first he could not see their house, though, as they neared it, his eyes seemed to wander round the entire horizon: limited in range, however, by the fact that they were mounting quite steeply. But Nell led the way through the rabbit and snake paths, first to the spring, then upwards once more; and there, needless to say, the house was. Earlier that afternoon, they had already toiled up and down several times with the baggage. The earlier occupants had been sturdy folk; men and women alike; aboriginals.

It was somewhere near the spring that Nell, this time, made her possibly crucial declaration.

"I've run away," she said, as if previously she had been afraid to speak the words. "Take care of me."

They entered.

When they had been lugging in the food and the blankets and the cressets and the pans, he had of policy refrained from even glancing at the walls of the house; but what could it matter now? For the glorious and overwhelming moment at least? And, judging by recent experience, the moment might even prove a noticeably long moment. Time might again stand still. Time sometimes did if one had not expected it.

Therefore, from as soon as they entered, he stared round at intervals quite brazenly, though not when Nell was looking at him, as for so much of the time she was now doing.

The upshot was anti-climax: here was not the stark, familiar bedroom in the rectory, and Stephen realized that he had not yet acquired points, or areas, of reference and comparison. He was at liberty to deem that they might never be needed.

Nell was ordering things, arranging things, even beginning to prepare things: all as if she had been a *diplomée* of a domestic college; as if she had been blessed with a dedicated mamma or aunt. After all, thought Stephen, as he watched her and intercepted her, her appearance is largely that of an ordinary modern girl.

He loved her.

He turned his back upon her earlier curious intimations. She had run away from it all; and had even stated as much, unasked and unprompted. Henceforth, an ordinary modern girl was what for him she should firmly be; though loyaler, tenderer, stronger than any other.

When, in the end, languishingly they went upstairs, this time they wrapped themselves in lovely new blankets, but Stephen was in no doubt at all that still there was only the one mark on her. Conceivably, even, it was a slightly smaller mark.

He would no longer detect, no longer speculate, no longer be anxious, no longer imagine. No more mortal marks and corruptions. For example, he would quite possibly never sleep in that room at the rectory again.

Thus, for a week, he counted the good things only, as does a sundial. They were many and the silken sequence of them seemed to extend over a lifetime. He recollected the Christian Science teaching that evil is a mere illusion. He clung to the thesis that time is no absolute.

Nell had the knack of supplementing the food he had purchased with fauna and flora that she brought back from the moor. While, at a vague hour of the morning, he lay long among the blankets, simultaneously awake and asleep, she went forth, and never did she return empty-handed, seldom, indeed, other than laden. He was at last learning not from talk but from experience, even though from someone else's experience, how long it really was possible to live without shops, without bureaucratically and commercially modified products, without even watered cash. All that was needed was to be alone in the right place with the right person.

He even saw it as possible that the two of them might remain in the house indefinitely: were it not that his "disappearance" would inevitably be "reported" by someone, doubtless first by Arthur Thread in the office, so that his early exposure was inevitable. That, after all, was a main purpose of science: to make things of all kinds happen sooner than they otherwise would.

Each morning, after Nell had returned from her sorties and had set things in the house to rights, she descended naked to the spring and sank beneath its waters. She liked Stephen to linger at the rim watching her, and to him it seemed that she disappeared in the pool altogether, vanished from sight, and clear though the water was, the clearest, Stephen surmised, that he had ever lighted upon. Beyond doubt, therefore, the little pool really was peculiarly deep, as Nell had always said: it would be difficult to distinguish between the natural movements of its ever-gleaming surface, and movements that might emanate from a submerged naiad. It gave Stephen special pleasure that they drank exclusively from the pool in which Nell splashed about, but, partly for that reason, he confined his own lustrations to dabblings from the edge, like a tripper. Stephen learned by experience, a new experience, the difference between drinking natural water and drinking safeguarded water, as from a sanitized public convenience. When she emerged from the pool, Nell each day shook her short hair like one glad to be alive, and each day her hair seemed to be dry in no time.

One morning, she washed her shirt and trousers in the pool, having no replacements as far as Stephen could see. The garments took longer to dry than she did, and Nell remained unclothed for most of the day, even though there were clouds in the sky. Clouds made little difference anyway, nor quite steady rain, nor drifting mountain mist. The last named merely fortified the peace and happiness.

"Where did you get those clothes?" asked Stephen, even though as a rule he no longer asked anything.

"I found them. They're nice."

He said nothing for a moment.

"*Aren't* they nice?" she inquired anxiously.

"Everything to do with you and in and about and around you is nice in every possible way. You are perfect. Everything concerned with you is perfect."

She smiled gratefully and went back, still unclothed, to the house, where she was stewing up everything together in one of the new pots. The pot had already leaked, and it had been she who had mended the leak, with a preparation she had hammered and kneaded while Stephen had merely looked on in delighted receptivity, wanting her as she worked.

He had a number of books in his bag, reasonably well chosen, because he had supposed that on most evenings at the rectory he would be retiring early; but now he had no wish to read anything.

He conjectured that he would care little if the capacity to read somehow faded from him. He even went so far as to think that, given only a quite short time, it might possibly do so.

At moments, they wandered together about the moor; he, as like as not, with his hand on her breast, on that breast pocket of hers which contained his original and only letter to her, and which she had carefully taken out and given to him when washing the garment, and later carefully replaced. Than these perambulations few excursions could be more uplifting, but Stephen was wary all the same, knowing that if they were to meet anyone, however blameless, the spell might break, and paradise end.

Deep happiness can but be slighted by third parties, whosoever, without exception, they be. No one is so pure as to constitute an exception.

And every night the moon shone through the small windows and fell across their bed and their bodies in wide streaks, oddly angled.

"You are like a long, sweet parsnip," Stephen said. "Succulent but really rather tough."

"I know nothing at all," she replied, "I only know you."

The mark below her shoulder stood out darkly, but, God be praised, in isolation. What did the rapidly deteriorating state of the walls and appurtenances matter by comparison with that?

But in due course, the moon, upon which the seeding and growth of plants and of the affections largely depend, had entered its dangerous third quarter.

Stephen had decided that the thing he had to do was take Nell back quickly and quietly to London, and return as soon as possible with his reinvigorated car, approaching as near as he could, in order to collect their possessions in the house. The machine would go there, after all, if he drove it with proper vigor; though it might be as well to do it at a carefully chosen hour, in order to evade Harewood, Doreen, and the general life of the village.

He saw no reason simply to abandon all his purchases and, besides, he felt obscurely certain that it was unlucky to do so, though he had been unable to recall the precise belief. Finally, it would seem likely that some of the varied accessories in the house might be useful in Stephen's new life with Nell. One still had to be practical at times, just as one had to be firm at times.

Nell listened to what he had to say, and then said she would do whatever he wanted. The weather was entirely fair for the moment.

When the purchased food had finally run out, and they were supposedly dependent altogether upon what Nell could bring in off the moor, they departed from the house, though not, truthfully, for that reason. They left everything behind them and walked down at dusk past Burton's Clough to the village. Stephen knew the time of the last bus which connected with a train to London. It was something he knew wherever he was. In a general way, he had of course always liked the train journey and disliked the bus journey.

It was hard to imagine what Nell would make of such experiences, and of those inevitably to come. Though she always said she knew nothing, she seemed surprised by nothing either. Always she brought back to Stephen the theories that there were two kinds of knowledge; sometimes of the same things.

All the others in the bus were old age pensioners. They had been visiting younger people and were now returning. They sat alone, each as far from each as space allowed. In the end, Stephen counted them. There seemed to be eight, though it was hard to be sure in the bad light, and with several pensioners already slumped forward.

There were at least two kinds of bad light also; the beautiful dim light of the house on the moor, and the depressing light in a nationalized bus. Stephen recalled Ellen Terry's detestation of all electric light. And of course there were ominous marks on the dirty ceiling of the bus and on such of the side panels as Stephen could see, including that on the far side of Nell, who sat beside him, with her head on his shoulder, more like an òrdinary modern girl than ever. Where could she have learned that when one was traveling on a slow, ill-lighted bus with the man one loved, one put one's head on his shoulder?

But it was far more that she had somewhere, somehow learned. The slightest physical contact with her induced in Stephen a third dichotomy: the reasonable, rather cautious person his whole life and career surely proved him to be, was displaced by an all but criminal visionary. Everything turned upon such capacity as he might have left to change the nature of time.

The conductor crept down the dingy passage and sibilated in

Stephen's ear. "We've got to stop here. Driver must go home.
Got a sick kid. There'll be a reserve bus in twenty minutes. All
right?"

The conductor didn't bother to explain to the pensioners. They
would hardly have understood. For them, the experience itself
would be ample. A few minutes later, everyone was outside in
the dark, though no one risked a roll call. The lights in the bus
had been finally snuffed out, and the crew was making off, aclank
with the accoutrements of their tenure, spanners, and irregular
metal boxes, and enameled mugs.

Even now, Nell seemed unsurprised and unindignant. She, at
least, appeared to acknowledge that all things have an end, and
to be acting on that intimation. As usual, Stephen persuaded her
to don his heavy sweater.

It was very late indeed, before they were home; though Stephen
could hardly use the word now that not only was Elizabeth gone,
but also there was somewhere else, luminously better—or, at least,
so decisively different—and, of course, a new person too.

Fortunately, the train had been very late, owing to signal trouble,
so that they had caught it and been spared a whole dark night
of it at the station, as in a story. Stephen and Nell had sat together
in the buffet, until they had been ejected, and the striplighting
quelled. Nell had never faltered. She had not commented even
when the train, deprived of what railwaymen call its "path," had
fumbled its way to London, shunting backwards nearly as often
as running forwards. In the long, almost empty, excursion-type
coach had been what Stephen could by now almost complacently
regard as the usual smears and blotches.

"Darling, aren't you cold?" He had other, earlier sweaters to
lend.

She shook her head quite vigorously.

After that, it had been easy for Stephen to close his eyes almost
all the way. The other passenger had appeared to be a fireman
in uniform, though of course without helmet. It was hard to
believe that he would suddenly rise and rob them, especially as
he was so silently slumbering. Perhaps he was all the time a
hospital porter or a special messenger or an archangel.

On the Benares table which filled the hall of the flat (a wedding
present from Harewood and poor Harriet, who, having been

engaged in their teens, had married long ahead of Stephen and Elizabeth), was a parcel, weighty but neat.

"Forgive me," said Stephen. "I never can live with unopened parcels or letters."

He snapped the plastic string in a second and tore through the glyptal wrapping. It was a burly tome entitled *Lichen, Moss, and Wrack. Usage and Abusage in Peace and War. A Military and Medical Abstract.* Scientific works so often have more title than imaginative works.

Stephen flung the book back on the table. It fell with a heavy clang.

"Meant for my brother. It's always happening. People don't seem to know there's a difference between us."

He gazed at her. He wanted to see nothing else.

She looked unbelievably strange in her faded trousers and the sweater Elizabeth had made. Elizabeth would have seen a ghost and fainted. Elizabeth really did tend to faint in the sudden presence of the occult.

"We are not going to take it to him. It'll have to be posted. I'll get the Department to do it tomorrow."

He paused. She smiled at him, late though it was.

Late or early? What difference did it make? It was not what mattered.

"I told you that I should have to go to the Department tomorrow. There's a lot to explain."

She nodded. "And then we'll go back?" She had been anxious about that ever since they had started. He had not known what to expect.

"Yes. After a few days."

Whatever he intended in the first place, he had never made it clear to her where they would be living in the longer run. This was partly because he did not know himself. The flat, without Elizabeth, really was rather horrible. Stephen had not forgotten Elizabeth for a moment. How could he have done? Nor could Stephen wonder that Nell did not wish to live in the flat. The flat was disfigured and puny.

Nell still smiled with her usual seeming understanding. He had feared that by now she would demur at his reference to a few days, and had therefore proclaimed it purposefully.

He smiled back at her. "I'll buy you a dress."

She seemed a trifle alarmed.

"It's time you owned one."

"I don't own anything."

"Yes, you do. You own me. Let's go to bed, shall we?"

But she spoke. "What's this?"

As so often happens, Nell had picked up and taken an interest in the thing he would least have wished.

It was a large, lumpy shopping bag from a craft room in Burnham-on-Sea, where Elizabeth and he had spent an unwise week in their early days. What the Orient was to Harriet, the seaside had been to Elizabeth. Sisters-in-law often show affinities. The shopping bag had continued in regular use ever since, and not only for shopping, until Elizabeth had been no longer mobile.

"It's a bag made of natural fibers," said Stephen. "It belonged to my late wife."

"It smells, It reminds me."

"Many things here remind *me*," said Stephen. "But a new page has been turned." He kept forgetting that Nell was unaccustomed to book metaphors.

She appeared to be holding the bag out to him. Though not altogether knowing why, he took it from her. He then regretted doing so.

It was not so much the smell of the bag. He was entirely accustomed to that. It was that, in his absence, the bag had become sodden with dark growths, outside and inside. It had changed character completely.

Certainly the bag had been perfectly strong and serviceable when last he had been in contact with it; though for the moment he could not recollect when that had been. He had made little use of the bag when not under Elizabeth's direction.

He let the fetid mass fall on top of the book on the brass table.

"Let's forget everything," he said. "We still have a few hours."

"Where do I go?" she asked, smiling prettily.

"Not in there," he cried, as she put her hand on one of the doors. He very well knew that he must seem far too excitable. He took a pull on himself. "Try *this* room."

When Elizabeth had become ill, the double bed had been moved into the spare room. It had been years since Stephen had slept in that bed, though, once again, he could not in the least recall how many years. The first step towards mastering time is always to make time meaningless.

It was naturally wonderful to be at long last in a fully equipped deep double bed with Nell. She had shown no expectation of being invited to borrow one of Elizabeth's expensive nightdresses. Nell was a primitive still, and it was life or death to keep her so. He had never cared much for flowing, gracious bedwear in any case; nor had the wonder that was Elizabeth seemed to him to need such embellishments.

But he could not pretend, as he lay in Nell's strong arms and she in his, that the condition of the spare room was in the least reassuring. Before he had quickly turned off the small bedside light, the new marks on the walls had seemed like huge inhuman faces; and the effect was all the more alarming in that these walls had been painted, inevitably long ago, by Elizabeth in person, and had even been her particular domestic display piece. The stained overall she had worn for the task, still hung in the cupboard next door, lest the need arise again.

It was always the trouble. So long as one was far from the place once called home, one could successfully cast secondary matters from the mind, or at least from the hurting part of it; but from the moment of return, in fact from some little while before that, one simply had to recognize that, for most of one's life, secondary matters were just about all there were. Stephen had learned ages ago that secondary matters were always the menace.

Desperation, therefore, possibly made its contribution to the mutual passion that charged the few hours available to them.

Within a week, the walls might be darkened all over; and what could the development after *that* conceivably be?

Stephen strongly suspected that the mossiness, the malady, would become more conspicuously three-dimensional at any moment. Only as a first move, of course.

He managed to close his mind against all secondary considerations and to give love its fullest license yet.

Thread was in the office before Stephen, even though Stephen had risen most mortifyingly early, and almost sleepless. It was a commonplace that the higher one ascended in the service, the earlier one had to rise, in order to ascend higher still. The lamas never slept at all.

"Feeling better?" Thread could ask such questions with unique irony.

"Much better, thank you."

"You still look a bit peaky." Thread was keeping his finger at the place he had reached in the particular file.

"I had a tiresome journey back. I've slept very little."

"It's always the trouble. Morag and I make sure of a few days to settle in before we return to full schedule."

"Elizabeth and I used to do that also. It's a bit different now." Thread looked Stephen straight in the eyes, or very nearly.

"Let me advise, for what my advice is worth. I recommend you to lose yourself in your work for the next two or three years at the least. Lose yourself completely. Forget everything else. In my opinion, it's always the best thing at these times. Probably the only thing."

"Work doesn't mean to me what it did."

"Take yourself in hand, and it soon will again. After all, very real responsibilities do rest in this room. We both understand that quite well. We've reached that sort of level, Stephen. What we do nowadays, *matters*. If you keep that in mind at all times, and I do mean at *all* times, the thought will see you through. I know what I'm talking about."

Thread's eyes were now looking steadily at his finger, lest it had made some move on its own.

"Yes," said Stephen, "but you're talking about yourself, you know."

Stephen was very well aware that the sudden death some years before of Arthur Thread's mother had not deflected Thread for a day from the tasks appointed. Even the funeral had taken place during the weekend; for which Thread had departed on the Friday evening with several major files in his briefcase, as usual. As for Thread's wife, Morag, she was a senior civil servant too, though of course in a very different department. The pair took very little leave in any case, and hardly any of it together. Their two girls were at an expensive boarding school on the far side of France, almost in Switzerland.

"I speak from my own experience," corrected Thread.

"It appears to me," said Stephen, "that I have reached the male climacteric. It must be what's happening to me."

"I advise you to think again," said Thread. "There's no such thing. Anyway you're too young for when it's supposed to be. It's not till you're sixty-three; within two years of retirement."

Thread could keep his finger in position no longer, lest his arm fall off. "If you'll forgive me, I'm rather in the middle of something. Put yourself absolutely at ease. I'll be very pleased to have another talk later."

"What's that mark?" asked Stephen, pointing to the wall above Thread's rather narrow headpiece. So often the trouble seemed to begin above the head. "Was it there before?"

"I'm sure I don't know. Never forget the whole place is going to be completely done over next year. Now do let me concentrate for a bit."

As the time for luncheon drew near, another man, Mark Tremble, peeped in.

"Glad to see you back, Stephen. I really am."

"Thank you, Mark. I wish I could more sincerely say I was glad to *be* back."

"Who could be? Come and swim?"

Stephen had regularly done it with Mark Tremble and a shifting group of others; usually at lunchtime on several days a week. It had been one of twenty devices for lightening momentarily the weight of Elizabeth's desperation. The bath was in the basement of the building. Soon the bath was to be extended and standardized, and made available at times to additional grades.

"Very well."

Stephen had at one time proposed to tear back; to be with Nell for a few moments; perhaps to buy that dress: but during the long morning he had decided against all of it.

His real task was to put down his foot with the establishment; to secure such modified pension as he was entitled to; to concentrate, as Thread always concentrated; to depart.

He had not so far said a word about it to anyone in the place.

The two seniors changed in the sketchy cubicles, and emerged almost at the same moment in swimming trunks. There seemed to be no one else in or around the pool that day, though the ebbing and flowing of table tennis were audible through the partition.

"I say, Stephen. What's that thing on your back?"

Stephen stopped dead on the wet tiled floor. "What thing?"

"It's a bit peculiar. I'm sure it wasn't there before. Before you went away. I'm extremely sorry to mention it."

"What's it look like?" asked Stephen. "Can you describe it?"

"The best I can do is that it looks rather like the sort of thing you occasionally see on trees. I think it may simply be something stuck on to you. Would you like me to give it a tug?"

"I think not," said Stephen. "I am sorry it upsets you. I'll go back and dress. I think it would be better."

"Yes," said Mark Tremble. "It does upset me. It's best to admit it. Either it's something that will just come off with a good rub, or you'd better see a doctor, Stephen."

"I'll see what I can do," said Stephen.

"I don't feel so much like a swim, after all," said Mark Tremble. "I'll dress too and then we'll both have a drink. I feel we could both do with one."

"I'm very sorry about it," said Stephen. "I apologize."

"What have *you* been doing all day?" asked Stephen, as soon as he was back and had changed out of the garments currently normal in the civil service, casual and characterless. "I hope you've been happy."

"I found this on the roof." Nell was holding it in both her hands; which were still very brown. It was a huge lump: mineral, vegetable, who could tell? Or conceivably a proportion of each.

"Your father would be interested."

Nell recoiled. "Don't talk like that. It's unlucky." Indeed, she had nearly dropped the dense mass.

It had been an idiotic response on Stephen's part; mainly the consequence of his not knowing what else to say. He was aware that it was perfectly possible to attain the roof of the building by way of the iron fire ladder, to which, by law, access had to be open to tenants at all hours.

"I could do with a drink," said Stephen, though he had been drinking virtually the whole afternoon, without Thread even noticing, or without sparing time to acknowledge that he had noticed. Moira, the colored girl from the typing area, had simply winked her big left eye at Stephen. "I've had a difficult day."

"Oh!" Nell's cry was so sincere and eloquent that it was as if he had been mangled in a traffic accident.

"*How* difficult?" she asked.

"It's just that it's been difficult for me to make the arrangements to get away, to leave the place."

"But we *are* going." He knew it was what she was thinking about.

"Yes, we are going. I promised."

He provided Nell with a token drink also. At first she had seemed to be completely new to liquor. Stephen had always found life black without it, but his need for it had become more habitual during Elizabeth's illness. He trusted that Nell and he would, with use, wont, and time, evolve a mutual equilibrium.

At the moment, he recognized that he was all but tight, though he fancied that at such times he made little external manifestation. Certainly Nell would detect nothing; if only because presumably she lacked data. Until now, he had never really been in the sitting room of the flat since his return. Here, the new tendrils on the walls and ceiling struck him as resembling a Portuguese man of war's equipment; the colored, insensate creature that can sting a swimmer to death at thirty feet distance, and had done so more than once when Elizabeth and he, being extravagant, had stayed at Cannes for a couple of weeks. It had been there that Elizabeth had told him finally she could never have a child. Really that was what they were doing there, though he had not realized it. The man of war business, the two victims, had seemed to have an absurd part in their little drama. No one in the hotel had talked of anything else.

"Let's go to bed *now*," said Stephen to Nell. "We can get up again later to eat."

She put her right hand in his left hand.

Her acquiescence, quiet and beautiful, made him feel compunctious.

"Or are you hungry?" he asked. "Shall we have something to eat first? I wasn't thinking."

She shook her head. "I've been foraging."

She seemed to know so many quite literary words. He gave no time to wondering where exactly the forage could have taken place. It would be unprofitable. Whatever Nell had brought in would be wholesomer, inestimably better in every way, than food from any shop.

As soon as she was naked, he tried, in the electric light, to scrutinize her. There still seemed to be only the one mark on her body, truly a quite small mark by the standards of the moment, though he could not fully convince himself that it really was contracting.

However, the examination was difficult: he could not let Nell realize what exactly he was doing; the light was not very powerful, because latterly Elizabeth had disliked a strong light anywhere, and he had felt unable to argue; most of all, he had to prevent Nell seeing whatever Mark Tremble had seen on his own person, had himself all the time to lie facing Nell or flat on his back. In any case, he wondered always how much Nell saw that he saw; how much, whatever her utterances and evidences, she analyzed of the things that he analyzed.

The heavy curtains, chosen and hung by Elizabeth, had, it seemed, remained drawn all day; and by now the simplest thing was for Stephen to switch off what light there was.

Nell, he had thought during the last ten days or ten eons, was at her very best when the darkness was total.

He knew that heavy drinking was said to increase desire and to diminish performance; and he also knew that it was high time in his life for him to begin worrying about such things. He had even so hinted to Arthur Thread; albeit mainly to startle Thread, and to foretoken his, Stephen's, new life course; even though any such intimation to Thread would be virtually useless. There can be very few to whom most of one's uttered remarks can count for very much.

Nonetheless, Nell and Stephen omitted that evening to arise later; even though Stephen had fully and sincerely intended it.

The next morning, very early the next morning, Nell vouchsafed to Stephen an unusual but wonderful breakfast—if one could apply so blurred a noun to so far-fetched a repast.

Stephen piled into his civil service raiment, systematically noncommittal. He was taking particular trouble not to see his own bare back in any looking glass. Fortunately, there was no such thing in the dim bathroom.

"Goodbye, my Nell. Before the weekend we shall be free."

He supposed that she knew what a weekend was. By now, it could hardly be clearer that she knew almost everything that mattered in the least.

But, during that one night, the whole flat seemed to have become dark green, dark gray, plain black: patched everywhere, instead of only locally, as when they had arrived. Stephen felt that the walls, floors, and ceilings were beginning to advance towards one another. The knickknacks were dematerializing most speedily. When life once begins to move, it can scarcely be prevented from setting its own pace. The very idea of intervention becomes ridiculous.

What was Nell making of these swift and strange occurrences? All Stephen was sure of was that it would be unwise to take too much for granted. He must hew his way out; if necessary, with a bloody axe, as the man in the play put it.

Stephen kissed Nell ecstatically. She was smiling as he shut the door. She might smile, off and on, all day, he thought; smile as she foraged.

By that evening, he had drawn a curtain, thick enough even for Elizabeth to have selected, between his homebound self and the events of the daylight.

There was no technical obstacle to his retirement, and never had been. It was mainly the size of his pension that was affected; and in his new life he seemed able to thrive on very little. A hundred costly substitutes for direct experience could be rejected. An intense reality, as new as it was old, was burning down on him like clear sunlight or heavenly fire or poetry.

It was only to be expected that his colleagues should shrink back a little. Nonetheless, Stephen had been disconcerted by how far some of them had gone. They would have been very much less concerned, he fancied, had he been an acknowledged defector, about to stand trial. Such cases were now all in the day's work: there were routines to be complied with, though not too strictly. Stephen realized that his appearance was probably against him. He was not sure what he looked like from hour to hour, and he was taking no steps to find out.

Still, the only remark that was passed, came from Toby Strand, who regularly passed remarks.

"Good God, Stephen, you're looking like death warmed up. I should go home to the wife. You don't want to pass out in this place."

Stephen looked at him.

"Oh God, I forgot. Accept my apology."

"That's perfectly all right, Toby," said Stephen. "And as for

the other business, you'll be interested to learn that I've decided
to retire."

"Roll on the day for one and all," said Toby Strand, ever the
vox populi.

Mercifully, Stephen's car had been restored to a measure of
health, so that the discreet bodywork gleamed slightly in the
evening luster as he drove into the rented parking space.

"Nell, we can leave at cockcrow!"

"I forgot about buying you that dress."

He was standing in his bath gown, looking at her in the wide
bed. The whole flat was narrowing and blackening, and at that
early hour the electric light was even weaker than usual.

"I shan't need a dress."

"You must want a change sometime."

"No. I want nothing to change."

He gazed at her. As so often, he had no commensurate words.

"We'll stop somewhere on the way," he said.

They packed the rehabilitated car with essentials for the simple
life; with things to eat and drink on the journey and after arrival.
Stephen, though proposing to buy Nell a dress, because one never
knew what need might arise, was resolved against dragging her
into a roadside foodplace. He took all he could, including, sur-
reptitiously, some sad souvenirs of Elizabeth, but he recognized
plainly enough that there was almost everything remaining to be
done with the flat, and that he would have to return one day to
do it, whether or not Nell came with him. In the meantime, it
was difficult to surmount what was happening to the flat, or to
him. Only Nell was sweet, calm, and changeless in her simple
clothes. If only the nature of time were entirely different!

"You'll be terribly cold."

She seemed never to say it first, never to think it.

He covered her with sweaters and rugs. He thought of offering
her a pair of his own warm trousers, but they would be so hopelessly
too wide and long.

Islington was a misty marsh, as they flitted through; Holloway
pink as a desert flamingo. The scholarly prison building was
wrapped in fire. Finsbury Park was crystal as a steppe; Manor
House deserted as old age.

When, swift as thoughts of love, they reached Grantham, they turned aside to buy Nell's dress. She chose a rough-textured white one, with the square neck outlined in black, and would accept nothing else, nothing else at all. She even refused to try on the dress and she refused to wear it out of the shop. Stephen concurred, not without a certain relief, and carried the dress to the car in a plastic bag. The car was so congested that a problem arose.

"I'll sit on it," said Nell.

Thus the day went by as in a dream: though there are few such dreams in one lifetime. Stephen, for sure, had never known a journey so rapt, even though he could seldom desist from staring and squinting for uncovenanted blemishes upon and around the bright coachwork. Stephen recognized that, like everyone else, he had spent his life without living; even though he had had Elizabeth for much of the time to help him through, as she alone was able.

Northwards, they ran into a horse fair. The horses were everywhere, and, among them, burlesques of men bawling raucously, and a few excited girls.

"Oh!" cried Nell.

"Shall we stop?"

"No," said Nell. "Not stop."

She was plainly upset.

"Few fairs like that one are left," said Stephen, as he sat intimately, eternally beside her. "The motors have been their knell."

"Knell," said Nell.

Always it was impossible to judge how much she knew.

"Nell," said Stephen affectionately. But it was at about that moment he first saw a dark, juicy crack in the polished metalwork of the bonnet.

"Nell," said Stephen again; and clasped her hand, always brown, always warm, always living and loving. The huge geometrical trucks were everywhere, and it was an uncircumspect move for Stephen to make. But it was once more too misty for the authorities to see very much, to take evidence that could be sworn to.

The mist was more like fog as they wound through Harewood's depopulated community. Harewood really should marry Doreen as soon as it becomes possible, thought Stephen, and make a completely new start in life, perhaps have a much better type of youngster, possibly and properly for the cloth.

Stephen was struck with horror to recollect that he had forgotten

all about the costly book which had been almost certainly intended
for Harewood, and which Harewood would be among the very
few fully to appreciate and rejoice in. The book had not really
been noticeable at first light in the eroding flat, but his lapse
perturbed Stephen greatly.

"A fungus and an alga living in a mutually beneficial relationship," he said under his breath.

"What's that?" asked Nell.

"It's the fundamental description of a lichen. You should know
that."

"Don't talk about it."

He saw that she shuddered; she who never even quaked from
the cold.

"It's unlucky," she said.

"I'm sorry, Nell. I was thinking of the book we left behind,
and the words slipped out."

"We're better without the book."

"It wasn't really our book."

"We did right in leaving it."

He realized that it had been the second time when, without
thinking, he had seemed ungracious about the big step she had
taken for him: the second time at least.

Therefore, he simply answered, "I expect so."

He remained uneasy. He had taken due care not to drive past
the crumbling rectory, but nothing could prevent the nondelivery
of Harewood's expensive book being an odious default, a matter
of only a few hundred yards. To confirm the guilt, a middle-aged
solitary woman at the end of the settlement suddenly pressed both
hands to her eyes, as if to prevent herself from seeing the passing
car, even in the poor light.

The ascending track was rougher and rockier than on any of
Stephen's previous transits. It was only to be expected, Stephen
realized. Moreover, to mist was now added dusk. At the putative
Burton's Clough, he had to take care not to drive over the edge
of the declivity; and thereafter he concentrated upon not colliding
with the overgrown stony waymark. Shapeless creatures were beginning to emerge which may no longer appear by daylight even
in so relatively remote a region. Caution was compelled upon
every count.

Thus it was full night when, somehow they reached the spot

where the track seemed simply to end—with no good reason supplied, as Stephen had always thought. Elizabeth would have been seriously upset if somehow she had seen at such a spot the familiar car in which she had taken so many unforgettable outings, even when a virtual invalid. She might have concluded that at long last she had reached the final bourn.

The moon, still in its third quarter, managed to glimmer, like a fragrance, through the mist; but there could be no visible stars. Stephen switched on his flash, an item of official supply.

"We don't need it," said Nell. "Please not."

Nell was uncaring of cold, of storm, of fog, of fatigue. Her inner strength was superb, and Stephen loved it. But her indifference to such darkness as this reminded Stephen of her father, that wonderful entity, whom it was so unlucky ever to mention, probably even to think of. Nonetheless, Stephen turned back the switch. He had noticed before that he was doing everything she said.

As best he could, he helped her to unload the car, and followed her along the narrow paths through the damp heather. Naturally, he could not see a trace of the house, and he suddenly realized that, though they struggled in silence, he could not even hear the gently heaving spring. They were making a pile at the spot where the house must be; and Nell never put a foot wrong in finding the pile a second, third, and even fourth time. Much of the trip was steep, and Stephen was quite winded once more by his fourth climb in almost no moonlight at all, only the faint smell of moonlight; but when, that time, he followed Nell over the tangled brow, the mist fell away for a moment, as mist on mountains intermittently does, and at last Stephen could see the house quite clearly.

He looked at Nell standing there, pale and mysterious as the moonlight began to fade once more.

"Have you still got my letter?"

She put her hand on her breast pocket.

"Of course I have."

They re-entered the house, for which no key was ever deemed necessary. It might be just as well, for none was available.

Stephen realized at once that what they were doing was moving into the house pretty finally; not, as he had so recently proposed, preparing to move out of it in a short time. It was clear that once

Nell truly and finally entered one's life, one had simply to accept the consequences. Stephen could perceive well enough that Nell was at every point moved by forces in comparison with which he was moved by inauthentic fads. Acquiescence was the only possibility. The admixture in Nell of ignorance and wisdom, sometimes even surface sophistication, was continuously fascinating. In any case, she had left familiar surroundings and completely changed her way of life for him. He must do the same for her without end; and he wished it.

The moonlight was now insufficient to show the state of the walls or the curiously assorted furnishings or the few personal traps he had omitted to bear to London. Stephen had worn gloves to drive and had not removed them to lug. He wore them still.

Nonetheless, when he said, "Shall we have a light now?" he spoke with some reluctance.

"Now," said Nell. "We're at home now."

He fired up some of the rough cressets he had managed to lay hands on when he had borrowed the sottish Jarrold's Land-Rover.

Nell threw herself against him. She kissed him again and again.

As she did so, Stephen resolved to look at nothing more. To look was not necessarily to see. He even thought he apprehended a new vein of truth in what Nell had said on that second day, still only a very short time ago, about her father.

Nell went upstairs and changed into the dress he had bought her. She had done it without a hint, and he took for granted that she had done it entirely to give pleasure. In aspect, she was no longer a part of nature, merging into it, an oread. Not surprisingly, the dress did not fit very well, but on Nell it looked like a peplos. She was a sybil. Stephen was scarcely surprised. There was no need for him to see anything other than Nell's white and black robe, intuitively selected, prophetically insisted upon; quite divine, as ordinary normal girls used to say.

When he dashed off his gloves in order to caress her, he regarded only her eyes and her raiment; but later there was eating to be done, and it is difficult, in very primitive lighting, to eat without at moments noticing one's hands. These particular hands seemed at such moments to be decorated with horrid subfusc smears, quite new. Under the circumstances, they might have come from inside Stephen's driving gloves; warm perhaps, but, like most modern products, of no precise or very wholesome origin. If ineradicable, the marks were appalling; not to be examined for a single second.

When Nell took off her new dress, Stephen saw at once (how else but at once?) that her own small single mark had vanished. She was as totally honied as harvest home, and as luscious, and as rich.

Stephen resolved that in the morning, if there was one, he would throw away all the souvenirs of Elizabeth he had brought with him. They could be scattered on the moor as ashes in a memorial garden, but better far. The eyes that were watching from behind the marks on the walls and ceilings and utensils glinted back at him, one and all. The formless left hands were his to shake.

In the nature of things, love was nonpareil that night; and there was music too. Nell's inner being, when one knew her, when one really knew her, was as matchless as her unsullied body. Goodness is the most powerful aphrodisiac there is, though few have the opportunity of learning. Stephen had learned long before from the example of Elizabeth, and now he was learning again.

Time finally lost all power.

The music became endlessly more intimate.

"God!" cried Stephen suddenly. "That's Schumann!" He had all but leapt in the air. Ridiculously.

"Where?" asked Nell. Stephen realized that he was virtually sitting on her. He dragged himself up and was standing on the floor.

"That music. It's Schumann."

"I hear no music."

"I don't suppose you do."

Stephen spoke drily and unkindly, as he too often did, but he knew that everything was dissolving.

For example, he could see on the dark wall the large portrait of Elizabeth by a pupil of Philip de Laszlo which had hung in their conjugal bedroom. The simulacrum was faint and ghostly, like the music, but he could see it clearly enough for present purposes, dimly self-illuminated.

He had taken that picture down with his own hands, years and years ago; and the reason had been, as he now instantly recalled, that the light paintwork had speedily become blotched and suffused. They had naturally supposed it to be something wrong with the pigments, and had spoken between themselves of vegetable dyes and the superiorities of Giotto and Mantegna. Stephen had hidden the festering canvas in the communal basement storeroom, and had forgotten about it immediately. Now he could see it perfectly well, not over the bed, but in front of it, as always.

"Come back," said Nell. "Come back to me."

The music, which once, beyond doubt, had been the music of love, was dying away. In its place, was a persistent snuffling sound, as if the house from outside, or the room from inside, was being cased by a wolf.

"What's that noise? That noise of an animal?"

"Come back to me," said Nell. "Come back, Stephen." Perhaps she was quite consciously dramatizing a trifle.

He had gone to the window, but of course could see nothing save the misleading huge shapes of the flapping birds.

He went back to the bed and stretched out both his hands to Nell. He was very cold.

Though there was almost no light, Nell grasped his two hands and drew him down to her.

"You see and hear so many things, Stephen," she said.

As she spoke, he had, for moments, a vision of a different kind.

Very lucidly, he saw Nell and himself living together, but, as it might be, in idealized form, vaguely, intensely. He knew that it was an ideal of which she was wonderfully capable, perhaps because she was still so young. All that was required of him was some kind of trust.

Held by her strong hands and arms, he leaned over her and faltered.

"But whatever animal is that?" he demanded.

She released his hands and curled up like a child in distress. She had begun to sob.

"Oh, Nell," he cried. He fell on her and tried to reach her. Her muscles were as iron, and he made no impression at all.

In any case, he could not stop attending to the snuffling, if that was the proper word for it. He thought it was louder now. The noise seemed quite to fill the small, low, dark, remote room; to leave no space for renewed love, however desperate the need, however urgent the case.

Suddenly, Stephen knew. A moment of insight had come to him, an instinctual happening.

He divined that outside or inside the little house was Nell's father.

It was one reason why Nell was twisted in misery and terror. Her father had his own ways of getting to the truth of things. She had said so.

Stephen sat down on the bed and put his hand on her shoulder. Though he was shivering dreadfully, he had become almost calm. The process of illumination was suggesting to him the simple truth that, for Nell too, the past must be ever present. And for her it was, in common terms, the terms after which he himself was so continuously half-aspiring, a past most absurdly recent. How could he tell what experiences were hers, parallel to, but never meeting, his own?

It would be no good even making the obvious suggestion that they should dwell far away. She could never willingly leave the moor, even if it should prove the death of her; no more than he had been able all those years to leave the flat, the job, the life, all of which he had hated, and been kept alive in only by Elizabeth.

"What's the best thing to do, Nell?" Stephen inquired of her. "Tell me and we'll do it exactly. Tell me. I think I'm going to dress while you do so. And then perhaps you'd better dress too."

After all, he began to think, there was little that Nell had ever said about her father or her sister which many girls might not have said when having in mind to break away. He would not have wanted a girl who had no independent judgement of her own family.

The process of insight and illumination were serving him well, and the phantom portrait seemed to have dissipated completely. The snuffling and snorting continued. It was menacing and unfamiliar, but conceivably it was caused merely by a common or uncommon but essentially manageable creature of the moors. Stephen wished he had brought his revolver (another official issue), even though he had no experience in discharging it. He could not think how he had omitted it. Then he recollected the horrible furred-up flat, and shuddered anew, within his warm clothes.

For the first time it occurred to him that poor Elizabeth might be trying, from wherever she was, to warn him. Who could tell that Harriet had not made a miraculous recovery (she was, after all, in touch with many different faiths); and was not now ready once more to accept him for a spell into the life at the rectory?

Nell was being very silent.

Stephen went back to the bed.

"Nell."

He saw that she was not in the bed at all, but standing by the door.

"Nell."

"Hush," she said. "We must hide."

"Where do we do that?"

"I shall show you." He could see that she was back in her shirt and trousers; a part of the natural scene once more. Her white dress glinted on the boards of the floor.

To Stephen her proposal seemed anomalous. If it really was her father outside, he could penetrate everywhere, and according to her own statement. If it was a lesser adversary, combat might be better than concealment.

Nell and Stephen went downstairs in the ever more noisy darkness, and Nell, seemingly without effort, lifted a stone slab in the kitchen floor. Stephen could not quite make out how she had done it. Even to find the right slab, under those conditions, was a feat.

"All the houses have a place like this," Nell explained.

"Why?" inquired Stephen. Surely Nell's father was an exceptional phenomenon? Certainly the supposed motion of him was akin to no other motion Stephen had ever heard.

"To keep their treasure," said Nell.

"You are my treasure," said Stephen.

"You are mine," responded Nell.

There were even a few hewn steps, or so they felt to him. Duly it was more a coffer than a room, Stephen apprehended; but in no time Nell had the stone roof down on them, almost with a flick of the elbow, weighty though the roof must have been.

Now the darkness was total; something distinctly different from the merely conventional darkness above. All the same, Stephen of all people could not be unaware that the stone sides and stone floor and stone ceiling of the apartment were lined with moss and lichen. No doubt he had developed sixth and seventh senses in that arena, but the odor could well have sufficed of itself.

"How do we breathe?"

"There is a sort of pipe. That's where the danger lies."

"You mean it might have become blocked up?"

"No."

He did not care next to suggest that it might now be blocked deliberately. He had already made too many tactless suggestions of that kind.

She saved him the trouble of suggesting anything. She spoke in the lowest possible voice.

"He might come through."

It was the first time she had admitted, even by implication, who it was: outside or inside—or both. Stephen fully realized that. It was difficult for him not to give way to the shakes once more, but he clung to the vague possibilities he had tried to sort out upstairs.

"I should hardly think so," he said. "But how long do you suggest we wait?"

"It will be better when it's day. He has to eat so often."

It would be utterly impossible for Stephen to inquire any further; not at the moment. He might succeed in finding his way to the bottom of it all later. He was already beginning to feel cramped, and the smell of the fungi and the algae were metaphorically choking him and the moss realistically tickling him; but he put his arm round Nell in the blackness, and could even feel his letter safe against her soft breast.

She snuggled back at him; as far as circumstances permitted. He had only a vague idea of how big or small their retreat really was.

Nell spoke again in that same lowest possible voice. She could communicate, even in the most pitchy of blackness, while hardly making a sound.

"He's directly above us. He's poised."

Stephen mustered up from his school days a grotesque recollection of some opera: the final scene. The Carl Rosa had done it: that one scene only; after the film in a cinema near Marble Arch. Elizabeth had thought the basic operatic convention too far-fetched to be taken seriously; except perhaps for Mozart, who could always be taken seriously.

"I love you," said Stephen. No doubt the chap in the opera had said something to the like effect, but had taken more time over it.

Time: that was always the decisive factor. But time had been mastered at last.

"I love *you,*" said Nell, snuggling ever closer; manifesting her feeling in every way she could.

Curiously enough, it was at the verge of the small, lustrous pool that Stephen's body was ultimately found.

A poor old man, apparently resistent to full employment and even to the full security that goes with it, found the corpse, though, after all those days or weeks, the creatures and forces of the air and of the moor had done their worst to it, or their best. There was no ordinary skin anywhere. Many people in these busy times would not even have reported the find.

There were still, however, folk who believed, or at least had been told that the pool was bottomless; and even at the inquest a theory was developed that Stephen had been wandering about on the moor and had died of sudden shock upon realizing at what brink he stood. The coroner, who was a doctor of medicine, soon disposed of that hypothesis.

Nonetheless, the actual verdict had to be open; which satisfied nobody. In these times, people expect clear answers; whether right or wrong.

Harewood, almost his pristine self by then, inquired into the possibility of a memorial service in London, which he was perfectly prepared to come up and conduct. After all, Stephen was an OBE already, and could reasonably hope for more.

The view taken was that Stephen had been missing for so long, so entirely out of the official eye, that the proper moment for the idea was regrettably, but irreversibly, past.

The funeral took place, therefore, in Harewood's own church, where the father and the grandfather of both the deceased and the officiant had shepherded so long with their own quiet distinction. People saw that no other solution had ever really been thinkable.

Doreen had by now duly become indispensible to the rector; in the mysterious absence of Stephen, to whom the rector had specifically allotted that function. At the funeral, she was the only person in full black. Not even the solitary young man from the Ministry emulated her there. It had not been thought appropriate to place Stephen's OBE on the coffin, but during the service the rector noticed a scrap of lichen thereon which was different entirely, he thought, from any of the species on the walls, rafters, and floors of the church. Performing his office, Harewood could not at once put a name to the specimen. The stuff that already lined the open grave was even more peculiar; and Harewood was more than a little relieved when the whole affair was finally over, the last tributes paid, and he free to stumble back to Doreen's marmite toast, and lilac peignoir. The newest number of the *Journal* had come in only just before, but Harewood did not so much as open it that evening.

As Stephen's will had been rendered ineffective by Elizabeth's decease, Harewood, as next of kin, had to play a part, whether he felt competent or not, in winding everything up. Fortunately, Doreen had been taking typing lessons, and had bought a second-hand machine with her own money.

The flat was found to be in the most shocking state, almost indescribable. It was as if there had been no visitors for years; which, as Harewood at once pointed out, had almost certainly been more or less the case, since the onset of Elizabeth's malady, an epoch ago.

A single, very unusual book about Harewood's own speciality was found. It had been published in a limited edition: a minute one, and at a price so high that Harewood himself had not been among the subscribers.

"Poor fellow!" said Harewood. "I never knew that he was really interested. One can make such mistakes."

The valuable book had of course to be disposed of for the benefit of the estate.

Stephen's car was so far gone that it could be sold only for scrap; but, in the event, it never was sold at all, because no one could be bothered to drag it away. If one knows where to look, one can see the bits of it still.

FRANK BELKNAP LONG
The Horror from the Hills

1

THE COMING OF THE STONE BEAST

IN A long, low-ceilinged room adorned with Egyptian, Graeco-Roman, Minoan and Assyrian antiquities a thin, careless-seeming young man of twenty-six sat jubilantly humming. As nothing in his appearance or manner suggested the scholar—he wore gray tweeds of Ivy League cut, a pin-striped blue shirt with a buttoned-down collar and a ridiculously brilliant necktie—the uninitiated were inclined to regard him as a mere supernumerary in his own office. Strangers entered unannounced and called him "young man" at least twenty times a week, and he was frequently asked to convey messages to a non-existent superior. No one suspected, no one dreamed until he enlightened them, that he was the lawful custodian of the objects about him; and even when he revealed his identity people surveyed him with distrust and were inclined to suspect that he was ironically pulling their legs.

Algernon Harris was the young man's name and postgraduate degrees from Yale and Oxford set him distinctly apart from the undistinguished majority. But it is to his credit that he never paraded his erudition, nor succumbed to the impulse—almost irresistible in a young man with academic affiliations—to put a Ph.D. on the title page of his first book.

It was this book which had endeared him to the directors of the Manhattan Museum of Fine Arts and prompted their unanimous choice of him to succeed the late Halpin Chalmers as Curator of Archeology when the latter retired in the fall of the previous year.

In less than six months young Harris had exhaustively familiarized himself with the duties and responsibilities of his office and was becoming the most successful curator that the museum had ever employed. So boyishly ebullient was he, so consumed with investigative zeal, that his field workers contracted his enthusiasm as though it were a kind of fever and sped from his presence to trust their scholarly and highly cultivated lives to the most primitive of native tribes in regions where an outsider was still looked upon with suspicion, and was always in danger of bringing down the thunder.

And now they were coming back—for days now they had been coming back—occasionally with haggard faces, and once or twice, unfortunately, with something radically wrong with them. The Symons tragedy was a case in point. Symons was a Chang Dynasty specialist, and he had been obliged to leave his left eye and a piece of his nose in a Buddhist temple near a place called Fen Chow Fu. But when Algernon questioned him he could only mumble something about a small malignant face with corpsy eyes that had glared and glared at him out of a purple mist. And Francis Hogarth lost eighty pounds and a perfectly good right arm somewhere between Lake Rudolph and Naivasha in the Anglo-Egyptian Sudan.

But a few inexplicable and hence, from a scientific point of view, unfortunate occurrences were more than compensated for by the archeological treasures that the successful explorers brought back and figuratively dumped at Algernon's feet. There were mirrors of Graeco-Bactrian design and miniature tiger-dragons or too-tiehs from Central China dating from at least 200 B.C., enormous diorite Sphinxes from the Valley of the Nile, "Geometric" vases from Mycenaean Crete, incised pottery from Messina and Syracuse, linens and spindles from the Swiss Lakes, sculptured lintels from Yucatan and Mexico, Mayan and Manabi monoliths ten feet tall, Paleolithic Venuses from the rock caverns of the Pyrenees, and even a series of rare bilingual tablets in Hamitic and Latin from the site of Carthage.

It is not surprising that so splendid a garnering should have elated Algernon immoderately and impelled him to behave like a college junior at a fraternity-house jamboree. He addressed the attendants by their names, slapped them boisterously upon their shoulders whenever they had occasion to approach him, and went roaming haphazardly about the building immersed in ecstatic reveries. So far indeed did he descend from his pedestal that even the directors were disturbed, and it is doubtful if anything short of the arrival of Clark Ulman could have jolted him out of it.

Ulman may have been aware of this, for he telephoned first to break the news mercifully. He had apparently heard of the success of the other expeditions and hated infernally to intrude his skeleton at the banquet. Algernon, as we have seen, was humming, and the jingling of a phone-bell at his elbow was the first intimation he had of Ulman's return. Hastily detaching the receiver he pressed it against his ear and injected a staccato "What is it?" into the mouthpiece.

There ensued a silence. Then Ulman's voice, disconcertingly shrill, forced him to hold the receiver a little further from his ear. "I've got the god, Algernon, and I'll be over with it directly. I've three men helping me. It's four feet high and as heavy as granite. Oh, it's a strange, loathsome thing, Algernon. An unholy thing. I shall insist that you destroy it!"

"What's that?" Algernon raised his voice incredulously.

"You may photograph it and study it, but you've got to destroy it. You'll understand when you see what—*what I have become!*"

There came a hoarse sobbing, whilst Algernon struggled to comprehend what the other was driving at.

"It has wreaked its malice on me—on me. . . ."

With a frown Algernon re-cradled the receiver and began agitatedly to pace the room. "The elephant-god of Tsang!" he muttered to himself. "The horror Richardson drew before—before they impaled him. It's unbelievable. Ulman has crossed the desert plateau on foot—he's crossed above the graves of Steelbrath, Talman, McWilliams, Henley and Holmes. Richardson swore the cave was guarded night and day by hideous yellow abnormalities. I'm sure that's the phrase he used—abnormalities without faces—subhuman worshippers only vaguely manlike, in thrall to some malign wizardry. He averred they moved in circles about the idol on their hands and knees, and participated in a rite so foul that he dared not describe it.

"His escape was a sheer miracle. He had displayed extraordinary courage and endurance when they had tortured him, and it was merely because they couldn't kill him that the priest was impressed. A man who can curse valiantly after three days of agonizing torture must of necessity be a great magician and wonder-worker.

But it couldn't have happened twice. Ulman could never have achieved such a break. He is too frail—a day on their cross would have finished him. They would never have released him and decked him out with flowers and worshipped him as a sort of subsidiary elephant-god. Richardson predicted that no other white man would ever get into the cave alive. And as for getting out. . . .

"I can't imagine how Ulman did it. If he encountered even a few of Richardson's beast-men it isn't surprising he broke down on the phone. 'Destroy the statue!' Imagine! Sheer insanity, that. Ulman is evidently in a highly nervous and excitable state and we shall have to handle him with gloves."

There came a knock at the door.

"I don't wish to be disturbed," shouted Algernon irritably.

"We've got a package for you, sir. The doorman said for us to bring it up here."

"Oh, all right. I'll sign for it."

The door swung wide and in walked three harshly-breathing, shabbily dressed men staggering beneath a heavy burden.

"Put it down there," said Algernon, indicating a spot to the rear of his desk.

The men complied with a celerity that amazed him.

"Did Mr. Ulman send you?" he demanded curtly.

"Yes, sir." The spokesman's face had formed into a molding of relief. "The poor guy said he'd be here himself in half an hour."

Algernon started. "What kind of talk is that?" he demanded. "He doesn't happen to be a 'guy' but I'll pretend you didn't say it. Why the 'poor'? That's what I'm curious about."

The spokesman shuffled his feet. "It's on account of his face. There's something wrong with it. He keeps it covered and won't let nobody look at it."

"Good God!" murmured Algernon. "They've mutilated him!"

"What's that, sir? What did you say?"

Algernon collected himself with an effort. "Nothing. You may go now. The doorman will give you a dollar. I'll phone down and tell him."

Silently the men filed out. As soon as the door closed behind them Algernon strode into the center of the room and began feverishly to strip the wrappings from the thing on the floor. He worked with manifest misgivings, the distaste in his eyes deepening to disgust and horror as the massive idol came into view.

Words could not adequately convey the repulsiveness of the thing. It was endowed with a trunk and great, uneven ears, and two enormous tusks protruded from the corners of its mouth. But it was not an elephant. Indeed, its resemblance to an actual elephant was, at best, sporadic and superficial, despite certain unmistakable points of similarity. The ears were *webbed and tentacled,* the trunk terminated in a huge flaring disk at least a foot in diameter, and the tusks, which intertwined and interlocked at the base of the statue, were as translucent as rock crystal.

The pedestal upon which it squatted was of black onyx: the statue itself, with the exception of the tusks, had apparently been chiseled from a single block of stone, and was so hideously mottled and eroded and discolored that it looked, in spots, as though it had been dipped in sanies.

The thing sat bolt upright. Its forelimbs were bent stiffly at the elbow, and its hands—it had human hands—rested palms upward on its lap. Its shoulders were broad and square and its breasts and enormous stomach sloped outward, cushioning the trunk. It was as quiescent as a Buddha, as enigmatical as a sphinx, and as malignantly poised as a gorgon or cockatrice. Algernon could not identify the stone out of which it had been hewn, and its greenish sheen disturbed and puzzled him.

For a moment he stood staring uncomfortably into its little malign eyes. Then he shivered, and taking down a woolen scarf from the coatrack in the corner he cloaked securely the features which repelled him.

Ulman arrived unannounced. He advanced unobtrusively into the room and laid a tremulous hand on Algernon's shoulder. "Well, Algernon, how are you?" he murmured. "I—I'm glad to get back. Just to see—an old friend—is a comfort. I thought—but, well it doesn't matter. I was going to ask—to ask if you knew a good physician, but perhaps—I—I . . ."

Startled, Algernon glanced backward over his shoulder and straight into the other's eyes. He saw only the eyes, for the rest of Ulman's face was muffled by a black silk scarf. "Clark!" he exclaimed. "By God, but you gave me a start!"

Rising quickly, he sent his chair spinning against the wall and gripped his friend affectionately by the shoulders. "It's good to see you again, Clark," he said, with a warm cordiality in his voice. "It's good—why, what's the matter?"

Ulman had fallen upon his knees and was choking and gasping for breath.

"I should have warned you not to touch me," he moaned. "I can't stand—being touched."

"But why . . ."

"The wounds haven't healed," he sobbed. "*It* doesn't want them to heal. Every night it comes and lays—the disk on them. I can't stand being touched."

Algernon nodded sympathetically. "I can imagine what you've been through, Clark," he said. "You must take a vacation. I'll have a talk with the directors about you tomorrow. In view of what you've done for us I'm sure I can get you at least four months. You can go to Spain and finish your *Glimpses into Pre-History*. Paleontological anthropology is a soothing science, Clark. You'll forget all about the perplexities of mere archeological research when you start poking among bones and artifacts that haven't been disturbed since the Pleistocene."

Ulman had gotten to his feet and was staring at the opposite wall.

"You think that I have become—irresponsible?"

A look of sadness crept into Algernon's eyes. "No, Clark." I think you're merely suffering from—from non-psychotic, very transitory visual hallucinations. An almost unbearable strain can sometimes produce hallucinations when one's sanity is in no way impaired, and considering what you've been through. . . ."

"What I've been through!" Ulman caught at the phrase. "Would it interest you to know precisely what they did to me?"

Algernon nodded, meeting the other's gaze steadily.

"Yes, Clark. I wish to hear everything."

"They said that I must accompany Chaugnar Faugn into the world."

"Chaugnar Faugn?"

"That is the name they worship *it* by. When I told them I had come from the United States they said that Great Chaugnar had *willed* that I should be his companion.

" 'It must be carried,' they explained, 'and it must be nursed. If it is nursed and carried safely beyond the rising sun it will possess the world. And then all things that are now in the world, all creatures and plants and stones will be devoured by Great Chaugnar. All things that are and have been will cease to be, and

Great Chaugnar will fill all space with its Oneness. Even its Brothers it will devour, its Brothers who will come down from the mountains ravening for ecstasy when it calls to them.' They didn't use precisely that term, because 'ecstasy' is a very sophisticated word, peculiar to our language. But that's the closest I can come to it. In their own aberrant way they were the opposite of unsophisticated.

"I didn't protest when they explained this to me. It was precisely the kind of break I had been hoping for. I had studied Richardson's book, you see, and I had read enough between the lines to convince me that Chaugnar Faugn's devotees were growing a little weary of it. It isn't a very pleasant deity to have around. It has some regrettable and very nasty habits."

A horror was taking shape in Ulman's eyes.

"You must excuse my levity. When one is tottering on the edge of an abyss it isn't always expedient to dispense with irony. Were I to become wholly serious for a moment, were I to let the— what I believe, what I know to be the truth behind all that I'm telling you coalesce into a definite construction in my mind I should go quite mad. Let us call them merely regrettable habits.

"I guessed, as I say, that the guardians of the cave were not very enthusiastic about retaining Chaugnar Faugn indefinitely. It made—depredations. The guardians would disappear in the night and leave their clothes behind them, and the clothes, upon examination, would yield something rather ghastly.

"But however much your savage may want to dispose of his god the thing isn't always feasible. It would be the height of folly to attempt to send an omnipotent deity on a long journey without adequate justification. An angered god can take vengeance even when he is on the opposite side of the world. And that is why most barbarians who find themselves saddled with a deity they fear and hate are obliged to put up with it indefinitely.

"The only thing that can help them is a legend—some oral or written legend that will enable them to send their ogre packing without ruffling its temper. The devotees had such a legend. At a certain time, which the prophecy left gratifyingly indefinite, Chaugnar Faugn was to be sent out into the world. It was to be sent out to possess the world to its everlasting glory, and it was also written that those who sent it forth should be forever immune from its anger.

"I knew of the existence of this legend, and when I read

Richardson and discovered what a vile and unpleasant customer the god was I decided I'd risk a trip across the desert plateau of Tsang."

"You crossed on foot?" interrupted Algernon with undisguised admiration.

"There were no camels available," assented Ulman. "I made it on foot. On the fourth day my water ran short and I was obliged to open a vein in my arm. On the fifth day I began to see mirages—probably of a purely hallucinatory nature. On the seventh day"—he paused and stared hard at Algernon—"on the seventh day I consumed the excrements of wild dogs."

Algernon shuddered. "But you reached the cave?"

"I reached the cave. The—the faceless guardians whom Richardson described found me groveling on the sands in delirium a half-mile to the west of their sanctuary. They restored me by heating a flint until it was white-hot and laying it on my chest. If the high priest hadn't interfered I should have shared Richardson's fate."

"Good God!"

"The high priest was called Chung Ga and he was devilishly considerate. He took me into the cave and introduced me to Chaugnar Faugn.

"You've Chaugnar there," Ulman pointed to the enshrouded form on the floor, "and you can imagine what the sight of it squatting on its haunches at the back of an evil-smelling, atrociously lighted cave would do to a man who had not eaten for three days.

"I began to say very queer things to Chung Ga. I confided to him that Great Chaugnar Faugn was not just a lifeless statue in a cave, but a great universal god filling all space—that it had created the world in a single instant by merely expelling its breath, and that when eventually it decided to inhale, the world would disappear. 'It also made this cave,' I hastened to add, 'and you are its chosen prophet.'

"The priest stared at me curiously for several moments without speaking. Then he approached the god and prostrated himself before it. 'Chaugnar Faugn,' he intoned, 'the White Acolyte has confirmed that you are about to become a great universal god filling all space. He will carry you safely into the world, and nurse you until you have no further need of him. The prophecy of Mu Sang has been most gloriously fulfilled.'

"For several minutes he remained kneeling at the foot of the idol. Then he rose and approached me. 'You shall depart with Great Chaugnar tomorrow,' he said. 'You shall become Great Chaugnar's companion and nurse.'

"I felt a wave of gratitude for the man. Even in my befuddled state I was sensible that I had achieved a magnificent break. 'I will serve him gladly,' I murmured, 'if only I may have some food.'

"Chung Ga nodded. 'It is my wish that you eat heartily,' he said. 'If you are to nurse Great Chaugnar you must consume an infinite diversity of fruits. And the flesh of animals. Red blood—red blood in Chaugnar's staff. Without it my god would suffer tortures no man could endure. It is impossible for a man to know how great can be the suffering of a god.'

"He tapped a drum and immediately I was confronted with a wooden bowl filled to the brim with pomegranate juice.

" 'Drink heartily,' he urged. 'I have reason to suspect that Chaugnar Faugn will be ravenous tonight.'

"I was so famished that I scarcely gave a thought to what he was saying and for fifteen minutes I consumed without discrimination everything that was set before me—evil-smelling herbs, ewe's milk, eggs, peaches and fresh blood of antelopes.

"The priest watched me in silence. At last when I could eat no more he went into a corner of the cave and returned with a straw mattress. 'You have supped most creditably,' he murmured, 'and I wish you pleasant dreams.'

"With that he withdrew, and I crawled gratefully upon the mat. My strength was wholly spent and the dangers I still must face, the loathsome proximity of Great Chaugnar and the possibility that the priest had been deliberately playing a part and would return to kill me, were swallowed up in a physical urgency that bordered on delirium. Relaxing upon the straw I shut my eyes, and fell almost instantly into a deep sleep.

"I awoke with a start and a strange impression that I was not alone in the cave. Even before I opened my eyes I knew that something unspeakably malign was crouching or squatting on the ground beside me. I could hear it breathing in the darkness and the stench of it strangled the breath in my throat.

"Slowly, very slowly, I endeavored to rise. An unsurpassably ponderous weight descended upon my chest and hurled me to the ground. I stretched out my hand to disengage it and met with an iron resistance. A solid wall of something cold, slimy and implacable rose up in the darkness to thwart me.

"In an instant I was fully awake and calling frantically for assistance. But no one came to me. And even as I screamed the wall descended perpendicularly upon me and lay clammily upon my chest. An odor of corruption surged from it and when I tore at it with my fingers it made a low, gurgling sound, which gradually increased in volume till it woke echoes in the low-vaulted ceiling.

"The thing had pinioned my arms, and the more I twisted and squirmed the more agonizingly it tightened about me. The constriction increased until breathing became a torture, until all my flesh palpitated with pain. I wriggled and twisted, and bit my lips through in an extremity of horror.

"Then, abruptly, the pressure ceased and I became aware of two blinking, fish-white eyes glaring truculently at me through the darkness. Agonizingly I sat up and ran my hands over my chest and arms. My fingers encountered a warm wetness and with a hideous clarity it was borne in on me that the thing had been feasting on my blood! The revelation was very close to mind-shattering. I was on my feet in an instant, trying desperately not to succumb to panic, but knowing, deep in my mind, that it would be a losing battle.

"A most awful terror was upon me, and so unreasoning became my desire to escape from that fearsome, vampirish obscenity that I retreated straight toward the throne of Chaugnar Faugn.

"It loomed enormous in the darkness, a refuge and a sanctuary. The wild thought came to me that if I could scale the throne and climb upon the lap of the god the horror might cease to molest me. Maligant beyond belief it undoubtedly was. But I refused to credit it with more than animalistic intelligence. Even in that moment of infinite peril, as I groped shakingly toward the rear of the cave, my mind was evolving a conceit to account for it.

"It was undoubtedly, I told myself, some cave-lurking survival from the age of reptiles—some atavistic and predatory abnormality that had experienced no necessity to advance on the course of evolution. It is more than probable that all backboned animals above the level of fishes and amphibians originated in Asia, and

I had recklessly conveyed myself to the hoariest section of that primeval continent. Was it after all so amazing that I should have encountered, in a dark and inaccessible cave on a virtually uninhabited plateau, a reptilian predator endowed with the rapacity of that most hideous of blood-sucking animals—the vampire bat of the tropics?

"It was a just-short-of-destructive conceit and it sustained me and made my desperate groping for some kind of certainty seem the opposite of wasted until I reached the throne of Great Chaugnar. I fear that up to that instant my failure to suspect the truth was downright idiotic. There was only one adequate explanation for what had occurred. But it wasn't until I actually ascended the throne and began to feel about in the darkness for the body of Chaugnar that the truth rushed in upon me.

"Great Chaugnar had forsaken its throne! It had descended into the cave and was roaming about in the darkness. In its vampirish explorations it had stumbled upon my sleeping form, and had felled me with its trunk so that it might satisfy its thirst for blood with quick and hideous ferocity.

"For an instant I crouched motionless upon the stone, screaming inwardly, feeling the darkness tightening about me like a shroud. Then, quickly, I began to descend. But I had not lowered more than my right leg when something ponderous collided with the base of the throne. The entire structure shook and I was almost hurled to the ground.

"I refuse to dwell on what happened after that. There are experiences too revolting for sane description. Were I to tell how the horror began slowly, to mount, to recount at length how it heaved its slabby and mucid vastness to the pinnacle of its throne and began nauseatingly to breathe upon me, the slight uncertainty I now entertain as to my sanity would be dispelled in short order.

"Neither shall I describe how it picked me up in its corpse-cold hands and began detestably to maul me, and how I nearly fainted beneath the foulness which drooled from its mouth. Eventually it wearied of its malign sport. After sinking its slimy black nails into my throat and chest until the pain became almost unbearable, it experienced a sudden access of wrath and hurled me violently from the pedestal.

"The fall stunned me and for many minutes I lay on my back on the stones, dimly conscious only of a furtive whispering in the

darkness about me. Then, slowly, my vision cleared and under
the guidance of some nebulous and sinister influence my eyes
were drawn upward until they encountered the pedestal from
which I had fallen and the enormous, ropy bulk of Chaugnar
Faugn loathsomely waving his great trunk in the dawn.

"It isn't surprising that when Chung Ga found me deliriously
gibbering at the cavern's mouth he was obliged to carry me into
the sunlight and force great wooden spoonfuls of revivifying wine
down my parched throat. If there was *anything* inexplicable in
the sequel to that hideous nightmare it was the matter-of-fact
reception which he accorded my story.

"He nodded his head sympathetically when I recounted my
experiences on the throne, and assured me that the incident
accorded splendidly with the prophecies of Mu Sang. 'I was afraid,'
he said, 'that Great Chaugnar would not accept you as its companion and nurse—that it would destroy you as utterly as it has
the guardians—more of the guardians than you might suppose,
for a god is not motivated by our kind of expediency.'

"He studied me for a moment intensely. 'No doubt you think
me a superstitious savage, a ridiculous barbarian. Would it surprise
you very much if I should tell you that I have spent eight years
in England and that I am a graduate of the University of Oxford?'

"I could only stare at him in stunned disbelief for a moment,
but so unbelievable and ghastly had been the coming to life of
Chaugnar Faugn that lesser wonders made little impression on
me and my incredulity passed quickly. Had he told me that he
had an eye in the middle of his back or a tail twenty feet long
which he kept continuously coiled about his body I should have
evinced little surprise. I doubt indeed if anything short of a
universal cataclysm could have roused me from my dazed acceptance of revelations which, under ordinary circumstances, I
should have dismissed as preposterous.

" 'It astonishes you perhaps that I should have cast my lot with
filthy primitives in this loathsome place and that I should have
so uncompromisingly menaced your countrymen.' A wistfulness
crept into his eyes. 'Your Richardson was a brave man. Even
Chaugnar Faugn was moved to compassion by his valor. He gave
no cry when we drove wooden stakes through his hands and
impaled him. For three days he defied us. Then Chaugnar tramped
toward him in the night and set him at liberty.

" 'You may be sure that from that instant we accorded him every consideration. But to return to what you would undoubtedly call my perverse and atavistic attitude. Why do you suppose I chose to serve Chaugnar?'

"His recapitulation of what he had done to Richardson had awakened in me a confused but violent resentment. 'I don't know,' I muttered. 'There are degrees of human vileness—'

" 'Spare me your opprobrium, I beg of you,' he exclaimed. 'It was Great Chaugnar speaking through me that dictated the fate of Richardson. I am merely Chaugnar's interpreter and instrument. For generations my forebears have served Chaugnar, and I have never attempted to evade the duties that were delegated to me when our world was merely a thought in the mind of my god. I went to England and acquired a little of the West's decadent culture merely that I might more worthily serve Chaugnar.

" 'Don't imagine for a moment that Chaugnar is a beneficent god. In the West you have evolved certain amiabilities of intercourse, to which you presumptuously attach cosmic significance, such as truth, kindliness, generosity, forbearance and honor, and you quaintly imagine that a god who is beyond good and evil and hence unamenable to your 'ethics' can not be omnipotent.

" 'But how do you know that there *are* any beneficent laws in the universe, that the cosmos is friendly to man? Even in the mundane sphere of planetary life there is nothing to sustain such an hypothesis.

" 'Great Chaugnar is a terrible god, an utterly cosmic and unanthropomorphic god. It is akin to the fire mists and the primordial ooze, and before it incarned itself in Time it contained within itself the past, the present and the future. Nothing was and nothing will be, but all things are. And Chaugnar Faugn was once the sum of all things that are.'

"I remained silent and a note of compassion crept into his voice. I think he perceived that I had no inclination to split hairs with him over the paradoxes of transcendental metaphysics.

" 'Chaugnar Faugn,' he continued, 'did not always dwell in the East. Many thousands of years ago it abode with its Brothers in a cave in Western Europe, and made from the flesh of toads a race of small dark shapes to serve it. In bodily contour these shapes resembled men, but they were incapable of speech and their thoughts were the thoughts of Chaugnar.

" 'The cave where Chaugnar dwelt was never visited by men, for it wound its twisted length through a high and inaccessible crag of the mysterious Pyrenees, and all the regions beneath were rife with abominable hauntings.

" 'Twice a year Chaugnar Faugn sent its servants into the villages that dotted the foothills to bring it the sustenance its belly craved. The chosen youths and maidens were preserved with spices and stored in the cave till Chaugnar had need of them. And in the villages men would hurl their first-borns into the flames and offer prayer to their futile little gods, hoping thereby to appease the wrath of Chaugnar's mindless servants.

" 'But eventually there came into the foothills men like gods, stout, eagle-visaged men who carried on their shields the insignia of invincible Rome. They scaled the mountains in pursuit of the servants and awoke a cosmic foreboding in the mind of Chaugnar.

" 'It is true that its Brethren succeeded without difficulty in exterminating the impious cohorts—exterminating them unspeakably—before they reached the cave, but it feared that rumors of the attempted sacrilege would bring legions of the empire-builders into the hills and that eventually its sanctuary would be defiled.

" 'So in ominous conclave it debated with its Brothers the advisability of flight. Rome was but a dream in the mind of Chaugnar and it could have destroyed her utterly in an instant, but having incarned itself in Time it did not wish to resort to violence until the prophecies were fulfilled.

" 'Chaugnar and its Brothers conversed by means of thought-transference in an idiom incomprehensible to us and it would be both dangerous and futile to attempt to repeat the exact substance of their discourse. But it is recorded in the prophecy of Mu Sang that Great Chaugnar spoke *approximately* as follows:

" 'Our servants shall carry us eastward to the primal continent, and there we shall await the arrival of the White Acolyte."

" 'His Brothers demurred. "We are safe here," they affirmed. "No one will scale the mountains again, for the doom that came to Pompelo will reverberate in the dreams of prophets till Rome is less to be feared than moon-dim Nineveh, or Medusa-girdled Ur."

" 'At that Great Chaugnar waxed ireful and affirmed that it would go alone to the primal continent, leaving its Brothers to cope with the menace of Rome. "When the time-frames are dissolved I alone shall ascend in glory," it told them. "All of you I shall devour before I ascend to the dark altars. When the hour of my transfiguration approaches you will come down from the mountains cosmically athirst for That Which is Not to be Spoken of, but even as your bodies raven for the time-dissolving sacrament I shall consume them."

" 'Then it called for the servants and had them carry it to this place. And it caused Mu Sang to be born from the womb of an ape and the prophecies to be written on imperishable parchment, and into the care of my fathers it surrendered its body.'

"I rose gropingly to my feet. 'Let me leave this place,' I pleaded. 'I respect your beliefs and I give you my solemn word I will never attempt to return. Your secrets are safe with me. Only let me go—'

"Chung Ga's features were convulsed with pity. 'It is stated in the prophecy that you must be Chaugnar's companion and accompany it to America. In a few days it will experience a desire to feed again. You must nurse it unceasingly.'

" 'I am ill,' I pleaded. 'I can not carry Chaugnar Faugn across the desert plateau.'

" 'I will have the guardians assist you,' murmured Chung Ga soothingly. 'You shall be conveyed in comfort to the gates of Lhasa, and from Lhasa to the coast it is less than a week's journey by caravan.'

"I realized then how impossible it would be for me to depart with Great Chaugnar. 'Very well, Chung Ga,' I said. 'I submit to the prophecy. Chaugnar shall be my companion and I shall nurse it as diligently as it desires.'

"There was a ring of insincerity in my speech which was not lost on Chung Ga. He approached very close to me and peered into my eyes. 'If you attempt to dispose of my god,' he warned, 'it's Brothers will come down from the mountains and tear you indescribably.'

"He saw perhaps that I wasn't wholly convinced, for he added in an even more ominous tone, 'It has laid upon you the mark and seal of a flesh-dissolving sacrament. Destroy it, and the sacrament will be consummated in an instant. The flesh of your body will turn black and melt like tallow in the sun. You will become a seething mass of corruption.' "

Ulman paused, a look of unutterable torment in his eyes. "There isn't much more to my story, Algernon. The guardians carried us safely to Lhasa and a fortnight later I reached the Bay of Bengal, accompanied by half a hundred ragged, gaunt-visaged mendicants from the temples of obscure Indian villages. There was something about our caravan that had attracted them. And all during the voyage from Bengal to Hongkong the Indian and Tibetan members of our crew would steal stealthily to my cabin at night and look in on me, and I had never before seen human faces quite so distorted with superstitious terror.

"Don't imagine for a moment that I didn't share their awe and fear of the thing I was compelled to companion. Continuously I longed to carry it on deck and cast it into the sea. Only the memory of Chung Ga's warning and the thought of what might happen to me if I disregarded it kept me chained and submissive.

"It was not until weeks later, when I had the Indian and most of the Pacific Ocean behind me, that I discovered how unwise I had been to heed his vile threats. If I had resolutely hurled Chaugnar into the sea the shame and the horror might never have come upon me!"

Ulman's voice was rising, becoming shrill and hysterical. "Chaugnar Faugn is an awful and mysterious being, a repellent and obscene and lethal being, but how do I know that it is omnipotent? Chung Ga may have maliciously lied to me. Chaugnar Faugn may be merely an extension or distortion of inanimate nature. Some hideous *process,* as yet unobserved and unexplained by the science of the West, may be noxiously at work in desert places all over our planet to produce such fiendish anomalies. Perhaps parallel to protoplasmic life on the earth's crust is this other aberrant and hidden life—the revolting sentiency of stones that aspire, of earth-shapes, parasitic and bestial, that wax agile in the presence of man.

"Did not Cuvier believe that there had been not one but an infinite number of 'creations,' and that as our earth cooled after its departure from the sun a succession of vitalic phenomena appeared on its surface? Conceding as we must the orderly and continuous development of protoplasmic life from simple forms, which Cuvier stupidly and ridiculously denied, is it not still conceivable that another evolutionary cycle may have preceded the one which has culminated in us? A non-protoplasmic cycle?

"Whether we accept the planetesimal or the three or four newer theories of planetary formation it is permissible to believe that the earth coalesced very swiftly into a compact mass after the segregation of its constituents in space and that it achieved sufficient crustal stability to support animate entities one, or two, or perhaps even five billion years ago.

"I do not claim that life *as we know it* would be possible in the earliest phases of planetary consolidation, but is it possible to assert dogmatically that beings possessed of intelligence and volition could not have evolved in a direction merely parallel to the cellular? Life as we know it is complexly bound up with such substances as chlorophyll and protoplasm, but does that preclude that possibility of an evolved sentiency in other forms of matter?

"How do we know that stones can not think; that the earth beneath our feet may not once have been endowed with a hideous intelligence? Entire cycles of animate evolution may have occurred on this planet before the most primitive of 'living' cells were evolved from the slime of warm seas.

"There may have been eons of—experiments! Three billion years ago in the fiery radiance of the rapidly condensing earth who knows what monstrous shapes crawled—or shambled?

"And how do we know that there are not survivals? Or that somewhere beneath the stars of heaven complex and hideous processes are not still at work, shaping the inorganic into forms of primal malevolence?

"And what more inevitable than that some such primiparous spawn should have become in my eyes the apotheosis of all that was fiendish and accursed and unclean, and that I should have ascribed to it the attributes of divinity, and imagined in a moment of madness that it was immune to destruction? I should have hurled it into the depths of the seas and risked boldly the fulfillment of Chung Ga's prophecy. For even had it proved itself omnipotent and omniscient by rising in fury from the waves or summoning its Brothers to destroy me I should have suffered indescribably for no more than a moment."

Ulman's voice had risen to a shrill scream. "I should have passed quickly enough into the darkness had I encountered merely the wrath of Chaugnar Faugn. It was not the fury but the forbearance of Chaugnar that has wrought an uncleanliness in my body's flesh, and blackened and shriveled my soul, till a furious hate has grown up in me for all that the world holds of serenity and joy."

Ulman's voice broke and for a moment there was silence in the room. Then, with a sudden, convulsive movement of his right arm he uncloaked the whole of his face.

He was standing very nearly in the center of the office and the light from its eastern window illumed with a hideous clarity all that remained of his features. But Algernon didn't utter a sound, for all that the sight was appalling enough to revolt a corpse. He simply clung shakingly to the desk and waited with ashen lips for Ulman to continue.

"It came to me again as I slept, drinking its fill, and in the morning I woke to find that the flesh of my body had grown fetid and loathsome, and that my face—my face . . ."

"Yes, Clark, I understand." Algernon's voice was vibrant with compassion. "I'll get you some brandy."

Ulman's eyes shone with an awful light.

"Do you believe me?" he cried. "Do you believe that Chaugnar Faugn has wrought this uncleanliness?"

Slowly Algernon shook his head. "No, Clark. Chaugnar Faugn is nothing but a stone idol, sculptured by some Asian artist with quite exceptional talent, however primitive he may have been in other respects. I believe Chung Ga kept you under the influence of some potent drug until he had—had cut your face, and that he also hypnotized you and suggested every detail of the story you have just told me. I believe you are still actually under the spell of that hypnosis."

"When I boarded the ship at Calcutta there was nothing wrong with my face!" shrilled Ulman.

"Conceivably not. But some minion of the priest may have administered the drug and performed the operation on shipboard. I can only guess at what happened, of course, but it is obvious that you are the victim of some hideous charlatanry. I've visited India, Clark, and I have a very keen respect for the hypnotic endowments of the Oriental. It's ghastly and unbelievable how much a Hindoo or a Tibetan can accomplish by simple suggestion."

"I feared—I feared that you would doubt!" Ulman's voice had risen to a shriek. "But I swear to you . . ."

The sentence was never finished. A hideous pallor overspread the archeologist's face, his jaw sagged and into his eyes there crept a look of panic fight. For a second he stood clawing at his throat, like a man in the throes of an epileptic fit.

Then something, some invisible force, seemed to propel him backward. Choking and gasping he staggered against the wall and threw out his arms in a gesture of frantic appeal. "Keep it off!" he sobbed. "I can't breathe. I can't . . ."

With a cry Algernon leapt forward, but before he reached the other's side the unfortunate man had sunk to the floor and was moaning and gibbering and rolling about in a most sickening way.

2

THE ATROCITY AT THE MUSEUM

ALGERNON HARRIS emerged from the B. M. T. subway at the Fifty-ninth Street and Fifth Avenue entrance and began nervously to pace the sidewalk in front of a large yellow sign, which bore the discouraging caption: "Buses do not stop here." Harris was most eager to secure a bus and it was obvious from the expectant manner in which he hailed the first one to pass that he hadn't the faintest notion he had taken up his post on the wrong side of the street. Indeed, it was not until four buses had passed him by that he awoke to the gravity of his predicament and began to propel his person in the direction of the legitimate stop-zone.

Algernon Harris was abnormally and tragically upset. But even a man trembling on the verge of a neuropathic collapse can remain superficially politic, and it isn't surprising that when he ascended into his bus and encountered on a conspicuous seat his official superior, Doctor George Francis Scollard, he should have nodded, smiled and responded with an unwavering amiability to the questions that were shot at him.

"I got your telegram yesterday," murmured the president of the Manhattan Museum of Fine Arts, "and I caught the first train down. Am I too late for the inquest?"

Algernon nodded. "The coroner—a chap named Henry Weigal—took my evidence and rendered a decision on the spot. The condition of Ulman's body would not have permitted of delay. I never before imagined that—that putrefaction could proceed with such incredible rapidity."

Scollard frowned. "And the verdict?"

"Heart failure. The coroner was very positive that anxiety and shock were the sole causes of Ulman's total collapse."

"But you said something about his face being horribly disfigured."

"Yes. It had been rendered loathsome by—by plastic surgery. Weigal was hideously agitated until I explained that Ulman had merely fallen into the hands of a skillful Oriental surgeon with sadistic inclination in the course of his archeological explorations. I explained to him that many of our field workers returned slightly disfigured and that Ulman had merely endured an exaggeration of the customary martyrdom."

"And you believe that plastic surgery could account for the repellent and gruesome changes you mentioned in your night-letter—the shocking prolongation of the poor devil's nose, the flattening and broadening of his ears. . . ."

Algernon winced. "I must believe it, sir. It is impossible sanely to entertain any other explanation. The coroner's assistant was a little incredulous at first, until Weigal pointed out to him what an unwholesome precedent they would set by even so much as hinting that the phenomenon wasn't pathologically explicable. 'We would play right into the hands of the spiritualists,' Weigal explained. 'An officer of the police isn't at liberty to adduce an hypothesis that the district attorney's office wouldn't approve of. The newspapers would pounce on a thing like that and play it up disgustingly. Mr. Harris has supplied us with an explanation which seems adequately to cover the facts, and with your permission I shall file a verdict of natural death.' "

The president coughed and shifted uneasily in his seat, "I am glad that the coroner took such a sensible view of the matter. Had he been a recalcitrant individual and raised objections we should have come in for considerable unpleasant publicity. I shudder whenever I see a reference to the Museum in the popular press. It is always the morbid and sensational aspects of our work that they stress and there is never the slightest attention paid to accuracy."

For the moment Doctor Scollard was silent. Then he cleared his throat, and recapitulated, in a slightly more emphatic form, the question that he had put to Algernon originally. "But you said in your letter that Ulman's nose revolted and sickened you—

that it had become a loathsome greenish trunk almost a foot in length which continued to move about for hours after Ulman's heart stopped beating. Could—could your operation hypothesis account for such an appalling anomaly?"

Algernon took a deep breath. "I can't pretend that I wasn't astounded and appalled and—and frightened. And so lost to discretion that I made no attempt to conceal the way I felt from the coroner. I could not remain in the room while they were examining the body."

"And yet you succeeded in convincing the coroner that he could justifiably render a verdict of natural death!"

"You misunderstood me, sir. The coroner *wanted* to render such a verdict. My explanation merely supplied him with a straw to clutch at. I was trembling in every limb when I made it and it must have been obvious to him that we were in the presence of something unthinkable. But without the plastic surgery assumption we should have had nothing whatever to cling to."

"And do you still give your reluctant assent to such an assumption?"

"Now more than ever. And my assent is no longer reluctant, for I've succeeded in convincing myself that a surgeon endowed with miraculous skill could have affected the transformation I described in my letter."

"Miraculous skill?"

"I use the word in a merely mundane sense. When one stops to consider what astounding advances plastic surgery has made in England and America during the past decade it is impossible to disbelieve that the human frame will soon become more malleable than wax beneath the scalpels of our surgeons and that beings will appear in our midst with bodies so grotesquely distorted that the superstitious will ascribe their advent to the supernatural.

"And we can adduce *more* than a surgical 'miracle' to account for the horror that poor Ulman became without for a moment encroaching on the dubious domain of the superphysical. Everyone knows how extensively the ductless glands regulate the growth and shape of our bodies. A change in the quantity or quality of secretion in any one of the glands may throw the entire human mechanism out of gear. Terrible and unthinkable changes have been known to occur in the adult body during the course of diseases involving glandular instability. We once thought that human beings invariably ceased to grow at twenty-one or twenty-two, but we now know that growth may continue till middle age, and even till the very onset of senility, and that frequently such growth does not culminate in a mere increase in stature or in girth.

"Doubtless you have heard of that rare, and hideously deforming glandular malady acromegaly. It is characterized by an abnormal over-growth of the skull and face, and the small bones of the extremities, and its victims become in a short time tragic caricatures of humanity. The entire face assumes a more massive cast but the over-growth is most pronounced in the region of the jawbones. In exceptional cases the face has been known to attain a length of nearly a foot. But it is not so much the size as the revolting primitiveness of the face which sets the victims of this hideous disease so tragically apart from their fellows. The features not only grow, but they take on an almost apelike aspect, and as the disease advances even the skull becomes revoltingly simian in its confor-mation. In brief, the victims of acromegaly become in a short while almost indistinguishable from very primitive and brutish types of human ancestors, such as *Homo neanderthalensis* and the unmentionable, enormous-browed caricature from Broken Hill, Rodesia, which Sir Arthur Keith has called the most unqualifiedly repulsive physiognomy in the entire gallery of fossil men.

"The disease of acromegaly is perhaps a more certain indication of man's origin than all the 'missing links' that anthropologists have exhumed. It proves incontestably that we still carry within our bodies the mechanism of evolutionary retrogression, and that when something interferes with the normal functioning of our glands we are very apt to return, at least physically, to our aboriginal status.

"And since we know that a mere insufficiency or superabundance of glandular secretions can work such devasting changes, can turn men virtually into Neanderthalers, or great apes, what is there really unaccountable in the alteration I witnessed in poor Ulman?

"Some Oriental diabolist merely ten years in advance of the West in the sphere of plastic surgery and with a knowledge of glandular therapeutics no greater than that possessed by Doctors Noel Paton and Schafer might easily have wrought such an abom-ination. Or suppose, as I have hinted before, that no surgery was involved, suppose this fiend has learned so much about our glands that he can send men back and back through the mists of time—

back past the great apes and the primitive mammals and the carnivorous dinosaurs to their primordial sires! Suppose—it is an awful thought, I know—suppose that some creature closely resembling what Ulman became was *once* our ancestor, that a hundred million years ago a gigantic batrachian shape with trunk-like appendages and great flapping ears paddled through the warm primeval seas or stretched its leathery length on banks of Permian slime!"

Mr. Scollard turned sharply and plucked at his subordinate's sleeve. "There's a crowd in front of the Museum," he muttered. "See there!"

Algernon started, and rising instantly, pressed the signal bell above his companion's head. "We'll have to walk back," he muttered despondently. "I should have watched the street numbers."

His pessimism proved well-founded. The bus continued relentlessly on its way for four additional blocks and then came so abruptly to a stop that Mr. Scollard was subjected to the ignominy of being obliged to sit for an instant on the spacious lap of a middle-aged stout woman who resented the encroachment with a furious glare.

"I've a good mind to report you," he shouted to the bus conductor as he lowered his portly person to the sidewalk. "I've a damn good mind . . ."

"Let it pass, sir." Algernon laid a pacifying arm on his companion's arm. "We've got no time to argue. Something dreadful has occurred at the Museum. I just saw two policemen enter the building. And those tall men walking up and down on the opposite side of the street are reporters. There's Wells of the *Tribune* and Thompson of the *Times,* and . . ."

Mr. Scollard gripped his subordinate's arm. "Tell me," he demanded, "did you put the—the statue on *exhibition?*"

Algernon nodded. "I had it carried to Alcove K. Wing C last night. After the inquest on poor Ulman I was besieged by reporters. They wanted to know all about the fetish, and of course I had to tell them that it would go on exhibition eventually. They would have returned every day for weeks to pester me if I hadn't assured them that we'd respect the public clamor to that extent at least."

"Yesterday afternoon all the papers ran specials about it. The *News-Graphic* gave it a front-page write-up. I remained at my office until eleven, and all evening at half-minute intervals some emotionally-overcharged numbskull would ring up and ask me when I was going to exhibit the thing and whether it really looked as repulsive as its photographs, and what kind of stone it was made of and—oh, God! I was too nervous and wrought-up to be bothered that way and I decided it would be best to satisfy the public's idiotic curiosity by permitting them to view the thing today."

The two men were walking briskly in the direction of the Museum.

"Besides, there was no longer any necessity of my keeping it in the office. I had had it measured and photographed and I knew that Harrison and Smithstone wouldn't want to take a cast of it until next week. And I couldn't have chosen a safer place for it than Alcove K. It's roped off, you know, and only two paces removed from the door. Cinney can see it all night from his station in the corridor."

By the time that Algernon and Mr. Scollard arrived at the Museum the crowd had reached alarming proportions. They were obliged to fight their way through a solid phalanx of excited men and women who impeded their progress with elbow-thrusting aggressiveness, and scant respect for their dignity. And even in the vestibules they were repulsed with discourtesy.

A red-headed policeman glared savagely at them from behind horn-rimmed spectacles and brought them to a halt with a threatening gesture. "You've got to keep out!" he shouted. "If you ain't got a police card you've got to keep out!"

"What's happened here?" demanded Algernon authoritatively.

"A guy's been bumped off. If you ain't got a police card you've got to . . ."

Algernon produced a calling-card and thrust it into the officer's face. "I'm the curator of archeology," he affirmed angrily. "I guess I've a right to enter my own museum."

The officer's manner softened perceptibly. "Then I guess it's all right. The chief told me I wasn't to keep out any of the guys that work here. How about your friend?"

"You can safely admit him," murmured Algernon with a smile. "He's president of the Museum."

The policeman did not seem too astonished. He regarded Mr.

Scollard dubiously for a moment. Then he shrugged his shoulders and stepped complacently aside.

An attendant greeted them excitedly as they emerged from the turnstile. "It's awful, sir," he gasped, addressing Mr. Scollard. "Cinney has been murdered—knifed, sir. He's all cut and mangled. I shouldn't have recognized him it if weren't for his clothes. There's nothing left on his face, sir."

Algernon turned pale. "When—when did this happen?" he gasped.

The attendant shook his head. "I can't say, Mr. Harris. It must've been some time last night, but I can't say exactly when. The first we knew of it was when Mr. Williams came running down the stairs with his hands all bloodied. That was at eight this morning, about two hours ago. I'd just got in, and all the other attendants were in the cloak room getting into their uniforms. That is, all except Williams. Williams usually arrives about a half-hour before the rest of us. He likes to come early and have a chat with Cinney before the doors open."

The attendant's face was convulsed with terror and he spoke with considerable difficulty. "I was the only one to see him come down the stairs. I was standing about here and as soon as he came into sight I knew that something was wrong with him. He went from side to side of the stairs and clung to the rails to keep himself from falling. And his face was as white as paper."

Algernon's eyes did not leave the attendant's face. "Go on," he urged.

"He opened his mouth very wide when he saw me. It was like as if he wanted to shout and couldn't. There wasn't a sound came out of him."

The attendant cleared his throat. "I didn't think he'd ever reach the bottom of the stairs and I called out for the boys in the cloak room to lend me a hand."

"What happened then?"

"He didn't speak for a long time. One of the boys gave him some whiskey out of a flask and the rest of us just stood about and said soothing things to him. But he was trembling all over and we couldn't quiet him down. He kept throwing his head about and pointing toward the stairs. And foam collected all over his mouth. It was ghastly."

" 'What's wrong, Jim?' I said to him. 'What did you see?'

" 'The worm of hell!' he said. 'The Devil's awful mascot!' He said other things I can't repeat, sir. I'm a God-fearing man, and there are blasphemies it's best to forget you ever heard. But I'll tell you what he said when he got through talking about the worm out of hell. He said: 'Cinney's upstairs stretched out on his back and there ain't a drop of blood in his veins.'

"We got up the stairs quicker than lightning after he'd told us that. We didn't know just what his crazy words meant, but the blood on his hands made us sure that something pretty terrible had happened. They kind of confirmed what we feared, sir—if you get what I mean."

Algernon nodded. "And you found Cinney—dead?"

"Worse than that, sir. All black and shrunken and looking as though he'd been wearing clothes about four sizes too large for him. His face was all *gone*, sir—all eaten away, like. We picked him up—he wasn't much heavier than a little boy—and laid him out on a bench in Corridor H. I never seen so much blood in my life—the floor was all slippery with it. And the big stone animal you had us carry down to Alcove K last night was all dripping with it, 'specially its trunk. It made me sort of sick. I never like to look at blood."

"You think someone attacked Cinney?"

"It looked that way, Mr. Harris. Like as if someone went for him with a knife. It must have been an awful big knife—a regular butcher's knife. That ain't a very nice way of putting it, sir, but that's how it struck me. Like as if someone mistook him for a piece of mutton."

"And what else did you find when you examined him?"

"We didn't do much examining. We just let him lie on the bench till we got through phoning for the police. Mr. Williamson did the talking, sir." A look of relief crept into the attendant's eyes. "The police said we wasn't to disturb the body further, which suited us fine. There wasn't one of us didn't want to give poor Mr. Cinney a wide berth."

"And what did the police do when they arrived?"

"Asked us about a million crazy questions, sir. Was Mr. Cinney disfigured in the war? And was Mr. Cinney in the habit of wearing a mask over his face? And had Mr. Cinney received any threatening letters from Chinamen or Hindoos? And when we told them no, they seemed to get kind of frightened. 'If it ain't murder,' they

said, 'we're up against something that ain't natural. But it's got
to be murder. All we have to do is get hold of the Chinaman.' "

Algernon didn't wait to hear more. Brushing the attendant
ungratefully aside he went dashing up the stairs three steps at a
time. Mr. Scollard followed with ashen face,

They were met in the upper corridor by a tall, loose-jointed
man in shabby, ill-fitting clothes who arrested their progress with
a scowl and a torrent of impatient abuse. "Where do you think
you're going?" he demanded. "Didn't I give orders that no one
was to come up here? I've got nothing to say to you. You're too
damn nosy. If you want the lowdown on this affair you've got to
wait outside till we get through questioning the attendants."

"See here," said Algernon impatiently. "This gentleman is president of the Museum and he has a perfect right to go where he
chooses."

The tall man waxed apologetic. "I thought you were a couple
of newspaper Johns," he murmured confusedly. "We haven't
anything even remotely resembling a clue, but those guys keep
popping up here every ten minutes to cross-examine us. They're
worse than prosecuting attorneys. Come right this way, sir."

He led them past a little knot of attendants and photographers
and fingerprint experts to the northerly part of the corridor.
"There's the body," he said, pointing toward a sheeted form which
lay sprawled on a low bench near the window. "I'd be grateful if
you gentlemen would look at the poor lad's face."

Algernon nodded, and lifting a corner of the sheet peered for
an instant intently into what remained of poor Cinney's countenance. Then, with a shudder, he surrendered his place to Mr.
Scollard.

It is to Mr. Scollard's credit that he did not cry out. Only the
trembling of his lower lip betrayed the revulsion which filled him.

"He was found on the floor in the corridor about two hours
ago," explained the detective. "But the guy who found him isn't
here. They've got him in a straitjacket down at Bellevue, and it
doesn't look as though he'll be much help to us. He was yelling
his head off about something he said came out of hell when they
put him in the ambulance. That's what drew the crowd."

"You don't think Williams could have done it?" murmured
Algernon.

"Not a chance. But he saw the murderer all right, and if we

can get him to talk. . . ." He wheeled on Algernon abruptly. "You seem to know something about this, sir."

"Only what we picked up downstairs. We had a talk with one of the attendants and he explained about Williams—and the Chinaman."

The detective's eyes glowed. "The Chinaman? What Chinaman? Is there a Chinaman mixed up in this? It's what I've been thinking all along, but I didn't have much to go on."

"I fear we're becoming involved in a vicious circle," said Algernon. "It was your Chinaman I was referring to. Willy said you were laboring under the impression that all you had to do to solve this distressing affair was to catch a Chinaman."

The detective shook his head. "It's not as simple as that," he affirmed. "We haven't any positive evidence that a Chinaman did it. It might have been a Jap or Hindoo or even a South Sea Islander. That is, if South Sea Islanders eat rice!"

"Rice?" Algernon stared at the detective incredulously.

"That's right. In a bowl with long sticks. I'm no authority on et-eternalogy, but it's my guess they don't use chopsticks much outside Asia."

He went into Alcove K and returned with a wooden bowl and two long splinters of wood. "All those dark spots near the rim are blood stains," he explained, as he surrendered the gruesome exhibits to Algernon. "Even the rice is all smeared with blood." Algernon shuddered and passed the bowl to Scollard, who almost dropped it in his haste to return it to the detective.

"Where did you find it?" the president spoke in a subdued whisper.

"On the floor in front of the big stone elephant. That's where Cinney was killed. There's blood all over the elephant—if it's supposed to be an elephant."

"It isn't, strictly speaking, an elephant," said Algernon.

"Well, whatever it is, it could tell us what Cinney's murderer looked like. I'd give the toes off my left foot if it could talk."

"It doesn't talk," said Algernon decisively.

"I wasn't wisecracking," admonished the detective. "I was simply pointing out that that elephant could give us the lowdown on a mighty nasty murder."

Algernon accepted the rebuke in silence.

"There ain't no doubt whatever that a Chinaman or Hindoo

or some crazy foreigner sneaked in here last night, set himself down in front of that elephant and began eating rice. Maybe he was in a church-going mood and mistook the beast for one of his heathen gods. It kind of looks like an oriental idol—the ferocious-looking kind you sometimes see in Chinatown store windows."

Algernon smiled ironically. "But unquestionably unique," he murmured.

The detective nodded. "Yeah. Larger and uglier-looking, but a heathen statue for all that. I bet it actually was worshipped once. Hindu . . . Chinese . . . I wouldn't know. But it sure has that look."

"Yes," admitted Algernon, "it is indubitably in the religious tradition. For all its hideousness it has all the earmarks of a quiescent Eastern divinity."

"There ain't anything more dangerous than interfering with an Oriental when he's saying his prayers," continued the detective. "I've been in Chinatown raids, and I know. Now here's what I think happened. Cinney is standing in the corridor and suddenly he hears the Chinaman muttering and mumbling to himself in the dark. He's naturally frightened and so he rushes in with his pocketlight where an angel would be fearing to tread. The light gets in the Chinaman's eyes and sets him off.

"It's like putting a match to a ton of TNT to throw a light on a Chinaman when he's squatting in the dark in a worshipful mood. So the Chinaman goes for the kid with a knife. He feels outraged in a religious way, isn't really himself, thinks he's avenging an insult to the idol."

Algernon nodded impatiently. "There may be something in your theory, sergeant. But there's a great deal it doesn't explain. What was it that Williams saw?"

"Nothing but Cinney lying dead in the corridor. Nothing but Cinney looking up at him without a face and that awful heathen animal looking down at him with blood all over its mouth."

Algernon stared. "Blood on its mouth?"

"Sure. All over its mouth, trunk and tusks. Never seen so much blood in my life. That's what Williams saw. I don't wonder it crumpled the kid up."

There was a commotion in the corridor. Someone was sobbing and pleading in a most fantastic way a few yards from where the three men were standing. The detective turned and shouted out a curt command. "Whoever that is, bring him here!"

Came an appalling, ear-harassing shriek and two plainclothesmen emerged around a bend in the corridor with a diminutive and weeping Oriental spread-eagled between their extended arms.

"The Chinaman!" muttered Scollard in amazement.

For a second the detective was too startled to move, and his immobility somehow emboldened the Chinese to break from his captors and prostrate himself on the floor at Algernon's feet.

"You are my friend," he sobbed. "You are a very good man. I saw you in green-fire dream. In dream when big green animals came down from mountain I saw you and Gautama Siddhartha. Big green animals all wanted blood—all very much wanted blood. In dream Gautama Siddhartha said: 'They want you! They have determined they make you all dark fire glue.'

"I said, 'No! *Please,*' I said. Then Gautama Siddhartha let fall jewel of wisdom. 'Go to *museum.* Go to big *museum* round block, and big green animal will eat you quick. He will eat you quick— before he make American man dark fire glue.'

"All night I have sat here. All night I said: 'Eat me. *Please!*' But big green animal slept till American man came. Then he moved. Very quickly he moved. He gave American man very bad hug. American man screamed and big green animal drank all American man's blood."

The little Oriental was sobbing unrestrainedly. Algernon stooped and lifted him gently to his feet. "What is your name?" he asked, to soothe him. "Where do you live?"

"I'm boss big laundry down street," murmured the Chinaman. "My name is Hsieh Ho. I am a good man, like you."

"Where did you go when—when the elephant came to life?"

The Chinaman's lower lip trembled convulsively. "I hid back of big white lady."

In spite of the gravity of the situation Algernon couldn't repress a smile. The "big white lady" was a statue of Venus Erycine and so enormous was it that it occupied almost the whole of Alcove K. It was a perfect sanctuary, but there was something ludicrously incongruous in a Chinaman's seeking refuge in such a place.

One of the detectives, however, confirmed the absurdity. "That's where we found him, sir. He was lying on his back, wailing and groaning and making faces at the ceiling. He's our man, all right.

We'll have the truth out of him in ten minutes."

The chief sergeant nodded. "You bet we will. Put the bracelets on him, Jim."

Reluctantly Algernon surrendered Hsieh Ho to his captors. "I suggest you treat him kindly," he said. "He had the misfortune to witness a ghastly and unprecedented exaggeration of what Eddington would call the random element in nature. But he's as destitute of criminal proclivities as Mr. Scollard here."

The detective raised his eyebrows. "I don't get it, sir. Are you suggesting we just hold him as a material witness?"

Algernon nodded. "If you try any of your revolting third-degree tactics on that poor little man you'll answer in court to my lawyer. Now, if you don't mind, I'll have a look at Alcove K."

The detective scowled. He wanted to tell Algernon to go to hell, but somehow the inflection of authority in the latter's voice glued the invective to his tongue, and with a surly shrug he escorted the group into the presence of Chaugnar Faugn.

Sanguinary baptism becomes some gods. Were the gracious figures of the Grecian pantheon to appear to us with blood upon their garments we should recoil in horror, but we should think the terrible Mithra or the heart-devouring Huitzilopochitli a trifle unconvincing if they came on our dreams untarnished by the ruddy vintage of sacrifice.

Algernon did not at first look directly at Chaugnar Faugn. He studied the tiled marble floor about the base of the idol and tried to make out in the gloom the precise spot where Cinney had lain. The attempt proved confusing. There were dark smudges on almost every other tile and they were nearly all of equal circumference.

"Right there is where we found the corpse," said the detective impatiently. "Right beneath the trunk of the elephant."

Algernon's blood ran cold. Slowly, very slowly, for he feared to confront what stood before him, he raised his eyes until they were level with the detective's shoulders. The detective's shoulders concealed a portion of Chaugnar Faugn, but all of the thing's right side and the extremity of its trunk was hideously visible to Algernon as he stared. He spoke no word. He did not even move. But all of the blood drained out of his lips, leaving them ashen.

Mr. Scollard was staring at his subordinate with frightened eyes. "You act as though—as though—good God, man, what is it?"

"It has moved its trunk!" Algernon's voice was vibrant with

horror. "It has moved its trunk since—since yesterday. And most hideously. I can not be mistaken. Yesterday it was vertical—today it is in a slightly upraised position."

Mr. Scollard gasped. "Are you sure?" he muttered. "Are you absolutely certain that the trunk wasn't in that position when the god arrived here?"

"Yes, yes. Not until today. In the excitement no one has noticed it, but if you will call the attendants—wait!"

The president had started to do that very thing, but Algernon's admonition brought him up short. "I shouldn't have suggested that," he murmured in Scollard's ear. "The attendants mustn't be questioned. It's all to unutterably ghastly and inexplicable and—and mad. We've got to keep it out of the papers, seek a solution secretly. I know someone who may be able to help us. The police can't. That's obvious."

The detective was staring at them pityingly. "You gentlemen better get out of here," he said. "You aren't used to sights like this. When I was new at this game I made a lot of mistakes. I could hardly stand the sight of a dead man, for instance. Used to hurry things along when there was no real need for haste, which is just about the worst mistake you can make at the preliminary examination stage."

With an effort Algernon mastered his agitation. "You're right, sergeant," he said. "Mr. Scollard and I realize that this business is a little too disturbing for sane contemplation. So we'll retire, as you suggest. But I must warn you again that you'd better think twice about treating poor Hsieh Ho as a convicted murderer."

In the corridor he drew Mr. Scollard aside and conversed for a moment urgently in a low voice. Then he approached the detective and handed him a card. "If you want me within the next few hours you'll find me at this address," he said. "Mr. Scollard is returning to his home in Brooklyn. You'll find his telephone number in the directory, but I hope you won't disturb him unless something really grave turns up."

The detective nodded and read aloud the address on Algernon's card. "Dr. Henry C. Imbert, F.R.S., F.A.G.S."

"A friend of yours?" he asked impertinently.

Algernon nodded. "Yes, sergeant. The foremost American ethnologist. Ever hear of him?"

To Algernon's amazement the sergeant nodded. "Yes. I got kind of interested in eternalogy once. I was on a queer case about two years ago. An old lady got bumped off by a poisoned arrow and we had him in for a powwow. He's clever all right. He gave us all the dope soon as he saw the corpse. Said a little negro had done it—one of those African pygmies you read about. We followed up the tip and caught the murderer just as he was giving the little fellow a cyanide cigarette to smoke. He was a shrewd Italian. He got the pygmy in Africa, hid him in a room down on Houston Street and sent him out to rob and bump off old ladies. He was as spry as a monkey and could shinny up a drainpipe on the side of a house in ten seconds. If it hadn't been for Imbert we'd never have got our hands on the guy that owned him."

Mr. Scollard and Algernon descended the stairs together. But in the vestibule they parted, the president proceeding down the still crowded outer steps in the direction of a bus whilst Algernon sought his office in Wing W.

"When Imbert sees this," Algernon murmured, as he extracted a photograph of Chaugnar Faugn from his chaotically littered desk, "he'll be the most disturbed ethnologist that this planet has harbored since the Pleistocene Age."

3

AN ARCHEOLOGICAL DIGRESSION

THE FIGURE is totally unfamiliar," said Doctor Imbert. "Nothing even remotely resembling it occurs in Asian or African mythology."

He scowled and returned the photograph to his youthful visitor, who deposited it on the arm of his chair.

"I confess," he continued, "that it puzzles and disturbs me. It's preposterously archeological, if you get what I mean. It isn't the sort of thing that one would—imagine."

Harris nodded. "I doubt if I could have imagined it from scratch. Without imaginative prompting or guidance from someone who had actually set eyes on it, it would be very difficult to conceive of anything so—so—"

"*Racial,*" put in Doctor Imbert. "I believe that is the word you were groping for. That *thing* is a symbolic embodiment of the massed imaginative heritage of an entire people. It's a composite—

like the Homeric epics or the Sphinx of Giza. It's the kind of art manifestation you would expect a primitive people to produce collectively. It's so perversely diabolical and contradictory in conception that one can scarcely conceive of a mere individual anywhere in the world deliberately sitting down and creating it out of his own imagination. I will concede that an unusually gifted artist might be *capable* of imagining it, but I doubt if such an obscenity would ever form in the human brain without a *raison d'etre*. And no individual living in a civilized state would experience the need, the desire to imagine such a thing, and least of all, to give it objective expression.

"Mental illness, of course, might account for it, but the so-called interpretative reveries of psychotics are nearly always of predictable nature. Grotesque and absurd as they may sometimes be, certain images occur in them again and again and these images are definitely meaningful. They follow prescribed patterns, are crude and distorted representations of familiar objects and people. The morbidities out of which they arise have been studied and classified and a psychiatrist who knows his business can usually decipher them. If you have ever examined a batch of drawings from a mental institution you will have noticed how the same motifs occur repeatedly and how utterly *unimaginative* such things are from a sane and sophisticated point of view.

"It is of course true that the folk creations of primitive peoples usually embody or symbolize definite human preoccupations, but more boldly and imaginatively, and occasionally they depart from the predictable to such an extent that even our expert is obliged to throw up his hands.

"I have always believed that most of the major and minor monstrosities that figure so conspicuously in the pantheons of barbarian races—feathered serpents, animal-headed priests, grimacing sphinxes, etc., are synthetic conceptions. Let us suppose, for instance, that a tribe of reasonably enlightened barbarians is animated by the unique social impulse of cooperative agriculture and is moved to embody its ideals in some colossal fetish designed to suggest both fertility and brotherhood—in, let us say, a great stone Magna Mater with arms outstretched to embrace all classes and conditions of men. Then let us suppose that cooperative agriculture falls into disrepute and the tribe becomes obsessed by dreams of martial conquest. What happens? To an obbligato of tomtoms and war drums the Mother Goddess is transfigured. A spear is placed between her extended arms, the expression of her face altered from benignity to ferocity, great gashes chiseled in her cheeks, red paint smeared on her arms, breasts and shoulders and her ears lopped off. Let another generation pass and the demoniac goddess of war will be transformed into something else— perhaps into a symbol of the most abandoned kind of debauchery.

"In a hundred years the original fetish will have become a monstrous caricature, a record in stone of the thoughts and emotions of generations of men.

"It is the business of the ethnologist and the archeologist to decipher such records, and if our scientist is sufficiently learned and diligent he can, as you know, supply a reason for every peculiarity of configuration. Competent scholars have traced, in a rough way, the advance or retrogression of racial groups in ethical and esthetic directions merely by studying and comparing their object of worship and there does not exist a more fruitful science than idolography.

"But occasionally our ethnologist encounters a nut that he cannot crack, a god or goddess so diabolical or grotesque or loathsome in conformation that it is impossible to link it associatively with even the most revolting of tribal retrogressions. It is a notorious fact that human races are less apt to advance than circle back on the course of evolution, and that idols and fetishes that were originally conceived in a comparatively noble spirit very often become, in the course of time, embodiments of the bestial and the obscene. Some of the degraded objects of worship now employed by African bushmen and Australian aborigines may conceivably have been considerably less revolting ten or fifteen thousand years ago. It is impossible to predict the depths to which a race may descend and the appalling transformation which may occur in its 'sacred' imagery.

"And so occasionally we encounter shapes that we scarcely like to speculate about, shapes so *complicatedly* vile that they haven't even analogous counterparts in comparative mythology. Your fetish is of that nature. It is, as I say, preposterously archeological and it differs unmistakably—although I am willing to concede a superficial resemblance—from the distorted dream images conjured up by psychotics and surrealistic artists. Only racial dissolution and decay extending over wide wastes of years could, in my opinion, account for such a ghastly anomaly."

He leaned forward and tapped Algernon significantly upon the knee. "You haven't told me its history," he admonished. "Reticence is an archeologist's prerogative, and in our work it is always an asset, but for a young man you're almost abnormally addicted to it."

Algernon blushed to the roots of his hair. "I'm seldom actually reticent," he said. "At the Museum they all think I talk too much. I've an exuberant, officious way at times that positively appalls Mr. Scollard. But this affair is so—so outside all normal experience that I've been dreading to tax your credulity with a résumé of it."

Doctor Imbert smiled. "Your books reveal that you are a very cautious and honest scholar," he said. "I don't believe I'd be inclined to question the veracity of whatever you may choose to tell me."

"Very well," said Algernon. "But I must entreat that you suspend judgement until you've heard all of the evidence. One can adduce rational explanations for each of the incidents I shall describe, but when one views them in the sequence in which they occurred they resolve themselves into a devastatingly hideous enigma."

Very tersely, without self-consciousness or affectation, Algernon then related all that he knew and all that he surmised and suspected about the thing whose image spread defilement on the paper before him.

Doctor Imbert heard him out in silence. But his eyes, as he listened, grew bright with horror.

"I doubt if I can help you," he said, when Algernon was done. "This thing transcends all of my experience."

There ensued a silence. Then Algernon said in a tone of desperate urgency, "But what *are* we to do? Surely you've something to suggest!"

Doctor Imbert rose shakingly to his feet. "I have—yes. I know someone who can, perhaps, help. He's a recluse, a psychic—a magnificient intellect obsessed by mysteries and mysticisms. I put little faith in such things—to me it's a degradation. But I'll take you to him. I'll take you anyway. God knows you're in trouble—that is obvious to me. And this man may be able to suggest something. Roger Little is his name. No doubt you've heard of him. He used to be a criminal investigator. A good one—a psychologist—discerning, erudite, shrewd—no mere detective-novel sleuth."

Algernon nodded understandingly. "Let us go to him at once," he said.

4

THE HORROR ON THE HILLS

IT WAS while Algernon and Doctor Imbert were journeying in the subway toward Roger Little's residence in the Borough of Queens that the Horror was announced to the world. An account of its initial manifestation had been flashed from Spain at midday to a great American news syndicate and all of the New York papers had something about it in their evening editions. The *News-Graphic*'s account was perhaps the most ominously disturbing in its implications. A copywriter on that enterprising sheet had surmised that the atrocities were distinguished by something outré, something altogether inexplicable, and by choosing his diction with unusual care he had succeeded in conveying to his unappreciative readers a tingling intimation of shockingness, of terror.

Beneath half-inch headlines which read:

HIDEOUS MASSACRE IN THE PYRENEES

he had written:

"The authorities are completely baffled. Who would wish to assassinate fourteen simple peasants? They were found at sundown on the mountain's crest. All in a row they lay, very still, very pale—very silent and pale beneath the soft Spanish sky. All about them stretched new-fallen snow and beside them on the white expanse were marks, peculiar and baffling. Men do not make footprints a yard wide. And why were all the victims laid so evenly in a row? What violence was it that could deprive them of their heads, drain the blood from their bodies and lay them stark and naked in a row upon the snow?"

5

"SOMEONE HAS been murdered and so you wish my advice," murmured Roger Little wearily. "You wish the advice of a retired and eccentric recluse, well on in years, who has ceased to traffic with crime. I am quoting from a profile which did not appear in the *New Yorker*." He was staring into the fire and the bright radiance which streamed roomward from the grate so illumed the sharp outlines of his profile that Algernon was struck silent with awe.

"A positively Satanic presence," he murmured, to himself. "The exact facsimile of a sorcerer from the *Malleus Maleficarum*. They would have burned him in the Fifteenth Century."

"Murder," resumed Little, "has become a shabbily synthetic art and even the most daring masterpieces of the contemporary school are composed of inferior ingredients clumsily combined. Men no longer live in fear of the unknown, and that utter and absymal disintegration of soul which the wise still call psychic evil no longer motivates our major atrocities. Anger, jealousy, and a paltry desire for material gain are pitiful emotional substitutes for the perverse and lonely egoism which inspired the great crimes of the Twelfth, Thirteenth and Fourteenth Centuries. When men killed with the deliberate certainty that they were jeopardizing their immortal souls and when the human body was regarded as a tabernacle for something more—or less—than human the crime of murder assumed epic and unholy proportions. The mere discovery of a mutilated cadaver in an age when men still believed in something—at least in *something*—filled everyone with terror and with awe. Men, women and children took refuge behind barricaded doors and the more devout fell upon their knees, crossed themselves, lighted candles and chanted exorcisms.

"But in this decadent age when a human being is assassinated society merely shrugs its shoulders and relinquishes the sequel to the police. What have the police to do with a sacrament of evil in our midst? The sense of virtually immitigable evil, of stark unreasoning fear which murder once left in its wake, and the intense esthetic enjoyment which certain individuals derived from merely studying such crimes as works of perverse and diabolical art have no parallels in contemporary experience. Hence it is that all modern murderers commit commonplace crimes—kill prosaically and almost indifferently without any suspicion that they are destroying more than lives of their unfortunate victims. And people go calmly about their business and are apparently not displeased to rub shoulders with the unholy ones in theaters, restaurants and subways!"

Algernon shifted excitedly in his chair. "But the problem we bring to you is enmeshed in the supernatural more hideously than any atrocity of the Ages of Faith. It transcends normal experience. If you will listen while I . . ."

Little shook his head. "I have written books—many books—describing dozens of instances of possession, of return, of immolation, of divination, and of transformation. I have confirmed the reality of the *concubitus daemonum;* have proved incontestably the existence of vampires, succubi and lamias, and I have slipped not too unwillingly, into the warm and clinging arms of women five centuries dead."

He shuddered. "But what I have experienced in this very room is no more than a flickering shadow, swift-passing and obscurely glimpsed, of the horror that lurks Godlessly in undimensioned space. In my dreams I have heard the nauseous piping of its glutinous flutes and I have seen, terribly for an instant, the nets and trawls with which it angles for men."

"If you are convinced that such a horror exists . . ." Algernon began, but Little would not let him finish.

"My books have left most of my readers totally unconvinced, for it would disturb them to believe that I am not mentally unbalanced," he went on quickly.

"Erudite and brilliant, but as mad as Bruno when he was burned at the stake for refusing to keep his speculations about the nature of the physical universe to himself."

He rose passionately to his feet. "So I've definitely renounced the collection and correlation of facts," he said. "Hereafter I shall embody my unique convictions in the eloquent and persuasive guise of a fable. I shall write a novel. The art of fiction as a purveyor of essential truth has innumerable advantages which detached and impersonal utterance must of necessity lack. The fictioneer can familiarize his readers *gradually* with new and startling doctrines and avoid shocking them into a precipitous retreat into the shell of old and conventional beliefs. He can prevent them from succumbing to prejudice before they have grasped one-quarter of the truths he is intent upon promulgating. Then, too, the artist can be so much more persuasive and eloquent than the scientist, and it can never be sufficiently emphasized that eloquence is never so effective in convincing men that certain things which are obviously false are momentarily true as it is in inducing them to discover that which is ultimately true beneath all the distortions of reality which can leave reason stranded in minds dominated by wishful thinking and a deep-seated fear of the unknown. Human wishes and desires are so eloquent in themselves that certainly some eloquence must be used in combating them. And that is why the mere scientist is so hopelessly at a loss when he seeks to convert others to what he himself believes to be the truth.

"He doesn't perceive that new truths must be presented to the human mind vividly, uniquely, as though one were initiating a mystery or instituting a sacrament, and that every failure to so present them decreases the likelihood that they will gain proponents, and that an entire civilization may pass away before any one arises with sufficient imagination and sufficient eloquence to take truths which have been enunciated once or twice coldly and forgotten because of the repugnance with which the common man regards fact barely recited and to clothe them in garments of terror and splendor and awe and so link them with far stars and the wind that moves above the waters and the mystery and strangeness that will be in all things until the end of time."

Little's eyes were shining. "I have determined," he said, "to thrust aside the veil as fearlessly as Blake must have done when he wrote of a new heaven and a new earth, to fashion a garment so mind-beguiling in its beauty that the ultimate revelation will remain cloaked until a spell has been cast which will permit of no drawing back, no craven surrender to fear."

He stopped suddenly, as if sobriety and an awareness of his surroundings had returned with a blood-rush to his entranced brain. "I have raved, no doubt. Like Blake, like Poe, like Gerard De Nerval I am always dreaming dreams, seeing visions. And to wordly men, calm and objective toward everyday realities, skeptical of all else, such visions, such glimpses are wholly incomprehensible. And you, no doubt, are inwardly pitying me and wondering how offended I would be if you should get up abruptly and plead a pressing engagement elsewhere. But if you only knew.

"There are things from *outside* watching always, secretly watching our little capers, our grotesque pranks. Men have disappeared. You're aware of that, aren't you? Men have disappeared within sight of their homes—at high noon, in the sunlight. Malignant and unknowable entities, *fishers* from outside have let down invisible tentacles, nets, trawls, and men and women have been caught up in a kind of pulsing darkness. A shadow seems to pass over them, to envelop them for an instant and then they are gone. And others have gone mad, witnessing such things.

"When a man ascends a flight of stairs it does not inevitably follow that he will arrive at the top. When a man crosses a street or a field or a public square it is not foreordained that he will reach the other side. *I have seen strange shadows in the sky.* Other worlds impinging on ours? I know that there are other worlds, but perhaps they do not *dimensionally* impinge. Perhaps from fourth-, fifth-, sixth-dimensional worlds things with forms invisible to us, with faces veiled to us, reach down and take—instantaneously, mercilessly. Feeding on us perhaps? Using our brains for fodder? A few have glimpsed the truth for a terrifying instant in dreams. But it takes infinite patience and self-discipline, and years of study to establish waking contact, even for an instant, with the bodiless shapes that flicker appallingly in the void a thousand billion light years beyond the remotest of the spiral nebulae.

"Yet I—can do this. And you," he laughed, "come to me with a little mundane murder."

For an instant there was silence in the room. Then Algernon stood up, his face brightened by the flames that were still crackling in the grate. "You say," he exclaimed, "a little mundane murder. But to me it is more hideous, more alien to sanity and the world we know than all your cosmic trawlers, and 'intrusions' from beyond."

Little shook his head. "No," he said. "I cannot believe that you are not exaggerating. It is so easy for men of exceptional intelligence to succumb at times to the fears, dreads, forebodings of ordinary men. Imaginative in a worldly sense, but blinder and dumber than clods cosmically. I am sure that I could unravel your puzzle with the most superficial layer of my waking mind, the little conscious mind that is so weak, so futile to grapple with anything more disturbing than what the body shall eat and drink and wear."

"If I had not seen," said Algernon, speaking very deliberately, "a stone thing shift its bulk, doing what the inanimate has never done in all the ages man has looked rationally upon it, I would have seriously doubted your sanity. It would be dishonest for me to pretend otherwise."

"A stone, you say, moved?" For the first time Little's interest quickened and a startled look came into his eyes.

"Yes, in the shape in which something—nature primeval perhaps, in eons primeval—shaped it. Moved in the night, unwatched by me. When Chaugnar Faugn . . ."

He stopped, was silent. For from his chair Little had sprung with a cry, his face bloodless, a cry of terror issuing from his thin lips.

"What is the matter?" gasped Doctor Imbert, and Algernon turned pale, not knowing what to make of so strange an occurrence. For Little seemed wholly undone, a mystic gone so completely mad that a violent outburst was only to be expected and might well be repeated, if he were not placed under immediate restraint. But at last he sank again into the chair from which he had so shockingly arisen, and a trace of color returned to his cheeks.

"Forgive me," he murmured brokenly. "Letting go like that was inexcusable. But when you mentioned Chaugnar Faugn I was for an instant mortally terrified."

He drew a deep breath. "The dream was so vivid that my mind rejected instantly a symbolic or allegorical interpretation. That name especially—Chaugnar Faugn. I was certain that something, somewhere, bore it—that the ghastliness that took Publius Libo on the high hills was an actuality, but not, I had hoped, an actuality for us. Something long past, surely, a horror of the ancient world that would never return to . . ." He broke off abruptly, seemingly lost in thought.

"Tell me about it," he entreated, after a moment.

With bloodless lips Algernon related once again the history of Chaugnar Faugn as it had been related to him by Ulman, enhancing a little its hideousness by half-guesses and surmises of his own. Little listened in tight-lipped silence, his face a mask, only the throbbing of the veins on his temples betraying the agitation which wracked him. As Algernon concluded, the clock on the mantel, a tall, negro-colored clock with wings on its shoulders and a great yellow ocean spider painted on its opalescent face, struck the hour: eleven even strokes pealed from it, shattering the stillness that had settled for an instant on the room. Algernon shivered, apprehensive at the lateness of the hour, fearful that in his absence Chaugnar Faugn might move again.

But now Little was speaking, striving painfully to keep his voice from sinking to a whisper.

"I had the dream last Halloween," he began, "and for detail, color and somber, brooding menace it surpasses anything of the kind I have experienced in recent years. It took form slowly, beginning as a nervous move from the atrium of my house into a scroll-lined library to escape the sound of a fountain, and continuing as an earnest and friendly argument with a stout, firm-lipped man of about thirty-five, with strong, pure Roman features and the rather cumbersome equipment of a *legatus* in active military service. Impressions of identity and locale were so nebulous and gradual in their unfoldment as to be difficult to trace to a source, but they seem in retrospect to have been present from the first.

"The place was not Rome, nor even Italy, but the small provincial municipium of Calagurris on the south bank of the Iberus In Hispania Citerior. It was in the Republican age, because the province was still under a senatorial proconsul instead of a *legatus* of the Imperator. I was a man of about my own waking age and build. I was clad in a civilian toga of yellowish color with the two thin reddish stripes of the equestrian order. My name was L. Caelius Rufus and my rank seemed to be that of a provincial quaestor. I was definitely an Italian-born Roman, the province of Calagurris being alien, colonial soil to me. My guest was Cnaeus Balbutius, *legatus* of the XII Legion, which was permanently encamped just outside the town on the riverbank. The home in which I was receiving him was a suburban villa on a hillside south of the compact section, and it overlooked both town and river.

"The day before I had received a worried call from one Tib. Annaeus Mela, edile of the small town of Pompelo, three days' march to the north in the territory of the Vascones at the foot of the mysterious Pyrenees. He had been to request Balbutius to spare him a cohort for a very extraordinary service on the night of the Kalends of November and Balbutius had emphatically refused. Therefore, knowing me to be acquainted with P. Scribonius Libo, the proconsul at Tarraco, he had come to ask me to lay his case by letter before that official. Mela was a dark, lean man of middle age, of presentable Roman features but with the coarse hair of a Celtiberian.

"It seems that there dwelt hidden in the Pyrenees a strange race of small dark people unlike the Gauls and Celtiberians in speech and features, who indulged in terrible rites and practices twice every year, on the Kalends of Maius and November. They lit fires on the hilltops at dusk, beat continuously on strange drums and horribly all through the night. Always before these orgies people would be found missing from the village and none of them were ever known to return. It was thought that they were stolen for sacrificial purposes, but no one dared to investigate, and eventually the semi-annual loss of villagers came to be regarded as a regular tribute, like the seven youths and maidens that Athens was forced to send each year to Crete for King Minos and the Minotaur.

"The tribal Vascones and even some of the semi-Romanized cottagers of the foothills were suspected by the inhabitants of Pompelo of being in league with the strange dark folk—*Miri Nigri* was the name used in my dream. These dark folk were seen in Pompelo only once a year—in summer, when a few of their number would come down from the hills to trade with the merchants. They seemed incapable of speech and transacted business by signs.

"During the preceding summer the small folk had come to trade as usual—five of them—but had became involved in a general scuffle when one of them had attempted to torture a dog for pleasure in the forum. In this fighting two of them had been killed and the remaining three had returned to the hills with evil faces. Now it was autumn and *the customary quota of villagers had not disappeared.* It was not normal for the Miri Nigri thus to spare Pompelo. Clearly they must have reserved the town for some terrible doom, which they would call down on their unholy Sabbathnight as they drummed and howled and danced outrageously on the mountain's crest. Fear walked through Pompelo and the edile Mela had come to Calagurris to ask for a cohort to invade the hills on the sabbath night and break up the obscene rites before the ceremony might be brought to a head. But Balbutius had laughed at him and refused. He thought it poor policy for the Roman administration to meddle in local quarrels. So Mela had been obliged to come to me. I enheartened him as best I could, and promised help, and he returned to Pompelo at least partly reassured.

"Before writing the proconsul I had thought it best to argue with Balbutius himself, so I had been to see him at the camp, found him out and left word with a centurion that I would welcome a call from him. Now he was here and had reiterated his belief that we ought not complicate our administration by arousing the resentment of the tribesmen, as we undoubtedly would if we attempted to suppress a rite with which they were obviously in ill-concealed sympathy.

"I seemed to have read considerable about the dark rites of certain unknown and wholly barbaric races, for I recall feeling a sense of monstrous impending doom and trying my best to induce Balbutius to put down the sabbath. To his objections I replied that it had never been the custom of the Roman people to be swayed by the whims of the barbarians when the fortunes of Roman citizens were in danger and that he ought not to forget the status of Pompelo as a legal colony, small as it was. That the good-will of the tribal Vascones was little to be depended upon at best, and that the trust and friendship of the Romanized townsfolk, in whom was more than a little of our own blood after three generations of colonization, was a matter of far greater importance to the smooth working of that provincial government on which the security of the Roman imperium primarily rested. Furthermore, that I had reason to believe, from my studies, that the apprehensions of the Pompelonians were disturbingly well-founded, and that there was indeed brewing in the high hills a monstrous doom which it would ill become the traditions of Rome to countenance. That I would be surprised to encounter laxity in the representatives of those whose ancestors had not hesitated to put to death large numbers of Roman citizens for participation in the orgies of Bacchus and had ordered engraved on public tablets of bronze the *Senatus Consultum de Bacchanalibus.*

"But I could not influence Balbutius. He went away courteously but unmoved. So I at once took a reed pen and wrote a letter to the proconsul Libo, sealing it and calling for a wiry young slave—a Greek called Antipater—to take it to Tarraco.

"The following morning I went out on foot, down the hill to the town and through the narrow block-paved streets with high whitewashed dead-walls and gaudily painted shops with awnings.

The crowds were very vivid. Legionaries of all races, Roman colonists, tribal Celtiberi, Romanized natives, Romanized and Iberized Carthaginians, mongrels of all sorts. I spoke to only one person, a Roman named AEbutius, about whom I recall nothing. I visited the camp—a great area with an earthen wall ten feet high and streets of wooden huts inside, and I called at the *praetorium* to tell Balbutius that I had written the proconsul. He was still pleasant but unmoved. Later I went home, read in the garden, bathed, dined, talked with the family and went to bed—having, a little later, a nightmare *within the dream* which centered about a dark terrible desert with cyclopean ruins of stones and a malign presence over all.

"About noon the next day—I had been reading in the garden— the Greek returned with a letter and enclosure from Libo. I broke the seal and read: 'P. SCRIBONIVS L. CAELIO. S. D. SI. TV. VALES. VALEO. QVAE. SCRIPSISTI. AVDIVI. NEC. ALIAS. PVTO'.

"In a word, the proconsul agreed with me—had known about the Miri Nigri himself—and enclosed an order for the advance of the cohort to Pompelo at once, by forced marches, in order to reach the doom-shadowed town on the day before the fatal Kalends. He requested me to accompany it because of my knowledge of what the mysterious rites were whispered to be, and furthermore declared his design of going along himself, saying that he was even then on the point of setting out and would be in Pompelo before we could be.

"I lost not a second in going personally to the camp and handing the orders to Balbutius, and I must say he took his defeat gracefully. He decided to send Cohors V, under Sextus Asellius, and presently summoned that *legatus*—a slim, supercilious youth with frizzed hair and a fashionable fringe of beard-growth on his under jaw. Asellius was openly hostile to the move but dared not disregard orders. Balbutius said he would have the cohort at the bridge across the Iberus in an hour and I rushed home to prepare for the rough day and night march.

"I put on a heavy paenula and ordered a litter with six Illyrian bearers, and reached the bridge ahead of the cohort. At last, though, I saw the silver eagles flashing along the street to my left, and Balbutius—who had decided at the last moment to go along himself—rode out ahead and accompanied my litter ahead of the troops as we crossed the bridge and struck out over the plains toward the mystic line of dimly glimpsed violet hills. There was no long sleep during all the march, but we had naps and brief halts and bites of lunch—cakes and cheese. Balbutius usually rode by my litter in conversation (it was infantry, but he and Asellius were mounted) but sometimes I read—M. Porcius Cato *De Re Rustica*, and a hideous manuscript in Greek, which made me shudder even to touch or look at but of which I can not remember a single word.

"The second morning we reached the whitewashed houses of Pompelo and trembled at the fear that was on the place. There was a wooden amphitheater east of the village, and a large open plain on the west. All the immediate ground was flat, but the Pyrenees rose up green and menacing on the north, looking nearer than they were. Scribonius Libo had reached there ahead of us with his secretary, Q. Trebellius Pollio, and he and the edile Mela greeted us in the forum. We all—Libo, Pollio, Mela, Balbutius, Asellius and I—went into the curia (an excellent new building with a Corinthian portico) and discussed ways and means, and I saw that the proconsul was with me heart and soul.

"But Balbutius and Asellius continued to argue and at times the discussion grew very tense. Libo was an utterly admirable old man, and he insisted on going into the hills with the rest of us and seeing the awful revelations of the night. Mela, ghastly with fright, promised horses to those of us who were not mounted. He had pluck—for he meant to go himself.

"It is impossible even to suggest the stark and ghastly terror which hung over this phase of the dream.

"Surely there never was such evil as that which brooded over the accursed town as the sinking sun threw long menacing shadows amidst the reddening afternoon. The legionaries fancied they heard the rustling of stealthy, unseen and ominously deliberate presences in the black encircling woods. Occasionally a torch had to be lighted momentarily in order to keep the frightened three hundred together, but for the most part it was a dreadful scramble through the dark. A slit of northern sky was visible ahead between the terrible, cliff-like slopes that encompassed us and I marked the chair of Cassiopeia and the golden powder of the Via Lactea. Far, far ahead and above and appearing to merge imperceptibly into the heavens, the lines of remoter peaks could be discerned, each capped by a sickly point of unholy flame. And still the distant, hellish drums pounded incessantly on.

"At length the route grew too steep for the horses and the six of us who were mounted were forced to take to our feet. We left the horses tethered to a clump of scrub oaks and stationed ten men to guard them, though heaven knows it was no night nor place for petty thieves to be abroad! And then we scrambled on— jostling, stumbling and sometimes climbing with our hands' help up places little short of perpendicular. Suddenly a sound behind us made every man pause as if hit by an arrow. It was from the horses we had left, and it did not cease. They were not neighing but *screaming.* They were screaming, mad with some terror beyond any this earth knows. No sound came up from the men we had left with them. Still they screamed on, and the soldiers around us stood trembling and whimpering and muttering fragments of a prayer to Rome's gods, and the gods of the East and the gods of the barbarians.

"Then there came a sharp scuffle and yell from the front of the column which made Asellius call quaveringly for a torch. There was a prostrate figure weltering in a growing and glistening pool of blood and we saw by the faint flare that it was the young guide Accius. He had killed himself because of the sound he had heard. He, who had been born and bred at the foot of those terrible hills and had heard dark whispers of their secrets, knew well why the horses had screamed. And because he knew, he had snatched a sword from the scabbard of the nearest soldier—the centurion P. Vibulanus—and had plunged it full-length into his own breast.

"At this point pandemonium broke loose because of something noticed by such of the men as were able to notice anything at all. *The sky had been snuffed out.* No longer did Cassiopeia and the Via Lactea glimmer betwixt the hills, but stark blackness loomed behind the continuously swelling fires on the distant peaks. And still the horses screamed and the far-off drums pounded hideously and incessantly on.

"Cackling laughter broke out in the black woods of the vertical slopes that hemmed us in and around the swollen fires of the distant peaks we saw prancing and leaping the awful and cyclopean silhouettes of things that were neither men nor beasts, but fiendish amalgams of both—things with huge flaring ears and long waving trunks that howled and gibbered and pranced in the skyless night. And a cold wind coiled purposively down from the empty abyss, winding sinuously about us till we started in fresh panic and struggled like Laocoön and his sons in the serpent's grasp.

"There was terrible sights in the light of the few shaking torches. Legionaries trampled one another to death and screamed more hoarsely than the horses far below. Of our immediate party Trebellius Pollio had long vanished, and I saw Mela go down beneath the heavy caligae of a gigantic Aquitanian. Balbutius had gone mad and was grinning and simpering out an old Fescennine verse recalled from the Latin countryside of his boyhood. Asellius tried to cut his own throat, but the sentient wind held him powerless, so that he could do nothing but scream and scream and scream above the cackling laughter and the screaming horses and the distant drums and the howling colossal shapes that capered about the demon-fires on the peaks.

"I myself was frozen to the helplessness of a statue and could not move or speak. Only old Publius Libo the proconsul was strong enough to face it like a Roman—Publius Scribonius Libo, who had gone through the Jugurthine and Mithridatic and social wars—Publius Libo three times praetor and three times consul of the republic, in whose atrium stood the ancestral forms of a hundred heroes. He and he alone had the voice of a man and of a general and triumphator. I can see him now in the dimming light of those horrible torches, among that fear-struck stampede of the doomed. I can hear him still as he spoke his last words, gathering up his toga with the dignity of a Roman and a consul: '*Malitia vetus—malitia vetus est—venit—tandem venit. . . .*'

"And then the wooded encircling slopes burst forth with louder cackles and I saw that they were slowly moving. The hills—the terrible living hills—were closing up upon their prey. The Miri Nigri had called their terrible gods out of the void.

"Able to shriek at last, I awoke in a sea of cold perspiration.

"Calagurris, as you probably know, is a real and well-known town of Roman Spain, famed as the birthplace of the rhetorician Quintilianus. Upon consulting a classical dictionary I found Pompelo also to be real, and surviving today as the Pyrenean village of Pampelona."

He ceased speaking, and for a moment the three men were silent. Then Algernon said: "The Chinaman had a strange dream

too. He spoke of the horror on the mountains—of great things
that came clumping down from the hills at nightfall."

Little nodded. "Mongolians as a rule are extremely psychic,"
he said. "I have known several whose clairvoyant gifts were superior
to a yoga adept's often astounding feats of precognition."

"And you think that Hsieh Ho's dream was a prophecy?"
whispered Imbert.

"I do. Some monstrous *unfettering* is about to take place. That
which for two thousand years has lain somnolent will stir again
and the 'great things' will descend from their frightful lair on the
Spanish hills drawn cityward through the will of Chaugnar Faugn.
We are in propinquity to the primal, hidden horror that festers
at the root of being, with the old, hidden loathsomeness which
the Greeks and Romans veiled under the symbolical form of a
man-beast—*the feeder, the all.* The Greeks knew, for the horror
left its lair to ravage, striding eastward in the dawn across Europe,
wading waist-deep in the dark Ionian seas, looming monstrous at
nightfall over Delos, and Samothrace and far-off Crete. A nimbus
of starfoam engirdled its waist; suns, constellations gleamed in its
eyes. But its breath brought madness, and its embrace, death. The
feeder—the all."

The telephone bell at Little's elbow was jangling disconcertingly.
Stretching forth a tremulous hand he grasped the receiver firmly
and laid it against his cheek. "Hello," he whispered into the
mouthpiece. "What is it? Who is speaking?"

"From the Manhattan Museum." The words smote ominously
upon his ear. "Is Mr. Algernon Harris there? I phoned Doctor
Imbert's house and they gave me this number."

"Yes, Harris is here." Little's voice was vibrant with apprehension. "I'll call him."

He turned the instrument over to Algernon and sank back
exhaustedly in his chair. For a moment the latter conversed in a
low tone; then an expression of stunned incredulity appeared on
his face. His hand shook as he put back the receiver and tottered
toward the fireplace. For an instant he stood staring intensely into
the coals, his fingers gripping the mantel's edge so tightly that his
knuckles showed white. When he turned there was a look of utter
consternation in his eyes.

"Chaugnar Faugn has disappeared," he cried. "Chaugnar Faugn
has left the museum. No one saw him go and the idiot who

phoned thinks that a thief removed him. Or possibly one of the attendants. But *we* know how unlikely that is."

"I'm afraid we do," Little said, grimly. "I am to blame." Algernon went on quickly. "I should have insisted they patrol the alcove. I should have at least explained to them that someone might try to steal Chaugnar Faugn, even if Ulman's story had to be kept from them."

He shook his head in helpless frustration.

"No . . . no . . . that would have done no good. A watchman would have been utterly impotent to cope with such a horror. Chaugnar Faugn would have destroyed him hideously in an instant. And now it is loose in the streets!"

He walked to the window and stared across the glittering harbor at the darkly looming skyline of lower Manhattan. "It is loose over there," he cried, raising his arm and pointing. "It is crouching in the shadows somewhere, alert and waiting, preparing to . . ." He broke off abruptly, as if the vision his mind had conjured up was too ghastly to dwell upon.

Little rose and laid a steadying hand on Algernon's arm. "I haven't said I couldn't help," he said. "Though Chaugnar Faugn is a very terrible menace it isn't quite as omnipotent as Ulman thought. It and its brothers are incarnate manifestations of a very ancient, a very malignant hyperdimensional entity. Or call it a principle, if you wish—a principle so antagonistic to life as we know it that it becomes a spreading blight, as destructive as a nest of cancer cells would be if cancer could be transplanted by surgical means into healthy tissue, and continue to grow and proliferate until every vestige of healthy tissue has been destroyed. But it is a cancer whose growth I can at least retard. And if I am successful I can send it back to its point of origin beyond the galactic universe, can cut it asunder forever from our three-dimensional world. Had I known that the horror still lurked in the Pyrenees I should have gone, months ago, to *send it back*. Yes, even though the thought of it now fills me with a loathing unspeakable, I should have gone.

"I am not," he continued, "a merely theoretical dreamer. Though I am by temperament disposed toward speculations of a mystical nature, I have forged a very concrete and effective weapon to combat the cosmic malignancies. If you'll step into my laboratory I'll show you something which should restore your confidence in the experimental capacity of the human mind when there is but one choice confronting it—to survive or go down forever into everlasting night and darkness."

6

THE TIME-SPACE MACHINE

ROGER LITTLE'S laboratory was illumed by a single bluish lamp imbedded in the concrete of its sunken floor. An infinite diversity of mechanisms lined the walls and sprawled their precise lengths on long tables and dangled eerily from hooks set in the high, domed ceiling; mechanisms aglitter in blue-lit seclusion, a strange, bizarre foreglimpse into the alchemy and magic of a far-distant future, with spheres and condensers and gleaming metal rods in lieu of stuffed crocodiles and steaming elixirs.

All of the contrivances were arresting, but one was so extraordinary in size and complexity that it dominated the others and riveted Algernon's attention. He seemed unable to drag his gaze from the thing. It was a strange agglomeration of metallic spheres and portions of spheres, of great bluish globes surrounded by tiny clusters of half-globes and quarter-globes, whose surfaces converged in a most fantastic way. And from the globes there sprouted at grotesque angles metallic crescents with converging tips.

To Algernon's excited imagination the thing wore a quasi-reptilian aspect. "It's like a toad's face," he muttered. "Bulbous and bestial."

Little nodded. "It's a triumph of mechanical ugliness, isn't it? Yes it would have been deified in Ancient Greece—by Archimedes especially. He would have exalted it above all his Conoids and Parabolas."

"What function does it perform?" asked Algernon.

"A sublime one. It's a time-space machine. But I'd rather not discuss its precise function until I've shown you how it works. I want you to study its face as it waxes non-Euclidean. When you've glimpsed a fourth-dimensional figure you'll be prepared to concede, I think, that the claims I make for it are not extravagant. I know of no more certain corrective for an excess of skepticism. I was the *Critique of Pure Reason* personified until I looked upon a *skinned sphere*—then I grew very humble, reverent toward the great *Suspected*.

"Watch now." He reached forward, grasped a switch and with a swift downward movement of his right arm set the machine in motion. At first the small spheres and the crescents revolved quickly and the large spheres slowly; then the large spheres literally spun while the small spheres lazed, and then both small spheres and large spheres moved in unison. Then the spheres stopped altogether, but only for an instant, while something of movement seemed to flow into them from the revolving crescents. Then the crescents stopped and the spheres moved, in varying tempo, faster and faster, and their movement seemed to flow back into the crescents. Then both crescents and spheres began to move in unison, faster and faster and faster, until the entire mass seemed to merge into a shape paradoxical, outrageous, unthinkable—a sphenoid with a non-Euclidean face, a geometric blasphemy that was at once isosceles and equilateral, convex and concave.

Algernon stared in horror. "What in God's name is that?" he cried.

"You are looking on a fourth-dimensional figure," said Little soothingly. "Steady now."

For an instant nothing happened; then a light, greenish, blinding, shot from the center of the crazily distorted figure and streamed across the opposite wall, limning on the smooth cement a perfect circle.

But only for a second was the wall illumed. With an abrupt movement Little shot the lever upward and its radiance dimmed, and vanished. "Another moment, and that wall would have crumbled away," he said.

With fascination Algernon watched the outrageous sphenoid grow indistinct, watched it blur and disappear amidst a resurgence of spheres.

"That light," cried Little exultantly, "will send Chaugnar Faugn back through time. It will reverse its decadent *randomness*—disincarnate and disembody it, and send it back forever."

"But I don't understand," murmured Algernon. "What do you mean by *randomness*."

"I mean that this machine can work havoc with entropy!" There was a ring of exaltation in Little's voice.

"Entropy?" Algernon scowled. "I'm not sure that I understand.

I know what entropy is in thermodynamics, of course, but I'm not sure . . ."

"I'll explain," said Little. "You are of course familiar with the A B C's of Einsteinian physics and are aware that time is *relatively* arrowless, that the sequence in which we view events in nature is not a cosmic actuality and that our conviction that we are going somewhere in time is a purely human illusion conditioned by our existence on this particular planet and the limitations which our five senses impose upon us. We divide time into past, present and future, but in reality an event's sequence in time depends wholly on the position in space from which it is viewed. Events which occurred thousands of years ago on this planet haven't as yet taken place to a hypothetical observer situated billions and billions of light years remote from us. Thus, cosmically speaking, we can not say of an event that it has happened and will never happen again or that it is about to happen and has never happened before, because "before" to us is "after" to intelligences situated elsewhere in space and time.

"But though our familiar time-divisions are purely arbitrary there is omnipresent in nature a principle called entropy which, as Eddington has pointed out, equips time with a kind of empirical arrow. The entire universe appears to be 'running down.' It is the consensus of astronomical opinion that suns and planets and electrons are constantly breaking up, becoming more and more *disorganized*. Billions of years ago some mysterious dynamic, which Sir James Jeans has likened to the Finger of God, streamed across primeval space and created the universe of stars in a state of almost perfect integration, welded them into a system so highly organized that there was only the tiniest manifestation of the random element anywhere in it. The random element in nature is the uncertain element—the principle which brings about disorganizations, disintegration, decay.

"Let us suppose that two mechanical men, robots, are tossing a small ball to and fro, to and fro. The process may go on indefinitely, for the mechanical creatures do not tire and there is nothing to make the ball swerve from its course. But now let us suppose that a bird in flight collides with the ball, sends it spinning so that it misses the hand of the receiving robot. What happens? Both robots begin to behave grotesquely. Missing the ball, their arms sweep through the empty air, making wider and wider curves and they stagger forward perhaps, and collapse in each other's arms. The random, the uncertain element has entered their organized cosmos and they have ceased to function.

"This tendency of the complex to disintegrate, of the perfectly-balanced to run amuck, is called entropy. It is entropy that provides time with an arrow and, disrupting nebulae, plays midwife to the birth of planets from star-wombs incalculable. It is entropy that cools great orbs, hotter than Betelgeuse, more fiery than Arcturus through all the outer vastnesses, reducing them to sterility, to whirling motes of chaos.

"It is the random element that is slowly breaking up, destroying the universe of stars. In an ever widening circle, with an ever increasing malignancy—if one may ascribe malignancy to a force, a tendency—it works its awful havoc. It is analogous to a grain of sand dropped into one of the interstices of a vast and intricate machine. The grain creates a small disturbance which in turn creates a larger one, and so on *ad infinitum.*

"And with every event that has occurred on this earth since its departure from the sun there has been an increase of the random element. Thus we can legitimately 'place' events in time. Events which occurred tens of thousands of years ago may be happening *now* to intelligences situated elsewhere, and events still in the offing, so to speak, may exist already in another dimension of space-time. But if an earth-event is very disorganized and very decadent in its contours even our hypothetical distant observer would know that it has occurred very late in the course of cosmic evolution and that a series of happier events, with less of the random element in them, must have preceded it in time. In brief, that sense of time's passing which we experience in our daily lives is due to our intuitive perception that the structure of the universe is continuously breaking down. Everything that 'happens,' every event, is an objective manifestation of matter's continuous and all-pervasive decay and disintegration."

Algernon nodded. "I think I understand. But doesn't that negate all that we have been taught to associate with the word 'evolution?' It means that not advancement but an *inherent* degeneration has characterized all the processes of nature from the beginning of time. Can we apply it to man? Do you mean to suggest . . ."

Little shrugged. "One can only speculate. It may be that medieval theology wasn't so very wrong after all—that old Augustine and the Angelic Doctor and Abelard and the others surmised correctly, that man was once akin to the angels and that he joined himself to nature's decay through a deliberate rejection of heaven's grace. It may be that by some mysterious and incomprehensibly perverse act of will he turned his face from his Maker and let evil pour in upon him, made of himself a magnet for all the malevolence that the cosmos holds. There may have been more than a little truth in Ulman's identification of Chaugnar with the Lucifer of medieval myth."

"Is this," exclaimed Imbert reproachfully, "a proper occasion for a discussion of theology?"

"It isn't," Little acknowledged. "But I thought it desirable to outline certain—possibilities. I don't want you to imagine that I regard the intrusion of Chaugnar Faugn into our world as a scientifically explicable occurrence in a facilely dogmatic sense."

"I don't care how you regard it," affirmed Algernon, "so long as you succeed in destroying it utterly. I am a profound agnostic as far as religious concepts are concerned. But the universe is mysterious enough to justify divergent speculations on the part of intelligent men as to the ultimate nature of reality."

"I quite agree," Little said. "I was merely pointing out that modern science alone has very definite limitations."

"And yet you propose to combat this . . . this horror with science," exclaimed Imbert.

"With a concrete embodiment of the concepts of transcendental mathematics," corrected Little. "And such concepts are merely empirically scientific. I am aware that science may be loosely defined as a systematized accumulation of tendencies and principles, but classically speaking, its prime function is to convey some idea of the nature of reality by means of an inductive logic. Yet our mathematical physicist has turned his face from induction as resolutely as did the medieval scholastics in the days of the Troubadours. He insists that we must start from the universal assumption that we can never know positively the real nature of anything, and that whatever 'truth' we may deduce from empirical generalities will be chiefly valuable as a kind of mystical guidepost, at best merely roughly indicative of the direction in which we are traveling; but withal, something of a sacrament and therefore superior to the dogmatic 'knowledge' of Nineteenth Century science. The speculations of mathematical physicists today are more like poems and psalms than anything else. They embody concepts wilder and more fantastic than anything in Poe or Hawthorne or Blake."

He stepped forward and seized the entropy-reversing machine by its globular neck. "Two men can carry it very easily," he said, as he lifted it a foot from the floor by way of experiment. "We can train it on Chaugnar Faugn from a car."

"If it keeps to the open streets," interjected Algernon. "We can't follow it up a fire-escape or into the woods in a car."

"I'd thought of that. It could hide itself for days in Central Park or Inwood or Van Cortland Park or the wider stretches of woodland a little further to the north but still close to the city. But we won't cross that bridge until we come to it." His expression was tense, but he spoke with quiet deliberation. "We could dispense with the car in an emergency," he said. "Two men could advance fairly rapidly with the machine on a smooth expanse.

"We must make haste," he continued, after a moment. "It's my chauffeur's day off, but I'll take a taxi down to the garage and get the car myself." He turned to Algernon. "If you want to help, locate Chaugnar Faugn."

Algernon stared. "But how . . ." he gasped.

"It shouldn't be difficult. Get in touch with the police—Assistance and Ambulance Division. Ask if they've received any unusually urgent calls, anything of a sensational nature. If Chaugnar has slain again they'll know about it."

He pointed urgently toward a phone in the corner and strode from the laboratory.

7

A CURE FOR SKEPTICISM

When Algernon had completed his phone call he lit a cigarette very calmly and deliberately and crossed to where Doctor Imbert was standing. Only the trembling of his lower lip betrayed the agitation he was having difficulty in controlling. "There have been five emergency calls," he said, "all from the midtown section— between Thirty-fifth and Forty-eighth Streets."

Imbert grew pale. "And—and deaths?"

Algernon nodded. "And deaths. Two of the ambulances have just returned."

"How many were killed?"

"They don't know yet. There were five bodies in the first ambulance—three men, a woman and a little girl—a negress. All horribly mutilated. They've gone wild over there. The chap who spoke to me wanted to know what I knew, why I had phoned—he shouted at me, broke down and sobbed."

"God!"

"There's nothing we can do till Little gets back," Algernon said.

"And then? What do you suppose we can do then?"

"The machine . . ." Algernon began and stopped. He couldn't endure putting the way he felt about Little's machine, and the doubts he had entertained concerning it into words. It was necessary to believe in the machine, to have confidence in Little's sagacity—supreme confidence. It would have been disastrous to doubt in such a moment that a blow would eventually be struck, that Little and his machine together would dispose, forever, of the ghastly menace of Chaugnar Faugn. But to defend such a faith rationally, to speak boldly and with confidence of a mere intuitive conviction was another matter.

"You know perfectly well that Little's mentally unbalanced," affirmed Imbert, "that it would be madness to credit his assertions." He gestured toward the machine. "That thing is merely a mechanical hypnotizer. Ingenious, I concede—it can induce twilight sleep with a rapidity I wouldn't have thought possible—but it is quite definitely three-dimensional. It brings the subconscious to the fore, the subconscious that believes everything it is told, induces temporary somnolence while Imbert whispers: 'You are gazing on a fourth-dimensional figure. You are gazing on a fourth-dimensional figure.' Such deceptions aren't difficult to implant when the mind is in a dreamlike state."

"I'd rather not discuss it," murmured Algernon. "I can't believe the figure we saw was wholly a deception. It was too ghastly and unbelievable. And remember that we both saw the same figure. I was watching you at the time—you looked positively ill. And mass hypnotism is virtually an impossibility. You ought to know that. No two men will respond to suggestion in the same way. We *both* saw a four-dimensional figure—an outrageous figure."

"But how do you know we both saw the same figure? We may

easily have responded differently to Little's suggestion. Group hypnotism is possible in that sense. I saw something decidedly disturbing and so did you, but that doesn't prove that we weren't hypnotized."

"I'll convince you that we weren't," exclaimed Algernon. "A time-space machine of this nature isn't theoretically inconceivable, for physicists have speculated on the possibility of reversing entropy in isolated portions of matter for years. Watch now!"

Deliberately he walked to the machine and shot the lever upward.

8

WHAT HAPPENED IN THE LABORATORY

ALGERNON RAISED himself on his elbow and stared in horror at the gaping hole in the wall before him. It was a great circular hole with jagged edges and through it the skyline of lower Manhattan glimmered nebulously, like an etching under glass. His temples throbbed painfully; his tongue was dry and swollen and adhered to the roof of his mouth.

Someone was standing above him. Not Imbert, for Imbert wore spectacles. And this man's face was destitute of glitter, a blurred oval faultlessly white. Confusedly Algernon recalled that Little did not wear spectacles. This, then, was Little. Little, not Imbert. It was coming back now. He had sought to convince Imbert that the machine wasn't a mechanical hypnotizer. He had turned it on and then—Good God! What had happened then? Something neither of them had anticipated. An explosion! But first for an instant they had seen the figure. And the light. And he and Imbert had been too frightened—too frightened to turn it off. How very clear it was all becoming. They had stood for an instant facing the wall, too utterly bewildered to turn off the light. And then Little had entered the room, and had shouted a warning—a frenzied warning.

"Help me, please," exclaimed Algernon weakly.

Little bent and gripped him by the shoulders. "Steady, now," he commanded, as he guided him toward a chair. "You're not hurt. You'll be all right in a moment. Imbert, too, is all right. A piece of plaster struck him in the temple, gave him a nasty cut, but he'll be quite all right."

"But—what happened?" Algernon gestured helplessly toward the hole in the wall. "I remember that there was an explosion and that—you shouted at me, didn't you?"

"Yes, I shouted for you to get back into the room. You were standing too close to the wall. Another instant and the floor would have crumbled too and you'd have had a nasty tumble—a tumble from which you wouldn't have recovered."

He smiled grimly and patted Algernon on the shoulder. "Just try to calm down a bit. I'll get you a whiskey and soda."

"But what, precisely happened?" persisted Algernon.

"The light decreased the wall's *randomness,* sent it back through time. I warned you that the wall would crumble if the light rested on it for more than an instant. But you had to experiment."

"I'm sorry," muttered Algernon shamefacedly. "I fear I've ruined your apartment."

"Not important, really. It's eery, of course, having all one's secrets open to the sky, but my landlord will rectify that." He gazed at Algernon curiously. "Why did you do it?" he asked.

"To convince Imbert. He said the machine was merely a mechanical hypnotizer."

"I see, Imbert thought I was rather pathetically 'touched.' "

"Not exactly. I think he wanted to believe you . . ."

"But couldn't. Well, I can't blame him. Five years ago I would have doubted too—laughed all this to scorn. I approve of skeptics. They're dependable—when you've succeeded in convincing them that unthinkable and outrageous things occasionally have at least a pragmatic potency. I doubt if even now Imbert would concede that this is an entropy-reversing machine, but you may be sure his respect for it has grown. He'll follow my instructions now without hesitation. And I want you to. We must act in unison, or we'll be defeated before we start."

Algernon began suddenly to tremble. "We haven't an instant to lose," he exclaimed. "I got in touch with the police just before you came back—they're sending out ambulance calls from all over the city. Chaugnar has begun to slay—" Algernon had risen and was striding toward the door.

"Wait!" Little's voice held a note of command. "We've got to wait for Imbert. He's downstairs in the bathroom dressing his wound."

Reluctantly, Algernon returned into the room.

"A few minutes' delay won't matter," continued Little, his voice surprisingly calm. "We've such a hideous ordeal before us that we should be grateful for this respite."

"But Chaugnar is killing now," protested Algernon. "And we are sitting here letting more lives . . ."

"Be snuffed out? Perhaps. But at the same instant all over the world other lives are being snuffed out by diseases which men could prevent if they energetically bestirred themselves." He drew a deep breath. "We're doing the best we can, man. This respite is necessary for our nerves' sake. Try to view the situation sanely. If we are going to eradicate the malignancy which is Chaugnar Faugn we'll need a surgeon's calm. We've got to steel our wills, extrude from our minds all hysterical considerations, and all sentiment."

"But it will kill thousands," protested Algernon. "In the crowded streets . . ."

"No," Little shook his head. "It's no longer in the streets. It has left the city."

"How do you know?"

"There has been a massacre on the Jersey coast—near Asbury Park. I stopped for an instant in the *Brooklyn Standard* office on my way up from the garage. The night staff's in turmoil. They're rushing through a sensational morning extra. I found out something else. There's been a similar massacre in Spain! If we hadn't been talking here we'd have known. All the papers ran columns about it—hours ago. They're correlating the dispatches now and by tomorrow everyone will know of the menace. What I fear is mass hysteria."

"Mass hysteria?"

"Yes, they'll go mad in the city tomorrow—there'll be a stampede. Unreasoning superstition and blind terror always culminate in acts of violence. Hundreds of people will run amuck, pillage, destroy. There'll be more lives lost than Chaugnar destroyed tonight."

"But we can do something. We must."

"I said that we were merely waiting for Doctor Imbert." Little crossed to the eastern window and stared for a moment into the

lightening sky. Then he returned to where Algernon was standing.
"Do you feel better?" he asked. "Have you pulled yourself together?"

"Yes," muttered Algernon. "I'm quite alright."

"Good."

The door opened and Imbert came in. His face was distraught
and of a deathly pallor, but a look of relief came into his eyes
when they rested on Algernon. "I feared you were seriously hurt,"
he cried. "We were quite mad to experiment with—with that
thing."

"We must experiment again, I fear."

Imbert nodded. "I'm ready to join you. What do you want us
to do?"

"I want you and Harris to carry that machine downstairs and
put it into my car. I'll need a flashlight and a few other things.
I won't be long. . . ."

9

THE HORROR MOVES

"WE MUST overtake it before it reaches the crossroads," shouted
Little.

They were speeding by the sea, tearing at seventy miles an hour
down a long, white road that twisted and turned between ramparts
of sand. On both sides there towered dunes, enormous, majestic,
morning stars aglitter on the dark waters intermittently visible
beyond their seaward walls. The horseshoe-shaped isthmus extended for six miles into the sea and then doubled back toward
the Jersey coast. At the point where it changed its direction stood
a crossroad, explicitly sign-posted with two pointing hands. One
of these junctions led directly toward the mainland, the other into
a dense, ocean-defiled waste, marshy and impregnable, a kind of
morass where anything or anyone might hide indefinitely.

And toward this retreat Chaugnar fled. For hours Little's car
had pursued it along the tarred and macadamized roads that fringe
the Jersey coast—over bridges and viaducts and across wastes of
sand, in a straight line from Asbury Park to Atlantic City and
then across country and back again to the coast, and now down

a thin terrain lashed by Atlantic spray, deserted save for a few ramshackle huts of fishermen and a vast congregation of gulls.

Chaugnar Faugn had moved with unbelievable rapidity, from the instant when they had first encountered it crouching somnolently in the shadows beneath a deserted bathhouse at Long Branch and had turned the light on it and watched it awake to the moment when it had gone shambling away through the darkness its every movement had been ominous with menace.

Twice it had stopped in the road and waited for them to approach and once its great arm had raised itself against them in a gesture of malignant defiance. And on that occasion only the entropy machine had saved them. Its light Chaugnar could not bear, and when Little had turned the ray upon the creature's flanks the great obscene body had heaved and shuddered and a ghastly screeching had issued from its bulbous lips. And then forward again it had forged, its thick, stumpy legs moving with the rapidity of pistons—carrying it over the ground so rapidly that the car could not keep pace.

But always its tracks had remained visible, for a phosphorescence streamed from them, illuming its retreat. And always its hoarse bellowing could be heard in the distance, freighted with fury and a hatred incalculable. And by the stench, too, they trailed it, for all the air through which it passed was acridly defiled—pungent with an uncleanliness that evades description.

"It is infinitely old," cried Little as he maneuvered the car about the base of a sea-lashed dune. "As old as the earth's crust. Otherwise, it would have crumbled. You saw how the bathhouse crumbled—how the shells beneath its feet dissolved and vanished. It is only its age that saves it."

"You had the light on it for five minutes," shouted Algernon. His voice was hoarse with excitement. "And it still lives. What can we do?"

"We must corner it—keep the light directed at it for—many minutes. To send it back we must decrease the random element in it by a billion years. It has remained substantially as it is now for at least that long. Perhaps longer."

"How many years of earth-time does the machine lop off a minute?" shouted Imbert.

"Can't tell exactly. It works differently with different objects. Metals, stone, wood all have a different entropy-rhythm. But roughly, it should reverse entropy throughout a billion years of earth-time in ten or fifteen minutes."

"There it is!" shouted Algernon. "It's reached the crossroads. Look!"

Against a windshield glazed with sea mist Imbert laid his forehead, peering with bulging eyes at the form of Chaugnar, phosphorescently illumed a quarter-mile before them on the road, and even as he stared, the distance between the car and the loathsome horror diminished by fifty yards.

"It isn't moving," cried Little. He had half risen from his seat and was gripping the wheel as though it were a live thing. "It's waiting for us. Turn on the light, sir. Quick! for God's sake! We're almost on top of it!"

Algernon fell upon his knees in the dark and groped about for the switch. The engine's roar increased as Little stepped furiously upon the accelerator. "The light, quick!" Little almost screamed the words.

Algernon's fingers found the switch and thrust it sharply upward. There ensued the drone of revolving spheres. "It's moving again. God, it's moving!"

Algernon rose shakingly to his feet. "Where is it?" he shouted. "I don't see it!"

"It's making for the marshes," shouted Little. "Look. Straight ahead, through here." He pointed toward a clear spot in the windshield. Craning hysterically, Algernon described a phosphorescent bulk making off over the narrowest of the bisecting roads.

With a frantic spin of the wheel, Little turned the car about and sent the speedometer soaring. The road grew narrower and more uneven as they advanced along it and the car careened perilously. "Careful," Algernon called out warningly. "We'll get ditched. Better slow up."

"No," cautioned Little, his voice sharp with alarm. "We can't stop now."

The light from the machine was streaming unimpeded into the darkness before them.

"Keep it trained on the road," shouted Little. "It would destroy a man in an instant."

They could smell the mud flats now. A pungent, salty odor of stagnant brine and putrescent shellfish drifted toward them, whipped by the wind. A sickly yellow light was spreading sluggishly in the eastern sky. Across the road ahead of them a turtle shambled and vanished hideously in a flash.

"See that?" cried Little. "That's how Chaugnar would go if it wasn't as old as the earth."

"Be ready with the brakes," Algernon shouted back.

The end of the road had swept into view. It ran swiftly downhill for fifty yards and terminated in a sandy waste that was half submerged at its lower levels. The illumed bulk of Chaugnar paused for an instant on a sandy hillock. Then it moved rapidly downward toward the flats, arms spread wide, body swaying strangely, as though it were in awe of the sea.

Little steered the car to the side of the road and threw on the brakes. "Out—both of you!" he shouted.

Algernon descended to the ground and stood for an instant shakingly clinging to the door of the car. Then, in a sudden access of determination, he sprang back and began tugging at the machine, whilst Imbert strove valiantly to assist him.

There came a bellow from the great form that was advancing into the marsh. Algernon drew close to Little, and gripped him firmly by the arm. "Hadn't we better wait here?" he asked, his voice tight with strain. "It seems to fear the sea. We can entrench ourselves here and attack it with the light when it climbs back."

"No," Little's reply was emphatic. "We haven't a second to waste. It may—mire itself. It's too massive to flounder through the mud without becoming hopelessly bogged down. We'll drive it forward into the marsh."

Resolutely he stopped and beckoned to his companions to assist him in raising and supporting the machine. Dawn was spreading in the east as the three men staggered downward over the sandy waste, a planet's salvation in the glittering shape they carried.

Straight into the morass they went, quaking with terror but impelled by a determination that was oblivious to caution. From Chaugnar there now came an insistent screeching and bellowing, a noise that smote so ominously on Algernon's ear that he wanted, desperately, to drop the machine and head back toward the car. But above the obscene bellowings of the horror rose Little's voice in courageous exhortation. "Don't stop for an instant," he cried. "We must keep it from circling back to the road. It will turn in a moment. It's sinking deeper and deeper. It will have to turn."

Their shoes sank into the sea-soaked marsh weeds, while luridly across the glistening morass the greenish light from the machine, effacing everything in its path save the mud itself, which bubbled and heaved, made younger in an instant by ten thousand years. And then, suddenly, the great thing turned and faced them.

Knee-deep in the soft mud it turned, its glowing flanks quivering with ire, its huge trunk malignly upraised, a flail of flame. For an instant it loomed thus terribly menacing, the soul of all malignancy and horror, a cancerous cyclops oozing fetor. Then the light swept over it, and it recoiled with a convulsive trembling of its entire bulk. Though half mired, it retreated swayingly, and its bellows turned to hoarse gurglings, such as no animal throat had uttered in all earth's eons of sentient evolution.

And then, slowly, it began to change. As the light streamed over and enveloped it, it began unmistakably to shrivel and darken.

"Keep the light steady," Little cried out, his voice tremulous with concern, his features set in an expression of utter revulsion.

Algernon and Imbert continued to advance with the machine, as sickened as Little was by what they saw but supported now by the disappearance of all uncertainty as to the truth of Little's claims.

And now that which had taken to itself an earth-form in eons primordial began awfully to disincarn and before their gaze was enacted a drama so revolting as to imperil reason. A burning horror withdrew from its garments of clay and retraced in patterns of unspeakable dimness the history of its enshrinement. Not instantly had it incarned itself, but by stages slow and fantasmal and sickening. To ascend, Chaugnar had had to feast, not on men at first, for there were no men when it lay venomously outspread on the earth's crust, but on entities no less malignant than itself, the spawn of star-births incalculable. For before the earth cooled she had drawn from the skies a noxious progeny. Drawn earthward by her holocaust they had come, and relentlessly Chaugnar had devoured them.

And now as that which had occurred in the beginning was enacted anew these blasphemies were disgorged, and above the dark wrack defilement spread. And at last from a beast-shape to a jelly Chaugnar passed, a jelly enveloped in darting filaments of corpse-pale flame. For an instant it moved above the black marsh, as it had moved in the beginning when it had come from beyond the universe of stars to wax bestial in the presence of Man. And then the flames vanished and nothing remained but a cold wind blowing across the estuary from the open sea.

Little let out a great cry and Algernon released his hold on the machine and dropped to his knees on the wet earth. Imbert, too, relinquished the machine but before doing so he shot back the lever at its base.

Only for an instant did the victory go unchallenged. For before the spheres on the machine had ceased to revolve, before even the light had vanished from the gleaming waste, the malignancy that had been Chaugnar Faugn reshaped itself in the sky above them.

Indescribably it loomed through the gray sea-mists, its bulk magnified a thousandfold, its long, dangling trunk swaying slowly back and forth.

For an instant it towered above them, glaring venomously. Then, like a racer, it stooped and floundered forward and went groping about with its monstrous hands for the little shapes it hated. It was still groping when it dimmed and vanished into the depth of the hazy, dawn-brightened sky.

10

LITTLE'S EXPLANATION

It was the fifth day since Chaugnar Faugn had been sent back through time. Algernon and Little sat in the latter's laboratory and discussed the destruction of the horror over cups of black coffee.

"You think, then, that the last manifestation we saw was a kind of spectral emanation, without physical substance."

"Not wholly, perhaps," replied Little. "An odor of putrefaction came from it. I should regard the phenomenon as a kind of tenuous reassembling rather than an apparition in a strict sense. Chaugnar had been incarnate for so long in the hideous shape with which we are familiar that its disembodied intelligence could reclothe itself in a kind of porous mimesis before it returned to its hyperdimensional sphere. So rapidly did our machine reverse entropy that perhaps tiny fragments of its terrestrial body survived, and these, by a tremendous exercise of will, it may have reassembled and, figuratively, *blown up*. That is to say, it may have taken these tiny fragments and so increased their porosity beyond the normal porosity of matter that they produced the cyclopean apparition we saw. All matter, you know, is tremendously porous, and if I could remove all the 'vacuums' from your body you would shrink to the size of a pin-head."

Algernon nodded, and was silent for a moment. Then he stood up, laid his coffee cup on the windowsill and crossed to where Little was sitting. "We agreed," he said, "that we wouldn't discuss Chaugnar further until . . . well, until we were in a little calmer frame of mind than we were a few days ago. It was a wise decision, I think. But I'm now so certain that what we both witnessed was not an illusion that I must insist you return an *honest* answer to two questions. I shall not expect a comprehensive and wholly satisfying explanation, for I'm aware that you are not completely sure yourself as to the exact nature of Chaugnar. But you have at least formed an hypothesis, and there are a good many things you haven't told me which I've earned the right to know."

"What do you wish to know?" Little's voice was constrained, reluctant.

"What destroyed the horror in the Pyrenees? Why were there no more massacres after—after that night?"

Little smiled wanly. "Have you forgotten the pools of black slime which were found on the melting snow a thousand feet above the village three days after we sent Chaugnar back?"

"You mean . . ."

Little nodded. "Chaugnar's kin, undoubtedly. They accompanied Chaugnar back, but left like their master, a few remainders. Little round pools of putrescent slime—a superfluity of rottenness that somehow resisted the entropy-reversing action of the machine."

"You mean that the machine sent entropy-reversing emanations half across the world?"

Little shook his head. "I mean simply that Chaugnar Faugn and its hideous brethren were *joined together* hyperdimensionally and that we destroyed them simultaneously. It is an axiom of virtually every speculative philosophy based on the newer physics and the concepts of non-Euclidean mathematics that we can't perceive the real *relations* of objects in the external world, that since our senses permit us to view them merely three-dimensionally we can't perceive the hyperdimensional links which unite them.

"If we could see the same objects—men, trees, chairs, houses—on a fourth-dimensional plane, for instance, we'd notice connections that are now wholly unsuspected by us. Your chair, to pick an example at random, may actually be joined to the window-ledge behind you or . . . to the Woolworth Building. Or you and I may be but infinitesimally tiny fragments of some gigantic monster occupying vast segments of space-time. You may be a mere excrescence on the monster's back, and I a hair of its head—I speak metaphorically, of course, since in higher dimensions of space-time there can be nothing but analogies to objects on the terrestrial globe—or you and I and all men, and everything in the world, every particle of matter, may be but a single fragment of this larger entity. If anything should happen to the entity you and I would *both* suffer, but as the monster would be invisible to us, no one—no one equipped with normal human organs of awareness—would suspect that we were suffering because we were parts of *it*. To a three-dimensional observer we should appear to be suffering from different causes and our invisible hyperdimensional *solidarity* would remain wholly unsuspected.

"If two people were thus hyperdimensionally joined, like Siamese twins, and one of them were destroyed by a machine similar to the one we used against Chaugnar Faugn, the other would suffer effacement at the same instant, though he were on the opposite side of the world."

Algernon looked puzzled.

"But why should the link be invisible? Assuming that Chaugnar Faugn and the Pyrenean horrors were hyperdimensionally joined together—either because they were parts of one great monster, or merely because they were *one* in the hyperdimensional sphere, why should this hyperdimensional connecting link be invisible to us?"

"Well—perhaps an analogy will make it clearer. If you were a *two* instead of a three-dimensional entity, and if, when you regarded objects about you—chairs, houses, animals—you saw only their length and breadth, you wouldn't be able to form any intelligible conception of their relations to other objects in the dimension you couldn't apprehend—the dimension of *thickness*. Only a portion of an ordinary three-dimensional object would be visible to you and you could only make a mystical guess as to how it would look with another dimension added to it. In that, to you, unperceivable dimension of thickness it might join itself to a thousand other objects and you'd never suspect that such a connection existed. You might perceive hundreds of flat surfaces about you, all disconnected, and you would never imagine that they formed one object in the third dimension.

"You would live in a two-dimensional world and when three-dimensional objects intruded into that world you would be unaware of their true objective conformation—or relatively unaware, for your perceptions would be perfectly valid so long as you remained two-dimensional.

"Our perceptions of the three-dimensional world are only valid for that world—to a fourth-dimensional or fifth- or sixth-dimensional entity our conceptions of objects external to us would seem utterly ludicrous. And we know that such entities exist. Chaugnar Faugn was such an entity. And because of its hyperdimensional nature it was joined to the horror on the hills in a way we weren't able to perceive. We can perceive connections when they have length, breadth and thickness, but when a new dimension is added they pass out of our ken, precisely as a solid object passes out of the ken of an observer in a dimension lower than ours. Have I clarified your perplexities?"

Algernon nodded. "I think—yes, I am sure that you have. But I should like to ask you another question. Do you believe that Chaugnar Faugn is a transcendent world-soul endowed with a supernatural incorporeality, or just—just a material entity? I mean, was Ulman's priest right and was Chaugnar an incarnation of the Oneness of the Brahmic mysteries, the portentous all-in-all of theosophists and occultists, or merely a product of physical evolution on a plane incomprehensible to us?"

Little took a long sip of coffee and very deliberately lowered his head, as though he were marshaling his convictions for a debate. "I believe I once told you," he said at last, "that I didn't believe Chaugnar could be destroyed by any agent less transcendental than that which we used against it. It certainly wasn't protoplasmic or mineral, and no mechanical device not based on relativist concepts could have effected the dissolution we witnessed. An infra-red ray machine, for instance, or a cyclotron would have been powerless to send it back. Yet despite the transcendental nature of even its carnate shell, despite the fact that even in its earth-shape it was fashioned of a substance unknown on the earth and that we can form no conception of its shape in the multi-dimensional sphere it now inhabits, it is my opinion that it is inherently, like ourselves, a circumscribed entity—the spawn of remote worlds and unholy dimensions, but a creature and not a creator, a creature obeying inexorable laws and occupying a definite niche in the cosmos.

"In a way we can never understand it had acquired the ability to roam and could incarn itself in dimensions lower than its own. But I do not believe it possessed the attributes of deity. It was neither beneficent nor evil, but simply amorally virulent—a vampire-like life form from beyond the universe of stars strayed by chance into our little, walled-in three-dimensional world. One unguarded gate may be standing ajar . . ."

"But do you believe that it actually made a race of men to serve it—that the Miri Nigri were fashioned from the flesh of primitive amphibians?"

Little frowned. "I don't know. Conditions on the cooling earth two billion years ago may once have been such that creations of that nature antedated the process of biological evolution with which we are familiar. And we may be sure that Chaugnar Faugn with its inscrutable endowments could have fashioned men-shapes had it so desired—could have fashioned them even from the planktonlike swarms of small organisms which must have drifted with the tides through the ancient oceans."

Little lowered his voice and looked steadily at Algernon. "Some day," he murmured, "Chaugnar may return. We sent it back through time, but in five thousand or a hundred thousand years it may return to ravage. Its return will be presaged in dreams, for when its brethren stirred restlessly on the Spanish hills both I and Hsieh Ho were disturbed in our sleep by harbingers from beyond. Telepathically Chaugnar spoke to sleeping minds, and if it returns it will speak again, for Man is not isolated among the sentient beings of earth but is linked to all that moves in hyperdimensional continuity."

T. E. D. KLEIN
Children of the Kingdom

"Mischief is their occupation, malice their habit, murder their sport, and blasphemy their delight."
　　　　　　　—Maturin, *Melmoth the Wanderer*

"They are everywhere, those creatures."
　　　　　　　—Derleth, *The House on Curwen Street*

"It taught me the foolishness of not being afraid."
　　　　　　　—rape victim, New York City

ON A certain spring evening several years ago, after an unsuccessful interview in Boston for a job I'd thought was mine, I missed the last train back to New York and was forced to take the eleven-thirty bus. It proved to be a "local," wending its way through the shabby little cities of southern New England and pulling into a succession of dimly lit Greyhound stations far from the highway, usually in the older parts of town—the decaying ethnic neighborhoods, the inner-city slums, the ghettos. I had a bad headache, and soon fell asleep. When I awoke I felt disoriented. All the other passengers were sleeping. I didn't know what time it was, but hesitated to turn on the light and look at my watch lest it disturb the man next to me. Instead, I looked out the window. We were passing through the heart of yet another shabby, nameless city, moving past the same gutted buildings I'd been seeing all night in my dreams, the same lines of cornices and rooftops, empty windows, gaping doorways. In the patches of darkness, familiar shapes seemed strange. Mailboxes and fire hydrants sprouted like tropical plants. Yet somehow it was stranger beneath the streetlights, where garbage cast long shadows on the sidewalk, and vacant lots hid glints of broken glass among the weeds. I remembered what I'd read of those great Mayan cities standing silent and abandoned in the Central American jungle, with no clue to where the inhabitants had gone. Through the window I could now see crumbling rows of tenements, an ugly red-brick housing project,

653

some darkened and filthy-looking shops with alleys blocked by iron gates. Here and there a solitary figure would turn to watch the bus go by. Except for my reflection, I saw not one white face. A pair of little children threw stones at us from behind a fortress made of trash; a grown man stood pissing in the street like an animal, and watched us with amusement as we passed. I wanted to be out of this benighted place, and prayed that the driver would get us through quickly. I longed to be back in New York. Then a street sign caught my eye, and I realized that I'd already arrived. This was my own neighborhood; my home was only three streets down and just across the avenue. As the bus continued south I caught a fleeting glimpse of the apartment building where, less than half a block away, my wife lay awaiting my return.

Less than half a block can make a difference in New York. Different worlds can co-exist side by side, scarcely intersecting. There are places in Manhattan where you can see a modern high-rise, with its terraces and doormen and well-appointed lobby, towering white and immaculate above some soot-stained little remnant of the city's past—a tenement built during the Depression, lines of garbage cans in front, or a nineteenth-century brownstone gone to seed, its brickwork defaced by graffiti, its front door yawning open, its hallway dark, narrow, and forbidding as a tomb. Perhaps the two buildings will be separated by an alley; perhaps not even that. The taller one's shadow may fall across the other, blotting out the sun; the other may disturb the block with loud music, voices raised in argument, the gnawing possibility of crime. Yet to all appearances the people of each group will live their lives without acknowledging the other's existence. The poor will keep their rats, like secrets, to themselves; the cooking smells, the smells of poverty and sickness and backed-up drains, will seldom pass beyond their windows. The sidewalk in front may be lined with the idle and unshaven, men with T-shirts and dark skins and a gaze as sharp as razors, singing, or trading punches, or disputing, perhaps, in Spanish; or they may sit in stony silence on the stoop, passing round a bottle in a paper bag. They are rough-looking and impetuous, these men; but they will seldom leave their kingdom for the alien world next door. And those who inhabit that alien world will move with a certain wariness when they find themselves on the street, and will hurry past the others without meeting their eyes.

* * *

My grandfather, Herman Lauterbach, was one of those people who could move in either world. Though his Brooklyn apartment had always seemed a haven of middle-class respectability, at least for as long as I knew him, whatever refinements it displayed were in fact the legacy of his second wife; Herman himself was more at home among the poor. He, too, had been poor for most of his life—a bit of a radical, I suspect—and always thought of my father, his son-in-law, as "nothing but a goddamn stuffshirt" simply because my father had an office job. (As his beloved daughter's only child I was spared such criticisms, although I'm sure he found my lackluster academic career a disappointment and my chosen field, The Puritan Heritage, a bore.) His attitude never changed, even when, nearing seventy, having outlived two exasperated wives, he himself was forced to don a necktie and go to work for the brother of an old friend in a firm that manufactured watch casings.

He had always been a comical, companionable man, fond of women, jokes, and holidays, but forty-hour weeks went hard with him and soured his temper. So did the death of my mother the following year. Afterward, things were not the same; he was no longer quite so endearing. One saw a more selfish side, a certain hardness, like that of a child who has grown up in the street. Yet one inevitably forgave him, if only because of his age and lack of consequence, and because there still hung about him a certain air of comedy, as if it was his doom to provide the material for other people's anecdotes. There was, for example, his violent altercation with the driver of a Gravesend Bay bus, which my grandfather had boarded in the belief that it went to Bay Ridge; and then there was the episode in Marinaro's Bar, where jokes about the Mafia were not taken lightly. Several weeks later came a highly injudicious argument with the boss's son, less than half his age, over the recent hike in transit fares for senior citizens, and whether this entitled my grandfather to a corresponding increase in pay. Finally, when the two of them nearly came to blows over an equally minor disagreement—whether or not the city's impending bankruptcy was the fault of Mayor Beame, whom my grandfather somewhat resembled—everyone agreed that it was time for the old man to retire.

For the next three years he managed to get by on his modest savings, augmented by Social Security and regular checks from my father, now remarried and living in New Jersey. Then, sud-

denly, his age caught up with him: on May 4, 1977, while seated
in his kitchen watching the first of the Frost-Nixon interviews
(and no doubt shaking his fist at the television set), he suffered a
major stroke, toppled backward from his chair, and had to be
hospitalized for nearly a month. He was, at this time, eighty-three
years old.

Or at least that was what he admitted to. We could never
actually be sure, for in the past he'd been known to subtract as
much as a decade when applying for a job, and to add it back,
with interest, when applying for Golden Age discounts at a local
movie house. Whatever the case, during his convalescence it became clear that he was in no shape to return to Brooklyn, where
he'd been living on the third floor of a building without elevators.
Besides, like his once-robust constitution, the neighborhood had
deteriorated over the years; gangs of black and Puerto Rican youths
preyed on the elderly of all races, especially those living alone,
and an ailing old widower was fair game. On the other hand, he
was not yet a candidate for a nursing home, at least not the
elaborate kind with oxygen tents and cardiographs attached. What
he needed was a rest home. As his doctor explained in private to
my wife and me on our second visit, my grandfather was by no
means permanently incapacitated; why, just look at Pasteur, who
after a series of fifty-eight strokes had gone on to make some of
his greatest discoveries. ("And who knows?" the doctor said, "maybe
granddad'll make a few discoveries of his own.") According to
the prognosis he was expected to be on his feet within a week or
two. Perhaps before that time he would have another stroke; likely,
though, it would come later; more than likely it would kill him.
Until then, however, he'd be alert and responsive and sufficiently
ambulant to care for himself: he would not be walking with his
usual speed, perhaps, but he'd be walking.

My grandfather put it more succinctly. "What the hell you think
I am," he said, voice gravelly with age, when the question of a
rest home was raised, "some vegetable in a wheelchair?" Struggling
to sit up in bed, he launched into an extended monologue about
how he'd rather die alone and forgotten on Skid Row than in a
"home"; but for all its Sturm und Drang the speech sounded
curiously insincere, and I had the impression that he'd been
rehearsing it for years. No doubt his pride was at stake; when I
assured him that what we had in mind was not some thinly
disguised terminal ward, nor anything like a day-care center for

the senile and decrepit, but rather a sort of boardinghouse where he could live in safety among people his own age, people as active as he was, he calmed down at once. I could see that the idea appealed to him; he had always thrived on conversation, jawboning, even aimless chatter, and the prospect of some company—especially that of fellow retirees with time on their hands—was an inviting one. The truth is, he'd been lonely out in Brooklyn, though of course he would never have admitted it. For my part I was feeling rather guilty; I hadn't come to see him as often as I should have. From now on, I told him, things would be different: I would find him a place in Manhattan, a place where I could visit him once or twice a week. I'd even take him out to dinner, when I got the chance.

He appeared to think it over. Then—for my sake, I think (and somehow I found this horribly depressing)—he screwed his face into a roguish grin, like a small boy boasting to an adult. "Make sure there are plenty of good-looking dames around," he said, "and you got yourself a deal."

The following weekend, with this qualified blessing in mind, Karen and I set about looking for a place. The press had recently brought to light a series of scandals involving various institutions for the aged, and we were particularly anxious to find a reputable one. By Saturday afternoon we'd discovered that many of the private homes were more expensive than we'd counted on—as much as two or three hundred dollars a week—and that in most of them the supervision was too strict; they resembled nothing so much as tiny, smiling prisons. Grandfather would never stand for being cooped up inside all day; he liked to wander. Another, run by nuns, was comfortable, clean, and open to non-Catholics, but its residents were in no condition to feed themselves, much less join in human conversation. These were the unreclaimables, lapsed into senescence; my grandfather, we hoped, would seem positively vigorous beside them.

Finally, early Sunday evening, on the recommendation of a friend, we visited a place on West 81st Street, scarcely a dozen blocks from where we lived. It was called, somewhat optimistically, the Park West Manor for Adults, even though it was rather less than a manor house and nowhere near the park. The owner was a certain Mr. Fetterman, whom we never actually met; it later turned out that he, too, was a bit of a crook, though never in ways that directly affected us. I gather from my wife, who, as

accountant for a publishing firm, has always had a better head
for business, that the home was part of some statewide franchise
operation with vague ties to local government. According to the
agreement—common, she informs me—my grandfather's rent was
to be paid for out of his now-meager savings; when they were
depleted (as, indeed, they would be in a year or so) the cost would
be borne by Medicaid for the rest of his life.

The building itself, of dirty red ornamental brick, occupied the
south side of the street between Broadway and Amsterdam Avenue,
a block and a half from the Museum of Natural History. It
consisted of two wings, each nine stories tall, connected by a
narrow, recessed entranceway several steps down from the sidewalk.
The place seemed respectable enough, though at first sight it was
not particularly impressive, especially at the end of the day, with
the sun sinking behind the Hudson and long shadows darkening
the block. The pavement in front of the building had recently
been torn up for some kind of sewer work, and huge brown metal
pipes lay stacked on either side like ammunition. My wife and I
had to step across a series of planks to reach the front door. Inside
it, just before the lobby, was an alcove with a battered wooden
desk, behind which, seemingly stupefied with boredom, sat a
wrinkled old black man in a guard's uniform—the sort of man
one sees at banks these days, ineffectually directing people to the
appropriate tellers. He nodded and let us pass through. No doubt
he thought he recognized us; it's said that, to whites, all blacks
look alike, and years in various city classrooms have convinced
me that the reverse is true as well.

The lobby wasn't much of an improvement. Like most lobbies,
it was dim, depressing, and cold. The rear wall was lined by a
mirror, so that, on entering, my wife and I found ourselves
confronted by a rather discouraged-looking little couple approaching from across the room, the woman frowning at the man, no
doubt for some trifling thing he had just said, the man glancing
with increasing frequency at his watch. To the couple's left ran
a long, ornate mantelpiece overhanging a blank expanse of wall
where a fireplace should have been. Grouped around this non-
existent fireplace were half a dozen caved-in leather chairs and a
pair of dusty rubber plants sagging wearily in their pots, their
leaves reflected in the mirror and, on a smaller scale, in the
painting hanging just above the mantel: a framed reproduction of
Rousseau's *Children of the Kingdom,* the primitive figures peering

out at us like a ring of ghosts, their faces pale and impassive against the violets, reds, and greens of the surrounding jungle. The colors were faded, as if from having been stared at by generations of residents.

It was the dinner hour. The lobby was deserted; from somewhere to the right came the sound of voices and the clank of pots and plates, accompanied by a scraping of chairs and the smell of boiled meat. We moved toward it, following the right-hand corridor past a series of turns until we came to a pair of wooden doors with windows in the top. Karen, boldened by fatigue, pushed her way through. Before us stretched the dining room, barely more than half filled, the diners grouped around tables of various shapes and designs. It reminded me of the mess hall at summer camp, as if my fellow campers had aged and withered right there in their seats without ever having gained appreciably in size. Even the waiters looked old: a few, hurrying up the aisles, still sported oily black pompadours, but most looked as if they could easily have traded places with the people they served. White hair was the rule here, with pink skull showing through. This was as true for the women as the men, since by this age the sexes had once more begun to merge; indeed, like babies, the individuals in the room were hard to tell apart. Nor were they any more inclined than children to disguise their curiosity; dozens of old pink heads swiveled in our direction as we stood there in the doorway. We were intruders; I felt as if we'd blundered into a different world. Then I saw the expectation in their faces, and felt doubly bad: each of them had probably been hoping for a visitor, a son or daughter or grandchild, and must have been keenly disappointed by every new arrival that was not the one awaited.

A small, harried-looking man approached us and identified himself as the assistant manager. He looked as if he was about to scold us for having arrived during dinner—he, too, probably assumed we were there to visit someone—but he brightened immediately when we explained why we'd come. "Follow me," he said, moving off at a kind of dogtrot. "I'll show you the place from top to bottom." In the noise and hubbub of the dining room I hadn't caught his name, but as soon as he started toward the nearest exit, my wife and I in tow, a plaintive chorus of "Mr. Calzone" arose behind us. He ignored it and pushed on through the door; I suppose he was glad of the diversion.

We found ourselves in the kitchen, all iron pots and steam,

with cooks in white T-shirts and white-jacketed waiters shouting
at one another in Spanish. "This used to be kosher," shouted
Calzone, "but they cut all that out." I assured him that my
grandfather liked his bacon as well as the next man. "Oh, we
don't give 'em bacon too often," he said, taking me literally, "but
they really go for the pork chops." My wife seemed satisfied, and
nodded at the dishwashers and the ranks of aluminum cabinets.
As for me, I wasn't sure just what to look for, but am happy to
report I saw no worm-eggs and not one dead cat.

Calzone was as good as his word. From the kitchen he conducted
us "up top" to the ninth floor via a clanging old elevator of the
self-service type, with the numbers beside the buttons printed so
large—in raised numerals nearly an inch high—that even a blind
man could have run it. (Its speed was such that, had one of the
home's frailer residents preferred to take the stairs, she would
probably have arrived in time to meet us.) The rooms on the
ninth floor, most of them unoccupied, were shabby but clean,
with private bathrooms and plenty of closet space. Grandfather
would have nothing to complain about. In fact, with its boarders
all downstairs at dinner, the place seemed more a college dormitory
than an old-folks' home. Aside from the oversized elevator panel
and the shiny new aluminum railings we'd noticed everywhere—
in easy reach of stairways, tubs, and toilets—about the only
concession to age appeared to be a sign-up sheet my wife came
across on a bulletin board in the second-floor "game room," for
those who wished to make an appointment at some community
medical center over on Columbus Avenue.

Our tour ended with the laundry room in the basement. It was
hot and uncomfortable and throbbed with the echoes of heavy
machinery, like the engine room of a freighter; you could almost
feel the weight of the building pressing down on you. The air
seemed thick, as if clogged with soapsuds, and moisture dripped
from a network of flaking steam pipes suspended from the ceiling.
Against one side stood four coin-operated dryers, staring balefully
at four squat Maytag washers ranged along the opposite wall. One
of the washers, in the farthest corner, appeared to be having a
breakdown. It was heaving back and forth on its base like something frantic to escape, a pair of red lights blinking in alarm above
the row of switches. From somewhere in its belly came a frenzied
churning sound, as if the thing were delivering itself of a parasite,
or perhaps just giving birth. A man in a sweat-stained T-shirt was

on his knees before it, scowling at an exposed bit of circuitry where a panel had been removed. Beside him stood an open tool kit, with tools scattered here and there across the concrete floor. He was introduced to us as Reynaldo "Frito" Ley, the building's superintendent, but he barely had time to look up, and when he did the scowl stayed on his face. "She acting up again," he told the assistant manager, in a thick Hispanic accent. "I think somebody messing with the 'lectric wire." Reaching around back to the wall, he yanked out the plug, and the machine ground noisily to a halt.

"Maybe it's rats," I said, feeling somewhat left out. He looked at me indignantly, and I smiled to show that I'd been joking.

But Calzone was taking no chances. "Believe me," he said quickly, "that's one thing they don't complain about." He ran a hand through his thinning hair. "Sure, I know, this building ain't exactly new, and okay, maybe we'll get a little bitty roach now and then, that's only natural. I mean, you're not gonna find a single building in the whole damned city that hasn't got one or two of them babies, am I right? But rats, never. We run a clean place."

"Rats not gonna bother my machines," added the superintendent. "They got no business here. Me, I think it was *los niños*. Kids."

"Kids?" said my wife and I in unison, with Calzone half a beat behind.

"You mean children from the neighborhood?" asked Karen. She had just been reading a series about the revival of youth gangs on the West Side, after more than a decade of peace. "What would they want in a place like this? How could the get in?"

He shrugged, "I don't know, lady. I don' see them. I only know is hard to keep them out. They all the time looking for money. Come down here, try to get the quarters from machines. No good, so they got to break something—cut up hoses in the back, pull the plug. . . . That kind, they do anything."

Calzone stepped between them. "Don't worry, Mrs. Klein. It's not what you're thinking. What Frito means is, on weekends like this you get people coming in to visit relatives, and sometimes they bring the little kids along. And before you know it the kids are getting bored, and they're running up and down the halls or playing in the elevator. We're trying to put a stop to it, but it's nothing serious. Just pranks, that's all." Moving to the door, he opened it and ushered us outside. Behind us the superintendent appeared rather annoyed, but when my wife looked back questioningly he turned away. We left him sulking in front of his machine.

"Craziest thing I ever head of," muttered Calzone, as he led us back to the elevator. "The kids in this neighborhood may cause a bit of trouble now and then, but they sure as hell ain't causing it in here!" The elevator door slid shut with a clang. "Look, I'm not gonna lie to you. We've had our share of problems. I mean, who hasn't, right? But if we've had any break-ins here it's the first time *I've* ever heard of it. Fact is, we've just beefed up our security, and there's no way anyone from outside's getting in. Believe me, your granddad's gonna be as safe here as anywhere else in New York."

Since that very morning's *Times* had carried the story of a wealthy widow and her maid found strangled in their East 62nd Street town house, these words were hardly reassuring.

Nor was my wife's expression when we got out of the elevator. She nudged me with her elbow. "I'd hate to think what the security was like before they beefed it up," she said. Calzone pretended not to hear.

The first battalions of old men and women were marching unsteadily from the dining room as the two of us bid him goodbye. "Come back again and I'll show you our new TV lounge," he called after us, retiring to his little office just beyond the stairs. As soon as he'd closed the door, I approached a pair of well-fed-looking old women who were shuffling arm-in-arm across the lobby. The stouter one had hair as blue as the veins that lined her forehead. Gazing up at me, she broke into a slightly bewildered smile.

I cleard my throat. "Pardon me, but would you two ladies say this is a safe place to live? I mean, from the standpoint of the neighborhood?"

Silence. The smile, the gaze, never wavered.

"Mrs. Hirschfeld doesn't hear so good," explained the other, tightening her grip on the woman's arm. "Even with the new battery you have to shout a little." She spoke with her eyes cast demurely downward, avoiding mine. Her hair was tied in a coquettish little bun. Who knows, I thought, Grandfather might like her. She told me her name was Mrs. Rosenzweig. She and Mrs. Hirschfeld were roommates. "Elsie's very happy here," she said, "and me, I can't complain. Three years already we've been here, and never any trouble." The lashes fluttered. "But of course, we never go outside."

They moved off together toward the elevator, leaning on one another for support. "Well, what do you think?" I asked my wife, as we headed for the exit in front.

She shrugged. "He's your grandfather."

Emerging from the lobby, we found ourselves once more in the presence of the guard, slumped glassy-eyed behind his desk. Here he is in the flesh, I thought, Calzone's beefed-up security. He nodded sleepily to us as we passed.

Outside, dusk had fallen on the block. To the west lay the familiar trees and benches of Broadway, with TV showrooms, banks, and Chinese restaurants. Copperware and cappuccino-makers gleamed in Zabar's window; Sunday browsers chatted by a bookstall on the corner. "Anyway," I said, "it's better than Brooklyn." But when we turned east I wasn't so sure. The building next door was a six-story tenement ribbed with fire escapes and a crumbling succession of ledges. On the front stoop, beneath a rust-stained "No Loitering" sign, sat a conclave of bored-looking young men, one with a gold earring, one fiddling with the dial of a radio as big as an attaché case. I wished we didn't have to walk past them.

"They look like they're posing for a group photo," I said hopefully, taking my wife's hand.

"Yeah —Attica, Class of 1980."

We moved by them silently, drawing hostile glares. Behind us, with a blare of trumpets, the radio exploded into "Soul Soldier." Another group of teenagers was gathered in front of a closed-up shop on the corner of 81st and Amsterdam. "Checks Cashed," a corrugated metal sign proclaimed, and below it, on a faded piece of cardboard taped inside the window, "Food Stamps Sold Here." The place was dark and empty, the window gray with dust.

Snap out of it, I told myself, the neighborhood's not so bad. Just another culture or two, that's all it was, and no worse here than where I lived, half a mile farther uptown. I noted the ancient public library, a shoe-repair shop, a pawnshop with guitars and watches in the window, a place where Haitian magazines were sold, a Puerto Rican social club, a shop whose sign read "Barber" on one side and "Barbería" on the other. Several *bontanicas,* shut for the day behind steel gates, displayed windows full of painted plaster figures: Jesus, and Mary, a bearded black man brandishing a snake, an angel with a dagger in his hand. All wore haloes.

Still, the people of the neighborhood did not. The crime rate, in fact, had been climbing that year, and while Park West Manor seemed as good a place as any for my grandfather, I had doubts about the safety of the block. As my wife and I walked home that night, heading up Columbus with the lights of Sunday traffic in our eyes, I thought of the old brick building receding behind us into the shadows of West 81st, and of the doorways, stoops, and street corners surrounding it where unsmiling black youths waited like a threat. I worried about whether they might somehow sneak inside, and about all the damage they might cause—although in view of what actually occurred, these fears now seem, to say the least, rather ironic.

Wednesday, June 8, 1977

If heaven is really populated by the souls of the dead, with their earthly personalities and intellect surviving intact, then the place must be almost as depressing as an old-folks' home. The angels may handle their new wings with a certain finesse, and their haloes may glow bright as gold, but the heads beneath them must be pretty near as empty as the ones I saw the first time I visited my grandfather at Park West Manor. Around me, in the game room, old men and women played leisurely hands of canasta or poker or gin, or sat watching in silence as two of their number shuffled round a pool table, its worn and faded surface just above the spectators' sight. One old man stood talking to himself in the corner; others merely dozed. Contrary to my expectations, there were no twinkle-eyed old Yankee types gathered round a checkerboard puffing corncob pipes, and I looked in vain for bearded Jewish patriarchs immersed in games of chess. No one even had a book. Most of those in the room that day were simply propped up in the lounge chairs like a row of dolls, staring straight ahead as if watching a playback of their lives. My grandfather wasn't among them.

If I sound less than reverent toward my elders, there's a good reason: I am. No doubt I'll be joining their ranks some day myself (unless I'm already food for worms, knocked down by an addict or a bus), and I'll probably spend my time blinking and daydreaming like everyone else. Meanwhile, though, I find it hard to summon up the respect one's supposed to feel for age. Old people have always struck me as rather childish, in fact. Despite their reputation, they've never seemed particularly wise.

Perhaps I just tend to look for wisdom in the wrong places. I remember a faculty party where I introduced myself to a celebrated visiting theologian and asked him a lot of earnest questions, only to discover that he was more interested in making passes at me. I once eavesdropped on the conversation of two well-known writers on the occult who turned out to be engaged in a passionate argument over whether a Thunderbird got better mileage than a Porsche. I bought the book by Dr. Kübler-Ross, the one in which she interviews patients with terminal cancer, and I found, sadly, that the dying have no more insight into life, or death, than the rest of us. But old people have been the biggest disappointment of all; I've yet to hear a one of them say anything profound. They're like the ninety-two-year-old Oxford don who, when asked by some deferential young man what wisdom he had to impart after nearly a century of living, ruminated a moment and then said something like, "Always check your footnotes." I've never found the old to be wiser than anyone else. They've never told me anything I didn't know already.

But Father Pistachio . . . Well, maybe he was different. Maybe he was onto something after all.

At first, though, he seemed no more than an agreeable old humbug. I met him on June 8, when I went to visit Grandfather. It was the spring of '77, with the semester just ending; I had Wednesday afternoons free, and had told Grandfather to expect me. We had installed him in Park West the previous weekend, after collecting some things from his Brooklyn apartment and disposing of the rest. At one-thirty today, unable to find him in his bedroom on the ninth floor, I'd tried the TV lounge and the game room, both in vain, and had finally gone downstairs to ask Miss Pascua, a little Filipino woman who worked as the administrative secretary.

"Mr. Lauterbach likes to spend his time outdoors," she said, a hint of disapproval in her voice. "We let them do what they want here, you know. We don't like to interfere."

"I understand."

"He's doing very well, though," she went on. "He's already made a lot of friends. We're very fond of him."

"Glad to hear it. Any idea where he might be?"

"Well, he seems to have hit it off with some of the local people. They sit out there and talk all day." For a moment I pictured him in dignified conversation with some cronies on a sunny Broadway bench, but then she added: "I'd try looking for him one block down, on the other side of Amsterdam. He's usually on a stoop out there, sitting with a bunch of Puerto Ricans."

I walked out frowning. I should have known he'd do something like that. When you gave him a choice between the jungle to the east—with its fire escapes, its alleyways, its rat-infested basements—and the tamer pastures of Broadway, Broadway didn't have a chance.

The spot he'd picked was a particularly disagreeable one. It was just up the block from an evil-looking bar called Davey's (since closed down by the police), a little bit of Harlem on the West Side: the sort of place where you expect a shoot-out every Saturday night. The buildings beside it were ancient with grime; even the bricks seemed moist, and the concrete foundations were riddled with something curiously like wormholes. I passed a doorway full of teenaged boys who should have been in school. They were hunched furtively against the wall, lighting something out of sight, while others shot craps on the sidewalk, striking poses out of Damon Runyon. In the dim light of an open first-floor window, heavy shapes moved back and forth. A man in dark glasses hurried toward me, angrily dragging a child by the arm. The child said something—he couldn't have been more than five—and as the man passed by he scowled and muttered back, "Don't tell me 'bout your mother, your mother's a goddamn whore!" Already I was beginning to feel depressed. I was glad Karen hadn't come.

My grandfather was three stoops in from the corner, seated beside a large black woman easily twice his weight. On the railing to his right, perched above his shoulder like a raven, sat another old man, with skin like aged parchment and a halo of white hair. He was dressed in black trousers and a black short-sleeved shirt, with the white square of a priest's collar peeking out above it like a window. His mouth was half concealed behind a shaggy white moustache, and the sole incongruous touch was the unnatural redness of his lips, almost as if he were wearing lipstick. On his lap lay a white paper bag.

Grandfather smiled when he saw me, and got to his feet. "Where's that pretty wife of yours?" he asked. I reminded him that Karen was at work. He looked puzzled. "What, *today?*"

"It's Wednesday, remember?"

"My God, you're right!" He broke into astonished laughter. "It felt just like a Sunday!"

I alluded to the trouble I'd had finding him. Here he was, hiding in the shadows, when only one block over—east to the museum, west to Broadway—there were plenty of comfortable benches in the sun.

"Benches are for women," he replied, with a conviction that allowed of no argument—just as, in some long-vanished luncheonette of my childhood, he'd told me, "Straws are for girls." (What does it say about him that he believed this? And what does it say about me that since that time I've never used a straw?)

"Besides," he said, "I wanted you to meet my friends. We get together here because the Father lives upstairs." He nodded toward the old man, but introduced the woman to me first. Her name was Coralette. She was one of those wide, imperturbable creatures who take up two seats or more on the subway. It was impossible to guess her age, but I could hear, each time she spoke, the echoes of a girlhood in the South.

The man was introduced as "Father Pistachio." This was not his name, but it was close enough. My grandfather never got his names or facts exactly right. Perhaps this had something to do with his general rebelliousness. It was certainly not a product of his age, for it had existed as long as I'd known him; half the time, in fact, he confused me with my father. Yet the names he thought up for most people were insidiously appropriate, and often stuck. Father Pistachio was one; I never saw the man without a white paper bag in his hand or, as it was now, crumpled in his lap— a bag that had been filled with those obscene-looking little red nuts, whose dye so stained his lips that he might have passed for some inhabitant of Transylvania.

But he wasn't Transylvanian; nor was he, despite my grandfather's introduction, a Puerto Rican. "No, no," he said quickly, looking somewhat pained, "you no understand, my friend, I say *Costa* Rica my home. Paraíso, Costa Rica. City of Paradise."

My grandfather shrugged. "So if it was paradise, what are you doing up here with an *alter kocker* like me?"

Coralette seemed to find this irresistibly funny, though I suspect the Yiddish escaped her. Pistachio smiled, too.

"My dear Herman," he said, "one is not permitted to stay forever in Eden." He winked at me, and added: "Besides, Paraíso just a name. Paradise *here*, in front of your face."

I nodded dutifully, but could not help noticing the darkened corridor behind him, the graffiti on the crumbling bricks and, just above his head a filthy window box from which a dead brown ivy plant and two long snakelike tendrils drooped. I wished he'd picked a more convincing spot.

But he was already quoting the authorities for support. "Buddha, he say, 'Every day is a good day.' Jesus Christ say, '*El Reino del Padre*—the Kingdom of the Father—is spread upon the earth, but men are blind and do not see it."

"Yeah, where he say that?" asked Coralette. "Ain't in no Bible *I* ever read."

"Is in the one I read," said Pistachio. "The Gospel According to Thomas."

My grandfather chuckled and shook his head. "Thomas," he said, "always this Thomas! That's all you ever talk about."

I knew that Bible talk had always bored my grandfather to tears—he'd said so more than once—but this rudeness seemed uncharacteristic of him, especially to a man he'd known so short a time. Seating myself against the opposite railing, facing the old priest, I searched my mind for more congenial subjects. I forgot exactly what we talked of first—the unseasonably warm weather, perhaps—but I do recall that twice again there were references to some private dispute between the two of them.

The first time, I believe, we'd been talking of the news—of the start of Queen Elizabeth's Silver Jubilee, in fact, which my wife and I had watched on TV the night before. Coralette appeared uninterested in the story, but it brought a curious response from Father Pistachio—"I could tell you of another queen"—and an immediate dismissal from my grandfather: "Oh, stop already with your queen!" The second time came much later, and only after the conversation had taken a number of circuitous turns, but once again the starting point was an item from the previous night's news: in this case the repeal of Miami's gay rights ordinance (*"Faygelehs,"* my grandfather snapped, "they oughta send 'em back where they came from!"), which had led to a discussion of Florida in general. Pistachio expressed an interest in settling there eventually—somehow he was under the impression that more than half its citizens spoke Spanish—but my grandfather had had a grudge against the place ever since, during the '20s, he'd made the mistake of investing in some real estate "just off the Everglades" and had lost his shirt. "Hell," he fumed, "they were selling land down there that was still underground!"

I let that one go by me; I could never have touched it. But it did bring a kind of response: Coralette, who read the *Enquirer* each week as religiously as she read the Bible, reported that a colony of derelicts had been discovered living "unnergroun' " in the catacombs below Grand Central Station. (Six months later the story would resurface in the *Times*.) There were as many as forty of these derelicts, pale, frightened, and skinny, subsisting on garbage and handouts from people in the street but spending most of their time down below, amid the steam pipes and the darkness. "Now some folks be wantin' the city to clear 'em outa there," she said, "but it don't make no difference to me. Fact is, I feels kinda sorry for 'em. They just a bunch o' poor, homeless men."

Pistachio sighed, stirred once again by some private memory. "All men are homeless," he said. "We have journeyed for so many year that—"

"Enough with the journey!" said my grandfather. "Can't we ever talk about anything else?"

Hoping to forestall an argument, I tried to change the subject yet again. I had noticed a fat little paperback protruding from Pistachio's back pocket, with *Diccionario* printed at the top. "I see you like to come prepared," I said, pointing to the title.

He gave a shrug both courtly and ambiguous, in true Old World style. "Is for my book," he said. His voice was modest, but there'd been a hint of capitals in it: "My Book."

"You're writing something?" I asked.

He smiled. "Is already written. More than forty years ago I finish it. Then I write it over in Latin, then in *portugués*. Now I am retired, write in English."

So that was why he'd come up north—to work on a translation of his book. It had already been published (at his own expense, he admitted) in Costa Rica and Brazil. The English title, itself the work of almost three days, was to be "A New and Universal Commentary on the Gospel According to Thomas, Revised in Light of Certain Excavations."

"I write it just before I leave the Order," he explained. "It say all I ever want to say. If I live long enough, *si Dios quiere,* I pray that I may see my book in the seven major languages of the world."

This struck me as a shade optimistic, but I didn't want to risk insulting him. He was obviously an extreme case of the proverbial one-book author.

"Who knows," he added, with a nod to my grandfather, "maybe we even do the book in Yiddish."

Grandfather raised his eyebrows and pointedly looked away. I could see that he had heard all this before.

"I gather that it's some sort of religious tract," I said, trying to sound interested. "The Puritans used to go in for that sort of thing. Treatises on doctrine, damnation, the Nativity—"

He shrugged. "Is about a *natividad,* but not the one you think. Is about *natividad* of man."

"Ain't no big mystery in that," said Coralette. "Ain't none of us so different from the monkeys and the lizards and the worms. Lawd done made us outa earth, just like the Bible say. Made each and ever' one of us the same." Reaching back, she took Father Pistachio's dictionary and worked a finger back and forth against the glossy surface of its cover. Soon a little roll of dirt and rubbed-off skin, gray-black in color, had accumulated beneath it; whereupon, taking my own hand between her two much broader ones, she rubbed my fingertip against the same surface. The same material appeared, the same color.

"See?" she said triumphantly. "We's all of us God's clay."

I never got to ask Father Pistachio his own views on the subject because by this time three o'clock had passed and the older children of the neighborhood, released from Brandeis High, were accumulating on the sidewalk before us like Coralette's gray-black matter. My grandfather got unsteadily to his feet just as a trio of teenaged girls swept up the steps, followed by a boy with a pirate's bandana and the straggly beginnings of a moustache. Not one of them was carrying a schoolbook. For a moment Coralette remained where she'd been sitting, blocking half the entranceway, but then she, too, sighed heavily and made as if to stand. I gathered that this was the usual hour for the group to break up.

"I say farewell for now," said Father Pistachio. "Is time for me to go upstairs to sleep. Tonight I work a little on my book." I helped him down from his perch, amazed at how small and fragile he seemed; his feet had barely been able to reach the landing.

"Come on," I said to Grandfather, "I'll walk you back." I told the others that I hoped to see them again. I half believe I meant it.

My grandfather appeared to be in a good mood as we headed

up 81st. I, too, was feeling good, if only from relief that he'd adjusted so readily to his new situation. "This life seems to be agreeing with you," I said.

"Yeah, things are always easier when you got a few friends around. That colored girl is good as gold, and so's the Father. He may not speak good English, but I'm telling you, he's one smart cookie. I almost wonder what he sees in me."

I had to admit it seemed an unlikely friendship: a self-professed scholar—a man of the cloth—keeping company with someone, in Whittier's phrase, "innocent of books" and of religion, the one equipped with little English, the other with no Spanish at all. What queer conversations those two old-timers must have had!

"You'll have to come by more often," Grandfather was saying. "I could tell he took to you right away. And he's dying to meet Karen."

"Oh? Why's that?"

"I don't know, he said she sounded interesting."

"That's funny, I wonder why he'd . . ." I paused; I had had a sudden suspicion. "Hey, did you by any chance happen to mention where she works?"

"Sure. She's with that big publishing outfit, isn't she? Something to do with books."

"That's right. *Account* books! She's in the billing department, remember?"

He shrugged. "Books are books."

"I suppose so," I said, and let the matter drop. Inside, though, I was wincing. Poor old Pistachio! No wonder he'd taken such an interest in us: the old geezer probably thought we'd help him sell his book! The truth was, of course, that using Karen as an "in" to the publishing world was like trying to break into Hollywood by dating an usher; but I saw no reason to tell this to Pistachio. He would find out soon enough. Meanwhile, he'd be a good friend for my grandfather.

" 'Course, he does go on a bit about that book of his," Grandfather was saying. "He'll talk your ear off if you let him. Some of the theories he's got . . ." He shook his head and laughed. "Know what he told me? That the Indians are a long-lost tribe of Israel!"

I was disappointed; I had heard that one too many times before. It had become something of a joke, in fact, like the Hollow Earth theory and Bigfoot. I didn't mind Pistachio's having a few crackpot

notions—at his age he was entitled to believe what he pleased—
but couldn't he have been just a bit more original? The long-lost-
tribe routine was old hat. Even my grandfather seemed to regard
it as a joke.

But typically, he'd gotten it all wrong.

Saturday, June 11

"Is no one safe today," said Father Pistachio. It was a statement,
not a question. "Is the same even for an old man like me. Two
nights ago I am followed home by six, seven boys. Maybe, in the
dark, they do not see I wear the collar of a priest. I think they
are getting ready to push me down, but I am lucky. God, He
watches. Just as I am asking myself if it is wise to call for help,
a car of the police comes slowly up the street, and when I turn
around the boys are gone."

"*Po*-lice?" sniffed Coralette. "I don't have no use for them *po*-
lice. Kids ain't scared o'them no more, and the law don't mean
a thing. Station's sittin' right up there in the middle of 82nd
Street, just a block away, and you ever see the house right next
door to it? Hmmph! Wouldn't want no daughter o' *mine* livin'
there—not these days. Blocks 'round here ain't fit for walkin'
down."

"Aw, come on," said my grandfather, "that's no way to talk.
Brooklyn's ten times worse than this, believe me. The way I see
it, if you're gonna sit inside all day you may as well be dead."

At this moment we, too, were sitting inside, round a greasy
little table at Irv's Snack Bar near the corner of 81st and Amsterdam, sipping our afternoon coffee and talking crime, New
York's favorite subject. Irv and his wife would let the old folks
sit for hours, so Grandfather's friends came here often, especially
on weekends, when the stoop of Pistachio's building was occupied
by teenagers. Occasionally the blare of their radios penetrated the
snack bar's thin walls, along with the pounding rhythms of soul
music from the jukebox inside Davey's, just across the street.
Saturday nights began early around here, at least when the weather
was warm; even at noontime the noise was almost incessant, and
continued through the weekend. I don't know how anyone could
stand it.

"My cousin's step-sister up on 97th, she say things just as bad
up there. Say they's a prowler in the neighborhood." The metal

chair sagged noticeably as Coralette shifted her weight. "Some kinda pervert, she say. Lady downstairs from her—Mrs. Jackson, down in 1-B—she hear her little girl just a cryin' out the other night, and see the light go on. Real late it was, and the chile only seven years old. She get up and go into the chile's room to see what happened. Window's wide open to let in the breeze, but she ain't worried, 'cause they's bars across it, like you got to have when you's on the groun' floor. But that chile, she shakin' fit to die. Say she wake up and they's a boy standin' right by her bed, just a lookin' down at her and doin' somethin' evil to hisself. She give a holler and reach for the light, and he take off. Wiggle hisself right out the window, she say. Mrs. Jackson, she look, but she don't see nothin', and she think the chile be havin' bad dreams, 'cause ain't nobody slippery enough to get through them bars. . . . But then she look at the wall above the window, and they's some kinda picture drew up there, higher than the little girl could reach. So Mrs. Jackson know that what the chile say is true. Chile say she seen that boy standin' there, even in the dark. Say it was a *white* boy, that's what she say, and mother-naked, too, 'cept for somethin' he had on over his head, somethin' real ugly like. I tell you, from now on that chile gwin' be sleepin' wid the light on!"

"You mean to say steel bars aren't enough these days?" I laughed, but I'm not sure why; we, too, lived on the ground floor, and not so far from there. "That's all Karen has to hear. She'll be after me again about moving to a more expensive place." I turned to Grandfather. "Do me a favor, don't mention this to her, okay?"

"Of course," he said. "You don't want to go around scaring women."

Father Pistachio cleared his throat. "I would like very much to meet this Karen someday. . . ."

"No question about it," I assured him. "We're going to get the two of you together real soon. Not today, though. Today she's busy painting."

My grandfather squinted at his watch, a souvenir of his years with the watch-casing firm. "Uh oh, speak of the devil, I have to get back. She's probably up there already."

My wife had gotten permission to repaint part of Grandfather's bedroom wall, as well as a few pieces of furniture salvaged from his former apartment. She was convinced she did such things better without my help, and that I would only get in the way—a belief which I'd encouraged, as I was in no hurry to join the two of them. I much preferred to sit here in the snack bar, eating jelly doughnuts and tracing patterns in the sugar on the table. Besides, there were some questions I wanted to ask Father Pistachio. Later, Karen and I were taking Grandfather out to eat, to celebrate his first successful week at the Manor. He'd told us it would be a welcome change.

"I'm looking forward to a decent meal tonight," he was saying, as he got up from his chair. He placed an unsteady hand on my shoulder. "These grandchildren of mine really know how to treat an old man!"

Making his way to the counter, he insisted on paying for my doughnuts and coffee, as well as for the Sanka he'd been restricted to since his stroke. "And give me some quarters, will you, Irv?" he asked, laying another dollar down. "I gotta do some wash, spruce up my wardrobe. My grandchildren are taking me out tonight—someplace swanky." Suddenly a doubt arose; he looked back at me. "Hey, I'm not going to have to wear a tie, am I?"

I shook my head. "It's not going to be *that* swanky!"

"Good," he said. "Just the same, I think I'll wear the socks with the monograms on 'em, the ones your mother gave me. You never can tell who you may be sitting next to." He bid the three of us good-bye, nodded to the counterman—"Take care, Irv, say hello to *Mrs.* Snackbaum for me"—and shuffled out the door.

Irv scratched his head. "I keep tellin' him, my name's Shapiro!"

Across the street the music had grown louder. I could feel the throb of the bass line through the soles of my shoes, and the air rang with grunting and screeching. I was glad I'd stayed inside.

Until now I'd avoided bringing up Pistachio's book. With Grandfather gone it was easier. "I understand," I said, "that you have some rather novel theories about the Indians and the Jews."

His face wrinkled into a grin. "Indian, Jew, Chinese, Turk—is all come from the same place."

"Yes, I remember. You said that's what you deal with in your 'Commentary,' "

"*Exactamente.* Is all there in the Gospel, for those who understand. Thomas, he is very clear, tell you all you want to know. Is through him I discover where man come from."

"Okay, I'll bite. Where *does* he come from?"

"Costa Rica."

The grin remained, but the eyes were absolutely earnest. I waited in vain for a punchline. Beside him Coralette nodded sagely, as if she'd heard all this before and was convinced that it was true.

"That sounds just a little unlikely," I said at last. "Man first walked erect somewhere in East Africa, at least that's what I've always read. They've got it all mapped out. Asia and Europe were next, and then across the Bering Strait and down into America. That was where the Indians came from: they kept on spreading southward till they'd covered the New World."

Pistachio had been listening patiently, mumbling "Yes . . . yes . . ." to himself as he searched his pockets for nuts. Finding one, he split it apart and studied it with the quiet satisfaction of a man contemplating a good cigar. At last he looked up. "Yes," he said, "all this I too have heard, from the time I am *estudiante*. But is all wrong. Is—how you say?—backward. Truth, she is far more strange."

The old man had gotten a faraway look in his eyes. Coralette pushed heavily to her feet and, mumbling excuses, waddled off upon some errand. I could see that it was lecture-time.

For the next half hour or so, as I sipped at still another cup of coffee, while the music from across the street grew steadily more primitive and the afternoon sunlight crept by inches up the wall, Pistachio gave me a short course in human history. It was an idiosyncratic one, to say the least, based as it was on certain Indian myth patterns and a highly selective reading of some fossil remains. According to his theory, the first men had evolved in the warm volcanic uplands of Central America, somewhere in the vicinity of Paraíso, Costa Rica—which was, by sheer coincidence, his own home town. For eons they had dwelled there in a city now gone but for the legends, one great happy tribe beneath a wise and all-powerful queen. Then, hundreds of millennia ago, threatened by invaders from the surrounding jungle—apparently some rival tribe, though I found his account here confusing—they had suddenly abandoned their city and fled northward. What's more, they hadn't paused for rest; as if still in the grip of some feverish need to escape, the tribe had kept on moving, streaming up through the Nicaraguan rain forests, spreading eastward as the land widened before them, but also pressing northward, ever northward, through what was now the United States, Canada, and Alaska, until the more adventurous pushed past the edge of the continent, crossing into Asia and beyond.

I listened to all this in silence, trying to decide just how seriously to take it. The whole thing sounded quite implausible to me, an old man's harmless fantasy, yet like a Velikovsky or a Von Däniken he was able to buttress his argument with a wide array of figures, facts, and names—names such as the Ameghino brothers, a pair of prominent nineteenth-century archeologists who'd advanced a theory similar to his, but with their own home, Argentina, as the birthplace of mankind. I looked them up the next day in the school library and discovered that they'd actually existed, though their theories had reportedly been "held in disrepute" since the late 1880s.

The name that came up most often, however, was that of Saint Thomas himself. I looked him up as well. His "Gospel" isn't found in standard Bibles, but it's featured in the ancient Gnostic version (an English translation of which, published here in 1959, is on the desk beside me as I write). I should add, by way of a footnote, that Thomas has a special link with America: when the Spaniards first arrived on these shores in the sixteenth century they were shocked to find the Aztecs and other tribes practicing something that looked rather like Christianity, complete with hell-fire, resurrections, virgin births, and magic crosses. Rather than admit that their own faith was far from unique, they theorized that Saint Thomas must have journeyed to the New World fifteen hundred years before, and that the Indians were merely practicing a debased form of the religion he had preached.

Somehow Pistachio had managed to scrape together all these queer old theories, folk tales, and fancies into a full-blown explanation of the human race—or at least that's what he claimed. He assured me that none of it conflicted with present-day Catholic doctrine, but then, I doubt he cared a fig for Catholic doctrine; he was obviously no normal priest. It was clear that, like a certain James character, he had "followed strange paths and worshipped strange gods." I wish now that I'd asked him what order he was from. I wonder if he left it voluntarily.

Yet at the time, despite my skepticism, I found the old man's sincerity persuasive. Moved by his description of the vast ante-diluvian city, with its pyramids, towers, and domes, and carried along by the sound of his voice as he traced man's hasty march across the planet, I could almost picture the course of events as if it were a series of tableaux. It had, I must admit, a certain grandeur: the idyllic tropical beginnings, a civilization sleeping through the centuries of peace, and then, all at once, the panicky flight from an army of invaders and the sudden dramatic surge northward—the first step in a global migration which would see that great primitive tribe break up, branching into other tribes that spread throughout the continent, wave upon wave, to become the Mochicas, the Chibchas, and the Changos, the Paniquitas, Yuncas, and Quechuas, the Aymaras and Atacamenos, the Puquinas and Paezes, the Coconucas, Barbacoas, and Antioquias, the Nicaraguan Zambos and Mosquitos, the Chontals of Honduras, the Maya and the Trahumare of Guatemala and Mexico, the Pueblo and the Navaho, the Paiute and the Crow, the Chinook and the Nootka and the Eskimo. . . .

"Let me get one thing straight," I said. "You're telling me that this accounts for all the races of mankind? Even the Jews?"

He nodded. "They are just another tribe."

So Grandfather had gotten it backward. According to Pistachio, the Israelites were merely a long-lost tribe of Costa Rican Indians!

"But how about family records?" I persisted. "Train tickets, steamship passages, immigration forms? I know for a fact that my family came over here from Eastern Europe."

The old man smiled and patted me on the shoulder. "Then, my son, you have made a circle of the world. Welcome home!"

The elevator shuddered to a halt and I stepped out onto the ninth floor. There was an odor of paint in the hall outside Grandfather's door. I knocked, but no one answered. When there was no response the second time, I pushed my way inside. None of the residents' doors were ever locked, old people being notoriously prone to heart attacks and fainting spells, strokes, broken hips, and other dislocations requiring immediate assistance. Though the supervision here was generally lax, absence from a meal without prior notice brought a visit from the staff. The previous summer, in a locked apartment in the middle of the Bronx, the body of an old man had lain alone and undiscovered for months until, riddled with maggots and swollen to four times its size, it had literally seeped through the floor and into the apartment below. That fate, at least, my grandfather would be spared.

His room, at the moment, was empty, but a radio whispered softly in the corner, tuned to some news station, and I saw my wife's handiwork in the freshly painted nightstand and armoire. I was admiring the job she'd done on the molding round the window when the two of them walked in, looking somewhat out of sorts. I asked them what was the matter.

"It's that laundry room," said Karen. "Only three of the washers are working, and we had a few slowpokes ahead of us. And of course your gallant old grandfather insisted that some women behind us go first, and we ended up waiting till everybody else was done. We just got the clothes in the dryer five minutes ago."

"Now, now," said Grandfather, "it'll just be a few minutes more, and then we can get this show on the road." He turned up the radio, an ancient white plastic Motorola, and for the next half hour we listened to reports of Mrs. Carter's South American tour, South Moluccan terrorists in Holland, and increasingly hot weather in New York. Soon he stretched and began fiddling sleepily with his pipe, which, as long as I'd known him, he'd never been able to keep lit. My wife saw some spots she'd missed beneath the window. I picked up the laundry bag and headed down the hall, attempting to look useful. When the elevator arrived I pressed the lowest button, marked by a "B" as big as my thumb.

Minutes later, when the door slid open once again, I felt momentarily disoriented. Outside the world still lay in daylight; down here, now that the machines were not in use, the corridor was gloomy and silent. It reminded me of a hospital at midnight, tiled walls receding into the distance while, down the middle of the ceiling, a line of dim, caged safety-bulbs made spots of illumination separated by areas of shadow.

The door to the laundry room would normally have stood within the light, but the bulb just above it was missing, leaving that section of the hall somewhat darker than the rest. Opening the door, I reached inside and groped for the light switch while my face was bathed by waves of steamy air. The superintendent's office must have been just beyond the farther wall, because I could hear, very faintly, the drumbeat of some mambo music. Then the fluorescent lights winked on, one after the other, with a loud, insect-like buzzing, but beneath it I could still make out the beat.

I recognized the broken washer at once. It was the unit in the corner at the back, the one that had been out of order weeks ago. Its electrical wire, coiled beside it, had been messily severed near the end, while another length still dangled from the socket in the wall. Evidently Frito had already attempted some repairs, for the unit had been pushed out of line, nearly two feet toward the center of the room. Beneath it, now exposed to view, lay a wide, semicircular drainage hole that extended, from the look of it, hundreds of feet down to some place Coleridge might have dreamed of, where waters flowed in everlasting night. No doubt the machines emptied into an underground spring, or one of those rivers that are said to run beneath Manhattan; only last winter the *Times* had written up a Mercer Street man who fished through a hole in his basement, pulling up eyeless white eels from a subterranean stream.

Leaning over, I caught a whiff of sewage, and could see, very dimly, the swirl of blackish current down below. Within it, outlined against the overhead lights, floated the reflection of my own familiar face, distorted by the movement of the water. It brought back memories of my honeymoon at a Catskill resort where, near the woods, an abandoned well lay covered by a moss-grown granite slab. When workmen lifted it aside my wife and I had peered into the hole, and for an instant had seen, there in the water, a pair of enormous frogs staring back at us, their pale bodies bloated like balloons. Suddenly they blinked, turned their bottoms up, and disappeared into the inky depths.

The dryer regarded me silently with its great cyclopean eye. The fluorescent lights buzzed louder. On the wall someone had scratched a crude five-pointed shape halfway between a holly leaf and a hand. I stuffed Grandfather's laundry into the bag and hurried from the room, happy to get out of there. Before closing the door, I switched the lights off. In the darkness, more clearly now, I heard the drumming. Where *was* Frito, anyway? He should have been spending less time on the mambo and more on the machines.

Grandfather appeared to be dozing when I got back to his room, but as soon as I stepped inside he looked up, seized the laundry bag, and dumped it on his bed. "Got to have my lucky socks!" he said, searching through a collection of the rattiest looking underwear I'd ever seen.

"Where's my skirt?" asked Karen, peering over his shoulder.

"You're wearing it," I said.

"No, I mean the one I had on first—that old summer thing I use for painting. It got filthy, so I stuck it in with Grandfather's stuff."

I knew the one she meant—a dowdy old green rag she'd had since college. "I must have left it in the dryer," I said, and walked wearily back down the hall. The elevator hadn't moved since I'd left it.

Yet someone had gotten to the laundry room ahead of me; I

saw light streaming under the door, and heard the distant music and a stream of Spanish curses. Inside I found Frito, shoulders heaving as he strained to push the broken washer back against the wall. He looked very angry.

He turned when I came in, and nodded once in greeting. "You give me hand with this, yes? This thing, she weigh six hundred pound."

"How'd you manage to move it out here in the first place?" I asked, eyeing the squat metal body. Six hundred seemed a conservative guess.

"Me?" he said. "I didn't move it." His eye narrowed. "Did *you?*"

"Of course not, I just thought—"

"Why I do this for, huh? Is no reason. Must have been *los niños*. They do anything."

I pointed to the severed wire. "And kids did that? Looks more like rats to me. I mean, look at it! It looks *gnawed*."

"No," he said, "I tell you once already, rats not gonna bother my machine. They try and eat through this stuff, they break their fuckin' teeth. Same with the cement." He stamped vehemently upon the floor; it sounded sturdy enough. " 'Leven year I'm in this place, and never any trouble till a couple weeks ago. I want to buy a lock, but Calzone says—"

But my eye had just been caught by a blob of faded green lying crumpled in the shadow of the dryer by the wall. It was Karen's skirt. Leaving the superintendent to his fulminations, I went to pick it up. I grasped the edge of the cloth—and dropped it with a cry of disgust. The thing was soaking wet, and, as I now saw, it had been lying in a puddle of milky white fluid whose origin seemed all too apparent. About it hung the sour odor I'd smelled before.

"Ugh!" I said. I made a face. I wasn't going to take this back upstairs. Let Karen believe it was lost. Gingerly I prodded it across the floor with my foot and kicked it down the drainage hole. It flashed green for a moment, spreading as it fell, and then was lost from sight in the blackness. I thought I saw the oily waters stir.

Frito shook his head. *"Los niños,"* he said. "They getting in here."

My eye followed the glistening trail that led from the dryer to the hole. "That's not kids," I said. "That's a grown man living in the building. Come on, let's get this covered up before somebody falls through." Bracing myself, I put my shoulder to the machine and pushed. Even when the superintendent joined me it was difficult to budge; it felt like it was bolted to the floor. At last, as metal scraped on concrete with an ugly grating sound, we got the thing back into line.

Just before leaving the room, I looked back to see Frito crouched by the coils of electric cord, glumly poking at the strands of wire that twisted like claws from the end. I sensed that there was something missing, but couldn't decide what it was. With a final wave I stepped into the hall, my mind already on dinner. Behind me, aside from the buzzing of the lights, the place was absolutely silent.

Wednesday, June 15

My grandfather was long overdue for a haircut; he'd last had one in April, well before his stroke, and his hair was beginning to creep over the back of his collar, giving him the appearance of an aged poet or, as he maintained, "an old bum." I'd have thought that he'd be pleased to get it trimmed, and to idle away an afternoon at the barber's, but when I arrived to pick him up in the lobby of the Manor he looked weary and morose.

"Everything's slowing down," he said. "I guess I must be feeling my age. I looked at my face in the mirror when I got up this morning, and it was the face of an old man." He ran his fingers through his hair, which had long ago receded past the top of his head. "Even my hair's slowing down," he said. "Damned stuff doesn't grow half as fast as it used to. I remember how my first wife—your grandmother—used to say I looked distinguished because my hair was prematurely gray." He shook his head. "Well, it's still gray, what's left of it, but it sure as hell ain't premature."

Maybe he was depressed because, after a lifetime of near-perfect health, he'd finally encountered something he couldn't shake off; though the doctor considered him recovered, the stroke had left him weak, uncoordinated, and increasingly impatient with himself. Or maybe it was just the weather. It was one of those heavy, overcast spring days that threaten rain before nightfall and, in the coming weeks, a deadly summer. As we strolled outside the air was humid, the sky as dark as slate. Beneath it earthly objects— the tropical plants for sale outside a florist's shop, an infant in

red shorts and halter with her ears already pierced, the gaudy
yellow signboard of La Concha Superette—stood out with unnatural clarity, as if imbued with a terrible significance.

"My legs feel like they're ready for the junk heap," said Grandfather. "My mind'll probably go next, and then where will I be?"

He was, in fact, walking even more slowly than usual—he'd
stumbled on the planks across the sewage ditch, and I'd had to
shorten my steps in order to stay by his side—but I assured him
that he had a few good decades left. "If worst comes to worst,"
I said, "you've still got your looks."

This brought a snort of derision, but I noticed that he stood a
little straighter. Screwing up his face, he thrust his hands into his
pockets like some actor in a 1930s Warner Brothers' movie.
"Nobody wants a man with a mug like mine," he said, "except
maybe somebody like Mrs. Rosenzweig."

"Well, there you are." I remembered the little old woman with
the deaf roommate. "See? There's someone for everyone." He
shook his head and muttered something about its not being right.
"Not right?" I said. "What's the matter? Saving yourself for some
pretty little blonde?"

He laughed. "There aren't any blondes where I live. They're all
old and gray like me."

"So we'll get you someone from the neighborhood."

"Stop already with the dreaming! The closest thing you'll find
around here is some colored girl with dyed blond hair."

"Here's one that looks white enough," I said, tapping on the
glass. We had reached the Barbería/Barbershop, where an adver-
tising placard in the window, faded by the sun, showed a beefy
Mark Spitz look-alike, hair aglisten with Vitalis, attempting to
guess the identity of a sinuous young woman who had just crept
up behind him. Covering his eyes with two pale, finely manicured
hands, she was whispering, "Guess who?" That unwarranted question mark annoyed me.

The shop's front door was open to let in a nonexistent breeze,
and the smell of rose water, hair tonic, and sweat hung nostalgically
in the doorway. There was only one barber inside, fluttering over
a burly *latino* who sat glowering into the mirror, somehow retaining
his dignity despite the clumps of shiny black hair that covered
his shoulders like fur. Portraits of Kennedy, Pope John, and some
unidentified salsa king beamed down at us through a talcum-
powder haze. Seating himself by the magazine rack, my grandfather

reached instinctively for the *Daily News,* realized he'd already seen it, and passed it on to me. Bored, I scanned the headlines—Spain holding its first free elections in forty-one years, two derelicts found dead and blinded in a men's room at Grand Central Station, James Earl Ray returned to prison following an escape—while Grandfather stared doubtfully at a pile of Spanish-language magazines on the lower shelf. Moments later I saw him frown, lean forward, and extract from beneath the pile a tattered, thumb-stained *Hustler,* which he opened near the middle. His expression changed, more in shock than delight. "Mmmph," he said, "they never had stuff like this back in Brooklyn." Suddenly remembering himself, he shut the magazine. I could see he was embarrassed. "You know," he said, "it's silly for you to sit around here all afternoon. I'll be okay on my own."

"Fine," I said. "We can meet later for coffee." Karen wouldn't be home till after her Wednesday-evening class, and I had plenty of errands to do.

Outside, the sky had grown even darker. As I started up Amsterdam, I could see shopkeepers rolling up their awnings. Davey's Tavern, on the corner ahead, was already noisy with patrons, while soul music, drunks, and broken beer bottles spilled out upon the pavement in front. An overturned garbage can disgorged its contents into the gutter; a few feet past it the opening to a sewer was clogged with bread crusts, wormy lettuce leaves, and pools of curdled cream. "Peewee, huh?" a man on the sidewalk was shouting. He wore greasy overalls and a sleeveless T-shirt dark with perspiration. "Hey, nigger, why they callin' you Peewee for? You needs some o' what I got?" He began digging drunkenly at his fly while the small, goateed man he'd been shouting at hurried toward a nearby car, muttering threats to "get me somethin' an' bust that nigger's ass."

I was just crossing the street to avoid the inevitable fight when I heard my name called. It was Father Pistachio, lounging calmly on his stoop just around the corner from the scene of action and grinning at me beneath his halo of white hair. In truth I'd been hoping to avoid him as well: I just didn't have the time today for another history lesson. Resolving that our meeting would be brief, I waved and circled warily in his direction. He seemed to be alone.

"Where's your friend?" I asked, declining his invitation to sit down.

"Coralette? She call me up this morning, all *dolorosa,* tell me she have trouble in the building where she live. Something about Last Rites. I tell her I am a priest, I can give the Last Rites, but she say is all right, she going to be asking her minister. Then someone else is having to use the telephone—Coralette, you know, she live in a hotel, is not a nice place at all—and so there is no more time for talking. She tell me she will come by later, though. Maybe you will still be here."

"I doubt it," I said. "I really can't stay. I've got to join my grandfather in a little while."

"Ah, yes." The old man smiled. "Herman, he say he gain twenty pound Saturday night at the restaurant. Say he have the best time of his life. And I am thinking to myself, Is good to know that some young people today still have respect for the old."

I nodded uneasily, hoping he wasn't leading up to another request to meet Karen. I hated to keep putting him off.

"Maybe soon you and your wife will be my guests for dinner," he went on. "Real Costa Rican food. How you like that?"

I sighed and said I'd like it very much.

"Good, good." He was visibly pleased. "I am just upstairs. And after I make the dinner, I show you what is to be in my book. Charts, maps, pictures—you understand? *Las ilustraciones.* Some I have already in the first edition, published in Paraíso. I bring it for you next time, yes?"

I said that would be fine.

All this time we had been hearing music from around the corner. Now, suddenly, came the sounds of a scuffle: a taunt, a scream, sporadic bursts of laughter from the crowd.

Pistachio shook his head. "Is a shame. Men, they just want to fight."

"Some men," I said. "But our great-great-granddaddies don't seem to have gone in for it much, at least according to you. They sound pretty cowardly, in fact—pulling up stakes when another tribe showed up, running off like a bunch of kids, leaving the city behind. . . . Sounds to me like they gave up without a fight."

I suppose I was needling him a bit, but it didn't seem to faze him.

"I think you do not understand," he said. "I never say it is another tribe. Is another *raza,* maybe, another people. One cannot be sure. No one knows where they are from. No one knows their name. Maybe they are what God make before He make a man.

Legend say that they are soft, like God's first clay, but that they love to fight. Quick like the piranha, and impossible to kill. No use to hit them in the head."

"Oh? Why's that?"

"Is hard to say. Many different stories. In one the Chibcha tell, is because they have something on the face. Flat places, ridges, things like little hooks. Back of head, she is like the front; all look much the same. Me, I think this mean they wear a special thing to cover the head in war." He made a kind of helmet with his hands. "See? This way you cannot hurt them, cannot keep them out. They go where they want, take what they want. Break into the city, steal the food, carry many captives to their king. The lucky ones they kill."

"They don't sound like very nice people."

He gave a short, unmerry laugh. "Some Indians say that they are devils. Chibcha say they are the children of God, but children He make wrong. Is no pity inside them, no love for God or man. When God see that they will not change, He try to get rid of them. They are so strong. He have to try one, two, three times! Chibcha call them *Xo Tl'mi-go,* 'The Trice Accursed.' "

I'm quoting here from memory and my spelling is approximate at best; whatever it was that he actually said, it was unpronounceable. My eyes were held by his plump little red-stained lips, which worked up and down when he talked and which continued to do so even now, as he paused to stuff another nut between them. The fight-sounds down the block had momentarily subsided, but then I heard the jangle of breaking glass—for me, even at a distance, the most unnerving and ugly of sounds—and I realized that the battle was still very much in progress. I'd swear that at one point I could hear the echoes of a faraway war cry; but maybe it was just the effect of the story.

The story—an Indian legend, he claimed—seemed to have been cooked up by a committee of primitive tribesmen sitting round a fire trying to scare themselves. It told of the invaders—clearly a bad bunch, given to all manner of atrocities—and of God's repeated attempts to exterminate them.

"First, they say, God curse the women, make them all *estériles,* barren. But is no good; is not enough. The men, they leave the jungle, raid the city, carry off its women from their bed. As long as they find women, they are still breeding."

"So then God curses the men, right?"

"Exactamente!" Raising a finger dramatically, he leaned toward
me and lowered his voice, though there was no one else around.
"God, He make their *penes* drop off. Their manhood. But again
it is no good. Even this is not enough. The fighting, the raiding,
she goes on as before. The women, they are taken from the city
and—" Here a disapproving little clucking sound, "—just as
before."

"But how could they keep on breeding without their, uh . . ."

He gave another one of those all-purpose Latin shrugs, which
seemed terribly enigmatic but may just have been embarrassed.
"Oh," he said vaguely, "they find a way." He picked a sliver of
pistachio from his teeth and stared at it a moment. "But is hard
to guess what is truth here, what is *fábula.* Is not history, you
know. Is only a story the Indians tell. *Un cuento de hadas."*

A fairy tale—yes, that's exactly what it was. A prehistoric fairy
tale.

"Well," I said, "I guess you can't blame our ancestors for running
away. Those outsiders don't sound like the kind of people you
want to hang around with. What happened, they take over when
the others moved out?"

The old man nodded. "City, she is theirs now. Belong to them.
For sport they pull her down—every temple, every tower, every
brick. Soon they are making ready to go after the others; is time
to breed again, time to bring back food, women, captives for the
sacrifice. And now, just before they leave, God make His final
curse: He seal their eyes close, every one, forever. No more can
they follow the tribe of our fathers. For them, is no more sunlight,
no more day. One by one they crawl back to the jungle. One by
one they are lost. All of them are dead now, dead and in the
earth for two hundred thousand year. Paraíso, she is built upon
the place where bodies lie. Farmers turn their bones up with the
plow, grind them up for meal. All are *cenizas* now—dust and
ashes."

That certainly sounded final enough, I thought. *Exeunt the
villains.* At least the fairy tale had a happy ending. . . .

"But hold on," I said, "what if these fellows survived even a
third curse? I mean, the first two didn't even slow them down,
they adapted right away. And it's not as if losing your sight were
a sentence of death. Who's to say the smart ones didn't stick
around? Their children could be down there in the jungle right
this minute, trying to figure out where all the women went!"

"You think perhaps they are hoping to make a new raid on Paraíso?" The old priest smiled wanly. "No, my friend. The last of them die off down there two hundred thousand year ago. Their story, she is over. *Se termino.*" He clapped his hands. "Now the tribes of man, they are far more interesting. My book tells how they learn to read the stars, build ships, make fire. . . ."

But I wasn't listening. I was thinking once again of those great Mayan cities, Tikal and Copán and the rest, standing silent and deserted in the middle of the jungle—as if, without warning, one afternoon or in the dead of night, all of their inhabitants had simply disappeared, or walked away, or fled.

I wasn't sure just where those cities lay, but I knew they were nowhere near Paraíso.

My grandfather sat waiting for me in the snack bar, lacquered and perfumed and shorn. "You shoulda seen the fight," he said as I settled into my chair. "Those colored boys can really take a beating. Damn thing would still be going on if it wasn't for the weather." He nodded toward the window, against which heavy drops of rain were splattering like gunfire.

For the next few minutes he regaled me with a description of the fight, which he'd viewed from the doorway of the barbershop. The shop itself had disappointed him—"four seventy-five," he said ruefully, "I could've cut my own hair for less than that!"—but its magazines had been a revelation. "It's unbelievable," he said, "they're showing *everything* nowadays. And you could see their faces!"

"What, are you kidding?" Maybe I hadn't heard right. "You mean to say you spent your time looking at the faces, instead of—"

"No, no, I didn't mean that! What the hell you take me for?" He leaned forward and lowered his voice. "What I'm saying is, you could tell who these gals *were.* You'd recognize 'em if you saw 'em on the street. In my day, if some floozie took her clothes off in a magazine, they made damn sure they blocked her eyes out first. Or maybe they'd show you the back of her head. But you hardly ever got to see the face."

I was going to ask him where he'd been living the past twenty years, but he was staring behind me and beginning to get up. I turned to see Coralette squeezing through the door. She saw us and moved ponderously toward our table, shaking rain from her umbrella as she came. "Lawd," she said, "if this ain't just the worst day I ever see!" Heaving herself into a seat, she sighed and shook her head. "Trouble, jus' no end o' trouble."

Coralette, it turned out, was a resident of the Notre Dame Hotel, which stood beside a drug rehabilitation center on West 80th Street. I had passed beneath its awning several times; it was a shabby little place, notable only for the grandiosity of its name and for a Coke machine that all but filled its lobby. Coralette's room was on the second floor, by the rear landing. Across the hall lived a tall, ungainly young black girl, a former addict who'd been enrolled in one of the programs at the building next door. The girl was severely retarded, with impaired speech and a pronounced mongoloid cast to her features, yet according to the scandalized Coralette she spent most of her time with a succession of men—criminals and fellow addicts, to judge by their appearance—from the s.r.o. hotels uptown. Occasionally she would bring one of these men back with her; more often she was out all night, and would return home in the morning barely able to report where she had been.

This spring had seen a change in her. She had stopped going out, and had taken to spending the nights in her room, although it was several weeks before the older woman had realized it. "She been in there all the time," said Coralette, "only I figured she away 'cause I don't never see no light under the door. Then one night I's on the way to the bathroom and hears her voice, but she ain't sayin' nothin'. . . . At first I think maybe she sick, or cryin' out in her sleep. But then I hears this movin' around, and I know she got somebody in there with her. I hears the two of 'em again on my way back. They makin' a lot o' noise, but they ain't talkin', if you knows what I mean."

The noise had been repeated on succeeding nights, and once Coralette had walked by when the visitor apparently was sleeping, "snorin' fit to kill." A few weeks later she had heard somebody coming up the stairs, followed by the closing of the door across the hall. "Now I ain't nosy," she declared, "but I did take me a peek through the keyhole when he pass. Didn't see much, 'cause the light out in the hall and it was dark as sin, but look to me like he didn't have no trousers on."

One night in April she'd encountered the girl outside the bathroom. "She lookin' sorta sick—say she think she got some sorta worm in her—so I asks her to come on in and rest herself. I got me a hot plate, so I cooks up a can o' black bean soup. Poor chile don't even know enough to say thank you, but she drink it all right down. 'Fore she go I asks her how she feelin', and she say she a whole lot better now. Say she think she gwin' be my frien'. Got herself a bran' new boyfrien', too. Sound like she real proud of herself."

For the past two weeks no one had seen her, though from time to time Coralette had heard her moving about in the room. "Sound like she alone now," Coralette recalled. "I figured she was finally settlin' down, takin' that treatment like she s'posed to. But then today the lady from the center come and say that girl ain't showed up for a month."

They had tried her door and found it locked. Knocking had brought no response; neither had an appeal from Coralette. Several other tenants had grown nervous. Finally the manager had been summoned; his passkey had opened the door.

The room, said Coralette, had been a shambles. "They was some kinda mess high up on the walls, and you got to hold your nose when you go in." The girl had been found near the center of the room, hanging naked from the light fixture with a noose around her neck. Oddly, her feet had still been resting on the floor; she must have kept her legs drawn up while dying.

"I guess that boy of hers done left her all alone." Coralette shook her head sorrowfully. "Seems a shame when you think of it, leavin' her like that, 'specially 'cause I recollect how proud she had been. Say he was the first white boyfrien' she ever had."

Wednesday, June 29

As one who believes that mornings are for sleeping, I've always tried, both as a student and a teacher, to schedule my classes for later in the day. The earliest I ever ride the subway is ten or ten-thirty A.M., with the executives, the shoppers, and the drones. One morning just before my marriage, however, returning home from Karen's house downtown, I found myself on the subway at half-past seven. Immediately I knew that I was among a different class of people, virtually a different tribe; I could see it in their work clothes, in the absence of neckties, and in the brown bags and lunch pails that they carried in place of briefcases. But it took me several minutes to discern a more subtle difference: that, instead of the *Times,* the people around me were reading (and now and then moving their lips to) the *Daily News.*

This, as it happens, was my grandfather's favorite—nay, only—reading matter, aside from an occasional racing form. "You see the story on page nine?" he demanded, waving the paper in my face. On an afternoon as hot as this I was grateful for the breeze. We were seated like three wise men, he, Father Pistachio, and I, on the stoop of Pistachio's building. I had joined them only a moment before and was sweating from my walk. Somehow these old men didn't mind the heat as much as I did; I couldn't wait to get back to my air conditioner.

"Recognize this?" said my grandfather, pointing to a photo sandwiched between a paean to the threatened B-1 bomber and a profile of Menachem Begin. "See? Bet you won't find this in your fancy-shmancy *Times!*"

I squinted at the photo. It was dark and rather smudged, but I recognized the awning of the Notre Dame Hotel.

"Wow," I said, "we'll have to send this down to Coralette." Last week, totally without warning, she had packed her bags and gone to stay with a sister in South Carolina, crossing herself and mumbling about "white boys" who were smashing the lights in her hall. I'd had to get the details from Grandfather, as my wife and I had been upstate last week. I hadn't even had a chance to say good-bye.

"I don't know," said Grandfather, "I'm not so sure she'd want to read this."

The article—"Watery Grave for Infant Quints"—was little more than an extended caption. It spoke of the "five tiny bodies . . . shrunken and foul-smelling" that had been discovered in a flooded area of the hotel basement by Con Ed men investigating a broken power line. All five had displayed the same evidence of "albinism and massive birth defects," giving the *News* the opportunity to refer to them as "the doomed quintuplets" and to speculate about the cause of death; "organic causes" seemed likely, but drowning and even strangulation had not been ruled out. "Owing to decomposition," the article noted, "it has not been possible to determine the infants' age at the time of death, nor whether they were male or female. Caseworkers in the Police Department's newly revamped Child Welfare Bureau say that despite recent budget cutbacks they are tracking down several leads."

"Pretty horrible," I said, handing the paper back to my grandfather. "I'm just glad Karen doesn't read things like this."

"But I have brought for you a thing she may like." Father Pistachio was holding up a slim orange book bound in some sort of shiny imitation cloth. It had one of those crude, British-type spines that stick out past the edges of the cover: obviously a foreign job, or else vanity press. This book, as it happened, was both. It was the Costa Rican edition of his "Commentary on Saint Thomas."

"Is a present," he said, placing it reverently in my hand. "For you, also for your wife. I inscribe it to you both."

On the flyleaf, in trembly, old-fashioned script, he had written, *"To my dear American friends: With your help I will spread the truth to all readers of your country,"* and, beneath it, *" 'We wander blind as children through a cave; yet though the way be lost, we journey from the darkness to the light.'—Thomas xv:i."*

I read it out loud to Karen after dinner that night while she was in the kitchen washing up. "Gee," she said, "he's really got his heart set on getting that thing published. Sounds to me like a bit of a fanatic."

"He's just old." I flipped through the pages searching for illustrations, since my Spanish was rusty and I didn't feel like struggling through the text. Two Aztecs with a cornstalk flashed past me, then drawings of an arrowhead, a woolly mammoth, and a thing that resembled a swim-fin. *"El guante de un usurpador,"* the latter's caption said. The glove of a usurper. It looked somehow familiar; maybe I'd seen one at the YMCA pool. I turned past it and came to a map. "See this?" I said, holding up the book. "A map of where your ancestors came from. Right on up through Nicaragua."

"Mmm."

"And here's a map of that long-lost city—"

"Looks like something out of *Flash Gordon*," She went back to the dishes.

"—and a cutaway view of the main temple."

She peered at it skeptically. "Honey, are you sure that old man's not putting you on? I'd swear that's nothing but a blueprint of the Pyramid at Giza. You can find it in any textbook, I've seen it dozens of times. He must have gotten hold of a Xerox machine and—Good God, what's that?"

She was pointing toward a small line drawing on the opposite page. I puzzled out the caption. "That's, um, let me see, *'La cabeza de un usurpador,'* the head of a usurper. . . . Oh, I know, it must be one of the helmets the invaders wore. A sort of battle mask, I guess."

"Really? Looks more like the head of a tapeworm. I'll bet he cribbed it from an old bio book."

"Oh, don't be silly. He wouldn't stoop to that." Frowning, I drifted back to the living room, still staring at the page. From the page the thing stared blankly back. She was right, I had to admit. It certainly didn't look like any helmet I'd ever seen: the alien proportions of the face, with great blank indentations where the eyes should be (unless those two tiny spots were meant for eyes), the round, puckered "mouth" area with rows of hooklike "teeth. . . ."

Shutting the book, I strolled to the window and gazed out through the latticework of bars. Darkness had fallen on the street only half an hour before, yet already the world out there seemed totally transformed.

By day the neighborhood was pleasant enough; we had what was considered a "nice" building, fairly well maintained, and a "nice" block, at least our half of it. The sidewalk lay just outside our windows, level with the floor on which I stood. Living on the bottom meant a savings on the rent, and over the years I'd come to know the area rather well. I knew where the garbage cans were grouped like sentries at the curbside, and how the large brass knocker gleamed on the reconverted brownstone across the street. I knew which of the spindly little sidewalk trees had failed to bud this spring, and where a Mercedes was parked, and what the people looked like in the windows facing mine.

But it suddenly occurred to me, as I stood there watching the night, that a neighborhood can change in half an hour as assuredly as it can change in half a block. After dark it becomes a different place: another neighborhood entirely, coexisting with the first and separated by only a few minutes in time, the first a place where everything is known, the other a place of uncertainty, the first a place of safety, the other one of—

It was time to draw the curtains, but for some reason I hesitated. Instead, I reached over and switched off the noisy little air conditioner, which had been rattling metallically in the next window. As it ground into silence, the noise outside seemed to rise and fill the room. I could hear crickets, and traffic, and the throb of distant drums. Somewhere out there in the darkness they were snapping their fingers, bobbing their heads, maybe even dancing;

yet, for all that, the sound struck me as curiously ominous. My eyes kept darting back and forth, from the shadows of the lamp-posts to the line of strange dark trees—and to that menacing stretch of unfamiliar sidewalk down which, at any moment, any-thing might walk on any errand.

Stepping back to adjust the curtains, I was startled by the movement of my own pale reflection in the glass, and I had a sudden vision, decidedly unscientific, no doubt inspired by that picture in the book: a vision of a band of huge white tapeworms, with bodies big as men, inching blindly northward toward New York.

Wednesday, July 6

"It was awful. *Awful.*"

"You're telling me! Musta been a real nightmare."

I folded my paper and sat up in the chair, straining to hear above the hum of the fan. The lobby was momentarily deserted, except for an old man dozing in the corner and two old women leafing through a magazine; a third sat numbly by their side, as if waiting for a bus. In the mirror I could see Miss Pascua and Mr. Calzone talking in the office just behind me. They were keeping their voices low.

"You've heard the, uh, details?"

"Nope. Just what I read in yesterday's *News*. Oh, sure, they're all talking about it back in the kitchen. You know how the guys are. Most of 'em got interviewed by the police, and they think they're on *Kojak*. But nobody knows much. I ain't seen Mrs. Hirschfeld all week."

"Her daughter came and took her Monday morning. I doubt if she'll be coming back."

I'd had the same impulse myself last night, when I'd first heard of the incident. I had telephoned my grandfather and asked him if he wanted to move out. He'd sounded angry and upset, but he'd expressed no desire to leave. The Manor, he'd decided, was as safe as anywhere else. A new guard had been hired for the entranceway, and tenants had been told to lock their doors.

"They haven't finished with the room yet," Miss Pascua was saying. "They keep marching through here with their bags and equipment and things. Plus we've got the Con Ed men downstairs. It's a real madhouse."

"And Mrs. Rosenzweig?"

"Ah, the poor thing's still at Saint Luke's. I was the one who telephoned the police. I heard the whole thing."

"Yeah? Bad, huh?" He sounded eager.

"Absolutely awful. She said she was fast asleep, and then something woke her up. I guess it must've been pretty loud, because you know what a racket the air conditioner makes."

"Well, don't forget, *she's* not the one who's got problems there. Her hearing's pretty sharp."

"I guess it must be. She said she could hear somebody snoring. At first, though, she didn't think anything of it. She figured it was just Mrs. Hirschfeld in the next room, so she tries to get back to sleep. But then she hears the snoring getting louder, and it seems to be coming *closer*. She calls out, 'Elsie, is that you?' I mean, she was confused, she didn't know what was going on, she thought maybe Mrs. Hirschfeld was walking in her sleep. But the snoring doesn't stop, it just keeps getting closer to the bed. . . ."

Across the lobby the elevator door slid open with an echoing of metal; several old men and women emerged. I was about to stand, until I saw that Grandfather wasn't among them. He had never been on time in his life.

"That's when she starts getting scared—"

Miss Pascua leaned forward. Above the mantel to my left, the figures in the painting stood frozen gravely at attention, as if listening.

"—because all of a sudden she realizes that the sound's coming from *more than one place*. It's all around her now, like there are dozens of sleepwalkers in the room. She puts out her hand, and she feels a face right next to hers. And the mouth is open—her fingers slide all the way in. She said it was like sticking your hand inside a tin can: all wet and round, with little teeth around the edge."

"Jesus."

"And she couldn't scream, because one of them got his hand over her face and held it there. She said it smelled like something you'd find in the gutter. God knows where he'd been or what he'd been doing. . . ."

My eyebrows rose skyward; I'm sure I must have started from my chair. If what Miss Pascua said was true, I knew *exactly* where the culprit had been and what he'd been doing. I almost turned around and called out to the two of them, but instead I remained silent. There'd be time enough to tell someone later; I would go to the authorities this very afternoon. I sat back, feeling well pleased with myself, and listened to Miss Pascua's voice grow more and more excited.

"I guess she must've thrashed around a lot, because somehow she got free and yelled for Mrs. Hirschfeld to come help her. She's screaming, 'Elsie! Elsie!' "

"A lot of good that'll do her! The old broad's deaf as a post."

"Sure, she'd sleep through anything. Right there in the next room, too. But poor old Mrs. Rosenzweig, she must've got them mad with all her yelling, because they hit her—hard. Oh, you should've seen her face! And they wrapped their arms around her neck and, do you know, they almost strangled her. She was just lying there, trying to breathe, and then she felt some others yank the sheet and blanket down, then they turned her on her stomach and pushed her face into the pillow, and she could feel their hands on her ankles, hauling her legs apart—the nightgown was actually ripped right up the side—and then another one of them pulled it up over her waist. . . ."

Miss Pascua paused for breath. "Jesus," said Calzone, "don't it make you just want to—" He shook his head. "It musta been the blacks. No one else coulda done a thing like that. I mean, to them one woman's the same as any other, they don't care how old she is, or if she's maybe got a handicap or something, just so long as she's white. You know, they caught this guy over on 76th Street, in one of them welfare hotels, he was going around with a stocking over his head—"

The elevator door slid open and my grandfather stepped out. He waved and started across the lobby. Behind me Miss Pascua had interrupted the other's story and was plunging breathlessly on, as if impatient to reach the climax of her own.

"And then, she says, there was this soft, scratching sound, real close to her ear. She says it was like someone rubbing his hands together from the cold. That's when—Well, it sure doesn't sound like any rape I ever heard of. All she'd keep saying was it felt like getting slapped. I mean it, that's just what she said."

My grandfather had reached me in time to overhear this. "God," he whispered, shaking his head, "it's absolutely unbelievable, isn't it? A woman that age—a poor defenseless blind woman. . . ."

"And the most horrible thing of all," Miss Pascua was saying, "she told me that the whole time, with all the things they did to her, they never spoke a single word."

Age-yellowed eyes opened infinitesimally wider. Wrinkled heads turned slowly as I passed. The second floor was crowded that day; I felt as if I were striding through a world of garden gnomes: old folks on the benches by the elevator, old folks standing motionless in the hall, old folks in listless conversation round the doorway to the game room. These were the same ones who congregated in the lobby each morning, waiting for the mailman to arrive, and who began gathering outside the dining room hours before mealtime. Now they had drifted up here, unmindful of the heat, to partake of what little drama yet remained from the events of Sunday night.

I was glad my grandfather wasn't one of them. At least he still got out. I'd said goodbye to him only a minute or two ago when, following the usual coffee and conversation with Pistachio, he'd retired upstairs for his afternoon nap. I hadn't told him about my suspicions, or what I intended to do. He would never have understood.

It wasn't hard to find where Mrs. Rosenzweig had been living; that end of the corridor had been screened off from the rest behind a folding canvas partition, the sort of thing hospitals use to screen the sick from one another and the dead from those alive. A small knot of residents stood chatting in front, as if waiting to see some performance inside. They regarded me with interest as I approached; I suppose that during the past few days they'd been treated to a stream of detectives and police photographers, and took me for another one.

"Have you caught them yet?" one of the ladies demanded.

"Not yet," I said, "but there may be one very good lead."

Indeed, I intended to supply it myself. I must have sounded confident, because they moved respectfully aside for me, and I heard them repeating to each other, "A good lead, he says they have a good lead," as I made my way around the screen.

Mrs. Rosenzweig's door was ajar. Sunlight flooded the room through an open window. Inside, two beefy-looking men sat perspiring over a radio, listening to a Yankees game. Neither of them was in uniform—one wore a plaid short-sleeve shirt, the other just a T-shirt and shorts—but the former, the younger of the two, had a silver badge hanging from his shirt pocket. They had been laughing about some aspect of the game, but when they saw me in the doorway their smiles disappeared.

"You got a reason to be here, buddy?" asked the one with the badge. He got up from the windowsill where he'd been sitting.

"Well, it's nothing very important." I stepped into the room. "There's something I wanted to call to your attention, that's all. Just in case you haven't already considered it. I was downstairs earlier today, and I overheard a woman who works here saying that—"

"Whoa, whoa, hold it," he said. "Now just slow down a second. What's your interest in all this anyway?"

Above the clamor of the radio (which neither of them made a move to turn down) I explained that I'd been visiting my grand-father, who lived here at the Manor. "I come by almost every week," I said. "In fact, I even had a slight acquaintance with Mrs. Rosenzweig and her roommate."

I saw the two cops exchange a quick glance—*Oh my God,* I thought, *what if these bastards think I did it?*—but the attack of paranoia proved short-lived, for I watched their expressions change from wary to indifferent to downright impatient as I told them what Miss Pascua had said.

"She said something about a foul smell, a sort of 'gutter smell.' And so it just occurred to me—I don't know, maybe you've checked this out already—it occurred to me that the logical group of suspects might be right outside." I pointed through the open window, toward the gaping brown sewage ditch that stretched along the sidewalk like a wound. "See? They've been working down there for at least a month or so, and they probably had access to the building."

The man in the T-shirt had already turned back to the game. The other gave me a halfhearted nod. "Believe me, mister," he said, "we're checking out every possibility. We may not look like it to you, but we do a pretty thorough job."

"Fine, that's fine, just so long as you intend to talk to them—"

The man in the T-shirt looked up. "We *do,*" he said. "It's being done. Thank you very much for coming forward. Now why don't you just give my partner here your name, address, and phone number in case we have to contact you." He reached out and turned up the volume on the radio.

Laboriously the other one took down the information; he seemed far more concerned with getting the spelling of my name right than with anything else I'd had to say. While he wrote I looked around the room—at the discolorations in the plaster, the faded yellow drapes, a lilac sachet on the bureau, a collection of music boxes on a shelf. It didn't look much like the scene of a crime, except for strips of black masking tape directing one's attention to certain parts of the walls and floor. Four strips framed the light switch, another four an overturned table lamp, presumably for guests. Beside it stood a clock with its dial exposed so that a blind person could read it. The bed, too, was bordered by tape, the sheet and blanket still in violent disarray. With sunlight streaming in it was hard to imagine what had happened here: the old woman, the darkness, the sounds. . . .

Snapping shut his notebook, the younger cop thanked me and walked with me to the door. Beyond it stood the canvas screen, blocking out the view, though in the space between the canvas and the floor I could see a line of stubby little shoes and hear the shrill chatter of old ladies. Well, I told myself, maybe I didn't get to play Sherlock Holmes, but at least I've done my duty.

"We'll call you if there's anything we need," said the cop, practically shutting the door in my face. As it swung closed I saw, for the first time, that there were four strips of masking tape near the top, around a foot square, enclosing a familiar-looking shape.

"Wait a second," I said. "What's that?"

The door swung back. He saw where I was pointing. "Don't touch it," he said. "We found it there on the door. That tape's for the photographer and the fingerprint guys."

Standing on tiptoe, I took a closer look. Yes, I had seen it before—the outline of a crude, five-pointed holly leaf scratched lightly into the wood. The scratch marks extended outward from the shape in messy profusion, but none penetrated inside.

"You know," I said, "I saw the same thing a few weeks ago on the wall of the laundry room."

"Yeah, the super already told us. Anything else?"

I shook my head. It wasn't till hours later, back in the solitude of my apartment, that I realized I had seen the shape in still another place.

They say the night remembers what the day forgets. Pulling out the crudely bound orange book, I opened it to one of the drawings. There it was, that shape again, in the outline of the flipper-like gauntlets which Pistachio claimed his *usurpadores* had worn.

I got up and made myself some tea, then returned to the living room. Karen was still at her Wednesday-evening class, and would not be back till nearly ten. For a long time I sat very still, with the book open on my lap, listening to the comforting rattle of the air conditioner as it blotted out the night. One memory kept intruding: how, as a child, I liked to take a pencil and trace around the edges of my hand. This shape, I knew, is one that every child learns to draw.

I wondered what it would look like if the child's hands were webbed.

Wednesday, July 13

Certain things are not supposed to happen before midnight. There's a certain category of events—certain freak encounters and discoveries, certain crimes—for which mere nighttime doesn't seem quite dark enough. Only after midnight, after most of the world is asleep and the laws of the commonplace suspended, only then are we prepared for a touch, however brief, of the impossible.

But that night the impossible didn't wait.

The sun had been down for exactly an hour. It was twenty minutes after nine o'clock. My grandfather and I were sitting edgily in his room, listening to news on the radio and waiting for the weather to come on. The past three days had been exceptionally hot, but tonight there was a certain tension, that feeling of impending rain. In the window beside us churned an antiquated little air conditioner, competing with the blare of soul and salsa from the street below. Occasionally we could see flashes of heat lightning far away to the north, lighting up the sky like distant bombs.

We were waiting for Father Pistachio, who was already several minutes late. I had promised to take both of them to an evening flute recital at Temple Ohav Sholom on 84th Street, on the other side of Broadway. There'd be a lot of old people in attendance, or so Grandfather believed. According to his calculations, the "boring part"—that is, the actual flute playing—would be over soon, and with a little luck the three of us would arrive just in time for the refreshments. I wondered if Pistachio was going to show up in his priest's collar, and what they'd make of it at the temple.

The radio announced the time. It was nine twenty-two.

"What the hell's keeping him?" said my grandfather. "We really ought to be getting over there. The ladies always leave early." He got up from the bed. "What do you think? This shirt look okay?"

"You're not wearing any socks."

"What?" He glared down at his feet. "*Oy gevalt,* it's a wonder I remember my own name!" Looking extremely dejected, he sat back on the bed but immediately jumped up again. "I know where the damn things are. I stuck them in with Esther Feinbaum's wash." He began moving toward the door.

"Wait a second," I said. "Where are you going?"

"Downstairs. I'll be right back."

"But that's ridiculous! Why make a special trip?" I fought down my exasperation. "Look, you've got plenty of socks right there in your drawer. Karen just bought you some, remember? The others'll wait till tomorrow."

"They may not be there tomorrow. Old Esther leaves 'em hanging down by the dryers. She doesn't like to have men in her room!" He grinned. "Anyway, you don't understand. They're my lucky socks, the ones your mother made. I had 'em washed special for tonight, and I'm not going without 'em."

I watched him shuffle out the door. He seemed to be aging faster, and moving slower, with each passing week.

"The time," said the radio, "is nine twenty-five."

I went to the window and looked down. Plenty of people were out on the sidewalk, drinking or dancing or sitting on the stoop, but there was no sign of Pistachio. He had said someting about bringing me some "new proof" of his theory, and I tried to imagine what it could be. A rabbi with a Costa Rican accent, perhaps, or a *Xo Tl'mi-go* skull. Or maybe just a photo of the back of his own head. I stood there while the wind from the air conditioner blew cold against my skin, watching heat lightning flash in the distance. Then I sat down and returned to the news. Karen would be on her way home, just about now, from her class up at Lehman in the Bronx. I wondered if it was raining up there. The radio didn't say.

Nine munutes later it happened. Suddenly the lights in Grandfather's room dimmed, flickered, and died. The radio fell silent. The air conditioner clattered to a halt.

I sat there in the darkness feeling faintly annoyed. The first thing that crossed my mind, I remember, was that somehow, perhaps in opening one of the dryers, Grandfather had inadvertently triggered a short circuit. Yes, I thought, that would be just like him!

In the unaccustomed silence I heard a frightened yell, then another, coming from the hall. They were joined, in a moment, by shouts from down in the street. Only then did I realize that more than just the building was affected. It was the whole city. We were having a blackout.

Still, even then, it seemed a minor annoyance. We'd had many such episodes before, in summers past, and I thought I knew what to expect. The city's overloaded current would dip momentarily; lights would flicker, clocks lose time, record players slow so that the voices turned to growls—and then, a few seconds later, the current would come back. Afterward we'd get the usual warnings about going easy on appliances, and everyone would turn his air conditioner down a degree or two. Perhaps this time the problem might be a little more severe, but it was still nothing to get excited about. Con Ed would fix things in a moment. They always had. . . .

Already it had grown hot inside the room. I switched the lamp on and off, on and off, with that sense of incomprehension and resentment one feels when a familiar object, something that's supposed to work, suddenly and mysteriously does not. Well, well, I thought, The Machine Stops. I went to the window, opened it, and peered into the darkness. There were no streetlights to be seen, and the sidewalk below me was almost invisible; it was as if I were looking down upon a courtyard or a river, though I could hear a babble of excited voices down there, voices and pounding feet and slamming doors. Buildings I could see a little better, and all of them looked dead, massive black monoliths against a black sky, with the moon just a sliver on the horizon. Across the water New Jersey was still lit, its brightness reflected in the Hudson, but here the only light came from the files of cars moving tentatively up Amsterdam and Broadway. In the glow of their headlights I could see faces at the windows of some of the other buildings, gazing out as I was, with varying degrees of wonder or curiosity or fear. From the street below came the sound of breaking glass.

It roused my sense of urgency, that sound. I wasn't worried about Karen—she'd get home okay—and no doubt old Pistachio, if he hadn't left yet, would have the sense to sit tight till the lights came on again.

But Grandfather was another story. For all I knew the old fool
was trapped down there in a pitch-black laundry room without a
single sound or ray of light to guide him. Perhaps he was unable
to locate the door; perhaps he was terrified. I had to get down
there to him. Feeling my way to the night table, I pocketed a
book of matches from beside his pipe rack and moved slowly
toward the hall.

Outside I could hear the residents shouting to one another from
their doorways, their voices querulous and frightened. "Frito!"
they were shouting. "Where's Frito?" Blindly I continued toward
the stairs, inching my way across the polished floor. "Frito? Is
that Frito?" an old lady called out as I passed. She sounded on
the edge of panic. Immediately others up and down the hall took
up the cry. "Frito, is it a blackout?" "Frito, do you have a
flashlight?" "Frito, I want to call my son!"

"For God's sake, stop it!" I shouted. "I'm not Frito—see?" I
lit a match in front of my face. It probably made me look like
a cadaver. "Now just stay in your rooms and keep calm," I said.
"We'll get the lights on for you as soon as we can."

I felt my way past the elevator, now useless, and went on until
I'd reached the top of the stairs, where I lit another match. The
first step lay just beneath my foot. Holding onto the metal railing,
I started down.

As a boy I'd been afraid of the dark—or, more specifically, of
monsters. I knew they only inhabited the world of movies, but
sometimes in the dark it would occur to me that I, too, might
be performing, all unwittingly, in a movie, perhaps even in the
dread role of victim. There were two things movie victims never
did, at least (alas) in my day: they never swore, and they never
uttered brand names. Knowing this, I'd hit upon an ingenious
way to keep my courage up. Whenever I was forced to brave the
darkness, whether in the celler or the attic or even my own room,
I'd chant the magic words *"Fuck"* and *"Pepsi-Cola"* and I knew
that I'd be safe.

Somehow, though, I doubted that these words—or any words,
in any tongue—would still be so effective. Magic wasn't what it
used to be; I would simply have to put one foot in front of the
other and take my chances.

Echoes of voices floated up the stairwell—cries for assistance,
for candles, for news. Others were calling out to friends. At each
floor the cries would get louder, diminishing again as I passed on

toward the next. While I descended I kept a tight grip on the railing, nervously feeling my way around the landings where the railing came to an end. The eighth floor disappeared behind me, and the seventh; I counted them off in my head. The sixth . . . The fifth . . . Passing the fourth floor, I saw a moving light on the stairway beneath and heard footsteps advancing upward. Then the light veered through a doorway and was lost from sight. One floor down I heard Calzone's voice and saw a flashlight beam receding down the hall. "No, you can't go *nowhere*," he was shouting, "it's blacked out all the way to Westchester. Con Ed says they're working on it now. They'll get it all fixed up before too long." I hoped he was right.

As I passed the second floor I began to hear a noise which, at the time, I couldn't identify: a hollow, rhythmic, banging noise from down below, like someone hammering on a coffin. I couldn't even tell where it was coming from, unless from the wall itself, for the hammering became louder as I continued my descent, reaching its loudest point almost midway between the two floors— after which, unlike the voices, it began growing fainter again. By the time I reached the first floor it was lost amid the noises from the street.

They were having a festival out there, or a riot. I could hear shouts, laughter, and Latin music from some battery-driven tape deck. I also heard the shattering of glass, and what I first mistook for gunshots, but which I later realized were only firecrackers left over from the Fourth. Despite the clamor outside, the lobby wore an air of desolation, like an abandoned palace in time of war. As I rounded the stairs I caught a glimpse of its high, mirrored wall and, in it, dim reflections of the rubber plants, the mantelpiece, the sagging, empty chairs. The room was illuminated by a lantern that flickered in the alcove in front. Nearby stood the new security guard, talking to a group of shadowy figures in the doorway. I remember wondering whether he'd be called upon to keep the neighborhood at bay tonight, and whether he'd be able to do so.

But at the moment that didn't seem important. Finding the railing again, I continued downward. The lantern light vanished with a turn in the stairs, and I found myself once more in total darkness. Already the first floor's noise seemed far behind; my footsteps, deliberate as they were, echoed softly from the walls. Seconds later I felt the railing end, and knew I'd reached the landing. Here I paused for breath, fingers pressed against the rough concrete. The air was suffocating; I felt as if I were chin-deep in warm water, and that if I stepped forward I would drown. Digging into my pocket, I found a match and, like a blind man, lit it. Walls leapt into view around me. I felt better now—though for a moment an old warning flashed through my mind about people smothering in locked vaults because they'd lit matches and burned up their oxygen. Silly, I thought, it's nothing but a basement— and proceeded down the final flight of steps.

At last my feet touched bottom. I lit another match and saw, ahead of me, the narrow corridor stretching into darkness. As I followed it, I listened. There was no sound. The match burned my fingers and I dropped it. "Grandfather?" I called, in the half-embarrassed voice of one not sure of a response. "Grandfather?" I thought I heard a stirring from farther down the hall, like something being scraped across a cement floor. "It's okay, I'm coming!" Lighting still another match, I made my way toward the door to the laundry room. Even at this distance I could smell the moist, sweet laundry smell and, beneath it, something sour, like a backed-up drain. *Sewer men,* I thought, and shook my head.

When I was still a step or two away, the match went. Blindly I groped for the door. I could hear someone on the other side, scrabbling to get out. At last my fingers found the knob. "It's okay," I said, turning it, "I'm here—"

The door exploded in my face. I went down beneath a mob of twisting bodies pouring through the doorway, tumbling out upon me like a wave. I was kicked, tripped over, stepped on; I struggled to rise, and felt, in the darkness, the touch of naked limbs, smooth, rubbery flesh, hands that scuttled over me like starfish. In seconds the mob had swept past me and was gone; I heard them padding lightly up the hall, heading toward the stairs.

Then silence.

I lay back on the floor, exhausted, unable to believe it was over. I knew that, in a little while, I would not be able to believe it had happened at all. Though they'd left the stench of sewage in my nostrils, the gang—whatever they were, wherever they had gone—already seemed a crazy dream born of the darkness and the heat.

But Grandfather was real. What had they done to him? Trembling, head spinning, I staggered to my feet and found the doorway to the laundry room. Inside I lit one last match. The floor shone wet and slippery; the four washers lay scattered across it like children's discarded toys. There was no sign of my grandfather.

Hours later, when they pulled him from the elevator stalled midway between the first and second floors—Frito with his crowbar, Calzone holding the light—all my grandfather would say (feebly waving the two little pieces of dark cloth as if they were trophies) was, "I found my socks."

Karen, all this time, was fifty blocks uptown.

At nine-thirty she and her friend Marcia had been driving home in Marcia's little white Toyota, returning from their evening class at Lehman. There'd been an obstruction at 145th Street, and Marcia had turned south onto Lenox Avenue, past the Lenox Terrace project and the blocks of ancient brownstones. Though the traffic was heavy tonight, they were making good time; a mile ahead, at Central Park, they would be turning west. The air inside the car was hot and stuffy, but they kept the doors locked and the windows rolled up tight. This was, after all, the middle of Harlem.

Suddenly, as if some child had yanked the plug, the lights went out.

Marcia's foot went instinctively to the brakes; the car slowed to a crawl. So did the cars in front and behind. A few, elsewhere, did not. From somewhere up ahead came a grinding crash and the sound of tearing metal. Horns blared, bumpers smashed against bumpers, and the traffic rolled to a standstill. Beyond the unmoving line of headlights there was nothing but darkness.

But all at once the darkness was filled with moving shapes.

"Oh my God," said Marcia. "Look!"

Up and down the blackened street, hordes of figures were rushing from the houses, cheering, clapping, arms waving, as if they'd been waiting all their lives for this moment. It reminded the women of a prison break, an end of school, a day of liberation. They saw one tall, gangling figure burst through a doorway and dash into the street directly in front of them. Suddenly, in sheer exuberance, he bounded high into the air, feet kicking like a ballet dancer's, and sailed clear across the hood of the car, landing moments later on the other side and disappearing into the night. Karen never got to see his face, but there was one image she'd remember long afterward, whenever the blackout was discussed: the image of those two white sneakers dancing high above the beam of the headlights, six feet in the air, as if somehow released, not just from man's law, but from the law of gravity as well.

It was nearly one o'clock, and I still couldn't reach her.

I was sitting in Grandfather's room with the phone cradled in my lap. Beside me the old man lay snoring. I had put him to bed only a few minutes before but he'd already fallen asleep, exhausted from his ordeal in the elevator. There would be no sleep for me, though: I was too worried about Karen, and events outside the window only made me worry more. I heard hoarse shouts, the shattering of glass, and gangs of youths passing unseen in the streets below, bragging to each other about the jewelry, clothes, and radios they'd robbed. On Amsterdam Avenue a crowd had formed in front of the pawnshop, and three dark burly men, naked to the waist, were struggling to tear down the metal security gate that stretched across the window and the door. Others, holding flashlights, were egging them on. There were distant fires to the north, and sirens, and the echoes of explosions. I was almost beginning to think of myself as a widower.

Suddenly, on my lap, the phone began to ring. (Telephones were not affected by the power failure, being part of a separate electrical system.) I snatched it to my ear before Grandfather awoke.

"Goddammit, Karen, where the hell *were* you all this time? I've been trying you for hours. Couldn't you at least have picked up a phone—"

"I couldn't," she said. "Honestly. I haven't been near a phone all night."

Her voice sounded far away. "Where are you now," I said, "at Marcia's? I tried there, too."

"Believe it or not, I'm up here at the Cloisters."

"What?"

"It's true—the castle's right behind me, completely dark. I'm in a phone booth near the parking lot. There's a whole bunch of people up here, it's really beautiful. I can see stars I've never seen before."

For all her seeming rapture, I thought I detected a thin edge of hysteria in her voice—and when she told me what had happened, I understood why.

She and Marcia had spent the first part of the blackout sitting terrified in their car, watching things go to pieces around them.

Store windows were being smashed, doors broken down; people were running past them waving torches. Others hurried back and forth along the avenue in a travesty of Christmas shopping, their arms weighed down with merchandise. Amid such activity those trapped within the cars had been ignored, but there'd been a few bad moments, and help had been slow to arrive. With stoplights out all over the city and traffic tied up everywhere at once, the accident had cost them nearly an hour.

Even when the line of cars began rolling again, they made little speed, creeping through the dark streets like a funeral cortege, their headlights providing the sole illumination—though here and there the eastern sky across the Harlem River seemed to glow with unseen fires. As they drew farther south the crowds grew thicker, crowds who made no effort to move aside for them. More than once their way was blocked by piles of burning refuse; more than once a fist would pound against the car door and a black face would glare fiercely through the window. Continuing in their present course seemed madness, and when some obstruction several blocks ahead seemed likely to halt them a second time, Marcia turned up the first wide thoroughfare they came to, 125th Street, and drove west in the direction of the Hudson, narrowly avoiding the bands of looters stockpiling food crates in the center of the street. At Riverside Drive, instead of resuming their way south, on impulse they had headed in the opposite direction, eager to get as far from the city as they could. They had driven all the way to Fort Tryon Park, at the northern tip of the island.

"We've both had a chance to calm down now," she added. "We're ready to start back. Marcia's getting tired, and both of us want to get home. We're going to take the West Side Highway all the way to 96th, so we shouldn't have any problems. But I swear to God, if we see another black I hope we hit him!"

I said I hoped that wouldn't be necessary, and made her promise to call me as soon as she got home. I was going to spend the night here in Grandfather's room.

After hanging up, I turned back to the action in the street below. Over on Amsterdam the crowd had succeeded in pulling down the pawnshop's metal gate. The large display window had already been stripped bare; glass littered the sidewalk. Now they were lined up in front of the shop like patrons at a movie theater, patiently awaiting their turn to file inside and take something. It was clear that the ones at the end of the line were not going to find much left. They passed the time by breaking the shards of glass into smaller pieces. The sound reminded me, somehow, of films I'd seen of Nazi Germany. It set my teeth on edge.

Suddenly there was a cry of *"Cuidado!"* and the crowd melted away. A minute passed, and then, like twin spaceships from another world, a pair of blue-and-white police cars rolled silently up the avenue, red lights whirling on their roofs. They paused, and from each car a searchlight beam swept dispassionately over the ruins of the shop. Then the searchlights were switched off, and the cars moved on, unhurried and silent. The crowd returned moments later. The sound of breaking glass continued through the night.

There were thousands of similar stories that night. There was the story of the man who pulled up before an appliance store in a rented truck and carted off a whole block of refrigerators; and the story of the twelve-year-old black boy who walked up to a white woman on the street and nearly strangled her when he tried to wrench a string of pearls from her neck; and the story, repeated many times, of mobs racing through the aisles of five-and-tens, stealing ribbons, erasers, spools of thread, shoes that didn't fit— anything they could lay their hands on, anything they saw. For months afterward the people of the poorer black sections of Brooklyn were forced to do their shopping miles from home because the stores in their own neighborhoods had been destroyed. By the time the blackout was over, nine million people had gone a day without electricity, three thousand had been arrested for looting with thousands more unpunished, and a billion dollars in damages had been lost.

But amid the statistics and postmortems, the newspaper stories and police reports, there were other reports—"unsubstantiated rumors," the *Times* called them—of roaming whites glimpsed here and there in the darker corners of the city, whites dressed "oddly," or undressed, or "emaciated" looking, or "masked," terrorizing the women of the neighborhood and hiding from the light. A woman in Crown Heights said she'd come upon a "white boy" thrusting his hand between her infant daughter's legs, but that he'd run away before she got a look at him. A Hunts Point girl swore that, minutes after the blackout began, a pack of "skinny old men" had come swarming up from the basement of an abandoned building and had chased her up the block. At the Astoria Boulevard subway stop near Hell Gate, an electrical worker had heard someone—a woman or a child—sobbing on the tracks where, hours before, a stalled train had been evacuated, and had seen, in his flashlight's beam, a group of distant figures fleeing through the tunnel. Hours later a man with a Spanish accent had telephoned the police to complain, in broken English, that his wife had been molested by "kids" living in the subway. He had rung off without giving his name. A certain shoppingbag lady, subject of a humorous feature in the *Enquirer,* even claimed to have had sexual relations with a "Martian" who, after rubbing his naked groin, had groped blindly beneath her dress; she had a long history of alcoholism, though, and her account was treated as a joke. The following September the *News* and the *Post* ran indignant reports on the sudden hike in abortions among the city's poor—but then, such stories, like those of climbing birth rates nine months later, are part and parcel of every blackout.

If I seem to credit these stories unduly—to dwell on them, even—it's because of what had happened to me in the basement, at the start of the blackout, and because of another incident, far more terrible, which occurred later that night. Since then some years have elapsed; and now, with Karen's permission, I can speak of it.

The two of them had driven back without mishap. Marcia had left Karen off in front of our apartment and had waited till she got inside. After all that they had been through that night, the neighborhood seemed an oasis of safety. There'd been stores broken into on Columbus, but our block, by this time, was relatively quiet. It was 2:15 A.M.

Unlocking the door, Karen felt her way into the kitchen and, with some difficulty, located a dusty box of Sabbath candles, one of which she lit on the top burner of the stove. A thin white stream of candle wax ran, wormlike, down her hand; she stood the candle upon a saucer to protect the rug. Moving slowly so that the flame would not go out, she walked into the bedroom, pausing to open the window and let some air into the room. She noticed, with some irritation, that it was already halfway open; someone had been careless, and it wasn't her. She would have to remember to mention it to me when she called. The phone was there before her on the night table. Carefully, in the flickering light, she dialed Grandfather's number.

I had been nodding off, lulled by the rhythm of Grandfather's snoring, when the telephone jerked me awake. For a moment I forgot where I was, but then I heard Karen's voice.

"Well," she said, "here I am, safe and sound, and absolutely exhausted. One thing's good, at least I won't have to go to work tomorrow. I feel like I could use a good twelve hours' sleep, though it'll probably be pretty unbearable in here tonight without the air conditioner. There's a funny smell, too. I just took a peek in the refrigerator, and all that meat you bought's going to spoil unless— *Oh God, what's that?*"

I heard her scream. She screamed several times. Then there was a thud, and then a jarring succession of bangs as the phone was dropped and left dangling from the edge of the table.

And then, in the background, I heard it: a sound so similar to the one coming from the bed behind me that for one horrifying second I'd confused the two.

It was the sound of snoring.

Nine flights of stairs and a dozen blocks later I stumbled from the darkness into the darkness of our apartment. The police had not arrived yet, but Karen had already regained consciousness, and a candle burned once more upon the table. A two-inch purple welt just below her hairline showed where, in falling, she had hit the table's edge.

I was impressed by how well she was bearing up. Even though she'd awakened alone in the dark, she had managed to keep herself busy: after relighting the candle and replacing the telephone, she had methodically gone about locking all the windows and had carefully washed the stickiness from her legs. In fact, by the time I got there she seemed remarkably composed, at least for the moment—composed enough to tell me, in a fairly level voice, about the thing she'd seen drop soundlessly into the room, through the open window, just as another one leaped toward her from the hall and a third, crouched gaunt and pale behind the bed, rose up and, reaching forward, pinched the candle out.

Her composure slipped a bit—and so did mine—when, six hours later, the morning sunlight revealed a certain shape scratched like a marker in the brick outside our bedroom window.

Six weeks later, while we were still living at her mother's house in Westchester, the morning bouts of queasiness began. The tests came back negative, negative again, then positive. Whatever was inside her might well have been mine—we had, ironically, decided some time before to let nature take its course—but we took no chances. The abortion cost only $150, and we got a free lecture from a Right to Life group picketing in front. We never asked the doctor what the wretched little thing inside her looked like, and he never showed the least inclination to tell us.

Wednesday, February 14, 1979

" 'Young men think that old men are fools,' " said Mrs. Rosenzweig, quoting with approval one of my grandfather's favorite sayings, " 'but old men *know* that young men are fools.' " She pursed her lips doubtfully. "Of course," she added, "that wouldn't apply to you."

I laughed. "Of course not! Besides, I'm not so young anymore."

It had been exactly a year since I'd last seen her; having arrived today with a big red box of Valentine's Day chocolates for her, I was glad to find her still alive—and still living at the Manor. Despite the night of terror she'd suffered back in '77, she had returned here as soon as she'd been discharged from the hospital, believing herself too old for a change of scene, too old to make new friends. The Manor was her home, and she was determined to stay.

Here, inside her own room, it was virtually impossible to tell that she was blind (just as I had been fooled the first time I'd met her); habit had taught her the location of every article, every piece of furniture. But elsewhere in the building, with her former roommate, Mrs. Hirschfeld, no longer there to lean on, she'd felt helpless and alone—until my grandfather'd acted the gentleman. He had befriended her, made her feel secure; they had walked along Broadway together, traded stories of the past, and kept each other company through the long summer afternoons. For a while, he had replaced Mrs. Hirschfeld in her life; she had replaced poor old Father Pistachio in his. . . .

"Did I ever show you what Herman gave me?" Unerringly she picked a small round object from the shelf beside her and began winding a key in its base. It appeared to be a miniature globe of the world, with a decal on the base proclaiming *"Souvenir of Hayden Planetarium."* When she set it back on the shelf, it played the opening bars of "Home Sweet Home."

"That's very nice."

The music ran on a few seconds more, then died in the air. The old woman sighed.

"It was nice of you to bring that chocolate. That's just the kind of thing your grandfather would have done. He was always very generous."

"Yes," I said, "he was. He never had much, but he was devoted to his friends."

The chocolate—in fact, the visit itself—had been my way of commemorating this day. It was the first anniversary of his death.

He had died following another stroke, just as the doctors had predicted—one of the few times in his life that he'd acted according to prediction. It had happened after dinner, while he'd been sitting in the game room with several of his cronies, laughing heartily at one of his own jokes. Laughter, Svevo tells us, is the only form of violent exercise old men are still permitted, but perhaps in this case the violence had been too much. Rushed to the hospital, he had lingered less than a week. I don't believe his end was a hard one. His last words are unrecorded, which is probably just as well—what are anyone's last words, after all, except a curse, a cry for help, or a string of nonsense?—but the last words I ever heard him say, and which have now become a family legend, were addressed to a young intern, fresh out of med school, who had come to take his blood pressure. During this process the old man had remained silent—speaking had become extremely difficult—and his eyes were closed; I assumed he was unconscious. But when the intern, putting away his instruments, happened to mention that he had a date waiting for him that night as soon as he got off work, my grandfather opened his eyes and said, in what was little more than a whisper, "Ask her if she's got a friend for me."

And Father Pistachio—he, too, is gone now, gone even before my grandfather. Although he has never been listed as such, he remains, as far as I'm concerned, the only likely fatality of the 1977 Blackout. It appears that, at the moment the power failed, he'd been on his way to visit Grandfather and me in the Manor, a short walk up the street. Beyond that it's impossible to say, for no one saw what happened to him. Maybe, in the darkness, he got frightened and ran off, maybe he had a run-in with the same gang that attacked me, maybe he simply fell down a rabbit hole and disappeared. I have one or two suspicions of my own— suspicions about the Blackout itself, in fact, and whether it was really Con Ed's fault—but such speculations only get my wife upset. All we really know is that the old man vanished without a trace, though Grandfather later claimed to have seen a white paper bag lying crumpled and torn near the stoop of Pistachio's house.

As for his effects, the contents of his room, I am not the one to ask—and the one to ask is dead. Grandfather was supposed to have gone over and inquired about them, but he told me he'd been "given the runaround" by the superintendent of the building, a gruff Puerto Rican man who understood almost no English. The super had maintained that he'd given all Pistachio's belongings to the *"policía,"* but I wouldn't be surprised if, in fact, he'd kept for himself the things he thought of value and had thrown away the rest. Still, I like to pretend that somewhere, in a storeroom down the dusty corridors of some obscure city department, hidden away in some footlocker or cubbyhole or file shelf, there lies the old priest's great work—the notes and maps and photos, the pages of English translation—complete with all the "new material" he'd hinted of.

One thing, at least, has survived. The super, a religious man (or perhaps just superstitious), had held back one of Pistachio's books, believing it to be a Bible, and this he allowed my grandfather to take. In a sense he was right, it was a Bible—the 1959 Harper & Row edition of *The Gospel According to Thomas,* which now stands on my desk looking very scholarly next to the cheap Spanish version of his "Commentary." The book holds little interest for me, nor is it particularly rare, but I find it makes an excellent memento of its former owner, thanks to the hundreds of annotations in Pistachio's crabbed hand: tiny comments scribbled in the margins, *"sí!"* and *"indudable!"* and even one *"caramba!"* along with some more cryptic—"Ync." and "Qch." and "X.T."— and pages and pages of underlinings. One passage, attributed to Christ himself, was actually circled in red ink:

Whoever feels the touch of my hand shall become as I am, and the hidden things shall be revealed to him. . . . I am the All, and the All came forth from me. Cleave a piece of wood and you will find me; lift up a stone and I am there.

Beneath it he had written, *"Está hecho."* It is done.

I was feeling depressed as I said goodbye to Mrs. Rosenzweig. Though I agreed to visit her again soon, privately I doubted I'd be back before next year. Coming here aroused too many painful memories.

Outside, the world looked even bleaker. It was not yet 5:00 P.M., and already getting dark. We'd had below-freezing temperatures throughout the week and the pavement was covered with patches of snow. Turning up my collar against the icy wind, I headed up the block.

Now, one of the hoariest clichés of a certain type of cheap fiction—along with the mind that "suddenly goes blank," and the fearful town where everyone "clams up" when a stranger arrives, and the victimized industrialist who won't go to the police because "I don't want the publicity," and the underworld informer who says "I know who did it but I can't tell you over the phone"— along with these is the feeling of "being watched." One's flesh is supposed to crawl, one's hair to stand on end; one is supposed to have an "indefinable sense" that one is under scrutiny. The truth is not so mystical. In the course of my life I have stared, and stared hard, at thousands of people who, were they the least bit sensitive, would have shivered or turned or perhaps even jumped in the air. None has ever done so. For that matter, I've undoubtedly been glared at by hundreds of people in my time without ever realizing it.

This time was the same. I was standing on the corner of 81st and Amsterdam, hunching my shoulders against the cold and waiting impatiently for the light to change. My mind was on the clean new restaurant across the street that advertised "Dominican and American Cuisine," right where Davey's Tavern used to stand. *How nice,* I said to myself. *Things are looking up.*

The light changed. I took one step off the curb, and heard something crackle underfoot. That was why I happened to look down. I saw that I had stepped upon a little mound of pistachio shells, red against the snow, piled by the opening to a sewer.

And I froze—for there was something in the opening, just beside my shoe: something watching intently, its face pressed up against the metal grating, its pale hands clinging tightly to the bars. I saw, dimly in the streetlight, the empty craters where its eyes had been—empty but for two red dots, like tiny beads—and the gaping red ring of its mouth, like the sucker of some undersea creature. The face was alien and cold, without human expression, yet I swear that those eyes regarded me with utter malevolence—and that they recognized me.

It must have realized that I'd seen it—surely it heard me cry out—for at that moment, like two exploding white stars, the hands flashed open and the figure dropped back into the earth, back to that kingdom, older than ours, that calls the dark its home.

RAY BRADBURY
Frost and Fire

1

DURING THE night, Sim was born. He lay wailing upon the cold cave stones. His blood beat through him a thousand pulses each minute. He grew, steadily.

Into his mouth his mother with feverish hands put the food. The nightmare of living was begun. Almost instantly at birth his eyes grew alert, and then, without half understanding why, filled with bright, insistent terror. He gagged upon the food, choked and wailed. He looked about, blindly.

There was a thick fog. It cleared. The outlines of the cave appeared. And a man loomed up, insane and wild and terrible. A man with a dying face. Old, withered by winds, baked like adobe in the heat. The man was crouched in a far corner of the cave, his eyes whitening to one side of his face, listening to the far wind trumpeting up above on the frozen night planet.

Sim's mother, trembling now and again, staring at the man, fed Sim pebble-fruits, valley-grasses and ice-nipples broken from the cavern entrances, and eating, eliminating, eating again, he grew larger, larger.

The man in the corner of the cave was his father! The man's eyes were all that was alive in his face. He held a crude stone dagger in his withered hands and his jaw hung loose and senseless.

Then, with a widening focus, Sim saw the old people sitting in the tunnel beyond this living quarter. And as he watched, they began to die.

Their agonies filled the cave. They melted like waxen images, their faces collapsed inward on their sharp bones, their teeth protruded. One minute their faces were mature, fairly smooth,

719

alive, electric. The next minute a dessication and burning away
of their flesh occurred.

Sim thrashed in his mother's grasp. She held him. "No, no,"
she soothed him, quietly, earnestly, looking to see if this, too,
would cause her husband to rise again.

With a soft swift padding of naked feet, Sim's father ran across
the cave. Sim's mother screamed. Sim felt himself torn loose from
her grasp. He fell upon the stones, rolling, shrieking with his new,
moist lungs!

The webbed face of his father jerked over him, the knife was
poised. It was like one of those prenatal nightmares he'd had again
and again while still in his mother's flesh. In the next few blazing,
impossible instants questions flicked through his brain. The knife
was high, suspended, ready to destroy him. But the whole question
of life in this cave, the dying people, the withering and the insanity,
surged through Sim's new, small head. How was it that he understood? A newborn child? Can a newborn child think, see, understand, interpret? No. It was wrong! It was impossible. Yet it was
happening! To him. He had been alive an hour now. And in the
next instant perhaps dead!

His mother flung herself upon the back of his father, and beat
down the weapon. Sim caught the terrific backwash of emotion
from both their conflicting minds. "Let me kill him!" shouted the
father, breathing harshly, sobbingly. "What has he to live for?"

"No, no!" insisted the mother, and her body, frail and old as
it was, stretched across the huge body of the father, tearing at his
weapon. "He must live! There may be a future for him! He may
live longer than us, and be young!"

The father fell back against a stone crib. Lying there, staring,
eyes glittering, Sim saw another figure inside that stone crib. A
girl-child, quietly feeding itself, moving its delicate hands to procure
food. His sister.

The mother wrenched the dagger from her husband's grasp,
stood up, weeping and pushing back her cloud of stiffening gray
hair. Her mouth trembled and jerked. "I'll kill you!" she said,
glaring down at her husband. "Leave my children alone."

The old man spat tiredly, bitterly, and looked vacantly into the
stone crib, at the little girl. "One-eighth of *her* life's over already,"
he gasped. "And she doesn't know it. What's the use?"

As Sim watched, his own mother seemed to shift and take a
tortured, smokelike form. The thin bony face broke out into a

maze of wrinkles. She was shaken with pain and had to sit by him, suddering and cuddling the knife to her shriveled breasts. She, like the old people in the tunnel, was aging, dying.

Sim cried steadily. Everywhere he looked was horror. A mind came to meet his own. Instinctively he glanced toward the stone crib. Dark, his sister returned his glance. Their minds brushed like straying fingers. He relaxed somewhat. He began to learn.

The father sighed, shut his lids down over his green eyes. "Feed the child," he said, exhaustedly. "Hurry. It is almost dawn and it is our last day of living, woman. Feed him. Make him grow."

Sim quieted, and images, out of the terror, floated to him.

This was a planet next to the sun. The nights burned with cold, the days were like torches of fire. It was a violent, impossible world. The people lived in the cliffs to escape the incredible ice and the day of flame. Only at dawn and sunset was the air breath-sweet, flower-strong, and then the cave peoples brought their children out into a stony, barren valley. At dawn the ice thawed into creeks and rivers, at sunset the day fire died and cooled. In the intervals of even, livable temperature the people lived, ran, played, loved, free of the caverns; all life on the planet jumped, burst into life. Plants grew instantly, birds were flung like pellets across the sky. Smaller, legged animal life rushed frantically through the rocks; everything tried to get its living down in the brief hour of respite.

It was an unbearable planet. Sim understood this, a matter of hours after birth. Racial memory bloomed in him. He would live his entire life in the caves, with two hours a day outside. Here, in stone channels of air he would talk, talk incessantly with his people, sleep never, think, think and lie upon his back, dreaming; but never sleeping.

And he would live exactly eight days.

The *violence* of this thought! Eight days. Eight *short* days. It was wrong, impossible, but a fact. Even while in his mother's flesh some racial knowledge of some strange far wild voice had told him he was being formed rapidly, shaped and propelled out swiftly.

Birth was quick as a knife. Childhood was over in a flash. Adolescence was a sheet of lightning. Manhood was a dream, maturity a myth, old age an inescapably quick reality, death a swift certainty.

Eight days from now he'd stand half-blind, withering, dying, as his father now stood, staring uselessly at his own wife and child.

This day was an eighth part of his total life! He must enjoy every second of it. He must search his parents' thoughts for knowledge.

Because in a few hours they'd be dead.

This was so impossibly unfair. Was this all of life? In his prenatal state hadn't he dreamed of *long* lives, valleys not of blasted stone but green foliage and temperate clime? Yes! And if he'd dreamed then there must be truth in the visions. How could he seek and find the long life? Where? And how could he accomplish a life mission that huge and depressing in eight short, vanishing days?

How had his people gotten into such a condition?

As if at a button pressed, he saw an image. Metal seeds, blown across space from a distant green world, fighting with long flames, crashing on this bleak planet. From their shattered hulls tumbled men and women.

When? Long ago. Ten thousand days. The crash victims hid in the cliffs from the sun. Fire, ice and floods washed away the wreckage of the huge metal seeds. The victims were shaped and beaten like iron upon a forge. Solar radiations drenched them. Their pulses quickened, two hundred, five hundred, a thousand beats a minute. Their skins thickened, their blood changed. Old age came rushing. Children were born in the caves. Swifter, swifter, swifter the process. Like all this world's wild life, the men and women from the crash lived and died in a week, leaving children to do likewise.

So this is life, thought Sim. It was not spoken in his mind, for he knew no words, he knew only images, old memory, an awareness, a telepathy that could penetrate flesh, rock, metal. Somewhere along the line, they *had* developed telepathy, plus racial memory, the only good gifts, the only hope in all this terror. So thought Sim, I'm the five-thousandth in a long line of futile sons? What can I do to save myself from dying eight days from now? Is there escape?

His eyes widened, another image came to focus.

Beyond this valley of cliffs, on a low mountain lay a perfect, unscarred metal seed. A metal ship, not rusted or touched by the avalanches. The ship was deserted, whole, intact. It was the only ship of all these that had crashed that was still a unit, still usable. But it was so far away. There was no one in it to help. This ship, then, on the far mountain, was the destiny toward which he would grow. There was his only hope of escape.

His mind flexed.

In this cliff, deep down in a confinement of solitude, worked a handful of scientists. To these men, when he was old enough and wise enough, he must go. They, too, dreamed of escape, of long life, of green valleys and temperate weathers. They, too, stared longingly at that distant ship upon its high mountain, its metal so perfect it did not rust or age.

The cliff groaned.

Sim's father lifted his eroded, lifeless face.

"Dawn's coming," he said.

2

MORNING RELAXED the mighty granite cliff muscles. It was the time of the Avalanche.

The tunnels echoed to running bare feet. Adults, children pushed with eager, hungry eyes toward the outside dawn. From far out, Sim heard a rumble of rock, a scream, a silence. Avalanches fell into the valley. Stones that had been biding their time, not quite ready to fall, for a million years let go their bulks, and where they had begun their journey as single boulders they smashed upon the valley floor in a thousand shrapnels and friction-heated nuggets.

Every morning at least one person was caught in the downpour.

The cliff people dared the avalanches. It added one more excitement to their lives, already too short, too headlong, too dangerous.

Sim felt himself seized up by his father. He was carried brusquely down the tunnel for a thousand yards, to where the daylight appeared. There was a shining insane light in his father's eyes. Sim could not move. He sensed what was going to happen. Behind his father, his mother hurried, bringing with her the little sister, Dark. "Wait! Be careful!" she cried to her husband.

Sim felt his father crouch, listening.

High in the cliff was a tremor, a shivering.

"Now!" bellowed his father, and leaped out.

An avalanche fell down at them!

Sim had accelerated impressions of plunging walls, dust, confusion. His mother screamed! There was a jolting, a plunging.

With one last step, Sim's father hurried him forward into the day. The avalanche thundered behind him. The mouth of the cave, where mother and Dark stood back out of the way, was choked with rubble and two boulders that weighed a hundred pounds each.

The storm thunder of the avalanche passed away to a trickle of sand. Sim's father burst out into laughter. "Made it! By the Gods! Made it alive!" And he looked scornfully at the cliff and spat. "Pagh!"

Mother and sister Dark struggled through the rubble. She cursed her husband. "Fool! You might have killed Sim!"

"I may yet," retorted the father.

Sim was not listening. He was fascinated with the remains of an avalanche afront of the next tunnel. Blood trickled out from under a rise of boulders, soaking into the ground. There was nothing more to be seen. Someone else had lost the game.

Dark ran ahead on lithe, supple feet, naked and certain.

The valley air was like a wine filtered between mountains. The heaven was a restive blue; not the pale scorched atmosphere of full day, nor the bloated, bruised black-purple of night, a-riot with sickly shining stars.

This was a tide pool. A place where waves of varying and violent temperatures struck, receded. Now the tide pool was quiet, cool, and its life moved abroad.

Laughter! Far away, Sim heard it. Why laughter? How could any of his people find time for laughing? Perhaps later he would discover why.

The valley suddenly blushed with impulsive color. Plant life, thawing in the precipitant dawn, shoved out from most unexpected sources. It flowered as you watched. Pale green tendrils appeared on scoured rocks. Seconds later, ripe globes of fruit twitched upon the blade-tips. Father gave Sim to his mother and harvested the momentary, volatile crop, thrust scarlet, blue, yellow fruits into a fur sack which hung at his waist. Mother tugged at the moist new grasses, laid them on Sim's tongue.

His senses were being honed to a fine edge. He stored knowledge thirstily. He understood love, marriage, customs, anger, pity, rage, selfishness, shadings and subtleties, realities and reflections. One thing suggested another. The sight of green plant life whirled his mind like a gyroscope, seeking balance in a world where lack of time for explanations made a mind seek and interpret on its own. The soft burden of food gave him knowledge of his system, of energy, of movement. Like a bird newly cracking its way from a shell, he was almost a unit, complete, all-knowing. Heredity and telepathy that fed upon every mind and every wind had done all this for him. He grew excited with his ability.

They walked, mother, father and the two children, smelling the smells, watching the birds bounce from wall to wall of the valley like scurrying pebbles and suddenly the father said a strange thing:
"Remember?"
Remember what? Sim lay cradled. Was it any effort for them to remember, when they'd lived only seven days!
The husband and wife looked at each other.
"Was it only three days ago?" said the woman, her body shaking, her eyes closing to think. "I can't believe it. It is so unfair." She sobbed, then drew her hand across her face and bit her parched lips. The wind played at her gray hair. "Now it is my turn to cry. An hour ago it was you!"
"An hour is half a life."
"Come," she took her husband's arm. "Let us look at everything, because it will be our last looking."
"The sun'll be up in a few minutes," said the old man. "We must turn back now."
"Just one more moment," pleaded the woman.
"The sun will catch us."
"Let it catch me then!"
"You don't mean that."
"I mean nothing, nothing at all," cried the woman.
The sun was coming fast. The green in the valley burnt away. Searing wind blasted from over the cliffs. Far away where sun bolts hammered battlements of cliff, the huge stone faces shook their contents; those avalanches not already powdered down, were now released and fell like mantles.
"Dark!" shouted the father. The girl sprang over the warm floor of the valley, answering, her hair a black flag behind her. Hands full of green fruits, she joined them.
The sun rimmed the horizon with flame, the air convulsed dangerously with it, and whistled.
The cave people bolted, shouting, picking up their fallen children,

bearing vast loads of fruit and grass with them back to their deep hideouts. In moments the valley was bare. Except for one small child someone had forgotten. He was running far out on the flatness, but he was not strong enough, and the engulfing heat was drifting down from the cliffs even as he was half across the valley.

Flowers were burnt into effigies, grasses sucked back into rocks like singed snakes. Flower seeds whirled and fell in the sudden furnace blast of wind, sown far into gullies and crannies, ready to blossom at sunset tonight, and then go to seed and die again.

Sim's father watched that child running, alone, out on the floor of the valley. He and his wife and Dark and Sim were safe in the mouth of their tunnel.

"He'll never make it," said father. "Do not watch him, woman. It's not a good thing to watch."

They turned away. All except Sim, whose eyes had caught a glint of metal far away. His heart hammered in him, and his eyes blurred. Far away, atop a low mountain, one of those metal seeds from space reflected a dazzling ripple of light! It was like one of his intra-embryo dreams fulfilled! A metal space seed, intact, undamaged, lying on a mountain! There was his future! There was his hope for survival! There was where he would go in a few days, when he was—strange thought—a grown man!

The sun plunged into the valley like molten lava.

The little running child screamed, the sun burned, and the screaming stopped.

Sim's mother walked painfully, with sudden age, down the tunnel, paused, reached up, broke off two last icicles that had formed during the night. She handed one to her husband, kept the other. "We will drink one last toast. To you, to the children."

"To *you*," he nodded to her. "To the children." They lifted the icicles. The warmth melted the ice down into their thirsty mouths.

3

ALL DAY the sun seemed to blaze and erupt into the valley. Sim could not see it, but the vivid pictorials in his parents' minds were sufficient evidence of the nature of the day fire. The light ran like mercury, sizzling and roasting the caves, poking inward, but never penetrating deeply enough. It lighted the caves. It made the hollows of the cliff comfortably warm.

Sim fought to keep his parents young. But no matter how hard he fought with mind and image, they became like mummies before him. His father seemed to dissolve from one stage of oldness to another. This is what will happen to me soon, thought Sim in terror.

Sim grew upon himself. He felt the digestive-eliminatory movements of his body. He was fed every minute, he was continually swallowing, feeding. He began to fit words to images and processes. Such a word was love. It was not an abstraction, but a process, a stir of breath, a smell of morning air, a flutter of heart, the curve of arm holding him, the look in the suspended face of his mother. He saw the processes, then searched behind her suspended face and there was the word, in her brain, ready to use. His throat prepared to speak. Life was pushing him, rushing him along toward oblivion.

He sensed the expansion of his fingernails, the adjustments of his cells, the profusion of his hair, the multiplication of his bones and sinew, the grooving of the soft pale wax of his brain. His brain at birth as clear as a circle of ice, innocent, unmarked, was, an instant later, as if hit with a thrown rock, cracked and marked and patterned in a million crevices of thought and discovery.

His sister, Dark, ran in and out with other little hothouse children, forever eating. His mother trembled over him, not eating, she had no appetite, her eyes were webbed shut.

"Sunset," said his father, at last.

The day was over. The light faded, a wind sounded.

His mother arose. "I want to see the outside world once more . . . just once more. . . ." She stared blindly, shivering.

His father's eyes were shut, he lay against the wall.

"I cannot rise," he whispered faintly. "I cannot."

"Dark!" The mother croaked, the girl came running. "Here," and Sim was handed to the girl. "Hold to Sim, Dark, feed him, care for him." She gave Sim one last fondling touch.

Dark said not a word, holding Sim, her great green eyes shining wetly.

"Go now," said the mother. "Take him out into the sunset time. Enjoy yourselves. Pick foods, eat. Play."

Dark walked away without looking back. Sim twisted in her

grasp, looking over her shoulder with unbelieving, tragic eyes. He cried out and somehow summoned from his lips the first word of his existence:

"Why . . . ?"

He saw his mother stiffen. "The child spoke!"

"Aye," said his father. "Did you hear what he said?"

"I heard," said the mother quietly.

The last thing Sim saw of his living parents was his mother weakly, swayingly, slowly moving across the floor to lie beside her silent husband. That was the last time he ever saw them move.

4

THE NIGHT came and passed and then started the second day. The bodies of all those who had died during the night were carried in a funeral procession to the top of a small hill. The procession was long, the bodies numerous.

Dark walked in the procession, holding the newly walking Sim by one hand. Only an hour before dawn Sim had learned to walk.

At the top of the hill, Sim saw once again the far off metal seed. Nobody ever looked at it, or spoke of it. Why? Was there some reason? Was it a mirage? Why did they not run toward it? Worship it? Try to get to it and fly away into space?

The funeral words were spoken. The bodies were placed upon the ground where the sun, in a few minutes, would cremate them.

The procession then turned and ran down the hill, eager to have their few minutes of free time running and playing and laughing in the sweet air.

Dark and Sim, chattering like birds, feeding among the rocks, exchanged what they knew of life. He was in his second day, she in her third. They were driven, as always, by the mercurial speed of their lives.

Another piece of his life opened wide.

Fifty young men ran down from the cliffs, holding sharp stones and rock daggers in their thick hands. Shouting, they ran off toward distant black, low lines of small rock cliffs.

"War!"

The thought stood in Sim's brain. It shocked and beat at him.

These men were running to fight, to kill, over there in those small black cliffs where other people lived.

But why? Wasn't life short enough without fighting, killing? From a great distance he heard the sound of conflict, and it made his stomach cold. "Why, Dark, why?"

Dark didn't know. Perhaps they would understand tomorrow. Now, there was the business of eating to sustain and support their lives. Watching Dark was like seeing a lizard forever flicking its pink tongue, forever hungry.

Pale children ran on all sides of them. One beetlelike boy scuttled up the rocks, knocking Sim aside, to take from him a particularly luscious red berry he had found growing under an outcrop.

The child ate hastily of the fruit before Sim could gain his feet. Then Sim hurled himself unsteadily, the two of them fell in a ridiculous jumble, rolling, until Dark pried them, squalling, apart.

Slim bled. A part of him stood off, like a god, and said, "This should not be. Children should not be this way. It is wrong!"

Dark slapped the little intruding boy away. "Get on!" she cried. "What's your name, bad one?"

"Chion!" laughed the boy. "Chion, Chion, Chion!"

Sim glared at him with all the ferocity in his small, unskilled features. He choked. This was his enemy. It was as if he'd waited for an enemy of person as well as scene. He had already understood the avalanches, the heat, the cold, the shortness of life, but these were things of places, of scene—mute, extravagant manifestations of unthinking nature, not motivated save by gravity and radiation. Here, now, in this stridulant Chion he recognized a thinking enemy!

Chion darted off, turned at a distance, taunting:

"Tomorrow I will be big enough to kill you!"

And he vanished around a rock.

More children ran, giggling, by Sim. Which of them would be friends, enemies? How could friends and enemies come about in this impossible, quick life time? There was no time to make either, was there?

Dark, knowing his thoughts, drew him away. As they searched for food, she whispered fiercely in his ear. "Enemies are made over things like stolen foods; gifts of long grasses make friends. Enemies come, too, from opinions and thoughts. In five seconds you've made an enemy for life. Life's so short enemies must be made quickly." And she laughed with an irony strange for one so young, who was growing older before her rightful time. "You

must fight to protect yourself. Others, superstitious ones, will try
killing you. There is a belief, a ridiculous belief, that if one kills
another, the murderer partakes of the life energy of the slain, and
therefore will live an extra day. You see? As long as that is
believed, you're in danger."

But Sim was not listening. Bursting from a flock of delicate
girls who tomorrow would be tall, quieter, and who day after that
would become shapely and the next day take husbands, Sim caught
sight of one small girl whose hair was a violet-blue flame.

She ran past, brushed Sim, their bodies touched. Her eyes, white
as silver coins, shone at him. He knew then that he'd found a
friend, a love, a wife, one who would a week from now lie with
him atop the funeral pyre as sunlight undressed their flesh from
bone.

Only the glance, but it held them in mid-motion, one instant.

"Your name?" he shouted after her.

"Lyte!" she called laughingly back.

"I'm Sim," he answered, confused and bewildered.

"Sim!" she repeated it, flashing on. "I'll remember!"

Dark nudged his ribs. "Here, *eat*," she said to the distracted
boy. "Eat or you'll never get big enough to catch her."

From nowhere, Chion appeared, running by. "Lyte!" he mocked,
dancing malevolently along and away. "Lyte! I'll remember Lyte,
too!"

Dark stood tall and reed slender, shaking her dark ebony clouds
of hair, sadly. "I see your life before you, little Sim. You'll need
weapons soon to fight for this Lyte one. Now, hurry—the sun's
coming!"

They ran back to the caves.

5

ONE-FOURTH OF his life was over! Babyhood was gone. He was
now a young boy! Wild rains lashed the valley at nightfall. He
watched new river channels cut in the valley, out past the mountain
of the metal seed. He stored the knowledge for later use. Each
night there was a new river, a bed newly cut.

"What's beyond the valley?" wondered Sim.

"No one's ever been beyond it," explained Dark. "All who tried to reach the plain were frozen to death or burnt. The only land we know's within half an hour's run. Half an hour out and half an hour back."

"No one has ever reached the metal seed, then?"

Dark scoffed. "The Scientists, they try. Silly fools. They don't know enough to stop. It's no use. It's too far."

The Scientists. The word stirred him. He had almost forgotten the vision he had in the moments before and after birth. His voice was eager. "Where are the Scientists?"

Dark looked away from him, "I wouldn't tell you if I knew. They'd kill you, experimenting! I don't want you joining them! Live your life, don't cut it in half trying to reach that silly metal thing on the mountain."

"I'll find out where they are from someone else, then!"

"No one'll tell you! They hate the Scientists. You'll have to find them on your own. And then what? Will you save us? Yes, save us, little boy!" Her face was sullen; already half her life was gone.

"We can't just sit and talk and eat," he protested. "And *nothing* else." He leapt up.

"Go find them!" she retorted acidly. "They'll help you forget. Yes, yes," she spat it out. "Forget your life's over in just a few more days!"

Sim ran through the tunnels, seeking. Sometimes he half imagined where the Scientists were. But then a flood of angry thought from those around him, when he asked the direction to the Scientists' cave, washed over him in confusion and resentment. After all, it was the Scientists' fault that they had been placed upon this terrible world! Sim flinched under the bombardment of oaths and curses.

Quietly he took his seat in a central chamber with the children to listen to the grown men talk. This was the time of education, the Time of Talking. No matter how he chafed at delay, or how great his impatience, even though life slipped fast from him and death approached like a black meteor, he knew his mind needed knowledge. Tonight, then, was the night of school. But he sat uneasily. Only *five* more days of life.

Chion sat across from Sim, his thin-mouthed face arrogant.

Lyte appeared between the two. The last few hours had made

her firmer footed, gentler, taller. Her hair shone brighter. She smiled as she sat beside Sim, ignoring Chion. And Chion became rigid at this and ceased eating.

The dialogue crackled, filled the room. Swift as heartbeats, one thousand, two thousand words a minute. Sim learned, his head filled. He did not shut his eyes, but lapsed into a kind of dreaming that was almost intra-embryonic in lassitude and drowsy vividness. In the faint background the words were spoken, and they wove a tapestry of knowledge in his head.

He dreamed of green meadows free of stones, all grass, round and rolling and rushing easily toward a dawn with no taint of freezing, merciless cold or smell of boiled rock or scorched monument. He walked across the green meadow. Overhead the metal seeds flew by in a heaven that was a steady, even temperature. Things were slow, slow, slow.

Birds lingered upon gigantic trees that took a hundred, two hundred, five thousand days to grow. Everything remained in its place, the birds did not flicker nervously at a hint of sun, nor did the trees suck back frightenedly when a ray of sunlight poured over them.

In this dream people strolled, they rarely ran, the heart rhythm of them was evenly languid, not jerking and insane. The grass remained, and did not burn away in torches. The dream people talked always of tomorrow and living and not tomorrow and dying. It all seemed so familiar that when Sim felt someone take his hand he thought it simply another part of the dream.

Lyte's hand lay inside his own. "Dreaming?" she asked.

"Yes."

"Things are balanced. Our minds, to even things, to balance the unfairness of our living, go back in on ourselves, to find what there is that is good to see."

He beat his hand against the stone floor again and again. "It does not make things fair! I hate it! It reminds me that there is something better, something I have missed! Why can't we be ignorant! Why can't we live and die without knowing that this is an abnormal living?" And his breath rushed harshly from his half-open, constricted mouth.

"There is purpose in everything," said Lyte. "This gives us purpose, makes us work, plan, try to find a way."

His eyes were hot emeralds in his face. "I walked up a hill of grass, very slowly," he said.

"The same hill of grass I walked an hour ago?" asked Lyte.

"Perhaps. Close enough to it. The dream is better than the reality." He flexed his eyes, narrowed them. "I watched people and they did not eat."

"Or talk?"

"Or talk, either. And we always are eating, always talking. Sometimes those people in the dream sprawled with their eyes shut, not moving a muscle."

As Lyte stared down into his face a terrible thing happened. He imagined her face blackening, wrinkling, twisting into knots of agedness. The hair blew out like snow about her ears, the eyes were like discolored coins caught in a web of lashes. Her teeth sank away from her lips, the delicate fingers hung like charred twigs from her atrophied wrists. Her beauty was consumed and wasted even as he watched, and when he seized her, in terror, he cried out, for he imagined his own hand corroded, and he choked back a cry.

"Sim, what's wrong?"

The saliva in his mouth dried at the taste of the words.

"Five more days . . ."

"The Scientists."

Sim started. Who'd spoken? In the dim light a tall man talked. "The Scientists crashed us on this world, and now have wasted thousands of lives and time. It's no use. It's no use. Tolerate them but give them none of your time. You only live once, remember."

Where were these hated Scientists? Now, after the Learning, the Time of Talking, he was ready to find them. Now, at least, he knew enough to begin his fight for freedom, for the ship!

"Sim, where're you going?"

But Sim was gone. The echo of his running feet died away down a shaft of polished stone.

It seemed that half the night was wasted. He blundered into a dozen dead ends. Many times he was attacked by the insane young men who wanted his life energy. Their superstitious ravings echoed after him. The gashes of their hungry fingernails covered his body.

He found what he looked for.

A half dozen men gathered in a small basalt cave deep down in the cliff lode. On a table before them lay objects which, though unfamiliar, struck harmonious chords in Sim.

The Scientists worked in sets, old men doing important work, young men learning, asking questions; and at their feet were three small children. They were a process. Every eight days there was an entirely new set of scientists working on any one problem. The amount of work done was terribly inadequate. They grew old, fell dead just when they were beginning their creative period. The creative time of any one individual was perhaps a matter of twelve hours out of his entire span. Three quarters of one's life was spent learning, a brief interval of creative power, then senility, insanity, death.

The men turned as Sim entered.

"Don't tell me we have a recruit?" said the eldest of them.

"I don't believe it," said another, younger one. "Chase him away. He's probably one of those warmongers."

"No, no," objected the elder one, moving with little shuffles of his bare feet toward Sim. "Come in, come in, boy." He had friendly eyes, slow eyes, unlike those of the swift inhabitants of the upper caves. Gray and quiet. "What do you want?"

Sim hesitated, lowered his head, unable to meet the quiet, gentle gaze. "I want to live," he whispered.

The old man laughed quietly. He touched Sim's shoulder. "Are you a new breed? Are you sick?" he queried of Sim, half seriously. "Why aren't you playing? Why aren't you readying yourself for the time of love and marriage and children? Don't you know that tomorrow night you'll be almost grown? Don't you realize that if you are not careful you'll miss all of life?" He stopped.

Sim moved his eyes back and forth with each query. He blinked at the instruments on the table top. "Shouldn't I be here?" he asked.

"Certainly," roared the old man, sternly. "But it's a miracle you are. We've had no volunteers from the rank and file for a thousand days! We've had to breed our own scientists, a closed unit! Count us! Six! Six men! And three children! Are we not overwhelming?" The old man spat upon the stone floor. "We ask for volunteers and the people shout back at us, 'Get someone else!' or 'We have no time!' And you know why they say that?"

"No." Sim flinched.

"Because they're selfish. They'd like to live longer, yes, but they know that anything they do cannot possibly insure their *own* lives any extra time. It might guarantee longer life to some future offspring of theirs. But they won't give up their love, their brief youth, give up one interval of sunset or sunrise!"

Sim leaned against the table, earnestly. "I understand."

"You do?" The old man stared at him blindly. He sighed and slapped the child's arm gently. "Yes, of course, you do. It's too much to expect anyone to understand, any more. You're rare."

The others moved in around Sim and the old man.

"I am Dienc. Tomorrow night Cort here will be in my place. I'll be dead by then. And the night after that someone else will be in Cort's place, and then you, if you work and believe—but first, I give you a chance. Return to your playmates if you want. There is someone you love? Return to her. Life is short. Why should you care for the unborn to come? You have a right to youth. Go now, if you want. Because if you stay you'll have no time for anything but working and growing old and dying at your work. But it is good work. Well?"

Sim looked at the tunnel. From a distance the wind roared and blew, the smells of cooking and the patter of naked feet sounded, and the laughter of young people was an increasingly good thing to hear. He shook his head, impatiently, and his eyes were wet.

"I will stay," he said.

6

THE THIRD night and third day passed. It was the fourth night. Sim was drawn into their living. He learned about that metal seed upon the top of the far mountain. He heard of the original seeds— things called "ships" that crashed and how the survivors hid and dug in the cliffs, grew old swiftly and in their scrabbling to barely survive, forgot all science. Knowledge of mechanical things had no chance of survival in such a volcanic civilization. There was only NOW for each human.

Yesterday didn't matter, tomorrow stared them vividly in their very faces. But somehow the radiations that had forced their aging had also induced a kind of telepathic communication whereby philosophies and impressions were absorbed by the newborn. Racial memory, growing instinctively, preserved memories of another time.

"Why don't we go to that ship on the mountain?" asked Sim.

"It is too far. We would need protection from the sun," explained Dienc.

"Have you tried to make protection?"

"Salves and ointments, suits of stone and bird-wing and, recently, crude metals. None of which worked. In ten thousand more lifetimes perhaps we'll have made a metal in which will flow cool water to protect us on the march to the ship. But we work so slowly, so blindly. This morning, mature, I took up my instruments. Tomorrow, dying, I lay them down. What can one man do in one day? If we had ten thousand men, the problem would be solved. . . ."

"I will go to the ship," said Sim.

"Then you will die," said the old man. A silence had fallen on the room at Sim's words. Then the men stared at Sim. "You are a very selfish boy."

"Selfish!" cried Sim, resentfully.

The old man patted the air. "Selfish in a way I like. You want to live longer, you'll do anything for that. You will try for the ship. But I tell you it is useless. Yet, if you want to, I cannot stop you. At least you will not be like those among us who go to war for an extra few days of life."

"War?" asked Sim. "How can there be war here?"

And a shudder ran through him. He did not understand.

"Tomorrow will be time enough for that," said Dienc. "Listen to me, now."

The night passed.

7

It was morning. Lyte came shouting and sobbing down a corridor, and ran full into his arms. She had changed again. She was older, again, more beautiful. She was shaking and she held to him. "Sim, they're coming after you!"

Bare feet marched down the corridor, surged inward at the opening. Chion stood grinning there, taller, too, a sharp rock in either of his hands. "Oh, there you are, Sim!"

"Go away!" cried Lyte savagely whirling on him.

"Not until we take Sim with us," Chion assured her. Then, smiling at Sim. "*If* that is, he is with us in the fight."

Dienc shuffled forward, his eye weakly fluttering, his birdlike hands fumbling in the air. "Leave!" he shrilled angrily. "This boy is a Scientist now. He works with us."

Chion ceased smiling. "There is better work to be done. We go now to fight the people in the farthest cliffs." His eyes glittered anxiously. "Of course, you will come with us, Sim?"

"No, no!" Lyte clutched at his arm.

Sim patted her shoulder, then turned to Chion. "Why are you attacking these people?"

"There are three extra days for those who go with us to fight."

"Three extra days! Of living?"

Chion nodded firmly. "If we win, we live eleven days instead of eight. The cliffs they live in, something about the mineral in it that protects you from radiation! Think of it, Sim, three long, good days of life. Will you join us?"

Dienc interrupted. "Get along without him. Sim is my pupil!"

Chion snorted. "Go die, old man. By sunset tonight you'll be charred bone. Who are you to order us? We are young, we want to live longer."

Eleven days. The words were unbelievable to Sim. Eleven days. Now he understood why there was war. Who wouldn't fight to have his life lengthened by almost half its total. So many more days of living! Yes. Why not, indeed!

"Three extra days," called Dienc, stridently, "*if* you live to enjoy them. If you're not killed in battle. *If. If!* You have never won yet. You have always lost!"

"But this time," Chion declared sharply, "we'll win!"

Sim was bewildered. "But we are all of the same ancestors. Why don't we all share the best cliffs?"

Chion laughed and adjusted a sharp stone in his hand.

"Those who live in the best cliffs think they are better than us. That is always man's attitude when he has power. The cliffs there, besides, are smaller, there's room for only three hundred people in them."

Three extra days.

"I'll go with you," Sim said to Chion.

"Fine!" Chion was very glad, much too glad at the decision.

Dienc gasped.

Sim turned to Dienc and Lyte. "If I fight, and win, I will be half a mile closer to the Ship. And I'll have three extra days in which to strive to reach the Ship. That seems the only thing for me to do."

Dienc nodded, sadly. "It *is* the only thing. I believe you. Go along now."

"Good-bye," said Sim.

The old man looked surprised, then he laughed as at a little joke on himself. "That's right—I won't see you again, will I? Good-bye, then." And they shook hands.

They went out, Chion, Sim, and Lyte, together, followed by the others, all children growing swiftly into fighting men. And the light in Chion's eyes was not a good thing to see.

Lyte went with him. She chose his rocks for him and carried them. She would not go back, no matter how he pleaded. The sun was just beyond the horizon and they marched across the valley.

"Please, Lyte, go back!"

"And wait for Chion to return?" she said. "He plans that when you die I will be his mate." She shook out her unbelievable blue-white curls of hair defiantly. "But I'll be with you. If you fall, I fall."

Sim's face hardened. He was tall. The world had shrunk during the night. Children packs screamed by hilarious in their food-searching and he looked at them with alien wonder: could it be only four days ago he's been like these? Strange. There was a sense of many days in his mind, as if he'd really lived a thousand days. There was a dimension of incident and thought so thick, so multicolored, so richly diverse in his head that it was not to be believed so much could happen in so short a time.

The fighting men ran in clusters of two or three. Sim looked ahead at the rising line of small ebon cliffs. This, then, he said to himself, is my fourth day. And still I am no closer to the Ship, or to anything, not even—he heard the light tread of Lyte beside him—not even to her who bears my weapons and picks me ripe berries.

One-half of his life was gone. Or a third of it—If he won this battle. *If.*

He ran easily, lifting, letting fall his legs. This is the day of my physical awareness, as I run I feed, as I feed I grow and as I grow I turn eyes to Lyte with a kind of dizzying vertigo. And she looks upon me with the same gentleness of thought. This is the day of our youth. Are we wasting it? Are we losing it on a dream, a folly?

Distantly he heard laughter. As a child he'd questioned it. Now he understood laughter. This particular laughter was made of climbing high rocks and plucking the greenest blades and drinking the headiest vintage from the morning ices and eating of the rock-fruits and tasting of young lips in new appetite.

They neared the cliffs of the enemy.

He saw the slender erectness of Lyte. The new surprise of her neck where if you touched you could time her pulse; the fingers which cupped in your own were animate and supple and never still; the . . .

Lyte snapped her head to one side. "Look ahead!" she cried. "See what is to come—look only ahead."

He felt that they were racing by part of their lives, leaving their youth on the pathside, without so much as a glance.

"I am blind with looking at stones," he said, running.

"Find new stones, then!"

"I see stones—" His voice grew gentle as the palm of her hand. The landscape floated under him. Everything as like a fine wind, blowing dreamily. "I see stones that make a ravine that lies in a cool shadow where the stone-berries are thick as tears. You touch a boulder and the berries fall in silent red avalanches, and the grass is very tender. . . ."

"I do not see it!" She increased her pace, turning her head away.

He saw the floss upon her neck, like the small moss that grows silvery and light on the cool side of pebbles, that stirs if you breathe the lightest breath upon it. He looked upon himself, his hands clenched as he heaved himself forward toward death. Already his hands were veined and youth-swollen.

Lyte handed him food to eat.

"I am not hungry," he said.

"Eat, keep your mouth full," she commanded sharply, "so you will be strong for battle."

"Gods!" He roared, anguished. "Who cares for battles!"

Ahead of them, rocks hailed down, thudding. A man fell with his skull split wide. The war was begun.

Lyte passed the weapons to him. They ran without another word until they entered the killing ground.

The boulders began to roll in a synthetic avalanche from the battlements of the enemy!

Only one thought was in his mind now. To kill, to lessen the life of someone else so he could live, to gain a foothold here and live long enough to make a stab at the ship. He ducked, he weaved, he clutched stones and hurled them up. His left hand held a flat stone shield with which he diverted the swiftly plummeting rocks. There was a spatting sound everywhere. Lyte ran with him, encouraging him. Two men dropped before him, slain, their breasts cleaved to the bone, their blood springing out in unbelievable founts.

It was a useless conflict. Sim realized instantly how insane the venture was. They could never storm the cliff. A solid wall of rocks rained down. A dozen men dropped with shards of ebony in their brains, a half dozen more showed drooping, broken arms. One screamed and the upthrust white joint of his knee was exposed as the flesh was pulled away by two successive blows of well-aimed granite. Men stumbled over one another.

The muscles in his cheeks pulled tight and he began to wonder why he had ever come. But his raised eyes, as he danced from side to side, weaving and bobbing, sought always the cliffs. He wanted to live there so intensely, to have his chance. He would have to stick it out. But the heart was gone from him.

Lyte screamed piercingly. Sim, his heart panicking, twisted and saw that her hand was loose at the wrist, with an ugly wound bleeding profusely on the back of the knuckles. She clamped it under her armpit to soothe the pain. The anger rose in him and exploded. In his fury he raced forward, throwing his missiles with deadly accuracy. He saw a man topple and flail down, falling from one level to another of the caves, a victim of his shot. He must have been screaming, for his lungs were bursting open and closed and his throat was raw, and the ground spun madly under his racing feet.

The stone that clipped his head sent him reeling and plunging back. He ate sand. The universe dissolved into purple whorls. He could not get up. He lay and knew that this was his last day, his last time. The battle raged around him, dimly he felt Lyte over him. Her hands cooled his head, she tried to drag him out of range, but he lay gasping and telling her to leave him.

"Stop!" shouted a voice. The whole war seemed to give pause.

"Retreat!" commanded the voice swiftly. And as Sim watched, lying upon his side, his comrades turned and fled back toward home.

"The sun is coming, our time is up!" He saw their muscled backs, their moving, tensing, flickering legs go up and down. The dead were left upon the field. The wounded cried for help. But there was no time for the wounded. There was only time for swift men to run the gauntlet home and, their lungs aching and raw with heated air, burst into their tunnels before the sun burnt and killed them.

The sun!

Sim saw another figure racing toward him. It was Chion! Lyte was helping Sim to his feet, whispering helpfully to him. "Can you walk?" she asked. And he groaned and said, "I think so." "Walk then," she said. "Walk slowly, and then faster and faster. We'll make it, I know we will."

Sim got to his feet, stood swaying. Chion raced up, a strange expression cutting lines in his cheeks, his eyes shining with battle. Pushing Lyte abruptly aside he seized upon a rock and dealt Sim a jolting blow upon his ankle that laid wide the flesh. All of this was done quite silently.

Now he stood back, still not speaking, grinning like an animal from the night mountains, his chest panting in and out, looking from the thing he had done, to Lyte, and back. He got his breath. "He'll never make it," he nodded at Sim. "We'll have to leave him here. Come along, Lyte."

Lyte, like a cat-animal, sprang upon Chion, searching for his eyes, shrieking through her exposed, hard-pressed teeth. Her fingers stroked great bloody furrows down Chion's arms and again, instantly, down his neck. Chion, with an oath, sprang away from her. She hurled a rock at him. Grunting, he let it miss him, then ran off a few yards. "Fool!" he cried, turning to scorn her. "Come along with me. Sim will be dead in a few minutes. Come along!"

Lyte turned her back on him. "I will go if you carry me."

Chion's face changed. His eyes lost their gleaming. "There is no time. We would both die if I carried you."

Lyte looked through and beyond him. "Carry me, then, for that's how I wish it to be."

Without another word, glancing fearfully at the sun, Chion fled. His footsteps sped away and vanished from hearing. "May he fall and break his neck," whispered Lyte, savagely glaring at his form as it skirted a ravine. She returned to Sim. "Can you walk?"

Agonies of pain shot up his leg from the wounded ankle. He nodded ironically. "We could make it to the cave in two hours, walking. I have an idea, Lyte. Carry me." And he smiled with the grim joke.

She took his arm. "Nevertheless we'll walk. Come."

"No," he said. "We're staying here."

"But why?"

"We came to seek a home here. If we walk we will die. I would rather die here. How much time have we?"

Together they measured the sun. "A few minutes," she said, her voice flat and dull. She held close to him.

The black rocks of the cliff were paling into deep purples and browns as the sun began to flood the world.

What a fool he was! He should have stayed and worked with Dienc, and thought and dreamed.

With the sinews of his neck standing out defiantly he bellowed upward at the cliff holes.

"Send me down one man to do battle!"

Silence. His voice echoed from the cliff. The air was warm.

"It's no use," said Lyte, "They'll pay no attention."

He shouted again. "Hear me!" He stood with his weight on his good foot, his injured left leg throbbing and pulsating with pain. He shook a fist. "Send down a warrior who is no coward! I will not turn and run home! I have come to fight a fair fight! Send a man who will fight for the right to his cave! Him I will surely kill!"

More silence. A wave of heat passed over the land, receded.

"Oh, surely," mocked Sim, hands on naked hips, head back, mouth wide, "surely there's one among you not afraid to fight a cripple!" Silence. "No?" Silence.

"Then I have miscalculated you. I'm wrong. I'll stand here, then, until the sun shucks the flesh off my bone in black scraps, and call you the filthy names you deserve."

He got an answer.

"I do not like being called names," replied a man's voice.

Sim leaned forward, forgetting his crippled foot.

A huge man appeared in a cave mouth on the third level.

"Come down," urged Sim. "Come down, fat one, and kill me."

The man scowled seriously at his opponent a moment, then lumbered slowly down the path, his hands empty of any weapons.

Immediately every cave above clustered with heads. An audience for this drama.

The man approached Sim. "We will fight by the rules, if you know them."

"I'll learn as we go," replied Sim.

This pleased the man and he looked at Sim warily, but not unkindly. "This much I will tell you," offered the man generously. "If you die, I will give your mate shelter and she will live as she pleases, because she is the wife of a good man."

Sim nodded swiftly. "I am ready," he said.

"The rules are simple. We do not touch each other, save with stones. The stones and the sun will do either of us in. Now is the time—"

8

A TIP of the sun showed on the horizon. "My name is Nhoj," said Sim's enemy, casually taking up a handful of pebbles and stones, weighing them. Sim did likewise. He was hungry. He had not eaten for many minutes. Hunger was the curse of this planet's peoples—a perpetual demanding of empty stomachs for more, more food. His blood flushed weakly, shot tinglingly through veins in jolting throbs of heat and pressure, his rib cage shoved out, went in, shoved out again, impatiently.

"Now!" roared the three hundred watchers from the cliffs. "Now!" they clamored, the men and women and children balanced, in turmoil on the ledges. "Now! Begin!"

As if at a cue, the sun arose. It smote them a blow as with a flat, sizzling stone. The two men staggered under the molten impact, sweat broke from their naked thighs and loins, under their arms and on their faces was a glaze like fine glass.

Nhoj shifted his huge weight and looked at the sun as if in no hurry to fight. Then, silently, with no warning, he snapped out a pebble with a startling trigger-flick of thumb and forefinger. It caught Sim flat on the cheek, staggered him back, so that a rocket of unbearable pain climbed up his crippled foot and burst into nervous explosion at the pit of his stomach. He tasted blood from his bleeding cheek.

Nhoj moved serenely. Three more flicks of his magical hands and three tiny, seemingly harmless bits of stone flew like whistling birds. Each of them found a target, slammed it. The nerve centers of Sim's body! One hit his stomach so that ten hours' eating almost slid up his throat. A second got his forehead, a third his neck. He collapsed to the boiling sand. His knee made a wrenching sound on the hard earth. His face was colorless and his eyes, squeezed tight, were pushing tears out from the hot, quivering lids. But even as he had fallen he had let loose, with wild force, his handful of stones!

The stones purred in the air. One of them, and only one, struck Nhoj. Upon the left eyeball. Nhoj moaned and laid his hands in the next instant to his shattered eye.

Sim choked out a bitter, sighing laugh. This much triumph he had. The eye of his opponent. It would give him . . . Time. Oh, gods, he thought, his stomach retching sickly, fighting for breath, this is a world of time. Give me a little more, just a trifle!

Nhoj, one-eyed, weaving with pain, pelted the writhing body of Sim, but his aim was off now, the stones flew to one side or if they struck at all they were weak and spent and lifeless.

Sim forced himself half erect. From the corners of his eyes he saw Lyte, waiting, staring at him, her lips breathing words of encouragement and hope. He was bathed in sweat, as if a rain spray had showered him down.

The sun was now fully over the horizon. You could smell it. Stones glinted like mirrors, the sand began to roil and bubble. Illusions sprang up everywhere in the valley. Instead of one warrier Nhoj he was confronted by a dozen, each in an upright position, preparing to launch another missile. A dozen irregular warriors who shimmered in the golden menace of day, like bronze gongs smitten quivered in one vision!

Sim was breathing desperately. His nostrils flared and sucked and his mouth drank thirstily of flame instead of oxygen. His lungs took fire like silk torches and his body was consumed. The sweat spilled from his pores to be instantly evaporated. He felt himself shriveling, shriveling in on himself, he imagined himself looking like his father, old, sunken, slight, withered! Where was the sand? Could he move? Yes. The world wriggled under him, but now he was on his feet.

There would be no more fighting.

A murmur from the cliff told this. The sunburnt faces of the high audience gaped and jeered and shouted encouragement to their warrior. "Stand straight, Nhoj, save your strength now! Stand tall and perspire!" they urged him. And Nhoj stood, swaying lightly, swaying slowly, a pendulum in an incandescent fiery breath from the skyline. "Don't move, Nhoj, save your heart, save your power!"

"The Test, The Test!" said the people on the heights. "The test of the sun."

And this was the worst part of the fight. Sim squinted painfully at the distorted illusion of cliff. He thought he saw his parents; father with his defeated face, his green eyes burning, mother with her hair blowing like a cloud of gray smoke in the fire wind. He must get up to them, live for and with them!

Behind him, Sim heard Lyte whimper softly. There was a whisper of flesh against sand. She had fallen. He did not dare turn. The strength of turning would bring him thundering down in pain and darkness.

His knees bent. If I fall, he thought, I'll lie here and become ashes. Where was Nhoj? Nhoj was there, a few yards from him, standing bent, slick with perspiration, looking as if he were being hit over the spine with great hammers of destruction.

"Fall, Nhoj! Fall!" thought Sim. "Fall, fall! Fall so I can take your place!"

But Nhoj did not fall. One by one the pebbles in his half-loose left hand plummeted to the broiling sands and Nhoj's lips peeled back, the saliva burned away from his lips and his eyes glazed. But he did not fall. The will to live was strong in him. He hung as if by a wire.

Sim fell to one knee!

"Ahh!" wailed the knowing voices from the cliff. They were watching death. Sim jerked his head up, smiling mechanically, foolishly as if caught in the act of doing something silly. "No, no," he insisted drowsily, and got back up again. There was so much pain he was all one ringing numbness. A whirring, buzzing, frying sound filled the land. High up, an avalanche came down like a curtain on a drama, making no noise. Everything was quiet except for a steady humming. He saw fifty images of Nhoj now, dressed in armors of sweat, eyes puffed with torture, cheeks sunken, lips peeled back like the rind of a drying fruit. But the wire still held him.

"Now," muttered Sim, sluggishly, with a thick, baked tongue between his blazing teeth. "Now I'll fall and lie and dream." He said it with slow, thoughtful pleasure. He planned it. He knew how it must be done. He would do it accurately. He lifted his head to see if the audience was watching.

They were gone!

The sun had driven them back in. All save one or two brave ones. Sim laughed drunkenly and watched the sweat gather on his dead hands, hesitate, drop off, plunge down toward sand and turn to steam halfway there.

Nhoj fell.

The wire was cut. Nhoj fell flat upon his stomach, a gout of blood kicked from his mouth. His eyes rolled back into a white, senseless insanity.

Nhoj fell. So did his fifty duplicate illusions.

All across the valley the winds sang and moaned and Sim saw a blue lake with a blue river feeding it and low white houses near the river with people going and coming in the houses and among the tall green tress. Trees taller than seven men, beside the river mirage.

"Now," explained Sim to himself at last, "Now I can fall. Right—into—that—lake."

He fell forward.

He was shocked when he felt the hands eagerly stop him in mid-plunge, lift him, hurry him off, high in the hungry air, like a torch held and waved, ablaze.

"How strange is death," he thought, and blackness took him.

He wakened to the flow of cool water on his cheeks.

He opened his eyes fearfully. Lyte held his head upon her lap, her fingers were moving food to his mouth. He was tremendously hungry and tired, but fear squeezed both of these things away. He struggled upward, seeing the strange cave contours overhead.

"What time is it?" he demanded.

"The same day as the contest. Be quiet," she said.

"The same day!"

She nodded amusedly. "You've lost nothing of your life. This is Nhoj's cave. We are inside the black cliff. We will live three extra days. Satisfied? Lie down."

"Nhoj is dead?" He fell back, panting, his heart slamming his ribs. He relaxed slowly. "I won. I won," he breathed.

"Nhoj is dead. So were we, almost. They carried us in from outside only in time."

He ate ravenously. "We have no time to waste. We must get strong. My leg—" He looked at it, tested it. There was a swath of long yellow grasses around it and the ache had died away. Even as he watched, the terrific pulsings of his body went to work and cured away the impurities under the bandages. It *has* to be strong by sunset, he thought. It *has* to be.

He got up and limped around the cave like a captured animal. He felt Lyte's eyes upon him. He could not meet her gaze. Finally, helplessly, he turned.

She interrupted him. "You want to go on to the ship?" she asked, softly. "Tonight? When the sun goes down?"

He took a breath, exhaled it. "Yes."

"You couldn't possibly wait until morning?"

"No."

"Then I'll go with you."

"No!"

"If I lag behind, let me. There's nothing here for me."

They stared at each other a long while. He shrugged wearily.

"All right," he said, at last. "I couldn't stop you, I know that. We'll go together."

9

THEY WAITED in the mouth of their new cave. The sun set. The stones cooled so that one could walk on them. It was almost time for the leaping out and the running toward the distant, glittering metal seed that lay on the far mountain.

Soon would come the rains. And Sim thought back over all the times he had watched the rains thicken into creeks, into rivers that cut new beds each night. One night there would be a river running north, the next a river running northeast, the third night a river running due west. The valley was continually cut and scarred by the torrents. Earthquakes and avalanches filled the old beds. New ones were the order of the day. It was this idea of the river and the directions of the river that he had turned over in his head for many hours. It might possibly—Well, he would wait and see.

He noticed how living in this new cliff had slowed his pulse, slowed everything. A mineral result, protection against the solar radiations. Life was still swift, but not as swift as before.

"Now, Sim!" cried Lyte.

They ran. Between the hot death and the cold one. Together, away from the cliffs, out toward the distant, beckoning ship.

Never had they run this way in their lives. The sound of their feet running was a hard, insistent clatter over vast oblongs of rock, down into ravines, up the sides, and on again. They raked the air in and out their lungs. Behind them the cliffs faded into things they could never turn back to now.

They did not eat as they ran. They had eaten to the bursting point in the cave, to save time. Now it was only running, a lifting of legs, a balancing of bent elbows, a convulsion of muscles, a slaking in of air that had been fiery and was now cooling.

"Are they watching us?"

Lyte's breathless voice snatched at his ears above the pound of his heart.

Who? But he knew the answer. The cliff peoples, of course. How long had it been since a race like this one? A thousand days? Ten thousand? How long since someone had taken the chance and sprinted with an entire civilization's eyes upon their backs, into gullies, across cooling plain. Were there lovers pausing in their laughter back there, gazing at the two tiny dots that were a man and woman running toward destiny? Were children eating of new fruits and stopping in their play to see the two people racing against time? Was Dienc still living, narrowing hairy eyebrows down over fading eyes, shouting them on in a feeble, rasping voice, shaking a twisted hand? Were there jeers? Were they being called fools, idiots? And in the midst of the name-calling, were people praying them on, hoping they would reach the ship?

Sim took a quick glance at the sky, which was beginning to bruise with the coming night. Out of nowhere clouds materialized and a light shower trailed across a gully two hundred yards ahead of them. Lightning beat upon distant mountains and there was a strong scent of ozone on the disturbed air.

"The halfway mark," panted Sim, and he saw Lyte's face half turn, longingly looking back at the life she was leaving. "Now's the time, if we want to turn back, we still have time. Another minute—"

Thunder snarled in the mountains. An avalanche started out small and ended up huge and monstrous in a deep fissure. Light rain dotted Lyte's smooth white skin. In a minute her hair was glistening and soggy with rain.

"Too late, now," she shouted over the patting rhythm of her own naked feet. "We've got to go ahead!"

And it was too late. Sim knew, judging the distances, that there was no turning back now.

His leg began to pain him. He favored it, slowing. A wind came up swiftly. A cold wind that bit into the skin. But it came from the cliffs behind them, helped rather than hindered them. An omen? he wondered. No.

For as the minutes went by it grew upon him how poorly he had estimated the distance. Their time was dwindling out, but they were still an impossible distance from the ship. He said nothing, but the impotent anger at the slow muscles in his legs welled up into bitterly hot tears in his eyes.

He knew that Lyte was thinking the same as himself. But she flew along like a white bird, seeming hardly to touch ground. He heard her breath go out and in her throat, like a clean, sharp knife in its sheath.

Half the sky was dark. The first stars were peering through lengths of black cloud. Lightning jiggled a path along a rim just ahead of them. A full thunderstorm of violent rain and exploding electricity fell upon them.

They slipped and skidded on moss-smooth pebbles. Lyte fell, scrambled up again with a burning oath. Her body was scarred and dirty. The rain washed over her.

The rain came down and cried on Sim. It filled his eyes and ran in rivers down his spine and he wanted to cry with it.

Lyte fell and did not rise, sucking her breath, her breasts quivering.

He picked her up and held her. "Run, Lyte, please, run!"

"Leave me, Sim. Go ahead!" The rain filled her mouth. There was water everywhere. "It's no use. Go on without me."

He stood there, cold and powerless, his thoughts sagging, the flame of hope blinking out. All the world was blackness, cold falling sheaths of water, and despair.

"We'll walk, then," he said. "And keep walking, and resting."

They walked for fifty yards, easily, slowly, like children out for a stroll. The gully ahead of them filled with water that went sliding away with a swift wet sound, toward the horizon.

Sim cried out. Tugging at Lyte he raced forward. "A new channel," he said, pointing, "Each day the rain cuts a new channel. Here, Lyte!" He leaned over the floodwaters.

He dived in, taking her with him.

The flood swept them like bits of wood. They fought to stay upright, the water got into their mouths, their noses. The land swept by on both sides of them. Clutching Lyte's fingers with insane strength, Sim felt himself hurled end over end, saw flicks of lightning on high, and a new fierce hope was born in him. They could no longer run—well, then they would let the water do the running for them.

With a speed that dashed them against rocks, split open their shoulders, abraded their legs, the new, brief river carried them. "This way!" Sim shouted over a salvo of thunder and steered frantically toward the opposite side of the gully. The mountain where the ship lay was just ahead. They must not pass it by. They fought in the transporting liquid and were slammed against the far side. Sim leaped up, caught at an overhanging rock, locked Lyte in his legs, and drew himself hand over hand upward.

As quickly as it had come, the storm was gone. The lightning faded. The rain ceased. The clouds melted and fell away over the sky. The wind whispered into silence.

"The ship!" Lyte lay upon the ground. "The ship, Sim. This is the mountain of the ship!"

Now the cold came. The killing cold.

They forced themselves drunkenly up the mountain. The cold slid along their limbs, got into their arteries like a chemical and slowed them.

Ahead of them, with a fresh-washed sheen, lay the ship. It was a dream. Sim could not believe that they were actually so near it. Two hundred yards. One hundred and seventy yards.

The ground became covered with ice. They slipped and fell again and again. Behind them the river was frozen into a blue-white snake of cold solidity. A few last drops of rain from somewhere came down as hard pellets.

Sim fell against the bulk of the ship. He was actually touching it. Touching it! He heard Lyte whimpering in her constricted throat. This was the metal, the ship. How many others had touched it in the long days? He and Lyte had made it!

Then, as cold as the air, his veins were chilled.

Where was the entrance?

You run, you swim, you almost drown, you curse, you sweat, you work, you reach a mountain, you go up it, you hammer on metal, you shout with relief, and then—you can't find the entrance.

He fought to control himself. Slowly, he told himself, but not too slowly, go around the ship. The metal slid under his searching hands, so cold that his hands, sweating, almost froze to it. Now, far around to the side. Lyte moved with him. The cold held them like a fist. It began to squeeze.

The entrance.

Metal. Cold, immutable metal. A thin line of opening at the sealing point. Throwing all caution aside, he beat at it. He felt his stomach seething with cold. His fingers were numb, his eyes were half frozen in their sockets. He began to beat and search and scream against the metal door. "Open up! Open up!" He staggered. He had struck something. . . . A *click!*

The air lock sighed. With a whispering of metal on rubber beddings, the door swung softly sidewise and vanished back.

He saw Lyte run forward, clutch at her throat, and drop inside a small shiny chamber. He shuffled after her, blankly.

The air-lock door sealed shut behind him.

He could not breathe. His heart began to slow, to stop.

They were trapped inside the ship now, and something was happening. He sank down to his knees and choked for air.

The ship he had come to for salvation was now slowing his pulse, darkening his brain, poisoning him. With a starved, faint kind of expiring terror, he realized that he was dying.

Blackness.

He had a dim sense of time passing, of thinking, struggling, to make his heart go quick, quick. . . . To make his eyes focus. But the fluid in his body lagged quietly through his settling veins and he heard his pulses thud, pause, thud, pause and thud again with lulling intermissions.

He could not move, not a hand or leg or finger. It was an effort to lift the tonnage of his eyelashes. He could not shift his face even, to see Lyte lying beside him.

From a distance came her irregular breathing. It was like the sound a wounded bird makes with his dry, unraveled pinions.

She was so close he could almost feel the heat of her; yet she seemed a long way removed.

I'm getting cold! he thought. Is this death? This slowing of blood, of my heart, this cooling of my body, this drowsy thinking of thoughts?

Staring at the ship's ceiling he traced its intricate system of tubes and machines. The knowledge, the purpose of the ship, its actions, seeped into him. He began to understand in a kind of revealing lassitude just what these things were his eyes rested upon. Slow. Slow.

There was an instrument with a gleaming white dial.

Its purpose?

He drudged away at the problem, like a man underwater.

People had used the dial. Touched it. People had repaired it. Installed it. People had dreamed of it before the building, before the installing, before the repairing and touching and using. The dial contained memory of use and manufacture, its very shape was a dream-memory telling Sim why and for what it had been built. Given time, looking at anything, he could draw from it the knowledge he desired. Some dim part of him reached out, dissected the contents of things, analyzed them.

This dial measured time!

Millions of hours of time!

But how could that be? Sim's eyes dilated, hot and glittering. Where were humans who needed such an instrument?

Blood thrummed and beat behind his eyes. He closed them.

Panic came to him. The day was passing. I am lying here, he thought, and my life slips away. I cannot move. My youth is passing. How long before I can move?

Through a kind of porthole he saw the night pass, the day come, the day pass, and again another night. Stars danced frostily.

I will lie here for four or five days, wrinkling and withering, he thought. This ship will not let me move. How much better if I had stayed in my home cliff, lived, enjoyed this short life. What good has it done to come here? I'm missing all the twilights and dawns. I'll never touch Lyte, though she's here at my side.

Delirium. His mind floated up. His thoughts whirled through the metal ship. He smelled the razor-sharp smell of joined metal. He heard the hull contract with night, relax with day.

Dawn.

Already—another dawn!

Today I would have been fully grown. His jaw clenched. I must get up. I must move. I must enjoy this time.

But he didn't move. He felt his blood pump sleepily from chamber to red chamber in his heart, on down and around through his dead body, to be purified by his folding and unfolding lungs.

The ship grew warm. From somewhere a machine clicked, automatically the temperature cooled. A controlled gust of air flushed the room.

Night again. And then another day.

He lay and saw four days of his life pass.

He did not try to fight. It was no use. His life was over.

He didn't want to turn his head now. He didn't want to see Lyte with her face like his tortured mother's—eyelids like gray ash flakes, eyes like beaten, sanded metal, cheeks like eroded stones. He didn't want to see a throat like parched thongs of yellow grass, hands the pattern of smoke risen from a fire, breasts like dessicated rinds and hair stubbly and unshorn as moist gray weeds!

And himself? How did *he* look? Was his jaw sunken, the flesh of his eyes pitted, his brow lined and age-scarred?

His strength began to return. He felt his heart beating so slow that it was amazing. One hundred beats a minute. Impossible. He felt so cool, so thoughtful, so easy.

His head fell over to one side. He stared at Lyte. He shouted in surprise.

She was young and fair.

She was looking at him, too weak to say anything. Her eyes were like tiny silver medals, her throat curved like the arm of a child. Her hair was blue fire eating at her scalp, fed by the slender life of her body.

Four days had passed and still she was young . . . no, younger than when they had entered the ship. She was still adolescent.

He could not believe it.

Her first words were, "How long will this last?"

He replied, carefully, "I don't know."

"We are still young."

"The ship. Its metal is around us. It cuts away the sun and the things that came from the sun to age us."

Her eyes shifted thoughtfully. "Then, if we stay here—"

"We'll remain young."

"Six more days? Fourteen more? Twenty?"

"More than that, maybe."

She lay there, silently. After a long time she said, "Sim?"

"Yes."

"Let's stay here. Let's not go back. If we go back now, you know what'll happen to us . . . ?"

"I'm not certain."

"We'll start getting old again, won't we?"

He looked away. He stared at the ceiling and the clock with the moving finger. "Yes. We'll grow old."

"What if we grow old—instantly. When we step from the ship won't the shock be too much?"

"Maybe."

Another silence. He began to move his limbs, testing them. He was very hungry. "The others are waiting," he said.

Her next words made him gasp. "The others are dead," she said. "Or will be in a few hours. All those we knew back there are old."

He tried to picture them old. Dark, his sister, bent and senile with time. He shook his head, wiping the picture away. "They may die," he said. "But there are others who've been born."

"People we don't even know."

"But, nevertheless, *our* people," he replied. "People who'll live only eight days, or eleven days unless we help them."

"But we're *young,* Sim! We can *stay* young!"

He didn't want to listen. It was too tempting a thing to listen to. To stay here. To live. "We've already had more time than the others," he said. "I need workers. Men to heal this ship. We'll get on our feet now, you and I, and find food, eat, and see if the ship is movable. I'm afraid to try to move it myself. It's so big. I'll need help."

"But that means running back all that distance!"

"I know." He lifted himself weakly. "But I'll do it."

"How will you get the men back here?"

"We'll use the river."

"*If* it's there. It *may* be somewhere else."

"We'll wait until there *is* one, then. I've got to go back, Lyte. The son of Dienc is waiting for me, my sister, your brother, are old people, ready to die, and waiting for some word from us—"

After a long while he heard her move, dragging herself tiredly to him. She put her head upon his chest, her eyes closed, stroking his arm. "I'm sorry. Forgive me. You have to go back. I'm a selfish fool."

He touched her cheek, clumsily. "You're human. I understand you. There's nothing to forgive."

They found food. They walked through the ship. It was empty. Only in the control room did they find the remains of a man who must have been the chief pilot. The others had evidently bailed out into space in emergency lifeboats. This pilot, sitting at his controls, alone, had landed the ship on a mountain within sight of other fallen and smashed crafts. Its location on high ground had saved it from the floods. The pilot himself had died, probably of heart failure, soon after landing. The ship had remained here, almost within reach of the other survivors, perfect as an egg, but silent, for—how many thousand days? If the pilot had lived, what a different thing life might have been for the ancestors of Sim and Lyte. Sim, thinking of this, felt the distant, ominous vibration of war. How had the war between worlds come out? Who had won? Or had both planets lost and never bothered trying to pick up survivors? Who had been right? Who was the enemy? Were Sim's people of the guilty or innocent side? They might never know.

He checked the ship hurriedly. He knew nothing of its workings, yet as he walked its corridors, patted its machines, he learned from it. It needed only a crew. One man couldn't possibly set the whole thing running again. He laid his hand upon one round, snoutlike machine. He jerked his hand away, as if burnt.

"Lyte!"

"What is it?"

He touched the machine again, caressed it, his hand trembled violently, his eyes welled with tears, his mouth opened and closed, he looked at the machine, loving it, then looked at Lyte.

"With this machine—" he stammered, softly, incredulously. "With— With this machine I can—"

"What, Sim?"

He inserted his hand into a cuplike contraption with a lever inside. Out of the porthole in front of him he could see the distant line of cliffs. "We were afraid there might never be another river running by this mountain, weren't we?" he asked, exultantly.

"Yes, Sim, but—"

"There *will* be a river. And I *will* come back, tonight! and I'll bring men with me. Five hundred men! Because with this machine

I can blast a river bottom all the way to the cliffs, down which the waters will rush, giving myself and the men a swift, sure way of traveling back!" He rubbed the machine's barrellike body. "When I touched it, the life and method of it burnt into me! Watch!" He depressed the lever.

A beam of incandescent fire lanced out from the ship, screaming.

Steadily, accurately, Sim began to cut away a riverbed for the storm waters to flow in. The night was turned to day by its hungry eating.

The return to the cliffs was to be carried out by Sim alone. Lyte was to remain in the ship, in case of any mishap. The trip back seemed, at first glance, to be impossible. There would be no river rushing to cut his time, to sweep him along toward his destination. He would have to run the entire distance in the dawn, and the sun would get him, catch him before he'd reach safety.

"The only way to do it is to start *before* sunrise."

"But you'd be frozen, Sim."

"Here." He made adjustments on the machine that had just finished cutting the riverbed in the rock floor of the valley. He lifted the smooth snout of the gun, pressed the lever, left it down. A gout of fire shot toward the cliffs. He fingered the range control, focused the flame end three miles from its source. Done. He turned to Lyte. "But I don't understand," she said.

He opened the air-lock door. "It's bitter cold out, and half an hour yet till dawn. If I run parallel to the flame from the machine, close enough to it, there'll not be much heat, but enough to sustain life, anyway."

"It doesn't sound safe," Lyte protested.

"*Nothing* does, on this world." He moved forward. "I'll have a half-hour start. That should be enough to reach the cliffs."

"But if the machine should fail while you're still running near its beam?"

"Let's not think of that," he said.

A moment later he was outside. He staggered as if kicked in the stomach. His heart almost exploded in him. The environment of his world forced him into swift living again. He felt his pulse rise, kicking through his veins.

The night was cold as death. The heat ray from the ship sliced across the valley, humming, solid and warm. He moved next to it, very close. One misstep in his running and—

"I'll be back," he called to Lyte.

He and the ray of light went together.

In the early morning the people in the caves saw the long finger of orange incandescence and the weird whitish apparition floating, running along beside it. There was muttering and moaning and many sighs of awe.

And when Sim finally reached the cliffs of his childhood he saw alien peoples swarming there. There were no familiar faces. Then he realized how foolish it was to expect familiar faces. One of the older men glared down at him. "Who're you?" he shouted. "Are you from the enemy cliff? What's your name?"

"I am Sim, the son of Sim!"

"Sim!"

An old woman shrieked from the cliff above him. She came hobbling down the stone pathway "Sim, Sim, it *is* you!"

He looked at her frankly bewildered. "But I don't know you," he murmured.

"Sim, don't you recognize me? Oh, Sim, it's me! Dark!"

"Dark!"

He felt sick at his stomach. She fell into his arms. This old, trembling woman with the half-blind eyes, his sister.

Another face appeared above. That of an old man. A cruel, bitter face. It looked down at Sim and snarled. "Drive him away!" cried the old man. "He comes from the cliff of the enemy. He's lived there! He's still young! Those who go there can never come back among us. Disloyal beast!" And a rock hurtled down.

Sim leaped aside, pulling the old woman with him.

A roar came from the people. They ran toward Sim, shaking their fists. "Kill him, kill him!" raved the old man, and Sim did not know who he was.

"Stop!" Sim held out his hands. "I come from the ship!"

"The ship?" The people slowed. Dark clung to him, looking up into his young face, puzzling over its smoothness.

"Kill him, kill him, kill him!" croaked the old man, and picked up another rock.

"I offer you ten days, twenty days, thirty more days of life!"

The people stopped. Their mouths hung open. Their eyes were incredulous.

"Thirty days?" It was repeated again and again. "How?"

"Come back to the ship with me. Inside it, one can live forever!"

The old man lifted high a rock, then, choking, fell forward in an apoplectic fit, and tumbled down the rocks to lie at Sim's feet.

Sim bent to peer at the ancient one, at the raw, dead eyes, the loose, sneering lips, the crumpled, quiet body.

"Chion!"

"Yes," said Dark behind him, in a croaking, strange voice. "Your enemy. Chion."

That night two hundred men started for the ship. The water ran in the new channel. One hundred of them were drowned or lost behind in the cold. The others, with Sim, got through to the ship.

Lyte awaited them, and threw wide the metal door.

The weeks passed. Generations lived and died in the cliffs, while the scientists and workers labored over the ship, learning its functions and its parts.

On the last day, two dozen men moved to their stations within the ship. Now there was a destiny of travel ahead.

Sim touched the control plates under his fingers.

Lyte, rubbing her eyes, came and sat on the floor next to him, resting her head against his knee, drowsily. "I had a dream," she said, looking off at something far away. "I dreamed I lived in caves in a cliff on a cold-hot planet where people grew old and died in eight days."

"What an impossible dream," said Sim. "People couldn't possibly live in such a nightmare. Forget it. You're awake now."

He touched the plates gently. The ship rose and moved into space.

Sim was right.

The nightmare was over at last.